PRAISE FOR STEVE LEWIS

The Marmalade Files

'The book's blurb says it's a romp through the "dark underbelly of politics" and for once the blurb doesn't lie' – news.com.au

'It's a fair bet that Canberra insiders and those beyond will drive themselves close to hallucination trying to figure out whether they are reading a tantalisation of fact or a facsimile of fiction' – Tony Wright, *Sydney Morning Herald*

'There is an eerie ring of reality' – *Daily Telegraph*

'A fast-paced political thriller that will appeal to any cynical observer of Australian politics' – *Adelaide Matters*

'Two prominent and seasoned Australian political journos have given us the best antidote to our current political drudgery by writing a delicious farce which will have you guessing who might be who. It's gripping and funny' – *Manly Daily*

'Cynical, opinionated, lively gallop through the landscape of contemporary Australian politics' – *Sydney Morning Herald*

'a joy-ride through an all too recognisable federal parliament heaving with a cast that, initially at least, seems only slightly blurred by gender reassignment … Will it fill you with hope? Probably not. But it's definitely fun' – *Weekend Australian*

The Mandarin Code

'A cracking read' – Tony Abbott

'Intelligent, rollicking entertainment' – *The Australian*

'This is fiction, but truth lurks behind every corner of it' – *Canberra Times*

The Shadow Game

Steve Lewis arrived in Canberra in late 1992, and spent the next two decades tormenting the nation's political elite. He worked for the *Australian Financial Review* and *The Australian*, and was national political correspondent for News Corp's big-selling metropolitan dailies. Along with Chris Uhlmann, Steve is one of the creative forces behind the global smash TV thriller *Secret City*, and is developing a suite of political and spy thrillers for the screen. He is the author of *Stand & Deliver*, a lively account of the National Press Club's fifty-year history, and works as a senior adviser to Newgate Communications.

Chris Uhlmann is one of Australia's best known and most respected political broadcasters. He began his career in journalism at the *Canberra Times* as the world's oldest copy-kid, after failed stints as a student priest, storeman and packer and security guard. He cohosted 666 ABC Canberra's breakfast program before switching to federal parliament and becoming the ABC's political editor. He has anchored the flagship current affairs programs *AM* and *7.30*, and in 2008 he won a Walkley Award for broadcast interviewing. He is now the political editor at Nine News.

Their books *The Marmalade Files* and *The Mandarin Code* (Books 1 and 2 of this volume) are the inspiration behind the TV series *Secret City*, which has screened to acclaim on Foxtel in Australia and Netflix internationally.

Carol Ann, 27/3/19

SECRET CITY

THE CAPITAL FILES

Enjoy! Canberra, the secret city. Good luck with the writing....

STEVE LEWIS
CHRIS UHLMANN

Like all works of fiction, this story was inspired by events in the real world, but it is a work of fiction and none of the main characters in this book really exist and, more importantly, none of the acts attributed to these fictional characters ever took place. So please do not interpret anything that happens in this book as a real event that actually happened or that involved any person in the real world (whether living or now deceased).

HarperCollins*Publishers*

Secret City: The Capital Files was first published in three separate volumes
by HarperCollins*Publishers* Australia Pty Limited:
The Marmalade Files in 2012
The Mandarin Code in 2014
The Shadow Game in 2016
This combined and abridged edition published in 2018
ABN 36 009 913 517
harpercollins.com.au

HarperCollins*Publishers*
Level 13, 201 Elizabeth Street, Sydney NSW 2000, Australia
Unit D1, 63 Apollo Drive, Rosedale, Auckland 0632, New Zealand
A 53, Sector 57, Noida, UP, India
1 London Bridge Street, London, SE1 9GF, United Kingdom
Bay Adelaide Centre, East Tower, 22 Adelaide Street West, 41st floor, Toronto,
  Ontario M5H 4E3, Canada
195 Broadway, New York NY 10007, USA

A catalogue record for this book is available
from the National Library of Australia

ISBN 978 1 4607 5721 5 (paperback)
ISBN 978 1 4607 1145 3 (ebook)

Cover design by Hazel Lam, HarperCollins Design Studio
Cover image by shutterstock.com
Typeset in Baskerville by Kirby Jones
Author photograph by Gary Ramage, News Ltd
Printed and bound in Australia by McPherson's Printing Group
The papers used by HarperCollins in the manufacture of this book are a natural, recyclable product made from wood grown in sustainable plantation forests. The fibre source and manufacturing processes meet recognised international environmental standards, and carry certification.

For Flint, Harry, Rosie and Charlie. My love forever.

For Gai Marie, sursum corda.

Long is the way and hard, that out of Hell leads up to light.
John Milton

CONTENTS

BOOK ONE

THE MARMALADE FILES

Canberra, June 16, 2011

It was a brutal morning, the mercury well below zero, the sun still in a foetal position. Canberra was snap frozen in a harsh winter embrace, the freeze lying like frosted glass across the national capital, yet to wake from its slumber.

The time was nudging 6.30am.

Harry Dunkley, a press gallery veteran with an instinct for trouble, nursed a thermos of coffee and a grade-three hangover as he coaxed his '97 LandCruiser along the sweeping lake road. Despite a layer of thermal clothing and a heater cranked to high, the cold bit hard as he turned right towards the muddy waters of Lake Burley Griffin.

Harry's face, still handsome despite an encroaching fifty-third birthday, wore the signs of a morning-after-the-night-before. And some night it had been. The press gallery's Mid Winter Ball, the one night of the year when politicians and journalists could enjoy that rarest of commodities in the capital – camaraderie.

Dunkley had unquestionably enjoyed himself, drinking too much of a good red – a 2006 Barossa shiraz, from memory. He'd chatted with the odd MP – one minister getting in his ear about a particularly embarrassing moment in Cabinet – before stumbling onto the dance floor for a late-night embrace with a Liberal staffer that threatened to get out of control.

But while the night had been spirited, Dunkley's mind had been focused on something more tantalising than a romp with a political starlet – the scent of a cracking yarn.

The phone call had come a few days earlier, in the middle of a particularly rowdy Question Time, as a hunted prime minister tried to fend off some well-aimed darts from a baying opposition. Dunkley was only half interested in the staged pantomime when his phone rang, its face illuminating with a distinctive Canberra number: 6261-1111. The Department of Foreign Affairs and Trade – DFAT – full of diplomats and policy wonks, many with multiple foreign languages under their university-educated belts.

3

What does DFAT want? Dunkley had wondered. He'd turned the volume down on his TV, anticipating a routine blast from one of DFAT's media nazis.

'Harry Dunkley? You don't know me, and you don't need to know my name – yet – but I have something for you, if you're interested.' The voice was cultured, with an accent polished, Dunkley had suspected, by a life serving successive Australian governments in various exotic locations and shitholes around the globe. There had been enough in those few words to prick Dunkley's interest.

And so now, as most of Canberra's population snuggled under their doonas, Dunkley idled his LandCruiser down a narrow dirt track off Lady Denman Drive. His destination: Yarramundi Reach, a lonely clip of land tucked away at the north-western end of Lake Burley Griffin.

In recent times the Reach had become a well-known gay beat for those who liked it rough and discreet. Word around parliament was that a small cabal of MPs, including at least one shadow minister, had been spotted picking up late-night trade, but Dunkley, like most in the press gallery, really didn't give a toss. 'Each to their own, mate,' he'd told a member of the ALP dirt unit when he'd come knocking with salacious details.

Now, in the early shadows of the day, nothing much stirred. Through a thin mist, a four-man rowing crew was slicing across the lake, their oars in rhythmic harmony. Further across the water, somewhere near the imperious High Court, several hot-air balloons climbed in a languid arc.

Dunkley slowed the LandCruiser to a crawl. The instructions had been specific: drive past the timber toilet block to a small clearing near the lake's fringe; be there at 6.45am. But whom was he meeting?

Unusually for Dunkley, he was on time; in fact, he was a few minutes early. He stepped out of the car's warmth, stamping his feet on the frosted ground.

Suddenly he heard the thud of a car door, maybe fifty metres away on the other side of a grove of eucalypts near the shoreline.

He walked in the direction of the sound; steady, not too fast. Through the trees he caught sight of a late-model dark-coloured European sedan – a Mercedes, he guessed. It reversed and then accelerated down a dirt track in the direction of Lady Denman. 'What the ...' Dunkley muttered, scrambling towards the departing vehicle, wondering whether he'd been tricked. He managed to glimpse its rear numberplate: blue with a distinctive DC stamp. A member of the diplomatic corps.

Close to the point the vehicle had driven off from, propped up on a picnic table so he could not miss it, was an A3-sized manila envelope. It bore a single, ironic marking – 'Embassy of Taiwan'.

From a distance, it appeared to be a fast-moving caterpillar, strung out for fifty metres or so, all blinking lights and lycra. Canberra's notorious early-morning cyclists were well versed in the art of riding two abreast and getting right up the noses of motorists. Dunkley eased off the throttle, uncertain about overtaking even though the road was near empty. 'C'mon, boys, get a move on ...'

He cast a sideways glance at the A3 envelope, anxious to prise open its secrets. He was five minutes from a cheerful joint in Yarralumla that served a decent latte and Spanish omelette. Most importantly, at this time of day, the cafe would be near deserted, perhaps hosting just a few hardy souls who'd ventured out to pick up the papers or get an early gym fix.

Pulling into the carpark, Dunkley could see a waitress setting up outside tables. Surely you jest, he thought.

Ensconcing himself inside near the window, he unwrapped one of the morning papers he'd brought with him, glancing at its headlines until his coffee arrived and he was sure it was safe to turn to the business at hand without interruption. His fingers stopped drumming the table and eagerly opened the envelope.

Three faces stared at him in glossy black-and-white. Two were Asian – Chinese, he guessed, given the Mao caps – and the other belonged to a Caucasian man in his early twenties with long sideburns and thick wavy hair. From the generous lapels on the man's open-necked shirt, Dunkley reckoned the photo dated back to the late 1970s.

Despite the passage of time, there was no mistaking that face with its trademark toothy smirk. 'Bruce Leonard Paxton.' Dunkley took a swig of his double-shot latte and turned the photo over, seeking confirmation. There was none. But he was sure the young face gazing up at him belonged to the man who had improbably risen through the Labor ranks to be crowned minister for defence.

A former poster boy for one of Australia's biggest blue-collar unions – the Construction, Forestry, Mining and Energy Union – Paxton was in his mid-fifties and had been the Member for Brand, a Labor seat on Perth's southern flank, for the past fifteen years. It wasn't listed on his CV, but he was also the least educated person ever to have been sworn in as the minister for Australia's proud defence services.

5

The appointment had brought jeers from the opposition, and with some justification. Paxton was the epitome of the Labor career man, a former union heavy who had been a fearsome figure in the wild west, cutting his teeth as a paid thug with the notorious Building Workers Industrial Union. He had left school at fifteen, the moment he was legal, and through a family contact landed a job almost immediately in the building sites around Perth, shovelling sand and shit, and learning to talk fast.

After a few years labouring and doing odd jobs for men who worked hard and drank wildly, he'd joined up with the local ALP – or, more correctly, the BWIU had paid his dues and directed him to the Rockingham branch.

His career had really taken off though when he'd switched allegiances and risen to become state secretary of the United Mineworkers Federation, then in the process of wielding its muscle across the state, particularly in the Pilbara, where the first riches of the mining boom were being exploited by hungry entrepreneurs. In the early 1990s the UMF merged with the BWIU to become a more potent force – the CFMEU.

Paxton and another union thug, Doug Turner, had forged a tag team that ran amok, taking on bosses and union rivals alike. It was during one of their escapades that Paxton mysteriously lost his left hand, claiming to be the victim of an industrial accident. 'Fucking drop saw took it clean off,' he would say over an ale, seeking to impress whoever cared to listen.

Instead of getting the prosthesis recommended by a team of specialists, he had a hook fitted in place of his missing hand. He famously paraded it on the front page of the *West Australian*, grinning maniacally beneath the cheeky headline 'Hook or Crook?'. He was dubbed Captain by adoring unionists and the unique look only served to build on the already menacing Paxton mystique.

After a decade and a half of union power, Paxton was persuaded to move into federal parliament. A safe seat was found, the Labor incumbent bought off with the promise of a diplomatic posting to the Holy See. Paxton came to Canberra masquerading as a workers' hero – 'Hawkie without the charisma' was the view of more than a few Labor colleagues – and set about using the skills he'd honed during his union career to build support within the Caucus.

He was forced to cool his heels during the long years in opposition, finding the travel between the west and Canberra a burden on family life, an argument he used to justify various dalliances with female staffers. 'Well, I do support fucking affirmative action,' he joked when quizzed by his colleagues on his unusually high female-to-male staff ratio.

In Canberra he toned down his wild man image by replacing the hook with a black-gloved prosthesis. But he kept the hook in his office and was rumoured to put it on behind closed doors whenever he faced a particularly tough meeting.

Now Harry Dunkley stared at the youthful facsimile of the minister. A single photo with no identifying inscription. Someone was trying to damage Paxton, of that he was sure. But who? And why?

Tilting the photo, he noticed a faint marking at its top right-hand edge, hard to see except in a certain light. 'Acacia.' The name meant nothing to Dunkley but he suspected it carried some significance. He slid the image back into its envelope and then into his leather shoulder bag, a gift from his daughter, Gaby. His hangover had receded, the caffeine taking hold.

Dunkley was ready to look the world in the eye, to take on the latest political travesty. As for the photo of Bruce Paxton, he had no idea what it meant – but he knew whom to ask to find out.

Canberra, June 16

Catriona Bailey peered down the barrel of the television camera and felt a trickle of sweat form on her upper lip. She was beginning to feel the strain and hated herself for it.

The foreign minister had slept fitfully, catching not much more than an hour's rest between two and three, which wasn't enough, even for her. She usually lived on four hours a night, finding it sufficient to keep up her inhuman work pace.

But two days ago a magnitude-eight earthquake had struck north-west China, killing hundreds and injuring thousands. That alone was enough to spark media interest, but the fact that a small number of Australians were missing – including a child – meant the domestic media was in hyper-drive.

And that was a great opportunity.

The Department of Foreign Affairs and Trade had set up a crisis centre and a hotline, and the minister was where she felt most comfortable: feeding the 24/7 news cycle. But keeping pace with the news had eaten into the few hours a day she normally set aside for rest.

In truth, DFAT wouldn't usually establish a crisis centre when so few Australians were at risk, but Bailey, typically, had demanded it. She also demanded half-hourly updates from local consular officials, hourly briefings from her staff on the Chinese and international reaction, telephone calls with every Chinese official imaginable and regular contact with her former academic colleagues to practise tricky local pronunciations.

She then regurgitated this information in dozens of interviews on every radio and TV program in the land. No audience was too small; no request went unanswered.

In an earlier life, Bailey had been a gifted Chinese scholar, fluent in Mandarin, and one of the youngest people ever appointed a professor at the Australian National University. She had a work ethic that bordered on the demented, burning through staff and earning her the sobriquet Attila the Hen.

She was also utterly awkward – 'socially autistic', her colleagues claimed – but worked hard at contriving a common touch, deploying idioms she imagined were in routine public use; unfortunately, since everything she learned came from books, much of her information was dated, resulting in constructions like, 'Come on, cobber, that's a bodgie piece of analysis. I am fully seized of the need for China to engage with the councils of the world and, in due season, it will.'

A long-time member of the Labor Party, Bailey had ditched academia in the '90s for a tilt at a seat in Sydney's west. Once elected, her relentless work ethic and fixation with being in the media saw her rise further and faster than anyone had imagined possible, especially given how few in Labor's ranks liked her.

'She is in the party but not of it,' critics would say.

But the public loved her, every card seemed to fall her way and, eleven years after entering parliament, she became the country's first female prime minister.

As PM, she was Australia's equivalent of Princess Di, feted like a rock star, every women's glossy clamouring to dress her for its cover, a one-woman political phenomenon whose approval ratings soared into the stratosphere. For a while, at least.

The descent was just as swift. A little over two years later her party abandoned her. She suffered the indignity of being the first prime minister to be dumped without being given the opportunity to contest an election. And that burned deep within. She became driven by revenge.

Now she was foreign minister and believed she could climb back to the top. She would do it the way she did it the first time: bypassing the party and talking directly to the people – her people – every hour of every day. And she would not stop, no matter who or what stood in her way.

*

It was 10.30pm and the tiredness was definitely catching up with Catriona Bailey.

Her day had begun with a 6.30am interview on Sydney radio station 2GB, moving on to News Radio and a quick ABC News 24 spot, back to commercial TV, then an appearance on Sky. And now, a dozen interviews later, she was fronting up to *Lateline*.

Bailey had found the previous interview a trial and had trouble concentrating, which was rare for her. She'd spilled a glass of water while being made up and had a headache from hell. It seemed difficult to write notes on her briefing papers. Naturally, she pressed on, and now was being beamed live across Australia.

TONY JONES: Foreign Minister, what can you tell us about the missing Australians?

CATRIONA BAILEY: Well, Tony, minutes before this interview I got off the phone to our ambassador in Beijing who informed me that we have four embassy staff on the ground in Qinghai province. You will be aware that the epicentre of the quake was in Yushu, which is about 772 kilometres from the provincial capital, Xining. Which is about two thousand kilometres by rail from Beijing. So let's be frank: it's a long way, cobber, that's just a fact. And the infrastructure and communications are badly damaged, so we haven't yet been able to ascertain the whereabouts of the four Australians, but I can assure you we are sparing no effort.

Bailey began to feel light-headed and her left arm was weirdly heavy. Maybe she should have had lunch, or dinner. She had to work hard to stay focused, and she feared tripping over some of the regional details.

JONES: So you don't have any new information?

Bailey hated to admit that she didn't – and wasn't about to.

BAILEY: Now, Tony, I said we are doing everything we can, employing every resource. I have demanded that the Chinese spare no effort in assisting us to locate our citizens.

As soon as the words left her tongue, which now felt thick in her mouth, Bailey realised her mistake.

JONES: You demanded? Foreign Minister, the Chinese have 400 confirmed dead, 10,000 injured, hundreds of thousands homeless. And you are demanding that they look for a few Australians?

BAILEY: I mean ... I said ... I have asked, of course ... but I ...

The television lights started to swirl before Bailey's eyes and then everything went black. She fell face down on the gleaming white oval-shaped desk.

JONES: Minister? Minister? For God's sake, someone at the Canberra end give her a hand!

Canberra, June 16

Brendan Ryan's plump figure lay propped up in bed with the remnants of a light snack scattered across his blanket – an empty Coke bottle, a packet of chips and three chocolate bar wrappers. The dietary habits of the Labor powerbroker were as slothful as his brain was sharp.

At thirty-eight, Ryan was considered the best Labor strategist in a generation and was already the party's most powerful factional warlord. A grateful new prime minister had appointed him a junior minister with some defence responsibilities, and his star was rising fast. A centre-left patriot and a fervent admirer of the United States, his sights were set on a seat in Cabinet.

The phone broke into his dreams of future glory.

'Freak Show's had a heart attack.'

'What?'

'Freak Show ... Bailey ... The bitch just seized up on *Lateline*, halfway through an interview ... it was brilliant. Turn on the television.'

It was the familiar voice of Sam Buharia, the don of the New South Wales Right, a fellow senator who played politics with all the subtlety of a Somalian warlord.

Ryan reached for the remote, and flicked on the ABC.

Tony Jones was scarlet-faced, reliving the moments before the foreign minister's collapse. And then the ABC replayed her seizure.

10

'Jesus,' Ryan muttered as he watched the minister slump forward. 'I'll call you back,' he told Buharia, not waiting for a response. He dropped the phone onto the bed.

Would Catriona Bailey die and finish the work that Ryan had started more than a year ago when he'd decided to kill her off as prime minister?

'Please, God, be merciful, let the bitch die quickly,' he entreated. He had long since lost any respect for the former leader who had all but destroyed the party he loved through her self-centred and anarchic use of power.

Ryan had been instrumental in her downfall, just months before a general election. And she had not had the decency to go quietly, instead making a public show of recontesting and winning her seat.

Thanks to Bailey's shenanigans, their election campaign had been a debacle. In the end, the major parties had been locked on the same number of seats and Labor only clawed its way back into office by stitching together a shaky alliance of independents and Greens. With parliament so finely balanced every vote was vital and Bailey had forced the prime minister to give her foreign affairs, threatening to sit as an independent if he refused.

Ever since, she had used Australian foreign policy as a vehicle to promote herself, looking for high-profile crises to exploit, parading on the world stage and making statements without consultation – some as baffling as they were damaging to Australia's international standing. She was a lone wolf, only interested in her own status; a publicity-seeking missile despised by her colleagues but still liked by the public.

'I call it the Bailey paradox,' Ryan would say. 'The further you get from the cow the more you like her.' Ryan's capacity for hate was legendary, and Bailey rated top of the pops on his list of foes.

Well, hopefully it would all be over soon. He began to ponder possible candidates to fill the inevitable Foreign Ministry vacancy. 'Me, maybe.'

Then his blood ran cold as a single word ricocheted through his brain: by-election!

Canberra, June 17

Harry Dunkley considered it indecent for a journalist to be anywhere near a newsroom before ten. And yet on this Friday morning at the fag end of a long and eventful week, he was dragging himself into the office and it was barely 9am.

Dunkley had no choice this morning, though. He'd been on the receiving end of a bracing phone call from *The Australian*'s chief of staff and told to haul his arse into work. A big political yarn was running and he was trailing the pack. Catriona Bailey had nearly snuffed it on national television the night before and the media had gone into overdrive. Everyone but Dunkley, who had gone to bed early and then slept in, switching his BlackBerry to silent as he tried to shake off an exhausting week.

There used to be an unwritten political armistice about reporting national politics – Fridays would be light duties only, with most senior gallery hands retiring to the better restaurants of Canberra for a lunch that often stretched into the weekend.

Those days were a distant dream. The rise of online technology and social media was changing the fabric of journalism. Dunkley's great love – print – was on the guillotine. Today's media was full of bits and bytes of bulldust, digital opinion stretching as far as the eye could see. Decent long-range reporting had given way to instant, shrill sensationalism, while newsrooms – roaring on the high-octane needs of a 24/7 product – were demanding more and more from their best reporters. The daily news had no beginning and no end; it was now just one continuous loop with every last gram of information shovelled into the machine.

Dunkley could sympathise with politicians who grumbled about the incessant demands of the rapacious media. But he had no idea what to do about it, any more than they did.

Arriving at his desk, he punched the speed dial to the Sydney conference room of *The Australian*, where the phone was answered by the familiar bark of editor-in-chief Deb Snowdon.

'And just where has our esteemed political editor been for the last eleven hours while our competitors have been towelling us with the story of the year.'

'I turned off my phone. I missed it. So can we dispense with the ritual flogging and get on with today?'

Snowdon, the first woman to storm and then command the male citadel of the national broadsheet, wouldn't let it go easily, but after a few more insults the conference call got back to business and the team hammered out a plan of attack. Dunkley didn't bother to mention the potential story about Paxton. After all, he had little to go on – just a single black-and-white pic. With the Bailey story occupying everyone's attention, the Paxton lead would be filed in the to-do list. Dunkley sensed it was a bigger story than that, but it demanded time. Plenty of it, and that, for now, was in short supply.

Canberra, June 17

'I don't care what you say, I am not fucking going!'

Martin Toohey's voice – agitated and defiant – could be heard in the corridor outside his office. By contrast, the response from his chief of staff was muted, but stern.

'Prime Minister, this government hangs by a thread and a by-election loss to the Coalition would see it fall. I agree Bailey is a bitch who almost single-handedly destroyed our party when *you* let her run it. But we survived by swallowing our pride and giving Bailey the ministry she wanted. We survived by putting together an alliance of Greens and independents to keep our fingernail grip on power. And if we survive another two years we might just win government in our own right again. For reasons best known to the sad bastards in Bailey's electorate, she is still popular there. If we are to survive we must win that by-election. Which means you must visit Catriona Bailey in hospital.'

Martin Toohey hated arguing with George Papadakis because he so often lost. The two men stared at each other, falling into a silent battle of wills.

The prime minister and his chief of staff had been friends for more than thirty years, harking back to their student politics days at the Royal Melbourne Institute of Technology.

Toohey would readily admit that Papadakis outgunned him, and most people, intellectually. The first-generation son of Greek immigrants, Papadakis had toiled in the family's grocery shop even as he blitzed his way through school.

He'd left RMIT to specialise in economics and public policy at the Australian National University. Entering Treasury as a graduate he had marched through the ranks to first assistant secretary level before leaving to become chief of staff to a newly elected Victorian Labor premier.

There he had helped replant Labor's economic credentials in the wasteland of the Cain–Kirner era, and developed an unrivalled reputation for having that rarest combination of gifts: the ability to devise good public policy and the political nous to implement it. He had returned to Canberra, as a deputy secretary in Treasury, when Labor won its first federal election in twelve years. It was his dream job. The hardest thing he had ever done was abandon it to guide the campaign of his old friend. And he did it for one reason only: because the party he loved stood on the precipice of electoral annihilation. His mission was simple: to protect the prime minister and drag Labor back from the abyss.

Of medium height, Papadakis had begun to go bald early and now sported just a half-crescent of short black-grey hair. He was round-faced and his body was heading in the same direction, thanks to a love of fine food and wine, and a grim determination never to exercise. 'God gave us brains so we could make and take the lift,' he would say.

Although he was not physically imposing, ministers quailed when he summoned them. His authority was unquestioned and the prime minister knew he was right about visiting Bailey. But every now and then he had to make a stand to remind himself that he was running the country. Though he lacked Papadakis's intellect he knew his political instincts were often better and he loved nothing more than those rare times he was proven right at the expense of his friend.

Toohey was tall, handsome and looked younger than his fifty-four years. He still had more than a hint of athleticism about him from his brief stint as a ruckman for Geelong West in the Victorian Football Association. He had learned to use his height and his deep baritone voice to great effect and was a passably good public speaker. He was no fool and knew his political strength lay in his union power base and his ability to get across a brief and sell it in the public market.

Toohey's path to power had been more politics than policy. He had followed the well-worn track from university politics to union organiser and then swiftly risen through the ranks to lead the oldest right-wing union in the country: the Australian Workers' Union.

Preselection for a safe Labor seat followed, but as he neared the top he was forced to make a dreadful choice: continue to support a good mate as Labor leader, and undoubtedly be led to defeat again, or throw in his lot with Catriona Bailey and possibly win office.

Bailey did not have the Caucus base to take the leadership on her own and neither did Toohey. What galled him was that he had more support than Bailey, but she was far more popular where it counted – in the electorate.

He knew the old saying in Australian politics: the very worst day in government is better than the very best in opposition. So Toohey backed Bailey, destroyed his old friend, and won government.

For a while, despite Bailey's astonishing personal weirdness, Toohey believed she might be a political genius and that they could be a formidable tag team, making the kind of changes that would lift them into the Labor pantheon with Hawke and Keating. But after a few months in power, he began to see how bad his judgement had been.

Bailey was chaos. She could not focus on one idea at a time, and with every finger-snap announcement entire tracts of the public service would have to scramble to make policy sense of it. As PM, she made grand pronouncements in public which had to be retro-fitted behind closed doors. Her advisers were too young and too green to corral her and correct her mistakes. And her determination to micro-manage meant she got buried in the weeds and lost sight of the big picture. 'She is like a lighthouse and a microscope,' one minister complained. 'Endlessly sweeping the horizon and then focusing for a millisecond on some trivial detail.'

And Bailey's language was absolute, allowing no easy path for retreat when things went pear-shaped.

The bureaucracy – which initially hailed a Labor prime minister after what many saw as the dark years of the Howard era – quickly grew to despise her and dubbed her TB, which handily stood for both a virulent disease and 'The Bitch'.

But the bureaucratic disdain was trumped by the hatred she engendered in her Cabinet and Caucus. They were sidelined and routinely subjected to the sharp edge of Bailey's tongue. She abused and ridiculed those who dared question her, and her colleagues began to dream of her demise. But while her poll numbers remained sky-high that day seemed a long way off.

For two years, the public had remained her best friend, despite increasing whispers of Napoleonic behaviour. Like the time a departmental head had been ordered to return from a summer holiday in the US because the PM demanded a brief on her desk 'within a week', only for it to sit, untouched, in her in-tray for a month. Or when a senior Bailey adviser spent a frustrating day chasing the PM around Australia after being summoned for an urgent meeting, eventually ending up in Darwin, close to midnight, without even a toothbrush, and the PM refusing to speak with her.

For a time, Bailey's constant stream of reviews and announcements had given the impression of a dynamic government, but the smokescreen had eventually blown away to reveal an empress without clothes.

Six months before the election, Bailey's poll numbers collapsed and Labor hardheads feared they would become the first government in eighty years to be turfed out after just one term.

Martin Toohey, the loyal deputy, began to contemplate the unthinkable – capping the PM.

15

When the execution came, it was over in a heartbeat. Once the possibility of knifing Bailey became a reality, almost the entire Labor Caucus wanted to get its hands on the blade – she was gone in less than twenty-four hours.

But she wasn't really gone, winning her western Sydney seat of Lindsay comfortably and demanding the foreign affairs portfolio as compensation.

Toohey despised Bailey. But he was trapped. He knew it and Papadakis knew it. He finally broke the silence.

'Okay, I'll go,' he seethed. 'But I'm not taking flowers.'

Beijing, February 16

Weng Meihui brushed back her long black hair and glanced at her delicate features in the mirror. She pulled her silk robe tighter and wondered if he would remember her. What was he like now? Would she have the same old feelings? Or had too much changed?

She remembered how she used to tease him when they were locked in each other's embrace, whispering in his ear, *'Dà Xióng Mao.'* My giant panda. He had loved it. It would titillate him and spur him to greater heights of passion.

They used to joke about how they were bridging the East–West divide, forging closer diplomatic ties, working together for global peace.

He had trusted her – he was so foolish and naive.

When had they first met? Was it 1979 or 1980? Perhaps as he strolled through the Forbidden City as she relayed facts to tourists about the history of the Imperial Palace, or on a walk around Tiananmen Square. Those years had blurred into one, back when the People's Republic was emerging from decades of darkness, from the bloodied cloak the Gang of Four had bound tightly around China's citizens. The first flush of Deng Xiaoping's reforms had been taking hold, giving hope to a nation that had endured the iron-fist rule of its communist dictators for thirty years.

For the first time since the Kuomintang had been swept from power, China had been open to foreign investment, eager for hard currency, and the West had responded, sending delegations to size up the business opportunities in a land of almost one billion people. Diplomatic relations were being restored with Western powers – the United States and Britain – with Australia, too, coming along for the ride.

Those first delegations had experienced a country which preached socialist equality but which in reality had stagnated economically, many of its people too hungry and too scared to protest against the ruling clique.

But these intrepid Western explorers had also sniffed the huge opportunities that lay ahead, as an emerging middle class grew in a marketplace the likes of which the world had never known.

And they'd been introduced to razor-sharp young Chinese officials like Weng Meihui. Tibetan by birth, Weng's parents had turned their backs on their country and cast their lot with the Chinese after the 1950 'liberation'. Her father had risen to become assistant governor, earning the wrath of the global 'Free Tibet' movement which dubbed him the 'Puppet of Beijing'. He'd been rewarded with a plum job in the communist capital and had broken the final link with his homeland by changing his family name.

Weng Meihui had been recruited as soon as she'd graduated from Peking University with a double major in international relations and classic Chinese literature. Her handlers had joked among themselves that she was perfectly suited to the tasks they had in mind for her, because 'betrayal ran in the blood' of her family.

She'd been sent straight to the Ministry of Culture – a prized posting – as one of a small group of multilingual officers who would act as escorts for the growing numbers of Westerners eager to sample the delights of the East.

Though clever and confident, she'd been recruited as much for her good looks as for her brains – not to mention her willingness to do whatever was required by her superiors to satisfy loose Western morals and to prise open loose Western lips.

It had been in this crucible of capitalism, communism, opportunism and sin that their sweet, sexy, impossible relationship had been forged. Both parties had known that each could only give so much, no more. Now, reminiscing in the dim glow of a Beijing night as she dressed for dinner, Weng Meihui wondered just how mutual that understanding had been.

Still tangled in reverie, she stepped delicately from the car, the door held open for her by the attentive concierge. Almost absentmindedly, she entered the fashionable restaurant – and pulled up short. There he was. A little older, a little more padding, but he still took her breath away. A giddy cocktail of lust, affection and regret surged to her head and heart, forcing her to stare at the floor for a long moment while she regained her composure. By the time she steeled herself to raise her eyes, he had discovered her. Pretending a cool she did not possess, Weng Meihui took her seat across the table from him, and so began a long, slow, painfully erotic dinner flirtation, destined to end only one way.

It was a little after 11.30pm when the limo pulled up outside the St Regis, still Beijing's best hotel. He stretched and stifled a yawn as he wandered through the lobby towards his fifth-floor room, glad to be rid of the minders who usually accompanied him.

It had been a wonderful evening, the formal dinner giving way to a few hours of intimacy, just the two of them, alone, again.

He had surprised himself over dinner, using his toes to first stroke, then part, her slim legs, teasing her to distraction, all the while carrying on a diplomatic discussion with a level head. He had learned a thing or two since those young, impetuous days. But as the seemingly interminable formalities had finally plodded to their conclusion, he'd felt the old habits of subterfuge stir. Negotiating wordlessly, they'd arrived separately at her room.

She had changed into her silk robe, opening the door to him silently. He quietly closed it behind him, then pressed her against the wall, holding her hands above her head as he kissed her – at first gently, then, as his blood rose, with increasing passion. She met his flicking tongue with her own and arched forward to press her breasts against his ample shirtfront.

Lying alone now on his hotel bed, he allowed his eyes to shut, weariness overtaking his body as he mentally flicked through his marathon twenty-four hours – a long flight and a day full of meetings, then that dinner that would have been deadly dull but for the fact that she was there, seated across the table and looking like heaven. He drifted off with a toothy grin – she had made it all worthwhile, every moment of it.

Canberra, June 17

Draped in a fur stole and a clinging black evening gown, Ben Gordon was impossible to miss.

An imposing six feet and two inches, he perched at the bar of the Atlantic, sipping a messy-looking cocktail. He had retained the Nordic good looks of his youth and his body had not yet succumbed to the middle-aged spread of so many his age. But he resembled nothing so much as a character from *Priscilla, Queen of the Desert*, Harry Dunkley thought, and was perhaps the least convincing transvestite in Australia.

As Dunkley approached, Gordon looked up and smiled through several layers of carefully applied hooker-red lipstick. The rest of his face was buried behind a thick layer of makeup, a crimson rouge giving extra definition to his angular features.

'Dunkie!' he squealed, a tad too loudly, as he rose to meet his friend. Every eye in the darkened room locked on the pair.

Gordon tottered across to him, his size eleven feet crammed into black Jimmy Choos that added several inches to his frame. A Gucci handbag the size of a rucksack was slung over his right forearm.

He planted a kiss, and about a centimetre of lipstick, on Dunkley's cheek. 'Hi, Ben.'

'Dunkie, you know better, it's Kimberley,' Gordon chided him, before launching into a monologue that Dunkley knew would have to be endured for five or so minutes before sensible conversation could begin.

'You never call. It's been what, two months? And don't tell me you're busy because you can always make time for your very best friends ...'

The recital gave Dunkley time to reflect on their friendship. They had first met thirty years ago at Sydney University's rugby club when Dunkley was a handy fly-half and Gordon the kind of hard-hitting lineout-jumping lock that coaches dream of. Both could have played in the top grades but they'd plumped for the more leisurely pleasures of fourth grade, where serious training gave way to serious drinking.

While Dunkley was enrolled in the soft-ply humanities – majoring in politics and English – Gordon was immersed in pure mathematics and linguistics. He passed both with honours. But work was scarce and he'd racked up thirty job applications before he finally landed a position as an analyst with the nation's domestic spy agency, the Australian Security Intelligence Organisation. After several years compiling files on mostly harmless citizens who had strayed into ASIO's orbit, he'd transferred into the bowels of the most secretive building in Canberra: the Defence Signals Directorate.

Nestled on the western end of the Defence precinct at Russell Hill, DSD stood out from the rest of the Lego blocks dumped on the hillside by virtue of its menacing hi-tech perimeter fence. Inside was Australia's listening post, the nation's electronic eavesdropping centre And it was where senior bureaucrats and ministers went when they wanted to have secure video-link conversations with their counterparts in the US and UK.

Gordon was the best analyst in the DSD. He made sense of raw data and had specialised first in Indonesia and later engaged with the emerging giant of China. He was fascinated by the mega-nation of 1.3 billion people, millions of them exiled to rural ghettos and thousands languishing in prisons for not much more than the crime of questioning Beijing's iron-fisted rule. He was particularly interested in China's push into the Asia–Pacific neighbourhood, where it was buying favour with nations small and large.

Outsiders sometimes wondered how Ben managed to hold one of the highest level security clearances – AUSTEO: Australian Eyes Only – given his unusual lifestyle.

For Ben the answer was easy.

'The security clearance tries to uncover areas where you might be compromised, some weakness that might leave you exposed to being blackmailed,' he would say. 'How can someone blackmail me for being a trannie if I dress like this in the cafeteria every day?' It was a compelling argument.

'So, what do you really want?' The change of tone shook Dunkley out of his mental meanderings.

'I've got a photo we need to talk about.'

Gordon's eyes narrowed. 'Well, we're not discussing it here. You have a look that tells me this is serious. I do my best serious business at Caph's in Manuka. Table at the back facing the entrance. Meet me in twenty minutes … I'll leave first.'

And with that, Gordon finished his cocktail and strode out, all purpose and intent, albeit in a pair of killer high heels.

Caph's, a downbeat joint in the cafe district of nearby Manuka, was unusually empty for this time of night, with just a few lonely souls scattered among its numerous tables. Ben Gordon, though, was taking no chances.

'Take the battery out of your BlackBerry.'

Dunkley followed the command, knowing that Gordon's knowledge of electronics and espionage left little room for argument. Ben had told him that an everyday mobile phone could be turned into a listening and tracking device, without much effort. And in Canberra, with its endless conspiracies and political intrigues, it paid to be ultra-cautious. Besides, Dunkley needed the advice of his long-time friend. The black-and-white photo was starting to trouble him. Bruce Paxton was easy, but who were the two Asian men?

Dunkley eased the photo out of its envelope and discreetly placed it in front of Gordon. His friend studied the photo carefully for a moment then lifted his gaze.

'Jesus, Harry, where did you get this?'

Before Dunkley had a chance to answer, Gordon spoke again. 'Acacia … you have no idea, do you?'

Dunkley stared at him blankly.

20

'It's the top-secret marking for ASIS, our international spooks. You are playing with dynamite. And you're also in serious breach of the Crimes Act.'

Gordon looked down at the photo again. He seemed shocked, Dunkley thought. And worried. The reaction heightened Dunkley's excitement. Somewhere in this photo was a cracker of a yarn.

'Zhou Dejiang! My, you have snared a big one.'

'And just who is Zhou Dejiang?'

'Harry, I thought a political junkie like you would know about our Chinese friend. He's one of the bigwigs in the Politburo, the head of China's Ministry for State Security. Their top spy. He was at one stage considered a candidate to become president, but there was some falling-out a few years ago, some mini-scandal that the Chinese were desperately keen to cover up. He may have got too close to the Americans or the Taiwanese … anyway, his career stalled for a while but for the past few years he's been in charge of ensuring the Chinese population plays within the rules – the rules that its leaders decide upon, of course.'

Gordon stared at the photo a moment longer. Dunkley could see it was triggering a grim series of connections in his friend's mind.

'Remember that unrest in Tibet a year or two ago? Maybe forty or fifty monks were killed, rounded up like dogs. We heard reports of one isolated monastery being raided by Chinese soldiers who cut out the eyes of monks they believed were orchestrating protests against Beijing. Mr Zhou was in charge of all that.

'Harry, you are not playing with a nice guy. Zhou Dejiang is a nasty piece of work, even by the standards of the goons who've made their way up to the higher ranks of the Communist Party. So, what can you tell me?'

Dunkley fiddled with a beer that had lost its froth, then filled Ben Gordon in on the story: the DFAT phone call, the lakeside rendezvous, the car with diplomatic numberplates, the Embassy of Taiwan envelope on the picnic table.

'So– now we have two out of the three,' he concluded. 'Bruce Paxton and Zhou Dejiang. What do you reckon it means?'

Gordon took a sip of his house white. Gone was his flirtatious manner; he was now deadly serious. 'That phone call from DFAT could have come from anywhere. I could make that number flash on your phone with fifteen dollars worth of kit from Tandy Electronics. I wouldn't say that it's not our friends in Foreign Affairs, but we can't be certain that it is. It could have been ASIS, ONA; it could even be Defence intel – there are plenty of boffins in my agency who could masquerade as an intern at the White House if they wanted to. Of course, it could always be a spook attached to a foreign embassy.

'I don't know about the links between Bruce Paxton and Zhou Dejiang, I'll have to sniff around on that. But I do know that Paxton is hated by the military top brass and he, in turn, is paranoid about being spied on.' Gordon paused, instinctively scanned the room, and continued.

'Paxton thinks there are forces inside his department determined to bring him down. Remember, he's the first defence minister in a long time prepared to stand up to the hierarchy and call their bluff on their demands for more and more billions of dollars to splurge on the latest hi-tech gear from France or the States. He's on a one-man waste-watch campaign and the CDF and his sidekicks don't like it one little bit. The shouting matches, I am reliably informed, have been doozies.

'As for the third gentleman in your photo, he has a passing resemblance to Xiu Jeng, the former Chinese ambassador to Washington, but I would have to check that more thoroughly.'

Gordon locked eyes with Dunkley. 'Look, Harry, I don't know exactly what you've got, but there's a rich history there. Some very powerful people are gunning for Paxton. And if some of the bigwigs around town catch up with him, he could be toast.'

Dunkley was sceptical. Paxton might be a professional scumbag, but he was no fool. He had outwitted many people over the decades to advance his career and given the finger to those who'd deemed him too thick to make it in the caged ring of federal politics. Dunkley had spent too many years with some of the most conniving minds in the business to question Paxton's ability to survive.

'Doubt me if you like, Harry, but Paxton is in the sights of some very powerful people. And the fact that you have this photo means they want him gone. We need to find out who we're playing with. You mind if I borrow it for a few days?'

'No worries. I've already scanned it into our system and I was going to ask you to keep it in your safe.'

Dunkley felt the tingle of excitement that always came when he was onto a big yarn. And having Ben's help was a godsend. He knew too that he could trust Ben, his friend for nearly thirty years – and the man who wore the sharpest dresses in Australian intelligence.

Canberra, June 18

The morning sun was just visible through a thick fog as the prime ministerial car approached the main entrance of Canberra's public hospital, the vanguard of a small procession that included two parliamentary secretaries and a clutch of advisers. Despite the hour, a gaggle of journalists was on hand to form a loose guard of honour.

The bulletproof glass distorted the outside world but Martin Toohey recognised several straightaway. 'Christ, those bloodsuckers ...'

Across from the entrance, a half-dozen satellite trucks were parked on the hospital grounds, beaming live footage of the prime minister's arrival to a national audience. Although it was Saturday, the networks had been broadcasting since 6am, trying to turn a moment of hard news into a continuous reel of infotainment.

The crews had been told that Toohey would have nothing to say. What they would get in several hours of broadcasting was one shot, endlessly repeated, of several white cars pulling up and the prime ministerial entourage solemnly proceeding into the hospital, ignoring the media demands.

But that was not the point. In the world of twenty-four-hour news, what was happening was often secondary to 'being there'. The networks and the news channels had their best-known anchors in position outside the hospital. In a country where not much happens, the near death of a foreign minister – and former national leader – was show-stopping stuff, even for a public that mainly despised politicians. Catriona Bailey was a celebrity and Australia had all too few.

So the semi-famous anchors in the studio would cross to the really famous anchors in front of the hospital and they would reminisce and speculate. About every half-hour they would replay the final moments of Bailey's fateful *Lateline* interview, now an internet sensation. In between they would host guests who had some level of expertise in politics or health or, even better, some personal association with the stricken foreign minister.

The ABC went for foreign-policy wonks and academics, while Sky plumped for political insiders and journalists from *The Australian*. But it was the commercial stations that, as always, showed real enterprise. Already this morning, an executive producer at Nine had sacked one of his underlings because Seven's *Morning Glory* had beaten his *Wakey Wakey* to Bailey's primary-school teacher.

Felicity Emerson had appeared on a stool next to the king of morning television, Peter Thompson, affectionately known nationwide as Thommo. She had regaled the audience with a heart-warming story about how a poor but socially aware six-year-old Bailey had offered her battered teddy to the Red Shield Appeal in place of money she didn't have.

'So she always had a deep social conscience,' Thommo prompted Emerson.

'Oh yes,' Emerson beamed, warming to the task of embroidering the past, 'and I remember saying at the time, that girl will do great things.'

Nine was already starting a long way behind Seven in this story because the nation knew that Thommo and Bailey shared a special friendship, struck years before she had become prime minister.

Together they had dived the Barrier Reef to highlight the threat of global warming and had shamed the former Coalition government into spending more money on cancer research. Bailey was an official member of the exclusive *Morning Glory* family.

Now, about fifty metres from the media melee, Toohey got a text message.

Mate, consider it personal favour if u stop 4 a chat,
Thommo

'Fuck,' seethed Toohey. 'The bastard will make me pay if I don't talk to him and everyone else will crucify me if I do.

'We'll plough through the pack and deal with the consequences later. We've got the reasonable defence that this is too solemn a moment for us to be doing doorstops.'

A wall of light and sound – the flash of cameras, the shouts of reporters, the whirr of motor drives – bombarded him as he emerged from the car.

'Prime Minister, a moment ...'

'How are you feeling today, PM?'

'Do you regret knifing her?' came Thommo's familiar voice. A question designed to provoke a reaction.

Toohey didn't blink. His face was grim determination as he walked through the hospital doors, leaving the baying crews in his wake.

Moments later an awkward group formed around Bailey's bed. She lay still, pale, a drip in her arm, a monitor measuring out the slow beat of her heart.

Toohey asked the obligatory question of her specialist. 'How's she doing?'

'Not good. It will be touch and go.'

Toohey surprised his colleagues with his response: 'Can you please give me a moment alone with her?'

Confused looks were exchanged, but everyone was quietly relieved to be able to leave the room.

As the group moved out of earshot, Toohey looked down on his fallen colleague.

'You selfish bitch.'

Canberra, June 19

Kimberley Gordon had bought her two-level townhouse in 'the Paris end' of Kingston four years earlier, regretting none of the significant outlay. Enterprising agents regularly told her – at the time *him* – that she could sell for a handsome mark-up, but Gordon was having none of it. She needed some stability in her private life, which had swung between disaster and catastrophe for much of the twenty-five years since she'd left Sydney.

She'd arrived in the national capital in late 1985 after a five-hour drive down the Hume, negotiating two rainstorms and the treachery of a single-lane highway that snaked around Lake George.

She'd gone straight to work in ASIO, surprised and delighted that her peculiar blend of talents and obsessions could be put to good use in the national interest. She'd spent years building up her credentials and skills, proving to her superiors that she could be trusted with the nation's most sensitive matters, even while wearing the most revealing of dresses. She was a fastidious worker and was now far too valuable for DSD to let go.

On this late Sunday morning, the apartment filled with the scent of fresh lilies from the nearby Bus Depot markets, Gordon poured a black coffee from her Diadema espresso machine before firing up her impressive network of computers.

'Thunderbirds are go!' she quietly encouraged herself.

Though she owned one of the most expansive private databases and most secure networks of computers in Australia, the task seemed daunting. She was starting with just two names – Bruce Paxton and Zhou Dejiang – plus a mystery third man and the Acacia marking. It was an intriguing cocktail, one that had immediately captured her imagination, and one that would have been far easier to understand if she could have accessed the DSD's vast data banks. But working on a project like this at the directorate was a huge no-no – every keystroke was logged and employees who breached the strict security protocols would be quickly shown the door. Or worse.

First, Zhou Dejiang, Gordon thought. An impressive CV sprang to life, courtesy of Gordon's access to Chinese data and her fluency in Mandarin. Much of it was already known to her; she had memorised the names and spouses of most of the top ranks of the Chinese Politburo – the murderers and torturers who controlled the daily lives of the mighty nation's 1.3 billion folk.

Okay, thought Gordon, we know about his upbringing, his graduation from the University of Peking, a stint at London's School of Economics – his first taste of the West – his return to Beijing and ascension to the upper levels of the communist regime. But what was the photo trying to say? What were his links with Paxton? Where did they start and where did they lead?

Gordon punched in 'Bruce Paxton' to see what would emerge and wasn't disappointed when a lengthy list was displayed on her main screen. Database One was doing its job, uploading line after line of information about Paxton's career in the United Mineworkers and his first taste of notoriety when a march on the West Australian parliament got out of hand and Paxton and a few of his cronies ended up in the back of a paddy wagon on the way to an overnight stay in Perth Central.

Another coffee was needed to get the brain into gear. Even security analysts succumbed to the lazy vibe of Sunday mornings. Gordon was making slow progress, but patience and diligence were the keys to good intelligence gathering. The most valuable breakthroughs rarely came without hour upon hour of often tedious research and mind-numbing checking. This task would be no different.

Zhou Dejiang and Bruce Paxton – what *was* the link? And the mystery third face in the photo? That would need another kind of software: face recognition technology. Australia's intelligence community – flush with funds after 9/11 – had invested heavily in this software breakthrough. The Australian Federal Police, ASIS, ASIO and even some of the states had rolled it out. Gordon had been impressed when shown how it worked and had managed to persuade a contact at the AFP to 'lend' her a shadow program.

Now it was time to put this sucker into action. Harry Dunkley, she knew, had been making inquiries of his own about Zhou Dejiang, but the two had made little headway on the third face.

The original pic lay on the table before her. She scanned it and highlighted the face of the unknown third man before revving up the application. The minutes ticked by, the software refusing to give up the man's identity.

Yet another fill of coffee – and when Gordon returned the screen had frozen on two images. The scan of the original photo and a match.

Zheng Wang. The name meant nothing to Gordon and, irritatingly, the program had spat out only those two words. She keyed them into another database and an immediate jumble of information appeared.

Gordon scrolled through page after page, none featuring accompanying photos. After a fruitless thirty minutes, she made a note of the file before closing down her computer network.

She made for her hall cupboard, a splendid seventeenth-century French piece crafted from solid oak, to grab a scarf and her favourite cashmere jacket.

A walk in the brisk Canberra air was called for, to clear the head and get the circulation flowing in feet that had been cramped by a new pair of Tods.

She would deliver the name of the third man to Dunkley, let her friend take on the quest to find the meaning in it, while she focused on the more pressing task of chasing down the link between China's top spy and Australia's defence minister.

Canberra, March 31

She had nipples like bullets and was not afraid to flaunt them.

Emily Brooks was a warrior of the hard right whose hatred of the Greens was surpassed only by the contempt she had for moderates in her own party. The self-appointed patron saint of the Liberals' 'harden-the-fuck-up' faction, Brooks was a disciple of Thatcher and Reagan. But when it came to the bedroom, she knew no ideology.

'So, how was your day, my little meister of spin?' she asked of tonight's conquest, a smallish man with an extended ego.

They had arrived separately at her mock-Tudor apartment – a five-minute drive from Parliament House – saying little before shaking off their clothing.

'Very productive, Emily. We managed to get the 6pm yarn away in record time.' He poured another glass of pinot gris, studying her form in the semi-dark.

Brooks was nearly fifteen years his senior. But he cared not a jot. What she lacked in nubility, she more than made up for with erotic experience.

They had made love on the rug in front of her fireplace, careful not to stain the lovely handwoven piece that had been transported back to Australia after one of her jaunts to the third world. It was now approaching 10.30, time to turn on that communist broadcaster, the ABC, for the nightly dose of *Lateline*.

Brooks nonchalantly checked her Cartier watch. 'I had a productive day too. That leader of mine, what a wonderful political talent she is, don't you think?'

Her words dripped with sarcasm. Brooks, a Queensland senator, was known to bear a deep hatred of her leader, the very small-l Elizabeth Scott, who she considered had sold out the Liberals' 'tough love' philosophy for a limp-wristed pandering to inner-city elites. It was sending the party base feral – the federal director had recently shown Brooks deeply distressing secret focus-group polling. In the minds of ordinary voters there was now little discernible difference between the government and the opposition.

Martin Toohey might be hanging on by a thread as prime minister, but Scott was also failing to make inroads with the swinging voters the Coalition needed to regain the executive ministerial suites. Something had to give and Brooks, arch-conservative and master plotter, had her sights on the weakest link. It was the Darwinian way, after all. But she needed a loyal lieutenant – or better still, a gullible member of the fourth estate – to carry out her dirty work.

Stretched out on her Assyrian rug, his fingers clasping the stem of an expensive wineglass, looking cute and too buff for his own good, Brooks's lover would come in handy, in more ways than one.

Canberra, March 1

Forty-three pages of crap, every single fucking word. Bruce Paxton was furious with his top brass, incensed at being stuffed around by a Defence hierarchy that was used to getting its own way with ministers too easily dazzled by expensive military toys.

Two weeks ago – just before jetting out of Australia – Paxton had given his departmental secretary, Hugh Trounson, strict instructions to prepare an interim savings plan for the coming Budget. He wanted fair dinkum cuts too, not the cosmetic bullshit that Defence was used to serving up. He had hoped the bureaucracy would play ball. He needed help to find the considerable reductions required to meet the government's strict fiscal targets. Its grim determination to return to surplus by 2013 was not negotiable.

There were just nine weeks till the Budget, and Paxton was preparing for a showdown. The Budget razor gang had given him an ultimatum: either come forward with $15 billion in savings over the next four years, or we'll do it for you.

And, for once, those fiscal goons in Treasury and Finance, those economic nazis who pranced around Canberra pretending they owned the place, were in the driver's seat – and they weren't about to take their foot off the brake.

All ministers had been ordered to perform heroics with their portfolios. Savings, savings, savings – that was the mantra flowing through the bureaucracy as the Toohey government tried to dig itself out of a big hole by preaching the virtue of economic responsibility. And the Greens and independents were letting all their newfound power go to their heads, telling the prime minister that he should wind back some of the extravagant spending in Defence, which had been off limits since 9/11. 'Overblown balance-of-power shitheads,' Paxton liked to call them.

He leafed through the document again, took a gulp of his tea and grimaced, not for the first time that day. Defence had shirked it, big time.

'Jesus, Rhys, this really is kindergarten stuff. Do those bastards think I'm going to buy it? And Cabinet?'

Unlike his boss, Paxton's chief of staff, Rhys Smyth, combined street smarts with a tertiary education and had emerged as a valuable backroom operator in a portfolio that had chewed through eight ministers in fifteen years.

If he wasn't careful, Smyth sometimes thought, Bruce Paxton would end up as number nine. Smyth had been with Paxton from the day he was sworn in as defence minister. He'd been brought in as a troubleshooter, at the direct request of the PM, to help out Paxton, who many thought was in over his head. Since then, Paxton and Smyth had forged a close and trusting relationship, Paxton surprising Smyth and other senior players in the government by getting on top of the tough portfolio. Together they'd seen through the military bullshit, even insisting that the chief of the defence force, Air Chief Marshal Jack Webster, and his three-star companions revert to economy class for short-haul domestic flights. The brass had hated it. But this was their toughest fight yet.

A knock on the door interrupted the two men. 'Minister, the CDF and secretary are here to see you.'

'Tell them to wait. I want to keep them on edge a little longer.' Paxton stood up and loosened his tie. He knew the next thirty minutes would be ugly, but he wanted to show the two men that he meant business.

Both would be dressed impeccably, Paxton knew, Webster in four-star military splendour and Trounson – well, he took his fashion advice from his former boss, Paul Keating, that poser from Sydney who now spent his time ripping into the party he had once led.

'Fuck 'em,' Paxton said with resolve. He removed his black-gloved prosthesis and pulled his favourite hook from the desk drawer.

More and more it was clear to him that the defence of Australia was not just about life and death or protecting the citizenry from hostile foreign forces ... no, on many occasions, it seemed to be more about protecting a multi-billion-dollar industry that relied on gullible governments being sweet-talked into supporting massive projects and equipment deals. In the time he'd been in the portfolio, Paxton had marvelled at the ability of the military to sound convincing as they argued that the taxpayer must stump up for the latest hi-tech gadget, the latest weapon to kill. The two men about to enter his room were among the very best – true veterans who had been trained by some of the finest to either capture or destroy their minister.

The Defence regime had been out of control for years – Bruce Paxton was about to seize back the levers, for the sake of the Budget … Jesus, for the good of Australia.

'Gentlemen, take a seat, let's get down to business.' Paxton's gleaming hook caught the light from the window as he beckoned them in.

The CDF and secretary noted that the minister had dispensed with the usual pleasantries. It went downhill from there.

'I gave you firm orders to deliver a savings plan to me by the time I got back from OS – a serious savings plan outlining how Defence could deliver on the government's intention to shave half a per cent from department outlays over the course of the next year. Simple, right? A down payment, gentlemen, on what will be a much bigger return to the taxpayer. I wanted real savings, a sign from you that Defence is serious in meeting what the government is demanding of all departments.

'Instead, you deliver this crock of shit.

'Am I filthy? Yep. Will I stand for it? NO. NO. NO. Do not underestimate my resolve to extract a great big dividend from the Defence Department. Do not, for one minute.'

Paxton slammed his hook down on his desk, and a chip of wood arced over the heads of his guests. He paused, scooped up the Defence document and flung it across the room. The Defence men sat poised, unflinching in the face of this ministerial tirade. Their expressions never faltered. Paxton was on the warpath and in a foul mood, as they had anticipated. They were copping plenty of flak but had expected that; as with most skirmishes, the enemy would soon run out of ammunition.

'I wanted more than a rehash of previously announced plans. Yes, I know that when Bailey was PM she led the charge for a big increase in military spending. Yes, I know the White Paper called for a $130 billion expansion of our military capability. But that was two years ago and you knew then that it was bloody unrealistic.'

Paxton motioned to his chief of staff, who handed documents to the CDF and secretary.

Webster and Trounson read quietly and slowly, carefully avoiding any display of emotion. They were, after all, masters of the art of camouflage. But as they digested the words in front of them, their internal thermometers rose towards boiling point.

What the minister was proposing was preposterous, a major cutback to the $8 billion program to build three air-warfare destroyers and, even worse, the first serious hint of cuts to the $16 billion purchase of up to one hundred F-35s through the Joint Strike Fighter program.

Eventually they looked up, the CDF clearing his throat before carefully speaking his mind. 'Minister, you can't be serious. What you are proposing would, in my view – and I am sure Secretary Trounson would agree – it would compromise Australia's national security. And that, Minister – well, that is a very big call.'

'That's bullshit and you know it, Jack.' Paxton rarely called the CDF by his first name, but he was fired up. 'The bottom line is this. Budget cuts are inevitable, you know that as well as I do.'

Trounson spoke up. 'Minister, what about the build-up by China of its military assets in the Pacific? It's off the charts. It will have three aircraft carrier groups by 2025. It will control our trade routes. And Beijing is ploughing billions into the region, buying favour, acting as a kind of pan-regional financier. We don't want to leave ourselves exposed. The Americans are nervous, as you know, and so should we be.'

Paxton fixed the secretary with a hard stare. 'Why should we be nervous? Maybe it's time for some strategic realignment. China is our biggest trading partner. It makes more motor cars in a day than our fucking industry makes in a whole year. It has a middle class of some 200 million people and it's growing like topsy. Our future lies far more with China than it does with America.'

He was warming to a theme now. 'Perhaps the time is right for a shift in our thinking. The Americans have their hands full with Afghanistan, and Obama, for all his rhetoric, has scant interest in the Pacific. The Stars and Stripes ain't what it used to be, fellas.

'What I'm suggesting not only makes good sense from a Budget point of view, it will also send a clear message to the region – particularly to Beijing – that Australia is no longer interested in playing deputy sheriff to the US, to being its lickspittle in the Pacific. Do you understand?'

Paxton waved his hook menacingly as his words ricocheted around the room, so extraordinary the CDF and secretary could scarcely believe them. Was Paxton, Australia's minister for defence, really suggesting Canberra cosy up to Beijing at the expense of Washington? Was he suggesting that ANZUS, that proud strategic compact that had served the Americans and its two south Pacific partners so well for sixty years, was reaching its use-by date? For nearly twenty minutes, they listened as Paxton outlined a plan that, if it was allowed to proceed, would destroy Australia's seventy-year-old military alliance.

Shaken, the two men rose from their seats and collected their briefcases. They were too professional to show emotion but both of them were livid. They were used to the occasional dressing-down from a minister but Paxton's diatribe had gone too far. This was a declaration of war.

Canberra, April 1

Jonathan Robbie pondered his script. Every word had to count, and every word was counted. A small box at the top of the INews template on his computer screen remorselessly ticked off the seconds.

A word had to add something because it stole a fraction of a second. So none could be wasted, inappropriate or out of place. Those print profligates don't really appreciate words, Robbie thought. They have the luxury of too many of them.

Robbie worked in the most punishing place in media, as a senior political reporter for Channel Nine, one of Australia's three commercial TV news stations. The 6pm bulletin was still where most Australians got their news and each night 1.2 million of them tuned to Nine. The competition was fierce; more so now that advertising dollars were haemorrhaging to cable TV, free digital stations and new media. Everyone's profits were down, nobody knew what the future held and so the pressure for an ever bigger, attention-grabbing splash grew.

'I don't care what the fuck you write,' Robbie's news director would say. 'Just don't bore me with pointy-headed policy. Politics is about conflict. Cover the fight. And cover it first.'

Each night, if he made the cut against fatal crashes, crime, fires and heart-rending animal stories, Robbie had just ninety seconds to grab the nation by the balls.

Robbie was a latecomer to journalism. He didn't fall into it until he was thirty, and was hired by the *Daily Telegraph* as probably the world's oldest cadet. He'd never looked back, and made his name covering lurid crimes on the Sydney tabloid's police beat.

Then came an unusual approach. With the pending retirement of press gallery legend Laurie Oakes, Channel Nine came knocking, even though Robbie had never worked in TV and knew nothing about politics.

Desperate to maintain its dominance of the 6pm bulletin on the east coast, Nine had reset its news sensibilities to the shock and scandal end of the scale and gambled on someone with flair, someone who could take the piss and who knew how to sell stories to punters.

It was a challenge Robbie would have found hard to resist at any price. But the price on offer was breathtaking.

Robbie was no Laurie Oakes. All he cared about was making a splash, not accuracy. He found the competition in the press gallery brutal, and making the contacts he needed to break news took time he didn't have. He was prepared to cut corners to make an immediate impression. He was the press gallery version of a radio shock-jock.

Robbie never set out to make anything up – but near enough was always good enough. He would run on the mere sniff of a story, never waiting for a second source to confirm something that sounded good.

And tonight, ironically April Fools' Day, he had a yarn that would put a torpedo hole in the side of the opposition leader, Elizabeth Scott. He was about to break the news that a Canberra bureaucrat was a Liberal Party mole – leaking information to Scott to damage the Toohey government.

And, for once, he was pretty sure it was true – because he'd received plenty of help from inside her tent.

Canberra, June 22

The soft melody of Neil Young's 'After the Gold Rush' washed over him. Harry Dunkley loved the Canadian songsmith's music and his ventures into melancholy, a place he knew well. He was not about feeling sorry for himself but there were moments, quiet times like these, when he would reflect on what life had thrown up, on the regrets that gnawed away at him. With a glass of red in his hand, tired and frustrated after another day doing battle with a government of liars and schemers, intent on total control, the song brought on memories he fought to forget.

Sydney's State Theatre – 1992? '93? They'd held hands tight, in love for the first time, or was it the last? He'd promised a lifetime of happiness as they'd taken their vows, a garden wedding with a celebrant, some distant relative with a trilling voice that had given them the giggles.

But Belle had left the national capital four years ago for a life away from politics and the wreckage of their marriage. She'd grown bored with Canberra, bored with him, sick of eating alone in their Red Hill home with its neat brick-and-tile symmetry.

After she fled he'd gone looking to fill the hole, testing other bodies against his own, but casual flings had never satisfied him. Canberra was a city dedicated to the transient relationship, with its parliament full of cheating hearts and daily lies. His brief loveless efforts to satisfy a yearning that could not be met had convinced him he wanted none of it.

Besides, work had always been his deepest passion, his finest affair; he adored the constant calls for the 'splash' from the news desk, the need to stay a step ahead of the competition. The press gallery had once soared with an esprit de corps born of a conviction that it was defending democracy, taking on the bastards, fulfilling an important role in a free country. But these days the bureaus resembled bank offices with diligent tellers churning through work like automatons, counting the bucks, making it all tally, taking orders from the government of the day, waiting for the truck to back up.

Ah, he hated the soulless parade, the battery-hen mentality.

He knew he should stop wallowing and call his daughter. Gaby had left another message, this one a notch up on last week's. She needed his help with some university assignment and was unimpressed that he'd ignored her pleas, not for the first time. He began rehearsing an apology he'd learned so well. 'Sweetheart, sorry, so sorry …'

Why did his interactions with his daughter always make him feel like a lousy dad? He would lay down his life for her, his angel. She knew that. They shared a talent for teasing each other, sensing each other's vulnerabilities and only occasionally overstepping the mark. They revelled in secret word games and cryptic conversations outsiders could not follow. The connection with his daughter made him feel special. Alive. He loved her with all his flawed heart. But he didn't pick up the phone.

He gazed around his apartment, if it could be called that, located at the back of a blond-brick home in Canberra's inner south, a convenient drive to parliament along a twisting maze of back roads.

It was comfortable enough, one decent-sized bedroom and another, smaller, that doubled as storage space, not that he had much of value to store. Belle had done well from the settlement, leaving him with a suitcase of regrets. He treasured an old Olivetti, a gift from his first boss, a true legend of old-school journalism. A cigar-chomping, womanising, free-wheeling rascal who drank himself to death, leaving a legacy of great writing and even grander tales that were still fondly recounted by the old-timers down at the Press Club.

34

Harry was snapped from his reverie by his BlackBerry heralding a text message from Ben Gordon.

This gets more interesting by the hour, my friend. Let's stay on it. Kimberley x

---

Canberra, June 23

Another day, another chapter of the Bailey media circus. Each change in her condition, no matter how tiny, was being regurgitated on an endless 24/7 media loop. Dunkley's print rivals were devoting copious column centimetres to the story. Which meant that he too was trapped into feeding the daily beast. Half-heartedly he put the finishing touches to a tedious fifty-centimetre piece on what it meant for the future of the government, citing two constitutional experts and a former party hack.

He'd just filed when the phone rang, an immediately recognisable number lighting up the screen. It was Mr DFAT, the same cultured voice from ten days earlier. 'Afternoon, Mr Dunkley, trust you were intrigued by my little present?'

Intrigued? That was an understatement. Everything about you, mate, even your phone number, could be a lie, Dunkley reflected.

Gordon had already delivered some solid intel about Zhou Dejiang and Bruce Paxton – the date of their first meeting in Beijing, records of the various times they had met since. On the third man they just had two words: Zheng Wang.

'Nice to hear your voice again, whoever you may be,' Dunkley replied in a mocking tone. 'You wouldn't care to reveal your identity?'

'Not yet, Mr Dunkley. Some things are best done behind the cloak of anonymity. But I'm interested to find out if you've made any progress.'

What did Mr DFAT want? To damage the minister? Destroy the government? Or, as had happened before, to set Dunkley up for a fall? Gordon's warning about the internal jihad against Paxton meant Dunkley needed to be cautious.

'Well, I was interested to receive a 25-year-old pic of our defence minister with a senior official in the Chinese government, one Zhou Dejiang.'

'Very good, Mr Dunkley. And the other face in the photo?'

'I'm still working on that.' Dunkley wanted to give no hint of Gordon's involvement.

'The past always points to the future, Mr Dunkley – this case is no exception.'

And with that little homily, Mr DFAT hung up.

Dunkley was puzzled by his mysterious informant. In his long experience he had never come across anything quite like this. He was always careful, but knew he had to proceed more cautiously than usual. He was part of someone's game, but then journalists always are. He just needed a clearer idea of whom he was playing with. And what they wanted. He feared it was a deadly game and he didn't want to appear on the casualty list.

Dunkley had suspected he would have to delve way back into Paxton's past if he wanted to solve this puzzle, and Mr DFAT had just confirmed it. Happily, the looming five-week winter break meant he would have more time to pursue the defence minister. He was going to have to wear out some shoe leather – and he would take leave to do it. He would work in the old way, checking every detail. This yarn was not grist for the 24/7 mill. He glanced at his watch: 3.13pm That made it lunchtime in Perth.

Canberra, Four years before present

Elizabeth Scott had not just broken the glass ceiling, she had destroyed it. Born into a wealthy family on Sydney's moneyed North Shore, she had the talent to make the most of her privilege and, by forty-two, had amassed a personal fortune topping $100 million. *Business Review Weekly* tagged her 'Australia's most formidable business figure' and splashed her arresting image across its cover, her athletic body wrapped in the figure-hugging fencing gear she'd worn as an Olympian. With her chestnut hair spilling to the shoulders of her white jacket she looked dazzling and dangerous.

The business world was staggered when, in 2004, she had turned her hand to politics. Everyone immediately assumed she was on a relentless path to the Lodge.

But a seat in parliament had not come easy. She'd had to blast out a sitting member from the blue-ribbon electorate of Warringah on Sydney's northern beaches. So by the time she arrived in Canberra, Scott already had more enemies than most.

It was not until the spring of 2006, a year before his political demise, that John Howard elevated her to the newly created portfolio of Water and Climate Change, pleading with her: 'Elizabeth, just get me back in the environmental game.'

The nation was in the grip of a crippling drought, water restrictions biting deep and the bushfires coming savage and early. The steady pulse of suburbia quickened as fear grew that climate change posed a real and present danger. John Howard, tapped into the values and aspirations of middle Australia, had recognised the political danger of doing nothing. The doctors' wives were in revolt and he needed a safe pair of hands, a believer in climate science and, critically, someone the public would trust.

Elizabeth Scott had fitted the mould perfectly. But the Libs were starting well behind Labor, whose crafty new leader, Catriona Bailey, was using climate change as a totemic part of her pitch for the future. She had handed responsibility for the portfolio to one of her best, Martin Toohey.

Scott and Toohey had been catapulted into one of the most quirky relationships in politics, that of a minister and her shadow. One had all the resources of government at her disposal and her job was to manage a particular area of state. The other, with the aid of a handful of staffers, spent all his waking hours stalking and trying to destroy the minister.

The incestuous nature of politics meant they spent a good deal of time in each other's company, attending the same events and trudging to the same dismal dinners in all parts of the country. The close study Martin Toohey made of Scott's character during the long hours in her orbit convinced him that, despite her obvious brilliance, she would never cut it in politics. Her two fatal flaws were a lack of political judgement and impatience.

Their first meeting had been at the reception desk of the Embassy Motel in the inner-south Canberra suburb of Deakin. Scott could have easily afforded to buy a luxurious home, but preferred to let it be known that she stayed in cheap digs.

Now, as she checked in on a frigid Canberra afternoon, she was disturbed by a familiar voice. 'Minister, you must be lost. The Hyatt is on the other side of Parliament House.'

Scott knew who Toohey was, of course. The tall Victorian had been a player in federal politics for years. He had been a junior minister in the Keating government and had held a number of senior shadow ministries since. He was well liked and well regarded, considered a decent man by both sides of politics. But all agreed he lacked the venom needed to take leadership.

'Now it *is* clear that I'm slumming it,' Scott responded. 'But it's too late to move.'

'See you about.' And he'd sauntered off.

And see him about she did. The Embassy's staff played a long-running in-joke on them, rooming the two political up-and-comers next to each other whenever they were both in Canberra. Many a time, Scott would be fumbling with her room keys close to midnight when Toohey's familiar silhouette would come striding down the hall towards her.

'Night, Minister,' he would say. 'Hope that dreadful policy of yours doesn't keep you awake.'

Finally, forced to sit next to each other on a flight from Darwin to Melbourne, they'd started to chat properly. About the absurdity of the parliamentary lifestyle. About how much they missed their families. About the tribulations and humiliations of being a public figure.

In the final sitting week before the 2007 campaign was announced, Scott and Toohey had arrived at the Embassy at the same time.

'Well, it won't be long now. Howard has to announce soon,' Toohey said.

Scott agreed. 'Then it will be six weeks of hell before we're creamed.'

'Sounds like a reason to celebrate to me. How about a drink?'

Scott hesitated for a moment. 'Okay, but not here. And not somewhere we'll be seen.'

'I know a place in Woden,' said Toohey. 'Most federal MPs wouldn't even know it's a Canberra suburb. But you're buying because you're loaded.'

'Lead on,' she said.

Peking, Twenty-nine years before present

A gentle rain tapped on her umbrella, the first sign of impending winter. It fell softly on the ocean of people silently sweeping by on their bicycles. Young, alone and giddy with excitement, her first venture onto the streets of Peking was a dream come true.

For as long as she could remember she had wanted to stand here, to soak up the history, to be part of this great nation with its flawed, intricately embroidered history. She couldn't think of a time when she wasn't attracted to all things Chinese.

Perhaps the spark had been the tiny Ming vase her mother had treasured. She'd marvelled at its delicate beauty, strictly off limits to young, inquisitive hands. Much like China itself, a mystery of politics and geography during the long decades of diplomatic isolation until Nixon and Whitlam extended the Western hand of comradeship, just ten years earlier.

China had been at the centre of the world for thousands of years. A civilisation making wonders like gunpowder while the West fumbled in a more brutish age. That was why the recent decades of humiliation at the hands of the West had been so hard for it to bear. She understood that and was angered by the West's oafishness. She knew that when China woke, nations would shudder. And when it woke she wanted to be part of its journey back to its rightful place: the centre of the world.

'Hey, sweetie!' An Australian accent, harsh and unpleasant, broke her blissful peace.

'Remember me?' The man standing beside her was stocky, with thick wavy hair and a toothy grin. 'Dinner last night ... all that Chinese tucker and not a decent sweet-and-sour to be seen. Anyways,' he gestured to her camera, 'would you mind taking a snap of us?'

She noticed then the two Chinese men, both in their mid-twenties, and somehow vaguely familiar. Had they been at the embassy as well? There was one more, a beautiful woman standing slightly apart from the others, but clearly attached to the group.

'Okay, smile for the camera.' She dutifully took the snap of the three men with the Kodak she'd bought in Hong Kong and promised to make a copy for the loud Australian.

And she did, plus another which she gave to a friend she'd made at the Australian embassy.

Canberra, Four years before present

The Elbow Room had all the charm of a 1970s brothel, or at least what Elizabeth Scott imagined one would look like. It was not a place she would normally dream of visiting, nor did she think she would ever return.

The tawdry lace and satin lampshades ensured the dismal glow that escaped them stained the room rouge. The lounges were op-shop chic and so dilapidated she almost sank to the floor when she sat down.

'How in God's name did you discover this small corner of hell?' she asked.

'Yes, I like it too.' Martin Toohey, from habit, surveyed the room for familiar faces. 'It was owned by a mate I played footy with. But for some unfathomable reason he went broke. I come here because no one else in parliament does. Also, they don't play music so loud that you have to yell to be heard. And, frankly, you can barely see your hand in front of your face, so being recognised isn't an issue.'

He stared at her through the scarlet haze. She looked good in any light but in here the small flaws of age were erased. It struck him, as if for the first time, that she was dangerously attractive: high cheekbones, chestnut hair, haunting grey-blue deeply intelligent eyes. She was wearing a wraparound dress that clung to her tall, lithe athlete's frame. Add the magisterial grace of her movements and Toohey began to wonder at the wisdom of his 'let's have a drink' suggestion.

'I have a question.' He cleared his throat and sank deeper into the faux-leather chesterfield. 'You don't have to answer but I'm intrigued. Are you only in politics to be prime minister?'

'I'll tell you if you answer this: why didn't you push to be leader over Bailey? You had more support. Do you lack the ambition – or the guts – to lead?'

He bristled. 'Oh, this is the "Toohey's a weak bastard" editorial I read in *The Australian* once a month.'

'I didn't say that.'

'Yes, you did. And yes, I did have more support. But not enough. If we got locked in a stand-off then everyone would lose. I would like to be PM. I think I will be. One day. United we have a shot at winning government. If I'd held out, Labor would be the loser. I put my party first.'

'Sounds noble. Sounds like you have yourself convinced.'

'So you do think I'm weak. You, of course, the famously tough negotiator, would have held out for everything and won nothing. That's a terrorist's bargain.'

'I don't think you're weak.' Scott sipped a very ordinary red and shuddered. 'But I do think we're very different. Yes, you have to risk it all to win it all. And yes: I came here to be prime minister. Why would you be a politician if you didn't want that?'

'To do something for your country,' Toohey answered. 'To make a difference. To try and leave things a little better than you found them.'

'I want to do all those things. And I don't think you can do them in our system without being prime minister. And I wouldn't have budged with Bailey because I believe I would do a better job than her. Or you. In the end it's individuals who make a difference, not groups. History is made by the unreasonable man … or woman. I think Bailey understands that; she's certainly unreasonable.'

'No,' countered Toohey. 'Here, the mob counts. Your liberal individualism jars. You're like the First Fleet jailers: never comfortable in the land, always looking to the horizon and yearning to leave. Labor was made by the jailed. We pitched our tent here. And we understood that only by sticking together could people thrive. We are the unique Australian political project and we built the fairest society on earth, despite you.'

Scott always enjoyed a contest and Toohey was proving more interesting than she had imagined. She had thought him pleasant but glib. Good with a quick political line but without the depth to imagine the next sentence. Now she sensed another layer and, despite herself, felt a surge of excitement.

As he spoke, Toohey leaned across the too-small table and locked her in his gaze. He had gentle eyes. Hazel. Just a touch on the green side. Age had weathered him, but he wore it well. The lines around his eyes and mouth suggested he laughed a lot. If it was true that you got the face you deserved by fifty, then he was clearly decent, but sharpened by experience. As he became animated he emphasised points with his strong, finely shaped hands, and a faint hint of aftershave drifted across the table. It was a clean smell, like fresh linen. She was drawn into his eyes and, for almost the first time since she was a teenager, Scott felt her body contract with desire.

It startled her and she realised he had stopped talking and she had paused a heartbeat too long. In fencing, the error would have been fatal. This game was getting dangerous, and she loved dangerous games.

'Do you lot ever tire of reinventing the past?' She recovered like a champion. 'It's a fine speech for the True Believers, but please don't delude yourself. This nation is as much a product of my political ancestors as yours. Labor opposed Federation. And the social compact here is liberal, built on individual rights. A party that respects everyone, no matter what their race, colour or creed.'

Toohey was revelling in the contest. He hadn't had this debate in years. The pub and the argument reminded him of late nights at uni. And there was that other intoxicant of youth he realised he had been missing for a long time – the company of a beautiful woman.

He cleared his throat and tried to clear his head.

'Australia proved the value of the group. The land was hard and settlers had to band together to survive. Workers had to fight for every single right. We learned through bitter struggle that solidarity was our most powerful weapon. The group makes the weak powerful. And it makes the powerful tremble.'

Scott gave up on the red and leaned towards Toohey.

'You can murder millions in the name of the group, Martin. Hitler, Stalin, Mao, all of them championed the many over the individual. The bedrock of the West is the truly revolutionary idea of a personal, individual relationship with God. Our law is built on it. Erase it and everything is negotiable. Yet demolishing our Christian keystone has been the Left's great project for over a century. Congratulations! You succeeded. And put nothing tangible in its place. Is it any wonder we are morally adrift?'

'Don't pull the cheap debating trick of hitching me to the Left's worst ideas, Elizabeth. Nice sermon, but your party uses its precious heritage to justify hoarding the wealth of many in the hands of a few. Mine understands that individual rights have to be balanced with the common good. And I know the Church, I was part of it once. Religion is the best and worst of us. At its worst it has slaughtered legions of innocents across every generation.'

'It wasn't the Church that was responsible for the mass slaughter of the twentieth century, Martin,' Scott smiled. 'It was the messianic state.'

Toohey paused. This was too much fun.

'If I might offer one gratuitous piece of political advice,' he said. 'Your impatience to lead and determination to dominate will tear your party apart.'

'Clearly I don't agree with you – again.'

'Or me with you. But if there has to be a Liberal Party and someone has to lead it … then it might as well be you.'

'Thanks. And I think you would have been a much better Labor leader than Bailey. That woman is certifiable, Martin, and I'm afraid you will live to regret not manning up on that one.'

'You don't think I'm tough enough.'

'I didn't say that. I think … I think you're … surprising.'

Toohey reached across the table and cupped her cheek in his hand. It was an impulse. She could have resisted, but she didn't. She leaned forward and kissed him gently, her tongue flirting with his lips as she slowly pulled away. The cheap wine tasted intoxicatingly better on him.

She was breathless. Her entire body tingled, her head felt light and the rouge-tinted room swirled for a moment. She wanted more, but knew she couldn't have it. She stepped back from the edge and grabbed the lifeline.

'I'm married,' she said, holding up her left hand in evidence.

'Me too.'

'Pity.'

'Yep.'

They stared at each other through the gloom for a few breathless moments.

'It's late,' he said. 'Let's go.'

Canberra, July 11, 2011

It was just over three hundred paces from the press gallery lair of Harry Dunkley to the office of the Clerk of the House of Representatives, the keeper of one of the most sensitive documents in the House, the Register of Members' Interests.

The bound volumes, maintained in alphabetical order, contained reams of information about every member elected to the parliament. No one, not even the prime minister, was exempt. And every MP was required to regularly update her or his pecuniary interests, providing details of hospitality received, family trusts liquidated and shares bought and sold. For any journalist prepared to sift through a mountain of information, it was a potential goldmine. And Dunkley was prepared to do the hard yards.

It was a Monday morning and parliament had finally taken its winter break, so things had quietened considerably. Even the fuss about Catriona Bailey's collapse had died down now that she had been in hospital for some weeks with no change. Finally Dunkley could focus on the Paxton mystery.

He had made the requisite appointment to pore over the register. And he'd asked for a specific folio from a specific date – the N-O-P-Q folio from 1996. He had a hunch, but he needed some proof. It was too soon to start making calls that would only set hares running.

The clerk's assistant carried the material to an anteroom, where Dunkley was waiting. Five minutes was all it should take, he hoped. Leafing through the fifteen-year-old document, he quickly found the entry he was seeking, a few lines that gave some credence to his embryonic theory.

The property had been sold just after Bruce Paxton entered parliament, as Dunkley had expected. Now he needed to find out where the money had come from to buy it. And that would take time even the reduced daily grind wouldn't allow. So, after he knocked off the Newspoll splash for tomorrow's paper, he was taking a long break.

Canberra, July 11

As regular as a metronome, Justin Greenwich would wake early every second Monday with a knot deep in the pit of his stomach.

The opposition leader's press secretary knew that, later that day, *The Australian*'s political editor, Harry Dunkley, would receive several pages of raw data that could make or break political careers. Eventually, Dunkley would call Greenwich to give him a heads-up on the numbers. Then it was Greenwich's grim duty to relay them to Elizabeth Scott. And she didn't take bad news well.

For two months, Newspoll had been a horror story for Scott and the Coalition she led. The slide had begun after a disastrous overreach by

Scott. A Channel Nine story by Jonathan Robbie had shattered her credibility, revealing she had groomed a Finance Department official, Michael Hamilton, to give damaging evidence against the government at parliamentary hearings.

Hamilton was a Liberal mole who had been funnelling information to the opposition for years. But, typically, an impatient Scott had pushed him hard and Hamilton grew reckless, handing over highly sensitive material on a financial rescue package for building societies in the wake of the global meltdown.

An internal investigation flagged Hamilton to the Australian Federal Police. As they watched, he continued to shovel out information to Scott. But it got worse when, in his eagerness to please, Hamilton fabricated some facts to implicate the prime minister in dubious dealings with a building society based in Toohey's electorate of Corio.

In what Greenwich saw as a cruel twist, Robbie broke the Scott–Hamilton link on April Fools' Day. It caused a sensation.

Scott wasn't responsible for the fraud, but it didn't matter. Perceptions were everything in politics. The media crucified her and the story refused to die. The Coalition had been ahead of the government in the polls but its primary vote dropped five points once the story aired. That was nothing compared to what happened to Scott's personal rating – it plummeted twenty points in a fortnight.

One thing that had surprised Greenwich at the time the story broke was Scott's insistence on seeing the prime minister to apologise in person. Greenwich had gone with her, but all staff were banished from the room. He didn't have to cool his heels in enemy territory long because the meeting was over in less than five minutes. Scott had been visibly upset when she emerged from Toohey's office.

Greenwich's BlackBerry rang.

'How bad?'

'Depends.' Dunkley's voice was friendly and Greenwich knew he was trying to soften the blow. 'The primary vote is basically stable on 39. But of course that still gives Labor a lead on two-party preferred, 52–48.'

'Don't toy with me, Harry.' Greenwich's voice quavered. 'You know there's only one thing she cares about. How is she tracking on personal satisfaction?'

'Satisfied, 21 per cent; dissatisfied, 62 per cent.'

Greenwich's hands were sweating so much he could barely write and his brain struggled to digest the figures.

'Jesus wept. Down four points on last fortnight?'

'Yes.'

'Down four points on what you said was the lowest rating of any opposition leader in Newspoll history?'

'Yes, it's bad.'

'What's the splash?'

'Well, the splash is something else. But on Scott we have a breakout reviving the famous *Bulletin* front page on Howard.'

'"Why does this man bother?"'

'Well, to be accurate: "Why does this woman bother?".'

'Harry ...'

'Yes, Justin?'

'I hope you die a lonely, slow and painful death.'

'You have a good night too, mate. See you about.'

The sweat from Greenwich's palms had made a damp spot on his pad, smudging some of the figures. But he could not erase the horror of what they meant.

With the right leader, the opposition would have been well ahead of the weak Toohey government. But these numbers held only one message: Elizabeth Scott wasn't that leader.

Scott was in the adjoining office, waiting for her press secretary to deliver the numbers. He looked at his pad again and picked up his mobile. His fingers fumbled with the tiny keyboard as he punched out a text message. Then he grabbed his bag, hitting 'send' as he scurried for the door.

He was in the corridor when a familiar voice echoed down the hallway.

'You are JOKING! Justin, get in here. NOW!'

And for the first time in many years, Greenwich broke into a sprint as he made for the exit.

Canberra, June 6

Two sleek BMWs with darkened windows and reinforced exteriors snaked up the steep driveway. They approached the circular drive with military precision, coming to a halt a few steps from the imposing front entrance of the Commonwealth Club. Three men wearing dark suits and even darker don't-fuck-with-me stares quickly emerged from the vehicles.

It was over-the-top and Brent Moreton, the newly arrived United States ambassador to Australia, loved every minute of it. He checked his Seiko Velatura – a personal gift from the president – and stepped out into the brisk Canberra air. He was dead on time for his first meeting with the Alliance.

Ambassador to Australia was a mid-level posting by Washington standards, a chance for Moreton to work with one of America's closest and most trusted allies – even if it was a country that most Americans had never visited and knew little about. Moreton had accepted the job without hesitation, viewing it as a stepping stone to a more exciting and important posting – or possibly as an entree to a seat in Congress.

He'd found the work satisfying but hardly intoxicating. Relations between the superpower and its Pacific cousin were in good shape, despite the occasional flare-up over trade. Until now.

Moreton walked briskly along a thickly carpeted corridor before entering a discreetly luxurious sitting room overlooking the club's garden, with views through to the lake. Four men were waiting, one in military regalia, the other three in crisp business suits, each of them cradling a beer or glass of wine.

'Ambassador, so very nice of you to come to our little gathering.' Jack Webster, chief of the defence force and a decorated former pilot, had met the ambassador a number of times over the years, mostly in Washington, where the two would cross paths during the Australian–American Leadership Dialogue and other bilateral talkfests.

Both were men of patrician bearing who loved their flags with a passion; both were dyed-in-the-wool patriots for the cause.

'Ambassador, I think you know Tom …'

Thomas Heggarty, director-general of the Australian Secret Intelligence Service, offered an outstretched hand.

'And Richard.' Richard Dalton, the director-general of the Australian Security Intelligence Organisation, had clocked up a year on exchange at the FBI.

David Joyce, secretary of the Department of Foreign Affairs, stepped forward next. 'Mr Ambassador, you look well, this Canberra climate is obviously agreeing with you.'

'I don't mind these sub-zero temperatures, David, although Janet is finding it tough to maintain her Texan tan.' There were laughs all round.

'Okay, let's get down to business.' Webster spoke firmly. 'We'll get the dinner orders happening; after all, we don't want to be disturbed too often.'

'Correction, Jack, we don't want to be disturbed at all.'

The ambassador fixed the four Australians with a look so serious he could have been announcing a death in the family.

*

46

The men took their seats, brushing away a waiter. Moreton clasped his hands and studied them, confident they could be trusted.

He knew that Webster, Heggarty, Dalton and Joyce met regularly at the club, drawn together by a common desire to protect – indeed nurture – the relationship with the United States amid a worrying trend on both sides of politics to forge ever-closer ties with China. Within the senior ranks of the Commonwealth public service, they were known as the most strident supporters of the US relationship and had dubbed themselves 'the Alliance' as a nod to the formal treaties binding the two countries.

Their meetings were shrouded in Freemason-like secrecy. The members told no one, not even their wives, of the gatherings, but the serving US ambassador had a standing invitation to attend.

Several days earlier, Moreton had contacted Webster on his secure private line, seeking an urgent meeting with the Alliance. He wouldn't give the reason over the phone, except to say it was of the utmost importance.

Now the ambassador began. 'Gentlemen, two weeks ago, I was summoned to DC for what I imagined would be a routine debrief on my first few months in Canberra. It was far from it.

'When I arrived at the State Department, I was taken directly to Assistant Secretary Robert Hinds's office; as you know he's one of Hillary's confidants.

'Guys, this is where it gets real touchy. Your defence minister, Mr Paxton ...'

Moreton's voice trailed off as he considered how best to phrase the coming bombshell. He trained his eye on Webster, and cleared his throat.

'Our government, at the very highest level, fears Mr Paxton is way too close to the Chinese. Given that we share our intelligence with you, this jeopardises us as much as it does you. I have been sent with a very specific message. Fix it or your access to our intel ends.'

The mandarins sat stunned.

The US was threatening to end what the Australian defence and intelligence agencies treasured above all else: access to the best intel money could buy. Thousands of spies and analysts and a spy satellite network, the Secret Internet Protocol Router Network (SIPRNET), that was, in the words of former defence minister Robert Hill, 'the greatest repository of information that exists'.

Webster finally spoke. 'What evidence do you have?'

The ambassador narrowed his gaze. 'It seems the secretary of state heard it direct from your foreign minister.'

47

_____

Canberra, June 19

As she'd prepared for her *Lateline* interview, Catriona Bailey had carried the worrying signs of an impending stroke. All the things she'd put down to tiredness would have disturbed a trained eye: dropping the glass, the dizziness, the trouble she had understanding questions, the headache, the difficulty she had writing.

It was her addiction to galloping about the world to insert herself in the news cycle that was at the root of the problem. A punishing series of jaunts had seen her more rundown than usual and she had picked up the flu on her way back to Canberra. Typically defying orders to rest, she'd ploughed on until a fever forced her to bed. Her fever had broken, but a blood clot had formed in her heart and had been pumped out and up a vertebral artery that merged with another at the base of the brain to form the basilar artery.

Here the clot had lodged. It had cut the flow of oxygen-rich blood to the brain's junction box, the pons, which suffered catastrophic damage.

And so Bailey had collapsed and appeared to be unconscious and unreachable. But she was not. She had suffered a very particular type of stroke and the effect was coma-like, but not a coma.

What Bailey was experiencing was locked-in syndrome. She had been completely unconscious for over a day, but then she woke. Bailey found she could hear and think clearly but was unable to move a single muscle in her body, even to open her eyes. And there was the problem. Others afflicted by locked-in syndrome could alert doctors to their fate by blinking responses. But Bailey's eyes remained firmly shut. In any case, her doctors were consumed by the task of simply keeping her alive. Even the most astute neurologist would have struggled to diagnose what was going on in Bailey's brain at this stage of her illness.

The first words she'd heard on waking came from a familiar voice.

'You selfish bitch.'

It was Martin Toohey, the bastard who had stolen the only thing that mattered to her: her job. The man she would never forgive.

And the man who didn't know that she had already laid a landmine that would destroy him and bring down his government full of traitors.

That thought of revenge empowered and sustained her. If she could have smiled, she would have.

_____

Canberra, May 16

For nearly a century, the Brookings Institution had been at the heart of every serious policy tussle in the US. A brisk ten-minute walk from the White House, it had also achieved the near impossible: in blindingly partisan Washington, it had the respect of both the Democrats and Republicans.

For Catriona Bailey, Brookings was as familiar and welcoming as the United Nations headquarters in New York. She had been a regular visitor for thirty years. As a student in the 1970s, Bailey had courted contacts at Brookings as a hooker courts her clientele. Her proudest moment came in April 2008 when she returned to Brookings as prime minister of Australia, making her first trip overseas aboard the Boeing 737 the Howards had ordered six years before. She had chosen Brookings as the venue for her first serious foreign policy speech, a statement that she was sure would resonate around the globe.

Bailey wanted to recast the relationship between the US and China, and saw herself as a regional intermediary, the Kissinger of the Pacific. Her speech – an opus stretching nearly fifty minutes – outlined her views on how to manage the rise of China and refashion the post-World War II power settlements to ensure China was a stakeholder in all decisions affecting global security. She argued that conflict between the US and China was avoidable and that the 'Pacific century' should be marked by a close working relationship between the Americans and Chinese.

It was a bold foray into global affairs, and well received by the policy wonks at Brookings, who were delighted to see one of their own elevated into a position of serious influence. Over morning tea, the Washington intelligentsia helped to fuel the notion that Cate Bailey was the woman the West needed at this vital hour, when the power balance was shifting east. Some said she could be the most important leader of her generation, the Thatcher of her time, a murmur Bailey did nothing to dispel with the travelling Australian media pack.

But it was a special meeting after the speech that helped lift that day into the stratosphere. The US presidential primaries were in full swing and Bailey's office, together with the Australian ambassador, had called in every favour to get 'face-time' and, more importantly, picture opportunities, with each of the three key candidates: the Republican frontrunner John McCain and the two Democrats who were still locked in a bruising struggle, Barack Obama and Hillary Clinton.

In the end, Obama proved elusive, and Bailey had to settle for a thirty-minute phone conversation with the black superstar, something her staff later paid for dearly.

But Hillary – well, that was a different equation. Clinton was an old friend, a member of the sisterhood and a Brookings fellow traveller. She called in for a delightful forty-minute chat with Bailey after her 'rise of China' speech.

So chuffed was Bailey by Clinton's show of support that she made a minor faux pas during the photo opportunity when the obvious question was asked: 'Are you backing Mrs Clinton for president?'

Bailey got that goofy look on her face that always emerged when she knew she was cornered. Clinton had done her an enormous favour, but how could a new Australian PM express a preference in US domestic politics?

'Well, you know me ... we girls have to stick together.'

Clinton beamed, taking it as an endorsement, a sentiment shared by the travelling media pack. The PM's media minders were forced to spend hours hosing it down, claiming it was nothing more than an expression of friendship, not a signal of preference over Obama.

Three years after she had delivered that brilliant speech, Bailey was back and so much had changed. Officially, Bailey was in DC as the foreign minister to hear Clinton, as secretary of state, address Brookings on what the Arab Spring meant for US relations in the Middle East.

Unofficially, she had a very specific message she intended to deliver.

After Clinton's speech the two friends sat down in the same room where, in 2008, they had met in such different roles. The irony was not lost on either of them.

'Things didn't exactly turn out the way we expected,' quipped Clinton.

'No,' said Bailey. 'I certainly didn't see it coming, did you?'

'For a long time Bill was convinced that we would win, and so was everyone else who mattered ... but what can you do? It's history; Obama has been surprisingly gracious and this is a great job.'

'So is mine,' Bailey lied. Just the memory of being prime minister was enough to make her wince. And she suspected Clinton felt the same about missing out on becoming the leader of the free world.

'There's something we're concerned about, Cate.' Clinton seamlessly switched to business. 'We hear from our embassy that your defence minister is considering making big cuts. Our people are keen to ensure your commitment to the Joint Strike Fighter is rock solid.'

'Hillary, you know that's sacrosanct,' Bailey said. 'I made it a priority when I was prime minister and Toohey has publicly backed it.'

'We aren't concerned about you or Toohey. We're concerned about Paxton. Is he committed to the alliance? His public remarks are quite pro-China.'

'Paxton's from Western Australia. They all love China because it's making them rich. I'm sure his past … dalliances … were meaningless.'

'Dalliances?' The alarm in Clinton's voice was obvious, and Bailey closed the net.

'It was a long time ago. He was just a union official on one of those visits the Labor Left used to make to China. It was the first time I met him. He was introduced to a young Tibetan woman, Weng Meihui. She turned out to be working for Chinese intelligence.'

'And the nature of this relationship?' Clinton leaned closer.

'Well, she was very … persuasive.'

'You're telling me that Australia's defence minister had a sexual relationship with a Chinese spy?'

'He wasn't defence minister then. And he hadn't seen her for years …'

'Hadn't?'

'Until three months ago. February. They met again over dinner.'

'Are you sure? How do you know?'

'Because, Hillary, I hosted it.'

Bailey paused to allow her friend to fully absorb the revelation before continuing. 'Look, Hillary, I'm sure it isn't serious.'

'Cate, I'm not so sure.'

'Hillary, no …' For the next ten minutes, Bailey launched a strident defence of Paxton. For the record. But, as she left, she knew the damage had been done. The clock was now ticking.

Canberra, July 12

'Those bastards, those grubby, calculating bastards.'

Sam Buharia sat with a neat espresso, dumbfounded by the front page of *The Australian*.

He both hated the national broadsheet for its relentless campaigning against Labor, and admired it for its audacious use of power. Hate media central, the Greens called it. But this morning, Rupert's flagship had gone too far.

BAILEY IN COMA OUT-POLLS TOOHEY

In an act of rat-cunning Sussex Street would have been proud of, the *Oz* had included Catriona Bailey in its fortnightly Newspoll. And just to ram home the point, the paper had splashed it all over page 1. Gleefully.

Bailey was ten points ahead of Martin Toohey as preferred prime minister – even more so with Labor voters – and twenty points in front of opposition leader Elizabeth Scott.

The imagery was devastating. A half-dead politician out-polling the PM screamed that Toohey was a dead man walking. The only good news, if any could be extracted from this stinking turd of a front page, thought Buharia, was that the dropkick of an opposition leader was stone motherless dead. If she was leading Labor, he would have capped her months ago.

Killing off leaders was something of a sport for Buharia. He was the one who signed the death warrant, leaving his loyal lieutenants to push the bodies down the elevator shaft. He'd had a hand in putting down two New South Wales premiers and one prime minister, a record unique in Australian politics. Unfortunately, he didn't seem to equate semi-regular assassination with long-term brand damage.

He was almost single-handedly responsible for what people dubbed the New South Wales disease: the poll-driven approach to politics that focused on spin and had wrung the last juices of idealism out of Labor's marrow. What was left were the dry bones of a once great party.

Buharia was obsessed with polling, particularly the focus groups of six to eight people who were gathered as litmus tests of community sentiment. He did not understand that the idea was to lead that sentiment, not follow it. Buharia's favourite saying after any focus group was, 'The punters hate it, mate.' One negative focus group on an issue was enough for him to start demanding that the government abandon multi-million-dollar projects. Several months of bad results saw him orchestrating Cabinet reshuffles.

He had coveted power from an early age and graduated from playground racketeering to Labor politics with ease. He had a gift for arithmetic and soon discovered that a man who could deliver numbers in Labor was a man to be reckoned with. He cultivated ethnic community leaders who could swing large groups of their people into ALP branches at a moment's notice. These flying squads would arrive at a branch en masse, sign up as members and then vote whichever way Buharia wanted.

And so Buharia had risen through the ranks of his party to be New South Wales secretary by the age of thirty, continuing the tradition of colourful characters who had littered Labor's past all the way back to its 1891 origins. But he lacked subtlety and foresight. He failed to see that just winning power was not enough to sustain a government, or a party. In the end you have to stand for something.

Watching appalled from Victoria, Brendan Ryan noted, 'Buharia thinks a year is 365 contests for the 6pm news. He's all tactics and no strategy. And what he's done is lose us his state for a generation.'

Buharia quit his role as secretary for the sinecure of the Senate before the full horror of his work in New South Wales was apparent. There he could enjoy a long career in relative anonymity. And continue to pull strings behind the scenes.

After about two minutes of absorbing the Bailey headline – a reasonably in-depth study by his standards – Buharia picked up his mobile and hit autodial 1.

'Rupert's dogs are barking,' the current New South Wales state secretary spat as he picked up.

'Yes mate, but what do we do about it?'

Canberra, July 12

Kimberley Gordon had difficulty remembering the first time she'd felt different. She had wrestled with her gender for more than two decades. She often confided in Harry Dunkley, even though her old friend was clearly uncomfortable talking about it.

Gordon was the product of a safe middle-class upbringing – as Ben, she'd attended a GPS school, enjoyed strong academic results, had an excellent sporting record and an inquiring mind. Then, in her mid-twenties, she'd felt a yearning to feminise her life. At her core she knew that her internal wiring didn't match her exterior. Dunkley would console her by saying, 'Everyone wonders who they are, mate; it's just that, for you, the question is more profound.'

Ben had bottled these feelings up upon her arrival in Canberra, conforming to the regimented life of a bureaucrat, unwilling to stand out in a city that did everything in its power to fade into the landscape. And she did not want to cruel her chances of promotion. She spent eight years in the Defence Signals Directorate, learning from one of the best analysts the agency had produced, Trevor Harris, before she worked up the guts to reveal all.

Unfortunately, her timing was bad. Harris was working flat chat on a Friday evening to finish a top-secret briefing for the prime minister on an operation gone wrong in Iraq when Gordon bowled up and burst out with, 'Trev, I'm going to change my name and identity—'

'Yeah, sure,' Harris said, waving a hand to indicate he was busy.

Gordon had considered a full sex change and done the research on what was required; she had even chosen a pretty name – Kimberley. But she'd decided against meddling with nature and instead opted for the less extreme life of a transvestite. She'd be a cross-dressing transformer working in one of the most secretive and paranoid arms of government – all six feet two inches of him … make that her.

When Gordon arrived at the DSD office the Monday following her announcement to Harris, the first hurdle she confronted was security – they wouldn't let her in. Harris fielded an irate call from the chief guard.

'Trev, we have someone down here who claims to be Ben Gordon.'

'And?' said Harris.

'He's a she.'

'Oh fuck …'

'That's what I said.'

'I'll be down in a minute.'

At this point Harris realised he should have paid more attention to Gordon's change-of-identity announcement.

But Harris went in to bat for her, extolling her analytical skills as some of the best in the business. The security clearance had then been routine, less trouble than Gordon expected. Reluctantly, the DSD hierarchy had given its blessing.

Harris's only request was for Gordon to be discreet when at meetings with other sections of the intelligence community. 'No flirting,' he had insisted.

That wasn't an issue. However, Gordon's insistence on using the female bathroom had caused a near meltdown.

Fifteen years later and Kimberley Gordon's cross-dressing lifestyle was now as routine as Friday night drinks. The women had even accepted her using their bathroom (but were quietly thankful when the agency installed a 'gender neutral' toilet).

From her kitchen a kettle whistle sang, stirring Gordon from her thoughts. There is work to be done, Ms Analyst, she said quietly to herself. She had been putting in long hours at DSD and there'd been precious little time to pick up her project with Dunkley. She'd finally squeezed a half-day off.

Dressed in a casual outfit she referred to as 'Target Chic', she was preparing to spend the next few hours immersed in what she imagined would be largely historical trivia. With just a few computers and a cup of steaming chai for company.

Whenever Gordon hit a dead end in analysis her routine was to radically shift thinking. What made her the best in her trade was her ability to imagine another path. In her experience, too much focus on minutiae meant you could miss the big picture. The photo was a tiny part of the huge story that was Australia–China relations. So she would set it and her secret databases aside. Gordon would now tackle the problem by using 'open source' material. And she would start with the woman charged with leading Australia's side of the relationship.

'Catriona Bailey, Catriona Bailey, Catriona Bailey.' Line after mind-numbing line of information about Ms Bailey consumed the computer screen, mostly mundane facts about the foreign minister's early years in politics, her rise to the highest office in the land – and then her quick demise.

Gordon was more intrigued by several pages of information that outlined Bailey's trajectory as an academic at the Australian National University. She had built an impressive list of achievements before choosing a life in the helter-skelter of politics.

But nearly hidden among the reams of facts and figures was a nugget so golden that Gordon gasped and leaned forward, eyes trained on a single line. Bailey had been in Beijing for three months in the early 1980s. About the same time that Paxton had visited the Chinese capital.

Canberra, July 13

George Papadakis scanned the room and called the meeting to order. He felt like a Soviet general at Stalingrad, hoping to survive the latest setback in a long siege.

He had assembled his best war cabinet to map out a strategy on what he called the Bailey Affair.

In the room were the convenor of the Victorian Right, Brendan Ryan; his NSW counterpart, Sam Buharia; the National Secretary, Alistair Cook; and Dr Sarah Franklin, a constitutional wizard.

Franklin was there because Bailey's staunch refusal to die meant that they were now in uncharted waters. The foreign minister had been in a coma for several weeks and while she thankfully hadn't woken up, she also didn't appear to be going away.

'Sarah, how long do we have to wait before we can declare Bailey's seat vacant?' Papadakis asked.

'Unfortunately, there is no direct precedent to follow,' Franklin replied. 'But the Constitution suggests she has to sign a letter of resignation to the speaker of the House of Representatives.'

'For Christ's sake, she can't sign, she's a veggie,' roared Buharia, who was getting cranky surprisingly early in the conversation.

'If she can't sign we can get someone to act as her agent,' Franklin explained. 'But we need to be able to establish that we have her permission. That is, we need to prove that she wants to resign.'

Brendan Ryan weighed in. 'In case my colleague didn't make himself clear, she has been on life support for weeks now. She's in intensive care and not expected to recover.'

'And you are certain she's incapable of understanding what's going on?' Franklin asked.

'Let's assume she's plant life.' Ryan confirmed Buharia's assessment.

'Well, if she's absent from parliament for more than two months, the speaker can declare her position vacant. But let's be very clear on this. In the one hundred and eleven years of federal parliament in this country no member's position has ever been declared vacant because he or she was absent without leave'

'Jesus, there must be some sort of time limit on how long you can represent a seat without showing up in parliament,' moaned Buharia.

'Not really.' Franklin warmed to her task; she had spent a week buried in the finer points of procedure and practice. 'The longest leave of absence on record is Adair Blain, an independent member for the Northern Territory. And this might shed a bit of chilly light on the current state of affairs: he was captured by the Japanese at the fall of Singapore in 1942, and then re-elected unopposed in 1943, while he was a prisoner of war. When he finally walked into parliament on 26 September 1945, wearing his uniform, after two years as a POW, he received a standing ovation. He was then granted another two months leave to recover in hospital.'

A shudder went through the room. This was harder than anyone anticipated, but it was par for the course when dealing with Bailey.

'I swear this woman is like some kind of medieval curse on the party,' muttered Ryan.

'Indeed, but if there is no precedent, we will have to make one,' Papadakis said. 'Her specialists tell me there is no likelihood of recovery. We need to get that in writing, then we need to write to the speaker asking that her seat be declared vacant. And the speaker needs to say yes.'

'What if the House intervenes?' said Franklin. 'What if the independents, the Greens and the Coalition refuse to countenance the removal of a member at the behest of a party?'

'She was elected as a member of this party,' raged Buharia. 'She can't do her job from intensive care. We have a right to replace her.'

'You have no right to do anything of the sort,' snapped Franklin, irritated by the routine ignorance of the law she so often found in the senators and MPs who were charged with making it. 'There is no mention of political parties in the Constitution. There is no mention of the prime minister or Cabinet. The law puts great weight on the people's right to elect their representatives and on the right of those representatives to hold their place in parliament until the people remove them.'

'That may be so,' said Ryan, 'but I think that we should proceed as George advises. We should wait a decent amount of time, say a couple of weeks, and then put the advice of the specialists to the speaker and encourage him to make the call, no matter how the House feels about it. He is, after all, supposed to be one of us. And we should begin planning for a by-election now, which, God knows, is going to be almost impossible to win.'

'And while the Constitution might make no mention of the prime minister or Cabinet, they both exist,' said Papadakis. 'So, after a decent amount of time, the prime minister will announce that his foreign minister is incapacitated and incapable and we will have a Cabinet reshuffle. Alistair, get a team together to prepare for a by-election in Bailey's seat. I'll be fucked if I'm leaving that in the hands of that dropkick secretary of the New South Wales branch.'

Papadakis turned his attention to Buharia. He loathed the senator from New South Wales and rarely deigned to speak to him directly.

'Sam, is there anyone left in that festering cesspool you preside over who's not currently facing some kind of charge and is capable of winning a by-election?'

'I don't like your tone,' huffed Buharia.

'I don't like you. I don't like your branch. I don't like what you've done to our party. So we all have our crosses to bear,' snapped Papadakis. 'You were the clown who foisted Bailey on us in the first place. You backed her long after it was clear she was barking mad. You are the architect of this crisis and you would not be drawing breath if I had anything to do with it.'

'I didn't hear you complaining when we won the election, or for the two years she was untouchable in the polls. It's easy to be wise after the event, soft-cock.'

Ryan didn't like Buharia either, but he needed a working relationship. He intervened. 'Everybody calm down. We all need to work on this together. It's going to be tough enough without squabbling among ourselves. Let's do the research, find a candidate, and see if there's a single positive we can massage into a message.

'And let's look on the bright side. Bailey might die any day now.'

Canberra, July 15

It was a small obituary, tucked away on page 22 of *The Age*, a quarter-page of copy that most readers would ignore on their way to the crossword or TV guide.

Lifted from the *New York Times*, it traced the life of Walter Chang, a reclusive industrialist who had survived the brutal crackdown against capitalists during the Cultural Revolution, later emerging as a central player in China's economic awakening in the late 1970s.

According to the obit, Chang had 'played a key role in spearheading the first wave of Chinese mining investment in Canada and Australia through the state-owned investment vehicle, China International Trust and Investment Corp'. Dunkley pulled up suddenly, mid-sentence, doing his best not to spill coffee on a just-ironed business shirt. He reread the lines before reaching into his shoulder bag for the file he had already compiled on Paxton, a collection of notes and photocopies of documents and old press clippings.

And there it was. An article from the early 1980s taken from the business pages of the *West Australian*. Paxton and his UMF mates were running riot on building sites in what was then the very wild west. But a single line had struck Dunkley as odd the first time he'd read it.

> Union secretary Mr Bruce Paxton congratulated Guangzhou Mining for being a model employer in the WA mining sector.

And underneath it said:

> Guangzhou is a subsidiary of China's state-owned investment arm, China International Trust and Investment Corp, which is understood to be exploring offshore opportunities in Australia, as well as the US and Canada. Its chairman is Mr Zheng Tian, also known as Wally Chang, who has handed responsibility for the Australian venture to his son, Zheng Wang …

And now here, next to the obituary, was a photograph of the Red Capitalist and his son Wang – the very same man from the black-and-white photo.

Dunkley recalled the lines that Mr DFAT had uttered during their most recent phone conversation: 'The past always points to the future.'

Now, after weeks of fruitless searching, another piece of the jigsaw had fallen into place.

Dunkley knew that he needed to do a heap more digging, but it wasn't iron ore he was mining for. It was something much more valuable.

———————

Canberra, July 15

Catriona Bailey lay stricken on her hospital bed, her life measured by a battery of medical machinery. To the untrained eye she was beyond resurrection. But Amy McCallum's eye saw things that escaped everyone else.

Regarded as one of the nation's best neurologists, she had been called in from Melbourne to examine the foreign minister. Bailey had been unresponsive for weeks and the Canberra medical team had exhausted almost all possibilities. It seemed Bailey would never recover. But McCallum knew from long experience never to take appearances for granted.

She sat on Bailey's bed and began the ritual. She always assumed her patient could hear her.

'Hi, Ms Bailey, I'm Amy, a neurologist,' she started. 'You are in intensive care in Canberra Hospital. You have been here for a month after suffering a serious stroke. You are on life support. You were unconscious on arrival and showed no response to any stimulus. Your eyes have been closed the whole time and recently they have been taped down. I am going to open your eyes now. It shouldn't hurt.'

McCallum gently removed the tape, wiped the outside of Bailey's eyes and opened them.

'Okay, I want you to do something for me. Look left.'

And Bailey's eyes moved left. The nurse standing next to the bed gasped.

'Look right,' said McCallum.

Bailey's eyes moved right.

'Jesus,' whispered the nurse.

'Blink if you can hear me clearly and understand what I am saying.'

Bailey blinked.

'That's excellent, Ms Bailey. Let's try something else. I am going to get the nurse to hold your feet. Can you move your toes?'

Nothing. The nurse shook her head.

'All right. I am going to put my finger in your hand. Can you squeeze it?'

Nothing.

'Okay, I am going to touch your arm. I want you to blink once if you can feel it or twice if you cannot.'

Bailey blinked once.

'I'm going to touch your leg now; can you feel it?'

Bailey confirmed she could.

'Ms Bailey, I think I know what's happened. You have suffered a rare kind of stroke. The lower part of your brain has been damaged and that means you have no control over any part of your body, save your eyes. In fact your eye movement is very good. And because your pathways have not been damaged you can still feel your body. But it might be a long time before you can move.

'Your upper brain has not been damaged. That's a start. And since you can move your eyes you can talk to us and give us instructions. We just need you to learn a new language.'

Canberra, July 15

The two men sat in the darkened corner of the cafe, quietly talking. The orders had come through from DC; the risk of doing nothing was too great. The operation had begun.

Preparations had been completed, as instructed. It was time now to flick the executioner's switch.

It would be the usual modus operandi: a strategic leak to the *New York Times* or the *Washington Post*. It wouldn't be front-page stuff, but a mention in the world news pages was just as valuable. After all, the intended audience was very select.

The leak would come from 'senior Pentagon sources' and would point to the target's public statements that suggested a retreat from the commitment to buy stealth bombers. The quote would include a direct criticism of the minister, something that was rare. The intelligence-sharing agreement would be raised. Those in the know in Canberra would be left in no doubt that Washington was not pleased.

They had tried to warn him, several times in fact. Don't meddle with the alliance. But he'd ignored them, another cocky minister who thought he could play God and to hell with the consequences.

He'd set his course, ordering the department to begin the process of winding back the Joint Strike Fighter program, as if it was his decision alone to destroy what had taken years to construct. All those billions invested in the alliance, strengthening the common bonds that had withstood so much over the years. And it was never more important than now, in the fight against militant Islam, and the rise of the Asian superpower.

He was putting it all at risk, god damn him. Didn't he know, didn't he care, about this war? It was no longer defined in the old paradigm of armies rolling across countries and invading neighbours. It was no longer a fight over territory alone. This war wasn't being fought so much with guns and bombs as with ideology; it was about the struggle to establish a dominant culture. It was about the existential threat posed by an inscrutable enemy targeting a weakening West.

They would teach him what it meant to question the value of shared beliefs, to be unpatriotic. The target would not know what had hit him; the pincer movement would be deadly and swift. They didn't like to see their victims squirm for any longer than necessary.

They were human. Most of the time, anyway.

Canberra, July 18

BAILEY'S AWAKE!

The headline screamed from the front of Melbourne's *Herald Sun*, the country's biggest selling paper. The 100-point font was usually reserved for the declaration of war – or an AFL drug scandal.

Typically, it had a red 'Exclusive' tag splashed above the byline. And this time, the scoop really was a game changer.

Brendan Ryan stared dumbly at the page. Even his huge intellect struggled to deal with the story.

It told the remarkable tale of a foreign minister trapped inside a broken body, but whose mind was as sharp as a tack.

Given its parochial nature, the *Herald Sun* had devoted an almost absurd amount of space to the brilliant Carlton-based neurologist who had diagnosed Bailey. And, as a bonus, her husband had once trialled for St Kilda.

Amy McCallum was teaching Bailey to blink out words one letter at a time, using the technique first developed by the French doctors who'd treated the journalist Jean-Dominique Bauby, who'd gone on to dictate a book, *The Diving Bell and the Butterfly*.

Ryan read that paragraph over and over to let it sink in. Bailey was aware. She could communicate. That meant they would need her permission to get her out of parliament. Ryan didn't need words blinked out a letter at a time to tell him what the bitch would do.

'This woman is like the fucking Terminator,' he said out loud. 'Blow her fucking arms and legs off and her fucking eyes keep blinking.'

Canberra, July 19

The gentle nod of academia greeted Kimberley Gordon as she arrived at the Australian National University a shade after 3pm. The Crawford School of Economics and Government was a standout among ANU's faculties – a treasure chest of boffins, all experts in their field, and hardly a grey beard among them.

She eased her VW Polo into Crawford's carpark, nestling the hatchback next to an ageing Volvo station wagon caked in a thin film of dirt and a clichéd pastiche of left-wing bumper stickers. She'd lined up a meeting with an old friend, George Tiding, one of the best historians in the country and a walking encyclopedia with an amazing ability to delve into the ANU's vast archives.

Tiding beckoned Gordon into his compact office where he had a few notes ready.

'Catriona Bailey was seconded from here to the embassy in Beijing for a few months in 1982,' he said. 'The files suggest it was a short-term arrangement, probably at her insistence so she could practise her Mandarin.'

'Do you have the precise dates, George? That is really crucial.'

'I can get those for you. You wouldn't like to tell me why Ms Bailey's past is so important to you all of a sudden?'

'Let's just say she's come into my orbit. I'm chasing a hunch.'

'Okay, but you should know someone else is interested in Bailey's past, someone with an American accent.'

Gordon didn't flinch, but her mind was ticking fast.

Someone else was trawling the same waters.

Bailey. Paxton. China. What was the connection?

Canberra, July 19

Rarely had Canberra Hospital experienced such a media circus. News that Catriona Bailey had woken, like some modern-day Lazarus, had sparked a frenzy.

The networks had staked out all the entrances, fearful of missing an important visitor. The crush was causing mayhem with the routine arrivals of the injured and sick, not to mention the comings and goings of patients' families and friends. Once more, the fourth estate was busy disgracing itself. One enterprising reporter from Network Ten had borrowed her mum's nursing uniform in an audacious attempt to locate the stricken Bailey. A screaming match had ensued between Ten's chief of staff and hospital management.

The hospital's exasperated CEO had already dismissed an intensive care nurse for leaking the news of Bailey's condition to the *Herald Sun*. Now she had called a press conference in a desperate bid to wrest back control of her hospital. But as she stepped in front of the television lights she feared things were about to get worse.

'Ladies and gentlemen, thank you for coming.' (The CEO actually wished them all to hell.) 'We understand there is considerable public interest in the condition of the foreign minister and that is why I have invited her specialist, Dr Amy McCallum, to speak with you today. She will say a few words about Ms Bailey's condition and then answer your questions.'

A nervous McCallum stepped up to the podium and squinted through the lights at the packed room.

She outlined Bailey's locked-in syndrome and the blinking communication system the foreign minister was painstakingly learning. 'Ms Bailey has made it clear to me that she wants the public to understand her condition and she has only one request, which I will get to in a moment,' she said.

'Unfortunately, the prognosis for Ms Bailey is not good,' she went on. 'It is rare for people with this condition to survive for long. In 90 per cent of cases people do not live beyond four months following the trauma.'

In Parliament House, Martin Toohey and some senior staffers were watching the press conference live. At the words 'rare for people with this condition to survive for long', Toohey caught Papadakis's eye and lifted his own eyebrows hopefully. It was a brief moment of optimism.

'But there are exceptions,' McCallum continued. 'The French journalist Jean-Dominique Bauby lived fifteen months, long enough to see his book published.'

The media waited impatiently through the description of the disease. McCallum was full of great information, but most saw it as background that they could get later. She had lost them early with the words 'only has one request, which I will get to in a moment'.

The second McCallum paused and the CEO said 'Any questions?' the room exploded into a cacophony of 'What did she ask for?'

'It was an unusual request,' McCallum responded. 'I checked it with her and then she refused to say anything else.'

'What was it?' bellowed the room.

'"I only want to talk to Thommo."'

Five kilometres away, the blasphemy of the prime minister reverberated through the corridors of parliament.

Perth, July 20

Harry Dunkley cursed. He'd been warned about Perth drivers, those foot-to-the-floor hoons who practised death-roll gymnastics on the ribbons of asphalt dissecting their city, ignoring the safety of others.

He'd arrived from Canberra the night before, late, the 737 bucking like a frisky nag in the turbulence that had turned the trip across the Nullarbor into a white-knuckle adventure. It had taken two whiskies and a small bottle of G & T to calm the nerves.

It had been a decade or so since he'd last travelled west, ten years in which Australia's mining boom had transformed Perth into a city of millionaires. The capital's suburban wastelands were now teeming with shift workers who regularly took the two-hour commuter flight north to the Pilbara, where a cleaner could clear $125k working on a rig and a barely qualified tradie could demand and receive more than $175,000.

It was close to 11am when Dunkley arrived at Osborne Park, a semi-industrial suburb fifteen minutes out of the CBD. So this is where public servants come to die, he thought.

His appointment was with the blandly titled 'Processing Officer, Consumer Protection Branch, WA Department of Commerce'. A brisk-looking woman greeted him, sat him down and handed him the file in question: a faded folder labelled 'United Mineworkers Federation – Workplace Reform Association'. Dunkley felt a tremble of anticipation.

'I'll give you some time; be back in ten if that suits.'

'Yeah, that'd be great. Cheers.'

Inside the file he found a handful of papers stapled together in a timeline of sorts. The association had been incorporated in Perth on 15 March 1984 by a solicitor from Slater & Gordon, that well-known Labor law firm.

Dunkley leafed through the papers until he came upon a single sheet headed 'Form 1 – Associations Incorporation Act 1977 (Section 5(1)). Application for Incorporation of Association'.

To the average Joe it meant bugger all, but to Dunkley it was pure gold.

The purpose of the association was declared to be 'the development of a framework to achieve a safe workplace'. A noble aim, he thought.

There were two signatories to the account setting up the association, the names scribbled and faded with time, but to Dunkley they stood out like the proverbial: Bruce Paxton and Doug Turner.

Dunkley rocked back in the chair and heaved a deep sigh. The flight across Australia, that five-hour journey from hell, had been worth it.

The voice on the end of the line grated, a cross between a fishwife's and a bikie moll's. Jennifer Turner had clearly lived a hard life, and her voice held no expectation that it would get any easier. Harry Dunkley introduced himself and politely asked to speak with her husband.

'Ex-husband,' she shot back. 'What do you want with that useless slimebag?'

'I'm working on a profile on Bruce Paxton … you know, the federal defence—'

'I know all about Paxton. As I suspect my ex-husband does … but as to his whereabouts, the last time I heard he was somewhere in Asia, rooting his silly arse off.'

'Would you know where exactly?'

'No, I fuckin' wouldn't, and even if I did I'm not sure I'd tell you anyway.'

Dunkley quietly sighed and searched for any opening.

'Look, I really appreciate your time and I'm sorry to have disturbed you, but I've flown across from the east and I'm really hoping to … Well, would you know who could help me find your ex?'

A pause. 'You could try Jimmy Booth. He and Paxton and my scumbag ex go back a long way … I think he's still working for the union, the Mineworkers or whatever they're called now.'

'Many thanks, Mrs Turner. Really appreciate it.'

'Huh. If you do happen to find my former husband, tell him he's a fuckin' useless moron who owes the kids and me bigtime.'

And with that, Jennifer Turner slammed down the phone.

Eighty-two Royal Street, East Perth was a pleasant-looking place. It could have been the HQ for a medium-sized accounting firm or some other paragon of corporate virtue. Instead it was home to one of the most notorious groups of union thugs ever to march across Australia's industrial landscape.

Dunkley, himself a keen member of the journos' union, was dressed in his best blue-collar chic, intent on blending in with the bovver boys he was about to meet. He climbed an internal stairwell, passing a blue Eureka flag and a sign that screamed, 'The workers united will never be defeated.' Ah, such magnificent cliché, he thought.

Jimmy Booth, all gruff-and-paunch, looked to be in his mid to late fifties and was dressed in a dark T-shirt and sleeveless CFMEU vest. He commanded a small office open to all, barking instructions to fellow organisers and secretarial help. Dunkley knew from his research that Booth had been on the union payroll for nearly thirty years, a hired goon who could be relied on to take it up to the bosses and coppers when the CFMEU needed a stink. In the eyes of Perth's establishment, he was pure evil.

Right then, though, he was Dunkley's best hope of tracking down Doug Turner. That's if Booth gave a fuck, of course.

'Which paper did you say you worked for?'

'*The Australian*, Jimmy.'

'Ah, the fucking *Oz*, that right-wing shit sheet. They stitched me and the missus up good a few years back, claimed we were raking it in, living the high life on the Swan … Fucking Murdoch pricks.'

'I cover politics out of Canberra, try not to get too involved in what happens over here. I'm sorry you had a bad experience … Can I ask you a few questions perhaps about Doug Turner?'

'Like what fucking size his coffin should be?'

'Do you know where he is? Somewhere in Asia, I'm told.'

'Don't know, mate, haven't spoken with the prick for years. Last time I heard he was working at a fish-and-chip place down on the coast, Cottesloe maybe. Why're you interested in Dougie, anyway?'

'I'm trying to write a feature piece on Bruce Paxton. I thought Doug Turner might be able to help me piece a few things together.'

'Yeah, he and Paxton were thick as thieves once, and I do mean thieves, mate. You could try one of those organisations set up by Vietnam Vets: Turner was in 'Nam for a couple of years, never quite got over it, if you ask me. Now, if you'll excuse me, mate, we have corporate dogs to take on …'

Jimmy Booth, 120 kilos of pure trouble, was on his feet and preparing to lead his stormtroopers once more into battle. For the benefit of the working man, of course.

Canberra, July 26

It was the most powerful television network in the land, controlled by a clique of ego-driven men. And one token woman. On this crisp Tuesday morning, the board of Network Seven was holding a special meeting, the chairman ringing in from Venice where he and wife number four were attending the Biennale.

It was the middle of the night in Europe but this hook-up was worth every lost minute of sleep and every euro. Seven was sitting on the biggest television scoop of the year, and it was determined to milk every last opportunity, and advertising dollar, from it.

A team of network specialists had been flown to Canberra from Sydney, taking over half a dozen suites at the Hyatt. The bar tab alone would be enough to feed a small army. But this was of little concern as preparations began for the *Morning Glory* live broadcast from Catriona Bailey's hospital bed.

The first teaser for the public was a clip of Thommo making a pilgrimage to the hospital. Seven had filmed him standing solemnly beside Bailey's bed, patting her deathly pale hand.

'It's great to see you again,' he whispered. 'Blink if you're happy to see us.'

The camera was tight on Bailey's face. She blinked. The news that night showed what might have been a tear easing from the corner of Thommo's eye. He smiled and whispered, 'Thank you. The *Morning Glory* family is thinking of you and praying for you.'

It was pure TV gold and it ran, relentlessly, as a network promo.

Seven's ratings were piling ever higher as Thommo, working both ends of the day, reported every detail for the masses. The network's 6pm numbers reached an unheard-of two million by the end of the first week. Over at Ten and Nine, executives were having multiple seizures of their own.

A private hospital had agreed to Network Seven's request to set up a room for the live broadcast after Canberra Hospital said no. It was fitted out with state-of-the-art equipment, overseen by the best medical staff money could buy. Seven spent an equally obscene amount transforming the room into a television studio.

Friday night's news devoted several precious minutes to Bailey's transfer from Canberra Hospital to the luxurious private suite a few kilometres away. But everything was being geared towards the live breakfast broadcast slated for Monday, August 1. Entertainment pundits predicted an unprecedented audience when *Morning Glory* rose that day.

Medical, technical and computer experts had been hired by Seven to research and understand Bailey's condition, so that come the day of the program the best possible technology would be on hand to let Bailey communicate both with Thompson and, if possible, directly with the audience. Part of the reason the network had delayed the interview was that Bailey had to be tutored in the use of a tool called Dasher, developed by a professor of physics at Cambridge, which used probability to drive a computer system that did away with the keyboard. Its humble looks belied its genius.

The Dasher screen showed a simple yellow page with colour-coded letters of the alphabet lined up on the right-hand side: 'A' at the top and 'Z' at the bottom. As the cursor moved towards a letter, the letter would begin to jostle forward, as if the cursor was a magnet attracting a pin.

Once the first letter was selected the program began to predict what would come next: combinations of letters would appear behind the first, with the most likely growing in size near the cursor. Once the first word was selected the combinations would grow to include whole words. So if you selected 'Hello', for instance, the words 'how' and 'are' and 'you' would start to pour from the right of the screen.

Given the program worked by slight movements of a cursor, it was not a huge leap to make it respond to eye movements.

But Bailey had more problems than most in mastering the technology because her vocabulary was so eclectic and her style so verbose. She was a diligent student, though, and after five painstaking days she could write 140 characters a minute.

And then it struck one of the Seven producers. Twitter!

Canberra, July 27

It was the dead hour, between 3 and 4am, when those who inhabited the darkness had mostly gone home and those who began early were yet to rise. And those who lay awake filled the void with their hopes and fears.

Martin Toohey had few hopes and his many fears often kept him from sleep. So he was familiar with this dead spot in the Canberra night. He strained to hear a single note of human activity outside. But there was nothing: no cars on Adelaide Avenue, no voices in the distance, just the soft breathing of his wife beside him and the creaks of a Lodge that had seen too many sleepless prime ministers.

Toohey glanced at the bedside clock as it ticked off another minute of his existence: 3.35am.

The last twelve months, when he stood at the pinnacle of political success, had been the worst of all. He had not wanted to kill a prime minister to be prime minister and he feared the blood of Catriona Bailey would never wash from his hands. He knew the Australian people could never understand, or forgive, what seemed from afar to be an unprovoked act of political brutality.

The election had been a disaster, leaving him with a stench of illegitimacy he could not shake. And because every government decision had to be negotiated with the crossbench, he looked weak. Worst of all, the deal he had signed with the Greens, against the advice of Papadakis, was turning into an unmitigated disaster: all upside for them, all downside for Labor. The only bright spot in the whole sorry mess was that the opposition was hopelessly divided.

The office of prime minister had not hung so low in one hundred and ten years of Federation. The compromises Toohey had to make now were the most painful of his political life. And that destroyed his confidence and robbed him of his political gifts.

Some commentators now claimed that Toohey was an even more robotic and less effective communicator than the appalling Bailey. The party's pollsters had begun to worry aloud that people had stopped listening to him. If that was true, there could be no coming back.

If the opposition ever got its act together, his government was dead. The only question was when it would be buried.

Canberra, July 29

Four words that could last a lifetime: 'Give me a call.' It had taken five days for Doug Turner, tracked by Harry Dunkley via a Vietnam Vets' Facebook page, of all places, to make contact via email, but he was willing to chat – from the safe distance of overseas, anyway. Dunkley waited ten minutes then punched in the number Turner had provided. The journalist was armed with a swag of papers: ASIC searches, file notes from his trip to the Association's register and a potted history of Turner's corporate exploits. There were plenty of missing pieces, but at least he would be able to ask some sensible questions.

'Well, hello Australia. Mr Dunkley, I presume?' Doug Turner sounded remarkably chirpy.

'G'day Doug, nice to finally chat to you. As you know, I'm writing a profile piece on Bruce Paxton – the two of you go back a way?'

'You can say that again. I haven't seen or spoken to Bruce in, oh, ten or so years, maybe longer. What exactly did you want to know?'

'How he got into politics, his early influences, those years the two of you were involved in the Mineworkers union ...' Dunkley left the words hanging, urging a response. An eternity seemed to pass before Turner spoke, this time in a more serious tone.

'I can tell you about those times, sure.'

There was, however, a catch.

Turner had done his research too, and realised that Dunkley was, in his words, 'a reporter of some note'. In exchange for information about Paxton, Turner wanted justice, and he saw Dunkley as the vehicle to achieve it.

Four decades after serving in the shit and slime of Vietnam, Doug Turner was still seeking recognition for himself and his mates, those brave soldiers from the 2nd Battalion Royal Australian Regiment who'd carried out their orders diligently and had never wavered – even when the Vietcong were threatening to turn them into mincemeat and the body bags kept mounting up. No, the 2RAR kept its end of the bargain, Turner told Dunkley, fighting like mad men and defending the ANZAC honour, even when the Yanks had left them to their fate.

They'd been exposed to the worst excesses of the human spirit, seen enough senseless killing and brutality to make them question the essence of mankind, and lain awake wondering, 'Is this the night I die?' Yet when they returned to Australia, they were met by another vicious enemy: the cult of public opinion. At home they were treated like shit by anti-war bigots who'd lost faith in the campaign against Communism.

It was all too confusing for young men like Turner who'd expected sympathy and comfort, not the cold glare of an angry country at war with itself.

Turner had tried to retreat into normality, moving to the west, where he scored work on the same Perth building sites as another tearaway, Bruce Paxton. The two had forged a close bond, chasing women around Perth's seedy nightspots and watching each other's backs when their wild ride threatened to spiral out of control.

And what an exhilarating ride it had been! Paxton had looked after his mate as he climbed the greasy pole, securing Turner a junior organiser's role at the UMF while Paxton reached for the stars.

The work had been therapeutic, helping Turner cope during those long nights when he'd lie awake for hours, sweating and cursing, unable to shake off the memory of Vietnam and its deep unspoken terror. He knew he was suffering post-traumatic stress disorder but was equally keen to cover it up, afraid he would be deemed unfit for work. He'd descend on the weekends into a suburban funk, struggling to fill the role of loving husband and father.

He'd held it together as long as possible, even after Bruce Paxton announced that he was being parachuted into a safe Labor seat, bound for a cushy life in Canberra. Their partnership, it seemed, was over.

The last decade had been particularly harsh. Turner had fallen out with his family after lapsing into routine depression mixed with alcohol-fuelled bouts of aggression, his torment not helped when he was sacked by the CFMEU for failing to turn up to work five days in a row.

And that prick Paxton? Why, he'd scooted east with barely a farewell. Thanks-for-all-your-help-mate-now-fuck-off. A friendship sacrificed on the altar of one man's out-of-control ego. Well, Paxton could stick his political ambition where it fitted.

Turner had severed ties with Perth, escaping north to start afresh, working on a pearl lugger in Broome before drifting to the tourist-laden islands of Indonesia, where he hoped to hustle an honest living.

But the torment of Vietnam kept flooding back. The Department of Veterans Affairs had been miserly, offering him only a partial pension. The mere thought of those bureaucrats playing god with his life sent Turner into spasms of rage and yet more alcohol abuse. After everything he'd done for his country ...

He'd retreated into the semi-paranoid world of cyberspace, searching for similarly minded folk. With a few mates located via the internet, Turner established Vets for Justice. The group had grown several hundred strong, a diaspora of fed-up Australian veterans who wanted nothing more than their dignity restored and their story heard.

They had delivered demands to successive governments in Canberra, always meeting the same response: 'Case closed. Next.'

As for Paxton, when he became defence minister, Turner thought he could be trusted to set the past right, to look after those who'd been fucked over. He sent his old mate a long letter a few weeks after he'd been sworn in, congratulating him and asking if he would personally intervene to help the Vets out, give them some recognition.

71

'You know what I received back from him?' Turner rasped over the phone. 'A fucking form letter sent by his chief of staff ... not even a personal note. That's when I thought, mate, you'll get yours one day ...

'So, let's cut to the chase. You want info about Paxton, right? Well, no one knows more about his past than me, I reckon. I played the loyal fucking lieutenant for him and that other pack of bastards in head office. Did everything they asked me to do, and then some. I can give you chapter and verse – but first there's a few things I need.'

'We aren't in the business of paying for stories, Doug,' Dunkley gently informed him.

'I ain't talking about your money, Mr Dunkley. I don't want Rupert's cash, although I reckon he'd have a few shekels to spare. There's something far more important to me, a job that you could do to bring our campaign into the public eye. Tell me, does the Battle of Nui Le mean anything to you?'

Canberra, August 1

The *Morning Glory* team was used to punishing hours but the pre-production for the Catriona Bailey shoot was more complex and gruelling than any before. It would be worth it, though. It was Monday morning, 4am, and dozens of Seven technicians, producers and stars were gathering for the TV event of the year.

Thommo had spent the entire weekend working with Bailey in her hospital room and their encounters had been shot from multiple angles. Then they were edited down, to be rolled in once the show went live at 6am. The best bits would be recycled several times during the morning. The relationship between Thommo and Bailey would be highlighted as the program reclaimed the foreign minister as a much-loved member of the *Morning Glory* family.

The audience, of course, was part of the family. Viewers would feel they were bedside at the hospital, wallowing in the emotion of the moment and flicking through the family album of mawkish, air-brushed memories. And they would be invited to join the conversation online, sending messages and asking Bailey questions.

Messages of support had already been recorded from a bevy of politicians and celebrities, including the prime ministers of the United Kingdom, India and New Zealand, and the president of China. Angelina Jolie and Bono, too, had sent notes of encouragement. The coup would be a live cross to the US secretary of state, Hillary Clinton, a long-time friend of Bailey.

Each minute of the three-hour show would be rigidly choreographed and dramatised. An enormous amount of effort had gone into staging the 'first words' Bailey blinked. This, of course, was utter nonsense given that Bailey had barely shut up since she had been taught to use the Dasher eye-movement word processor. She had been issuing a steady stream of instructions to everyone at Seven, from the chairman to the makeup assistant, and had strong opinions on how the show should run.

The extravaganza kicked off at 6am with an establishing shot of Thommo outside the hospital.

'It's with a mixture of sorrow and joy that we join you this morning,' he began.

Cut to a ceiling camera showing Bailey lying on her hospital bed, attached to all manner of medical machinery.

'Part of me is cut up at seeing our mate Cate trapped inside her own body, unable to move.'

The camera slowly zoomed towards Bailey's bed.

'But another part of me knows that her mind is still soaring like an eagle.'

A close-up of Bailey's face from a camera mounted on the Dasher monitor filled the viewers' screens.

'She hasn't lost her great wit, her massive intellect or, most of all, her deep concern about us and this country.'

A wide two-shot of Thommo sitting beside Bailey's bed flashed up next. Then the camera came in for a mid-shot of Thommo.

'This morning, I guarantee you will shed a tear. But you will also laugh with and be inspired by Cate Bailey. It's been an extraordinary journey to this day ... but let's begin by remembering happier times.'

The opening bars of 'You've Got to Have Friends' played as exquisitely edited footage of Bailey in happier, healthier times rolled out into the lounge rooms of Australia.

Everything had been timed to the second, words and pictures telling a seamless story. By the time the nostalgic montage was finished the ground had been tilled for the first big bang.

'Cate, how do you feel?' whispered Thommo.

The director cut to a shot of Bailey's face, her eyes concentrating on the Dasher screen, urging the cursor to respond.

'B-o-n-z-e-r' appeared on the screen.

Outside the hospital, a small but growing band of hardy locals erupted in a cheer. The broadcast cut to a shot of them and Thommo's breakfast partner, Janelle 'Janny' Jeffries, who was positioned in the freezing cold in the hospital carpark, where a huge screen had been erected and the public invited to attend.

Janny leapt to her feet, clapping her mittened hands. The director cut back to a close-up of Thommo.

'That's our girl. That's our Cate,' he said, fighting back tears.

Days of effort had gone into considering that first question and Bailey had toyed with a number of responses. Most of them were ridiculously verbose and littered with medical terms she had imbibed from her specialist. She had been persuaded to keep the first message brief.

And then the single word had taken an hour to record, given Dasher was bewildered by the ancient ockerism.

The program's Twitter feed immediately spat out:

First words from hospital bed. Bailey says she's 'BONZER'.

It was re-tweeted by thousands and Bailey began trending around the nation. That chatter would be fed back into the program through the morning, amplifying the circular conversation.

The rest of the show was equally script-perfect.

The Chinese president announced that a panda cub born the week before would be named 'Cate Cate', in honour of a much-loved, fallen friend of the People's Republic.

The half-hour set aside for audience questions to Bailey's Twitter account went off, despite the producer's fears it would be dreary TV. Thommo and Janny were at their nonstop chatty best while Bailey dutifully plugged out the answers.

A highlight was a question from a young cancer sufferer who asked: 'Are you still angry at the prime minister for taking your job?'

'N-o. T-h-i-s h-a-s s-h-o-w-n m-e t-h-a-t n-o-t-h-i-n-g i-s m-o-r-e i-m-p-o-r-t-a-n-t t-h-a-n y-o-u-r h-e-a-l-t-h.'

Hillary Clinton burst into tears at the end of her interview with Thommo when he told her that Bailey had been closely following her trip to South Korea and was impressed by her steely determination to bring the errant North to heel.

'You hang in there, girl!' urged Clinton.

'I w-i-l-l H-i-l-l-a-r-y,' Bailey said.

Outside, the crowd had grown steadily all morning. Across the nation, the minute-by-minute breakdown of the ratings would show that the audience peaked at one million just after 7am and, more remarkably, stayed at that level until 9am.

The show had been designed to end with a bombshell. As the clock ticked towards 9am, Thommo leaned towards Bailey.

'Cate, you've shown us this morning that you are as sharp and talented as you always were. What do you want to do now?'

'I w-a-n-t t-o g-o b-a-c-k t-o w-o-r-k.'

Perth, August 1

A light breeze filtered through Perth's CBD, taming the temperature that was nudging twenty-five despite the season. Office workers strode purposefully along streets that bore triumphal evidence of the state's economic boom with cranes thrusting skywards and jackhammers assaulting the senses at every turn.

Ah, the joys of rampant capitalism, Dunkley thought, remembering the crooks who had run riot in the '80s, aided and abetted by a WA Labor government drunk on power and its proximity to great big chunks of cash. All those white-collar criminals – Bondy, Laurie Connell and their ilk – who had ripped off gullible shareholders before crashing back to earth and into jail. Now the mining giants were scrabbling over Indigenous land, reluctant to pay their fair share of tax and relentlessly gouging at the ancient landscape.

But it wasn't BHP or Rio Tinto that Dunkley was pursuing today. Entering the foyer of an unremarkable building, he scanned a directory and found his target, taking a lift to the offices of the Australian Electoral Commission, the bureaucracy responsible for maintaining the electoral roll and ensuring that, roughly every three years, around eleven million voters exercised their democratic right to put either Labor or the Coalition into power.

Dunkley introduced himself to an AEC officer who had already done some preliminary work. He was led to a desk where a pile of documents and files connected with the 1996 federal election lay in wait.

The election had been a watershed. John Winston Howard, the man once about as popular as herpes, had surged into office, sweeping away Paul Keating and his dwindling band of True Believers. It was an emphatic victory, one that would usher in another long period of Coalition rule. Labor had lost a humiliating thirty-one seats on the back of a 6.17 per cent swing. But in a rare bright moment for the ALP, Bruce

Leonard Paxton had fended off an enthusiastic Liberal candidate to take his seat in the House of Representatives, part of a Caucus reduced to a miserable forty-nine members of parliament.

And while there had been whispers about the way Paxton had made it to Canberra – whom he'd paid off, whom he'd fucked over along the way – for the most part the current defence minister's past had been left alone.

Until now. Until Dunkley had decided the minister's history was worthy of exhumation.

He started sifting through the electoral returns for 1995, trying to prise open the secrets of who'd been bankrolling Labor's WA branch. Nothing looked out of the ordinary: the pages were filled with blue-chip corporates who donated $50,000 or $100,000 every year to each of the major parties, seeking to remain scrupulously non-partisan. There were the standard big-ticket donations from the unions that stood to lose big-time under a Howard government, even though it was Keating and his sidekick Laurie Brereton who had taken on Labor's industrial wing, introducing enterprise bargaining.

The '95 returns gave way to 1996, a more solid-looking document reflecting the intensity of an election year. Both Labor and the Coalition had scored handsomely, Dunkley noted.

As he scanned page after page of mainly anodyne returns, a small item caught his eye. On 11 January 1996 – just weeks before Keating fired the election starter's gun – the CFMEU had made an $80,000 donation to the ALP. There was nothing sinister about that, but in brackets the words 'For the purpose of Bruce Paxton's campaign' had been added. And that, Dunkley knew, was highly unusual and needed further investigation.

Sydney, August 1

In his plush Paddington terrace, Jamie Santow sat entranced in front of his plasma flat-screen for nearly two hours, digesting every minute of the *Morning Glory* broadcast. He had just one focused thought: how could *GetSet!* get aboard the Bailey Express?

The 24-year-old university whiz-kid (double major in public relations and sociology) was the master of seizing the moment to promote himself and his online activist organisation by surfing waves of public emotion.

GetSet! rarely identified an original issue or put effort into a need that wasn't already on the political radar. No, that demanded spending real time and intellectual capital. It was best to leave that sort of slog to others and just turn up with *GetSet!* banners as the wave began to crest, claiming the credit

76

for any victory, moving seamlessly to the next media event and leaving any unresolved issues for the worker bees in specialist lobbies and the public service to sort out.

The beauty of Santow's progressive organisation was that it was virtual. Members could log into the state-of-the-art website, sign a petition on anything from live exports to climate change, watch their name and their issue appear on the front page, then log off and get on with their day.

The protest movement was no longer about storming the barricades, making placards and singing the 'Internationale'. Activism and outrage now came free, with minimal effort and instantaneous gratification. In a parody of Timothy Leary's famous '60s edict, the online protest anthem was 'Dial-in, whine-on, log-out'. *GetSet!* was the perfect political forum for an increasingly self-obsessed world.

It was Bailey's return-to-work bombshell that gave Santow the idea he was looking for. He would use *GetSet!*'s considerable clout to lobby for Bailey to continue as the foreign minister, working from her hospital bed. She would become the pin-up girl – er, person – for the differently abled lobby. If Bailey could work as foreign minister, then no one was barred from any job. She would inspire by example.

He assumed there might be a few practical difficulties for the government in having a foreign minister who could not travel, attend Cabinet, sit in parliament or Caucus, or even make international calls. But that was not his problem. He would simply do what he always did: make an emotional appeal and portray any hesitation by the government as evidence of prejudice.

What he really needed was a slogan. After about ten minutes of doodling, he settled on 'Reinstate Cate'. It was easy to chant, would look good on the *GetSet!* website and should fit nicely on T-shirts.

He picked up the phone to begin organising the first stunt. He knew Seven's commercial rivals would be loath to carry much of the *Morning Glory* broadcast, but neither could they ignore the huge political yarn. What they needed were fresh angles – and that was Santow's genius.

And what he really needed were some people in wheelchairs.

Sydney, August 1

Jonathan Robbie stood by the window gazing out at Sydney's hectic streets, a stiff whisky in his left hand, the television remote dangling from his right. Oh shit, he thought.

The *Australian Story* profile on opposition leader Elizabeth Scott had been as bloody as one of David Attenborough's wildlife documentaries.

The profile had been sold to Scott as an in-your-own-words half-hour of soft soap, a chance to humanise the Liberal leader and play down her image of immense privilege. Instead it had been a horror show. The first, and biggest, problem was timing. The story had largely been shot during the Michael Hamilton 'Bank-gate' scandal. The producer had even been shooting in Scott's office when Nine News went to air to reveal the public servant's links to the Liberal Party and his lies about the prime minister.

Among many unfortunate moments immortalised on video was Scott's press secretary's priceless response to the news item. 'How the fuck did that shallow bastard Robbie find that out?' muttered Justin Greenwich. 'I'll bet my right ball there's a rat in our ranks.'

The *Australian Story* producer had asked Robbie questions for an hour. And, towards the end, she'd invited him to comment on Scott's character. Finally he'd opined that Scott was 'heartless and cold-blooded' in her dealings with the deluded Hamilton.

Robbie had worried about that statement ever since and had even raised the matter once with Scott, asking whether she had considered what would happen to Hamilton. She had been adamant that he was a more than willing participant and that she viewed him as a whistleblower on what she honestly believed was an enormous scandal. She had no sympathy for Hamilton and was enraged by the damage his lie had done to her.

The call came at 8.34pm. Robbie knew without looking who was on the line. Elizabeth Scott.

'Jonathan, you complete moron. You are such a moron it's hard to know where to begin. "Heartless? Cold-blooded? Expendable?" He came to us, you dumb bastard. He was a suicide bomber.

'And you, you dumb prick. You had to parade your so-called scoop. To stand in judgement of me and impugn my character and pretend you're something more than a third-rate hack who screwed his way into a yarn. Yes, Jonathan, I know. Don't think I'm blind to who's making the bullets you fire. Do you honestly believe that I think you're smart enough to have worked that story out for yourself? Or done some real journalism?

'It will all come out in time. And your judgement will be shown to be completely fucked. And it won't be a matter of opinion, it will be a matter of fact.'

And so it went for fifteen uninterrupted minutes as Scott unloaded. She worked herself into a rage and unpicked every element of his character with expletive-laced flourishes. But as Scott's stream of invective began to run dry, she became introspective, mournful and self-pitying. Not knowing how to rebuild her shattered political capital was tearing her apart.

'I don't know what to do. Why is the police investigation taking so long? Why don't they release some of the information they have? If people could only see it they'd realise I'm telling the truth. I've half a mind to hold a press conference and release the emails, but then I'd probably be accused of interfering with a police investigation.'

Scott paused for the first time. 'What do you think I should do?' she said.

'Well, I wouldn't ask me,' Robbie spat back. 'Because some people think my judgement's fucked.'

Scott dropped her mobile on her kitchen table and stared blankly out the window, oblivious to the beauty of the ocean view.

For the first time ever she felt her life was beyond her control and it terrified her. Business success had come easily, but politics was an alien land full of unexpected dangers. Her mind wandered back over the horror of the past months, but her memories always ended at the same bitter encounter.

It was early April and she was standing in the prime minister's office in front of an enraged Martin Toohey.

'I respected you,' he said in a low and menacing tone.

'I never asked him to lie,' Scott said. 'He had good information about problems in your bank finance scheme; you know he did because you've been trying to hide it. That's fair game.'

'We were trying to save an entire industry and hundreds of jobs threatened by a financial crisis,' Toohey said. 'Yes, it was flawed but there is no perfect solution. And you wine and dine this attention-seeking partisan. You flatter him. You get him to overwind his story and then he publicly accuses me of being corrupt.

'You know me. You know that's a lie. But you let it stand for three days before it was blown out of the water. Mud sticks. You know that.'

Scott's voice quavered. 'He said he had an email that would be a bombshell. And then ... How could I be sure?'

'You didn't care if it was true or not. You were willing to let what little dignity I have left in public life be shredded because you saw a chance of charging to an election.'

'Martin, I—'

'Get out. I am done talking with you. Anything I ever have to say to you again you can read in the papers, watch on TV or cop in the parliamentary chamber.'

'Martin, I apologise.'

'Save it, you spoilt, selfish Tory bitch. Get out.'

Scott remembered being surprised as she turned to leave; she was used to confrontation but Toohey's words had cut deep.

Her personal standing in the polls had collapsed. And that meant that she was vulnerable. Her blood was in the water and the sharks were circling.

Canberra, August 6

On a quiet weekend with the sun streaming into her apartment, Kimberley Gordon loved to relax with a cloth and containers of polish and oil, smoothing the 1790s perfection of her Louis XVI dining table and admiring the artisan toil that had transformed rough lengths of timber into a work of elegance and beauty. She liked to recall her favourite Keating story: the Labor PM would keep his Cabinet colleagues and advisers waiting for hours if he got into a groove with one of his Napoleonic artefacts. Ah, the sheer bloody indulgence of it all.

Gordon's table had cost a packet, but she considered it the soundest of investments. 'You don't put a price on something of exquisite beauty,' she would explain to those friends who questioned the purchase.

The table served a practical purpose too, when she hosted dinner parties for her small but close coterie of friends. She loved experimenting with dishes she'd seen on *MasterChef*, redolent with the marvellous tang of faux celebrity. But this Saturday afternoon, gourmet experiences were not on the menu. Instead, Gordon was seeking a breakthrough in an increasingly complex project. While Harry Dunkley was off chasing shadows in the west, Gordon was focusing on the links between Bruce Paxton and Catriona Bailey.

She'd arranged a series of papers on the table, short bios and other material she'd prepared on Paxton and the two Chinese men in the photo. Somewhere in this jumbled maze were clues – but to what?

Okay, she told herself, think logically. Bailey had been in Beijing at the same time as Paxton, perhaps when the defence minister had first met Zhou Dejiang. Was it a chance meeting? Unlikely. The Chinese were masters at placing the right person in the right place at the right time, hoping to trip up their international visitors. But the only clue was the photo from thirty-odd years ago. What was it about the past that was now shaking the present?

Lately, the intelligence wires had been buzzing with news of a secret bust in Beijing – a woman named Lillian Chan had been recruited to entice Western diplomats into her sex-baited web, but instead was caught selling classified Chinese intel to the West. She faced a lengthy stint in one of China's rural gulags – a shameful end to what had been a promising career.

Had Paxton succumbed to the wiles of some other Chinese temptress? There was nothing firm in the files that Gordon had seen, just the odd suggestion here and there of a man whose moral compass had been shipwrecked for many a year.

Gordon was tossing theories around but they all seemed to lead nowhere. She'd come to a roadblock, the dreaded point that every security analyst fears. If she was going to find out what it all meant, she would need help. And that raised an immediate problem.

She knew whom to turn to – Charles Dancer, a senior DFAT official, the department's under-the-radar troubleshooter with access to the very best in intelligence. Dancer was the complete professional and Gordon knew him well. The problem? Perhaps Gordon knew him a little too well …

It had started as a fumbling encounter at the National Press Club in the heart of Canberra's bureaucratic district. The regular Thursday night blues crowd had shuffled in, joining a throng of public servants, to hear the Wah-Wahs, a decent outfit steeped in Buddy Guy licks, with a small but loyal following. Gordon had shown up around nine, hoping to meet up with some friends, including one Annie the Trannie, who was as fond of people-spotting as she was of music. That night did not disappoint – Annie gleefully pointed out a senior Liberal MP, an appalling man from Queensland, canoodling in a corner with a young male staffer in an embrace that Gordon suspected would find its way onto YouTube within days. Or into that special file held by the Liberal Party whip.

The NPC was rocking despite the lack of journalists – a fact that never ceased to amaze the management, who'd tried just about every trick imaginable to entice the press gallery into the club.

Three songs from the end, during a solid version of 'Little Queenie', Annie had grabbed Gordon and marched her onto the dance floor, straight into the arms of Charles Dancer.

'Bugger you, Annie,' Gordon thought, though she was secretly pleased to have been introduced to the suave, older Dancer. Even though, despite his name, the man appeared to have two left feet.

A flirtatious relationship had ensued, the two bonded by their unusual lifestyles and penchant for French period furniture. But after a number of years the magic had died and they'd agreed to go their separate ways. There was no hostility, but the few times they had bumped into each other – once at the Dendy during Canberra's annual film festival and another time at the home of a mutual friend – they'd felt awkward.

Well, thought Gordon, she was just going to have to put that to one side. She was in need of a helping hand and Dancer was among the very best in the business.

She'd chosen the Chairman and Yip, a still fashionable place that had been serving excellent Asian-infused plates for nearly two decades. It was a little pricey but Albert, the hunky manager, could be relied on to find a discreet table when asked.

The night air was brisk but bearable, and Gordon managed to snag a park almost opposite the restaurant. A good omen, she thought, as she spotted Albert through the window.

Dancer had beaten her by a few minutes and was already seated, glass in hand, when Gordon arrived at the table.

'Charles, you're looking well.'

'You too, Kimberley.'

A short silence ensued as they perused the menu and then ordered.

'So, Kimberley, why this secrecy? That was a very cryptic phone message you left.'

'Sorry about that. Look, I want to ask a favour … a purely professional favour,' Gordon added, a little clumsily.

Dancer's expression remained neutral.

'This has to remain hush-hush …'

'Kimberley, you can trust me. You of all people should know that.'

Dancer's tone was reassuring and after a quick half-glass of Riesling, Gordon felt relaxed enough to spill the beans.

'I'm working on Bruce Paxton …' She halted, sensing a slight shift in Dancer's usually impassive gaze.

'Go on …'

Gordon took another sip of wine, wondering how much to reveal to her old friend. 'Well, a colleague's come across some material which suggests he has some links with the Chinese. Trouble is, there's precious little in the records to confirm any history between Paxton and our Asian friends, and my efforts to dig into his past have so far drawn a blank.'

Dancer waited till a waiter had delivered plates of duck pancakes and steamed prawn dumplings before replying. 'Mr Paxton does indeed have an interesting past. In fact, I'm surprised that most of it remains hidden in the vault, so to speak.'

'What do you mean?'

'Let's just say he features in a few files that I'm aware of. I presume you know what I'm talking about?'

'I honestly don't, Charles.'

'You've not heard about the ... Marmalade Files?'

Gordon's surprised look left Dancer in little doubt that she really was in the dark.

'Heavens, Kimberley, I thought an experienced analyst like you would know all about them.' Dancer's voice held a hint of mockery. 'As you know, some years ago I was given a special role in the department, a job best described as Fix-it Man for our foreign service. An invisible diplomat, if you like.

'I was part of a small team, just the three of us, reporting directly to the department secretary. We took our orders from him and no one else. We were given the task of cleaning up our nation's diplomatic messes – and Kimberley, there have been more than a few. I'm not sure if you're aware of the incident back in 1996 when the government of Thailand came very close to making an official complaint over the behaviour of David Bleasdale?'

Gordon shook his head as she bit into a dumpling.

'Mr Bleasdale spent his years in Bangkok indulging his penchant for underage boys. It had been tolerated at previous postings, but the Thai government wanted to stamp out the growing number of paedophiles entering the country – and Bleasdale was among the grubbiest of the lot.

'I had to hot-foot it to Bangkok, arriving in the nick of time to negotiate a truce. We had a fair bit on their envoy in Sydney, a man whose sexual fantasies would test even the most experienced of hookers. Let's just say the two countries called it a draw.

'It was during this time that I learned of a cache of top-secret files buried deep in the bowels of DFAT.

'They contain the secrets that our government doesn't want the public – or even you, Kimberley – to know about. These are not mere accidents, either; these are atrocities that plumb the depths. File after file of secret intelligence, some of it ours, some of it from our American or British friends. All of it highly sensitive.

'You want to know about Mr Paxton, of course. Let me set the scene for you ...'

Paxton had first travelled to Beijing in 1980 as part of a Young Labor delegation, a regular trip for up-and-coming ALP stars. The delegations had become an annual event after Whitlam opened diplomatic ties with the communist state in 1972. Day-long ventures to the Great Wall, evening drinking sessions with some of the Politburo's more promising cadres, and the chance to learn about China's rich history and forge closer ties despite the political differences. But for some members of the Labor family, the emergence of China from its economic slumber also represented a golden opportunity to do business in the way they liked best – corruptly.

On his second visit, in 1982, Paxton had met some young Communists keen to forge closer ties with the West and to learn more about Australia and its awaiting opportunities.

'Kimberley, Bruce Paxton is a nasty piece of work. He is completely devoid of moral scruples. He would sell his mother to make a profit. Over the years he has been tailed on his trips to China, and not just by us …'

'What sort of things did he get up to?'

'You name it. Paxton doesn't mind experimenting. We followed him to Taipei a few times, kept track as he went from one brothel to another. The Chinese aren't dumb; we suspect they planted a few hookers of their own – communists and capitalists are the same between the sheets.'

'Charles, that's quite a tale. I guess I have one burning question – who do you have to fuck to see these Marmalade Files?'

Dancer clasped his hands before his chest, like a penitent in the confessional, and fixed Gordon with a seductive stare.

'I think I might be able to help you there.'

Canberra, August 8

It was a footnote in the history of the Vietnam War, but for Doug Turner and his brothers in arms it carried a special significance – even forty years later.

On the morning of 21 September 1971, troops from Australia and New Zealand were combing the steaming jungle near the village of Nui Le, on high alert for their nimble enemy, when they stumbled into a Vietcong stronghold. Despite calling in US air power, a protracted battle resulted in the death of five Australian diggers. Three of those soldiers were left on the battleground for hours as their comrades fought a desperate hand-to-hand battle. They may well have been left behind for good but for the heroics of two New Zealand troopers who ignored the enemy fire to retrieve the bodies.

'They were fucking heroes and now both of them are dead. One of them passed away just a few weeks ago; I got word from his brother who also served in Vietnam. The other took his own life in '95 – he'd suffered for years and, well, he just couldn't go on ...'

Turner's voice was quavering, this emotional flight into the past taking its toll. 'And you know what? They got diddly squat from their government, too. Sound familiar? Of course it does – those bastards across the ditch treated their vets just as shabbily as the pricks in Canberra.

'I reckon the Australian people should hear about these heroes, don't you, Harry? So here's the deal. You get your newspaper to write this up and I'll give you chapter and verse on my little mate ... what do you think?'

It was a story with real appeal. Dunkley needed little convincing – particularly as Turner held all the aces when it came to Paxton.

The following Saturday, squeezed between a spread on the current contagion felling global markets and a fluffy piece on Gen Y's spending habits, a longish article was published on page 7 of *The Australian*. It was headed 'Forgotten Kiwi Heroes: Vietnam Vets Who Risked All for Aussie Mates'.

Photos of the two men – taken several years earlier, before their descent into ill health – accompanied the story, which carried the byline 'Harry Dunkley'. It was a long way from his usual sniping political fodder, but he suspected it might turn out to be one of the most important pieces he'd had published.

In short order he received an email from Doug Turner.

Harry, an outstanding piece. It brought a tear to this old digger's eye. You kept your end of the bargain and I will keep mine. How soon can you hop on a plane to Bali?

Bali, August 11

Waves danced on black volcanic sands as villagers fossicked for valuable stones rubbed smooth by time and tide. On a steaming Thursday, Harry Dunkley lugged his overnight bag along a beach track toward Cucukan, a tiny village hidden away on Bali's east coast. The villagers eked out a modest living from fishing and small-scale farming, but also served the handful of expats who'd made this tropical hideaway their home: two Americans, a retired Dutch lawyer, the odd blow-in from Britain – and Doug Turner, running from his past.

The Vietnam veteran had stumbled on Cucukan and been captivated by its quaint charm. He'd told Dunkley about the goose farmer who daily led his flock along dirt roads, the traditional dances performed by young girls in ornate costume. He had also told Dunkley of the half-dozen villas nestled close to the beach, with sweeping views across the waters.

His was third from the left, as you looked from the ocean. Dunkley set out along the glistening sands, politely declining the attention of several hawkers. It was only a five-minute stroll to Turner's white-walled abode, but in this climate it felt longer.

Time for rock'n'roll, Dunkley thought. He was closing in on this yarn, he knew, but it was still proving elusive. Doug Turner was the key and Dunkley felt the tingle down his spine he always experienced whenever a big story was within reach.

A walkway veered through heady jasmine vines, past a swimming pool complete with recliners scattered around its edges. An outdoor table showed the remains of a late breakfast.

And standing in the doorway, dressed in a silk robe, with thinning hair and a whitish goatee, was Doug Turner. He gave Dunkley an impish grin.

'Welcome to paradise, Harry Dunkley. Nice of you to drop in.'

Over coffee, Turner offered up some more of his past, the wild days in the west, running rampant with Bruce Paxton, before the breakdown of his marriage, and the descent into a deep funk. 'This place,' Turner said, his arms sweeping the villa, 'was a godsend. Gave me a purpose, and that article, Harry, well that was something else. So, you got your notebook ready?'

Dunkley nodded. 'Yep , but I am going to need more than just your word against a minister's.'

Turner smiled. 'Harry, I was Paxton's bag man and I kept every fucking receipt.'

Canberra, August 11

It was dubbed Gareth's Gazebo, a sneering doff of the hat to Gareth Evans, the former foreign minister who reputedly packed two suitcases for his first trip to Canberra: one for his clothes, another for his ego.

Just a stone's throw from Parliament House, the headquarters of the Department of Foreign Affairs and Trade was officially known as the R.G. Casey Building. Its vast confines were home to more than a thousand of

Canberra's most cunning bureaucrats – and, in the Marmalade Files, some of Australia's best-kept secrets.

Charles Dancer was one of the select few who knew about, and had access to, the Marmalade Files. After all, some of his best work had made its way into the archives. Now, with the bulk of DFAT's employees winding down after another crazy day of diplomacy and paper-shuffling, Dancer fondled the keypad that would allow him to enter the file room's secret confines. It was just after 6.30pm and he had promised to update Kimberley Gordon later that night, over a quiet drink at the Realm.

A row of gleaming cabinets greeted him once he'd been approved by the special security screen, and within a minute he'd removed the file he wanted and was skimming its contents. He planned to copy what was needed and then get the hell out.

'Lord, Mr Paxton, you have been a busy boy ...' He flicked through the rich history of a man who'd been relentlessly tailed, spied on, tapped and surveilled, his eyes fixing on a particularly juicy few pages, including several photographs that gave graphic meaning to the word 'compromised'.

There were nine pages in total to be copied and placed back into the file. Everything neat and in perfect order. That was the goal of foreign diplomacy, wasn't it? To maintain the mirage of stability, to avoid the appearance of confrontation, even when things were turning to shit.

Charles Dancer, with his decades of hands-on experience, wasn't about to meddle with the DFAT golden rule.

Canberra, August 11

The bank of television screens in the prime minister's press office was blasting out a nonstop barrage of Bailey Mania – in the long winter break it was the only political story filling the void. Brendan Ryan and George Papadakis, two of the most powerful men in the country, stood impotent, shaking their heads in awe at the power of a political zombie who was tearing the heart out of their government. And at the ability of the media to keep talking about the same story for weeks.

Transfixed, they watched as a demonstration outside Bailey's hospital was beamed through to each of the four TV screens. A beautiful young woman in a wheelchair, wearing a *GetSet!* pullover, was demanding that Bailey be allowed to continue in her job.

'I know what it's like to have people discriminate against you because you are differently abled,' the young woman said. 'I think the Toohey government has a great opportunity to show leadership here. Catriona Bailey has proven she is capable and can communicate. She should stay on as foreign minister.'

'Won't that pose some practical difficulties?' asked an ABC journalist. 'She can't leave hospital. Which means she can't attend parliament or Cabinet and can't travel.'

'That's old-think,' snapped the young woman. 'That's can't do. Technology is the great leveller. Cate can communicate. The world can come to her. She can be a symbol for all the differently abled: we can all aspire to the dignity of work, if we are only allowed to. And if Toohey won't let that happen then it is a second betrayal. A greater betrayal than when he backstabbed her so he could become prime minister. He would be betraying all of us as well.'

'Sweet Mother of Jesus take me now,' muttered Ryan. He turned to Papadakis but was interrupted by an explosion of expletives from the next office.

'Fucking flaming bull's tits and rat's cocks!' The prime minister stormed though the door, incoherent with rage. 'Did you see that shit! If I sack her now it'll be like clubbing a one-flippered harp seal cub to death.'

'Or boiling a three-legged baby panda in tar,' Ryan offered.

'You're not helping!' roared Toohey. 'You two are supposed to be the geniuses – what do I do?'

Both Ryan and Papadakis were, for once, lost for words. The void was filled by the voice of *GetSet!*'s Jamie Santow, who had stepped up to the ABC microphone, exuding his all-too-familiar moral superiority.

'I think there is little left to say after those stirring words,' he began, then continued for another twenty minutes.

'The gauntlet has been cast. Will Martin Toohey take up the challenge?'

'I fucking hate that opportunistic little prick.' Toohey was seething.

'Maybe we're looking at it the wrong way,' Papadakis said.

'There's some way of looking at this other than it being one of the largest shit sandwiches in Australian political history?' Toohey asked.

'I'm with the PM,' Ryan shrugged. 'Except it isn't just a shit sandwich, it's a whole bain-marie full of turds.'

'We've been preparing for a by-election we probably can't win,' Papadakis explained. 'If we lose it, we lose government. But if, out of the vast generosity of our spirit, we keep Bailey, then the weight is back on the Coalition. They have to offer her a pair and we keep our majority in parliament. Imagine the outcry if they took advantage of Bailey's stroke to try and take control of the numbers in the House.'

'What if they say the country is ungovernable and they're doing it in the national interest?' Ryan said.

'Scott is a small-l liberal. She wouldn't do it. It would make her look like a monster and she's already got an image problem. It would kill her with her socially aware support base.'

'But what does it buy us?' Toohey seemed to have calmed down. 'We've already been compromised at every turn. This minority government is killing us. Everyone wins but us. All we get is three years of taking it up the arse followed by an eternity in opposition. Why should we try and hold on?'

'It buys us time. We survive,' Papadakis said. 'Something will change.'

'It better,' said Ryan.

Canberra, August 12

It held the same appeal as eating one's greens, attending Mass or getting the cane on a winter morning. Once a week, Martin Toohey was obliged to sit down with Greens's leader Randal Wade, thanks to the accord he'd signed to keep his government afloat.

It had quickly become the mark on his weekly calendar that he dreaded – the ordeal of having to endure lengthy sermons from a pretentious twat with a messiah complex.

The PM believed that Wade and other moralising hypocrites had arrived in an era tailor-made for their brand of fast-food activism. Elizabeth Scott had been right: the demise of Christianity in the twentieth century meant the West was adrift. With no agreed set of values, it ricocheted from one daft idea to the next, driven by the winds of emotion.

The profound irony was that the Greens despised Christianity, yet their brand of politics mimicked religion: their followers were the new Puritans, on a relentless quest to rid the West of its many vices. And, stripped to its core, their creed, like the Puritans' of old, was deeply misanthropic. In the end, the Greens believed people – poor people, anyway – were a pestilence on the face of the earth. They hated everything about the working class: their jobs, cars, houses, choice of food, sports; their drinking, smoking and gambling. So the Greens were determined to legislate these vices away – or make them really expensive.

The PM was in the middle of writing himself a memo to 'call ABC managing director and threaten to cut funding … again' when George Papadakis knocked.

'Mr Wade is here,' Papadakis said, with that cheese-eating grin he wore when he knew he'd spend the next thirty minutes watching his old friend being tortured.

'Martin!' Wade flounced across the room with his hand extended. 'I'm sure you look forward to our chats as much as I do. They are always so fruitful.'

'Sure,' Toohey said. 'Sit. What's on your mind?'

'Well, I don't need to tell you how upset the community is about live cattle exports, Martin. I have never seen so many outraged emails.'

'I agree a lot of people are upset,' Toohey said, emotionless. 'But emails are no measure of how the community feels.'

'I don't believe what we saw in those Indonesian slaughterhouses was at all complex. It was clearly animal cruelty, and you obviously agreed because you initially agreed to shut the industry down and did suspend exports for some weeks.'

'We overreacted,' Toohey shot back. 'Our advice was to move slowly, to shut some abattoirs, not the lot. But, driven by you, and our own Left, we made a mistake … again. We hadn't thought through what it meant for the diplomatic relationship with Indonesia, let alone an industry that employs thousands in northern Australia.'

'You saved many animals from being treated cruelly, Martin. Your first call was right. Those cattle have feelings and desires. What really is the difference between them and us?'

'The fact that I can understand how stupid the statement you just made is, and a cow can't.'

Papadakis shifted in his seat, just enough for Toohey to recognise that his friend was sending him a 'calm down' message.

Wade was taken aback by a tone he had never heard from Toohey before and he dialled up his own passion. 'Some of us believe you restarted something as evil as the slave trade,' he parroted.

Toohey wrestled with his temper. 'Only someone who believes human and animal life are equivalent could say that. And to be consistent you would then have to demand an end to all slaughter of animals for food everywhere, which I note the Greens are not doing. Should I ban the eating of all meat, Randal?'

'Of course not. Don't be absurd.'

'I'm not being absurd. But, mark my words, if we close the door on live exports then the militant vegetarians behind that campaign will turn their attention to the domestic meat market. How's the new vegan regime going, by the way?'

'Never felt better, you should try it. In time, I believe many more people will discover the benefits of not eating meat. And, no matter what your excuses, I am reintroducing my bill to ban live exports and I expect you to support it.'

'I won't be doing that. We've had this discussion; the matter is settled.' Toohey glanced at Papadakis. His expression did not change but his chief of staff got the message. Papadakis had often said that the Greens were never satisfied with compromise and always returned to the well for more.

'Perhaps you should reconsider,' Wade said. 'I know you have a big agenda when parliament resumes. I know you need to deliver some big reforms to show you can govern. I'm sure you wouldn't want to see any of that jeopardised.'

'Are you threatening me, Randal?'

'Of course not. I'm just saying that this is a core issue for us and we want it fixed.'

'It wasn't even on your radar until the ABC covered it.'

'We are not kidding about this, Martin. This is deadly serious.'

Toohey locked Wade in his gaze and willed him dead. He thought of several bitter responses but, out of the corner of his eye, he could see Papadakis silently urging him to keep his cool. He took a deep breath.

'Too bad. We've already done this. You put up your bill and got to parade your concern. We opposed it and you had the pleasure of attacking us as heartless animal torturers. Go ahead. Put your bill up again, but I am telling you now, we will never support it.'

'Then I will have to reconsider some of the other conversations we have had. My base is very angry about this. And I'm personally disappointed, Martin; I thought you'd see reason.'

There was a long pause as Wade left the room and closed the door. Papadakis broke the silence. 'Not exactly the way I'd hoped to end the week.'

Toohey was in no mood for banter. He drummed his fingers on his notepad for a small eternity as he struggled to regain his composure.

It was time to fight back.

'George,' Toohey sighed, 'I have tried, God knows, to hold this circus together. But that's it. I'm done with being the only one eating shit.' He picked up his mobile, scrolled through some names and dialled a man who made his skin crawl.

'Sam, it's Martin. I need your help.'

Canberra, August 12

This was the moment of truth, a slug-'em-out showdown between two Liberal heavyweights, the female equivalent of Ali versus Foreman. And just like the rumble in the jungle, only one of them would triumph.

Emily Brooks and Elizabeth Scott sat a metre apart in a corner of the opposition leader's office, a plunger of coffee and a tray of biscuits untouched between them. They were hardly friends at the best of times, but this afternoon, in an empty parliament, the hatred was electric.

'I think you will agree it's time for a change of tactics, Liz.' Brooks found it difficult to maintain a facade of respect when she spoke with her leader. She despised Scott's soft-left world view and saw it as a cancer on the party. (The only thing she hated more than Scott was the Welcome to Country. That politically correct nod to Indigenous history that Catriona Bailey had foisted on parliament.)

'How so?' Scott, typically, disagreed with Brooks. 'We went within one seat of winning an election against a first-term government. That's the first time that has happened in eighty years. Now the government is in disarray and we are well placed.'

'True, but that was all their doing, not yours, Liz. Labor committed the greatest act of self-harm since Federation in killing a prime minister six weeks before the poll. And they still won. They formed government. Don't forget that. And since then, you have managed what I thought was impossible. Your approval rating is worse than that joke of a PM's. We should be untouchable, but we aren't.'

The blood rose in Scott's face. She had a quick temper and Brooks could see she had to fight to keep her emotions in check.

'I think we both know how Jon Robbie came by his story, Emily. Scoops are usually delivered in manila folders; you clearly prefer a box.'

'I don't know what you're talking about. And isn't your highly offensive accusation missing the point? You made a play against the prime minister that fell apart in three days. The leak wasn't the problem, wherever it came from.'

'Get to the point.'

'You're the problem – you. Your foolish attempt to try and blast out Toohey shattered your credibility. It called your political judgement into question, again. It reinforced all the hesitations that the electorate has about you. I don't know if you can recover.'

'Are you threatening me? Is this a challenge?'

'No, it's a warning. This is your last chance. I could get the numbers tomorrow to spill your position; it's not as if our colleagues are that attached to you.'

Scott eyed Brooks carefully. 'What do you want?'

'I want you to refuse a pair for Catriona Bailey when parliament returns.'

'You want me to deny a pair to a woman on life support?'

'Yes.'

'It's indecent. I can't do it. And I won't.'

'Do it, or I'll find someone who will.'

'I'll be murdered in the media. It's well known that I have a godchild with cerebral palsy. And I'm the first female leader of the opposition. You know that I've made a stand to try and make politics more family friendly.'

'That's your problem.' Brooks stood up. 'I'll show myself out.'

That night Jonathan Robbie ran an 'exclusive' which foreshadowed plans for the Coalition to adopt an extreme position on pairs, which would include denying one to the wildly popular, bedridden foreign minister. The story included the classic non-denial: 'A spokesman for the opposition leader declined to comment.'

Within the hour Bailey had tweeted: 'Scott reaches a new low. This is the politics of the gutter and a direct attack on the disabled.'

Online polling ran at 90 per cent against the plan and by morning a *GetSet!* picket had formed outside Scott's electoral office.

The Liberal leader was trapped, faced with a diabolical choice — conscience or career.

Canberra, August 14

The photo was postcard perfect, the couple unmistakeable. It was a remarkable sight: Bruce Paxton and his Chinese Mata Hari enjoying dinner at the Green Tea House in Beijing.

Kimberley Gordon worked methodically through the pages Charles Dancer had lifted from the Marmalade Files, but their theme was clear after a few sentences. The man with one of the most sensitive portfolios in the Australian government had revisited a dalliance with a woman as dangerous as a fresh drift of snow on a steep mountain cliff.

93

No wonder Paxton was setting off alarm bells in Defence and beyond; the man had succumbed to the lures of one of China's best. Weng Meihui was a real piece of work, a magnificent asset for her communist masters. She had used her nubile charms, the intel suggested, to secure all sorts of secrets for the state.

Paxton and Weng had been first identified as a couple in 1982, but the relationship caused few concerns for the Australian embassy – Paxton was just a union bovver boy with a healthy libido. Any nuggets of pillow-talk he was feeding Weng would be of little consequence.

It was only after he was elected to parliament that his continued interest in Ms Weng became significant. The file notes suggested the two had sought each other's company whenever Paxton visited China – in 1997, 2000 and 2002. It was not clear if, or when, he had been compromised by Weng, but the file noted that his increased interest in a number of Pacific islands – Nauru and Tuvalu, especially – coincided with China's growing financial links with these tiny nations.

China was using its financial clout to try and broaden its political power base across the Pacific Rim as a counterweight to the might of the United States. Superpower against rising power. The Cold War might have ended, but a new one was beginning and the world was again feeling the wrath of hostile states.

Had Paxton become a willing envoy for the Chinese? Gordon wondered. Many men had betrayed their country either for money or for sex. Looking at the intelligence on Paxton, it appeared he may have succumbed to both.

The file duly noted that Paxton appeared to have backed off and kept Weng at a distance as his political career took off, with appointments to the shadow ministry and then as minister for defence. 'An eight-year hiatus has been observed by officers. Despite twice visiting Beijing over this period – in 2005 and then in 2008 as a guest of the Chinese government for the Beijing Olympics – BP did not meet with Weng.'

However, there was no doubting the relationship had been rekindled during Paxton's most recent visit to China at the beginning of the year. The photographs did not lie. Bruce Paxton had walked straight back into a honey trap.

It all seemed so convenient – a defence minister with a known weakness for women seated so close to a former consort. Who'd arranged this liaison? Was it a set-up, a deliberate ploy to compromise the minister?

Kimberley Gordon's mind was racing; she needed answers. Most of all, she needed to find out just who was aware of this dirty little secret.

Canberra, August 15

There were days, long thankless days, when George Papadakis felt like Winston Wolfe, the Harvey Keitel character from *Pulp Fiction*, always cleaning up after someone else's mess. The unbridled joy of helping run the nation would give way to the rank thought that being chief of staff to the prime minister was a lowly descent into the gutter minds of those MPs bent on a suicide mission.

Xavier Quinn, the gaffe-prone education minister, was one of the worst. But foot-in-mouth wasn't his only problem – his biggest liability was an inability to keep his penis in his trousers.

Why was it always the Catholics? Papadakis again gave quiet thanks for the Great Schism. The best thing his Greek Orthodox Church ever did was ditch those weirdo Latins in 1054. A thousand years on, it still looked like a good policy.

It seemed to Papadakis that Australian Catholics who had been endlessly fed messages during childhood that bodily things were bad reacted in one of two ways: they felt guilty all the time or they simply rebelled and rooted like the world was about to end.

Xavier Quinn was the worst kind: he paraded his faith in public and in private banged like a dunny door in a cyclone.

Papadakis's theological musings were interrupted by a knock on his door.

'You wanted to see me, George?' It was Quinn.

'Yes. Sit down.' Papadakis wasn't about to waste time on niceties. 'Minister, do you recall a meeting we had in this very office the day before you were sworn in?'

'Yes.' Quinn shifted in his seat.

'Then you will recall one key message I had you repeat before I agreed that you would be included in the ministry?'

'Yes.'

'What was it?'

'Don't screw the crew.'

Papadakis leaned forward. 'Well done, Minister. Yes, rule number one: don't screw the crew. Why? Because it causes more grief, more often, than you can possibly imagine. I don't care that you are serially unfaithful to your wife as long as you're careful, but Minister, screwing your chief of staff is a bad idea. It's a bad idea at any time, but it's a worse idea when she's married to the assistant national secretary.'

'That's bullshit, all bullshit. I won't sit here and be talked to like this by you. I know there are rumours about Connie and me but there always are when men and women work closely together. It's … a kind of sexism.'

'Please, Minister, you of all people can't mount a feminist argument. Though I'm not surprised you tried to because, frankly, you would mount a knothole in a tree. That's the problem. So save the denials for your wife. Your chief of staff is leaving your office today. I'm doing a straight swap with the industry minister's COS.'

'What – Clare Jones? No way. She's a muff-diver and she hates me.'

'I know, she was even less keen than you … until I told her that part of her job was to persecute you, with my blessing. That's all, thanks.'

Papadakis began making some notes as Quinn stood and shrank towards the door.

'Oh, and Minister.'

'What?'

'About the blow job from the prostitute in the back seat of that cab in Darwin …'

Quinn went white. 'Who knows about that?' he squeaked.

'Turns out the cab driver is a party member. And, happily, rather than posting the security camera footage on YouTube he sent it to me. It might come in handy one day. Now get the hell out of my office.'

Papadakis felt his spirit sink. That had been the easy meeting. He found it simple to punish people he had no regard for. A much harder task was asking good people to do difficult things. And David Joyce, the secretary of the Department of Foreign Affairs and Trade, was salt of the earth and a fine public servant.

Joyce had been transferred from leading ASIO to try to keep Cate Bailey under some kind of control. He'd done an outstanding job, single-handedly keeping Australia's precious foreign relations in some kind of order while his mad minister galloped from one country to the next in an endless quest to promote herself and her absurdly expensive ambition to win a seat on the United Nation's Security Council.

'George?'

Papadakis stood to meet his old friend. 'David, good to see you, mate. Would you like a coffee?'

'No, mate, thanks.'

'Have a seat. Look … I won't beat around the bush about your minister.'

'Yes, very sad. The department's, er, well … they didn't wish that on her. But I guess I'm here to hear about a replacement.'

'Not exactly.'

'You're not giving it to the trade minister who's acting in the job? The guy couldn't find Tasmania on a map.'

'Of course not.'

'Thank Christ. Who then?'

'You know things are … difficult … for us politically, what with the hung parliament and the loss of a vote in the chamber.'

'Yes.'

Papadakis could tell Joyce's finely tuned spook instincts had begun to tingle. The man knew something bad was about to happen.

'Well, Cate Bailey can communicate, she's remarkably popular and there is a big push from the disability lobby to let her keep her job.'

'You are fucking joking, George!' Joyce leapt to his feet. 'You can't do this to me! I had to babysit that hideous bitch for a year as she ran amok around the globe. Do you know how many disasters I averted? I'm surprised Mossad hasn't taken her out after she sold out Israel to woo Security Council votes from the Arab states. We threw a party in my office the night she was taken to hospital and invited half the Canberra diplomatic corps. The French bought Bollinger. We didn't leave till dawn.'

'David, it's only until we can think our way through this. You'll be running the show. How much damage can she do from a hospital bed?'

'Heaps!' Joyce's face was red. 'She's learned to text. She sends me about a hundred messages a day. And because she's borderline Asperger's she's memorised the mobile numbers of half the world's foreign ministers. She's bombarding them with her hare-brained ideas. She has to be stopped. I don't have the strength for this anymore. I'm fifty-six, I can take my super and run.'

'David … please. I will fix it, just give me a couple of weeks. I don't know how but I will fix it.'

'You'd better fix it or this country's rooted and I'm moving to New Zealand.'

'Just a few more weeks.'

'One month. Tops. After that find another idiot to do your bidding.'

'Thank you.'

Joyce slouched towards the door, opened it and stopped. 'What happened?'

'What do you mean?'

'What happened to Labor, George? You used to be a serious party. Now you're some kind of sad, faded circus act.'

Canberra, August 15

YOU GOOSE!

Sydney's *Daily Telegraph* liked to start the morning screaming, preferably at someone it hated.

Alongside the massive headline was a picture of Greens leader Randal Wade looking suitably foolish and startled, snapped opening the front door of his Point Piper mansion in his animal-patterned pyjamas.

The three paragraphs below the enormous headline went straight for the jugular.

Greens leader Randal Wade is under intense pressure to quit after being caught illegally buying *foie gras*, a ritzy French paste made from the livers of force-fed geese.

An outraged Lindy Byrne from Animals Australia said Wade, an avowed vegan, was a 'rank hypocrite'.

'Everyone knows foie gras is one of the cruellest foods in the world,' she said. 'And clearly he felt guilty about it because he has been trying to hide it. He has to go.'

The tabloid had detailed information linking Wade to the illegal importation and consumption of *foie gras*, including credit card bills, email trails and logs of phone calls. Someone clearly had access to private details that were very hard to get. The *Tele* pointed out that Wade had initially denied the story, but once presented with the wealth of detail had directed the paper to his lawyer. The lawyer had tried and failed to get an injunction preventing the story from being published.

The revelation was a double blow for Wade because in February the Australian Quarantine and Inspection Service had slapped an indefinite ban on the importation of poached and semi-cooked *foie gras* due to an outbreak of Newcastle disease in France.

So not only was Wade morally culpable in the eyes of his peers, he had deliberately broken the law. And as a senior AQIS source pointed out, Wade's selfishness was a direct threat to the environment.

'We didn't ban this stuff because it was the food of choice for wankers,' the source said. 'Newcastle disease is highly contagious. It could devastate

Australia's avian industry and kill native birds by the hundreds of thousands. This guy is a selfish, dangerous clown. And a criminal.'

In several inside pages the *Tele* took Wade apart. There was a novice's guide to the horrors of *foie gras*. It detailed how ducks and geese were caged and force fed several times a day – a mechanical feeder stuffed down their throats so a mixture of corn and oil could be pumped into their stomachs. This blew up their livers to ten times the normal size, which was where the name *foie gras* came from, meaning, literally, fat liver.

Finally, it detailed the cost of Wade's food perversion. Five hundred grams of poached whole goose *foie gras* retailed for $300. And it was usually eaten with champagne or a sweet wine like Sauternes or Monbazillac. An investigation of Wade's bin had unearthed an empty bottle of 1998 vintage Krug champagne, which retailed for $379. Also discovered was the butt of a Cohiba Espléndidos cigar, retailing for $83. The *Tele*'s total for one pre-dinner splurge was $762, a figure it said could feed a Mount Druitt family of four for more than a fortnight.

It was devastating.

Sam Buharia forensically examined the paper to ensure there was not a single fingerprint on it that could lead back to him.

No. Job done. A perfect crime. And the cunt wouldn't see the week out.

___

Canberra, August 15

It was one of Canberra's finest days, the clarity of the sky guaranteed to lift anyone's spirits. Unfortunately for Kimberley Gordon, she was locked in the confines of Defence's most secure facility and felt only the artificial climate of recycled air and harsh neon lighting. Adding to Gordon's grey mood, her boss had placed a series of files on her desk with firm instructions. 'I need answers tomorrow morning.'

Usually such an edict would be enough to stimulate her analytical brain into trying to solve whatever problem had been placed before her. But today she couldn't keep her mind on the job. Instead she was captivated by the mystery surrounding the pasts of Bruce Paxton and Catriona Bailey, pasts that, she was sure, were about to explode into the present.

And today there had been a significant development. Gordon's colleagues were intrigued by a smallish article buried in the world pages of the *New York Times*, quoting senior Pentagon sources who, according to the *Times*, were miffed by reports that Australia was about to pull back on the flagship Joint Strike Fighter program. One quote, in particular, stood out. 'A number of

99

recent decisions by Minister Paxton raise the question of his commitment to ANZUS.'

In diplomatic terms, it was a definite shot across the bow. It was rare for US sources to be directly critical of a close ally like Australia. Something big was going on. She didn't know what it was, but Gordon was sure that she and Dunkley were edging close to the epicentre.

It reminded her of the blunt message the Americans had sent in the lead-up to the dismissal of Gough Whitlam in November 1975. The head of the CIA had told his Australian counterpart that the US wanted Whitlam gone. Gordon was no raving leftie, but she could still recall her outrage and anger when, as a novice in the intelligence arena, she had first been alerted to the CIA's involvement in the Dismissal.

Why wasn't this on the history syllabus? Surely the Australian people were not so supine as to completely ignore this shameful episode?

For a while, Gordon had become obsessed with the issue, particularly after reading of the show trial of Christopher Boyce, the American who was sentenced to forty years imprisonment after being convicted of spying in 1977.

Boyce had learned that Pine Gap – the communications facility in the Northern Territory that America had promoted as a joint facility with Australia – was in reality a CIA project. Incredibly, Boyce claimed to have CIA cables outlining plans to dispose of the Whitlam government for fear that it would close Pine Gap. The CIA was profoundly concerned by Whitlam's socialism and his wooing of China.

Eventually arrested for leaking information to Russia, Boyce was thrown into jail and never given the chance to explain why the US would betray one of its closest allies.

Gordon had studied the case carefully and considered it the most egregious act of interference by a foreign government in Australia's sovereign affairs. She could recite word for word Whitlam's lament to parliament after the Dismissal: 'It is precisely because America is our principal ally that Australia must be satisfied that American agents are not acting in a manner contrary to our interests as a nation. Are we to let an ally get away with something that a rival would not be allowed to get away with? Alliances are not strengthened by covert operations or by condoning or covering up such covert operations.'

They were masterful and prescient words and they came flooding back as Gordon contemplated what she'd uncovered in the past few weeks – and what she suspected still remained hidden in the vault of secrecy.

Despite every keystroke at DSD being logged, Gordon was so enraged at the thought that the Americans were meddling in domestic politics – again – that her usual caution had cracked. She'd spent the last few hours trawling through the DSD's super-computers looking for clues, but had sought to cover her tracks by embedding her searches within existing DSD projects. Then she'd returned to the rote working day, confident in her ability to escape internal prying eyes.

Late that evening, logging on to her personal email account at home, Gordon hit the keyboard with a ferocity that surprised her, tapping out a few sentences to her friend.

> Charles, starting to look like shades of '75 here. What do our friends in DC think they are up to? Do they REALLY believe they can get away with it? Again! This is not the action of a friendly nation.
>   Kimberley

She hit send, then wrote a similar message to Harry for good measure, watching the emails disappear into the ether before closing the computer for the night. It was late and she was planning an early start tomorrow.

A few kilometres away, in a small, brightly lit room, two men monitored their PC screens. Just after 11pm, they logged a short email.

> Charles, starting to look like shades of '75 ...

———————

Sydney, August 15

Elizabeth Scott gazed at the ocean and breathed in a long draught of the chill salt air. The moon hung full and low, skimming light over the waves as they rolled towards Manly.

The crazies will be out tonight, she mused, sending me mad messages. Immediately, she tried to erase the image from her mind. She needed to think clearly and not about any of the thousand pieces of ephemera that crowded political life. No one, except those who had done the job, could ever imagine it. The workload was crushing, relentless and largely thankless. Constituents, local branch members, businesses, donors, colleagues, the media – everyone wanted a piece of you. No, everyone demanded it. And believed your time was theirs by right.

If they didn't get what they wanted the threats were never far away: 'Won't vote for you', 'Will challenge your preselection', 'Will tell the media' – or the new narcissism: 'Will write about it on Twitter.'

Scott was used to high-pressure jobs but found politics suffocating. You could never lash out in public, no matter how rudely you were treated, or how idiotic the complaint. The mask was always on, and it chafed.

She could still be herself on this porch, looking out to sea, when the rest of the family was asleep. She had loved this house from the moment she saw the ocean. In moments of despair she could feel her spirits rise as she was drawn into the uncluttered vastness of it.

'Why am I doing this to myself?' It was not the first time she'd asked the question but, right now, the answer was more remote than ever. She had given up her freedom to be locked in the spotlight of the most thankless job in public life: opposition leader.

From day one, everyone had questioned her motives.

'Only wants to be PM' was the default assessment. She'd been branded power-mad, dictatorial, heartless, politically inept and uncaring by people who knew nothing about her. She barely bothered to read opinion pieces anymore, so rote had the abuse become. And the cartoons. From the moment she'd stepped into politics she'd been drawn wearing a tiara with a silver spoon in her mouth, or dressed in a ballgown. That she had largely made her own wealth never seemed to matter. She came into public life as a spoiled rich girl cliché and she feared she'd never shake the image.

Yes, she was ambitious and that was never going to be sated in business. She was a nationalist and believed fiercely that Australia wasn't a lucky country. It had made its own luck and that luck would run out without good leadership. She had ideas and knew she could make a difference, if she ever got the chance.

But now that chance, like the night tide, was ebbing. Scott had made so many compromises that even she began to wonder if what people said about her was true: that there was nothing she wouldn't do to get to the Lodge.

And when she got there what would be left? A shell, echoing a cacophony of conflicting voices she had mimicked to talk her way to power.

She recalled one of the lines from her favourite play, *A Man for All Seasons*, where, in a debate between William Roper and Thomas More, Roper says he would cut down every law in England to get at the Devil.

'Oh?' said More. 'And when the last law was down, and the Devil turned round on you – where would you hide, Roper, the laws all being flat?'

In her six years in politics she had met only one person who really understood the terrifying dilemma of trying to balance conviction with the pursuit of power. He recognised something of himself in her, understood her conflicts, and knew she was a good person. Different from him, but good. It mattered so much to her that someone knew.

And the connection had been so strong it frightened her. But she couldn't talk to him anymore. Politics was killing all the things that she loved. She wondered if it would kill her. If, one day, she would sit on the porch, looking out to sea, and not be able to remember who she was.

Canberra, Four years before present

They'd been engulfed in silent uncertainty as the taxi drove them back to the Embassy Motel all those years ago.

It was a short fifteen minutes from the Elbow Room and they were both lost in the thoughts and emotions of the last hour.

Elizabeth Scott glanced at Martin Toohey as the streetlights tracked across his face. He was a decent man; flawed, as she was, but decent. She hoped he saw that in her.

They climbed the stairs to their second-floor rooms, which the hotel's staff, as usual, had ensured were next to each other.

Scott didn't want it to end – for the brief, flirtatious moments of understanding to evaporate into another lonely night in an empty hotel room.

She dropped her keys. Toohey swept them up and turned to her. He stepped closer than he needed to be. Much closer.

He put the keys in her hand and closed it, wrapping his fingers around hers. He stared into her eyes and Scott again felt that expectant tingle that had evaded her for years.

'It's … it's been just great. You are great. I can't tell you how important tonight was, how it felt to … just talk.' Toohey seemed to be finding it hard to focus; he seemed almost nervous.

'It was.' She didn't budge, didn't make a move towards the door. Half of her screamed, 'Ask me! Just ask me!'

'Well …' He shuffled on the spot. 'Early morning and everything. I should get some sleep. So should you. Not that you need it, you look just … just great.'

'You too. Goodnight.' She kissed him on the cheek, turned without looking back, opened the door to her room and walked in. Alone.

She rested against the door and heard the click of his door closing. Surely, she thought, this is the moment when I feel good about myself, when I congratulate myself for being faithful.

'So why do I feel so empty?' she said out loud. She surveyed the dreary decor and sighed. 'If this is what victory over sin feels like, God, then it's little wonder you lose so many battles.'

She threw her coat onto the bed. There was a knock and she could have sworn her heart actually stopped beating.

She opened the door on his goofy smile.

'On indulgence, Madam Speaker, I'm sure there was something else I wanted to say ... I just can't remember what.'

She threw her arms around him and they kissed.

'Jesus!' he exclaimed.

'Let's leave him out of this.'

The night was a blur of passion. Both knew it would be their first and last time together. And neither wanted to leave anything unexplored.

Canberra, August 17, 2011

Like many reporters his age, Harry Dunkley feared the great era of newspapers was coming to a close. Crusading editors who were prepared to send their charges into the field had been replaced by bean counters, hired to prune budgets and slash expenses.

There were only a handful of heroes left, and more sinners than saints. Christ, there were some days when Dunkley questioned whether there was any principle or honour left in his once noble profession, now seemingly controlled by the vapid minds of those who chased celebrity and preferred fluff and polemic over hard news.

But today, a bright winter's day in the national capital, Dunkley awoke with a sense that he was about to make history.

It was nearly a quarter to four and there was still no sign of the minister. Harry Dunkley paced the anteroom, waiting for the twenty minutes of valuable ministerial time he'd been allocated when he'd pushed Bruce Paxton for a meeting. Parliament was in full swing and Paxton was in the throes of his reform agenda, carving large chunks from the military's bulging arsenal of overpriced kit. Dunkley privately shared Paxton's zeal for taking on the defence establishment, but this was not about sentiment. He'd pumped himself up, written and then rewritten his notes and memorised the questions that needed to be fired at the minister.

An approaching swirl told him something was up, a flurry of bodies gliding by in the outside corridor and, finally, Bruce Paxton, minister for defence, swept in. He tensed up when he saw Dunkley, as if he suspected the next half-hour or so would prove as painful as extracting a tooth without anaesthetic.

'Righto, Mr Dunkley, what is it that couldn't wait?' Paxton got straight down to business. He'd taken a beating during Question Time and Dunkley noticed a slight twitch in his right shoulder, the sign of a man under severe pressure.

'Minister, for the past two months I've been researching your time with the CFMEU and the United Mineworkers—'

'Oh, terrific, mate, I'm flat chat trying to reshape Defence and you're about to give me a fucking history lesson.'

'More than a history lesson, Minister. In 1982, you made a trip to China. You were WA secretary of the Mineworkers at the time, correct?'

'If you say so, mate.'

'You made contact with Zhou Dejiang and Zheng Wang, two of China's up and comers. Mr Zhou is now in charge at the Ministry for State Security and Mr Zheng ... well, the son of the Red Capitalist has done very nicely out of his various business ventures.'

Paxton's face was impassive.

'One of those ventures was Guangzhou Mining. Zheng set that up in 1982, supported by his father and the Chinese government which deemed him a "safe" entrepreneur. He was a busy boy, Mr Zheng, establishing Guangzhou as one of the vanguard Chinese export companies. He took tentative steps at first, forging links with the West; there were various projects in Brazil, the US – and Western Australia.

'And that, Mr Paxton, is where you come in.'

'Really? How exactly?'

Dunkley took a deep breath. This was the key moment and he wanted to get it right.

'The United Mineworkers Federation Workplace Reform Association.' Dunkley spoke slowly, deliberately. He wanted to make sure that Paxton got it. From the slight grimace on his face, Dunkley gathered that he had.

'Guangzhou had big plans for its investments in WA – it was looking at iron ore, nickel and possibly gold. It had the backing of the Communist Party and an endless line of credit.

'You were briefed on those plans during another trip to China, late in 1983. At an informal dinner that Mr Zheng hosted for you and three others. You sought him out some time after this, didn't you? You wanted to talk turkey and, by all accounts, he was eager to listen. Zheng was keen to foster ties with those in the West who could help his business expand and you, a senior union figure, were exactly what he was looking for.'

Paxton interrupted. 'This is all very impressive, Mr Dunkley, but where's it leading? I'm running behind time thanks to the Coalition's brains trust … now, that's a contradiction in terms …' He smiled grimly.

'I know, Minister, but I need to spell this out. You made arrangements with Zheng, offered him a priceless deal — industrial peace, provided he gave you what you wanted: money. And he did.' Dunkley checked a figure on a page of his notes. 'To be precise, $385,900 paid into a Commonwealth Bank account held at the Northbridge branch in Perth. This was the account affiliated with the Workplace Reform Association, except its purpose wasn't to help the members of the UMF, was it? You wanted this money for much less noble purposes, like ensuring your re-election as state secretary.'

Dunkley's confidence was growing. He had documents to back every word. 'Then there was the house, the nice pad near Freo, all paid for by Guangzhou. And then — the big one. As if it wasn't bad enough using Chinese money to buy union elections and personal property, you channelled nearly $80,000 into your '96 campaign to win Brand. Those nice Community Voice newsletters, the endless mail-outs to voters, those sponsorships of the local netball and footy teams were all paid for by China Inc. And you never declared one red cent, did you?'

The two men stared at each other, each loath to blink first.

Dunkley felt a surge of excitement. He knew he had his man.

The minister started to clap slowly, with the heavy hand of sarcasm.

'Mr Dunkley, that is quite a story. It must have taken some time to piece it all together. I reckon you could enter that in the Walkleys — in the Best Fiction category. You might think yourself pretty fucking smart, but you can't prove one word!'

Dunkley reached into his bag, pulled out his digital recorder and placed it in front of the minister's snarling face. He turned up the volume before pressing play.

'Good morning, my name is Douglas William Turner, Vietnam veteran, 2RAR, and a former assistant state secretary with the CFMEU. For eight long years, I was a loyal bagman for Bruce Leonard Paxton. And I kept records of every transaction. Oh, and Bruce, if you're listening to this, you are a dead man ...'

_____

Canberra, August 18

George Papadakis didn't like surprises. And he really didn't like Bruce Paxton. For him, Paxton was another piece of garbage left over from the Bailey government that he didn't dare pick over in case something nasty crawled out.

And something very nasty had just crawled out.

The PM's chief of staff had taken the call after midnight, just as he was drifting off after another day of tragicomedy on the hill.

'George ... it's Bruce ... Bruce Paxton ...'

The defence minister was slurring his words, enough to confirm he'd been drinking most of the night. 'Something's come up, I need to meet with the PM tomorrow ... today, I mean ...'

'When you say "something", do you mean the Yanks have decided to give us the stealth bombers for free? Or do you mean something bad?'

'The second one, mate ... something bad, not pretty.'

'How "not pretty", Bruce?'

'That fucker Dunkley from the _Oz_ is out to get me,' Paxton whimpered.

Papadakis's blood ran cold. He despised most of the press gallery but he had a grudging admiration for Harry Dunkley. If he had something on Paxton, chances were it was real and dangerous.

Over a torturous hour-long call, Papadakis managed to wheedle all the details out of Paxton. And they were horrifying.

The meeting was scheduled for eight.

'Prime Minister, the defence minister is here to see you.'

Martin Toohey didn't bother rising to greet Paxton, who wore the crumpled look of a man facing his own mortality.

And Toohey and Papadakis weren't about to make it any easier. For ten drawn-out seconds, they said nothing, until the prime minister broke the silence, uttering just one word.

'Well?'

For several hours, Paxton had been rehearsing the lines that he hoped would save his ministerial career and steer him through this crisis. At 4am, the arguments had sounded convincing and he had even allowed himself to imagine that he, Papadakis and Toohey would emerge to fight this battle together.

But as he began to speak the dream evaporated, and all he could muster for the two most powerful men in the country was a barely audible, 'I'm fucked.'

'The prime minister and I have already established that. What we need to ensure, Bruce, is that we are not all as fucked as you.'

Papadakis's voice was as cold as the morning frost. But he could not completely abandon Paxton; after all, the government was hanging by a thread – Catriona Bailey remained in hospital and now a ministerial resignation loomed. Papadakis knew the resignation would have the media baying for blood.

The prime minister finally spoke. 'Bruce, this is what you're going to do. You will write a letter of resignation and say nothing to anyone until this story breaks. You will then retire to the backbench, but not from parliament. You will be looked after. If any legal expenses are incurred, the party will pay. It irks me to say this but we cannot afford the loss of even fools like you before the next general election.'

With that, Paxton rose and walked from the room, receiving not even a cursory farewell. He knew that he had no choice. He would draft the resignation letter as instructed. But even as he drifted from sight, past the security guard's cubicle, he was plotting. Plotting redemption and revenge. And not necessarily in that order.

Sydney, August 18

'SHAME MURDOCH, SHAME.' A small group of sloganeering protestors greeted Harry Dunkley as he arrived at News Limited's head office in the inner Sydney suburb of Surry Hills. The phone-hacking scandal had filtered Down Under, providing a platform for these professional agitators to ply their trade.

It was a shade after 10am. The drive from the national capital had taken nearly four hours, the last thirty kilometres a slow crawl along the M5. It had given Dunkley a chance to go through his strategy for explaining the import of the Paxton story to his editor and the company's fastidious inhouse lawyer. He had gone over its factual accuracy and, most importantly, the legal protection conferred by Doug Turner's statement, which backed up every piece of evidence Dunkley had gathered. In his mind, it was watertight.

But he knew there would still be a battle to get the go-ahead to publish.

He'd just ordered a coffee from the ground-floor cafe when his BlackBerry rang. It was Ben Gordon. Harry felt guilty – he'd noticed several missed calls from Gordon last night and this morning and still hadn't replied.

'Hey, Ben, sorry. I meant to call you back, but the last twenty-four hours have been busy.'

'Harry, where are you?'

'I'm in Sydney, mate, going to see the boss to discuss you know what.'

'We need to talk.' There was a hard edge to Gordon's voice, an urgency that snapped Dunkley out of his self-obsession.

'What's up?'

'We need to talk, not over the phone.'

'I'll be in Sydney all of today, maybe tomorrow as well. I'm sorry, Ben, I should have been in touch earlier but things have moved very quickly.'

'Harry, we need to talk, asap. There's a whole other side to this ...'

Dunkley saw Deb Snowdon, his editor, enter the cafe and head his way. 'Ben, mate, I've got to—'

'There's something else—'

'Harry!' For once Snowdon looked happy as she sat down beside him.

'Gotta go,' Dunkley said into the phone, his tunnel vision for the big scoop relegating his friend's plea for the moment.

He could just hear Ben on the other end, still talking. '... something about Bailey, Harry. Something unbelievable.'

Canberra, August 18

Brendan Ryan was alone, as usual. The Labor powerbroker liked to work late into the night, with only the light from his computer screen illuminating his apartment on State Circle, the road ringing the parliament.

He had shared the odd relationship in his thirty-eight years, but women usually found his introspection, intensity and lack of interest in anything but politics a turn-off. Coupled with an inability to tolerate people he considered dim – and that was most people – it didn't make him an engaging date.

From the time he was a teenager he had gone to bed well after midnight and risen late, but recently he'd found it hard to sleep at all. He was constantly anxious and his already poor health was worsening.

Everywhere the news was bad. It seemed as if the pillars on which he had built his life were all crumbling at once. The global financial crisis had accelerated the power shift from the West to the East and Ryan feared for the future.

The West had been on a suicide mission for a couple of hundred years, its most influential thinkers chipping away at its foundations, weakening its political structures. They'd killed off the Christian God, taken an axe to the hierarchy of ideas, demonised the past and opposed development. They were the vandals in Rome. And Rome was burning.

Never a fan of the European Union, Ryan feared its splintering monetary system would bring the entire enterprise undone. He could have taken a sadistic pleasure in seeing Europe, the source of many of the worst ideas in Western thought, go belly up. Except it would probably drag the United States down too. And for Ryan that would be an unalloyed catastrophe.

Ryan understood the flaws in the United States better than most, but believed that the post-World War II settlement guaranteed by US military might had delivered more good than evil. America had established and maintained the power structures that ensured prosperity.

So the shift in power from West to East disturbed Ryan. He hoped conflict could be averted, but deep in his soul he feared it couldn't. War was coming. In some ways it was already raging as, daily, China launched internet attacks. But it was only the beginning. War was coming and the West was weak.

At some stage in any life a man had to choose his friends. Ryan's were the US and Israel. Everyone else could go hang.

And Ryan had also chosen his great love: the Australian Labor Party. For Ryan, Labor was the supreme innovator in Australian political life, driving the projects that had delivered a just society: a living wage, public education, the pension, superannuation and universal medical care.

Now Labor was adrift. The same shallow ideas from the Left that were killing the West had infected and corroded his party. It had lost touch with its largely conservative blue-collar base as white-collar, inner-city lefties reinterpreted the party of Chifley and Curtin into some kind of endless gay Mardi Gras.

'If Chifley were alive today, the Left would have banned his fucking pipe,' Ryan muttered.

His party was broken and, for the first time in his life, Ryan didn't know how to fix it.

_____

Canberra, August 18

The night was deathly still as a light mist crept round a row of poplars laid bare by Canberra's long winter. It was just after 9pm and Telopea Park was empty and dark.

Kimberley Gordon liked it this way. She would often walk this lonely strip in the evening, finding its bracing cold and silence a perfect antidote to a frenetic day. The park was just a few minutes from her apartment, and after reaching its pathways she set her course towards the lake.

She could just pick out the distant chimes of the National Carillon, its bells ringing out Schubert's *Serenade*. The music of the Carillon usually soothed, but not tonight. Instead its mix of metal and melody only added to her growing sense of alarm.

Gordon had stepped out to try and make sense of what she knew – how a hundred jagged pieces of evidence pointed to an extraordinary conclusion.

The ring of her mobile, from inside her coat pocket, interrupted her thoughts. She ferreted out the phone but the number was unfamiliar and she didn't need the distraction anyway. What she needed was clear air and headspace.

Another thought had been nagging her, a fear that she had left her fingerprints as she pursued the key to this terrible secret.

She mentally marked out a series of possible missteps, privately chastising herself for being so stupid, so bloody amateur. First, she had used a work computer to download information – information locked in DSD's electronic vaults. She knew every keystroke would be logged, but had thought the risk worth taking. Then she had fired off a series of emails to Charles Dancer outlining her concerns about this deepening conspiracy.

She recalled how her home computer had slowed one night. And how she had heard two distinct clicks on the line during one of the dreaded phone calls to her mother. She'd been sloppy. Was she paying the price; was she being tracked through cyberspace? Were her phone calls being tapped? Had she, the hunter, become the hunted?

She shivered and pulled her cashmere coat tighter, hoping to ward off the cold and a growing sense of panic. She desperately wanted to share the intel with Dunkley, and looked forward to meeting with her friend.

She turned and quickened her pace, keen to put the park's darkness behind her.

A frightened possum scurried across her path and up a tree, its rasping cry piercing the quiet. Her heart missed a beat as she came to a sudden halt.

There was something else. An echo. A scuffle of shoes on the footpath nearby.

She was not alone.

_____

Sydney, August 19

The din of the garbage truck nearly tore a hole through Dunkley's sorry head. The paper-thin walls of the pub on Albion Street amplified the sounds of the early morning inner-city traffic. Dunkley blinked, staring at a damp spot on the ceiling before remembering why he was there. He stumbled out of bed, noticing the time – 7.17am – as he opened the door, fumbling for the newspaper he'd ordered.

He placed it on the bed as he reached for his BlackBerry, noticing six missed calls – three from the same number. Probably 2UE, he reckoned, wanting a chat about his scoop. He pushed the curtains back a few feet and unfurled the broadsheet to its full front-page splendour.

'DEFENCE MINISTER IN UNION SLUSH FUND SCANDAL' screamed the headline. Christ, thought Dunkley, marvelling at his page 1 handiwork. He really had plunged the knife in. He finished reading his splash before turning to the page 4 and 5 spread, which featured a graphic detailing Paxton's sordid dealings with the Chinese beside pictures of Doug Turner and Zheng Wang.

Just then his phone rang. It was the Canberra online desk, one of the early morning crew whose role was to deliver 'value-add' to the paper's daily coverage of national affairs.

'Woohoo, great fucking story, Harry, it's going off. Twitter is in meltdown and three opposition MPs have already called for Paxton to stand down ... Hold on, this has just come through from the prime minister's press office – I bet they're ecstatic with you – the minister is going to hold a presser in the Blue Room, 9am. What d'ya reckon? Will he walk the plank?'

Dunkley was pretty sure he would but couldn't be certain, given the precarious nature of the Toohey government. One thing was clear, though: Dunkley wouldn't be at the press conference to twist the blade a little deeper and to bask in the adulation and jealousy of his press gallery colleagues. He'd been at News Limited HQ until late, getting the lawyers to sign off on the final story. And then he'd spent the early hours celebrating. Now he needed to leg it back to the national capital for the critical follow-up – and to meet with Ben Gordon to discover what he'd found out that was so urgent.

Canberra, August 19

From the early hours of the morning the Coalition's shock troops had been carpet-bombing the airways, decrying the latest Toohey government scandal and demanding an early election.

The hard right's warrior queen, Emily Brooks, had been on to the ABC's News Radio from the moment she arrived at work. An interview was put to air just after 6am.

'This government is a sick joke and a disgrace – it has to go. The prime minister must sack his minister then drive to Government House and sack himself,' she fulminated. 'The people of Australia deserve better than this motley rabble, this poor excuse for a government. The Coalition is ready to take over, and the people are demanding it. The time for change is now.'

It took a few moments for the interviewer to be able to break into the diatribe.

'Surely the resignation of the minister will be enough. What will you do if the government carries on?'

'Shadow Cabinet has voted on this,' Brooks thundered. 'We will deny a pair to the foreign minister and block every piece of legislation. In the national interest we will shut this government down until it does the decent thing.'

'With respect,' the interviewer said, 'your leader, Elizabeth Scott, has repeatedly refused to back that tactic. Has she had a change of heart?'

'I'm quite certain she sees the sense of it now,' Brooks said.

Scott was scheduled to make an appearance on *Wakey Wakey* just after seven. She was equally strident in calling for an end to what she called 'the incompetent and illegitimate Toohey government'.

'If the prime minister does not call an election will you deny a pair to the foreign minister?' asked the all-too-pretty male presenter.

Scott paused. Her staff had told her that Brooks had already been trying to paint her into a corner. They were split on how she should respond. But Scott wasn't.

'No,' she said. 'There has to be some grace in public life. I will not deny a pair to a woman on life support. It would be monstrous … I cannot lead a party that does not observe the basic rules of human decency.'

The opposition leader had drawn a line in the sand. She would not concede to the demands of Brooks and her hard-right cronies. Scott had finally found the point beyond which she would not compromise.

She had set the scene for a showdown with Brooks at the joint party room meeting on Tuesday. She had made her choice and now the party would have to make its decision: back her or sack her.

_____

Lake George, August 19

For nearly two hours, the radio had played a steady loop of Bruce Paxton the Musical. The ABC had predictably gone wall to wall after the shock of the minister's resignation, made public in his press conference, calling in its political hotshots to interview anyone they could get their hands on. The high-rating commercial stations 2GB and 2UE had devoted large chunks of their morning line-up to the scandal too. That great court of public opinion – talkback radio – was in overdrive, with the punters evenly divided on whether Paxton should have walked the plank.

Dunkley had raised the temperature on the scandal during several radio interviews by phone while on the road, telling Melbourne's 3AW that there was 'more to come'. He'd regretted the comment immediately.

'What sort of stuff do you still have?' the broadcaster had asked, a reasonable question, but in truth Dunkley didn't know. He could only hope Ben Gordon had some dynamite in his kitbag. It had sounded like it on the phone yesterday. But Dunkley didn't know because he'd barely spoken to Ben in weeks. Journalism was a selfish business, but he'd make it up to his friend, his collaborator on this grand tale.

The shimmering haze of Lake George, flanked by a trail of giant wind turbines on its eastern edge, told Dunkley he was a half-hour from Canberra. The trip down the highway had flown, the adrenalin rush from the Paxton resignation acting like a turbo-charge for the rental car he was driving. Several times, he had felt like winding down the windows and shouting into the wind 'I AM FUCKING ALIVE', but the temperature had roared out its warning, and he'd timidly withdrawn.

He reached for his BlackBerry and hit speed dial for Ben Gordon. It rang six or seven times, before a strange voice answered.

'Who is this?' Harry asked.

'Senior Constable Chris Waters. And who might you be?'

Dunkley's mind was racing. He checked to make sure he'd rung Ben's number.

'I'm a friend of Ben Gordon's … is everything all right?'

'You want to tell me your name?'

'Harry Dunkley. Is everything all right?'

'Mr Dunkley, *The Australian*, right? I think it wise we meet in person. You're in Canberra?'

'Not yet. I'm about twenty-five minutes away, depending on traffic.'

'I'm in Woden, the main police station. You know where we are?'

Dunkley kept his voice calm, despite his rising alarm.

'Yep, I'll see you hopefully in half an hour.'

He hung up and wondered what on earth Ben had got himself into.

Canberra, August 19

Even while Bruce Paxton was singing his death hymn, journalists were receiving an email from the prime minister's media office.

Media alert. Courtyard. 10am.

The PM's courtyard in the full grip of a Canberra winter was a desolate, grey place; an empty square of frigid concrete. So there was method in George Papadakis's madness, scheduling a presser there. He would keep the journalists waiting until they couldn't feel their feet and hands, then send the PM out. Twenty minutes in they would want the ordeal to end as much as the nation's leader did.

Martin Toohey and his inner circle of trusted advisers had spent close to two hours war-gaming for the press conference, pausing only to watch Bruce Paxton's resignation.

'So, George, what'll be the first question?' Toohey asked.

'When are you going to resign?' Papadakis's reply was swift.

'You think?'

'PM, I know.'

'Do we have a good answer for that?'

'Depends on how you define good.'

'What about we run through all the bills that have successfully passed through parliament?' offered Dylan Blair, the largely useless media adviser.

'Dylan,' Papadakis said, 'do us all a favour and go down to Aussies and tell Dom we're going to need lots of coffee.'

'I'll have a long black,' said Toohey.

The PM turned to the rest of his troops. 'Seriously, what's the answer? Has he broken any laws?'

'Don't think so, PM. The AEC has a three-year statute of limitations on election donations – section 315 – and this happened nearly fifteen years ago,' said Sarah Franklin, the legal expert.

'But there's no statute of limitations on being stupid and, let's face it, corrupt.' Toohey stared out the window. 'Still, the loss of a minister should not mean the loss of a government. In our system we hold power as long as we hold the confidence of the House. And we have the numbers.'

'There's still a question mark over that, PM,' Papadakis said. 'The Coalition's lunar right is threatening to deny Bailey a pair. If that happens then we're in a much tougher place. You know Scott as well as any of us. Will she hold on that?'

'Who knows, and it's not today's main problem, although it'll come up in the litany of second-order issues we face.' He had a guilty flashback to their last meeting and regretted, again, his vicious parting words to her.

'Today we are the government. We have lost a minister, we have to admit fault on that. But we will not cut and run from government just because it's hard. Government is supposed to be hard.

'And let none of you forget, the Labor Party is the only party that takes the tough decisions for the national good. We can't let the Tories take the low road to glory, as they always do. We don't shirk the difficult reforms, the ones that Hawke and Keating and Gough made as they tried to craft a better Australia. So what's my opening line going to be?'

'Ladies and gentlemen, thanks for coming.' Toohey scanned the array of badly dressed journos and wondered why he always said that. As if they wouldn't come to feast on the carcass of his government.

'As you know, the defence minister has offered his resignation and I have reluctantly accepted it. It is a profound disappointment. However, Mr Paxton agrees with me that his behaviour, no matter how long ago it occurred, is not compatible with the standards I demand from my ministers. I recognise this is a blow for my government. But let me make myself perfectly clear. I intend that this government will go full term.

'Any questions?'

The prime minister was buried in cacophony as a dozen gallery journalists yelled in unison, hoping to get in the first question, sensing that blood would soon be spilled.

Toohey picked out the man he knew would get straight to the point, Jonathan Robbie, the headkicking number two from Channel Nine.

'Why won't you do the decent thing and resign?'

116

'The minister has done the decent thing and resigned. There is no reason for the government to follow on the basis of a misjudgement Bruce Paxton made long ago, before he was a member of parliament. While I enjoy the confidence of the parliament I am the prime minister and I intend to get on with doing my job. The decent thing for this country is to give it a decent future and I have always believed that only Labor can deliver that.'

The prime minister pointed to another inquisitor.

'Did Minister Paxton offer to resign from parliament?'

'Definitely not.'

'Should he?' yelled another.

'The former minister faces no charges. He has been convicted in the court of public opinion. He has paid a high price for that. He will continue to support this government from the backbench and work to clear his name. Michelle?'

The press gallery doyenne asked whether the PM was confident of his stricken foreign minister being given a pair by the Coalition.

'That is a question you should be putting to the opposition leader. My understanding is that she has committed to that on television this morning. Unfortunately, my experience in dealing with Ms Scott gives me no confidence that I can rely on her word.'

It went for thirty agonising minutes. Finally, Dylan Blair yelled, 'Last question.'

And then Toohey did something none of his staff had war-gamed.

'Finally, can I take this opportunity to say that from today our relationship with the crossbench will be recast. I am ending the formal agreement with the Greens. We will propose Labor bills – it is up to the Greens whether they support them, try to amend them or vote them down. The Greens' new leader can decide if she wants to back a progressive Labor government or if she wants to hand over the reins of power to the Coalition. That is a decision only she can make.'

With that, the prime minister turned on his heel and walked inside as a dozen voices yelled in his wake. Turning into his office, he shut the door and was greeted by a grinning Papadakis.

'Well, Martin, that was unexpected. Welcome back – I've missed you.'

Canberra, August 19

The last half-hour of Harry Dunkley's drive to the Woden Police Station was a blur, his mind racing like an out-of-control speedway rider, round and round and round. Had Ben Gordon been arrested for poking his nose into Commonwealth affairs at Dunkley's urging? Was he about to join Ben in a cell?

Senior Constable Chris Waters had left instructions at the front desk for Dunkley to be ushered through to his office as soon as he arrived. Within a few minutes, he was in an upstairs room being offered a cup of tea.

Dunkley's heart started to beat faster. Something was clearly wrong. He sensed that Ben wasn't just in trouble; it was worse. Far worse.

Waters seemed to confirm it when he sat down opposite him, looking as if he'd rather be anywhere else.

'Mr Dunkley, I'm sorry to inform you that Mr Gordon was found, close to 1am, at the southern end of Telopea Park, Kingston, near Wentworth Avenue. He was deceased. And while we don't have the autopsy results, it's pretty clear to us he was bashed and strangled.'

Dunkley was stunned. Ben Gordon, dead? It wasn't possible. 'How ... who found him? Why ...'

'Mr Dunkley, I'm not at liberty to provide too much detail at this stage, given the nature of the matter. I don't need to tell you that what appears to be another gay-bashing crime will need to be handled with the utmost sensitivity.'

Waters flicked open a folder, reading from some notes. 'I am told that you are the executor of Mr Gordon's estate ... I presume you know this?'

It took Harry a while to respond. It all seemed so unreal. 'Ben doesn't have much family, or at least family he was close to, and I agreed a decade or so back ... I never thought it would happen, though ...'

'I can get someone to show you through his apartment after we've signed some papers,' Waters said gently. 'The family has been notified of the death, and I believe his mother and sister are on their way to Canberra. You may prefer to speak with them first?'

'Not really. To be honest, I've only ever met them briefly.'

Dunkley struggled to think clearly. He prided himself on being able to stay calm in a crisis. But, until now, that had always been a crisis for someone else.

'Listen, Senior Constable, this is a great shock, a tragedy, but I have to get to work at Parliament House. Can I arrange to meet someone later at Kingston, say 7pm?'

'That can be arranged, sure.'

Dunkley left his details with Waters and departed in a daze. Ben dead? A gay bashing? Found around 1am? It didn't make sense. Ben had often told

Dunkley that he was too old to be chasing the sort of casual anonymous sex sought by those who visited Telopea Park at night.

Something didn't fit. He needed answers and a visit to Ben's Kingston apartment was a priority.

But it would have to wait until later. The biggest political yarn in years was going off on the hill and he needed to get back and reclaim ownership of it. His job was just about all he had left now.

Just after 7pm, a police car pulled up outside the Argyle Apartments and two constables got out of the vehicle. Harry Dunkley had arrived a few minutes earlier, still numbed by the news of Ben Gordon's death, but also determined to find out what had happened to his friend.

What had Ben meant when he said the Paxton stuff was 'bigger than you know, maybe much bigger'? And what had he said about Bailey? Had Ben told others? Or had their project been infiltrated? Had their phones been tapped, their computers accessed by prying eyes?

The two constables had the keys to the apartment and followed Dunkley as he led them across a courtyard to the entrance.

He needed to access, discreetly, Ben's safe, which he knew was in the spare bedroom. It possibly contained a clue to what Ben had discovered.

'Mind if I take a look in the spare room?'

The constables were nearing the end of a busy shift and as far as they were concerned, Dunkley, as executor of Gordon's estate, could have access to whatever he wanted – as long as they were done and dusted within half an hour.

Dunkley had looked up the code Ben had entrusted to him all those years ago and took little time to punch in the safe's combination, the door opening with a soft click.

Inside was a stack of documents, some jewellery, a leather pouch tied with a red ribbon and an old fob watch.

Dunkley leafed quickly through the pile of papers until he found a folder marked 'BP'. He checked to make sure he was still alone, then flicked through its contents.

There were the notes and clippings that Gordon had shown him or spoken to him about during their trek for the truth. But one item was missing, something that was maybe more valuable than all the other contents combined.

Someone had taken the original black-and-white photo which had kicked off this mad chase that had now claimed the life of his friend.

Dunkley vowed, then and there, that he would track the bastards down.

———————————

Canberra, August 23

Elizabeth Scott gazed up at the pictorial guard of honour, at the good men who had led the conservative forces through the last half-century. Menzies, Howard, Fraser – each a hero in his own way, all paid-up members of the Liberal pantheon.

She would join them one day, her black-and-white portrait emblazoned with the words 'First Female Liberal Leader'. But on this Tuesday morning, with her restless colleagues circling, Scott had more immediate things on her mind.

Most weeks, the meeting of the joint parties – the Liberals and Nationals – was a mundane affair, punctuated by jovial banter and the odd policy stoush. But today, a pressing question needed to be asked and answered. Would the Coalition back the government's request to give the stricken foreign minister, Catriona Bailey, a parliamentary pair? It was a vote that would help decide whether the Toohey government survived or not.

Scott was preparing to demand that her party back her judgement and say yes. It was a question of decency, she believed, but the shadow Cabinet had baulked when she'd sought its support. So she was going to take the issue directly to her colleagues. It was a rare thing to do – to ask the party room to vote on a question of parliamentary tactics – but these were not normal times.

The main hurdle was Emily Brooks, the hard-right warrior who had been courting the Nationals and the conservative flank of the Liberal Party, and whose tough-as-nails approach in the Senate and the media had been credited with bringing the Toohey government to its knees. In contrast, Scott knew there was growing unease with her own leadership style, and her failure to put sufficient distance between her small-l liberal view of the world and that of the discredited Labor brand.

So, she mused, it would come down to this: high principle versus brutal pragmatism. She would demand a vote to back her stance, with the implied threat of standing down if the party overruled her. It was a calculated, high-stakes gamble. But she didn't believe the Coalition would risk a leadership change when the Toohey government was on life support.

She was wrong.

The press gallery began getting a sense of the unfolding drama when the joint party meeting ran into its second hour. Then some MPs and senators started texting their media favourites with messages like 'Things not going well for Scott' and 'Unbelievable in here. Very heated.'

The television networks scurried to stake out the hallway outside the Coalition party room. They were joined by a gaggle of scribblers. The 24-hour broadcasters began to speculate that the leader had been rolled.

Finally, the doors opened and the Liberal whip emerged alone, to be immediately consumed by the media crush.

'Ladies and gentlemen, please,' he pleaded. 'I have a short statement and I won't be taking any questions.

'Today, after a debate on parliamentary pairs, Senator Emily Brooks moved a motion of no confidence in the leadership of Ms Elizabeth Scott. The ballot was tied. Ms Scott then stood down. Senator Brooks was elected leader.'

The gallery pack was dumbfounded. Scott had rolled the dice and lost. Like John Gorton in 1971, she had then done the honourable thing and resigned. The Scott experiment was over.

As the whip finished speaking, a triumphant Emily Brooks emerged from the party room, an entourage of beaming followers in tow. Half the journalists in the group split off to record the first words of the new leader while the others stayed poised to witness the bitterness of the vanquished.

Cameramen positioned themselves in front of Brooks while journalists bombarded her with questions.

'How do you feel?'

'I am honoured and humbled.'

'Do you feel sorry for Elizabeth Scott?'

'Ms Scott is a great Australian and will be a great member of my team.'

'How can a senator be leader of the opposition?'

'Read the Constitution. Nothing stops a senator from being opposition leader or prime minister. It is purely convention that the prime minister be a member of the House of Representatives. I will stay in the Senate until the general election is called, then I will resign and contest a lower house seat.'

'What does this mean for the prime minister?'

'His worst nightmare.'

Brooks exuded confidence – some would say cockiness – but no one questioned that she was a stone-cold political killer and that Toohey now faced a much tougher challenge.

Moments later Scott emerged with a couple of her staunchest supporters on either side. Her face was set, she looked tired, but she held her composure. The crushing pressure she had felt since taking the top job was gone. In its place was the bitter hollowness of loss, coupled with a primal sense of relief. 'What will you do now? Will you recontest?'

The question seemed almost to come out of a fog.

'I'm going to take my time and have a think about it.'

'Will you serve Emily Brooks on her front bench?'

'No, I won't.'

From his suite, Martin Toohey watched as Scott made her dignified way back to her office. It was only about seventy metres from the party room but she was slowed by the crush of media.

'The Via Dolorosa of loss,' he said as he watched her journey, feeling every pain-filled step. 'You're a better man than I am, Ms Scott.'

Later, after a muted press conference, as Scott returned to the opposition leader's office, she found that her staff was already packing. Her personal assistant tearfully smiled at her.

'The calls have started to flood in,' she said. 'Most of them congratulating you for showing some character and doing the right thing. They say it's rare in politics now and they've changed their opinion of you.'

'Pity they didn't tell Newspoll that,' Scott said, wearily opening her personal office door. Sitting in the middle of her desk was a magnificent vase of flowers.

'Those came a few minutes ago,' the assistant said. 'Here's the card.'

Scott opened the envelope and removed a card bearing the handwritten words of a verse from *Paradise Regained*.

For therein stands the office of a king,
His honour, virtue, merit and chief praise,
That for the public all this weight he bears.
Yet he who reigns within himself, and rules
Passions, desires, and fears is more a king...

She felt a lump grow in her throat as she read the beautifully familiar verse to the end. Her eyes glazed with tears. It was Martin Toohey's handwriting.

The assistant looked at the card.

'Who's it from?' she asked.

'Nobody you'd recognise.'

122

Canberra, August 24

Harry Dunkley scanned the rows of the mourning, uniform in their grief, and thought, What a pitiful crowd. Fewer than two dozen were seated in the spacious chapel.

In the front row, Gordon's mother and sister sat solemnly, eyes rimmed with red, occasionally speaking softly to each other. Behind them, Ben's small community of cross-dressing buddies huddled together in gloomy counterpoint, their too-short black skirts, killer heels and platter-sized hats almost grotesque in broad daylight, as if they'd staggered out of the bar scene in *Star Wars*.

In the second-last row, a man in a dark suit was sitting alone. His face was vaguely familiar. Dunkley made a mental note to seek him out when the service was over.

Ben's brother, Michael, had started to speak, welcoming the sparse crowd for what would be a short memorial. 'And the eulogy today will be delivered by Ben's oldest and dearest friend, Harry Dunkley ...'

Dunkley rose, feeling as if he was floating off the ground. He needed to get a grip. He had spent hours trying to write something meaningful, but still felt a guilty pang of inadequacy.

'I have spent my entire adult life crafting words ...' He paused and cleared his throat. 'Trying to find exactly the right phrase for exactly the right moment. But there are some places where words run out. I find myself in such a place now. I do not have the skill to find the right words to do justice to the life of my friend Ben Gordon. But I will try.

'Ben and I were friends for nearly thirty years, and from the moment we met, in the Manning Bar at Sydney Uni, we instinctively liked each other. Ben was the sort of friend who stuck with you through thick and thin, who could be counted on to help out if you got into a tussle on the rugby field, or if your life was turning to mud.

'He wrestled his whole life to come to terms with who he was, who he should be. He felt cheated by nature, and I never really realised until now what a heavy load that must have been for him. It would have crushed a lesser man, or woman.

'I do not know what Ben was meant to be. I just hope he was at peace with himself when he died. But I do know this. Ben was my friend and his love was as reliable and constant as starlight. No matter how profound or painful his struggles, he never wavered as a friend. If anything, I failed to be the kind of friend he needed and deserved. He had asked me for years to call him Kimberley and, to my shame, I find it hard. Even now.'

Dunkley paused. 'His death is hard to understand. The police report says it was another gay bashing in Canberra. That he died simply because he was the wrong kind of person in the wrong place at the wrong time.

'But I don't believe it ...' Dunkley glanced at his notes, composing himself before looking out into the crowd. He noticed that the man in the suit was weeping. He continued, turning his gaze to the plain white coffin draped with a garland of brightly coloured flowers.

'Ben Gordon was taken from us too early, a beautiful, brilliant man who strayed into the path of some evil, twisted mind. But his spirit, his irrepressible spirit, will live on. And I will not rest until I find out the truth ...' He fought back his own tears before uttering a word he had resisted for years: '... the truth of who killed our friend ... Kimberley, and why.'

Dunkley bowed his head for a moment. Then he looked to the crowd and noticed the man in the dark suit was gone.

Canberra, August 25

GETCHA!

It was a cheeky nod to one of the most famous newspaper headlines of all time, the 'GOTCHA' announcing the sinking of the *General Belgrano* by the Brits during the 1982 Falklands War.

Now another Murdoch tabloid had grabbed it. It wasn't a warship that had copped it, but Jamie Santow, that sanctimonious high priest of online outrage. And he'd taken it where it really hurt, condemned by the very medium on which he'd built a virtual empire.

One misdirected tweet from Santow to one of his co-conspirators at *GetSet!* had been sent to each of his hundred thousand followers.

The cripple crusade has gone off. Maybe we need to get some spastics on board 2. What u think mate?

Maybe there is a God after all, George Papadakis thought, as he scanned the tabloid that was otherwise full of dire news for the Toohey government.

Santow had desperately tried to lay the blame elsewhere, even suggesting his Twitter account had been hacked. But the twitterati were having none of it, and the calls for his resignation were getting louder by the tweet. In

124

a final act of online irony, one infuriated *GetSet!* member had kicked off a petition on the group's website to have Santow replaced – on the grounds he had brought the organisation into serious disrepute. There were already 1400 backers for this, and the numbers were building steadily.

The online beast of discontent that Santow had helped create was about to devour him.

Canberra, August 25

Emotionally shattered, physically drained. Harry Dunkley had been working on pure adrenalin for almost a week, trying to keep focused on the biggest political story of his life, while feeling overwhelmed by the loss of his friend and the shadow of guilt it had cast.

Dunkley closed down his PC, grabbed his keys and quietly slipped out of the parliamentary building. The time had clicked over to 8pm, the temperature barely registering above zero. Checking his watch, he calculated it would take him no more than ten minutes to reach the rendezvous.

Red Hill is one of the highest points in Canberra, and a favoured meeting place for fitness freaks who slog up its paths on foot or by bicycle. It is also a trysting place for lovers, particularly those seeking illicit liaisons away from the city's watching eyes. Dunkley had last been to its pinnacle a year ago, dining at Beyond Red with a shadow minister whose ambition outweighed his talent. Tonight food would have to wait.

A quarter past eight came and went, and the few vehicles that eased up the hill disgorged only hungry diners heading for the restaurant. A tune played on the CD, Jeff Buckley's 'Hallelujah', with its soft ode to lovers past. Canberra's night lights danced and an approaching vehicle flashed its high-beam twice. It was the signal.

Finally, after two months of intrigue and subterfuge, Dunkley was to meet Mr DFAT, the man who had initiated the downfall of Bruce Paxton.

A slim athletic man emerged from a late-model Citroën, his face partly obscured by a fur-lined hood. He walked the few metres to Dunkley's passenger door, checking to make sure no one was close by, and got in. He lowered his hood and looked straight into Dunkley's eyes.

'Well, well, the man at the funeral, second-last row, dark suit.'

'Not bad, Mr Dunkley.' The man offered a handshake. 'Charles Dancer. 'Might I say, you delivered a very nice eulogy.'

'Charles Dancer? I've been around this place for a very long time and I've never heard of you.'

'I'm flattered, I pride myself on being invisible.'

'I have one trivial question to start with,' Dunkley said. 'What was with the diplomatic plates and the Embassy of Taiwan envelope?'

'A man must have some fun, Mr Dunkley; it was a theatrical flourish, nothing more.'

'So why me? What was this all about? Why are you here now? And, not to put too fine a point on it, who the fuck killed my friend?'

'Correction, Mr Dunkley ... *our* friend. Kimberley and I were close, though we had a different kind of relationship to the one you shared. Perhaps a tad more fractious, too. So that answers the question of why I am here. And why I am risking a two-year stint in jail for breaching the Official Secrets Act.'

'You did that when you handed over a picture that came from an ASIS file.'

'I had permission to do that, from serious people – that's my job.'

'Why?'

'Because Bruce Paxton was a real and present danger to the realm. He threatened the alliance with the United States and he was clearly a security risk. And, Mr Dunkley, he was in bed with Chinese intelligence, literally.'

In the half-light of the car interior, Dunkley's confusion was apparent.

'Let me make it simple for you. While you chased one face in a thirty-year-old photo, our friend Kimberley was pursuing the other. And that man, Zhou Dejiang, introduced Paxton to one of his best – and most alluring – spies. From the Chinese perspective, it worked a treat,' Dancer said.

'Paxton had been compromised for thirty years. We would have let it pass ... but then he rekindled that relationship earlier this year. That dalliance in the Orient was the tipping point – how could we allow a defence minister like that to continue?'

'What do you mean *we*? Who is *we*?' Dunkley was getting annoyed. 'The prime minister? He gets to decide who serves, doesn't he? Who are you talking about?'

'I'm talking about the people who will be here as a half-dozen prime ministers come and go. The patriots who serve this country in silence and who defend its interests, and those of our allies.'

'Faceless bureaucrats and diplomats? Is that who you're talking about? Who else? The Yanks?'

'The Americans certainly had an interest in the lustful habits of Paxton. But theirs was a more fundamental concern, as was ours.'

'Which was?'

'The alliance, Mr Dunkley. Paxton was a risk to this country's security, pure and simple. He had already triggered major concerns in Washington with his plans to wind back the Joint Strike Fighter program. Added to that, he was sleeping with a skilled Mata Hari. That's some double act, I would say.'

'And did your employers and their mates kill Ben?'

Dancer seemed genuinely distressed. 'I'm as confused as you are about that. It doesn't make any sense. It's not … our style.'

'What about the Americans? They don't seem to have an issue with capping inconvenient people.'

'They are capable of it, certainly. But it's not usual. They'd do it in Pakistan maybe, or Colombia. But here, never, and we would not take it as the act of a friendly nation.'

'Who then? And what did Ben have that was so damaging that someone wanted him dead?'

'I want to know as badly as you do.'

'What if he had information that linked the United States and senior Australian bureaucrats to a plot to topple a democratically elected minister?' Dunkley asked. 'I would say that's pretty damaging, wouldn't you? People would want to keep him silent, wouldn't they?'

'Yes, they would, but believe me, there are other ways to discredit a story. And Kimberley had certain disadvantages when it came to credibility. We could have destroyed her easily. Worst case scenario, we'd plant kiddie pictures on her computers and have the police raid her house. Game over. That's also my job.'

'That's some job, your job.'

'This nation has many enemies, Mr Dunkley. I help guard it. You might not like my methods but you sleep soundly in your bed because people like me stand watch.'

Dunkley felt sudden rage boiling inside him.

'Even if it kills me, I will find out who killed Ben. Give me a number I can contact you on. This isn't the end of our conversation. It's the beginning.'

Canberra, August 26

The day dawned fine and mild in the national capital, the first sprigs of wattle signalling the approach of spring. Canberra had yielded to an uncommon beauty, the kind of day that explained the bush capital's allure.

From its lofty perch, the Australian flag that normally flew proud above the parliament hung limp, seemingly ashamed to unfurl its full banner to the skies. Perhaps it was a silent message to those men and women below who bickered and fought over the laws governing the nation. Because for the past fortnight the flag had stood sentinel over one of the most explosive – and tawdry – periods in the history of Australia's Federation.

Defence Minister Bruce Paxton had resigned in disgrace, his past finally catching up with him. Elizabeth Scott had rolled the dice and lost, another in the long line of opposition leaders to have been killed off by an impatient party room. The Toohey government was reeling as an energised Coalition engaged in bare-knuckle politics, led by Emily Brooks, one of the most effective street fighters the parliament had seen. 'A rabid rottweiler on steroids,' a Liberal colleague admiringly dubbed her.

The parliamentary pantomime had descended into pure farce as the resurgent Coalition tied the House of Representatives in procedural knots, refusing to grant a pair for the stricken foreign minister, Catriona Bailey.

'It's a joke. This is now a place where getting stuck in the dunny could see the government fall,' one long-serving Labor MP was heard to moan.

Only skilled manoeuvring by the leader of the House had seen the government survive. But the games in the chamber had dashed any chance of getting business done. It was political gridlock and some of the nation's most experienced commentators were predicting the government would fall by Christmas.

Martin Toohey's decision to rip up the accord with the Greens had contributed to the instability. Firm friends had turned into mortal enemies and the Greens' new leader – emboldened by a Newspoll showing the Greens' primary vote surging to 15 per cent – had launched a campaign targeting Labor's inner-city base ahead of the next election. That had set off a revolt by sections of the Labor Left, who were agitating for some kind of symbolic action to win back the luvvies.

'So what do we do now?' an exhausted Toohey asked George Papadakis, as the two sat in the prime ministerial suite, attempting to wash away some of the grime from the last fortnight.

'Pray, my friend. It won't work but nothing else we try does either.'

Canberra, August 26

It was 3am and the hospital was silent. The night staff went about their work, all quiet efficiency. In dim rooms, medical machinery softly hummed as patients dozed between rounds of routine monitoring.

In Room 43, Catriona Bailey was ignoring the hour, keeping watch as a battery of screens relayed unfolding world events. On CNN, Israel's prime minister was addressing a press conference. Bailey dashed off a tweet cautioning him against a pre-emptive strike on Iran's nuclear sites.

The foreign minister was by herself, but never alone, plugged into the outside world through a phalanx of wires and modules, plotting and scheming while the national capital slept.

She turned next to finessing the finishing touches on her latest 8000-word piece for *The Monthly*. In typically overblown prose, the essay, 'Renewing Labor', mapped out a path for her shattered party. She traced its fall to the malign influence of factional bosses and union warlords and said there was no choice but to hand it 'back to the people, where it belongs'.

What Labor needed most, she argued, was courageous leadership. By the man – or woman – made for the age. As usual, in closing, she threw in a religious allusion. 'A prophet is not someone who can see the future,' she wrote. 'It is someone who sees the present, with perfect clarity.'

She grinned, internally. *She* was the perfect political prophet for the global 24/7 internet age. Unsleeping, all-seeing and hard-wired into the virtual universe. This little effort would set the cat among the pigeons nicely.

Bailey now saw her life in messianic terms. She had been crucified by the party, and laid in the tomb. She had appeared to be dead – but was not.

The fuel that coursed through her veins and sustained her was revenge.

And she would rise. Again.

Canberra, August 26

The quiet ambience of the Tulip Lounge in Manuka was the perfect tonic for a wasted Harry Dunkley.

He collapsed into one of the feather-soft couches and thumbed through a generous cocktail menu, searching for something a little more serious than a Fluffy Duck. He finally reached a list of imported ales, most of which he had never heard of.

But this wasn't a social outing. He was waiting for a contact. *The* contact. In two decades covering the gory spectacle of national politics, there were few people he trusted more.

He and the contact had an unwritten agreement – Dunkley would call only in times of crisis. The last time the two had talked was a little over a year ago when Dunkley had rung to confirm a tip that Labor was preparing to dump Bailey as prime minister.

The journalist glanced at his watch, confirming that his contact was late. He was always late. But Dunkley wasn't going anywhere. He was searching for answers and suspected this was his best means of getting them. No one was better connected in Canberra, whether it be about the factional plays in Labor, the latest manoeuvrings within Defence or the musings of the US administration.

Almost an hour after the agreed appointment, the untidy figure of Brendan Ryan shambled up the stairs.

'Sorry, I was held up,' Ryan said, sweeping up the drinks menu with one hand as his other plunged into a bowl of nuts.

'No problems, mate. You've had a bit on lately.'

'You might say that. You can't accuse us of making politics boring.'

'Yep, you guys are good for journalism.'

They shared a small laugh and chased down the waiter.

The odd thing about Ryan, Dunkley mused, was that he was usually a vault. But once persuaded to talk, he seemed to enjoy it – and was a trove of information.

'Do you reckon you can hold on with the numbers in the House the way they are?'

'Well, right now Simmo is talking to that grubby Queensland Liberal, trying to persuade him to break ranks. He might do it too, 'cause he won't get preselected again.'

'But surely you can't win another election? You're gone – it's just a matter of time, isn't it?'

'Never make bold predictions, Harry, you know that. If we can endure, we can turn this around. Sure, it's like trying to land a spaceship on a snowflake, but that's the plan. And this new Liberal leader, she's a nasty piece of work … in time, people will grow to hate her.'

Ryan paused. 'Sorry about your friend, Harry.'

'Thanks, mate, that's really why I'm here.'

'I know.'

'How much do you know?'

'More than you, but not everything, not by a long chalk.'

'So tell me about the Yanks. It's been suggested they were behind the leak that destroyed Paxton. Are my sources solid?'

Ryan took a slow sip of beer. 'The Americans were concerned, mate. And they had every right to be. Our own people were deeply concerned.

Washington might have sped the process up, but Paxton was gone from the moment he hooked up with that Tibetan girl again. We simply couldn't afford a defence minister, with unfettered access to such sensitive information, so deeply compromised.'

Another scoopful of nuts disappeared into Ryan's mouth, then he continued.

'I don't know if he ever told the Chinese anything useful, but it doesn't really matter. That fucking fool was threatening our nation's ability to defend itself. He wanted to cut back Defence spending. And this at a time when we need to be expanding our military. We have to prepare, Harry, for future conflict – a war with China which, in my judgement, is inevitable. Our people had been dragging their feet on Paxton for nearly two months. Give the Americans credit, mate, they know how to finish the job.'

Dunkley digested the explosive information, realising he'd taken the wrong fork in the road. 'So I missed the big story. I followed the money and found a crook.'

'That's still a story. It's just not the most interesting one. But it had the desired effect. So thanks. Your country salutes you.' Ryan mockingly raised his glass.

'But weren't you concerned that getting rid of Paxton might bring the government down?'

'No, mate. We don't need Paxton as defence minister, we just need his vote in the parliament. Of course it was bloody embarrassing, but it was essential to secure the defence of the realm. Some things, my friend, are beyond politics.'

'Does the prime minister know about this?'

'No.'

Dunkley ordered two more beers, before turning back to Ryan.

'Who killed Ben?'

'I don't know for sure, but we suspect the Chinese.'

'Jesus, Brendan, that's bullshit. What possible reason could they have?'

'I can't prove this, but we suspect the Chinese were on to your friend and his little, er, theory. About Bailey.'

Ryan carefully scanned the surrounding lounges, before lowering his voice and continuing. 'Do you remember the phone call from Gordon last week? He said to you that there was something else he had to tell you. "Something unbelievable about Bailey."'

Dunkley was stunned. 'Mate, how do you know that?'

'We were listening, Harry, and clearly we weren't the only ones. We didn't move against Gordon because we wanted him to help you. From the start we knew he would. That's why you got the photo. And Harry ... I know you're wondering, but we've got it back, safe and sound where it belongs.'

'What was Ben going to tell me about Bailey?'

'Well, he did say "something unbelievable". And he was dead right. Didn't you ever think that the reason we gave for shafting that bitch was a bit thin? That she was a crazy control freak who was hard to work with? We've had maniacs in office before and lived with them. Name a PM who isn't hard to work with. Ask Gary Gray about Captain Whacky. Sure, Bailey was riding low in the polls. But if that was the reason for killing a prime minister, Toohey would have gone months ago.

'Don't forget our main problem in that abortion of an election campaign was that we couldn't explain to the Australian people why we dumped our leader. We were lucky that Scott's such a lousy politician or the Coalition would have hosed us.'

Ryan moved in close.

'We got rid of Catriona Bailey because she's a ... *spy*.'

Dunkley wore a what-the-fuck expression that could have been seen clear across the room.

'Harry, you look startled, but let me go on. She was recruited by the Chinese when she was a language student in Hong Kong in the early 1980s. Honkers was a rich breeding ground then for the Commies. And they really hit the jackpot.

'All the time that Bailey was working her way up through Labor ranks, building her contacts in Washington, she was also feeding intel back to Beijing. She pretended to take a hard line against China on human rights, but she was always acting in their interest. It was a convincing performance too. We – us and the Americans – only found out when it was too late.'

Dunkley struggled to absorb this impossible information. It was as if Ryan was speaking another language.

Outside, the orderly nature of the Canberra evening continued, a steady procession of public servants returning to their neat homes after another day performing the tasks necessary to keep the Commonwealth of Australia ticking over.

'I don't have any evidence that the Chinese killed Gordon,' Ryan conceded. 'But I do know that no one on our side did. I think the Chinese intercepted Gordon's call to you, panicked, and decided to act.'

Ryan fell into silence and Dunkley didn't know how to fill it. Finally, he spoke.

'Well, that's the most extraordinary tale I've ever heard, Brendan. But I could never write it ... unless I turned my hand to fiction.'

'Why not, mate?'

'Because ... nobody would ever believe me.'

BOOK TWO

THE
MANDARIN
CODE

Canberra, January, 2013

He woke in a knot of panic, the sheets stained with sweat. He'd not meant to sleep, for fear of the dark angels that had begun to haunt his dreams. His eyes flashed open to a void beyond black, and the still breath of midnight amplified his every heartbeat.

Canberra usually cooled with the sunset, but an unnatural heat lingered in this blast-furnace summer. A faint scent of smoke hinted at fire licking at the city's edges. The hour was nearly upon him.

Cradling a USB drive in his sticky palm, the Chinese national wondered how future generations would judge him. As a delusional zealot, or as a good man who'd tried to warn them?

Somewhere outside, a generator chugged its diesel drone. In the cramped cabin, the heavy, even breathing of his two roommates signalled they were asleep. It was time to move.

Six months earlier, he'd been sent to this strange, empty land to help build an ultra-secret frontline. Listed as Asset 53, he was one of China's revered cyber-warriors. But he was a rebel who longed for intellectual freedom, who yearned to break the shackles of the stultifying regime that choked its people as the old dynasties had once bound the feet of its women. He'd lost faith when they'd forced an abortion on his mother for the crime of conceiving a second child. The botched procedure had taken the one person whom he had loved unconditionally. So he'd made a vow – to work within the system just as long as it took to gather the weapons that he needed to destroy it.

And now he had them, his own personal arsenal, carried on a tiny memory stick that he placed, carefully, in his left trouser pocket.

He mentally rehearsed his escape route. Nine hundred and eighty-seven steps to freedom. He'd measured the distance in cyberspace: from the compound that was his home, feverishly being transformed into a new Chinese embassy, to the fortified front gates of the embassy of the United States.

Briefly, he'd contemplated defecting to the Australians, but the risk was too great. Having witnessed their kow-towing at the altar of China's wealth, he feared they would hand him back if pressure was applied. No, the Americans were his best hope, and he would buy his freedom with the evidence in his pocket and the trove of priceless information in his head.

Not glancing back, he stole out of the cabin to the expanse of the compound, hurrying to the shadows that would hide him from cameras on either side of the three-metre fence.

His heart beat a staccato pulse as he pushed a makeshift ladder into place and climbed to a narrow opening in the perimeter wire.

He leapt into the dark and landed with a crunch, his weight flattening the tinder-dry grass. The impact shuddered through his legs, and he rolled to cushion the fall, then took a breath to check his route.

Eucalypt bark, curled and brittle-dry, littered the ground. His every step would echo until he reached the concrete path. Slowly he navigated a glade of trees. A sticky web grabbed at his face and he stifled a gasp, clawing frantically at the gossamer threads wrapped across his cheeks. He froze. A creature slowly traced a path from his hairline to his temple. With a panicked flick he sent it to the bushes.

Exhaling, he continued towards the path that ran alongside the compound. Streetlights ahead marked a long avenue towards a city he had never seen. On his right, the dirt-block site that had been his home – his prison – for the past six months. A final stand of long grass, then he reached the path and forced his limbs into a steady jog. He knew he was not safe. He could not relax until the fortress of the building site was behind him.

The quiet was shattered by a harsh voice, familiar, ordering him to halt. *'Ting! Ting!'*

Two shadows emerged from the gloom, blocking the path. He turned, and raced into the unknown.

He charged across a road, a route he'd never intended to take. A hotel loomed on the right. Should he go there? No. His course was set. There was a bridge ahead, a well-lit route across the lake. This was his best chance. The city was there, on the other side. Freedom was there, on the other side. Could he lose his pursuers in this foreign place? He scanned his surroundings for signs of life, of help, but the street leading to the bridge was empty.

The footsteps were getting louder.

He was still young, and had once been athletic. But in the panic to avoid capture, he had sprinted the first hundred metres. Within a minute his muscles were burning more oxygen than his lungs could deliver and his body began to rebel.

Keep going.

The well-trained security men were closing on him, and were now only fifty metres away. His chest was lead-heavy as he pushed up the incline to the bridge.

The lights of the city teased him, called to him. He could feel the pursuers on his heels now. They would catch him in seconds.

There was no time to think, little time to act. With one final effort, he surged towards the bridge railing; pushing his hands down hard, he vaulted over the edge.

Four seconds of panic and a crack as his head met the water. His mother's face appeared, beckoning him to a better place.

Then everything went black.

Washington

Earle W Jackson III reclined in the sturdy leather chair, soaking up the majesty of the room, and considered the staggering improbability that he belonged in it. The three months since his election had passed in a blur of meetings and briefings that gave him few moments to reflect on the miracle of his becoming the forty-fifth president of the United States of America. In November's ballot, he'd shocked the fancied Democratic incumbent, winning with a populist blend of good ol' boy southern charm and homespun protectionism. Not since Truman's upset victory over Dewey in '48 had the White House welcomed such an unexpected occupant.

Now here he was in the Oval Office, the epicentre of world power, an unrivalled, near mythical place. The heart of the American empire. The new Rome.

Jackson turned to the three bay windows behind the desk carved from the timbers of the British ship, the *Resolute*. He looked through bulletproof glass to the South Lawn, dusted with snow, imagining the Republican lions who'd sat here before him, the weight of the world on their shoulders.

A cancelled phone call had given him exactly five minutes to himself. He slipped easily into one of his regular mind games, imagining how his favourite president might have reacted to the difficult challenge facing him. *What would Reagan do?* It was based on the question his strict Presbyterian mother had frequently asked him: 'What would Jesus do?'

Despite serving eight years as governor of Mississippi, he was ill-prepared for this role, leader of the free world, the most powerful man on the planet. Trained for a life of law, he had risen steadily, though unspectacularly, through the Republican ranks to chair the deeply conservative Rankin County, Mississippi district, and had been picked as an observer during the controversial 2000 Florida presidential re-count. He'd risen to public prominence in a referendum battle over the state flag: the last in the union to have the battle cross of the Confederacy emblazoned on it.

A 2001 court ruling had opened the door for civil rights activists and local businessmen to expunge the Civil War remnant from the standard. That outraged Jackson and he was a man made for the fight. A direct descendant of General Thomas 'Stonewall' Jackson, he was not about to stand by as his heritage was airbrushed to appease liberal do-gooders.

Never an original thinker, Jackson lifted his rallying cry from the National Rifle Association: 'You can have my flag when you peel it from my cold dead hands.' It appealed to and amplified the many prejudices that fortified his natural constituency. It also helped that the proposed alternative was a circle of stars, suspiciously similar to the European Union banner: 'The Euro fag flag', Jackson called it.

It was a fight he couldn't lose. The flag was retained with a two-thirds majority. Three years later, he was elected governor. His charisma, crisp good looks, folksy yet polished style of public speaking and impeccable conservative credentials were a heady cocktail and he emerged from the pack to storm the 2012 Republican primaries.

Jackson went into the presidential poll a rank underdog but he surprised the pundits, tapping into American trauma over the financial crisis and growing anxiety about the nation's diminishing global authority. The people were hungry for a return to past glories so that's what Jackson promised them.

In a twist on the Reagan 'Morning in America' campaign, Jackson's crusade anthem was the theme from *Star Wars* and his slogan the aspirational 'The Empire Strikes Back'. It was an aggressive mix of hope and xenophobia, which blamed outsiders and their liberal allies within the US for the nation's decline.

In a stroke of genius, Jackson built a cartoon version of a rising China to replace the Axis of Evil as America's new enemy-in-chief. He toured the rust belt, pointing to manufacturing jobs that had been 'stolen' by the emerging communist power. 'Every "Made in China" tag you see is a pink slip handed to an American worker' was his mantra on the stump. 'Every dollar you spend on foreign trinkets is money taken from American pockets and food taken from our children's mouths.' His campaign centrepiece was a solemn promise to declare China a 'currency manipulator' if he won office.

Against the advice of every sane Republican, that's what he did. And from day one in the Oval Office, his foreign policy battles began to rival his considerable domestic woes.

The president checked his watch. 'Lesley!' he bellowed.

His PA pounced on the intercom. 'Yes, Mr President?'

'Send in my eleven o'clock.'

Jackson stiffened as a high-powered group strode through the door: the cream of his national security team, accompanied by the secretary of Treasury. He already knew that the CIA and the State Department were in rare agreement: his decision to declare China a currency manipulator had knocked over a domino and others were falling.

China had responded belligerently. It declared currency to be a sovereign issue and called the US stance an act of aggression. It cancelled the annual meeting of the joint economic strategic dialogue and recalled its ambassador to Beijing for 'briefings'.

Eight Chinese warships had then sailed through the twelve-nautical-mile zone off the disputed Senkaku Islands, and the Japanese were threatening retaliation. China's riposte was to schedule missile tests for the Taiwan Strait, something it had not done for nearly two decades. There was no way of telling how far the sabre-rattling would go.

The president surveyed the room then motioned to the director of the Central Intelligence Agency.

'Mr President.' Travis Manning spoke as directed. 'As I explained in our last meeting, when I suggested we move slowly on the China front, the problem is that we don't yet have a clear idea of the temperament of the new leadership. At almost the same time you were elected, the Communist Party's 18th Congress appointed the people who will lead China for the next five years. As I said in January, we need time to let them settle in and for us to get some feel for just who we are dealing with. There's a growing view that this new team is more deeply nationalist, and more dangerous, than the last.'

'And as I told you, I am not going to break a pledge I made to the American people on my first day in office.' Jackson spoke more loudly than necessary, meeting reason with volume. His tone dropped as he searched for an argument. 'And for God's sake, Clinton declared China a currency manipulator in '94 and things didn't go to hell in a handbasket.'

The Treasury secretary jumped on the opening. 'Mr President, China's gross domestic product in '94 was $500 million. Ours was $7 trillion. Today, China's GDP is $9 trillion, closing on our $15 trillion. Based on these growth

141

rates, their economy will surpass ours before the end of the decade. And in 1994 we did about $10 billion worth of trade with China. Now it's over half a trillion and rising.

'In 1994 China was an insignificant player in the government bond market. It now owns more than $1 trillion worth of our bonds. To put that another way, Mr President, only the Federal Reserve controls more US government debt than China.'

'The point is: pissing them off is a bad idea,' interjected Manning. 'And there's more. George has come back from Beijing with some disturbing intel.'

George Blake, the CIA's Beijing station chief, was a hardened intelligence careerist, and he knew China, its nuances and instincts better than anyone.

'Sir, the new Chinese president, Meng Tao, was billed as continuing the market-oriented reform of Deng Xiaoping. But we have reason to believe his sympathies lie with the New Left, which is pushing back against growing inequality in China and wants the party to return to its Maoist roots.'

Blake reached into his folder for a briefing note and handed it to the president.

'We intercepted a conversation between Meng and one of his allies, Jiang Xiu. It's clear that they know your currency declaration is a domestic political ploy and could easily be negotiated in financial forums. But they see an opportunity to play Chinese public opinion against the US by painting us as an aggressor that's trying to strangle Chinese growth before it becomes a threat.'

Blake paused for a moment to allow Jackson to absorb the brief before continuing. 'China is mobilising its considerable assets – military, financial and virtual – opening the way for serious retaliation. I believe they will rub up against their neighbours to test our will. They might even be looking for an opportunity to roll back economic and social reform under cover of a "national emergency". We could be playing right into their hands. They sense we are weakened by a decade of war and economic decline. Sir, they are looking for an excuse to demonstrate that they are the rising global power.'

The secretary of state tagged in, determined to pressure Jackson into relenting.

'We urge you, Mr President.' Henry Wilenski leaned forward to press home his appeal. 'Make it plain, today, that you do not intend to proceed with the next steps of your currency declaration. Make a statement saying you won't be imposing tariffs and restrictions on Chinese goods. You can make a credible argument that your warning has been heeded and that talks should come before any more action.'

Jackson rose to his full 6 feet 3 inches and slammed both hands on the desk. 'Except that's not what I said. I said I would impose tariffs on Chinese goods within ninety days of the declaration if China did not lift the value of its currency and level the goddamn playing field.'

He turned his back on the group and looked out the window once more, the defiant gesture of an insecure man.

'Mr President, that would not be wise.' Wilenski was pushing hard. 'This will not help American workers and it threatens the peace at a time when we are in no shape to fight.'

Jackson raised his hand and turned to eyeball the group.

'I need to think about this,' he said. 'We'll talk again tomorrow. That's all for now. Thank you, gentlemen.'

Dismissed and disgruntled, the group shuffled out.

As the door closed, the president picked up his phone. 'Lesley, get Big Mac on the line.'

Canberra

They ran squealing down to the lake's turbid waters, a tangled knot of excited school children. The year six class from Sydney's inner west was on its annual pilgrimage to Canberra.

Fuelled on fast food and pre-teen adrenalin, they'd spent the morning at Questacon, mixing fantasy with science. It was now time for a picnic lunch on the shores of Lake Burley Griffin before continuing to the National Museum.

'Slow down and be careful. Watch the muddy banks,' a teacher bellowed.

Several errant boys were creeping stealthily towards a thicket by the water's edge, intent on slipping from the teachers' gaze, chasing those moments of freedom every schoolkid yearns for. Their ringleader, a tousle-haired blond with attitude beyond his years, spotted it first. Half submerged, the body was maybe ten metres from shore. He called his mates over to make sure he wasn't imagining things. From the bank, they couldn't see a head or even a pair of feet, but there was no mistaking that this was a corpse. Playtime was over.

Four hours later, the initial forensic examination had been completed. The body was an Asian male, likely aged in his thirties. Of slender build, he was clothed in plain trousers and a light-coloured shirt. A pair of joggers weighed down his spindly legs. And that was it. An initial search had turned up nothing else – no wallet, no ID, no jewellery or other personal items.

The task now fell to the morgue for a thorough examination of the body and to the water police for a sweep of the muddy inlet.

Like the capital, the lake was placid on the surface, but beneath its coffee-coloured water lurked hidden danger. The remnants of the eucalypts that once crowded the Molonglo riverbanks before the dam was built lay in wait below the lake's smooth skin: a trap for the unwary and the foolish.

A senior constable gazed out over Burley Griffin, its quiet waters now empty. He shook his head before turning to his colleagues.

'Christ, fellas, how do you find so many new ways to drown in this puddle?'

Beijing

Alone in his sanctuary, Jiang Xiu cradled a mug of green tea in one hand as he tapped an ink block with a favourite brush. A Chinese melody drifted in the background, a hymn of praise for the plum blossom of spring. Thick walls offered protection from the city and its suffocating barrage of sound, and he savoured the serenity of his early morning ritual, a rare respite from the burden of leadership.

In five days he would turn fifty-six, still young compared to the dinosaurs who stained the party's upper ranks. Curmudgeon communists, he called them.

For the past six months, Jiang had headed China's propaganda agency. His appointment as minister was part of a coup that had seen a number of his nationalist comrades elevated to the helm of the ruthless political machine that would rule this vast, ambitious empire for the next five years. Dubbed the Magnificent Seven, the Standing Committee of the Political Bureau of the Communist Party of China Central Committee had the destiny of 1.35 billion people in their grasp. They would not disappoint. And they would not relent.

Unlike many of his contemporaries, Jiang had started with nothing but the unbridled love of his mother. He was no princeling, no Maserati-driving poseur who'd leveraged the family name to earn his wealth. He despised nepotism, a cover for the weak and lazy. He had gained power through cunning and intellect, and through a fierce political drive first unleashed as an undergraduate at Jilin University, where he'd studied economics and international management. He'd garnered plaudits from party elders for his organisational skills, but he was also a keen student of China's compromised history, and was determined to forge a new era for the Middle Kingdom, to place it on its rightful path to global supremacy.

Now, in his small studio in House No 2, near the centre of Beijing, he dipped his brush into a pool of oily liquid. Two blank sheets of paper were set several feet apart on a long timber bench. Jiang's brush skimmed the first white sheet and left a perfect tracery of black.

Like dancing, rippling ribbons …

He loved calligraphy's tradition and grace, each stroke a link to the past. And with each practised touch, he recalled the words of his master: 'Deviation from the model is a failure.'

It was a dictum that applied to all of nature and politics. He had dabbled in Western philosophy and was struck by the parallel he saw with Plato's theory of forms: that this world was merely a copy of a perfect one. Jiang believed a universal template existed and his role as a politician was to make China the best replica of the model. Any deviation was a step towards chaos.

The only Western figure he respected, other than Plato, was Napoleon, a rare military leader gifted with great insight. 'Let China sleep, for when she wakes she will shake the world,' the French general had said.

China would certainly shake the world, as it had done through the ages, if Jiang could shake it awake. In the sweep of history, the West walked in the shadow of China's majestic past. China had gunpowder when the peasants of the West were still hurling stones at castle walls. All of mankind's great achievements had been conceived here, in the Middle Kingdom, the bridge between heaven and earth. For a millennium, China had been the envy of the world.

Then came the fall. The great indignity.

A familiar rage surged. Jiang's face tightened. He gripped his brush hard.

The West's interruption of China's ascendancy was an outrage. And it still awaited punishment for the century of humiliation that had begun in 1839 with the First Opium War. The West and its brutal lackey Japan had brought China to its knees – shackled, humbled and impoverished. It had been on the long march back since 1949.

Jiang flinched. Some memories were hard, painful, personal.

His mother had been celebrating her fifteenth birthday in her Nanking home in December 1937 when the Japanese invaded. They had stolen her childhood as they raped her. She witnessed the massacre of countless innocent Chinese, butchered by that evil force. She had spent every birthday since in mourning and her suffering was seared on her son's soul.

She had forged Jiang as a warrior, and he had spent his life readying for war.

Two lines, refined and flowing, perfectly intersected ...

He had disguised himself, playing the role of an acolyte of Deng Xiaoping, a market liberal. But he believed that the Chinese economy had to be managed like a bird in a cage, allowing the centrally planned system to define its limits. Yes, the cage could be made larger and, occasionally, other birds might be let in, but the bars ensured order.

China's growth, and the yearning of its fast-growing middle class for greater freedoms, had to be tightly controlled. The delusions of those who believed China could take its place at the helm of the new world order while relaxing its iron grip enraged him. Who were they, these free-market liberals preaching discredited Western ideals? The emergence of the internet had allowed this Western infection to spread. With Jiang's guidance, the Politburo would tame those who believed the future of China was more entwined with Coca-Cola and McDonald's than with Mao and the state.

Swift running script, an infinite power ...

Leaders often needed a crisis to precipitate decisive action and the 1997 Asian financial meltdown, which hit China hard, had offered Jiang – then a rising star within the Communist Party – the first opportunity to rein in those who sought to mimic the West. The shadow capitalism that China had pursued meant that many of its banks tottered as the meltdown struck. Jiang had been given responsibility – and unfettered power – to right the creaky financial system.

It was a challenge that he'd taken up with relish. He was dubbed the Dragon Titan for his zealous pursuit of regional officials who'd thought they could continue to operate with autonomy.

Smooth top-down vertical lines, mellow like pearl and jade ...

After three years, he'd been rewarded with appointment to the party's finance committee, a high-level role that gave him access to the upper echelons of the Politburo. He'd been determined to impress and had soon been charged with running one of China's biggest state-owned companies. He became a familiar name to the bankers from Wall Street and London who'd initially expected the same riches they'd milked by flogging off lazy, capital-starved enterprises from the former Eastern Bloc. But while Russia and its Soviet allies were easy pickings for these vultures, Jiang was formidable.

He married a sharp economic brain with determination and dogma. He championed the workers, arguing that China had a responsibility to ensure that its most vulnerable had the same rights as those who, through accident of birth or other connections, had risen to the top.

A curved arc, flexible and vivid ...

He was centre stage as China made giant strides to catch the West. He became associated with a group of conservatives, the 'New Left', who were convinced that the greatest threat was not from outside forces, but from those within the party who wanted China to become a pale imitation of America and Japan.

He was an ultra-nationalist who believed the adoption of Western ideas poisoned his country. Now he was able to make change. And exact revenge.

Not since its imperial glory had China possessed the wealth and the power to strike at her weakened foes. He would need resolve, but he was not alone. Other key figures on the committee shared his view. And that fool in the White House had conveniently opened the door. President Jackson's declaration that China was a currency manipulator represented an opportunity to push back. Hard.

The challenge was to take the Chinese people with him. To harness their sense of nationalism and direct their anger towards the West. Once that began he would pour oil on the fire. He would not stop until China emerged victorious.

And if the world had to be torn asunder and remade, then so be it.

Jiang stood back and admired his work, which spelled out Mao's revolutionary edict.

When the enemy advances, withdraw; when he stops, harass; when he tires, strike; when he retreats, pursue.

Canberra

The slightest of trembles. George Papadakis studied his hands for the telltale sign that one of the most powerful men in the nation was as nervous as a sixteen-year-old at a school formal.

He switched on his iPad, flicked to that journal of torment. It was nudging 6am and today marked the first Newspoll of the year. An election year. The numbers would not be a surprise because Papadakis, the prime minister's chief of staff, was always given a preview the night before the results went public. It was how *The Australian* interpreted the raw data that really mattered. How the views and prejudices of 1200 voters were spun, twisted, beaten up and spat out would dictate the sort of day that Martin Toohey and his minority Labor government would have.

Every radio and television station, every two-bit 'analyst' with a Twitter handle, would be waiting to wring Newspoll for every last drop. For just over two years, the broadsheet had used the fortnightly measure of the national pulse to persecute Labor. If the numbers fell, the *Oz* would boldly predict an imminent move against Toohey, despite there being no viable alternative. No change would be dubbed 'flat-lining', conjuring images of a government on life support. A miraculous rise was a 'dead-cat bounce' that briefly masked Labor's long-term, irreversible decline.

Since the last election, *The Australian* had not written one positive word about the minority government that had survived despite the conservative clique's ceaseless predictions of its imminent demise. The paper had glossed over the fact that the government's legislative agenda had scarcely missed a beat as Toohey deftly herded the hundred and fifty cats in the House of Representatives to relative order.

But as the online edition downloaded, Papadakis knew the latest numbers would tell their own devastating story without the paper applying the mix-master.

He plunged a half-cup of caffeine down his throat as he digested the horror.

TOOHEY HITS HISTORIC LOW

Support for the Toohey government has crashed with Labor's primary vote slumping below 30 per cent for the first time in Newspoll history.

Toohey, Papadakis's political soul mate, would be dead but for the fact that his only possible challenger, Catriona Bailey, remained stricken in a Canberra hospital eighteen months after being felled by a stroke during an interview on the ABC's *Lateline*.

The bastards at the *Oz* blithely ignored this inconvenient truth and kept including Bailey in their 'preferred prime minister' poll.

In further dire news for Martin Toohey, bed-ridden foreign minister Catriona Bailey remains an overwhelming favourite, outranking the prime minister as preferred leader by 44 per cent to just 17 per cent.

Mongrels.

The only sniff of good news was Emily Brooks's continuing struggle to gain traction. The opposition leader was paying a price for denying Bailey a parliamentary pair after her stroke stopped her attending parliament. Focus group testing showed Brooks rated as cold and heartless. Voters were turned off by her calculating approach and Tory grandees were murmuring that she'd have to soften her steely exterior.

The big winner in the poll was 'Other', which had climbed to 20 per cent as voters turned away from the major parties.

Papadakis glanced out at the courtyard.

Who can blame them? We are our own worst enemy.

The Toohey government had been the gift that kept giving for the press gallery. Any success was always trumped by spectacular own goals. Among a raft of contenders, the most extraordinary was Bruce Paxton's fall from ministerial grace. He had failed to declare that his first election campaign – way back in 1996 – had been funded in part by China Inc. That bombshell had nearly undone them.

Paxton, a one-time ally of Toohey, had initially accepted his demise, taking his place among the wasters and plodders on a surly backbench. He was thrown a few parliamentary crumbs and, for the most part, played the loyal foot soldier. But his mood changed when Toohey made it clear he would not be reinstated to the ministry.

He'd first sounded off to an ambitious press gallery newbie. Her story, 'Paxton Marks Toohey a Fail', was the first of many. Now he routinely threatened to resign from the Labor Caucus to sit on the crossbenches as an independent.

Despite his many failings, Paxton wasn't the government's biggest headache. That dubious honour went to Bailey who had an almost supernatural capacity to upstage the government. Her rock-star status had forced Toohey to retain her as foreign minister, despite her incapacity. And every time the PM was getting some traction, Bailey would steal the limelight.

It's like we're trapped in a B-grade horror movie being stalked by the Zombie Queen.

The diplomatic poseurs at the United Nations had made it worse by awarding Bailey a special peace prize based solely on the foreign minister's non-stop string of heartfelt tweets during the early months of the Syria crisis. Bailey's online tirade had achieved nothing. But it triggered favourable press – which was just the kind of 'action' those UN pretenders adored.

If she dies, we're dead at the by-election. Catch 22. I wish I'd stayed in Treasury.

Papadakis tried to calm the rage that pulsed within whenever he thought about Bailey. He turned back to his iPad. There was work to do. He had to think clearly to apply the finishing touches to a plan he and Toohey had been hatching for months.

They called it the Big Bang, their bid to break the cycle of dire news. To change the national conversation. To lay down a platform for an unlikely election win.

We can claw this back.

The truth was, Labor's own research matched the public polls. The party was heading for decimation. But the internal polling also showed there was a glimmer of hope amid the ruin. While it confirmed that barely 30 per cent of the population was prepared to vote Labor, a surprising 38 per cent still identified themselves as 'Labor voters'. If the Toohey government could win back its base it could be competitive.

We need to capture their imaginations and their hearts. To show that only we can deliver jobs and a fair go.

And that was what the Big Bang was designed to do. It was the ultimate circuit-breaker, a multi-pronged, multi-billion-dollar plan to boost jobs, skills, education and health.

Privately, Papadakis admitted its purpose was to dig the government out of a hole. But he also firmly believed it was visionary and 'Labor to the bootstraps'.

Its long-term cost was breathtaking, and only partly offset by cutting existing spending, particularly on defence. The real genius of the plan was the revenue stream tapped to fund it. The bulk of the money would flow from a yet-to-be-signed deal with a Chinese state-owned energy company. It had been two years in the making, driven by the PM and a trusted few in Cabinet.

It was unique. The Australian government would sign a 99-year lease ceding control over a massive gas-field just off Darwin to Sinopec, the world's fifth-largest company. It would give the Chinese what they coveted: real energy security through effective ownership of every step in the supply chain.

And it would give the Toohey government what it desperately needed: cash. Money was a big problem: revenues were falling, government spending kept rising and the treasurer, ridiculously, had staked Labor's economic reputation on a return to surplus this very year.

The beauty of the plan was that the gas-field was offshore and located in a territory, not a state. That meant all the bountiful tax revenues would flow directly to the Commonwealth, and as a bonus the Northern Territory would enjoy the benefits of massive investment. And the money would flow from the moment the deal was signed, with a $10 billion down-payment on the lease. Sinopec would then pay $1 billion a year, tied to inflation. At the end of the lease the site would revert to the Commonwealth, hopefully helping to combat the inevitable claims of 'selling off the farm'.

We will deliver a massive social dividend. Whitlam-on-steroids.

The beating heart of the Big Bang was a plan for universal mental health coverage. A Medicare-like set-up to cover a yawning gap in the health system. It would deliver to every family what the expensive advertising blitz would repeat ad nauseam: 'Peace of Mind'.

Even the economic hard-heads in the party agreed: the social benefits easily outweighed the cost. Secret focus-group testing showed that the punters loved the idea.

Papadakis scribbled small patterns as he pondered Toohey's grand vision. Sure, it was a high-wire gamble, Labor's last desperate chance, but its could work, could get the government back in the game.

And if Toohey stumbled? The Tories would ensure that there was no safety net to save him.

Canberra

Amanda Werner cast her eyes across the paperwork, straining to find a clue that would shed light on the mystery of this Asian corpse. Facts were proving elusive.

For nearly two years, Detective Sergeant Werner, a veteran of AFP and UN work in Cyprus, Timor-Leste, South Sudan and Afghanistan and now the chief coronial liaison officer for the ACT Police, had worked in this gleaming warehouse for the dead. It was designed to store up to one hundred bodies – ambitious, because most days in sleepy Canberra no more than a dozen lay on the slabs of polished steel.

The body had arrived the previous evening after its discovery by a group of schoolchildren visiting from Sydney.

Makes a change from PE and maths.

Werner had played spectator as the ACT's top forensic pathologist, with nearly thirty years experience in trying to tease secrets from the dead, had carried out the post-mortem examination five hours ago.

The cause of death was drowning. Although the man had suffered a blow to the head, consistent with falling from some height, the water in his lungs confirmed the head trauma had not been fatal. All the signs indicated that he had taken a tumble into the lake, most likely from Commonwealth Avenue Bridge.

But why?

There were no traces of alcohol in the body, so the chances that he'd been part of a group skylarking around the lake were slim.

Suicide?

That too was unlikely. A fall from either bridge could kill if the person landed awkwardly, but the structures weren't terribly high and didn't usually attract those wishing to end their lives.

The policewoman gazed out at the light industrial landscape of Phillip, the southern suburb that was home to the morgue. Late afternoon ho-hum. A salesman was closing a deal on a Hyundai, while the local office supplies outlet looked as if it was shutting early.

And here she was, troubled and restless, trying to commune with the dead.

'Amanda, are you there?' The voice of the front office clerk roused Werner from her reverie.

'What's up?'

'Two people to see you, from the Chinese embassy.' The clerk emphasised the name of the country as if she was swallowing a razor blade. 'They want to chat about a deceased Asian man.'

Chinese? Maybe that's one part of the puzzle solved.

Werner gathered up a few papers before walking to the foyer and extending her hand to a man dressed in an ill-fitting grey suit. She then turned to an attractive woman clad in a smart outfit.

The man spoke with a heavy accent, wrestling with his English.

'Hello. I am Zheng Dong, First Assistant Secretary, Embassy of China.' He looked uncomfortable and glanced at his companion.

'Weng Meihui. I am also from the embassy.'

Weng spoke with the faintest of accents, all diplomatic charm. She offered a warm smile.

Werner's practised eye studied the pair. Weng had the poise and beauty of a model. Tall for an Asian woman. Her face was open and friendly. Her age was elusive, but there were hints about her eyes that she was older than she appeared. The man did not look like a diplomat. His cheap suit could not disguise the hardness and athleticism of his body. Werner noted too the calluses and scars on his knuckles, the sign of someone who had spent years training in hand-to-hand combat. But it was his eyes that sent a chill through her. So black that the pupil vanished into the iris. An assassin's eyes.

'Ms Werner. The man who was found in the lake, dead. He is, we believe, a worker from the embassy. He was deeply troubled and not happy with living far from his home. Unfortunately it would appear that he took his own life. My colleague and I would like to see the body.' Zheng spoke politely, but Werner sensed a hint of menace beneath the civil veneer.

'Of course. Come with me.'

A few moments later, she drew back the cloth covering the unidentified body.

'Is this your man?'

Zheng nodded.

'The People's Republic of China has legal responsibility for this man, who was in Australia on a diplomatic passport. We will take the body with us. Now.'

Werner was on her turf and not about to give ground to visiting bureaucrats. They knew their rights and she knew hers.

'That may well be, Mr Zheng, but the body has not yet been cleared for release.'

Weng opened her elegant handbag and removed an envelope, offering another winning smile as she handed over an official letter from the embassy and a passport photograph of the dead man. 'We don't wish to cause any trouble. But we are the legal guardians of this man. His name is Lin An.'

Werner dug in. She wasn't to be taken for a fool.

'I'm sorry, but we haven't concluded the formal investigation. We can't allow bodies to leave the morgue without all the proper paperwork and procedures being completed. I'm sure you understand that, Mr Zheng, Ms Weng.'

The Chinese pair stole a quick glance at each other. Zheng was clearly displeased but clearly there would be no cutting corners, or getting around this green-eyed *gweilo*. Finally, Weng spoke.

'Thank you, Ms Werner. We appreciate your time and assistance. We ask respectfully that you check with your superiors about making arrangements for us to retrieve the body, once all proper procedures have been completed.'

'Of course, Ms Weng. If everything goes to order, the body should be available for consular pick-up in the next few days. But I stress this will depend on the final results of the forensics.'

With that, she led the two diplomats back to the foyer, shaking their hands as she bade them farewell. The slightest of grins ghosted across Zheng's face … or were Werner's sharp eyes deceiving her?

She returned to her office, preparing to make detailed notes of the visit. What she had not told the Chinese pair – and had not yet documented anywhere – was that the body had yielded one fascinating clue: a USB had been secreted in the man's intestine. It had shown up on the MT scan and the pathologist had retrieved it with one deft cut.

Werner opened a locked desk drawer and held a plastic bag up to the late afternoon light. The USB carried a single word, UNIS. It had 10GB of memory – and heaven knows what it contained on its digital circuit board.

Earlier, she'd plugged it into her PC. It was encrypted and that alone was fascinating. Now the visit by the Chinese diplomats had deepened her suspicion that there was an intriguing story behind this death. And that meant Werner needed to push matters up a very different chain of command from the routine coronial hierarchy.

She picked up the phone. She knew just the man to talk to.

Canberra

He paced the bare room, illuminated by a single fluorescent light that buzzed softly. His schoolboy error had left the knuckles on his right hand badly bruised and he counted himself lucky that no bones had broken. But he knew from long experience that his fingers would ache for days.

Never, never lose your temper.

That it was imperative to stay in control had been drilled into him. His instructors had been determined to instil discipline, to harness the unquenchable rage that coursed through their promising disciple. That needed to be managed. Directed. But never extinguished.

If he was honest, he would admit that he enjoyed these rare moments of letting go a little too much. The tools of his trade, strewn across the floor, were useful. But he always liked to get 'hands on' once the groundwork had been laid. And rage, too, could be a useful tool.

The bunker where he was working had not yet been completed; it would one day be an embassy storeroom. It required none of the artistry that would grace the rest of the mansion. Below ground level, it was a windowless concrete box with minimal ventilation.

The air had grown fetid as he'd worked. Others would have found it oppressive, but he felt exhilarated. He took a deep breath. The smell. It was one of the things he loved. The mud-like tone of fresh concrete mixed with stale sweat and the acidic tinge of urine. And the top note: the sweet, familiar tang of blood.

And fear.

Others scoffed but he had always known that fear had a smell. He had

154

been close to it all his life. His own fear, as a child, when his father's anger made the taste of his own blood routine.

Then the smell of his father's terror as he lay helpless before the blade as the rage that had been brewing exploded for the first time. That moment of sweet revenge had made him feel powerful, alive. Both his crude savagery and calm demeanour had shaken the police when they'd found him by the brutalised corpse.

It led the state to save him from execution. Instead they would train him, still a teenager, to be a special breed of foot soldier. Because the state knew that such men were valuable. That terror had its place.

The interrogator stopped rubbing his hand and returned his focus to the centre of the room where a shattered body was bound to an office chair. Builder's wire bit deeply into wrists with the subject's every agonised wrench. His white shirt was covered in blood and sick. His head flopped unconscious to the right, exposing the ragged flesh and cartilage that had once been his left ear.

A thread of spittle dribbled from split lips. The little fingers from both hands were missing: tossed on the floor near a kitchen cleaver, some pliers and several teeth. A hammer had crushed toes, smashed a kneecap and broken several ribs.

A welt just under the subject's left eye was beginning to swell. The interrogator knew his last ferocious blow had broken a cheekbone. And the subject had passed out, again.

Yet he had learned nothing of the incident that had so enraged his masters. The subject had shared a room with the traitor and seen and heard nothing on the night of the escape. It had been the same with the other one.

Both, it seemed, were innocents.

So what remained of his day's work was simply for pleasure.

'Wake up!' he barked, as he poured water over the battered head. Slowly a mind muddied by pain and terrorised by what a fellow human was capable of cleared enough to rouse from one nightmare to another.

His mouth tried to form a plea. A futile effort to evoke some pity.

'Please ...' His single word came out a guttural sob.

The interrogator felt the tingle of excitement that always came with the last desperate entreaty for life.

'I now understand you know nothing about the escape.' His voice was low, measured. 'But you need to know this. He betrayed his nation. And you. You are suffering because of him. Believe me, I will make it end. Soon.'

He dangled a blade before swollen eyes.

'Now, let's get rid of those pants.'

He emerged as early evening shadows were turning to night. It was warm, the air was clear, and birds chattered in the trees that surrounded the compound. In the nearby suburbs the mundane dinner-time rituals were well under way.

If anyone had been paying attention, they would have noticed that the lights that usually lit the building site had been extinguished.

The interrogator paused for a moment.

So quiet. Like the moment when death comes.

He was still astounded by the silence of this place, its proximity to nature, so different to the relentless noise of the city that he knew.

He motioned to the two men behind him who were labouring with the body. Another carried a plastic shopping bag, its contents heavy. They shuffled fifty metres to a trench that would form part of the foundations of the embassy's administrative wing.

The body was dumped next to another and the plastic bag thrown in alongside. The interrogator rubbed the aching knuckles of his right hand as he nodded to the men. Concrete flowed down the slipway of the mixer as a worker expertly guided the grey liquid over the small pile of human remains.

The half-dozen men looked at the interrogator only for instructions. Otherwise they steadfastly avoided his jet-black gaze and busied themselves with their appointed tasks.

He smiled as he lit a cigarette. Fear. He could not smell it mixed with this sweet night air or see it in the shadows that shrouded the faces of his peons.

But he knew it was there because they knew what he had done.

Canberra

Martin Toohey looked up from the mountain of paperwork piled on his desk. It was close to midday and the first pangs of hunger prompted thoughts of lunch. But the poached salmon would have to wait. Toohey was expecting a VIP visitor.

A quiet knock signalled his arrival. 'The ambassador to see you, Prime Minister.'

*

Brent Moreton had landed in Australia several years earlier and had quickly forged a reputation for telling it as it was. Or as the Americans wanted it to be. A charmer nonetheless, Moreton was highly regarded on the social circuit and his dinner invitations stretched out almost a year.

Toohey and Moreton had forged a solid relationship, despite their different world views. Both were professional advocates for their respective causes and when from time to time conflict between the Toohey government and the US arose, they were mature and sensible enough to work through it.

But the challenges were growing. China and America were amping up the rhetoric to a level not seen since the end of the Cold War. President Jackson seemed to be taking his cues from the Tea Party loonies who believed in guns, God and slashing government. His foreign policy was an extension of his domestic tub-thumping – his decision to declare China a currency manipulator was just the most significant of several early blunders.

And China was increasingly combative, testing its growing power and the will of the United States to confront it. Some think tanks had begun to speculate that conflict between the two powers was inevitable, and might occur sooner rather than later.

Toohey was trying to chart a middle course: needing both Chinese dollars *and* the security of the US alliance.

'The Switzerland of the Pacific,' one Canberra-based analyst had sneered.

Above all, the PM wanted to avoid being pushed into making an impossible choice between two rival powers. That made talks with the two nations' envoys a delicate dance between raindrops.

'Prime Minister, thanks for making the time to see me so quickly,' Moreton began. 'I want to bring you up to speed on events. The president has been ringing several world leaders – David Cameron, Angela Merkel, Shinzo Abe – and he would like to speak with you this evening.'

The ambassador paused as if searching for the right tone.

'We are increasingly concerned about the direction Beijing is heading. The new Chinese leadership seems determined to flex its muscles. It's as if we have gone back to the bad old days before Deng got his hands on the political and economic levers.'

Toohey began his practised tightrope walk.

'I'm not sure I share your pessimism, Brent. We've had two senior ministers visit China in the past month. Their feedback has been quite positive. The trade minister believes we are closer than ever to a free-trade deal, and that would be terrific not just for us but for this part of the world generally.'

'It would be quite a coup, I grant you that, Prime Minister. And yet China shows little interest in being part of our bid to free up trade across the entire region through our Trans-Pacific Partnership.'

Toohey knew exactly what the Chinese thought of that: another exercise in the US writing the rules and expecting Beijing to follow them.

'Well, we support it and are optimistic that China will too, one day,' Toohey lied.

The main game was yet to unfold and he left space for Moreton to fill.

'I'm not sure I share your optimism. But one thing is clear: what China is spending its money on. Its military. It admits to lifting defence spending 11 per cent this year to $120 billion. We think it's much more than that.'

Moreton had his brief well rehearsed.

'Their J-20 program is well advanced; the prototype stealth fighter they've been developing at Chengdu is not on par with ours, but it ain't far behind. China's air capability has moved ahead in leaps and bounds.'

The ambassador reached for a cup of tea before continuing.

'Our intelligence isn't as definitive on China's submarine program, but, Martin, they are putting together a very nice fleet. The Taiwan Strait is getting very crowded and they aren't pleasure craft out for a Sunday paddle.'

Toohey was trying to recall his latest briefing on the relative strengths of China's and America's military machines. Infuriatingly, he couldn't remember specifics, but he did know that Uncle Sam was well ahead. He sought to inject some common sense into the debate.

'Brent, you and I both know China is miles behind the US when it comes to military capability. You spend more than four times what China outlays on defence. Right now your country accounts for just under 40 per cent of the world's military spending. Even if they are hell-bent on catching up, it would take decades.'

Moreton leaned forward, determined to make his friend understand.

'Martin, they don't need to spend what we do right now to be a threat. They just have to have the kit to push out into the neighbourhood and push us back across the Pacific. And this new leadership is something else; it is much more aggressive than we expected. And not just in the real world. You have no doubt read the latest Five Eyes briefs on China's cyber-espionage activities?'

The ambassador left the words hanging, knowing Australia's genuine concern about the threat posed by Beijing's cyber-thieves. The prime minister's own emails had been stolen by the Chinese, and Toohey had only learned of this when the US alerted Australia to the audacious intrusion.

'We are entering a new phase in our relationship with China,' Moreton insisted. 'President Jackson is very concerned by the latest briefings.'

Toohey was worried about activities on both sides of the Pacific.

'Frankly, Brent, I am more than a little concerned by the tone out of Washington,' he responded. 'Declaring China a currency manipulator was a mistake. It would be better if your president let the calmer heads in his national security team prevail, rather than being dictated to by the Tea Party. It would be wise to take a step back on that. If China feels boxed in, it will retaliate. You are handing them a reason to do so. Stop yelling at China and start talking to it.'

Toohey almost immediately regretted the Tea Party line, realising that even if the ambassador secretly agreed he would be forced to come to his president's defence.

'We needed to send a shot across China's economic bow.' Moreton swiftly manned the president's barricade. 'For too long, they've been able to get away with using their fixed currency to damage our economy. We will not meekly sit back and allow Beijing to game the system. If they want to enjoy the benefits of the international economic road rules, they should abide by them.'

With a politician's instinct for seizing on just those words that served his argument, Toohey grasped the opening offered by Moreton.

'Australia wants everyone to obey the international rules that help ensure the peace, Brent. Because if we keep the peace we can all prosper. And if we accommodate China's rise we can guarantee the peace. If you attempt to ring-fence it, no good will come of it.'

He reached for a glass of water before continuing.

'Brent, I appreciate your concerns, but my government believes it is critical that China and the US attempt to forge a more constructive relationship. A true partnership. And that might mean that, occasionally, the US has to step back and give China space to mature. The twenty-first century rests on peace between your nations, and as a friend to both of you, that is our counsel.'

Toohey knew that the idea of the US taking a step back on anything wasn't one that had a lot of currency in Washington. But he believed that it was a powerful argument and one he intended to make as strongly as he possibly could.

The two men had been talking for close to twenty minutes when Moreton lifted the stakes.

'A free-trade deal is one thing. But Washington is very worried that you are about to get strategically entangled with China. Martin, we hear that a massive gas deal that involves effective Chinese ownership of Australian resources will be at the heart of your National Press Club address.'

Toohey was stunned. The China deal was top secret. Just a handful of people knew about the Northern Territory gas hub plan.

'As usual I am staggered by your intelligence.' Toohey was measuring each word and wrestling with his emotions. 'That plan is not yet finalised, and if and when it is I will act in the best interests of my nation.'

'Don't commit yourself to this, Prime Minister.' Moreton too was treading carefully. 'If you do, it will put us in a very awkward position.'

'Brent, I will promise you just this. I will do what is right for my country. And the party I lead. Labor has always been the party of big ideas, just like your Democrats. We owe our political success to our ability to marry good economic policies with progressive social reforms. That is what I intend doing.'

Moreton looked unconvinced and Toohey suspected the cable back to DC would be quite something.

'Martin, our friendship has endured for many decades. Australia has always been one of our closest allies, through good and bad. The president will be calling soon and I think our conversation has given you a good flavour of what is on his mind. He treasures this alliance and hopes he can count on you in what may well be difficult times ahead.'

'Always happy to talk.' But Toohey had run out of patience with the conversation and was keen to begin another with his chief of staff to try to track down the source of this latest damaging leak. 'And as a friend of America I will repeat the advice I have offered you.'

The ambassador had delivered his message and glanced at his Seiko Velatura before continuing. 'Your government has some big decisions ahead of it, my friend. Now, I must away. Lunch with the Brits awaits.'

He stalled at the door, and looked back.

'Prime Minister, don't forget who your mates are.'

Canberra

Charles Dancer sat Buddha-like, meditating, as the Canberra morning sun streamed into his home, a soft tune thrumming in the background. The sunlight played across a row of jade statues, sourced from back-alley dens in Laos and Cambodia. Asian paintings covered the walls, while a custom-made set of shelves tastefully showcased fertility figures, dolls and masks, all of it a reminder that he – ostensibly a dry-as-dust bureaucrat – had led a life of intrigue.

Dancer stretched and ended his yoga session. He poured a shot of black coffee, adding two sugars. For the past fifteen years, he'd lived in a bungalow close to the bustling village of Manuka, a few kilometres from the R.G. Casey Building, home to his official employer, the Department of Foreign Affairs and Trade.

Along with many of his colleagues, Dancer had a taste for the good life. He got a thrill whenever he came across a new treasure overseas and occasionally would leverage his status to ensure its smooth passage through Customs. His walk-in wardrobe reflected a refined taste in clothing. He seldom shopped at home, relying on regular international travel to maintain a steady supply of tailor-made suits and shirts. Recently, he'd experimented with internet shopping and was pleased with his first online purchases.

A lifetime of living alone, a steady and well-paid job with generous allowances, and the hand-me-down benefits of his parents' estate ensured financial security.

Dancer had followed a standard path into DFAT's ranks, graduating from the Australian National University with honours in International Relations, earning a special commendation for an insightful thesis on Australia's relationship with Indonesia. Hired through the graduate program – Class of '77 – Dancer was considered a stand-out among the many who, each year, jostled for one of the handful of positions on offer. He'd adapted easily to the departmental culture, had worked hard and been rewarded with a posting to Jakarta after just five years.

On the surface, he was a boilerplate public servant. Under the radar, he had been recruited by the Australian Secret Intelligence Service, and he'd become one of their very best.

Dancer was fastidious and uber-fit, enjoying long rides on a custom-made Kona that could whip down the narrow mountain trails that flanked the national capital. For thirty years he'd maintained a steady weight of 85 kilograms, underpinned by an obsession with healthy eating. While his wine cellar was graced with prized vintages, he drank in moderation and considered a hangover to be a sign of frailty.

On this crystal-cut morning in Canberra, however, the tastes and habits of Charles Dancer mattered little. He contemplated the USB that he'd been given by Amanda Werner.

His mate from the morgue had rung out of the blue. They'd first met in Afghanistan in 2008 when he was attached to a contingent sent in to track the faint footprints of Osama bin Laden. They'd forged a bond in the ancient war-torn wasteland, often sharing a non-alcoholic beer as an antidote to the daily assassinations and bombings. She'd explained, over a glass of wine, about the body in the lake and the visit from the Chinese embassy staff, their clumsy attempt to retrieve the corpse before the investigation had finished.

What they didn't know was that a memory stick had been retrieved from his stomach during the autopsy. Werner had used discretion to ensure there was no record of it on the official police file. She'd given Dancer brief details about the man – identified as Lin An – and a copy of the forensic notes.

According to the Chinese, Lin was a construction worker sent to Australia to help build the fortress-like embassy that was taking shape on the lake's edge, four hundred metres from the existing buildings. The story didn't fit though; his pallid body displayed none of the brawn or weathering you'd expect of a labourer exposed to Canberra's punishing climate.

Dancer fired up his MacBook Pro and slipped in the USB. As Werner had warned him, the file was encrypted. That reinforced the notion that Lin was not a labourer. Clicking through the unreadable documents, Dancer surmised it would take quite some time before they could be cracked.

And if Lin had locked it with keys that only he possessed?

Well, it would take a little longer.

Once opened, the file would have to be translated, although that would pose little trouble for Dancer who'd been stationed for several years in Beijing. Prior to his posting, he'd studied Mandarin at the RAAF School of Languages at Point Cook and graduated R4S4, the highest levels of reading and speaking.

Dancer had a particular passion for China and its rich and painful history. It was something he'd shared with Kimberley Gordon, a former security analyst with the Defence Signals Directorate whose death eighteen months before had left a searing wound.

Dancer had envied Gordon's courage in resolving her gender confusion because it had been very different for him. As a teenager in a strict Baptist home, Charles had fought the attraction that he felt for men. Denied it and himself. He could never admit it to his parents and his father's words still haunted him.

All mankind is depraved, sinful and lost.

He had quit his family's stern religion as soon as he left home. But it clung like a cancer on his soul. Dancer loathed himself and his homosexuality. He had grasped at relationships with women, but they'd ranged from the awkward to the embarrassing.

Eventually he had given in to his desires but only when he was far from home. Even in his late forties, he had never had a long-term love.

Until he met Kimberley. Then he was besotted. She seemed to offer an answer. Outwardly female, bodily male. For a while, they revelled in each other, liberating each other's yearnings. But, in time, Dancer's doubts and his self-loathing returned. Kimberley had fought to maintain their special bond, to try to get him to find peace with himself. But the relationship was doomed.

I pushed her away.

They avoided each other for more than a year before Kimberley had sought his help with a difficult job. He had been thrilled to hear from her. Tried to help her. To point her in the right direction.

And then she was killed.

More than once, Dancer had caught himself muttering 'For you, Kimberley …' as he set about some onerous task, trying not to douse himself in self-pity and blame.

Now, on a summer's day promising to soar into the high thirties, Dancer began to run the first pass of a decryption program over the USB. A nervous twinge whisked down his left arm, the anticipation of stumbling onto something big.

An hour later, Dancer had extracted a few shards of information from one of the hundreds of files on the memory stick. The lines of the decrypted code did not disappoint, confirming that Wade was right to be suspicious of the Chinese claim that the dead man, Lin An, was a labourer.

The first file was a dossier on Lin.

My, my, my …

Dancer had seen enough secrets in his time that he could usually cover his excitement with a studied indifference. It was something he practised, even in the isolation of his own home.

But this file showed that Lin was attached to one of China's most dangerous institutions: Unit 61398. The unit was an arm of the People's Liberation Army and the nerve centre of China's hacking empire, home to hundreds of cyber-warriors who'd launched assaults against corporations and countries.

Dancer had read top-secret files blaming China for infiltrating key assets in Australia. Rumour had it that the Australian Security Intelligence Organisation's director-general believed China was responsible for stealing the building plans of the new spy HQ on the edge of the Defence complex in Russell, a stone's throw from Lake Burley Griffin.

Dancer's mind was racing. The fact that a Chinese cyber-warrior, albeit a dead one, was in Canberra confirmed his worst suspicions about the real nature of the new embassy being built within cannon shot of Parliament House.

He weighed his options. Of course, he would present the information to his superiors. But that was no longer enough. He had watched with alarm as each warning issued by intelligence chiefs about the growing threat of China went unheeded by the pathetic Toohey government.

The people needed to know how *serious* the threat was. If they did, they would be horrified. And that would force the Toohey government into making the right decisions. To act in the national interest.

The best way to influence public opinion was through the mainstream media. Despite the rise of online news, tweeting and blogging, Dancer wanted to leak this information to the outside world the old-fashioned way.

First he had work to do. He saved the material from the USB onto a portable hard drive, then put it in a safe hidden behind an early Mapplethorpe. Next he uploaded a few lines from the document he had opened onto another memory stick, editing the raw data to ensure that it offered no more than a tantalising taste.

Dancer had a low regard for journalists, but there was one he trusted, the press gallery veteran Harry Dunkley. After Kimberley's death they had been drawn together by a deeply ironic intersection of work and shared affection for her.

Dunkley had been cool, even hostile at first. But his anger had eventually dissipated and he and Dancer had shared the odd bottle of wine as balm for their common grief.

Dancer flicked on his mobile and scrolled through an impressive contact list. Six rings later, a gruff voice answered.

'Well, well. Look who the cat's dragged in ...'

Fort Meade, Maryland

The steel door slid open with a sound like air rushing from a tyre valve and Matthew Sloan stood transfixed as it revealed a scene drawn from a childhood fantasy.

The chair of Australia's Parliamentary Joint Committee on Intelligence and Security had stepped onto the bridge of a spaceship that was immediately, eerily, familiar. The skin on Sloan's scalp tightened and his arms tingled with goose bumps.

The circular room was built on two levels. He'd stepped onto the upper deck where the focal point was a single high-backed chair on a raised platform. It looked towards a massive plasma screen that arced from floor to ceiling across both levels of the bridge. The screen displayed a satellite image of the world, with the United States dead centre. Also on the top deck, just below and in front of the captain's chair, was a command module where two senior crew sat monitoring a bank of computer screens. Three sets of stairs ran down to the lower deck where more crew clustered around duty stations dotted around the outer circle.

So, it was true. The US National Security Agency's Intelligence and Security Command's 'Information Dominance Centre' at Fort Meade, Maryland, had been designed as an exact replica of the bridge of a Constitution Class starship. To be specific, the USS *Enterprise*.

In the late 1960s, like so many Australian kids, Sloan had tuned in avidly each week to watch Captain Kirk and his crew boldly go where no man had gone before. Now he was one of a very privileged few to venture here. The Labor MP swelled with pride. He was the first Australian parliamentarian to be invited into the beating heart of the most sophisticated signals intelligence operation on Earth.

The main chair swivelled and an athletic-looking military man rose to greet him. General Dick Hargreaves was the longest-serving leader of the NSA and the inaugural commander of US Cyber Command. From this bridge he listened to the world's secrets and battled shadowy adversaries.

'Mr Sloan, I presume.' Hargreaves spoke with a gentle southern drawl. 'I am delighted that you could join us.'

'General, the pleasure and honour are mine.' Sloan glanced about the impossible room. 'This is extraordinary.'

'Yes, Matthew, the folks at Imagination in Hollywood helped us put it together. Our idea was we're going into a new area – information warfare and cyber – so how do we build *esprit de corps* and help the army think about this in a new light? We've got to get people energised about carrying out this mission. We've got to creatively inspire them to bring disparate data together to help secure our nation.'

'Forgive me for asking,' Sloan was still gawping, 'but is it true that the number on your car space here at Fort Meade is 007?'

Hargreaves laughed. 'That's correct. It shows you that the folks at NSA have a sense of humour. But I drive a Chevy pickup, not an Aston Martin.'

Both men chuckled and Sloan, knowing his time here would be strictly limited, moved to the main game.

'General, the reason I requested this meeting is so I might give my committee a proper feel for how you work. We're particularly interested in trying to replicate your cyber-war capabilities. We want America's assessment of the threats.'

The general pressed a button on a console in the armrest of his chair. The giant screen flicked to a flow chart headed 'NSA Operations'.

'NSA has two main tasks,' Hargreaves began. 'First, it collects, decodes, translates, analyses and disseminates foreign signals, or communications, for intelligence and counter-intelligence purposes and to support our military operations.

'NSA's second job is information assurance. That is, to prevent adversaries from gaining access to the nation's most sensitive secrets.'

The general punched the button again and the screen flicked to another diagram.

'Cyber Command's mission is three-fold: first, to defend the nation from cyber-attacks; second, to operate and defend the Defence Department's information networks; and, finally, to support our military combat commanders with the cyber-capabilities they need, including conducting full-spectrum military cyberspace operations, when directed, in order to enable our military actions across the air, land, sea, space and cyber domains. In short, Cyber Command's task is to ensure the military has freedom of action in cyberspace – and to deny the same to our adversaries.'

Sloan was already across a lot of the theory. What he wanted was an idea of how it worked in practice.

'So does all this help in a real-world war zone?'

Hargreaves shifted forward in his seat and Sloan could see this keeper of secrets was enjoying the chance to boast about his work.

'One of my proudest moments is how we responded in Iraq in '05 and '06. The casualties were mounting with a dozen allied soldiers being killed or wounded daily, driven by a surge in roadside bombings.

'We started collecting a much broader range of insurgent communications and then, crucially, compressing the time it took us to get actionable intelligence back into the hands of the end users. We successfully reduced that disconnect from about sixteen hours down to around one minute. We saved lives.'

Sloan wanted to talk about another kind of war. One waged in bits and bytes in the ether. One Australia was ill equipped to fight.

'General, how serious is the threat of cyber-war?'

166

'Matthew, I believe the rise of globalisation has made the world a more dangerous place. What keeps me awake at night is the threat of terrorist and cyber-attacks; those are the two threats where adversaries can reach far into the homeland and really hurt populations. Those risks are growing, and we need to be out in front of them.

'What we're seeing is more folks testing boundaries with mounting numbers of state-on-state cyber-probes and sometimes cyber-attacks. But the main risk is miscalculation. Assume one country believes it can hit your nation with a cyber-attack, and that it won't lead to physical conflict.

'But in launching that cyber-attack, suppose they knock down your stock exchange or temporarily disable your banking system, which is a very real possibility. And if they extend those attack vectors to take out power grids, transport systems and other infrastructure, there can be devastating consequences.

'Your government then feels it has to retaliate and we have an unpredictable chain reaction that could lead to outright war. In the virtual world no one knows where the red lines are.'

Sloan felt uneasy listening to this new doomsday scenario. Now he understood why the spooks he knew were paranoid, always glancing at the shadows in search of an enemy that might or might not exist.

'So how do we protect ourselves?' the MP asked.

The general's eyes wandered over his gleaming twenty-first-century war-room.

'When you think about success on the battlefield, you say your artillery has to be the best. Your armour has to be the best. Your infantry has to be the best. The same logic applies in the cyber-domain.'

Sloan had worked his way towards the one question that was keeping *him* awake at night.

'So who should Australia fear the most?'

The general caught Sloan's eye and didn't miss a beat: 'China.'

'Why?'

'You matter to China. You're a reliable source of what it needs to rise as the next superpower. But it sees you as tied to us, the current superpower, through ANZUS. That presents a problem. No matter what you say in public, in China's mind you can't straddle that divide forever. One day you'll have to make a choice.

'So China needs to know your deepest thoughts. The relationships at the heart of your leadership, right down to who is literally fucking whom, if you'll pardon my French. That's why they opened up your parliamentary

167

communications systems. When we found out about it we warned you. But we believe that they'd had access for a year.'

Sloan's heart sank. He was well aware of the damage. 'It was like an open-cut mine.'

'Indeed, and right now there's a warehouse full of Chinese analysts poring over every line of what they took, looking for weaknesses.'

'I don't doubt it.' Sloan shook his head.

'And since our president decided to muscle up to China on its currency manipulation we've been recording attacks on our systems every day that are off the charts. You could be in the line of fire, too.'

'Why? What have we done? If anything our government is doing too much to appease China.'

The general frowned. 'Yes, we've noticed that. But in the end, you're our ally. You have access to all this.' Hargreaves swept his right arm across the bridge. 'So that makes you a target.'

Suddenly the general rose from his chair. The audience was over. The spymaster had real work to do, but he had one last message to send. He leaned in close to deliver it.

'Matthew, if there is one thing that you should tell your government back in Canberra, it is this: the enemy is already through the gates.'

Canberra

Harry Dunkley rolled out of bed, the remnant of a dream already fading. It was nearly 7am and the press gallery veteran rubbed an ache in his hip, a reminder of too much rugby in his reckless youth.

The soft morning light cast a glow over the sleeping Celia Mathieson. She seemed to shine from within and looked younger than her thirty-two years. Her beauty and their fledgling relationship still astounded him.

They'd met in October when Mathieson, back in Canberra after eight years overseas, was hired by *The Australian* as a 'data journalist'. Dunkley had rolled his eyes when told of the new position, assuming it was something dreamed up by Gen Y back-office types.

Mathieson was the only daughter of one of Canberra's most senior mandarins, the fearsome Roger Mathieson – AO and all-round shit. He had bulldozed his way to the top of the public service, serving as deputy secretary in half a dozen agencies. Perhaps it was to escape from her father's long shadow that Celia had taken off overseas soon after graduating with honours in Advanced Computing from the Australian

National University. She'd only returned when her mother was diagnosed with breast cancer.

A month after she'd started at the *Oz*, Dunkley had enlisted her help to trawl through the entitlement records of every MP and senator. She'd taken her time completing the task but Dunkley had been astounded by her computer skills. He'd shouted her a joint byline on the subsequent story and asked her out for a drink after she'd given him a tantalising 'thank you' kiss that lingered a tad too long.

Their relationship had blossomed from spreadsheets to bedsheets and now, as Dunkley watched his sleeping angel, he felt the guilty lust of a man who couldn't quite believe his luck. He shook his head in wonder. What does she see in me?

He headed to the bathroom, splashing his face to wash the sleep from his eyes before examining last night's damage. He tried to convince himself he was still handsome despite the creased face that looked all its fifty-five years and offered a little too much history. Still, the first flourish of grey added a certain Clooney lustre, he thought.

He stifled a yawn as he opened the front door to collect the newspapers. He was always pleased to see real-world print resting with reassuring tactility on the porch.

But as he carried the five mastheads inside, he was dismayed by their meagre weight. The rise of the internet and changing reading habits were strip-mining advertising dollars from the old media by the millions. And as the cash dried up and profits shrank, the farewells for journalist colleagues were becoming routine. Every paper in the country was fighting for its survival, slashing costs as it shed hardcopy readers. Jesus, even his local newsagent was toying with scrapping the paper run.

'It's costing me money,' he'd told Dunkley recently as he'd settled his monthly account. 'I only do it 'cause of customers like you. And you're getting fewer every year.'

It had hit Dunkley like a punch. Something that he'd assumed would be a permanent feature of his life was about to vanish. That reassuring thud of paper on grass would soon, like the clink of the milk run, become a story that grandparents told to wide-eyed youngsters.

He quickly scanned the headlines to see if he'd been scooped by one of his colleagues in the blast furnace of the federal parliamentary press gallery, still the most competitive marketplace in journalism. Nope. Instead his rivals would be frothing over his own story – and, more importantly, so would their editors.

Despite nearly thirty years in the game, Dunkley still felt the same kid-in-a-toyshop thrill when he broke a yarn that would set the agenda. A tingle took hold as he gazed at the headline on page 1 of the national broadsheet:

TOOHEY IS TERMINAL

And the lede hit like a prizefighter.

> Labor risks electoral annihilation with just one in four voters backing the embattled Toohey government, secret internal ALP polling reveals.
>
> The credibility of Prime Minister Martin Toohey has also crashed.
>
> The polling shows voters in battleground seats in western Sydney and Brisbane have lost faith in the government's ability to manage the country.
>
> Labor insiders fear the party is beyond salvation and the public has stopped listening to the prime minister.
>
> 'They are waiting with baseball bats and chainsaws,' one senior source said. 'When the election is held, the streets will run red with our blood. Toohey's a great guy but this can't go on.'

Pointers promised more thrills inside, including a thundering editorial which boasted, once again, that the judgement of the *Oz* had been vindicated. A historical analysis revealed that Toohey was the least popular prime minister since Billy McMahon. The paper's caustic 'Cut and Paste' column amused itself with a series of quotes from the ABC and Fairfax ripped from Toohey's days of early promise, all designed to show the multiple delusions of the 'Love Media'.

And just to make sure that not a single reader was left in any doubt as to where the newspaper stood, *The Australian*'s chieftains had published a photo of a glowing opposition leader, Emily Brooks, as she left a function full of cheering Tory types, with the caption 'Headed for the Lodge'.

Dunkley flinched. He had no trouble going in hard with the facts, and Labor had brought most of its woes on itself. But he had rarely met a more objectionable individual than Brooks. While the country seemed poised to throw the government out, the punters weren't hungering for the alternative. Would Brooks be better able to provide the three key things Dunkley believed Australians craved from their leaders – predictability, certainty and competence?

Dunkley believed that at another time, under different circumstances, Toohey would have made a decent PM. But that was a fantasy. History had punched Toohey's card and before the end of the year his brief, unhappy term in office would be over.

The sun pouring through an eastward-facing window lit up a dust-covered Walkley Award, among a pile of other ill-treated honours on a cluttered shelf. The chaos of the Bailey–Toohey years had been the most successful of Dunkley's long career covering politics. Labor had been good for journalism and he'd led the pack.

So what.

No award could mask the pain that followed the death of Kimberley Gordon. It was only after she was gone that he realised how alone he really was and what a friend she had been.

Only now, in his budding relationship with Celia, had some of the pain begun to fade. But Dunkley knew he would always be tormented until he unravelled the mystery of Kimberley's death. And avenged it.

He was convinced her murder was linked to the former defence minister Bruce Paxton and his murky ties to China. Dunkley had asked for Kimberley's help with a photo that eventually implicated Paxton in electoral fraud. But she had turned up a more astonishing story: that Paxton and former prime minister, Catriona Bailey, had been courted by Chinese spies.

The allegation was unprovable, the evidence circumstantial at best. And he was well aware that spooks like Kimberley were naturally paranoid and prone to conspiracy theories. But Dunkley could not reconcile one undeniable fact: within hours of Kimberley stumbling onto the links between Bailey and Chinese intelligence, she was dead.

Someone knew what she knew and wanted it to die with her.

Every day he felt the weight of guilt. She had died helping him.

Dunkley had used his considerable investigative skills to try to track down the killer. All roads led to China, and he believed a third secretary, who had abruptly left the Chinese embassy in Canberra following Kimberley's death, was the key. Dunkley had taken long-service leave to follow the trail to Beijing, but turned up nothing.

So he'd come home and thrown himself back into his job with vigour. But the experience had hardened him against China. He'd written opinion pieces warning of the strategic risks that came with the opportunities of its rise, reminding Australia to remember who its real friends were. Since the Second World War, the United States had provided the security environment that had allowed China to flower peacefully. Dunkley doubted that China would be as benevolent when it was fully grown. Everything he saw confirmed his prejudice against a nation that seemed to be ever more aggressive in its dealings with its neighbours.

Dunkley's opinions were at odds with the prevailing view and drew much criticism. But he'd found some in Cabinet, Defence and Canberra's diplomatic community, including the Japanese ambassador, who were deeply grateful.

Later this morning, he had an appointment with an old contact. He'd received the call a day earlier, out of the blue, from someone who kept more secrets than a Catholic priest.

Canberra

The clean sheets felt pleasant against her skin, the fresh linen acting as a balm.

For eighteen months, Catriona Bailey had lain paralysed, her world reduced to a hospital room, the hum and whirr of life-support machines as familiar as her own voice had been.

This was her life, lungs, heartbeat. And her prison. Medical science had kept her alive, but every day was a battle against despair. The small things mattered, sustained her, like the daily change of linen.

Bailey would have descended into madness but for the wonders of the information age that liberated her mind and unshackled her from these life-giving machines. Sanity had come from the computer that turned her eye-movements into words, and the internet that allowed her brilliant mind to wander the world.

There was one other thing that sustained Bailey.

Revenge.

In the few quiet hours when she wasn't blinking commands or keeping up a steady stream of online banter, she was plotting the demise of the man responsible for her descent to in-patient: Martin Toohey.

It began with his smash-and-grab plot to steal her prime ministerial crown. Although she'd been tagged the Tungsten Lady, her downfall, swift and unexpected, had been devastating.

She was convinced her paralysis was directly linked to Toohey's treachery.

So the thought of making him pay for his duplicity sustained her. Hope, she'd learned, was a powerful elixir. With hope, miracles could happen.

I must believe I can walk again. Talk again.

Now, in the small hours of the Canberra morning, after finishing a discussion on Syria with her online disciples in the United States, she turned her mind to finding a cure for her condition. She scoured the internet for the latest information on anyone who had recovered from locked-in syndrome.

The gold standard was Kate Allatt, a forty-year-old who had almost completely recovered after two years. But Allatt was so rare as to be unique. Bailey feared she would never regain her old abilities.

But there has been progress.

Hours of painful therapy had seen some movement return to her hands. And as she tested the long disused muscles in her neck and back she felt that she would, before long, be able to sit upright.

Even better, the doctors believed she would soon be able to breathe unassisted. That meant she would be able to test whether the tracheotomy in her neck had done permanent damage to her voice box.

And if she could sit up, be taken off life support and speak she would be able to leave this room behind. She'd find liberation in a wheelchair, for her body and mind.

If it is humanly possible, I will triumph.

But time was pressing. An election was due later this year. She would take short-cuts if necessary, even if they were risky and untested.

Bailey needed to rise again, more quickly than was humanly possible. And when she achieved that, she would turn off Martin Toohey's life support.

Beijing

The seven men filed on stage, all purpose and swagger, dressed in identical dark suits with bold red ties. The recently elected Standing Committee of the Political Bureau of the party's Central Committee would be the ones to steer the nation through the next phase of its inexorable rise to the peak of global power. The audience of three hundred and seventy-six Communist Party central committee members was drawn from every corner of the republic, stacked with the people who really ran China. Regional governors sat beside generals who nodded sagely at those who ran state-owned enterprises. They had come together in the cavernous Great Hall of the People for the third plenum of the 18th Central Committee. Their task: to debate a five-year economic and strategic plan.

Jiang Xiu stood near the far left of the elite line-up, his number six stamped on the floor, and obediently followed his comrades as they answered the audience applause with soft handclaps of their own.

A surge of elation pulsed through him. His mother would have been so proud.

But Jiang knew this public forum was purely for show. The future direction of the nation had already been thrashed out behind heavy wooden doors, fortified to resist armies.

An hour earlier, the seven men had finished a secret meeting with no minders or notetakers, not even a servant to pour the tea. In power since November, the Standing Committee's first gatherings had been perfunctory administrative affairs. But today's meeting had been the first to test whether Jiang had correctly judged where the numbers and the will of his comrades lay.

Although technically one of the most junior of the seven, Jiang had led much of the debate, outlining his plans as the minister for propaganda.

He had been pushing hard for China to take an aggressive stance against the United States and its new president. The declaration of China as a currency manipulator was an insult that needed to be met with unshakeable resolution.

Jiang had known that the president was with him, as was one other. What had mattered was whether he could secure a fourth vote.

His opening monologue had analysed America's weaknesses: a military fatigued by a decade of war, a faltering economy still staggering from the financial meltdown. The US government was losing its grip and its people were dismayed.

And China was growing more powerful by the day. The delegations of heads of government, financiers and industrialists from around the globe were evidence of a shift in the world order. Wealth bought military might: China would soon launch its latest nuclear-powered submarine to patrol the disputed waters of the East China Sea.

Jiang had told his comrades that America had made a critical strategic error and that it was an opportunity that should be seized: immediately and forcefully.

'We need to press our advantage now, with all the means at our disposal – diplomatic, military and business – to put pressure on the United States,' he had said. 'We need to force it to publicly retreat from its pledge to pursue us as currency manipulators. If we can make the superpower take just one step back it will be a massive symbolic victory. A turning point in our history. A sign that China is now powerful enough to bring the US to heel. If they so much as blink, we have won.'

Jiang had studied the faces of his six comrades, trying to gauge whether his argument was cutting through. Two places to his left, Wu Weifang had coughed to indicate his intention to speak.

'My young friend is getting ahead of himself.' Wu was the oldest member of the Standing Committee and his opening remark was designed to make Jiang sound like an impulsive teenager. Wu was in charge of anti-terrorism and national security and, despite his age, was considered to be the most liberal of the magnificent seven.

'China must not make the mistake of the West and rush into battle, as the United States did in Iraq and Afghanistan. Patience is our ally. Daily we are growing more powerful, but now is not the time to provoke a conflict. What if we misjudge? If we are forced to retreat, this Standing Committee will lose face and credibility early in its tenure. We should push back, of course. But let's temper our response and bide our time.'

'Age does bring wisdom ... for some, Comrade Wu.' Jiang had locked on the elder statesman, his words laced with sarcasm. 'But we have waited for more than a century. Generations of our countrymen have lived and died in humiliation. I do not intend to join them. If we listen to you, we will be debating for another hundred years.'

It had been a risky play. Wu was highly regarded. But Jiang judged that others shared his impatience to demonstrate China's strength. His intention was to snatch power by isolating dissenting voices. He made his move.

'I believe that these extraordinary times demand the president's leadership.' He'd spoken slowly, turning to each member of the Standing Committee. 'I propose we establish a new National Security Committee which will direct the military and the police, with the president as its chair.

'Its aim will be to focus all our energies on responding to this unprovoked act of aggression. The committee would, of course, include Comrade Wu, as it will absorb his responsibilities. I propose that I be the third member because to prevail we will need to harness and direct the nationalist sentiment of our people.'

No one had spoken as the committee digested the audacious bid to strip Wu of his responsibilities and to hand unprecedented power to the president.

Wu had turned and pleaded with his leader.

'Comrade Meng, what is proposed is unwise. It is best that the seven of us deal with these matters and keep the arrangements that have worked so well for our predecessors ...'

The president had silenced Wu with a dismissive wave of his hand.

175

'I believe Comrade Jiang's proposal shows a wisdom well beyond his years.' Meng's words had been a deliberate rebuke to Wu, and acted as a warning to any committee member swayed by his argument.

'We did not provoke this confrontation, the Americans did. This new president is determined to humiliate us, to contain our growth. If we step back, America and its lap-dog Japan will step forward. Wavering will be seen as weakness: by our enemies and, as importantly, by our people. The question is: are we strong enough to seize this opportunity? I propose we vote on Comrade Jiang's proposal. Right now. And I support it.'

The president had raised his hand and searched the room for compliance. Jiang's hand had joined his leader's, and had been followed by the party secretary's. And, as the tension in the room had risen, so had a fourth hand. The chair of the central committee for Discipline Inspection had completed the majority.

Jiang had smiled, the long hours of preparation had not been wasted. Wu's voice would mean nothing on the new all-powerful National Security Committee, as he and the president were of one mind. This committee's plans would be settled before it met.

And when it acted, the world would shudder.

In the early evening, Jiang met President Meng. Alone.

'Have you organised the next steps as we discussed?' Meng asked.

'Yes, sir.' Jiang pushed a piece of paper across the desk. 'This is a map of our proposed expanded air defence identification zone. As you can see, it covers the Diaoyu Islands. We will demand that any commercial or military planes that intend to fly through it lodge their flight plans with us.'

'The Americans will have to test it.'

'I believe they will. We will be ready.'

'But there will also be other steps, on the water?'

'Yes, sir, as we discussed.'

'We must be careful. We cannot afford a full-scale confrontation with our enemy. Instead, the assassin's mace will be our weapon. We do not need to defeat the giant in battle but to wound and neutralise it.'

Jiang nodded.

'And call the North Korean Ambassador. I am sure Korea can be a useful partner in this enterprise.'

'Of course, sir. Anything else?'

'Zero Day. How is it progressing?'

Jiang looked down at his papers, as if seeking a file note. He'd expected the question but had hoped for better news before briefing his leader.

'It is proceeding, sir,' he eventually said. 'But you know better than anyone that it is our most sensitive program. We have an operational issue that has yet to be resolved. We are moving more slowly than we'd hoped, but I am confident Zero Day will proceed. As planned.'

'Very well, Mr Jiang. Remember, a tiger moves with stealth-like steps. We must leave no trace.'

Canberra

His eyes were piercing and black; his face bore the hint of a smile and a poise that carried across the centuries. Joseph Banks had been a man of wealth and influence, a child of the Enlightenment, whose intelligence was evident in this masterful portrait.

'What do you think of him, Harry?' Charles Dancer spoke with appreciation, keeping his gaze on the painting on the National Portrait Gallery wall. 'He was a giant of his age, one of the true fathers of this nation. And so superior to the pygmies who rule us now, don't you think?' He turned sharply, his gaze as intense as that of Banks.

'Charles, I didn't realise you were such a student of the arts,' Dunkley said. 'The dark arts maybe, but not the fine arts.'

'Very droll, Harry. I wanted you to soak up the history. You need to be able to put everything I'm about to tell you in perspective.'

Dancer gestured at the painting. 'Banks was a guardian of his age as we are guardians of this age. Our role is to hand on a better nation. To look to the long term, for the common good. Not to be captives of the moment, of the latest fad.'

The journalist wasn't sure what Dancer was driving at, what his agenda was. But he needed to settle one of his own.

'Why didn't you return my calls?' he challenged the secretive diplomat. 'You promised to help track down Kimberley's killer. You know I can't do it on my own.'

'Harry, please, let it go.' Dancer was examining the next portrait. 'It's a futile quest. It wasn't a single person who killed Kimberley, it was the ideology of an evil state. You should never have got her involved; neither of you was equipped for the task. You were innocents wandering into a war.'

'So why did you call now, Charles?'

'Harry, I have wrestled with what I'm about to tell you. My career has been about protecting the realm, without the public knowing about it.

'That is as it should be. Unlike you, I believe that nations need secrets. Bismarck knew that the sausage grinder of the state was best kept from public view. Traitors like Julian Assange would be jailed if I had my way.'

Dancer faced the reporter. 'But when a state is led by fools, sometimes the people need to be stirred. It's now clear that this government is not just incompetent, it's dangerous.

'It's blinded by Chinese wealth and intellectually crippled by its determination to stay in power. It can't be moved by wise counsel behind closed doors because the only thing that motivates it is public opinion. So the public needs to be warned that it's sleepwalking into disaster.'

'What "disaster"?' Dunkley's voice held a hint of disbelief.

Dancer was examining a poorly constructed painting of the brilliant but headstrong explorer Matthew Flinders.

'This government has absolutely no idea what it is dealing with and how dangerous China's rise is. It foolishly believes you can separate Chinese commerce from Chinese politics. But it's bartering with this country's soul. It's betting that there will never come a time when we will have to choose between prosperity and our traditional security pact with the United States.'

Passion flared in Dancer's eyes.

'China can never be a true and trusted friend, not now, not ever. Each step towards it is a step away from our real friends. And into a very dangerous future.'

He had stopped pretending an interest in the art and turned all his attention on Dunkley, taking a step towards the journalist. His voice became more intent.

'You know that now, Harry. Kimberley's death has taught you that much. It's perhaps given you a new perspective on China. I've been reading your opinion pieces. They're very good.'

'Well thanks, Charles. We at *The Australian* always aim to please the powers that be. And that only occasionally includes governments of the day.'

'Of course you do.' Dancer's laughter echoed around the empty room. 'And I can see that the government's feelings towards you are just as mixed. Anyway, let me tell you a story. Off the record, of course, and with absolutely no trace back to me.'

The reporter nodded: the ancient code – between a source and a scribe – would be honoured.

'Thank you. Okay, Harry, did you hear about the body that was dragged out of the lake four days ago? An Asian man, aged in his thirties, no ID?'

'Sorry Charles, but I've been too busy with national politics to focus on local life. I vaguely recall some mention on radio, though.'

'Yes, the police called for assistance in identifying him. At first, our man was a real John Doe.' Dancer's voice dropped and Dunkley stepped closer.

'But he was a Chinese national. Part of a team that's building the new Chinese embassy.'

The reporter was starting to get the sniff of a yarn.

'Was he an embassy official, Charles?'

'Yes and no. And that is part of the problem and the point of this sorry story. When Catriona Bailey was prime minister, she ticked off on a deal that allowed the embassy to be built in complete secrecy with an entirely Chinese workforce. Dozens of them were flown in on diplomatic visas. The site is off limits to everyone; not even unions or local government safety inspectors are allowed in. Only a select number of local suppliers can come and go but they are whisked in and out under close watch. Of course we've sent people in under the guise of being contractors, but frankly, Harry, that site is a black box to us.'

Dancer's voice rose in agitation.

'No prime minister with this nation's best interest at heart should ever have signed off on a project like that. And now it appears we may be paying a high price for Bailey's desperation to please Beijing.'

An elderly couple appeared, looked into the room for a moment, consulted a map of the gallery and disappeared. Dancer picked up the theme.

'Bailey's replacement, Martin Toohey, is just as bad. He's asleep at the wheel and his government is wilfully blind to the threat from China, especially from cyber-espionage and warfare. We've tried to warn them. The real and present danger this nation faces has been pressed home by officials at National Security Committee meetings. We've even shown the prime minister evidence that his own emails have been hacked, along with everyone else's in parliament. And what have they done to defend themselves? Nothing. The government doesn't seem to care that Australia is being attacked every day in the virtual world by a country that poses as our friend in the real world. We think our man, Lin An, was trying to alert us to the extent of that threat.'

'Do you know what he was up to? Or why he went for a swim?'

'We're not certain about anything. But we think he was trying to defect.'

'How do you know that, Charles?'

'Because we found this in his gut.'

Dancer discreetly opened his right hand. A memory stick lay across his palm.

'Jesus!'

'Indeed. I wanted to show you this, just to assure you there is potentially a very big story about our man in the lake. We're still analysing the material. But I reckon you have enough to get started.'

Canberra

A pair of white pillars embossed with gold numerals – the number '25' – framed a steep driveway. There was nothing else to tell guests they'd arrived at the Commonwealth Club.

Because if you didn't know where it was, you weren't meant to be there. The members of the Alliance who'd gathered in one of the club's discreet rooms on this long summer evening had no doubt that they belonged in the place. It was just one of their many certainties. They carried an unshakeable conviction that they were the sentinels of prosperity and freedom, mandarins who could outwit and would outlive the longest serving politician.

But the rock on which their grouping had been built, the security pact between Australia and the US, was under threat as the Toohey government wrestled with the rise of China, embracing the communist power in ever-closer economic and political ties. As power shifted from the West to the East, more quickly than they could have imagined, their meetings had taken on an urgent edge.

Just how urgent became clearer when the US ambassador to Australia, Brent Moreton, strode into the meeting, late and very pissed off.

He nodded curtly as he took his place beside chief of the defence force Jack Webster, throwing back a neat Scotch before slamming the table with his open palms. 'Gentlemen, we've got a fucking big problem.'

The envoy outlined the bones of a briefing he'd been given by one of his trusted Labor sources. 'Your prime minister is about to strike a deal with China that will make your country beholden to it. Forever.'

Webster, miffed at being out of touch, leapt in. 'How?'

'Toohey plans to sell off a gas-field in the Northern Territory to the Chinese in a desperate bid to buy votes for his re-election. The strategic stupidity of it is mind-blowing.'

The ambassador was having trouble maintaining his usually implacable manner.

'He is selling off your farm, gentlemen. And he doesn't understand that once he announces the deal, he will be a wholly owned subsidiary of China Inc. His political survival depends on them paying up. He will temper every action and every statement to ensure this deal holds until he gets to the other side of the election.'

Moreton rose and theatrically pounded a fist into his open palm, leaning towards the stunned mandarins. 'This will hover over Australia like the blade of a guillotine.'

Webster searched for a response. But it was David Joyce, secretary of the Department of Foreign Affairs and Trade, who leapt into the fray.

'The Japanese will go crazy,' Joyce said, incredulous and angry. 'They've been begging us to sign an energy security pact for years. It's their number one concern. They're already convinced we've abandoned them for China.'

Other doomsday scenarios played out.

'So we're going to set up a Chinese platform just off Darwin.' Thomas Heggarty, director-general of the Australian Secret Intelligence Service, began to imagine the possibilities offered to any spy chief worth his salt. 'If I was running China's Ministry of State Security, I would turn it into a listening post. Our ears for the entire region to our north are based at just three places: Cocos Island, Bamaga and Shoal Bay. Every one of them will be compromised and the Chinese could listen to every call from Hobart to Broome.'

The defence chief finally spoke. He was horrified. 'The range of our Jindalee over-the-horizon radar is a lot more than three thousand kilometres. Imagine what China could do? Jesus, they could monitor every RAAF and Qantas take-off and landing. And we plan to base more troops and more kit up north.'

'And more marines,' Moreton chipped in. 'They could monitor every movement, every joint exercise.'

Richard Dalton, director-general of the Australian Security Intelligence Organisation, saw the platform as an evil ark. 'When ASIO is asked for co-ordination comments for the Cabinet debate, we'll red flag it as a grave security risk.'

'Don't be so fucking naive, Richard. You won't be asked. None of us will be.' Webster was on his feet. 'This government is paranoid about high-level leaks and with good reason. Who among us would trust anyone in that Cabinet? Toohey won't talk to any but a select few before announcing this sell-out to China as a done deal.'

'So if they won't seek our advice, what are our options?' Dalton asked, reflecting the frustration of the room.

Webster was staring out the window as the lake caught the last glow of the sunset. He turned back to the room, placing a hand supportively on the ambassador's shoulder. 'This can *never* be allowed to happen.'

Canberra

Harry Dunkley's fingers hovered over his keyboard, attempting to coax a must-read yarn from a tangled mess of background material, off-the-record quotes and join-the-dots supposition.

He'd sold this exclusive hard, providing his editor with the barest of outlines, promising to file early enough to allow News Corp's lawyers time to hook their claws into his copy. He figured he had an hour, maybe one and a half, of scribbling and polishing time left.

He massaged a face that hadn't seen a razor for forty-eight hours. He liked to joke that he had a good head for print. He wasn't interested in joining those prima donnas who pranced around Sky News or ABC News 24, seeking to build their profiles as 'political analysts'. The ether was already full enough of bullshit. *This* was what he lived for. The thrill of the chase, the scent of a big splash that would cut through the vapid nonsense that passed for news these days.

Okay, now for the lede. Plenty of drama, plenty of grunt, make it tight and make it sing.

The body of a man dragged from Canberra's Lake Burley Griffin has been identified as one of a small army of workers flown in to build China's new embassy.

All the workers on the highly secretive building are Chinese nationals travelling on diplomatic passports and the site is immune from local laws under a deal struck with the Labor government.

The project's secrecy has prompted concerns over worker safety. Union and ACT government representatives are barred from the site and there appears little they can do to ensure no one is injured or killed.

Little is known of the dead man, Lin An, prompting intelligence officials to voice their concerns that the embassy site might pose a national security threat.

The mysterious death comes on the back of a spike in Chinese-based cyber-espionage against Australia.

182

> *The Australian* has learned that Cabinet's National Security Committee has been briefed twice in the past six weeks on 'specific threats' from Chinese cyber-units.
>
> And the emails of key government figures, including the prime minister, are understood to have been hacked. US intelligence officials alerted their Australian counterparts and provided evidence that China was the source of the attacks.
>
> Worried intelligence officials have accused the Toohey government of being 'asleep at the wheel'.

Dunkley sat back and studied his handiwork. Thirty years in the hard news business and he still got a thrill when it all came together, when the usual grind of daily journalism gave way to a big delicious fillet of prime news.

This was a story that mattered and could make it onto the international stage.

All he had to do now was weave in the quote from a 'senior national security official' that he hoped would get his copy a legal tick without it being gored to death.

> 'We are one step away from cyber-war. And yet this government seems intent on chasing China's cash at the expense of our national sovereignty,' a senior national security official told *The Australian*.
>
> 'Beijing is launching daily cyber-attacks against us, yet Mr Toohey says nothing. When will the government learn that you can't appease a dragon?'

Jesus, that should get some attention.

Dunkley read the draft a final time before checking his watch again: 4.12pm. He lined up his editor's email, cc-ed it to his chief of staff in Canberra, and then hit 'send', watching a story that he had lovingly chased and crafted over the past two days disappear.

He leaned back in his chair, a self-satisfied grin creasing his face. Then he wondered just how many prying eyes would read his sparkling prose before it was published online at midnight.

Canberra

It was the Ides of March, spring but still cool.

He lifted his finest purple robe above the dirt as he crossed the cobbled street. A rider slowed his horse as he recognised the pedestrian, and dipped his head in homage.

The familiar shape of the Theatre of Pompey hove into view. The Senate was in session and Caesar was due to address it.

As he strode towards the theatre, Tillius Cimber called out to him beseechingly.

'Caesar, please … I ask you again to consider the fate of my brother. I have gathered signatures from some of Rome's finest citizens pleading for his return.'

The emperor dismissed him with an imperious wave. 'I have told you before. The matter is settled.'

The petitioner's face hardened to a snarl as he dropped his scroll and dragged down Caesar's tunic, pinning his arms to his sides.

Within seconds the emperor was engulfed as a dozen conspirators emerged from the shadows, striking at his unprotected flesh with their blades.

The searing pain as the metal tore into his body.

One face leered from the crowd, plunging his dagger deeper than the rest.

'*Et tu, Brute?*'

With his final breath the emperor whispered three defiant words not recorded by history. '*Non occides ambitionem.*'

Catriona Bailey's eyes flashed open as the nightmare shook her awake. The face of her murderer was still vivid.

Her heart was racing. The nightmares were becoming more frequent. Even in waking, the hallucinations were sometimes so real that it was hard to separate dreams from reality.

Bailey's doctor had warned her that this might happen when she'd demanded a radical course of treatment to speed her recovery: a dangerous cocktail of Stilnox and Prozac.

'I strongly advise against it,' he had said. 'Yes, it might see a rapid improvement in your physical condition but you risk destroying your mind. There are a host of possible side effects and you could do permanent damage.'

She had dismissed his concerns.

Now, in her waking hours, Bailey could feel her body growing stronger. But sleep became a torment. And, sometimes, reality blurred.

'I had to do it, you know.'

Martin Toohey's voice startled her. He stepped from the shadows of her hospital room.

184

Why?

'Because you risked everything.'

You will pay. Soon.

Toohey's face vanished into the dark, and Caesar's last words echoed in her tormented mind.

You can't kill ambition.

_____

Canberra

Nguyen Thi Mai Loan pulled the latest copy of *Foreign Affairs* from her satchel as she crunched into another muesli bar. The whip-smart graduate student was pulling the graveyard shift, alone. It was 5.05am and a long night was nearly over.

She wondered whether eminent diplomatic careers usually started like this, waiting for dull consular calls to replace lost passports. Then she froze.

TEN CHINESE FISHERMEN OCCUPY SENKAKU ISLANDS

A tremor shot down her spine as she digested the Reuters newsflash scrolling across her monitor.

'Holy fuck,' she said, in an accent minted in Sydney's outer west.

Before being accepted into DFAT's prestigious graduate program, Nguyen had finished a PhD on the Chinese military. Part of that involved war-gaming scenarios that might escalate into armed conflict between China and the US. This was straight out of the textbooks.

Even the name of these benighted islands was a source of dispute. Japan called them the Senkakus, while China hailed them as the Diaoyu.

They were five uninhabited islands and three barren rocks lying around two hundred nautical miles south-west of Japan and the same distance east of China. The largest was just a tick over four square kilometres.

In the history of mankind, had there ever been so much dispute over such a useless pile of rocks? she wondered.

Both countries claimed the islands but Japan administered them and they had been an increasing source of tension ever since oil had been discovered nearby in 1968. But the bilateral relationship hit rock bottom when the Japanese government bought three of the islands from a Japanese family that had held their title. Asserting government control was supposed to reassure the Chinese that no one was about to do anything rash. That was not how the message was received.

The official Chinese response had been blunt. Its Foreign Ministry said Beijing would not 'sit back and watch its territorial sovereignty violated'. Relations had not improved when Shinzo Abe had been re-elected as Japan's prime minister, a man Beijing viewed as a dangerous nationalist whose instincts would be to try to contain China's growth.

Without warning, the Chinese had escalated the dispute by inventing what it called an 'air defence identification zone' covering the islands. It demanded all aircraft flying in the region lodge flight plans with China or face 'emergency defensive measures'.

So far, despite bluster from the US and Japan, there had been no breach of the airspace, but no one believed things would hold for long without China's resolve being tested.

So the fishermen's occupation meant only one thing: it was a government-sanctioned act of aggression. No matter how China's Foreign Ministry would spin it, the dragon was testing its power, daring the West to confront it or retreat.

Nguyen digested the news and what it meant. Less than a minute after viewing the newsflash she was on the phone to her boss.

An hour later the DFAT crisis centre was alive with a dozen senior officials poring over each shard of news. Secretary David Joyce had called in the PM's chief of staff. Around the globe similar departments were abuzz, no matter the time zone.

George Papadakis was dressed in a tracksuit and wore the expression of a man who believed international and domestic events were conspiring to make his life hell. He was beginning to take it all personally.

Joyce's mood was grimmer than usual. He was studying a cable and muttering. 'The bastards, do they really think we are fools?'

'What do we know for sure, David?' Papadakis and Joyce had been friends for years and Papadakis wasn't fazed by his mate's dog days.

'We know that ten Chinese fishermen went ashore on the largest island just before 3am, Beijing time.' Joyce hadn't lifted his head from the cable he was reading. 'The island is called Uotsuri Jima by the Japanese and Diaoyu Dao by the Chinese.'

Joyce put down his papers, took off his glasses and looked at the line of clocks on the crisis centre wall.

'If the timing seems odd, George, consider this. The fishermen announced on social media that they had taken the island within minutes of landing. They were well organised because Reuters had a newsflash out inside five minutes. That meant it lobbed into the US just after 2pm. Very decent of them. It ensures that every network has plenty of time to lead the story on the evening news.'

He handed his friend the cable he had been studying. 'Here's a one-page summary of the story so far.'

The brief began with an official statement from Beijing. The People's Republic did not sanction the actions of the fishermen but its leadership understood 'the genuine affront that all citizens feel at the illegal occupation of Chinese land by a foreign power'. The government could not be expected to contain 'the nationalist zeal' of a handful of its people.

It would work with the fishermen to try to get them to quit the island voluntarily, as a demonstration that China was a good international citizen. But China's claim over the island stood and the incident only served to highlight the need for a rapid resolution.

It didn't wash with the Japanese, or anyone else, who knew that, at the very least, the occupation had an official sanction.

The Japanese statement fairly shook with rage as it castigated China for an 'act of aggression'. It called on the Chinese government to remove the fishermen within forty-eight hours and carried a barely disguised threat: 'Japan does not rule out taking unilateral action to bring this invasion of its territory to an end.'

By contrast, the US State Department had issued a tempered response, calling for calm. It trotted out its long-held line: that the US did not have an official position on ownership of the islands.

However, America recognised that Japan administered the islands and that any attack on them would trigger the US–Japan bilateral security pact.

'But this isn't an attack or an official act of the Chinese government, is it, David?' Papadakis had some admiration for China's deft hand.

'That's the beauty of it,' Joyce said. 'The fishermen have asserted China's claim and given Beijing distance from it. Of course their government sanctioned it, and probably organised it. But we can't prove that. So now the ball is in the court of Japan and, most importantly, the US. What they do next is crucial.'

Joyce had served in China and had risen to become ambassador to the United States. Papadakis thought him the pre-eminent Australian diplomat of his age. This was what Joyce was the master of, looking at the pieces on the chessboard and analysing what was going through the players' heads. Then calculating a perfectly executed move of his own.

'George, never forget that any government, dictatorship or democratic, is also playing to a domestic audience. This move is an exercise in stirring Chinese nationalist sentiment, and focusing it outwards.

'Most people in the West don't understand how important public opinion is in China. They see a dictatorship and imagine it has absolute control over the masses. It doesn't. Tiananmen Square proved that public anger can turn inwards, on the government.

'So the role of the skilled propagandist is to harness and direct the people's mood. And whoever is the brains behind this knows his audience well. These fishermen will become national heroes and this cause will be elevated to the top of the nation's agenda. That will force the weak-kneed in the Chinese administration to side with the hard-liners. They have stirred the hornets, and they're headed our way.'

Papadakis looked at the wall map of the East China Sea with a growing sense of dread. 'So how will the US respond?'

'That is tough. My guess is State will want to fart-arse around drafting crafty statements while the Pentagon will demand a measured but proportionate and decisive response. And in the mix will be Republican firebrands in and out of Congress who think that a proportionate response is to nuke Beijing. The question, George, is what will you do?'

'Try and stay out of it.'

Joyce's face hardened.

'You might be able to buy a few weeks but you can't keep doing that forever, George. This is a tough choice, but the US is our ally. China is testing us. You might think that you can walk the tightrope between these powers, but you can't.'

Papadakis thought of the months that had gone into his plan to dig the Toohey government out of its electoral hole. It relied on Chinese finance. He just needed to nurse that deal to the other side of the election. He needed to buy time.

'Is it weak to want peace? Our country's prosperity, your kids' jobs – they depend on peace and doing business with China. We need to use our unique position to urge China and the US to see that escalating this dispute is in no one's interest. The bloody Yanks started this whole mess anyway when that redneck idiot in the White House declared China a currency manipulator. Why kick a fucking hornet's nest?'

'Everyone wants peace, mate.' Joyce was bent on trying to get Papadakis to make a stand. 'And I think we will have peace, but it won't be easy as the big powers come to a settlement. But we can't allow China to keep throwing its weight around with its neighbours or there will be no end to it. No one respects weakness.

'Leaving aside who started it, my advice is to fall in behind the United States when it decides to act. The Chinese are not going to stop doing business with us in the long run. They need us as much as we need them.'

'Your advice is noted but it's the short run that worries me.' Papadakis picked up his notes and headed for the door. He wasn't about to be backed into a corner by Joyce. He took another pace then stopped.

'Before I brief the PM, what's our own intelligence telling us?' he asked.

Joyce frowned and ran his hands through what remained of his hair.

'There's a Collins-class submarine in the area and it can see the camp set up by the fishermen,' he said. 'Hopefully it can also see the subs from China, the US and Japan that no doubt are there. The waters around that island will be like Hoddle Street at peak hour. The last thing we want is for a sub that we claim patrols only Australian waters to surface two hundred nautical miles off the coast of China.'

Papadakis groaned. 'Don't say that, David. Knowing our luck, we'll have rear-ended a Chinese sub by lunchtime.'

Canberra

Martin Toohey adjusted his Geelong jersey, upping the pace slightly and silently enjoying the laboured breathing of his walking companion. The prime minister was halfway through his daily constitutional, a brisk thirty-minute walk, and was determined to make every step count.

'I want to reach for the stars with this one, George. I really do.'

The PM turned to his chief of staff, who until recently had harboured a near pathological fear of physical exercise. But a medical check-up had given Papadakis a fright and for the past few weeks he'd joined his friend and boss whenever the two were in Canberra together.

It was a chance not only to walk off the previous night's dinner but to plot and scheme, to hatch a plan that might revive the dire fortunes of the Toohey government. Or, more likely, to debrief on the latest disaster, like the Chinese fishermen's recent occupation of the Senkakus and the diplomatic shitstorm that ensued.

In a week, Toohey would address the National Press Club and his speech would attempt to reboot the government and set the tone for the election year.

'We've got to turn things around next week, George, otherwise we'll be well and truly rooted.'

Toohey desperately needed a big cut-through statement. He wanted a speech that would stand the test of time, that would resonate through the ages like Paul Keating's seminal 1992 Redfern speech which captured the torment of Australia's indigenous community.

The two men were walking by the edge of Lake Burley Griffin, passing the Southern Cross Yacht Club, a quarter hour from the Lodge. It was 5.55am.

Two bodyguards walked ahead while a security car, with two more guards inside, tracked a discreet distance behind. The national capital was still layered in darkness; sunrise was half an hour off, but the first light was just beginning to paint the horizon.

Papadakis grunted as he contemplated the climb back up to State Circle.

'I know boss, I know.' He squeezed the words out between wheezing pants. 'James has got a first draft ready for you … to look at later this morning. He's taken me through a few sketches … and it isn't bad. Plenty of grist for the comrades … and a great mental health plan for the base. Future lies to our north … the looming Asian century … the innovative hub of Asia … that sort of stuff. Our best Treasury man is working on the numbers in strict confidence … word is that everything is fiscally sound … Jesus, Martin, can you slow down just a touch …'

The PM glanced across at his friend and confidant, smiling as he eased off, allowing him to draw level. Neither man looked a picture of fitness, but the competitor in Toohey enjoyed the rare feeling of superiority.

'Sorry, George. I get a bit carried away sometimes, don't I? That's what you love about me though, right?' Toohey playfully danced around Papadakis, giving his chief of staff a light jab to the arm as he skipped ahead.

The PM didn't notice that his senior security man had stopped until he was right next to him. Concern was furrowing the big man's face.

'Boss. We got to move. To parliament. Just got a call from the office. We have a crisis.'

George Papadakis put his mobile into a locker bearing his name then punched a six-digit code into the pad by the security door. It slid open, revealing an airlock and another door leading to Cabinet's hi-tech Situation Room.

The Howard government had dismissed a 'Sit Room' as indulgent but Catriona Bailey had embraced having her own Washington-style bunker, just metres from her office. So taxpayers had spent $35 million building her one.

That had caused a storm at Senate hearings with one Coalition senator describing the room as an extravagance built to 'feed the *West Wing* fantasies of the Labor leadership'.

Seventy-two thousand dollars had bought two long 'integrated' tables that abutted each other in the centre of the room, each with inbuilt computers and communications systems. The thirty German-built Wilkhahn 'FS' armchairs, covered with specially ordered green leather, had set taxpayers back $90,000.

Huge plasma television screens, run by technicians in the nearby communications room, covered both of the room's long walls. Mostly they were used for teleconferencing; there were secure locations in all the state capital cities where a minister or official could go to be beamed into the Sit Room. A dozen embassies and high commissions around the world were also fitted out for secure videoconferencing.

By convention, politicians sat on one side of the table, and defence, police and intelligence officials on the other. Only the politicians had voting rights; the officials were there to offer expert advice.

Lining the walls behind the main table were rows of chairs for other advisers. And, just as in the Cabinet room, there was a chair in each corner for a notetaker. Every word spoken was logged; each person at the main table was fitted with a microphone.

George Papadakis took his place just behind the PM's chair. He loved the Security Committee meetings because this was the real work of government and it was in this setting that Toohey shone.

If only the public could see how he performs when it really matters.

Toohey never wasted time, kept the meetings focused, issued orders that were clear and set realistic goals.

Now the prime minister strode into the room carrying a bundle of papers, the chatter about the table dying as he sat down.

'Welcome, everyone. Okay, what do we know? Eliza?' Toohey nodded to the head of Airservices Australia.

'Just before 6am this morning the entire air traffic control system on Australia's east coast went down. For thirteen minutes every plane in the air vanished from our sight.'

Eliza Stubbs paused as the plasma screens lit up, displaying a map of Australia overlaid with a sketch of the air traffic control network.

'The TAAATS system controls twenty-three radar towers, mostly on the east coast. There are two centres, Brisbane and Melbourne. So the network's split north and south, with Brisbane controlling the northern zone, Melbourne the southern.'

The image changed to a flow chart showing Airservices' security hierarchy.

'In each centre there are forty-two consoles, divided into groups to cover different sectors. And there are multiple back-ups to ensure a system failure cannot shut the whole show down. When the primary system in Melbourne failed at 5.47am, the duplicate system swung online automatically. It failed. So did our third layer of defence in Melbourne. We immediately moved to the contingency plan. There are ten consoles in Brisbane which are configured to take over from Melbourne in the case of catastrophic failure, and vice versa. When we switched them on, the system froze.'

The room was silent and Stubbs continued.

'Prime Minister, there is a one in ten million chance that all this could happen by accident. Chillingly, the crash occurred just before the 6am curfew in Sydney was lifted. So international and interstate flights into Sydney were starting their approaches to Kingsford Smith.

'We made radio contact with every plane and told them to hold their course if they were still en route or to switch to a pre-ordained emergency holding pattern if they were preparing to land.

'At exactly 6am all our systems returned.'

Stubbs's face was grey and there was a slight tremble in her voice as she finished.

'Prime Minister, we have no idea how it happened.'

Toohey tapped his pen on the desk as he digested the explosive news.

'Ted,' the prime minister turned to the ASIO deputy director-general who ran intelligence co-ordination, 'what do you think?'

'The official line has to be we don't know – because we don't,' Ted Spencer said. 'But I know what it looks like. This is an attack, not an accident. And because it was so contained I can only assume it's a shot across our bow. Someone is letting us know they own us.'

That observation resonated with the worst fears of the room.

'Who?' The prime minister scanned the brass, braid and suits across the table. 'Who would do this and why?'

Thomas Heggarty, head of ASIS, spoke. 'It's just about impossible to pin this stuff down. It could be a bored teenager in a bedroom in Tokyo. It might be a group of anarchists like Anonymous. But I don't think so.

'Something this sophisticated has to be state sponsored. And the disturbing thing is that this isn't trawling for information. This is an act of aggression. If this was happening in the real world under the old rules and someone bombed these installations, we would immediately declare it an act of war.'

Heggarty looked down at a note from a previous security committee meeting.

'We can't be sure who did this, Prime Minister, but you will recall our discussion on the massive increase in cyber-attacks on the US since it declared China a currency manipulator. We also know that there have been several attacks on US banks where the intent was not just to steal but to bring systems down.'

'Sure,' Toohey said. 'But we have good relations with Beijing. I have publicly called on the US to moderate its language on China. We have also, deliberately, been very guarded in taking sides on the Senkaku Islands dispute.'

'That's what we say, Prime Minister,' Heggarty continued. 'But yesterday the Chinese would have noted that the first rotation of US marines arrived in Darwin. Two hundred men from Lima Company, Third Battalion, Third Marine Regiment. As you know, they're here to stay as part of the US pivot to Asia and their ranks will swell to 2500 over time. They were welcomed by the US ambassador and the event knocked crocodiles off the front page of the *NT News*.'

David Joyce, the secretary of Foreign Affairs, interrupted. 'Yesterday the Chinese ambassador made a pointed reference to the marines' arrival at a function I attended. He said it appeared Australia had made an interesting choice. When I pressed him to elaborate, he noted an editorial in the *Global Times* that, intriguingly, was reprinted in the *China Daily*. It is in your papers.'

Toohey flicked through his briefs. It was a front-page editorial.

AUSTRALIA COULD BE CAUGHT IN SINO–US CROSSFIRE

Apparently, Australia aspires to a situation where it maximises political and security benefits from its alliance with the US while gaining the greatest economic interests from China. However, Prime Minister Toohey may be ignoring something – Australia's economic co-operation with China does not pose any threat to the US, whereas the Australia–US military alliance serves to counter China.

Australia surely cannot play China for a fool. It is impossible for China to remain detached no matter what Australia does to undermine its security. There is real worry in Chinese society concerning Australia's acceptance of an increased US military presence. Such psychology will influence the long-term development of the Australia–China relationship.

Toohey wasn't surprised that the *Global Times* would take such a hard line. The paper was the Chinese equivalent of Australia's radio shock jocks, always shaking its outraged nationalist fist at the world. But he knew enough about China's leadership to know Beijing was sending a serious message when this red-ragging rhetoric was reprinted as an editorial on the front page of the leading English-language daily.

'How many of you believe that the blackout was a warning shot from China?' he asked.

Every official raised their hand.

'Who is certain?'

All the hands went down.

'We can't go on maybes. Ladies and gentlemen, this is now your number-one priority. Throw everything you have at it. We need to know what happened. Who did it. And how we can stop it happening again. We'll meet this afternoon at two, sooner if there are any developments.'

Toohey began to gather his papers.

'Before you leave, Prime Minister,' the chief of the defence force, Jack Webster, was speaking, 'we haven't addressed the serious situation in the East China Sea, which you mentioned in passing earlier.'

Toohey could see that the usually cocksure defence chief was choosing his words diplomatically and wondered why a matter that wasn't on the agenda was being raised. He settled back into his seat.

'Yes, go on.'

'I think I speak for all agencies when I say we need to stand firmly beside Japan and our ally, the United States. When they act we need to act with them. Our one statement so far has simply been to call for calm. We have to speak with a stronger voice.'

Toohey ran his eyes along the line of officials. 'You guys been workshopping?' His tone was sardonic.

'That's our job, sir.' Webster met the prime minister's gaze with an icy stare. 'And to offer our professional advice. Our advice is to back our friends and the alliance that has served us so well.'

Toohey weighed his reaction and tried to calm his rising anger.

'You're right on two counts,' he said. 'We, the Security Committee, do need to discuss this issue and I do need to take firm action.'

He took a breath and took a plunge.

'Your advice has been noted. But it is my decision. So I want the officials to clear the room. This is a debate for committee members only.'

194

No one moved. No one could believe what was being asked. Only the Cabinet had been invited to stay. Even Papadakis looked stunned.

'Ladies and gentlemen,' the prime minister's voice was cold with authority, 'the military types among you should understand the difference between a request and an order. I said go. And I mean now.'

Canberra

It was 8am, a terrifying time for an old-school print journalist to be charging into the working day. But Harry Dunkley was on the hunt for a good yarn and a chief of staff to a Cabinet minister had suggested an early-morning 'off-the-record' chat.

Dunkley hadn't expected a coffee queue snaking around the cramped interior of Aussies Cafe and spilling outside. Fifteen minutes for a flat white! He sighed and gazed around the unique parliamentary nook.

Aussies sat at an intersection of corridors in the secure area of parliament. It was an epicentre of deal-making, a hub for people on the move.

The cafe's lease included a roped-off area with room for a dozen tables. Today, with the circus in full swing, every table was occupied. Lobbyists mingled with political staffers who ogled pretty young parliamentary aides who giggled at security hulks who glanced menacingly at anyone straying into their orbit. Journalists circled like starved seagulls around any minister trying to steal a few minutes of peace.

The queue had barely moved and Dunkley toyed with the unthinkable. *The Trough?*

No, Dunkley would rather skip coffee than retreat to the staff cafe on the other side of the building. His phone buzzed in his pocket. There was a message full of cryptic promise.

'Ten minutes. Usual place.'

It was a trusted source, who only mentioned 'usual place' when he had something juicy. Dunkley abandoned his miserable wait, fending off a few barbs from his gallery colleagues as he meandered through the crowd towards the Members' Hall, texting his coffee date. 'Mate, your turn to stand in the queue. I'll join you in twenty.'

After fifty metres, the corridor Dunkley was following widened to an expanse that bridged the gap between the House and Senate chambers. At its centre was a square pool made from a single piece of South Australian black granite. High above, a skylight revealed the massive flag flying above the parliament, its image reflected in the glossy blackness of the pool.

Dunkley chuckled as he recalled the parliament's architect explaining the thinking behind the small pond.

The sound of water trickling through the pool prevents the conversations of members of parliament from being overheard.

Except it was a thoroughfare. There were better places to share secrets.

Dunkley walked to a little-used lift, just past a glass walkway that led to the Senate chamber. The doors slid open and he hit 'M'.

Fifteen seconds later, a mechanical voice announced 'Mezzanine' and he stepped into one of parliament's legendary spaces.

Few people ventured to the meditation room to meditate. Few even knew where it was. A plaque declared the room was set aside for religious observance or quiet reflection. But most came here for illicit sex.

Several cubicles offered a measure of privacy, and Dunkley walked towards the furthest one. He contemplated a dubious stain on the blue lounge within, wondering if a DNA swab would link it to any minister.

A minute later, the lift doors opened again. He tensed then relaxed as a familiar shape emerged.

Brendan Ryan dumped himself on the lounge beside Dunkley. Over the years he'd morphed from a source for the journalist to almost a friend. He was finally in the job he'd always craved, minister for defence. Time was short.

'No notes, no tape. Just memorise.'

Jesus. Who's been fucked over now?

'NSC met half an hour ago. Earlier this morning, just before curfew finished, air traffic across Australia went down. Planes were flying blind, international and domestic. It could have been a disaster, but thankfully all landed safe. No one else in the media knows. It's all yours.'

'You're kidding? How long was it down?'

'According to Airservices, it was thirteen minutes. Exactly.'

'And there was no warning?'

'That's not the way it works when you want to launch a cyber-attack.'

'What?'

'A cyber-attack, Harry. An act of aggression. Looks like someone in Beijing decided that hacking into the PM's emails was just a warm-up.'

Dunkley glanced at Ryan, noticing the steady tapping of his index finger. For a seasoned political assassin, he seemed tense.

'You suspect China was behind this?' Dunkley asked. 'What proof have you got?'

'Harry, we ain't 100 per cent, but the view around the room was that China's the most likely culprit. Tom Heggarty confirmed there's been an increase in cyber-attacks by China since the US declared it a currency manipulator.'

Dunkley was trying to break things down into a series of mental dot points, wishing he could jot down a few notes.

'Brendan, this is dynamite. I'll work on it during the day, file for tomorrow's paper.'

'Mate, this is a twenty-first-century attack; you live in the 24/7 era. This is for your digital readers. They've got to get something for paying their subscriptions to Rupert. A lot of planes were involved and you can't be sure this story won't break elsewhere.'

Dunkley weighed his options. He hated publishing online without verifying every last fact. He could fight, but Ryan might give the yarn to someone else.

He'd knock this into shape and file asap, much as it pained him to give his competitors entree to the story before the evening presses rolled into action.

An hour later, *The Australian*'s website splashed with a stunning exclusive. It outlined the suspected cyber-attack and the hastily convened National Security Committee meeting before reaching a chilling conclusion: 'One senior source, familiar with the NSC discussion, said, "There was real fear in the room, and all roads lead to Beijing."'

———————————

Canberra

'Steady on the powder, love, you'll have me looking like a drag queen.'

Bruce Paxton was his usual gruff-and-grumble self, but he had a soft spot for the ABC's makeup artist.

The former defence minister had stepped into the press gallery bureau to be interviewed as part of the high-octane loop of commentary sparked by Harry Dunkley's story.

Reporters were pumping out reaction to the extraordinary news that Australia's air-traffic control system had been attacked.

The call had gone out for talking heads and Paxton was happy to oblige, as it allowed him to fill two of his favourite roles – discussing national security and pissing on Labor's bloated carcass.

He was still a member of the ALP, but in name only. Paxton had recast himself as a dissident. He was now Mr Dial-a-Quote and his bare-knuckle assaults inflicted deep bruises on his party.

As Paxton entered the studio, ABC News 24's political editor, Lyndal Curtis, looked up briefly from her notes. 'We'll go live in two minutes.'

Paxton sat impassively as a small team fussed around the studio, wiring him up while makeup gave his face a final dab. When it was time to play ball, he would not disappoint.

'Lyndal, the cyber-security white paper the Toohey government released in January was a sad joke. It offered no new money to fight on the twenty-first-century frontline and simply rebadged programs that were already funded.'

'So you are blaming the government for this?'

'My oath, I blame them. I wanted Defence to focus less on its big-ticket toys and more on the main game. Cyber-hacking and warfare are real threats. All Martin Toohey wants from Defence is to strip out a couple of billion to prop up his Budget. And he put Brendan Ryan in charge – what a mistake! He's a diabetic in a lolly shop. Ryan spends too much time sucking up to Washington and not enough looking after our national interest.'

Paxton was on a roll and Curtis lobbed another inviting question.

'Do you believe, as the national security team is reported to believe, that China is responsible for this?'

'Look, if you believed everything the brass said about China it would be banged up for dressing up as a dingo and taking Azaria Chamberlain. It could have been anyone, and remember, this is a cyber-attack, not hacking, which is usually the Chinese go. The point is we need better defences and we don't have them.'

Curtis shifted tack to the stand-off in the East China Sea.

'Well, on that, you won't get a cigarette paper between me and the PM, Lyndal.'

Paxton had long argued that it was high time Australia rethought its alliance with the United States and had been critical of Japan's determination to isolate China. The future, as he saw it, was for Australia to draw back from the US and encourage it to share power in the Pacific.

'I see that the prime minister has said that Australia has no view on the ownership of the islands and has urged all sides to act with care and solve the problem diplomatically.'

Paxton leaned forward and tapped his prosthetic left hand on the table.

'Let's not forget who started all this, that Tea Party tool, Earle Jackson. He decided to base his presidency on an ill-conceived attack on China, using US financial clout. I think the Chinese have every right to respond. In any event, this fishermen's convention on the Diaoyu Islands is not sanctioned by Beijing.'

'You mean the Senkaku Islands,' Curtis corrected him.

'No, I don't.'

It was some of Paxton's finest work. He ambled out of the studio feeling chuffed. As a sign that his interview had hit a nerve, the hallway outside the ABC was crammed with journalists from other networks, desperate for a Paxton grab they could call their own.

He was happy to repeat the performance, but kept it tight. A ComCar was waiting on the other side of parliament to whisk him to another appointment.

Fifteen minutes later, he arrived at the Thai embassy in nearby Yarralumla. He usually baulked at diplomatic functions, but had struck up a good relationship with the new Thai envoy. And a decent feed was on offer.

The fragrant smells of coriander, spiced beef and sweet sauces tantalised him as he passed an outdoor marquee. But he made a beeline for the drinks waiter, snatching a Hunter Valley white as he scoured the crowd for friendly faces.

Oh shit!

Ali Bakir, the Palestine Liberation Organization's apparently permanent representative in Canberra, was in close orbit. Paxton used to joke, when he was defence minister, that Bakir was a small bore, but could be used with lethal effect. Today, though, the last thing he wanted was a dissertation on the evils of the Jewish state.

He turned towards trestle tables laden with food and edged his way into the queue. He loaded his plate and carefully manoeuvred his way through the crowd with his head down until he guessed he was a safe distance from Bakir.

A gentle, familiar laugh. He froze.

It couldn't be.

He searched the crowd and there she was, in a tight circle of admiring envoys – laughing in that way that men found intoxicating.

The last time he'd heard that sweet sound was at the St Regis in Beijing. He'd just called room service, from memory.

She caught sight of him, dipped her head and turned, expertly exiting the conversation, leaving disappointed diplomats in her wake.

'What are you doing here?' Paxton's urgent whisper was part question, part rebuke.

'Good work for my government, Mr Paxton. I arrived just over a month ago.'

She smiled and old feelings stirred.

'It's nice to see you, Bruce.'

Weng Meihui's hand brushed his arm as she removed an imaginary piece of cotton from his suit.

'And ... us?' Paxton surprised himself with his words.

'That is for another day,' she said, another small ripple of laughter cutting like crystal through his heart. 'Today there is someone you need to meet.'

Weng guided Paxton to a man standing a few metres away.

'Mr Paxton, this is my husband, the new ambassador, Tian Qichen.'

———————

Washington

Earle Jackson scanned his copy of the Morning Book and frowned. The US president loved a good horror story, but this was terrifying. And all too real. It seemed as if the whole world was on edge, bad news overlapping ever more dire headlines.

The overnight watch team in the White House Situation Room had compiled a list of international flashpoints. The Middle East was its usual basket case. Baghdad was ablaze with daily suicide bombings, and the growing tide of Syrian refugees from the civil war was swamping Lebanon and other nervous neighbours. In Thailand the public was venting its anger while South America's incessant drug war was taking a heavy toll.

But it was the Pacific, the geographic arc that stretched from the Arctic to the archipelago of Indonesia, that troubled him most.

In the weeks since he had declared China a currency manipulator, a wave of real and virtual reprisals had washed like a tsunami from East to West.

China had reasserted its claim over 80 per cent of the South China Sea. But it was in the East China Sea that the real danger loomed. The fishermen who had invaded the Senkaku Islands were Chinese folk heroes, and Beijing was offering no solution on moving them.

It had taken an enormous effort to restrain the Japanese from retaliating. They had agreed to wait, but only after the US promised to issue a strong declaration in the United Nations in support of the Japanese being recognised as the 'administrators' of those troublesome rocks.

Jackson had been harangued by Japan's prime minister in a personal call. Shinzo Abe had made it crystal clear that his patience was running out. It was time for the US to show that its core alliances mattered. It was time to act. 'Weakness is provocative,' Abe had said, quoting Rumsfeld. 'And nothing is more provocative than a weak White House.'

The North Koreans, predictably, had decided to reboot their nuclear program and pull out of the five-party talks. The insane hermit kingdom, no doubt at the urging of the Chinese, was planning to test another missile that would track over South Korean airspace. The South was demanding more sanctions, but that was being blocked in the UN Security Council by China and Russia.

There were reports that Chinese nuclear submarines were patrolling the waters near Hawaii and the commander of the Pacific Fleet was demanding the right to engage 'the enemy' if the U-boats entered US territorial waters.

And through the portals of the internet, all-out war was raging as cyber-warriors armed themselves with ever more potent weapons. The number and scale of cyber-attacks on America and its allies had exploded, ranging from the frivolous to the dangerous. Government websites had been shut down by denial-of-service attacks. Wall Street's computers had been compromised, causing a run on US blue chips until trade had been suspended. In Utah, a sewage spill into a dam was being blamed on hackers who had apparently infiltrated the local water utility's SCADA operating system. In Washington, the Pentagon was reporting thousands of attempts a day to crack its formidable defences.

Jackson slurped a mug of cocoa and looked around the Situation Room, wondering if JFK had felt as impotent during the Bay of Pigs crisis in '61.

No, for all his faults, JFK never felt impotent.

It was Kennedy who had established the Sit Room following that disaster. A half-century later, the forty-fifth president was charged with mapping a path out of the mess that he'd helped create.

The surprisingly small room was crowded with nearly twenty people, including National Security Adviser Patrick Denton. The career diplomat was a rarity in Washington – he possessed impeccable Republican credentials and had enjoyed a stellar career in the State Department, that viper's nest of bleeding-heart Democrats.

Denton filled the long pause in the meeting caused by the president's demand that he be allowed time to properly digest the Morning Book.

'Mr President, we recommend a two-track response. We should make a stronger statement in support of Japan over the Senkakus. And we have to back that with action. We need to do something in the real world that reasserts our position as the dominant power in the Pacific and one that won't be played for a fool. Not to act only emboldens China and will invite another move designed to test our resolve.'

Denton knew this would play better with the president than the rest of his advice.

'But then, sir, we need to offer an olive branch to China over the currency war. We have to settle things down and seek a return to normal diplomatic relations.

'No one wants a conflict, and if things keep tracking the way they are going, the chances that either we or the Chinese will miscalculate are large. To be blunt, sir, America is in no shape for conflict in the Pacific. We need time to regather. We need to press the reset button.'

Jackson scanned the room, wanting to avoid the hard decision for a moment. He picked out Dick Hargreaves, another southerner and the four-star general who ran both the National Security Agency and Cyber Command.

'Dick, what do you think? How are we going to get around the Great Firewall of China?' The president chuckled at his little joke as if he had invented the term, jolting the room into forced mirth.

'Mr President, the number of cyber-strikes from China has gone off the charts. We are certain they have infiltrated – or at least positioned themselves ready to strike – key civilian and military targets. And Cisco is reporting a number of unidentified attacks on Tier 1 ISP networks which we suspect are coming from our red friends.'

Jackson snorted. 'Our red friends? Now that's an oxymoron if ever I heard one.'

'Yes, Mr President.' Hargreaves continued without losing a beat. 'We have not been sitting idle on this matter either.'

He lifted a folder onto the desk and opened it.

'Sir, Operation GENIE has managed to insert a number of weapons behind enemy lines, behind the Great Firewall, as you put it. In short, we have broken into some of China's military and civilian networks and placed covert implants within them. Those bugs will allow us to hijack computers and steal data. Or destroy it. I have a full brief here.

'China knows some of its systems are compromised. But we are certain they have no idea how deeply, because we have developed hardware, called

"Quantum", which allows us to jump the gap to computers that are not connected to the internet. We can now access, or bring down, some of China's most sensitive systems using covert radio waves. It is our most secret and lethal weapon.'

The general was clearly pleased with the capabilities of his computer army, but ended on a sober note.

'Our homeland is vulnerable to a serious Chinese attack – but Beijing understands that retaliation would be swift and potent. It boils down to how much damage we are each prepared to inflict on the other.'

Jackson ran his finger around the inside rim of his mug, collecting a rich foam of chocolate-coloured milk. He plunged his chubby digit into his mouth, disgusting at least half the people in the room.

'What you're telling me is that we're in a classic stand-off. It's the old American versus Commie mutual self-destruction scenario, ain't it? The goodies against the baddies.'

'That is essentially correct.' Hargreaves thought the analogy trite, but decided to leave it. 'China knows that we could do serious damage to its economy, to its infrastructure, through our cyber-weapons. Equally, they could unleash a cyber-attack on us that would do significantly more damage than 9/11. Mr President, there are no rules of engagement in cyberspace. Once it starts in earnest there is no telling where it will end.'

Jackson knew he couldn't avoid addressing the central question forever. He had to decide whether to press ahead with his plans to continue the currency war by imposing trade sanctions on China or seek some kind of negotiated settlement. Over the last few days he'd finally seen the wisdom of tempering his actions. This escalating fight was consuming all his administration's energy and his domestic agenda was being swamped.

'Ladies and gentlemen, I need a few moments alone. Can you give me the room?'

The request came as a surprise, but the brass and the bureaucrats dutifully obeyed their commander in chief.

With the room emptied, Jackson picked up the phone and dialled the one man in Congress he feared.

For Morgan McDonald, ignorance wasn't bliss, it was a career.

The Republican congressman and leader of the House, known universally as Big Mac, firmly believed that too much information got in the way of clear decision making and, judging by his success, his constituents agreed.

As a teen, McDonald had been horrified when his musical hero, Elvis, held his 1973 Aloha concert in Hawaii. In protest at the King's decision to perform outside continental USA, McDonald had burned his Elvis collection. His mother had counselled, 'It's still America, honey,' but that rang hollow to Big Mac's suspicious mind.

He had been a founding member of the 'Birthers', who claimed Barack Obama's birth certificate was a forgery. When a TV news anchor presented him with hard evidence that Obama was born in Hawaii, not Kenya, he immortally replied: 'Hawaii is not really America.'

That quote had gone viral and the Hawaiian governor was apoplectic. But he was a goddamned Democrat so it went down a treat with Big Mac's Tea Party base. As did his claim that when it came to foreign affairs he had never owned a passport and was reluctant to get one.

Big Mac neatly divided the world into allies and foes: at home and abroad. An ally did what you told them. Foes were everyone else. He liked to quote the Bible to back this view. 'Hell, Jesus said, "If you aren't with us, you are against us."'

Since the fall of the Berlin Wall, McDonald had been convinced that no state would ever again rival American power. But he watched the rapid rise of a new breed of communism in the East with growing dismay. He saw Beijing as way more cunning than Moscow.

Wolves who've wrapped themselves in the sheep's clothing of capitalism.

Big Mac was deeply offended by what he saw as China's manipulation of the market. While America had written the rules and exported riches and freedom to the far-flung corners of the globe, the communist state was gaming the system and building wealth to export its malign influence everywhere.

And they have us by the financial balls.

Beijing now owned more than a trillion dollars of US bonds and, in Big Mac's view, held the American economy hostage. He'd been staggered to learn that China might rise to become the world's largest economy by 2030. He wanted to bring the reds to heel, before it was too late.

We have seventeen years to corral this beast or it will kill us.

Big Mac became obsessed with stunting China's rise. He encouraged a two-pronged plan, which he'd developed with a few trusted cronies.

The first step was containment. Big Mac supported the creation of a new strategic block that included the USA, Japan, the Philippines, Taiwan, Indonesia, Malaysia, India, Vietnam and Australia.

Publically he called it the Asian Area of Co-operation and Peace, but privately it was the 'Dog Collar'. He would surround, isolate and choke the beast. As part of this pact, the US would respond to any incursion into the territorial waters of treaty members.

Despite some early promise, work on the treaty had stalled. So Big Mac set to work on the second prong of his plan: confrontation. He had confided it in a well-received secret briefing to his Pentagon pals during the presidential election campaign.

'We need to goad China into a fight with America before it acquires sufficient military strength to be a real threat. If it believes we are frustrating its financial growth, it will lash out as Japan did at Pearl Harbor. Once it does that, gentlemen, America should respond with devastating force.'

He had crafted the president's threat to declare China a currency manipulator and would ensure that his friend followed through. For too long, the US had been weak in the face of growing Chinese provocation and it was time to strike back.

'I don't want my kids to live in an America where everything is stamped "Made in fucking China".'

Some of his confidants worried that the US couldn't afford a long war, that Iraq and Afghanistan had demonstrated that it couldn't occupy a foreign country. Big Mac dismissed such weakness with a standard response: 'We ain't gonna occupy them, son, we gonna nuke 'em.'

And if that meant the end of the world through nuclear war?

'Well son, then that's God's will. Remember your Bible. The end of the world will bring about the second coming of Christ. Jesus will sort through the corpses and bring the Christians to eternal life. If that is to be, then I will be proud to be the disciple who made it happen.'

Big Mac was at his desk when the call came through. He listened for less than a minute, then exploded.

'Goddamn you as a coward, Earle Jackson. We made a deal. You made a sacred pledge to the American people. You will keep your promise no matter how hard the road seems. You will impose tariffs. You will bring China to heel. You will restore the empire. For if you do not, I'll give you four years of hell.'

Canberra

Tian Qichen angrily pointed at the small group opposite the front gates of his embassy.

'Why are they still here? Pestilence!' The Chinese ambassador spat out the words as his late-model BMW turned out of the driveway, the protesters just metres from his window.

Three women and a man were camped beneath a trio of banners accusing China of harvesting human organs and other abuses.

'Falun Gong has no right to be here.' Tian had arrived in Canberra five weeks earlier, excited at the prospect of becoming his country's representative in Australia. But he struggled to understand the country's tolerance of troublesome minorities, like the one that was a permanent fixture outside his embassy.

For the past decade, successive ambassadors had lobbied prime ministers and other figures in power to remove this embarrassment. Now Tian turned to his political counsellor. 'I want them gone within a month.'

His deputy nodded wearily, knowing the request was futile.

The ambassador flicked open a briefing note. He was heading to Parliament House for his first formal meeting with Prime Minister Martin Toohey.

The most important item was finalising the 99-year lease over the Northern Territory gas-field. The resource was valuable, but more important was the unambiguous signal that would ricochet across the Pacific when the deal was signed. Australia would be crossing a Rubicon by allowing effective foreign ownership of some of its key resources. This southern land would be tied, ever tighter, to the economic apron strings of China. The deal would bind the two nations in a long-term strategic embrace.

Tian looked out the window as the car purred up the road that climbed the outer edge of Parliament House. He smiled.

How will the United States and Japan respond?

He wondered why Australia clung to the American alliance like a national security blanket. The dependence was personified by the presence in Darwin of a battalion of US marines. That was also on his agenda.

As the BMW pulled up outside the ministerial wing, the PM's deputy chief of staff was waiting.

'Welcome, Mr Ambassador. Nice to see you. Please, this way.'

It was a short walk to the prime minister's office and the ambassador was ushered straight in. Martin Toohey and George Papadakis were waiting and effusively welcomed Tian and his counsellor.

Toohey had prepared a welcome gift – a package of rare green tea. 'Your favourite, I'm reliably informed. I've also arranged for some to share in our meeting today.' Toohey pointed to the tea service on the table placed between two comfortable chairs.

'Ah Mr Toohey, your diplomats have done good work.'

They laughed as they eased into each other's company.

'Please.' Toohey motioned to a chair. 'I apologise for the weather, Ambassador. Must be a difficult change, coming from your winter.'

'I have been through much worse. Three years in Egypt prepares one for even the most extreme heat.'

'That was the experience of our soldiers too – during the Second World War.'

'Yes, I imagine they would have suffered. I have read of the exploits of your 6th Division in battles with the Italians in Egypt. They fought with the British and they fought well.'

Toohey was impressed. This ambassador had done his homework.

Tian continued. 'Australian soldiers seem to make many expeditions to fight in foreign wars. But since the Second World War, always with America: in Vietnam, Iraq and Afghanistan.'

It was the neatest of verbal transitions, a move worthy of a chess grandmaster. Toohey had offered an opening and Tian had taken it, pivoting the conversation to the American alliance.

'Well, we are out of Iraq and in the process of withdrawing our troops from Afghanistan,' Toohey countered. 'They'll be out of that place by year's end. And then? Well, I fret for that country's future'

'Its future will be like its past, Prime Minister. Lawless. Tribal. Violent. It has driven out invaders for centuries. The British and the Soviets could not hold it, so why did the US believe that it could?'

Tian took a sip of his green tea, nodding approval at its familiar taste.

'But the Americans have a new interest. In Asia. And they will have a much warmer welcome in Darwin.'

This was the main game. Toohey had been expecting it.

'Your country should not fret the small stuff, Ambassador. Australia and the United States have shared joint military exercises for decades – and never has that encroached on our relations with your wonderful country. At times, we've told the Americans they've overstepped the mark – I remind you of John Howard's speech to the Asia Society in New York in 2006. Washington did not take kindly to that.'

Tian put down his tea and looked up at the large map of the world on the southern wall.

'You are right, of course, Prime Minister. But the strong economic and trade links we have built are no threat to America, while an increased American presence in the Pacific could be interpreted as a threat to us. You can understand that some of my colleagues might be concerned about a build-up of US troops in Darwin and increasing joint military exercises. Some don't necessarily view that as being the action of a country that is seeking a special relationship with China.'

Toohey sipped the green tea. It was bitter.

My move.

'And countries seeking that special relationship need to be fully open and transparent with each other. We are concerned about a recent serious security breach of our air-traffic control systems. There are signs that point back to China.'

Tian was impassive as he leaned forward to return his cup and saucer to the table.

'Yes, I have read the reports in *The Australian*. It seems to have a very negative view of our government.'

Toohey laughed, genuinely.

'*The Australian* has a very negative view of *my* government. Believe me, you get better press than I do.'

Tian's face held a trace of a smile. 'But it seems that some in your government believe we are acting as aggressors. It does disturb me that China is so often blamed without evidence. All countries are at risk from cyber-attacks. We believe the United States is behind many security breaches in our own systems.'

Toohey decided to open another delicate line of inquiry.

'We are also concerned about the rising tensions in the East China Sea. As you know, we take no position on who owns the disputed islands and have simply called for calm. But there is potential for this fishermen's occupation to be misinterpreted, to get out of hand.'

'Prime Minister, my government thanks you for your temperate response on this matter. You will appreciate that, just as you cannot control your newspapers, we cannot be held responsible for the zeal of some of our citizens. We are working on removing the fishermen, but they have become very popular at home. We ask for patience and believe the matter can be resolved.'

Toohey knew a long discussion on the disputed rocks would go nowhere. Besides, he was keen to nail down some outstanding issues concerning the gas deal.

'Mr Ambassador, happily most of our dealings are about issues of friendship and mutual benefit. We are very excited about the Northern Territory gas hub and George and I would like to discuss the details with you.'

Tian beamed. 'May I say that my superiors in Beijing view this agreement as a sign of a new maturity in our relationship.'

Twenty minutes later, Toohey and Tian ended what had been a mostly successful meeting.

'Mr Ambassador, I would be honoured if you would be my special guest when I give the speech at the National Press Club announcing the agreement.'

Tian clasped his hands as a smile creased his face. 'Of course, Prime Minister. I would enjoy that. Very much.'

The two men rose and shook hands. As the ambassador departed, Toohey turned to his chief of staff.

'What do you think? How did I go?'

'About a draw, I'd say. Got a bit interesting at the start but the two of you brought it back on track pretty well. You never know, you may get to like him.'

'I think I do like him, George.'

'But do you trust him?'

The PM gazed out at the courtyard's summer haze.

'About as much as I trust any member of Cabinet.'

Canberra

Tears streamed down Catriona Bailey's pallid face as she looked at the empty plastic cup resting in her trembling hand. It had taken all of her formidable willpower to lift it to her mouth and drink.

It was a liberation. After twenty months on life support, Bailey had been unshackled: from the ventilator that kept her lungs pumping; the catheters that drove her circulatory system; and the oxygen that flowed through the tracheotomy in her throat.

She was propped upright in her hospital bed, drinking alone and unassisted. That simple act had been a daydream just a few weeks ago. She put down the cup and slowly practised flexing and unflexing her fingers.

The slightest of movements made her feel powerful, alive.

Bailey recalled the moment she had awoken in hospital after her stroke. It was so horrifying she'd thought she was having a nightmare. She could hear the doctors, nurses and visitors coming and going from her room, could feel the weight of her body on the bed, the sheets that covered her and the tubes that cut into her. But she could not move, see or speak.

When I realised it wasn't a dream, I thought I would go mad.

She'd heard the whispered conversations, the doctors who'd measured her life in days and discussed harvesting her organs. And the sound of that hated voice: Martin Toohey.

That's when she'd decided to fight. To recover. To rise and destroy him. The thought of revenge had given her the will to live. To work again and continue her love affair with the public.

My people.

Bailey had lived out almost every moment of her working life in public. She maintained an almost continuous Twitter stream. But the very observant among her two million followers would have noted that recently she had stopped talking about every minute change in her condition.

And as her health had rapidly improved, she'd restricted visiting access to just her chief of staff.

When I return, no one will see me coming.

'Eight thousand fucking words!' Brendan Ryan shook his head as he scrolled through line after line of the pedestrian prose that marched off the *Guardian*'s online features page. The typically pseudo-intellectual babble carried the byline 'Catriona Bailey' and the headline:

TOOHEY CAN BRING PEACE IN THE PACIFIC

It began, as articles by Bailey almost always did, by quoting herself. 'In 2008 I coined the term "the age of non-polarity" to describe a world dominated not by one or two states but by dozens of actors.'

It rambled on through bloated sentences of tortured syntax, each stuffed with academic and biblical references, historical analogies and a dozen more verbal selfies before it got to the point.

We live in a dangerous time where the two largest actors on the world stage are locked in a rapidly escalating battle over who will build the international frameworks of the twenty-first century, frameworks that will replace the settlements struck and maintained by the United States after the Second World War. Both China and the United States are wrestling for the pen with which to write those settlements. I fear they might see the sword as being mightier.

Another thousand mind-numbing words on, Bailey stirred Australia into her witch's brew of an argument.

> Australia can use its privileged place as one of the United States' oldest allies and China's most reliable energy supplier to broker peace between the behemoths of the world stage by leveraging its role as a creative middle power.

Then came the *coup de grâce*, the point Bailey knew would run in the news and cause maximum grief.

> On my advice, Prime Minister Martin Toohey has been masterful in ensuring Australia does not get trapped into taking sides in the East China Sea islands dispute. But he can, and must, take a larger role. He must use our middle power status to immediately engage in shuttle diplomacy between the major powers to bring about an enduring peace and an agreed international framework in the Pacific. Or a 'Pax Pacifica', as I like to call it.

As a political professional, Ryan had a grudging admiration for Bailey. She was an evil genius. She knew her 'shuttle diplomacy' line would be parroted by the media the next time Martin Toohey stuck his head up for a press conference. Like all of Bailey's advice it sounded reasonable, but it was designed to put Toohey in an impossible position. If he demurred he would be portrayed as missing an opportunity for peace. But if he was mad enough to agree, it meant he would be out of the country for weeks on end during an election year. And that would cruel the minute chance he had of winning the poll.

Who am I kidding, he might as well go. Jesus Christ couldn't raise this party from the dead.

Ryan had orchestrated the coup that snatched the prime minister's mantle from Bailey and he was still proud of it as a clinically brilliant political assassination. But he had been very disappointed in Toohey. He was a decent man, but the public saw him as a devious back-stabber. Far worse in Ryan's eyes was that Toohey liked grand, expensive, centralised social planning. That cost money the Treasury didn't have and so he racked up debt and cut deeply into other areas, particularly Defence.

Ryan had plotted to bring down the former defence minister and left-wing fool, Bruce Paxton, in an effort to stop cuts that he believed were a threat to national security. But it had been futile. The prime minister was determined to bribe his way back to power and Defence was simply a cash cow to be milked.

Maybe losing the election was the best thing that could happen. What Ryan wanted to avoid was losing so badly that political recovery would take a generation.

He scrabbled in his desk drawer for a bar of chocolate as he tried to conjure a plan that would keep his party viable.

I'd back anyone against Toohey now as long as they could save some furniture.

'Minister?' His personal assistant was at the door.

'Yup.'

'The prime minister's chief of staff is here.'

The familiar stocky frame of George Papadakis ambled into the office and sat down with a thud. As usual, he was carrying the weight of the nation.

'Do you have any Scotch?' Papadakis asked theatrically.

'George, it's barely lunchtime.'

'Heroin then. I've just come from a meeting with the Chinese ambassador and can't face any more green tea. And I need something to dull the pain of trying to keep this shambles of a show on the road.'

Ryan liked Papadakis and didn't envy his job, but he was disappointed that this member of Labor's Right and old-school Treasury hard-head hadn't managed to rein in his profligate boss.

'I've got headaches of my own, mate. ERC wants more cash from Defence and we're down to the bone. As I've said many times, I'm concerned that we are compromising national security and—'

Papadakis held up his hand.

'Brendan, I know. I've heard your complaints many times and I have said, many times, that everyone has to take a hit. And you know that the mental health plan is close to the PM's heart and probably our only hope of victory at the election.'

Ryan had known he'd get no joy from Papadakis; he'd simply wanted to underline his growing concerns.

'So mate, apart from liquor and hard drugs, what's on your mind?'

'It's your political brain I need. You know how much the PM values your judgement, you're one of his trusted few. These leaks are killing us, Brendan. We expect them from the party, even Cabinet, but we're now being white-anted by someone in the intelligence community. The leak from the NSC is intolerable.'

Ryan rocked back in his chair and swung round to face the window.

'George, you know as well as I do that leaks are one of the symptoms of a government in decline. Leaks from the administration are as good as a death knock. If we can change our fortunes, then we might get back some semblance of order.'

Papadakis checked his watch and started to rise from his chair.

'I know. I just needed the walk. And a shoulder to cry on. Thanks, Brendan.'

'Hey, have you seen the *Guardian* feature by Bailey?'

Papadakis slumped back in his seat and groaned.

'What does the Zombie Queen want now?'

'She says Toohey should engage in shuttle diplomacy to ensure world peace.'

Papadakis was massaging his temples as he got up.

'Cocaine, that's what I need. I'll find someone in the NSW Right. One of them's bound to be a dealer.'

Canberra

From the top of Red Hill, Bruce Paxton soaked up the capital's charm. The city was greener than he'd expected after this summer from hell. Arterial roads carried loads of school children and harried mums, high-vis tradies and brow-beaten cabbies. But the byways wove in and out of the land's natural contours and suburbs vanished beneath the rising green of trees. In the distance, the majestic Brindabellas were a tapestry of green and violet beneath a sky of startling blue.

'Can you believe that a lot of Australians hate this place?' Paxton turned to Weng Meihui, also transfixed by the view.

'In my city there are few trees and the sky is black with smog,' she said, gazing out of the restaurant window. 'I love the space and the clarity of the air here.'

Paxton wrapped his right hand around a chilled glass of white and glanced at her face.

Why has she come back into my life? Now? After all this time?

His first instinct had been, 'This means trouble.' But now, as the afternoon waned, the memories came flooding back. Of nights wrapped in her tantalising, impossible embrace.

She teased him with a smile. 'What are you thinking, Bruce?'

'Don't mock me, but there's a line from a song I just love, by a bloke called Eric Clapton. Bit of a guitar god. He sang about a woman looking "wonderful tonight". And ...'

She leaned over and gently took his hands.

'Why don't you fix the bill?'

The key turned and the door to his apartment opened. He'd taken the precaution of doing a bit of cleaning up.

'So, here it is, the castle. Not much, but I like it.'

She sensed his apprehension, and gently stroked his arm. 'Just relax,' she reassured him.

He bent to the CD player and flicked through a messy pile, pulling out a Michael Bublé compilation some old flatmate had left behind. Personally, he couldn't stand the smug Canadian crooner, but women, he was told, loved him. A soft tune played, something about a woman making him feel young.

Now, that's appropriate.

He turned and leaned into her tight body, hungrily meeting her lips.

'It's been a—'

'Shhhh.' She cut him off as her fingers skilfully dealt with a row of buttons, releasing his shirt and easing it to the floor.

He stood in his singlet, arms crossed self-consciously.

'And off with that, too.'

Her nimble fingers reached firmly beneath the hem of the singlet, and she pulled it up so insistently that he had no choice but to raise his arms above his head.

The cloth covering his eyes, he started with surprise as he felt her soft, warm lips press again upon his own rougher mouth. She kissed him long and lusciously, and he luxuriated in her familiar yet exotic scent. Finally she released him, and he quickly shed his remaining clothes, all body consciousness lost as he urgently drew her to him.

Her fingers traced circles in his chest hair while she rested her head on his arm. The last vestiges of the day had disappeared, and her stomach purred with a mild hunger.

For the first time, she noticed a few sun spots on his neck.

'You need to take care of yourself,' she said, triggering a grunted response.

'Why, darling? Who's coming after me now?'

'No Bruce. I mean your skin.' She dabbed a small red blotch under his chin. 'There.'

'Oh, that. Too many years in the outfield, waiting for some bastard to hit the ball my way.'

Weng looked perplexed.

'Cricket, my love. Only game in the world that can last five days without a friggin' result.' He laughed at the sheer bloody idiocy of it.

Weng eased her body up on a pillow. 'Sounds like a meeting of the People's Congress. It can last five days, sometimes six, and all they do is rubber-stamp what has already been decided. The current Standing Committee is the worst we've ever had.'

Paxton had never heard Weng speak this way; normally she offered nothing but slavish praise for her masters.

'You're sounding a touch bolshie. Things not going so well for you out here?'

She raised herself on both elbows, suddenly serious.

'Bruce ... sometimes ...'

He noticed the slender trail of a tear.

'Mei ... what is it, my love?'

She sighed. 'Often I question what I have become. What I have done for my state. I used to believe in it and that made what I did bearable. But now I fear my country is lost. And I am lost with it.'

Paxton smoothed a lock of hair from her face.

'Well, you're not lost, you're with me. And I know what you are, Mei. I have always known. I didn't delude myself that you were attracted by my charms. But I've never told you anything that would compromise my country.'

'I know. Maybe that is why I love you.'

Paxton held her close as she continued.

'If I had my way, I'd replace all the generals and apparatchiks with the smartest graduates from the universities. Then I'd allow them to open China to the outside world, to really let a thousand flowers bloom. But President Meng seems intent on withdrawing into some nationalist past. We are regressing.'

Paxton could empathise. For the first time in many years he was questioning his own commitment to the great cause. He had played the loyal ALP foot soldier for nearly four decades and had never recoiled from a fight.

From the time he'd signed up as a member of the Rockingham branch in Perth, his dues paid by the Building Workers' Industrial Union, he'd obediently followed every instruction.

All the time he was climbing the greasy pole, from union bovver boy to minister of the crown, he'd had his eyes firmly on the prize. And now? He'd been fed to the wolves a year and a half ago, and for what? He'd broken no laws. Sure, he'd built a slush fund with some Chinese cash, but who in politics had clean hands when it came to that? He'd been dumped because the government was too weak and too gutless to fight.

'I believed in a great cause, the Labor Party. Now? I'm not sure what we stand for anymore. We seem to spend most of our time apologising for cock-ups. And when it does get hard, we cut and run.'

He paused and gazed at his Chinese princess.

'What went wrong, Mei?'

She kissed him. Gently.

'We got older,' she said. 'Now I have to go.'

Canberra

The convoy swept into the National Press Club, the prime ministerial limousine, C1, sandwiched between a pair of gleaming white security vehicles.

Several guards jumped from the cars, taking up positions on either side of C1. Advisers hurriedly grabbed notepads and iPhones.

On his soft leather seat, protected by bullet-proof glass and bodyguards trained to kill, Martin Toohey wrestled with the knot of his silk tie. Finally, he slipped off his seatbelt.

'Okay, George, time to rock-and-roll.'

Near the club entrance, a gaggle of environmentalists was protesting against what they saw as a pitifully low carbon emission target. One was dressed as a polar bear in a suit that looked as if it had been knocked up by his mum. A bedraggled koala lurked without menace. Both were suffering in the heat, and having trouble with the scansion of their chant.

'Five … five … will not keep us alive.'

The club was packed with journalists, lobbyists, bureaucrats and the Labor faithful. Toohey's office had primed the media with snippets from his speech, which had been billed as a game-changer. It was more than that – this was the Grand Final.

Strategically, the Chinese ambassador was seated at the main table, causing a flurry of activity among the snappers.

'Please everyone, switch your phones to silent.' The club's CEO reminded the room that Toohey's speech, just minutes away, was being broadcast live across the nation, on the ABC and Sky News.

In his seat, Toohey took a final gulp of water, brushed at his sleeve and gathered his notes. He walked to the podium and scanned the room as the NPC president made the introductions. The applause was generous.

Toohey got straight into stride.

'This election year is a contest for the future. A contest between the builders with the vision for a twenty-first-century nation and the wreckers who will drag us back to the past.

'Our mission, Labor's mission, is to build a better Australia, to build the jobs of the future and to invest in a fairer country.'

Toohey's presentation was mapped out as a series of steps. Each would be a news story in its own right. Toohey would make some admissions of fault in an effort to consign error to the past. Then there would be a run of headline moments that culminated with the big bang announcement.

The first declaration guaranteed a headline on its own.

'So that we are not dogged with speculation for the rest of the year, today I announce that the election will be held on Saturday, 14 September.'

There was a sharp intake of breath at the press tables, followed by frantic scribbling. Twitter went into overdrive.

This was unheard of, a prime minister giving away the natural advantage of keeping the election date a secret until the last moment. But it was just the start.

'A decent nation cares for those who cannot care for themselves. No one in our community is more vulnerable than those with a mental disability.

'Just last week in Penrith, I met Jody, a young single mother with three children. One, Michael, has a severe disability. Jody is only twenty-four and Michael's needs are so great that she has to care for him day and night. She does not have any family to offer respite.

'She told me that she lies awake at night worrying about what will happen to her son when she can't take care of him anymore.

'A fair Australia, a just Australia, a decent Australia, lends people like Jody and Michael a hand.

'So today I announce the most sweeping reform to mental health care since Federation. My government will legislate this term to secure the future of Jody and Michael and the thousands who struggle each day with this silent epidemic.

'Ladies and gentlemen, the Mental Health Justice Act will provide universal and lifetime cover for those, like Michael, who need our support.

'It will also provide generous respite care for mothers like Jody.

'This will not come cheap. In 2018, the first full year of the scheme, it will cost $6 billion ...'

At this point, the economics editors lowered their heads and began to scribble. Toohey could see it on their faces: here we go, yet another unfunded promise by Labor.

But the PM was ready for the pointy heads.

'... but it will be fully funded, through savings already booked from Defence, and by a unique agreement with the People's Republic of China.

'This afternoon the chief executive of Sinopec and I will sign a heads of agreement concerning the Medusa gas-field off the Northern Territory coast. The Medusa is the largest known gas reserve in the world.

'The agreement will give Sinopec a 99-year lease over the site. In addition to the usual company taxes and royalties, it has agreed to an immediate down payment of $10 billion and yearly leaseholder payments of $1 billion every year thereafter. All of that money will be put in trust to build a war chest for the Mental Justice package.

'So, $11 billion will flow from next financial year, after Sinopec signs the lease. We expect that to be finalised by late August.'

On the floor in front of the stage, two tables of journalists sat stunned. They were used to observing the first rough draft of history – but this was momentous.

Toohey was building to his punchline, which was aimed straight at Labor's core supporters. As he did, he noticed several of the journalists picking up their mobiles and checking messages that had flashed onto their screens.

Probably their editors gobsmacked by my plan.

'This program is Labor to the bootstraps. It tends to the weakest by leveraging our nation's bounty. And it delivers jobs. Ten thousand jobs in the construction phase and a thousand permanent jobs thereafter. It cements our place as an energy superpower and it builds even stronger ties with our neighbours in this Asian Century.

'Only Labor has the plan to deliver a fair go for Australia. Help for the weakest. Jobs for the rest. Prosperity for all.'

The prime minister finished his speech to rapturous applause. He acknowledged it with a nod and took a drink of water, readying himself for the queue of questioners.

The first came from Jonathan Robbie of Channel Nine. He wore a smug smile.

'Prime Minister, thank you for your speech. But I have just received extraordinary news. Catriona Bailey has tweeted a picture of herself. She's been taken off life support. Here ... can you see the picture? What is your response?'

218

That unspeakable cow.

'Jonathan, I could not be more delighted to hear that the foreign minister seems to be making a miraculous recovery. I am, quite literally, speechless. I look forward to seeing her soon.'

The next question was from News Ltd's Tom Shapiro, a young gun training to be a headkicker.

'Given the foreign minister's close links with China, will she play a big role in helping to make sure this deal is sealed?'

'Tom, I'm sure she will have a role to play, but this deal will be sealed by me. My office has all the necessary plans in place.'

Andrew Probyn, the *West Australian's* feisty political correspondent, was on his feet.

'PM, the foreign minister has just tweeted, congratulating you on picking up one of the ideas that came up at her 2020 forum. Is that true?'

You little Pommy prick!

'Andrew, more funding for mental health was a recommendation from the forum but I think you'll find that the detail of this plan is far wider in scope than anything that has come before. And, if I might take some credit for this, there is a big difference between having an idea and sealing a deal.'

The next three questions were all about Bailey, the gallery ignoring the detail of Toohey's tour de force.

Finally, Laura Tingle, the political editor from the *Australian Financial Review*, got the call and Toohey knew she hated Bailey at least as much as he did. She was also a serious economic journalist.

'PM, you've skated over an important element in funding this plan. The briefing notes suggest that by 2025 your funding model will be $1 billion a year short of paying for itself. And you plan to lift the Medicare levy to fund the shortfall.'

We hoped that would be a footnote, not a focus.

'You're right, Laura. The difference will be funded by lifting the Medicare levy by a modest 0.25 per cent. But that will not happen until 2020 and, even then, it will only add a few dollars a month to the costs of an average family. Again, I stress that cost will not come for seven years. I think you will agree, Laura, that is a modest charge for a safety net that will give everyone peace of mind.'

Phones were starting to light up again on the press tables.

The final question was from Paul Bongiorno, Ten's veteran political correspondent.

'PM. Bruce Paxton has just put out a press release saying he is quitting the Labor Party to sit on the crossbenches. Will that jeopardise the passage of your bill?'

Fuck me drunk, can't I have a second of clear air?

'Well, Paul, that is a surprise. But Bruce Paxton has spent his life trying to improve the lot of working men and women and I would be staggered if he did not see the merit in this plan. I will be seeking a meeting with him and briefing the other crossbench MPs soon.'

And with that the prime minister stepped down from the podium, ignoring the gift of a Mont Blanc pen and honorary Press Club membership.

A day that promised triumph and glory had turned to shit. Again.

Canberra

It's dubbed the 6pm index, a few minutes of primetime torture that can test the bravest.

Every night the prime minister and his inner sanctum gathered around a bank of television screens to see how they'd fared on the commercial networks.

Tonight was a disaster.

Network Seven led with exclusive footage of Catriona Bailey sitting serenely in a wheelchair, flanked by a deeply tanned neurosurgeon from Brisbane.

'This is close to miraculous. I've never had a patient show such steely determination to recover,' the neurosurgeon said. 'And, let me emphasise this, very few people suffering from Ms Bailey's condition ever get off life support. We hope that soon the foreign minister will be able to talk.'

On Nine, Laurie Oakes had scored an interview with Bruce Paxton, who was declaring his intention to be yet another thorn in the side of the Toohey government.

'I will treat every bill on a case by case basis,' Paxton advised. 'This government had better not take me for granted.'

Ten lacked the other networks' clout, so its bulletin, an hour earlier than the big two, had no exclusive, but Hugh Riminton reported that the prime minister's speech had been 'overshadowed' by the breaking news on Bailey and Paxton.

At 7pm, the ABC led with the 'serious reservations' being expressed by the Queensland and Western Australian governments about the gas hub plan. Both feared the Commonwealth's intervention would jeopardise projects planned for their states. And both were making noises about a vague constitutional problem that neither would elaborate on.

'What crap!' spat Papadakis. 'We have all the legal power we need to proceed in the Territory.'

'Mate,' Toohey sighed with the resignation of a man with low expectations. 'The longer I'm in this job, the more I wonder whether I have any power at all.'

Melbourne

The Toorak tram rumbled by as Matthew Sloan hustled along the footpath with the frantic resolve of a man who was late.

He had hated every minute of the Multicultural Communities Council meeting he'd just endured. Typically, minutes had piled into wasted hours in the drone of self-important speeches. The conclave of complaint was supposed to be finished by six, leaving him ample time for the 7.30 dinner rendezvous. It was now 7.50.

If only the public could gaze inside a member of parliament's life.

While the perception was of a life of privilege and taxpayer-funded travel, in truth the diary of an MP was larded with tedious speech nights and vapid community events. And meetings. Constituents, complainers, urgers and spivs all demanding time to whine.

But then there were the moments he lived for, the hidden pearls that made his job worthwhile.

As chair of the Parliamentary Joint Committee on Intelligence and Security, Sloan had access to some of the nation's deepest and most sensitive secrets.

It also meant he was feted by every embassy and enjoyed junkets across the world to meet with counterparts in exotic lands. He'd just returned from the US, where he'd been given a personal tour of Langley by the new head of the CIA. A framed photograph of Sloan arm in arm with the director now graced his office wall.

He was now within smelling distance of Bacash, one of Melbourne's best eateries and Sloan's favourite restaurant. Sloan loved the slate-grey interior, the crisp white tablecloths, the attentive staff and the exquisite menu. He could already taste the chargrilled calamari with chorizo.

Waiting for him at a corner table was Blake Cornwall, the political counsel at the United States embassy in Canberra. Dressed in a sharp dark-blue suit, Cornwall could have been a top-flight banker or lawyer waiting for a client. Instead he was effectively America's number-one operative in Australia, the CIA's eyes and ears who could even pull rank on the ambassador when it came to the big calls.

He rose to greet Sloan with a handshake.

'Sorry I'm late. Held up at the last event by a group of blowhards,' the MP apologised.

'Don't worry about it, Matthew.' Cornwall spoke in polished Bostonian tones. 'I've already ordered some starters and a decent bottle of white. It's really great to see you. How's Mary?'

'Really well. She asked me to pass on how touched she was when the ambassador wrote to her after her mother died.'

'He was saddened to hear about it, Matthew. As he often says, the bonds between our nations are so deep that we are essentially family.'

'Very true, Blake. And you know there is no stronger friend of the US than Australia.'

'Is that so?' Cornwall's smile vanished, his face turned to stone and his voice dropped.

'Then what the fuck are you pissants playing at in this gas deal with China?'

Sloan was stunned. He struggled to compose himself.

'It's … an economic compact, it's …'

'It's a sell-out. Yet another signal from your government that the old alliances are fading. You have forgotten who your friends are. Do you really believe that this region would be peaceful if we hadn't done the hard defensive yards? I went to the trouble of getting you a briefing from the head of the NSA. Do you know how rare that is? Are you so stupid that you missed the key message? Make no mistake on how this is being viewed in DC. By everyone. Hell, even the State Department and Pentagon agree: you're giving us the bird and we aren't about to sit quietly while you guys rat on us.'

'What are you suggesting, Blake … ending security agreements?'

'Use your imagination,' Cornwall said, as he threw his napkin on the table and rose to leave. 'And enjoy your dinner. Alone. I've ordered and paid. You guys should be used to that.'

Canberra

CABINET SPLIT ON CHINA DEAL

The Australian's splash was designed to erect a tombstone on the policy Martin Toohey and George Papadakis had meticulously crafted over the previous three months. A report on the mental health package was relegated to page 5. Predictably, the national broadsheet had seized on political divisions within the government over the gas mega-deal.

A 'senior source' claimed that most of Cabinet had been kept in the dark on the details of the package. There was deep disquiet about 'selling off the farm' to the Chinese and serious concern about how the proposed deal would be received by Australia's neighbours and its ally-in-chief, the United States.

The chief of staff had barely slept. Papadakis had left the office after watching a *Lateline* interview with Western Australia's Colin Barnett, who was in meltdown. The premier of the resource-rich state had accused the Commonwealth of stealing potential Chinese investment money and issued threats of a Constitutional challenge.

Throughout the long evening, Papadakis had been peppered with disturbing calls.

In Melbourne, his close friend Matthew Sloan had been monstered by the CIA's chief spook. The secretary of the Department of Foreign Affairs and Trade had been shirt-fronted by what he described as a 'hysterical' Japanese ambassador at a charity ball. The South Korean consul had ear-bashed the minister for trade and suggested that Labor had placed Australia on a perilous course, one that could jeopardise a planned free-trade agreement. Even the Israelis had briefly lifted their eyes from the Middle East to give their American friends a diplomatic hand. This time, it had been delivered with their usual shovel-to-the-head bluntness to a hapless parliamentary secretary.

Toohey stuck his head around Papadakis's door, holding his iPad.

'You know, I miss the old paper version of this rag because right now I'm off to the bathroom.'

'What the fuck do we do now?' Papadakis asked in despair.

'We stick to our guns, mate. This is a good program. You and I know that. We can't be knocked off course. So, what are your plans?'

'Maybe I'll tune into Alan Jones and get his calm, considered view on the foreign investment side of this. Just so my spirits can soar with the eagles.'

Canberra

Harry Dunkley drove north on Anzac Parade, slowing as he passed the Vietnam Forces National Memorial, monument to a time when folk, young and old, began to lose faith in government.

Straight ahead, the striking facade of the Australian War Memorial drew closer, its copper-green dome set against the moss-and-emerald forest of Mt Ainslie.

What is it about this shrine to the dead that I find so compelling?

Dunkley had spent countless hours at the War Memorial, absorbing the tragic history of a young nation that had lost too many to the horrors of war. It never failed to move him.

Charles Dancer had called again and asked that they meet in the First World War gallery, just off the main entrance. When Dunkley arrived, Dancer was contemplating a white landing boat, scarred with bullet holes from the day it approached the beach at Gallipoli.

'Imagine it, Harry ...' Dancer tried to conjure up century-old spirits. 'The boys in this open boat. And they were boys. The hellfire raining down on them. The noise. Friends dying beside them. Yet they go on, driven by a sense of duty. To their country. To each other.'

As Dancer turned to drive his message home, Dunkley could see this place also moved the shadowy diplomat. He was beginning to get a sense of what drove Dancer: he saw himself in the long line of warriors who'd guarded the nation.

'Never ever forget the sacrifice made over generations to ensure this country's stayed free,' Dancer stressed. 'People like Keating argue that the First World War wasn't our fight. Well, sometimes a fight chooses you. And the boys who died in that war perished in the belief they were fighting for a good cause.

'Their country, their friends, their way of life and maybe even quaint old notions of Empire. Those are things worth fighting for, Harry. Their sacrifice was noble and should be venerated. We can't look back from this distance and judge them. If they were following the wrong cause, it's the politicians and generals who should stand condemned by history. The foot soldiers were honourable men. Heroes.'

Dunkley walked to the bow of the boat to examine one of the ragged holes where a bullet from a Turkish Mauser had ripped through the metal of the hull, just above the waterline.

'You're sounding quite sentimental today, Charles. I like military history lessons. But I suspect that ain't the reason you called me here.'

'It's not history, Harry. War is always with us. It's sometimes hot, sometimes cold. Sometimes you see it and sometimes it's a secret war with invisible trenches. Right now the frontline is just over there.'

Dancer turned and pointed south, in the direction of the new embassy being built by the Chinese. He pulled a small handful of prints from his jacket pocket.

'Have a look at these, Harry. And yes, they are yours to keep – and publish.'

There were three photos, all aerial shots taken from directly above the new Chinese embassy compound.

'Jesus, how did you get these, Charles? A spy satellite?'

'Hardly.' He smiled. 'That kind of technology is a bit expensive. Actually, Defence finally put that RAAF hot-air balloon to good use. We tried a few times before the winds were on our side. It drifted right over the embassy site, and the Chinese were none too happy.'

Dunkley flicked through the colour pics, each showing a different aspect of the embassy compound. In one, three men in white overalls were shovelling inside a deep trench. A black pipe was being laid down the middle. The work looked difficult and dangerous.

'I'm assuming these guys don't have union cards.'

'I suspect you're right, Harry. The Chinese appear to have brought their OH&S habits from home. But we've had a close look at the work and, coupled with other pictures and information, we believe that site will mostly be used as a communications hub. It will gather and distribute intelligence.'

Dancer moved to examine a glass case displaying some of the hand weapons used in the First World War. He seemed taken by a vicious-looking trench knife that married a wickedly sharp blade with a knuckle-duster handle.

'If I'd been in the trenches I would have wanted one of those. Each war calls for new and better weapons, Harry. And in the current war our man in the lake was well equipped for battle.'

Dancer lowered his voice and Dunkley stepped closer to the case.

'As you know, Lin An came to Australia on a diplomatic passport; his occupation was listed as construction worker. Turns out he was a cyber-spy, one of China's best. He was attached to Unit 61398, an arm of the People's Liberation Army. Its headquarters have been tracked to a building in Shanghai.

'Harry, that building is the source of thousands of cyber-attacks launched by the PLA against dozens of countries and numerous corporations.'

'Charles, I'm no great shakes on computing, but can't you hack into a system from anywhere in the world? Like those teenage nerds who bring down New York banking systems from their bedrooms?'

Dancer tapped the glass case holding the array of weapons.

'All these things are harmless, Harry. Here behind the glass. They're made with deadly purpose but only become dangerous when they're wielded with deadly intent. But if I were to smash the glass, pick up a gun, load it and point it at you? Well, you'd get a whole new perspective on the weapon.'

'What's your point?'

'Computers are just another weapons system. To be dangerous they have to be operated by someone with evil intent. To be deadly they have to be able to breach the trenches and castle walls we build to defend ourselves. Our most precious secrets are very well defended. To get at those, Harry, you need someone to open the door.

'Lin An's memory stick reveals that the Chinese have managed to crack some of our most secure communications. Not everything. But given he was trying to defect, I assume the USB was just a taster. God knows what the Chinese have. If Lin An hadn't jumped the fence we would be none the wiser. And we still have no idea where the hole in our defences is.'

Dunkley pondered the menacing contents of the display case.

'So someone has broken the glass and is about to use our own weapons against us?'

'It would appear so. And the glass was broken from the inside.'

The next day, Dunkley's story about Lin An and the new Chinese embassy ran prominently on page one, accompanied by a trio of sharply detailed photos.

As Martin Toohey re-read the story, he subconsciously fiddled with the knot of his tie. George Papadakis recognised the sign that his boss was agitated.

'How come Dunkley knows more about our intelligence than I do?' the PM thundered. 'And why is it that someone in the intelligence community has decided to parade their concerns on his front page? That's a crime. If they have a beef, why don't they come to me?'

Papadakis gave voice to what they were both thinking.

'Maybe they're not on our side.'

Melbourne

It was closing on 7.30am when Alison Cox boarded the tram to Docklands and the ANZ's Melbourne office, headquarters for the bank's information systems. Cox was Manager, Network Behavioural Analysis – a job title that took a fair bit of explaining at dinner parties.

226

'We are the new vault walls,' she would say.

A small team was under her watch, charged with ensuring that tens of millions of dollars in daily transactions were secure. She'd been hired six months earlier, as part of a big push to bolster ANZ's defences against cyber-criminals.

It was nearly 7.45am when she walked into the office where the overnight traffic flows were already being analysed by her team.

She examined the summary sheet. 'Volumetric flows are normal.'

An hour and a half later, the first sign of trouble appeared. It was 9.11am when her team identified a spike in traffic on the internet banking system. It was manageable.

Two minutes later, her phone buzzed. 'Alison – my office, now please.'

Wendy Chang was ANZ's chief information officer, a brilliant analyst recruited to overhaul the bank's creaky security systems.

'What's happening with this uptick in traffic?' She was pointing to a graph on one of her computer screens that was blinking madly.

'Not certain at this stage, Wendy. It's certainly a big increase; we're monitoring and trying to isolate it now.'

Cox walked back to her office, stopping briefly to talk with a colleague about Thursday night drinks. The chat was interrupted by her deputy.

'You need to see this, Alison. It's going haywire.'

It was 9.45am. ANZ's internet banking system was being bombarded with wall-to-wall requests.

Customer service was starting to receive irate phone calls as frustrated customers tried and failed to log on to the bank's internet system, bogged down by a massive increase in traffic.

Cox's phone rang – it was her boss.

'What's going on?' Chang asked.

'It looks like a denial of service attack.' Cox furrowed her brow as she stared into the system diagnostics readout on her screen. 'And it's massive. Our computers can't keep pace. If it amps up any more they'll start to shut down.'

'God!' Chang had been at the bank for only a year and in that time had seen very few real cases of internet sabotage. She was taking no risks.

'I'm convening a high-priority incident team. Alison, I want you in the meeting room. Five minutes.'

Chang swung around to her computer. She clicked on her email, shaking out the stress in her shoulders before composing a note to ANZ senior management.

It was now 10am. Chang had convened her security team. There were six in the group and each had been through countless cyber-drills and exercises.

But this was the real deal.

'What's the latest on traffic volumes?'

Cox's 2IC had the data, and flicked across his iPad screen till he found the exact figure. 'It's up 189 per cent on daily average. We're adding extra capacity but it doesn't appear to be working ...'

'Wendy,' Cox leapt into the conversation. 'I've just had an alert from credit card transactions. They're in trouble, too.'

It was compounding. Chang was now seriously worried. The ANZ was under attack.

An ashen-faced Cox gasped and held up her iPad. Chang moved closer to see the information on the screen.

To her surprise it displayed a map of the Asia-Pacific region and a small blinking light was pulsing on a city to Australia's north.

Shanghai.

***

Canberra

George Papadakis's morning was shaken by an urgent call from the ANZ chairman.

'George, I'll be brief.' The chairman was agitated.

'In fifteen minutes we'll be issuing a formal statement to the ASX. It will announce that all of our systems have been shut down due to a technical issue with our servers. None of our customers will have access to their accounts or credit cards for the next twenty-four hours. We'll assure people that their money is safe and that normal service will resume as soon as possible.

'Now, George, I'm about to tell you something in the utmost confidence. Our systems have been attacked. We've been forced to shut them down. And we're genuinely concerned that if this news gets out it will shake customer confidence. I don't need to tell you what a run on the ANZ would mean for the entire financial system.

'We're trying to trace the origin of the attack but that's very hard as whoever is behind this has recruited zombie computers from around the world. But we know this much. It's very sophisticated and our guys believe that only a state would have the resources. Everyone here in Melbourne is pretty sure it's coming from China.'

Papadakis raced into the prime minister's office.

'PM ...' Papadakis was breathless. 'ANZ is shutting down internet banking ... a massive cyber-attack ... they think it's coming from China.'

Toohey looked exhausted.

'I just got off the phone to the head of the stock exchange. It's suspending trading and blaming it on some vague computer malfunction. It's not true. Their computers were overloaded by a denial of service attack. They think it's China too.'

The two men grappled with the bombshell.

'First air-traffic control, now this.' Toohey broke the silence. 'What could we have done to piss off the Chinese so much that they would do this? It just doesn't make sense.'

Papadakis responded cautiously. 'Well, maybe it's Beijing's way of declaring they don't like us straddling both sides of the street, cosying up to Chinese money while allowing American troops on our soil.'

'And if you're right, George, we're supposed to do what? Just roll over and cop it? Christ, I do that every day in this place. I'm jack of it. We need to send a message of our own.'

Toohey thumped his desk.

'Martin, what can we possibly do to cause them any kind of grief? And, importantly, what can we do that's deniable?'

The prime minister turned to his trusted lieutenant and smiled.

'George, get me the CFMEU.'

Canberra

The steel handcuffs dug into the soft flesh of wrists shackled to a medieval wooden truss. Leather straps bound his ankles, stretching his pale body into a naked 'X' framed in a rectangle. Livid red marks striped his back.

Jonathan Robbie was used to being flogged by parliamentarians but this was very different.

A riding crop lashed the journalist's buttocks, delivering a small dose of pleasure and plenty of pain.

'Arrrhhh!'

'Scream, bitch!' yelled his tormentor, whose ardour was growing with each whack.

Emily Brooks was a study in dominatrix chic. Thigh-high black boots tapered to six-inch silver-encased stiletto heels. Rock-hard muscles met a taut arse, bare save for the sliver of a lipstick-red leather thong. Her toned and tanned torso was also bare and a black studded bra scarcely contained breasts that seemed too pert for her forty-eight years. Her hands and arms were encased in over-the-elbow gloves that neatly matched the thong. A studded dog collar circled the opposition leader's neck.

Brooks paused to admire the criss-cross pattern she'd imprinted on her lover's flesh and searched for a patch of unmarked skin. She found her spot and delivered a diagonal welt from right hip to left thigh with, perhaps, an excess of enthusiasm.

'Shit! That really hurt,' yelped her increasingly unwilling accomplice. The pair had agreed on a safe word before the sex play began and now Robbie decided to tap the mat.

'Kittens!' he squealed.

'Oh, has the little petal had enough?' sneered Brooks. 'I was just getting warmed up.'

'I know, my love, but we did discuss this.' Robbie was struggling to get his hands free. 'You know I'm uncomfortable with the handcuffs. I prefer rope or stockings, so I can get loose if I have to. Right now I feel … well, trapped.'

'Don't you trust me, sweetie?' Brooks purred close to his ear.

The answer was no. He was terrified.

'Of course I trust you,' he lied. 'So "Kittens", my dear. Let me down.'

'But I can't do that just yet, Jonnie. I have something I want to talk about. And a special treat.'

'You want to chat? Let's get a coffee.'

'I needed your full attention, dear. I was very disappointed with your story on our asylum seeker policy. I thought it was a bit unfair. You made me sound like a monster.'

'Well, threatening to use the navy to sink asylum seeker boats is a touch extreme. I was tame by comparison with the others.'

'But you know I wouldn't do it. I just think we need to show some real steel to ensure no one makes that terribly unsafe journey. Sometimes what seems like cruelty is really the best way of saying I love you. So I'm disappointed in you, Jonnie, but don't worry, you'll get your special treat anyway.'

There was a dull buzz as something battery-powered was switched on.

'What's that?' Robbie's heart was pounding. 'What are you doing?'

Brooks strayed into his view with her hands behind her, looking at once both fearsome and coy.

'Just a little something I found in Fyshwick.' She slowly pulled her hands from behind her back.

'No, dear, no,' Robbie pleaded. 'You can't be serious. And this isn't funny. Kittens' … Kittens' playtime is over now!'

'My dear, playtime has just begun.'

'Noooooooooooooo!'

Canberra

Dean Hall dubbed it Operation Trojan Horse. The local head of the Construction, Forestry, Mining and Energy Union had been dreaming of this sweet moment for a year. Everything had been planned to the minute.

The Chinese embassy site had been off limits to the militant union, and that chafed. The Chinese had shipped in their own labour to build their new headquarters behind a wall of secrecy. Several aerial photos revealed China's low regard for workplace safety.

What fucking building site would wrap razor wire around its perimeter?

The Chinese had banned Australian workers from the site; not even the ACT's chief building inspector had been allowed to run the ruler over it. The gates were only ever opened to foreigners when the Chinese took delivery of building materials. This morning, the embassy had organised a delivery of blue metal. The supplier had been instructed to be at the front gate at 9.30am precisely. It was now 9.26.

The truck pulled up and the driver sounded the horn. The gate was unbolted and one of the Chinese security guards emerged. He recognised the driver, but motioned in Hall's direction and shook his head.

'He comes in while I unload, mate,' the driver shot back. 'New union rules.'

The goon looked suspiciously at Hall but went back to the gates and pushed them both open. The diesel engine rattled into gear and the truck rolled fifty metres inside the wire.

The union chief yelled into his mobile. 'Trojan Horse is go, go, go!'

The tarp covering the tipper was thrown back and twelve fearsome organisers leapt into action. Two ran to the gates and held them open while the rest fanned out across the compound.

Once the gates were secured a small convoy appeared from a hundred metres away, led by Channel Nine's live links van. Harry Dunkley was in the next car with a News Corp photographer.

Hall waited until the cameraman was out of the Nine van and rolling before he grabbed the loudhailer. It squealed into life.

'This site has been declared black!' he yelled. 'We believe there are serious breaches of occupational health and safety on this site and we're here to ensure that's rectified.'

A few Chinese workers tried to intervene but they were hopelessly outgunned.

A chant broke out from the brothers who had unfurled a giant CFMEU banner and were standing defiantly under its proud sail.

'Aussie jobs! Aussie jobs! Aussie jobs!'

Dunkley spotted a tough-looking Chinese national on the edge of the melee. He was dressed in a suit and talking into his mobile.

'Ray, take a few pics of him, please,' the reporter called to his snapper.

He edged closer, determined to try and ask a few questions while the union bovver boys were playing havoc with the bewildered Chinese workforce.

'Hey, mate! You got a moment?'

The tough guy shot Dunkley a lethal look with his jet-black eyes. Then he saw the snapper and turned and walked quickly into one of the half-finished buildings.

After thirty minutes of mayhem, Hall called the union members together for one last show of strength.

'We, the CFMEU, will never allow standards to be compromised. Too many workers have been killed in the ACT during the past few years due to lax occupational health and safety standards. The Chinese government should get this message: You play in Australia under our rules.'

The dirty dozen cheered and offered some last-minute fist-shaking for the cameras. Then they climbed aboard the tipper. A sandy-haired thug tilted his head to the skies and began to sing:

The workers' flag is deepest red
It shrouded oft our martyred dead ...

Just over a kilometre away, Martin Toohey and George Papadakis watched as the protest played out on Sky. They'd brushed off a minister's tap at the PM's door as they sat engrossed.

'Do you think he knows that China has a red flag and that it's already a workers' paradise?' Papadakis asked.

'I think the irony is lost on him.' Toohey couldn't recall when he had last enjoyed Sky's political coverage so much.

'The Chinese won't be happy about this,' Papadakis said.

'George, how can we be held responsible for the actions of a militant union?' Toohey couldn't suppress a laugh. Victories had been few and far between. 'Believe me, the CFMEU will be happy to take all the blame ...

and the credit. They'll be printing T-shirts with "Hall's Heroes" stamped on them before the end of the month.'

Papadakis shook his head in admiration. 'So, Prime Minister. The Senkakus have come to Yarralumla. Nice work.'

Canberra

The clip of shoes on the hard polished floor announced the arrival of the Chinese ambassador in the R.G. Casey building. He was greeted by a junior official waiting at the reception desk.

'Mr Joyce is expecting you, Ambassador.'

Tian Qichen offered a weak smile and nodded for the underling to lead the way. He was in no mood for banter. In his briefcase was a démarche: the highest form of official complaint from a foreign embassy to a host government. He'd been instructed to hand-deliver it to the secretary of the Department of Foreign Affairs and Trade and to protest in the strongest possible terms against the invasion of Chinese sovereign territory by union thugs. Australian–Sino relations were at their lowest ebb since Catriona Bailey had delivered a lecture in Mandarin to Peking University students, lamenting the treatment of Tibet.

In his fourth-floor office, DFAT secretary David Joyce, armed with an official statement from the prime minister's office, gazed through expansive windows to Parliament House, just up the hill, as he waited for the diplomat.

Joyce had known Tian for years. He'd performed his professional duty by welcoming the ambassador to Australia with a Sunday evening barbecue at his Forrest home. He quite enjoyed his company.

But the secretary knew this encounter would be bruising.

'Ambassador, very nice to see you. I hope you and Ms Weng are enjoying your first weeks in our country.'

Tian said nothing but placed his black briefcase theatrically on Joyce's desk and flicked its two locks open. Reaching inside, he removed a letter. A single sheet of paper was embossed with official Chinese government letterhead.

'Mr Joyce, I am sure you are aware of my government's strong displeasure concerning yesterday's events. They were unacceptable. Needless to say, they have done nothing to help negotiations over a free-trade deal.'

He glanced at the official letter as if seeking guidance.

'The embassy site is contaminated; its role has been compromised. The Chinese government is demanding another block of land suitable for our new building.'

Joyce had his own piece of paper, stamped with the Australian crest and signed by Martin Toohey. He decided to match Tian's theatrics and read some of it aloud.

'The prime minister says he regrets the incident and notes that the "actions of the workers were not sanctioned by anyone in government". But as a Labor prime minister he understands "the genuine affront that all decent union officials" would feel at what they saw as "illegal work practices on Australian soil by a foreign power".'

The ambassador immediately recognised the wording. It was almost a carbon copy of the language used by Beijing to describe the occupation of the Senkaku Islands by the Chinese fishermen.

Joyce lowered the paper and looked over his half-moon glasses at Tian.

'As for the land, Mr Ambassador, that is not within my gift. I will pass on your request to the prime minister and the National Capital Authority. But you should be aware that diplomatic land in the capital's dress circle is in short supply.'

The ambassador responded carefully. 'I came to Australia hoping to build on our excellent relationship, one that has proved very beneficial. The prime minister's announcement on the gas deal was evidence of this deepening friendship.'

'And we want to continue to enjoy a good relationship,' Joyce said. 'But, to be frank, some in our government believe that the recent attacks on our aviation and banking systems originated in China. If so, they would not be the actions of a friend.'

Tian looked out at the parliament building, its enormous flag stretched full in the late afternoon breeze.

'It is ironic, Mr Joyce. If what you say is true about the invasion of our embassy, then this truly is a land where the workers run the government.' He turned back to the secretary. 'I thought that was my country, not yours.'

Canberra

Our man in Canberra Dunkly on fire. Must be in line for Gold
Walkley. About time.

The fact Rupert Murdoch had misspelled his name couldn't dent Harry Dunkley's pride at featuring in a tweet from the great man. The reporter had been delivering a regular supply of white-hot scoops for the *Oz*.

234

Earning a commendation from News Corp's global chief was icing on a very tasty cake.

Harry had almost morphed into the very thing he loathed – a celebrity journalist – and was in fierce demand with voracious television and radio networks, always on the lookout for new talent. He'd become a darling of 2GB with the Sydney radio station's hosts clamouring to have him on their programs to buttress the network's 'Fortress Australia' mentality. Alan Jones had even asked him to front a 'Buy Back the Farm' campaign he was planning to launch the following week, an invitation Dunkley had politely declined.

Jones had then dangled a bigger carrot.

'Harry, I'm backing a new party – Australia First – that will run candidates in every electorate at the September election. You can be part of this – even become prime minister.'

Again, Dunkley demurred.

But it was true that public opinion was turning. The Lowy Institute's annual poll on Australian global attitudes showed that the nation was becoming more suspicious of China.

Dunkley's stories were tapping into old fears and prejudices. The internet was alive with the worst of the human spirit. Dark anonymous forces had established a blog with a subtle title 'The Yellow Peril'. Its motto? 'Revive White Australia'.

Dunkley fretted about the extreme end of this debate. In every interview he repeated the mantra that he was 'not anti-China'. But in his reflective moments he was pleased to be at the vanguard of those sounding the alarm over the rise of the communist nation and the shift of power from West to East.

And when he was honest with himself, he knew what was driving him.

They killed Kimberley.

He tugged a jacket over his shoulders and put a protective arm around his girlfriend as they left the Dendy cinema in Civic. It was closing on 9.30pm and Celia Mathieson had insisted on seeing the latest Ryan Gosling flick, an escapist fantasy that he'd found vapid.

'I liked it, Harry. Yeah, it wasn't *War and Peace*, but so what?' Celia suggested a quick bite at one of the restaurants along Bunda Street, but as they peered into Wagamama they saw the staff putting up the 'Closed' sign. It was an all-too-familiar scenario in the national capital, which lacked the big-city vibe of Sydney, Melbourne, even Brisbane.

Still, the silken touch of Celia's blouse as they strolled along the spine of this pretend CBD was compensation enough. Their relationship was still in its early phase: a few movies, a nice dinner, a picnic on the lake, several overnight stays in her Kingston apartment and a handful in his untidy pad.

Tonight offered similar promise.

'What about a drink, Cel? Cube should be open.'

'Ooh, you are being adventurous, old man. Didn't think you liked gay bars?'

'Ease up. I'm not your typical boring middle-aged hung-up male.'

She stopped and swung in front of him, blocking his path as she hooked a long lingering kiss on his lips. 'We'll see about that, Harry.'

Canberra

The pink brush with ivory inlay swept across her raven-black hair. A whiff of perfume – musky vanilla – roused a memory. Her first time with Bruce, three decades ago … they had been so young, and hadn't known how precious and fleeting that gift was.

Weng Meihui dabbed on makeup with the skill of an artisan and frowned. She turned on a harsh light and directed its glare towards her slender throat.

She was in her early fifties and still alluring to men. But this southern light troubled her. It revealed too much, highlighting every hint of age.

How long will I be of use to them?

The state had raised her, schooled her, trained her, employed her, housed and cared for her. She was lucky; she'd been chosen for her intellect as much as her physical appeal. And she had repaid their faith, every time, without question.

No man was her hero, and she was no one's servant. She was flint-tough, sharp-minded and had used her quick wit more than a few times to escape difficult situations.

There were two soft knocks at the door. 'May I come in?'

He was here. Her consort. Her partner. Their choice. Tian Qichen entered without waiting for her response.

'I was pleased when I heard that you would be accompanying me to Australia. How are you enjoying this place?' he asked.

She was unsure how to answer. After all, it had only been a matter of weeks and the assignment, still in its early stages, was not without its challenges.

He sensed her hesitation and stepped in to break the silence.

'Your mission with the parliamentarian has gone well. Beijing is pleased.'

Of course they are.

'Yes, I am happy that he decided to sit as an independent in the federal parliament.'

'Did he take much convincing?'

She hesitated. There were things that she needed to keep to herself.

He repeated the question. He'd moved closer, bringing with him a faint smell of mint and wax.

'Not much at all. He understood that sitting as an independent would allow him to leverage that position and put pressure on the prime minister. And remember, he is no special friend of the Americans,' Weng said.

Tian looked around the room as if searching for something. He turned back to her.

'You have feelings for him?'

Weng felt a tinge of shame.

'Of course not. This is my … profession.'

'And I have always admired you for that. You are very skilled and much respected.'

He moved even closer and reached out to stroke her hair. 'And very beautiful.'

'You are kind.' Weng turned to face him and smiled. 'But I am getting old and the light in this country does me no favours. Soon my country won't have any use for me.'

'You are too hard on yourself.' He grasped her hands.

'Don't.' She pulled away, surprised at the cold slap of her voice.

His face hardened.

'As you wish, Ms Weng.'

She rose from her chair and walked past him to the bathroom.

'Please, Ambassador, close the door on the way out.'

Sydney

The dashboard lights of the Mercedes SLK softly lit Elizabeth Scott's face as she negotiated the sweep left onto Manly Road. It was late and the call, though unexpected, had been welcome. They'd arranged to meet in a carpark just off the Spit Bridge, a short drive from her Manly home.

Scott had come close to quitting parliament after being dumped as opposition leader. Her husband had begged her to return to business, where she had made her fortune.

But Scott could not bear admitting failure. She believed she still had plenty to offer and was the best person to lead the Liberal Party, which was being dragged hard to the right by the odious Emily Brooks.

Redemption in the mainstream had come slowly for Scott, though she'd found to her surprise that she'd been quickly taken up by the luvvies of the Left, who saw her as the civilised face of conservative politics. These were the same people, of course, who had pilloried her every move when she'd led the Liberal Party.

What had really liberated her was being on the backbench. Better still, her willingness to act as a commentator on her party and leader had put her in high demand with the media. Now, eighteen months after her demise, opinion polls showed she was among the most recognised and popular politicians in the nation.

Scott had learned brutal lessons about politics and knew that it didn't pay to play fair. She had decided to exploit her wealth and had engaged a private investigator to comb through her rival's life.

Now the PI claimed to have hit paydirt.

Crossing the bridge, Scott turned left onto Parriwi Rd and into the carpark. She pulled up her convertible alongside a smart-looking Ford.

Thank God someone still buys Australian.

A middle-aged man limped from the car. His demeanour and clothing bore the unmistakeable stamp of the ex-copper. He opened the passenger's door of the Mercedes and climbed in.

'Nice set of wheels. I'm obviously not charging enough.'

Scott wasn't in the mood for small talk. 'What do you have for me?'

'Gold. Pure unadulterated gold.'

'Photos?'

'Better. Video.'

'How did …? No, don't tell me how. Just tell me what.'

'I'll tell you, love. I saw some strange shit in my time at Vice down the Cross, but this makes *Underbelly* look like an episode of *Lassie*.'

––––––––––

Canberra

'Welcome to the best Japanese restaurant in Canberra, Harry. Great to see you.'

Akito Mori's familiar shape framed the doorway. He was officially listed as the counsellor for public affairs at the Japanese embassy, but Dunkley

238

suspected he was the station chief for Japan's spy agency, the Cabinet Intelligence and Research Office, or Naicho.

He ushered Harry to the embassy's informal dining room, where Ambassador Satoki Tenaka was waiting, a glass of champagne in his hand. Dunkley smiled as he greeted the diplomat.

'Apologies for my lateness, Your Excellency, I was held up at work.'

'Harry, you know it's Satoki.' The ambassador bowed his head slightly as they shook hands. 'If you keep calling me Your Excellency, I will fear you have forgotten my name.'

Tenaka was of middle height and the flecks of grey in the thick hair framing his boyish face were the only hint of his more than sixty years. He had a storyteller's capacity to make the complexity of the world understandable and Dunkley looked forward to these dinners because he always learned something useful.

After several minutes of chat about family and work, Dunkley asked Tenaka to revisit a story he had told before, from his years as a junior diplomat in Singapore. The journalist wanted to have the history of China's rise clear in his head.

'The Chinese were fascinated by Singapore in the late '80s and early '90s and there were many delegations from Beijing,' Tenaka said. 'Deng Xiaoping was contemplating how to manage the growth of China. In Singapore he saw a state that had everything he wanted: one-party rule; no effective opposition; and, apparently, little corruption. But most important was the social harmony that was ensured because the people were wealthy. And that was the bargain he decided to strike with the Chinese people: "We will make you rich and you will obey us."'

The ambassador had exchanged his champagne for sake and he swallowed a mouthful from a delicate cup.

'So far it has worked, but the Chinese leaders are always wary of their people. They know they are one mistake away from internal unrest. So they need an external enemy to ensure the people focus their anger outwards.'

'And although we focus on the rhetoric aimed at the US or Australia,' Dunkley said, 'Japan is the country China has its major grievance with.'

Tenaka put down his cup.

'We fought two wars in fifty years between 1894 and 1945,' he said. 'In the first we humiliated the Qing Dynasty and became the major power in Asia.'

The ambassador took off his glasses and rubbed his eyes, as if he was recalling a personal, painful memory.

'The second war was from 1937 to 1945. We occupied China and ... many terrible things happen in war. Some in China think the Americans ended the battle too soon and that China's war with Japan is not settled. There is an anti-Japanese museum in Beijing and although we have apologised many, many times for the ... excesses ... it will never be enough for some.'

Dunkley had more than a little sympathy for China's anger. He had been horrified by what he had read about the Japanese occupation.

'Perhaps as many as twenty million Chinese died.' Dunkley knew he was treading on sensitive ground.

Tenaka put his glasses back on and met Dunkley's gaze.

'As I said, war is a terrible thing. More than two million of my people died in the Second World War. More than two hundred thousand died when the two atomic bombs were dropped. But America would argue that they ended a war that would have claimed many more lives. Was what they did right, Harry?'

That was a question Dunkley had contemplated many times: can brutality be justified for a greater good? He had no answer, just more questions.

'So is it just history that's driving this new nationalistic push from Beijing?' he asked.

'No. A large part of it is driven by economic concerns. China's growth is slowing. If the people do not feel the benefits of growth they will see only its costs, like huge damage to the environment and displacement of the population. They will become restless. Then there is the direct competition between our two nations for energy.'

Dunkley had spent enough hours at the Japanese ambassador's table to know that the ill-will between China and Japan wasn't a one-way street. Japan's foreign policy was aimed at getting the US to use its power to box China in and restrain its growth.

'Japan has its own grievances with China, doesn't it, Satoki?'

'Japan is only eight hundred kilometres from China. We can feel it. Its rubbish washes up on our shores; its pollution stains our skies. We have economic problems of our own and our key concern is also energy. Since Fukushima, things have got much worse. We import 75 per cent of our fuel. So we need secure suppliers, like Australia, and we need secure trade routes. Those routes run through the East China Sea. A rapacious China threatens all that. Never forget there are two powers in East Asia, Harry, and they are rivals.'

As usual, Mori had deferred to his boss and remained silent for much of the meal. He finally spoke.

'Things are very bad in the East China Sea, Harry. China is testing us. And we have the views of our own people to consider. We cannot be seen to retreat from Japanese land – it would bring down the government.'

Dunkley didn't doubt it. Tenaka dabbed his mouth with his napkin and pointed to a world globe on the mantelpiece that showed Japan and China facing outwards.

'And, thanks to the internet, the front line in this conflict is the whole world, as you point out in your many fine articles. But to be frank we are very disappointed with the response of your government both to the provocations we have suffered over the Senkakus and the virtual attacks on your own homeland. We wonder if China's wealth is blinding Australia's government to the very real and present dangers.'

Mori lowered his voice. 'The battle in Australia isn't confined to the internet. We were most interested in the pictures you published after the union raid on the new embassy. Do you remember this man?'

He handed over an enlarged version of the picture Dunkley had asked his snapper to take of the be-suited man inside the construction site.

'Yes, I remember him. He clearly wasn't mixing concrete. And he scarpered when I tried to front him.'

'We know him. He is attached to the Communist Party's Commission for Discipline Inspection. It is a secretive internal investigation unit that interrogates and disciplines party members. It operates independently of the police and is known for its brutality. This man is a Communist Party stormtrooper, Harry. His only role is as a torturer and a killer. So why is he here in Canberra?'

Harry looked long and hard at the picture.

'I have no idea.'

Sydney

Sydney's steamy heat engulfed Paul Mahoney as he emerged from the Great Southern Hotel. It was Friday afternoon and the ABC journalist had clocked off for a long lunch, only to be dragged back to the studio by a radio producer demanding that he file for *PM*.

'But I told you, I don't have a story,' he complained.

'And I told you, mate, right now I don't have a show. So get your arse back here and find one.'

'Bastard,' he said, after he was certain she'd hung up.

As he reluctantly entered the *PM* workspace in the first-floor newsroom, his phone rang. It was a number he hadn't seen in the months since he'd left Canberra on the promise of a bright future in TV in Sydney, only to be seconded to radio current affairs.

'Elizabeth Scott, what use do you have for a retired gallery hack?'

'Now Paul, you know you were always one of my favourites and I know you can be discreet,' she purred.

Mahoney knew the tone. He was being courted for a favour.

'Well, I hope you've got a story because I have a deadline that's just an hour away.'

'Oh, I do. But you didn't hear this from me.'

'Sure, what is it?'

'In twenty minutes a video will be posted on YouTube. I'm going to give you a headstart simply by telling you where to look.'

'I'm intrigued.'

'You will be more than intrigued. And, my dear, you'll owe me.'

Mahoney's mood improved immeasurably. And it soared when he saw the surprisingly graphic images of Emily Brooks and that Channel Nine grub Jonathan Robbie.

Oh, to be able to use the pictures …

Once again, he longed to work in the bright lights of television.

Washington

Big Mac wiped the crumbs from his lips and lifted a sheaf of papers. 'Nancy, how do I look?'

'Like a leader going into war, sir.'

Morgan McDonald was preparing for a press conference in the Capitol building and had been rehearsing the script with his press secretary. The Republican House leader was fired up, ready to rumble.

The Tea Party – the group of dissident far-right Republicans that McDonald controlled – was in revolt, and he wasn't about to make life any easier for President Earle Jackson.

He would teach that son of a bitch what it meant to go limp-wristed.

Big Mac led his entourage to the media conference room, a hundred metres from his office. It was nearing 4pm, and the press corps was getting restless, needing to prepare evening bulletins and newspaper articles.

McDonald used to hate the press, particularly the liberal media who'd given Nixon, Reagan and Bush Mk 1 and 2 such a hard time. Obama, by comparison, had been shown easy street even though his damned healthcare package threatened to bankrupt the Stars and Stripes.

In Big Mac's eyes, the *New York Times* was America's *Pravda*.

But he'd learned the importance of forging a good working relationship with the media to ensure his political message was spread as widely as possible.

'Okay … ready, fellas? Today I am here to announce that I am calling on President Jackson to take decisive action to ensure the United States can live within its financial means.

'America is a great world power. Our friends overseas need us now more than ever. But a weakened United States, beholden to the foreign dictates of countries that don't share our values and beliefs, cannot be allowed. That's what being in debt to the world means. As leader of the House Republicans, I will do everything within my power to ensure the US remains a force for good.

'When the president calls for the debt ceiling to be lifted, I appreciate that he believes he is acting to repair the damage inflicted on this country by the Democrats. But we can't do that without getting an assurance that big cuts to government spending are planned.

'I know that the deadline to resolve this, to prevent a government shutdown, is drawing close.

'So tonight I will call the president and offer him a ten-point plan. This has been thrashed out with other right-thinking Republicans. It is a sign of goodwill, that we are willing to compromise.

'But we will not compromise the supremacy of the United States in world affairs. I urge my friend Earle Jackson to reconsider his weak stand on Chinese currency manipulation. If he doesn't, all bets are off.'

Several hours later, President Jackson delivered a foreign policy speech to the right-wing hawks of the American Enterprise Institute. He began with some domestic house-cleaning.

'My friends in Congress are right when they say that we should not live beyond our means. But they are wrong to try and starve this government of funds. I will bring down the deficit, but that can't be done overnight.

'I have taken a call this evening from my ol' friend Big Mac … sorry, the House majority leader, and I have agreed to sit down and discuss his ten-point plan. Right now I pledge myself to this: government will be smaller. As a corresponding sign of goodwill, the House leader has offered to pass the debt-ceiling legislation through Congress tonight.

'As friends do, Big Mac and I have had our disagreements. But there is one thing where we see eye to eye: the United States of America should bow to no one.

'I will be honest and say that there are many voices in my government urging me to back off on my demand that China play by the international road rules. They say that we should accommodate the rising power in the East. But if we let China push us around now, what will the future hold? If I step back, China will step forward and, in the end, we will retreat right across the Pacific.

'So I make another pledge tonight. I will do everything in my power to ensure the best possible relationship with the Chinese leadership. I do believe that we can live together.

'But I will not kowtow to Beijing. Given China has done nothing to increase the value of its currency, I will be putting a plan to Congress to impose tariffs on a range of Chinese goods. It will begin with motor vehicles and television sets, but the longer China refuses to act, the more I will increase the scope of the tariffs.

'And tonight, in a sign of solidarity with our good friends in Japan, I have ordered two unarmed B-52s to fly over the Senkaku Islands. I also reaffirm that Japan is the rightful owner of these islands, now and forever.

'God bless our ally Japan. And God bless America.'

Beijing

Jiang Xiu pulled back from the TV screen and smiled. The Americans were practically doing his job for him.

The minister for propaganda had been urging his comrades to take an even more assertive stance. Some on the Standing Committee were still sceptical and were counselling restraint. But Jiang had been deploying all official channels to ensure his aggressive message was disseminated as widely as possible.

It was working. The *People's Daily* had become almost as strident as the *Global Times*, renowned for its anti-Western tirades. Chinese nationalist spirit was stirring. Anti-US and -Japan sentiment was bubbling nicely.

Online attacks against the US president had already been trending on China's own version of Twitter, Weibo. And now Earle Jackson had made a fatal error.

Jiang could not believe that Jackson had declared Japan the 'rightful owner' of the disputed islands. It was likely that this was a slip of the tongue, because it was not the official position of the United States. But words were missiles in diplomacy and Jiang had already ordered CCTV's general channel to run that grab on a continuous loop. It would be used to whip up public outrage.

Just as astoundingly, Jackson had telegraphed his next move. A worthy general did not do that. Jiang assumed the B-52s would make their pass over the islands at night. That gave him all day to urge his comrades into action.

All of China was watching. After today, all of the world would be watching. He picked up the phone.

'I need to see the president. This morning.'

Three hours later, Jiang entered the Hall of the Purple Light within the Zhongnanhai complex – the real seat of Chinese power.

Here, the past intersected with the future. An official led him into a splendid room of Qing dynasty furnishings. Their beauty papered over a dark stain on Chinese history. It was the last remnant of the Qing who had fought and lost the 1894 Sino–Japanese war, signing the unequal Treaty of Shimonoseki that ceded control of Taiwan to the Japanese. That had led to the annexation of the Diaoyu Islands.

The Middle Kingdom must not allow itself to be pushed around by inferior countries ever again.

Jiang waited patiently as President Meng concluded a meeting with several senior financial advisers.

'Mr President,' he began. 'You have seen for yourself that the United States is determined to stifle our legitimate territorial claim over the Diaoyu Islands. Now they threaten to send war planes into our airspace.

'Nothing we have done comes close to such provocative action. We cannot back down. We cannot display weakness. Our people need to see that our resolve is firm.'

The president clasped his hands. He had trained Jiang well, but the next steps were the most dangerous of all.

'Comrade Jiang, I know that you are anxious to see China rise, as I am. But we must not overreach. We cannot be seen to be the aggressors. Our response must be proportional to the affront.'

Jiang placed two folders on the table.

'Mr President, I have a proposal for you to consider.'

Western Pacific Ocean

Manny Sanchez pushed forward on the throttle and felt the surge of power as eight Pratt & Whitney TF33 engines spat into action.

Four hundred and fifty thousand pounds of aviation muscle lumbered down the runway on the mission signed off by President Jackson just two nights earlier. It was time to demonstrate support for one of the United States' most trusted friends.

It was late February and the easterlies were prevailing over the Pacific island of Guam, one of America's largest non-mainland military bases. Three hours to the north, a small outcrop of rocky islands had become the touchstone in an increasingly fraught political dance.

The US and China were at each other's throats, neither willing to cede ground as the battle between capitalism and communism reached fever pitch for the first time since the demise of the Soviet Union. Several well-credentialled analysts in Washington were suggesting a new Cold War might be developing.

Sanchez was wearing his 'sanitised' flight suit, the one with the badges of his beloved 69th Bomb Squadron hidden away, a precaution against identification if he was shot down. Two and a half years ago, Sanchez had taken a break from flying, responding to his wife's request following the birth of their son, Emanuel Jnr. But his new role of Air Training Exchange Officer had failed to quench his need for high-stakes flying action. He'd sought a return transfer to the 69th within a year.

Now, back in the B-52, he felt for the reassuring grip of his 9 millimetre, and turned to the sky.

It was pushing 2200 hours and the B-52 would climb east out of Andersen Air Force Base before turning north-west. Sanchez felt every crack in the 11,200-foot runway as the BUFF cranked towards 155 knots.

'Tommy. You ready, brother? Black hole ahead.' Sanchez spoke with the larrikin ease of an experienced pilot who lived by the motto: Work Hard, Play Harder. He and his co-pilot, Tom Danville, had flown many times out of Andersen, but those first few moments when the island's visual markers gave way to the black of the Pacific could still be disorienting.

The two pilots were joined in the cramped cockpit by Sam Meserve, the E-Dub. The electronic warfare officer was the butt of many jokes as the crew used humour to alleviate the tension of long flights to dangerous places. Meserve served another useful purpose – he was the in-house cook.

Tonight's mission was scheduled for just under seven hours. Two B-52 bombers would fly, unarmed, to the disputed islands where they would engage in a simulated weapons drop over the largest, Uotsuri Jima. They would then return to Guam, arriving at a scheduled 0500.

Sanchez listened as radio navigator Jim McCowan chatted with the step desk, taking in the latest weather forecast. Fine and light winds. The radio crackled as air-traffic control issued final instructions. 'ICER One Two. Climb and maintain nine block 10,000.'

Sanchez lifted the proud veteran of the skies from the tarmac, muttering a silent prayer as a single bead of sweat tracked down his back.

Huan Tun-jen impatiently paced the bridge of the *Changchun*. The newly minted ship of the People's Liberation Army Navy should have been further out in the East China Sea by now.

But the Luyang Class II Type 052C destroyer, commissioned just a month earlier, had been hampered by problems with its Ukrainian-made gas turbines. The engines should have been propelling the *Changchun* along at nearly 30 knots.

Instead, it was cruising at a modest 22. Huan was battling to contain his frustration. This mission was critical.

Twelve hours earlier, Ding Haichun, the political commissar of the PLAN's East China Sea Fleet, had rung with strict instructions. The *Changchun* would sail from its base at Zhoushan City where mechanics had been working around the clock. The engines should have been fixed. But time had run out and Huan was commander of a vessel whose speed was no better than China's outdated cruisers.

Not that he was anticipating conflict on the ocean itself. This mission would rely on the vessel's Active Phased Array Radar system and its ability to track enemy targets to a distance of 150 kilometres.

Manny Sanchez scanned his instrument panel, the steam gauges that had barely changed since the late '50s. He liked to explain to novices that BUFF, the affectionate name used by B-52 crews, stood for Big Ugly Fat Fucker, laughing at the comic crudity of an airframe that would be ninety-four years old at its scheduled retirement in 2046.

A flip-down computer screen gave him a read-out on their position, the GPS-aided moving map offering a picture of the globe. It also told him the last known positions of Chinese airframes, something he sensed would come in handy.

The FENCE check was perfect. The BUFF was flying at M.84, just over 600 mph. They were at FL28, the legal limit for an airframe that was non-reduced vertical separation minimum (RVSM) certified.

They were two hours out of Guam. Flying conditions were good and Sanchez would shortly declare 'due regard' with Tokyo Centre, allowing the plane to climb to 34,000 feet.

They would maintain contact with Tokyo. Up to a point.

Flying 'due regard' meant that Sanchez and his crew, and the other B-52 flying one mile behind and one thousand feet above, could do whatever was necessary to accomplish the mission.

The lead radar technician on the *Changchun* picked up the first blips of the American planes at 0032. He jotted down their position before relaying the information up the chain of command.

The aircraft were approaching the largest of the Diaoyu Islands and the radar nav had placed them at 25°46′N 123°31′E.

Despite the public declaration by President Jackson, Huan was still mildly surprised by America's blatant disregard for Chinese sovereignty. The *Changchun* was positioned fifty kilometres west of the Diaoyus, now sailing at 19 knots. The commander knew his instructions to the letter.

He checked his watch. In fifteen minutes, he would issue the first warning. Then he would log the position of the two enemy planes with the mainland.

'Sam, I'm looking forward to that chicken.'

Manny Sanchez appreciated good food and he liked to give the E-Dub a lift when he could. Staying positive was good for morale, but he knew the food would have to wait until the B-52 was heading home to Guam.

The two bombers were closing on the Senkaku Islands, their mission running smooth as silk. In a quarter-hour, they would begin the simulated mission over Uotsuri Jima. Thirty minutes of training exercises, then the return to Andersen. The mood was quiet and serious.

They were flying FL34, the thinner air allowing the planes to nudge up to M.88. Sanchez wanted to slow the BUFF in a few minutes, though, once they began their bombing exercises.

Just then, the E-Dub patched in. 'We've got early warning radar, Manny. Chinese.'

Sanchez wasn't surprised and he wasn't fazed.

The BUFF would maintain its position despite China's attempt to knock them off course. He had his orders. They weren't carrying munitions, they were in international airspace – the communists could go to hell.

Huan took the call from the mainland at 0049. The aircraft had ignored the early warning signals, as he'd expected. Such arrogance.

He placed the *Changchun* on a full war footing and waited for further instructions.

Just over 140 miles away, two of China's fourth-generation fighter jets, Shenyang J-11s, raced down the Ningbo runway. It would take them just fourteen minutes to intercept the enemy, to show the Americans that the world's most populous nation would no longer be pushed around by an arrogant imperial power.

'Motherfuckers!' Sanchez couldn't believe the Chinese fighter would make such a reckless move.

The two jets had appeared on the radar eight minutes ago, maintaining a discreet distance on either side of his plane, and out of visual sight. But he had been warned about Chinese aerial cowboys and one of the jets had broken formation to fly across the BUFF's airzone.

It was pure intimidation. Dangerous and irresponsible.

'He's flashing his wings.' Sanchez radioed through to the B-52 accompanying him, barking instructions to abort the training mission.

It was time to apply the speed brake, taking the BUFF over the falls. He dropped power and pushed the yoke forward. He applied the brake and buckled in for the rollercoaster ride that would take them almost into negative Gs. The BUFF would descend four thousand feet in a blink. And then?

Sanchez called back to Andersen. He was pulling out of the mission. He'd fly an oval-shaped race-track for a few minutes, then turn for the safety of home. He wouldn't risk a dogfight with an enemy who was clearly dosed.

'Time to leave. Tommy, let's bring this plane around. Nice and slow.'

Flying thirty thousand feet above the East China Sea, being pursued by a reckless daredevil from the PLA Air Force – that really wasn't in the training manual.

Manny Sanchez briefly closed his eyes, conjuring up an image of a laughing, trusting, loving three-year-old boy. Then, for the first time in a long while, the pilot reached for the cross around his neck and offered a silent prayer to the heavens.

_____

Canberra

Martin Toohey massaged his temples, trying to fend off the stress that was building in this early hour.

Christ! Is this how wars start?

For once, the screaming headline on news.com.au matched the gravity of the story, and Martin Toohey's apprehension grew with every word.

SECONDS FROM WAR: US, CHINA IN MID-AIR STOUSH

China and the United States came within moments of disaster last night in a high-stakes game of brinkmanship over the disputed Senkaku Islands.

Chinese warplanes confronted two unarmed B-52 bombers, a move that military experts said put the two powers one mistake from war.

Pentagon officials claim a 'reckless' act by one of the Chinese fighter planes forced the B-52 pilot to take emergency evasive action to avoid collision.

The prime minister flicked through the daily briefings on his desk. It was 6.20am and the leader's office was pulsing with the energy of forty staff.

In his office next door, George Papadakis looked more worry-worn than usual as he leafed through the same high-level briefings that had been prepared by the Office of National Assessments. They offered ominous warnings that the US–China stand-off could be the flashpoint for a regional confrontation. He bundled up his papers, grabbed his coffee mug and walked the short distance to greet his friend.

'One mistake now and this will go completely pear-shaped,' he said.

Toohey still had his head buried in the briefs. He looked up wearily.

'I gave the Canadian prime minister a call last night before this latest bloody escapade and he thinks Earle Jackson is the most dangerous president in our lifetime. The Tea Party has him by the balls and he's an ugly mix of stubborn and stupid.'

'And the Five Eyes intel is starting to paint a pretty chilling picture of this new Chinese leadership.' Papadakis pointed the PM to a file in his papers marked 'Analysis of the Standing Committee'. 'The president relies heavily on the head of his Propaganda Department, Jiang Xiu. He turns out to be an ultra nationalist.'

Toohey pulled out the brief and read its four pages. 'Gee ... we've managed to bug the leadership's phones.'

250

'Not us specifically, but the Americans have been pretty successful at getting a fix on the president – what he's contemplating and plotting.'

'Question is, where does that leave us? I don't want to get drawn into a pissing competition with the two biggest dicks on the planet.'

'We might not have much choice in this, Martin. The Americans will expect us to roll in behind them.'

'Mate, we can't afford that. We have to try and keep this dispute at arm's length. Just say enough to keep the Yanks happy and not so much that we piss off the Chinese.'

Papadakis rolled his eyes. 'That will take a level of skill that we haven't yet displayed.'

'Well, we'd better get this right. Our future depends on it. We'll keep our position non-committal as long as we possibly can. I intend to nurse this gas-hub deal to the other side of the election. Even if it evaporates the day after it.'

'And if we can't manage that? If conflict breaks out?'

Toohey leapt from his seat with a ferocity that startled Papadakis.

'Then, George, I will be a leader during a national security crisis. I will use fear to make the Australian people think twice before they change government. I'll win this election fair and square … or I'll use every dirty trick in the book. Just like my fucking opponents always do.'

Papadakis was shocked and disturbed. For all his faults, Toohey usually kept his cool. Now even that was breaking down.

A knock on the door interrupted a tense silence. 'Prime Minister, the Greens leader is here for her scheduled 7am meeting.'

Toohey groaned.

'From the absurd to the absolute fucking ridiculous.'

Kiirsty Stanford-Long was in her early thirties, a political vixen who'd schemed her way to the helm of the Senate's balance-of-power party. She was statuesque and shiny and had one of the parliament's sharpest tongues. In another life, Toohey might have found her alluring.

But he despised Stanford-Long's holier-than-thou approach to politics, so typical of her party of wowsers, environmental flat-earthers and do-gooders. Meetings with her always reminded Toohey of Whitlam's barb to the Victorian Left: 'You are pure in the way that eunuchs are pure.'

'Prime Minister.' Stanford-Long offered her hand. 'Thanks for seeing me, I know you have a very busy schedule.'

'Well Kiirsty, nothing is more important to me than the mental justice bill and I hope that we can rely on your support. The numbers will be tight and this is the kind of initiative that this country needs.'

'Martin, I'm delighted by the bill and the Greens have always supported legislation that seeks to improve the lives of Australians. Of course we support it, but I think that we have a historic opportunity here for more sweeping reform.

'As you know, one of the biggest contributing factors to depression is the abuse of alcohol. The Mental Health Commission's latest report was explicit on the link between excessive drinking and the growing number of people seeking help.'

Toohey could feel it coming: a Greens boondoggle that would, no doubt, nail him to the cross of a dog of a policy.

'What do you have in mind?'

'We have a once-in-a-generation chance to take the lead here, as we did with the plain packaging of tobacco.'

Stanford-Long lifted several sheets of paper from her bag.

'We've been working on this in the party room, with the help of the preventative health agency. It's bold. And I'm sure will be popular. Have a look at some of these pictures.'

The prime minister gazed down at what he hoped was a mock shot of a bloodied corpse lying across a car bonnet beneath three words blasted in large, prominent font.

DRINK. DRIVE. DEAD.

Toohey rubbed his brow, his headache building. 'Let me get this right. You want me to plaster every can of beer and every cask of wine in Australia with graphic shots of dead people. So every night when people sit down to relax with a harmless quiet ale they can be reminded that I've ruined one of the few pleasures they have left. That should go down a treat.'

Stanford-Long wore the expression of a pet cat that'd been chastised for bringing a dead rat into the home.

'I'm disappointed, Martin. I thought you'd see the wisdom of this. The bottom line is: we want this as part of the mental health package. Without it, the job is only half done. We are not going to support a bill that locks in failure.'

Toohey's temper was rising. 'That's what you said when you opposed our first emissions trading bill and allowed the global warming sceptics in the opposition to argue that not even the Greens thought it was any good. Because of that we lost a once-in-a-lifetime opportunity to get bipartisan support for action on climate change. That's what I call locking in failure.'

252

The prime minister paused and took a deep breath before continuing.

'Kiirsty, can I remind you that the last brainwave the Greens had – and that we foolishly accepted on the advice of closet activists in the Department of Health – was to ban foods with high salt content.'

Toohey was reliving what was clearly a painful moment.

'The problem was that the salt level was measured by every 100 grams. That saw Vegemite pulled from supermarket shelves. For a bloody month! No one eats 100 fucking grams of Vegemite on their toast! That's half a jar. And remember the tabloid headlines when it was discovered there was a black market in the stuff: "BOOTLEG KIDDIES".'

Toohey was getting red in the face and Papadakis briefly worried that the PM himself was getting too much salt in his diet. But he was just warming up. He stood up and paced the room. Stanford-Long was shocked into silence. For once.

'Then it got out that you and your mates in Health had been exchanging emails about kids' exercise. You proposed and they entertained the idea that we ban all contact sport for under-eighteens.

'And who found out about that? Who got the leak? I'll tell you who. Ray fucking Hadley. He only built his fucking first career on calling fucking football and his second fucking career on fucking me. It was the perfect storm. And the first thing I knew about it was when the shock jock broadcast it.'

Papadakis considered intervening. But Stanford-Long was flint-hard and was not going to be bludgeoned into changing her mind. Toohey could engage in bluster but she had what he needed. The numbers.

When Toohey finished shouting, her response was icy.

'Thanks for the history lesson, but both of those reforms would have succeeded if you hadn't gone to water. And the country would have been better for it. We are not turning on this. I look forward to your considered response.'

Stanford-Long gathered her papers and bag and stormed out. Papadakis turned to a still-fuming Toohey as the door slammed.

'Have I ever told you how much I admire your masterful way with women?'

Canberra

Emily Brooks had achieved what she had always courted. Worldwide fame. The online footage of her cavorting with journalist Jonathan Robbie had gone '*Gangnam Style*' viral.

Snippets of the sex tape had also aired round the clock on Australian TV. The images had been discreetly blurred, but what was left to the imagination only made it worse.

The warning at the end of every introduction was guaranteed to draw a crowd: 'The following story contains graphic sex scenes that might offend some viewers.'

Towards the end of each replay it became apparent, even through the blurred images, that the man wasn't having such a good time.

'Nooooooooooo!'

Online there were no constraints and the images were paraded in their uncut glory. On Twitter #SpankMeEmily had become the top trending Australian topic for the year.

Inevitably, the creative sexual escapades of two mostly consenting adults had been distilled to one predictable phrase: 'Bondage-gate'.

The left-wing blogs were ablaze with anger at the hypocrisy of a leader who made so much of her Christian values. Despite their commitment to advancing women's rights, when it came to Brooks all bets were off. Blog sites were littered with lewd and sexist references to the opposition leader.

Fairfax couldn't get enough of the story and the News Limited tabloids were in overdrive.

But *The Australian* decided to use the issue to launch one of its regular jihads on the ABC. It focused on the public broadcaster's 'ethics' in breaking the story when the media had traditionally avoided peering into politicians' private lives. An *Oz* editorial thundered that the story was driven by 'a blatant left-wing bias that infects the entire organisation'.

Channel Nine was in a position almost as uncomfortable as the one that its manacled reporter had endured. It couldn't ignore the story and yet its Canberra-based attack dog had a starring role. Its news stories focused on Brooks and referred only fleetingly to 'television journalist Jonathan Robbie'. The network put out a statement saying that Robbie was taking extended leave to recover from a lower back injury.

For Seven and Ten, 'Bondage-gate' was proof that, somewhere in the universe, there is a God. They camped outside Robbie's Deakin home and tried to doorstop him whenever his 1971 orange and black VH Valiant Charger pulled into the driveway.

But the real gold was mined when an eagle-eyed ABC crew, Dave McMeekin and Nick Haggarty, spotted Robbie's unmistakeable muscle car at the Deakin shops. Both hated Robbie from long days spent working with the bad-tempered and arrogant reporter in pool crews on overseas trips.

Their camera was waiting as Robbie emerged, decaffeinated soy cappuccino takeaway in hand, from a bustling Cafe D'Lish. McMeekin was shooting, Haggarty was carrying the sound boom and firing off questions.

'Jon, have you got a moment?'

'Piss off you bastards.' Robbie pushed past the camera.

'Mate, can you relive the experience for us …' Haggarty was grinning like a schoolboy.

'I've got nothing to say and you guys are invading my privacy.'

'It's a public place and … hey, why are you limping?'

'I'm a sick man.'

'We know, we saw that online.'

'Leave me alone, I have nothing to say.' Robbie lifted his pace but was clearly labouring. It was a long walk to the Valiant but the two hardened professionals had no trouble keeping pace under the weight of their gear. By the time Robbie was fumbling with the keys at the car door he was breathless and angry and the camera was half a metre from his face.

'Does that kinky stuff hurt?' Haggarty was running out of questions that could run on primetime.

'Fuck off, you vultures!' Robbie screamed as he slammed the door, upending the nancy-boy coffee he'd left on the roof. The V8 roared to life and its tyres squealed as he reversed and the crew retreated. Then, the footage would show, he appeared to veer towards the camera as he took off, laying down more rubber as he straightened at the last moment before extending his arm out the window, offering the middle finger of his right hand in a final defiant salute.

Emily Brooks was also under siege. But she remained tough and calm under pressure, refusing to resign and adamant that her party would have to sack her if it wanted her gone. Together with her press secretary, she devised a plan that might save her political skin. Brooks would make a statement to the parliament. The advantage was that she wouldn't have to face questions from the media. The downside was that she would have to face the scorn of the House of Representatives. And she would be beamed live to the nation, for as soon as she announced that she would seek the House's indulgence to make a personal statement, the networks decided to carry it live.

The chamber and its galleries were full when Brooks strode in with her carefully prepared speech. In the end, she'd decided that the best form of defence was attack. She would cast herself as the victim and only address the tricky question of her bondage session in passing.

Brooks began by theatrically turning on the press gallery, pointing her finger at representatives of each media outlet.

'*J'accuse* you ... and you ... and you ...' Brooks thundered. 'You seek to stand in judgement of me: as judge, jury and executioner. Today I open my own court and you are indicted. You are charged with a criminal invasion of privacy and the gross abuse of your privileged role as journalists. Our democracy has been damaged by your desperation to damage me.'

Brooks put on her glasses and turned to her speech like a QC checking a brief.

'Let's begin with the facts. I am a single woman in a relationship with a single man. We are consenting adults. I have broken no law. What was done occurred in the privacy of my own home. People can make their own judgement about what they have seen. All I ask decent Australians is to consider how they came to see it.'

Brooks's voice was strong and her hands steady as she turned the pages of her speech.

'Someone broke into my home. That is a crime. Someone installed not one but two video cameras in my bedroom. That is a crime. Someone videotaped me without my knowledge and then distributed the images without my consent. All those things are crimes. I ask the Australian people: how would you feel if the same thing happened to you? How would the members of this House feel?'

Brooks's gaze wandered slowly around the chamber, searching out those with interesting private lives.

There was a nervous shuffling. Some MPs who had been riveted by the Schadenfreude of Brooks's discomfort found pieces of paper that, all of a sudden, demanded urgent attention.

'But those crimes pale beside the moral bankruptcy of the media.' Brooks eyeballed the journalists in the gallery just a few metres above her. 'You trafficked these stolen goods and had the gall to demand that I, the victim, be made to stand trial.'

Brooks had memorised the final paragraphs of her speech and addressed the chamber with a confident air.

'But I will not be lectured to about morality by the media or my opponents. I will not. And after today I will not be answering questions about my private life. I have plenty of questions of my own about the media's role in a series of crimes. I have asked the police to investigate. Politics is a hard business and I play it hard. I expect no more and no less than is expected of others.'

It was a bravura performance and a throaty 'Hear, hear' followed Brooks as she gathered her papers and swept out.

After the speech the corridors rang with gossip as MPs of all political persuasions appraised Brooks's performance and her prospects. Even her enemies were impressed by the audacity of a speech aimed at morphing her from villain to victim. There was a grudging admiration, too, at her shifting the attack onto the media, something all politicians and most of the public enjoyed.

But some Coalition MPs told their Labor mates that they thought her leadership was doomed.

'We'll let Brooks take all the hits on opposing the mental health bill and then we'll dump her and have a new leader for the dash to the election,' one Coalition plotter said. 'Say what you like about her, she's tough. Elizabeth Scott would wave the bill through even though we can't afford it.'

For the first time in ages, Martin Toohey and George Papadakis looked forward to the evening news. The PM had ordered snacks and a good bottle of red. They were ready for showtime.

'Hurry up, George; you'll miss the start,' Toohey hollered at 5.58pm.

Papadakis bustled through the door to the opening strains of the Seven News theme. The sting promised extended coverage of 'Bondage-gate'.

Toohey and Papadakis rocked with laughter at the opening. Commercial TV news stories usually ran for ninety seconds, but a staggering three minutes was devoted to Robbie's encounter with the ABC.

'Stick that up your arse!' Toohey yelled at the television and then laughed himself red at his own wit. Wiping tears from his eyes, he turned to Papadakis.

'I've always hated that little shit and, no matter what happens to Brooks, this is the end of him. He'll never be able to set foot in the gallery again. The ABC just paid for itself. Let's give them more money.'

The next story, covering Brooks's speech, wasn't as good. The opposition leader had shown steel and pulled off a great performance in the most difficult of circumstances.

The third was a collection of vox pops, and opinion was split on whether Brooks should go. But everyone agreed Robbie was a grub. 'Like all journalists,' one woman added.

When the fun on Seven ended after ten glorious minutes, Toohey ran through the tapes of Nine and Ten. He switched to SBS live at 6.30. The entertainment only ended after the ABC's *7.30* devoted twenty minutes to the affair, including a side-slapping defence of Brooks by her deputy, the dour National Party leader, Charles Mayfield. The best exchange was, as always with Mayfield, unwitting.

'It's you lot at the ABC that should be ashamed,' Mayfield raged. 'You've been whipping this up into a frenzy.'

'Would you like to rephrase that?' a poker-faced Leigh Sales replied.

7.30's last story examined the reaction of the Christian lobby and it was clear many were struggling to defend Brooks, although the word 'forgiveness' was used a lot. Toohey was sorry when the program finally moved on to other news.

'How do we keep this going?' The prime minister, the usual whipping boy for the nightly news, wanted to drag out the Coalition's pain.

'We could have a few of the more crazy-brave MPs and senators drop some inflammatory remarks,' Papadakis said. 'We'll get the Victorian Right's online stooge to post some really appalling stuff. And there are all those fake Twitter accounts the national secretariat manages.'

Toohey had been schooled in the art of union 'shit sheets' since his early years in Labor and knew the best stuff needed imagination and flair.

'Yes all that. But we need something that will really bite. Call Robbie Swan and get the Sex Party to come out and say it applauds Emily Brooks for making bondage acceptable. And that as a result of her good work he hopes to see the basics of it taught in high school. That kind of third-party endorsement will screw with her base.'

Papadakis frowned at his boss.

'Sometimes you scare me, Martin.'

Toohey wasn't listening.

'And Black Ops, George. We don't want our fingerprints on it.'

Honolulu

Aubrey W Holland bristled with anger. His men, on a peaceful mission in international airspace, had been provocatively shadowed and put in harm's way.

The admiral's fury had been heard all the way to the White House.

From his base in Hawaii, the commander of Pacific Command controlled an area spanning half the world: from the blue waters of the US west coast to the western border of India. From Antarctica to the North Pole.

Within an hour of the B-52s returning to their base in Guam, shaken after their run-in with the Chinese fighter jets, Holland had issued a robust statement.

'The actions of those Chinese pilots were unnecessary, unprofessional and showed a lack of experience,' he'd thundered.

'As a leader I find it impossible to believe that they were not acting under orders. China is growing more aggressive by the day. It now claims most of the South China Sea and is involved in territorial disputes there with Vietnam, India and the Philippines. In the East China Sea it is threatening South Korea and Japan. Most of the world's trade passes through these waters.

'It has the posture of a country that is spoiling for a fight. It is now up to the leaders of all free nations to decide if they are prepared to let China rule the international waterways.'

Holland had personally briefed the president. He liked the steel that Earle Jackson had put back in America's spine. The admiral believed that it was overdue for the US to assert its rights of free passage on the high seas. Jackson agreed.

In a few hours time, the president would hold a press conference. And he wasn't promising words, he was promising action.

Canberra

Harry Dunkley's eyes lingered on the soft turquoise wings sketched on his lover's skin, the pair of butterflies tattooed below the curve of her hip. He mentally did the maths as she lay quietly sleeping: Celia Mathieson was gorgeous, feisty, whip-smart – and twenty-two years his junior.

He wondered what the social media wowsers – the Twitter mullahs who loved to stand in judgement – would make of this liaison.

Well, fuck 'em. This was 2013 and if he wanted to sleep with a 32-year-old then the self-appointed morality police could take a running jump.

Besides, he'd made enough sacrifices as he'd pursued his career. A marriage that had never got out of second gear had broken down; his ex, Belle, had fled the national capital, escaping to Sydney, then Byron. She had never come to grips with his commitment to political reporting, his 'fucking obsession with that fucking paper'.

His relationship with his daughter had also turned fractious. He'd all but ignored Gaby during the difficult final year of her degree, a double arts major. It hadnt't helped that he'd nearly missed her graduation, arriving half an hour late with the academic jamboree in full swing.

He wondered how she would respond to her dad having an affair with a woman a handful of years older than she was. He could hear her reproach in his head.

Disgusting!

Maybe it was better to keep his beautiful sleeping muse a secret. Besides, the only people who counted in this arrangement were the two of them. Celia was perfectly capable of deciding whether to throw herself, butterfly tattoo and all, into this relationship.

She isn't Lolita, for Christ's sake.

He checked his watch: 7.56am. It was a Wednesday and there was plenty to get on with. If only he could drag himself away from Ms Butterfly Wings.

He slipped out of bed and into the kitchen, filling the kettle. He was tuning into *AM* when his mobile rang, and he swiftly answered it before it woke Celia.

'Good morning, Harry.' It was a voice he didn't know.

'Hello. Who is this?'

'Someone who'd like to meet with you. Alone.'

'I usually like to know who I'm meeting.'

'I appreciate that, but I think you'd find our conversation interesting – and useful. I think Ben Gordon would probably appreciate it too.'

The mention of his friend's name triggered a familiar surge of emotion in Dunkley. Remorse. Guilt. Sadness.

Then there was a different feeling as a deft hand teased his lower torso, urging him back to bed. He turned to Celia, putting his index finger to his mouth.

'Okay, Mr Anonymous. Where and when?'

'Hansel and Gretel Cafe in Phillip. I'll meet you there in forty minutes.'

Dunkley felt a soft tug on his arm, a whisper of encouragement.

'Can we make it an hour, please?'

'Certainly, Harry. I'll be wearing a blue and white-checked shirt, glasses, sandy hair. Look forward to meeting you then.'

Dunkley was a few minutes late, and immediately spotted the sandy-haired man with the checked shirt, his head buried in a copy of that day's *Australian*.

The man folded the broadsheet before offering Harry a cautious smile, beckoning the reporter to join him.

'Harry, nice to finally meet you in person. Trevor Harris.' A freckled hand stretched out with a firm grip. 'Coffee?'

'Flat white, thanks.'

As Harris motioned to a waitress, Dunkley struggled to place him in Kimberley's circle of friends.

'Let me make it easy for you, Harry. I was Ben's immediate boss at DSD when he died … was killed. What was it? Eighteen months ago?'

'Kimberley's boss? What's your role at DSD?' Dunkley probed.

'So you called Ben "Kimberley"? I never really got the hang of that.' Harris shook his head with genuine regret before answering Dunkley's question.

'My former role was head of the Scientific and Technical Analysis branch. I spent quite a bit of time there, at DSD. About ten years all up. But I've been out of the agency coming up to six months now.'

There was a hesitancy in Harris that hinted at a larger story.

'Why did you leave?'

'Variety of reasons, a touch too complicated to discuss right now. You know the agency's in the process of being reorganised and will be integrated into the broader intelligence framework?'

'I've heard some stuff about it, although the secret society of spooks isn't really my speciality.'

'Really? I've read several of your recent pieces in *The Australian*. That article about "The Challenge of the Dragon" was quite perceptive, I thought. And well informed.'

Harris was fishing for Dunkley's intelligence sources and that was something he never discussed. He sipped his flat white, smiled and took a moment to soak up the cafe's ambience. He and Belle had been regulars at the company's original outlet in Manuka, introducing Gaby to the pleasure of frothy milk when she was tiny. The memory brought on a pang of nostalgia.

'So why am I really here?'

'Harry, first things first. I don't want to get into trouble; I don't want to breach the Secrets Act. I am most definitely not a whistleblower. But you need to know some things about our dead friend.'

He stole a quick glance around the cafe. No one was close enough to hear them over the background clatter. Still, Harris was taking no chances, and leaned further towards Dunkley.

'You only have part of the story of Ben's death. When I was informed of it, I assigned a colleague to close down his IT profile. It's usually a straightforward task – access the person's files, download any unfinished business to a common user hard drive, provide a report to management. To me. But Ben's profile was stubbornly hard to access. That's when I took over the task. Personally.

'Some interesting stuff came floating out. I found a Gmail address that he'd set up. You recall the email that Ben sent you, the one that referred to "shades of '75"?'

Dunkley looked blank. 'Can't say that I do.'

'Really, Harry? Ben sent you and another of his friends a very similar email – about twenty minutes apart – on Thursday, 15 August 2011.'

'I honestly don't recall receiving any email like that. I get literally hundreds of the buggers each day, but I reckon I'd remember something Kimberley sent me, particularly so close to when it happened. She was killed three days after that.'

Harris seemed to reflect for a moment, then reached into a green shopping bag. He took out an A4 sheet and placed it between them.

'Here it is.'

Harry
Starting to look like shades of '75. We really need to talk.
Call me
Kimberley

'Ben definitely sent it. I found it and made a copy. He meant you to have it and he sent it from a private account, so I'm not breaking any rules by giving it to you.'

Dunkley read the email several times before speaking.

'What does it mean?'

'Well, Harry, maybe it means you've been looking in the wrong direction.'

Canberra

A film of dust confirmed that the box had been undisturbed for a while, dumped in a corner of Harry Dunkley's cluttered garage. He'd all but forgotten this carton filled with bits and pieces recovered from Kimberley's apartment. As the executor of her estate, Dunkley had settled her will and filled the box with the items left to him. None had appeared to be of much value.

Had he, in his absent-minded grief, sought to consign its contents to history? Maybe. Now, eighteen months later, Dunkley had a reason to prise the box open.

Shades of '75? What was that about?

262

He carried the box into his flat and sliced the tape sealing it with a sharp kitchen knife. Celia had brewed a fresh pot of coffee and joined him at the dining table with two mugs. Dunkley worked his way through the top layer of job-related letters and piles of Christmas and birthday cards.

He examined each item in turn and continued digging till he reached the layer of books lining the bottom of the carton. Wedged tightly in a corner was a paperback version of Paul Kelly's *The Dismissal*.

'Kimberley was obsessed with the Whitlam government and hated John Kerr and Malcolm Fraser with a passion,' Dunkley explained to Celia.

'Malcolm Fraser's not so bad; he's the only Liberal I like.'

'Believe me, in 1975, you would have hated him.'

'Waaay before my time, grandad.'

Dunkley tensed at the reminder of the difference in their ages and looked more closely at the well-thumbed book. It had been bookmarked with an old plastic pass card at the opening page of a chapter titled 'The Security Crisis'. Mathieson gently kneaded Dunkley's shoulder as they both leaned forward to read two words scribbled in the page's margin.

Reg Withers.

'Who's that?' she asked.

'Reg Withers? He was the leader of the Senate when the Coalition blocked supply. Fraser's upper house henchman during the crisis in '75.'

Celia opened up her MacBook, keen to find out more.

'Surly-looking type, if you ask me. Harry, pass me that card ...'

Dunkley pushed the plastic bookmark across the table as he began to read the chapter's opening paragraphs. Like most political animals he found the Dismissal intriguing and somewhat unbelievable. But he'd forgotten the questions raised at the time about the role of the CIA in Whitlam's downfall.

'In the days preceding 11 November there were two major upheavals in Australia's system of government. The first was the political and constitutional crisis which covered the newspapers and engulfed the country,' Kelly wrote.

'The second was a security crisis that centred on the United States' communications base at Pine Gap near Alice Springs and the cover of American CIA agents operating in Australia. Only the tip of the security iceberg was ever apparent.'

Dunkley shivered.

'"Shades of '75."'

Then, it hadn't been the Chinese accused of meddling in domestic politics. It was the Americans. And they'd been charged with helping to bring down a democratically elected government.

'Harry?'

Dunkley looked up from the book. Mathieson was turning the card over in her hand.

'This is a crypto card. It's one part of a series of keys that you need to get into a highly secure Cloud archive.'

'A what? Can you speak slowly and in words of one syllable?'

'Sorry old man, I forgot.'

'Okay, that's twice now. You don't need to be nasty, miss.'

'The Cloud is a huge memory bank. Anyone can store documents in it. It means that you don't have to put everything on a hard drive and can access it from anywhere in the world. It's dead simple, Harry. Even you could do it on Google.'

Mathieson chuckled and Harry narrowed his eyes.

'Three times.'

'But this is much more secure. It plugs into the side of the computer and I'm pretty sure it works with Amazon Web Services. But I'll need the other keys – a username and a password – to get into it.'

Mathieson pulled a card reader from her computer bag and plugged it into one of her MacBook's USB ports. Then she pushed in the card and called up the Amazon Web Services page on her browser.

Dunkley was always amazed at the speed with which this digital native could navigate a world he found alien.

A few moments later a page opened with two empty boxes in it. The cursor blinked in the top one.

'Okay, so far so good, but we don't know the username.'

Dunkley pointed at the handwritten words on the page. 'Yes, we do.'

Mathieson typed 'Reg Withers' into the box, and hit the tab. The cursor jumped to the lower rectangle.

'Any idea of the password?'

'Not a clue.'

'Well, you don't get too many chances.'

Dunkley rifled through the book to see if Kimberley had left another handwritten key. There were none.

He turned to the front cover.

'Try "dismissal".'

Mathieson typed in the nine-letter word. 'The password you entered is incorrect' flashed in red.

'Bugger.'

'Next?'

264

'What else could it be?' Dunkley slapped his forehead. '1975? Kerr? Gough? Try "Whitlam".'

Again, the computer flashed 'The password you entered is incorrect', and this time it added 'You have one more attempt before this account is locked'.

'How long will it be locked?' Dunkley looked anxiously at Mathieson.

'I don't know, depends on how secure Kimberley wanted it to be. Could be five minutes. Could be an hour. Could be a day. Could be forever.'

Dunkley looked skyward. 'Jesus wept, Kimberley! You could have given us a few more clues.'

'Well, short of divine intervention, we better make this one work.'

Dunkley tried to put himself in Kimberley's shoes. She knew everything about the Whitlam government and its dramatic fall.

He turned and went back to the computer, staring at the two boxes that stood between them and Kimberley's trove. 'Reg Withers' filled the first. A West Australian tough guy. Loved to throw his weight around. Had a hard-arse nickname …

Dunkley's face lit up.

'Cel, try "Toecutter".'

'You sure?'

'Yes.'

She tapped out the letters carefully.

T-O-E-C-U-T-T-E-R.

The computer whirred for a second. And then the gates opened.

Canberra

The six ceramic panels sparkled in the artificial light. The ode to an ancient landscape now marked by the furrows of agriculture and scarred by industry ran the width of parliament's Mural Hall. It was Martin Toohey's favourite piece of art in this democratic cathedral, and he found it both humbling and inspiring.

'It's called "The Dreaming", isn't it?' A rich American baritone broke his concentration.

'Brent, good to see you. I didn't know that Australian art was your thing. And no, that's a common mistake; it's called "The River".'

The prime minister turned to shake the hand of the US ambassador, noticing at the same time that a small group was gathering on a nearby podium, meaning that he'd soon be required for official duties – the opening of an exhibition of Pacific Rim art.

'Of course, I can see that,' Brent Moreton said. 'And I'm no culture vulture, I'll admit that, Martin. But it pays to fly the flag – particularly when the office of the prime minister requests your presence at the cutting of a ribbon.'

'I didn't know you'd been leaned on to attend this event. Sorry.'

'Don't worry about it,' Moreton said. 'Besides, I wanted a quick chat. About something important.'

'What's on your mind? Presumably not the virtues of Polynesian art.'

'No, Prime Minister.' Moreton stepped closer. 'I wanted you to hear this from me first. The president plans to call you today, at 11am, if that's convenient.' Moreton didn't pause for confirmation.

'The United States is stepping up military plans for the East and South China Seas. We want our allies to back us and, in some cases, share the burden.'

Toohey knew he was about to cop a curve ball from the baseball-loving envoy.

'As part of the US pivot to the Pacific, the president will invite you to forward-base Australian forces on Guam. It would be a tremendous gesture of support for the alliance. It would open a raft of possibilities for joint training and allow a rapid response to natural disasters. We were thinking of a squadron of your Super Hornets which are already inter-operable with our forces there.'

The PM had been blindsided. 'We do that, my friend, and the Chinese will go ballistic. And I use the word deliberately. I have to go now but I can tell you that my initial reaction is a firm no.'

Moreton touched the PM's sleeve, halting his departure. 'You might like to reconsider that, Prime Minister. Because the president will formally announce his plan for a new Pacific partnership at a press conference in the White House. In four hours' time.'

Thirty minutes later, Toohey thundered into his office, calling for his chief of staff. 'George! The United States of god-forsaken America wants us to put planes on Guam to give the Chinese the idea that it's building a coalition of the willing, just in case they get any funny ideas. In a few hours Jackson will publicly invite us to help them with the regional heavy-lifting to bolster the US presence in Guam.'

'Shiiiitttttt! And if we don't?'

'The public declaration is designed to make this an offer we can't refuse. It doesn't pay to piss off the United States. But the Chinese will crucify us. They must know that.'

Toohey closed his eyes. He wore the mantle of national leadership with pride, but at times like these it threatened to overwhelm him.

'The Americans are trying to drag us into war, their war, again.' The prime minister offered his friend a weak smile as he slowly shook his head. 'George, they've got my balls in a vice.'

———————

Canberra

Weng Meihui slipped out of the embassy into the Canberra afternoon glare. She was keen to avoid the stares of the Falun Gong protesters and lowered her head as she turned left towards the lake.

Her hands gripped a bag containing a paperback: Tim Winton's *Cloudstreet*. She'd borrowed the novel from a colleague, Xiu Linjiang, to read on the plane from Beijing, taking his word that it contained 'great insight' into the Australian character.

How she had enjoyed the foray into the lives of two working-class families, desperate and dirt poor, drawn together by their daily effort to survive. It had reminded her of stories her mother told of growing up in the backstreets of Lhasa, the Tibetan capital, following the 1950 'liberation'.

She was returning the book and was keen to see how Xiu had been faring in the month since he'd arrived from the northern winter to work at the new embassy compound, installing communications equipment, he'd told her.

The compound was only four hundred metres from the embassy, but the workers' accommodation was very different to the luxury Weng enjoyed in her suite. They were housed in dongas and makeshift cabins, and kept under virtual house arrest.

Security had been further tightened since the drowning death of Lin An and the invasion by the Australian union thugs. The workers' weekly movie night at the embassy had been cancelled and communications with the homeland curtailed.

'A secure China must come first,' the ambassador had told Weng when she'd voiced concerns about the workers' loss of amenities.

Now she walked up the curved driveway off Alexandrina Drive as a cement-mixer rumbled past. The gates were open and she waved to the security attendant.

'Hello. I am Weng Meihui.' She flashed her official pass and looked around the busy site, taking in the drilling, clinking, hammering and shouting as a dozen workers laboured in the baking sun.

The attendant looked at her suspiciously, as if he was surprised to see a woman, particularly the ambassador's wife.

'Xiu Linjiang. Where will I find him?' Weng asked pleasantly.

'He's not here, madam.'

'Where is he?'

The attendant shuffled nervously. Weng sensed something was amiss.

'Mr ...' She checked his pass. '... Wong. Tell me where Xiu is, please.'

'Madam, I don't know. Please, I am just security on this gate.'

'Where is his room then? I want to return a book.' She took the paperback from her bag and showed it to him.

He pointed to a group of huts about eighty metres away. 'That one at the end,' he finally said. 'Upstairs.'

Weng walked into the compound, ignoring the wolfish stares of three labourers who were shovelling dirt into a long trench.

She arrived at the two-level cabin and climbed the set of external stairs, impatient now to complete her errand. There were two rooms on the upper level, the names of the occupants written in texta on the beige-coloured walls.

Xiu's name was on the furthest room, along with those of his two room-mates: Dong Mao and ... she froze. The third name was unmistakeable. Lin An.

She entered the room. It smelt of antiseptic. There were three bunks and each had been stripped of its sheets.

Weng placed the book on a bedside table and was turning to leave when she stopped. There was a small wardrobe made from flimsy-looking timber against the far wall. She walked over to it and opened the door.

Empty.

'Weng. Why are you here?'

His voice startled her. She turned. Zheng Dong loomed in the doorway.

'That book, Zheng. Xiu lent it to me. Do you know where he is?'

'He is gone.'

'Where?'

'Home, for good.'

'Why?'

'The compound has been compromised. His work has been suspended.'

'And the other one who was here?'

'Same.'

'Did either of them know what happened to Lin An?'

268

'No.'

'How do you know, Zheng?'

'Because I asked them.'

Canberra

Line after line of meaningless code. A jumble of computer-generated hieroglyphics, inverted numerals, symbols and squiggles. None of it made any sense.

Harry Dunkley's eyes ached as he tried to digest the mystifying mess. He was in a maze, with all the fun squeezed out.

'What do you make of this?'

He looked forlornly at Mathieson, hoping that her IT expertise would allow them to crack the next nut. She whistled and was wide-eyed in her appreciation.

'Harry, your friend didn't want to make it easy.'

'Yeah. Kimberley never liked to do things by halves. The question is, can you make sense of it?'

'I can do anything with the right level of persuasion.' She nudged him light-heartedly. 'Seriously, Harry, I don't know. This is a big job and decryption is not my speciality.'

Celia took a sip of Diet Coke. She had a newfound respect for Kimberley, who had been clearly more than just a pretty face.

'This is going to take serious time, Harry, just to get to first base. Obviously she wanted this stuff deep in the ether.'

Canberra

The long table was set just for two. The intimate setting magnified Weng Meihui's sense of isolation. The ambassador had insisted on dressing formally for this full moon dinner in a dark suit and tie, a spit of grease in his hair. Weng had thought about wearing a casual outfit but had reconsidered. The consequences of offending him were too great.

She'd spent weeks in this strange country, trying to adapt to its quirky customs and habits. It was hard, dry, confronting, beautiful. She knew she could learn to love this land of open spaces.

But something she could never enjoy were the dinners alone with her 'husband'. He had demanded they maintain their marital facade, warning her that prying eyes were everywhere.

269

She was practised in the art of small talk, usually able to beguile even the most unreceptive of men. But Tian was her greatest challenge – tedious, narrow-minded, controlling.

Recently a darker edge had invaded their dinners. He desired her, and that made their relationship increasingly awkward.

His first advances had been amusing as he'd fumbled to find the words to entice her to his bed. But his veneer of charm had evaporated when she'd resisted. Privately, he'd become aggressive and occasionally crude. He could remove all pretence of being the dutiful husband in a heartbeat.

Tonight she was also troubled by her visit to the compound. Troubled and frightened.

No one could shed light on the fate of Lin An's room-mates. She'd discreetly sounded out a secretary who made travel arrangements for the workers. 'I know nothing, Madam Weng,' had been the curt reply.

A curtain of silence had fallen. The state was capable of much. She suspected the men had been brutalised, but why?

Had they, too, sought to escape the compound? Were they hiding in this bland city?

'Good evening, Mei.' The ambassador's sudden appearance startled her. He reached for her hand and gently squeezed it.

'Good evening, Qichen. It's nice to see you. How was your day?'

'Productive, my dear. We are making good progress with the trade talks despite some difficulties over Australia's defence ties.'

He motioned to the butler. 'A whisky, neat, and wine for Ms Weng.'

Weng had not planned to drink alcohol, but did not contradict the ambassador. She was after answers. Wine would at least help lubricate the conversation.

'And you, my dear, what have you been doing today?' Tian asked the question with a slight smile.

How much has he been told?

'I had a good day. The plans for the exhibition are progressing well and I had coffee with Miss Lindwall from Britain and Mrs Toffey from Canada. Nice women and, like me, fairly new to this city.'

'That is good. Yes, the diplomatic community likes to look after its own. We are all strangers together.'

Tian contemplated his whisky. 'And you paid a visit to the compound, I hear.'

'Yes. The architecture is very nice.'

'The architecture? I had no idea of your interest in building design.'

270

'It is something I have been intrigued by … for some time …' Weng was stumbling. He was toying with her. She felt herself blushing.

He motioned to the table. 'Shall we?'

Weng took her place, the butler pulling her chair out from the table.

'Thank you.' Her smile masked an inner trembling.

Tian lifted his chopsticks and sampled an appetiser of salmon and rice. He fixed his gaze on Weng.

'Mr Zheng tells me you have an interest in Mr Xiu and his whereabouts.'

'He lent me a book. I was returning it. An Australian book, *Cloudstreet*.' Weng tried to sound calm and conversational.

Tian dragged a thin bone from his mouth, placed it on the side of his plate.

'I sent a cable to the office today about your visit to the compound. The commander will ring tomorrow on the secure phone.'

Where is this heading?

She nodded as she gripped her wine glass. A clatter from the kitchen startled her.

'You know …' Tian considered his words. 'There is the opportunity for us to make something of the next few years, together here in Canberra. The task is to follow the instructions we have been given. I don't recall you being asked to become an inquisitor, my dear.'

She tensed as he leaned towards her.

'I could make life very difficult for you, Mei. Or very good. It is your choice, my beloved wife.'

She had known too many men like Tian. When they couldn't get what they wanted through charm, they used blackmail. Or violence. They deluded themselves that this was power, when their desperation for sex made them weak.

Weng had spent her life gathering loose words from these men and knew her power over them. They swelled with pride after a conquest, like pumped-up peacocks. And they talked.

White light from the full moon washed through the room. Tian lit a cigarette and blew smoke across the bed, smug and pompous.

'My dear, would you care for a drink?'

'Yes, a cognac would be nice.'

Weng smiled at his absurd nakedness as he strutted across the room and poured the drinks. His weak chest, pot belly and reed-thin arms and legs were obscene in the moonlight. The brown liquid jiggled in the glasses as he returned to bed.

She leaned on his arm. 'I was just returning a book, you know. My curiosity got the better of me.'

Tian gazed out the window at the moon. 'It is best not to ask questions about things of which you know little.'

'Of course. I was just concerned.'

Weng knew she was on very dangerous ground. Tian's desire was tinged with contempt and when, inevitably, his lust was sated her life would be expendable. Those who sell their souls have always looked down on those who sell their bodies. She hoped her meek response would invite an answer that his arrogance could not resist.

'Those men failed in their duty. Lin An escaped and threatened the entire operation. An operation vital to our state. Known only to a trusted few.'

Her fingertips traced a line down his face.

'You must be one of the trusted few to be in charge of this very important mission.'

He snorted proudly.

She pushed a bit harder. 'And those men? What happened to them?'

'They are gone.'

'Home?'

'No, just gone. Anyone who fails in this mission will meet the same fate.'

Tian turned to face her.

'That includes you and me. Our leaders were displeased by the attack on the compound. We considered aborting the project but there is no sign our enemies know what we are doing. The rewards will be great.'

'What rewards?'

The ambassador gently ran the back of his hand over her breasts, sweeping upwards. His fingers rested on her neck. And tightened.

'You understand so little. You steal small secrets one at a time from feeble men. My mission is to know everything. That building will be our gateway to the West, to everything that they know. And Mei, we are already in.'

Canberra

It was closing on 7pm. Celia Mathieson had arranged to meet Harry Dunkley in his office and was tingling with excitement.

It had taken her a whole day to untangle just one of the documents in Kimberley's cloud, translating a mountain of IT mumbo-jumbo. There were still dozens of documents to unlock. She had a couple of pages of text and little idea what it meant.

Still, it was exhilarating to be working on a cloak-and-dagger project. She'd dashed off an email to Dunkley and couldn't wait to see his reaction when she unveiled her find.

Eureka! I've cracked the code on Kimberley's cloud! Will bring
up the booty tonight.
See you soon
Cel
PS. What is the Alliance?

The sun was low and the evening chatter of birds was rising as Mathieson walked towards parliament. Both houses were in session and there was a big story brewing about health reform.

A band of exercisers was jogging up a grass-covered slope and a few tourists were still wandering around the forecourt fountain as she crunched across red gravel to the building's front doors. She ignored the main entrance and skipped down a set of stairs on the left. At the bottom she pushed her way through a stainless-steel door to the security station known as Point One. Only pass-holders could enter this checkpoint, the only one staffed 24/7.

Mathieson scratched around for her pass as a bored security attendant watched *Sky*. Her bag and phone passed through the security X-ray. She followed, walking up a set of stairs to a pair of concertina doors that folded back as she approached. Beyond, a passageway opened to a vast tunnel system: a labyrinth of concrete and cables.

Mathieson loved the underground network of roads, one of the building's many secrets. During the day it bustled with a small army of technicians, chefs, labourers and tradies who kept the parliament functioning. But it emptied at night.

It was so easy to get lost down here that there were two lines painted on the floor, marking the way to the nearest lifts. A green line hooked left to the House of Representatives while red ran to the Senate.

Mathieson knew there was a longer path to a lift that emerged outside the News Corp bureau on the second floor. But it wasn't marked and she'd lost her way once before. Tonight she would follow Harry's advice. 'Stick to the red line'.

Her footsteps echoed along a concrete roadway as she passed locked storerooms, pallets of goods, parked electric cars and mysterious passageways.

'Level two,' a mechanical female voice announced when the lift arrived on the second floor.

She walked the long corridor to the News bureau, arriving to find Dunkley under the pump. He barely lifted his gaze, stabbing at the computer, word after word after word.

'Deadline, honey. Sorry.'

Oh great, I bust a gut to get this stuff and he's wrapped up in a ho-hum story.

'Sure, no probs. I can wait. What's the story anyway?'

'Harry, they need it now. Please.' The shrill voice of the bureau's harried chief of staff rang out.

'Harry, don't mean to hassle but can you give me an ETA?' Mathieson asked softly.

'Cel, sorry but I've got to write a comment after I finish the splash. Reckon I'm another hour; forty minutes, at least.'

'Sure.' She touched his arm. 'Could I just have a few minutes to discuss you know what?'

He looked up, a felt-tip pen in his mouth.

'Can't stop right now. I know I told you I'd be done and dusted by 7.30 but Toohey's in deep trouble. His mental health bill is lineball. And they've called an all-nighter.'

He shrugged, hoping Celia would sympathise with his plight.

She wanted to, but didn't. She'd been so excited by her progress with the files and had been dying to share her find with Harry. She felt ridiculously disappointed and suddenly exhausted.

'For fuck's sake, I've spent the best part of today getting this stuff ready for you and you can't even spare me a few minutes!' She threw an envelope on his desk. 'I'll see myself out.'

'Cel ...'

No time for others. Takes me for granted. Christ, I'm sounding like Mum.

She was fuming as she strode out, as angry with herself as with Harry. Close to tears, she was not in the mood to see anyone and headed towards the nearest lift.

'Basement,' the female voice intoned.

Three floors down, she entered the bowels of parliament. A pungent rotting smell was driven by a cold air-conditioning draught.

These were unfamiliar surrounds. She needed to get her bearings. These tunnels must follow the building footprint. So turn right, and walk to a road flanking the western edge. Then down the length of the building and right again, back to Point One.

There was something unsettling about this part of the underworld. Many of the lights had been switched off and pools of darkness loomed over openings in the passageway, to both the right and left.

She paced one hundred metres down the corridor. It closed to nothing.

Bugger you, Harry Dunkley.

She retraced her steps to the lift, and stopped.

Okay, you've done this before. I must hit a road that goes north. Soon.

Her pace quickened along a dim corridor as a mechanical bang bounced off concrete walls. She stopped. The tick of a clock above. It was 7.38pm. She looked around for signs of life. Nothing.

Get a grip, Celia. Anyway, I've got my phone.

She checked. No reception.

Slowly, she started walking again, drifting to the centre of the corridor to avoid the dark alcoves and recesses. 'No Entry' signs flanked her on either side. Above, a tangle of cables and pipes snaked along the ceiling, the arteries of the building.

An intersection loomed. East Terrace.

This is it.

The corridor was curved and dark. She couldn't see the end. Just a green-and-white 'Exit' sign in the distance. The lonely clip of her heels on concrete echoed eerily. She turned at the sound of a vehicle reversing, its mechanical beep amplified in the quiet, but saw nothing.

She turned back. Something was wrong. Two massive fire doors had swung shut, blocking her path. She reached for her phone. It showed 'SOS only'.

A tingle of fear shivered through her.

Taking a deep breath, she pushed hard against the heavy metal barriers, forcing them open. Ahead, black shadows. Had she triggered an alarm? The exit sign was maybe seventy metres away. She had a choice: walk through the gloom or return again to the lift.

The globe above flickered, then darkness engulfed her.

Canberra

George Papadakis had a PhD in economics and knew every nuance of the market economy. A former Treasury boffin, he had a peerless understanding of the complex algorithms of the nation's finances. But when it came to the simple maths of counting parliamentary heads, Dr Papadakis was lost.

That job fell to Alberto 'Burt' Crespo, Leader of the House and one of the best number-crunchers ever produced by Labor.

'Jesus, Burt, there are only one hundred and fifty MPs; why is this so hard?' Papadakis was flustered.

'Well, George, there aren't one hundred and fifty, for a start.' Crespo always carried a pad and was constantly making lists to keep track of the shifting sands of crossbench support. A pen was permanently lodged behind one ear.

'Bailey has been out of the equation for twenty months,' he explained. 'So that's one hundred and forty-nine. And since we bludgeoned the Tories into agreeing to pair her vote, the starting point is one hundred and forty-eight.'

Papadakis was determined to focus: the government's future relied on passing the mental health bills. Negotiations had stalled. In the last few hours Martin Toohey had declared that parliament would sit until the bill was done.

Angry MPs had rescheduled their Thursday night flights home. Debate and procedural manoeuvring were raging in a House that would probably sit all night.

'Okay.' Papadakis took a deep breath. 'One more time from the beginning.'

'We started this term with the Coalition and us locked on seventy-two votes each and there were six swinging votes on the crossbench: one Green and five independents.' Burt looked up from his pad and Papadakis nodded.

'We got the support of the Green and three of the independents to get seventy-six votes and form government. But after that every other vote has been negotiated on a bill-by-bill basis.'

'With you. Go on.' Papadakis knew that was the easy bit.

'But we had to supply a speaker, and he only votes when there is a tie. That's why we got a Coalition MP to rat and sit in the Chair. On any important tie, he always votes with us, but that's rare. On most bills, having him in the chair just strips one vote off them. So after that they had seventy-one to our seventy-two, with seven swinging votes.'

This was where Papadakis usually lost focus. Because behind each of these bland numbers was a long and usually painful story.

The deal to get the speaker was a prime example. They'd been lumped with one of the most unsavoury MPs ever to park his arse on the green leather of the Lower House. Labor's chances of survival rose in parliament, but fell in the electorate.

'George, are you with me?' Burt nagged.

'Yep, yep. Continue.'

'But then we lost Bailey. And the Coalition refused to pair her. For a while things were grim. But she whipped up public opinion and forced the Tories to grant her a pair. So on a good day we have our seventy-one, plus the Green, plus three independents. Which is seventy-five. And they usually get seventy-two when you add the independents who support them and subtract one to cover Bailey.'

'Excellent.'

'But then we lost Paxton to the crossbench.'

Papadakis rubbed his temples. Crespo was on a roll.

'Actually, I think we'll get Bruce. He's a genuine left-winger and thinks mental health is a matter of social justice.'

'That's great.' Papadakis's face brightened slightly.

'The Greens, on the other hand—'

Papadakis interrupted. 'Are extremist jihadists about as ready to compromise as al-Qaeda.'

'Yep, if they don't get plain packaging of alcohol, their MP will vote against the bills.'

Crespo flicked through the pages of his pad and frowned. He was a brilliant parliamentary strategist and had managed to herd the Lower House cats so well that the government's legislative program rarely missed a beat. But this bill was proving harder than most.

'But then there's the bad news.'

'That last bit wasn't the bad news?'

'No. All through that we still had the numbers. Right now, we have seventy-three at best, but so does the Coalition. Support from the crossbench is going to cost us. One of the independents is threatening to abstain and the others are shaky. George, the speaker is wavering. His electorate's up in arms about the deficit and this is a big call on the public purse. And they hate the China deal. A tie means we lose.'

'What about the rest of the crossbench menagerie?'

'Well, George, that's where it gets complicated.'

Canberra

Harry Dunkley had been hammering the keyboard solidly since Question Time, knocking out a splash, an inside lead and a 40-centimetre comment.

He was buggered, famished and in need of a drink. Or three. Most importantly, he owed Celia an apology. Finally, he closed down his PC.

He'd nearly left the bureau when he remembered the envelope Celia had thrown on his desk. He shoved it in his leather bag, reaching for his mobile to call his girlfriend, mentally rehearsing a well-worn apology.

Five rings and a familiar voice. 'Hi. You know the drill. Leave a message for Celia. Bye.'

Bugger.

Dunkley pushed the lift button, eager to escape parliament. As the doors closed, he pulled out the envelope.

'Notes from the Cloud' was written along the top of the first page.

He scanned the opening lines. It was mainly practical stuff, explaining how Celia had decrypted several megabytes of Kimberley's parting gift to the world.

Then a roll call of former mandarins jumped off the page. Leaders of Australia's defence and security establishment, going back decades. The names of several former US ambassadors, too.

All under the one heading.

The Alliance.

Three minutes later he was sitting in his LandCruiser in the Senate carpark. He turned on the interior light to read the rest of the material. His hands told him he needed a scotch.

Celia had done great work and Dunkley was keen to atone for his tardiness.

He started the engine and reached for his phone, hitting the 'redial' button as he drove out into the night.

'Hi. You know the ...'

Celia, don't do this to me. I'm sorry.

He eased into Parliament Drive then turned into Kings Avenue. He was five minutes from her apartment, a nice place on Kingston Foreshore that Daddy had bought. Celia had moved in when she'd returned to Canberra six months ago, ignoring her father's plea to move back home.

She'd given Harry a key to the place a few weeks back, when it appeared their relationship was becoming more than just lustful obsession.

He hit Celia's number again.

'Hi. You know ...'

Dunkley cursed himself.

Hell hath no fury like a woman ...

Except he hadn't scorned her. He'd simply been engrossed in knocking out a strong front-page yarn for the newspaper that had employed and sustained him for the past twenty-something years. He would make it up to her.

Was there a florist open this time of night?

No. And wilted carnations from the servo wouldn't do the trick. An apology on bended knee and praise for her detective work? Besides, they had work to do. Celia had uncovered material that would lead them – where?

The address was Kingston dress circle: Eastlake Parade. Third floor, views over the lake, tastefully furnished, fridge full of decent plonk, comfy bed. What more did a man need?

He opened the door, gently calling her name.

The lights to the apartment were on and the CD player was pumping out some Gen Y nonentity. And the entire place had been royally trashed.

She was curled up on a lounge, pale and scared. Her eyes were red-rimmed and she barely registered when he leaned down to kiss her cheek.

'Celia, what happened? Are you okay?'

Harry Dunkley hated coming to her parents' flash Forrest residence on two counts: her father, Roger, was just a decade older than he was, and Harry had touched up the pompous bureaucrat more than once.

But tonight Dunkley had swallowed his pride. A dozen calls to Celia's mobile had gone unanswered, and he'd arrived at Mathieson Manor just after 10pm.

'A beer, Harry?' Roger Mathieson was trying to be civil for the first time since he'd become aware of Dunkley's relationship with his daughter.

'Thanks … er … Roger. Much appreciated. Have you called the police?'

'Yes, they came and went in a half-hour.'

Dunkley knelt by Celia's side. She looked washed out and had barely said a word. She was trembling.

Her brother sat on a facing lounge, glaring through unfashionably long hair. Clearly, the family was pinning the blame on the journalist for whatever had happened.

Suddenly Celia gave off an exaggerated sigh and sat up. She pointed to a brightly coloured canvas covering most of one wall, an opus by an artist from the Pintupi people.

She whispered, so quietly he nearly missed it, 'He knew about it.'

Finally it was just the two of them. The rest of the Mathieson family had gone to bed, leaving Harry and Celia alone.

She was still subdued, avoiding his gaze. He was hungry for information but unsure how hard to push her. She reached for the safe grip of his hand.

'It was cold, Harry, cold and metallic. He placed it on my throat, not hard, more as a warning. I could barely see. I thought ...'

Her voice trailed off.

'Go on, Cel, tell me what happened.'

'Well, I stupidly took the lift near *The Age*'s office, down to the basement. I was pissed off with you, didn't want to see anyone.'

He stroked her arm encouragingly.

'I'm walking along, trying to get my bearings, thinking I was heading the right way. Then, all of a sudden, the lights went out.'

She shuddered. 'Then he was there. Right beside me in the dark. His voice was so calm and evil, as if he did this for a living. He told me if I screamed again it would be the last sound I made. I believed him.'

Celia reached for a whisky. It seemed to fortify her a little.

'He knew about what I'd been doing, Harry. The Cloud. The download. Everything.'

She was looking straight into his eyes.

'I was petrified. I saw an exit light down the hall, but he was blocking my way – he had a calm fury that scared me to pieces. He came right up to my face and that's when he mentioned the Nungurrayi. Oh Harry, he knew my family ... '

Celia began to quietly sob. 'I'm sorry. He knows too much – about me, us, my dad. I can't go on. Not with this. Not with you.'

Canberra

Emily Brooks dropped her head into her hands and ran her manicured nails through her coiffed hair.

'I hate the fucking National Party.'

She had once said that nothing a politician could do would surprise her, but eighteen months as opposition leader had given the lie to that boast. The astounding news from her press secretary had recalibrated her tragically low expectations of her colleagues.

Justin Greenwich had taken the call moments earlier. 'He's checked himself into hospital, claiming he's suffering nervous exhaustion and won't be able to vote.'

Dallas Bairstow was a New South Wales National Party MP who had spent his tender years as a boarder at Sydney's St Joseph's College. That was two strikes against him before he swung a bat, in Brooks's eyes.

Bairstow had all the afflictions that came with both his creeds. He was an agrarian socialist who was deeply suspicious of markets and foreign investment. He never saw a government dollar that couldn't be spent on subsidies for the bush. And he was a bleeding heart. His only redeeming feature, as far as his leader was concerned, was that his years in a Catholic boarding school had given him a pathological fear of homosexuality so he was vehemently opposed to gay marriage.

'So, Justin, why is he really in hospital?' Brooks made a note to ensure the Trade portfolio was taken from the Nationals, should she ever become prime minister.

'The Nats tell me his electorate has the highest rate of mental illness in Australia and that his people love Toohey's bill. He says he can't vote against it.'

Brooks grabbed her mobile, searched its contacts and punched the number of the Nationals' leader.

'Charles? Emily. Don't talk, just listen. Get your deputy and get a private car. Drive to Canberra Hospital. Find that weasel Bairstow. Bring him back. Then don't let him out of your sight until after the vote.'

Brooks paused as the National leader's protest could be heard through the earpiece of her phone.

'I really don't give a rat's arse how you do it. Just do it.'

She hung up and threw the mobile down in disgust.

'Okay, let's assume all our own numbers hold on this vote. Who else have we got?'

Greenwich stared at his dog-eared notebook and chewed the end of his pen.

'Well, the manager of opposition business assures me that, if pushed, the speaker will use his casting vote with us on this one. But it won't come to that. Counting Bailey's pair, no matter how you cut it, I reckon we come up one vote short.'

Brooks drummed her nails on the desk.

'Pull the pair,' she spat.

Greenwich pleaded with her. 'Boss, we can't. We were crucified in the media the last time we did that. You had to make a grovelling apology. And if the vote is tied, the speaker might still rat on us. So we'd lose twice.'

Brooks shuddered at the memory; she hated having to apologise for anything.

'Justin, let me make this clear. I am not opposing this bill just to make Martin Toohey's life a misery. I'm doing it because the nation can't afford it. Toohey's racking up the national credit card and the payment will fall due when he's well out of politics. What is proposed is far worse than just an attempt by Labor to buy itself another multibillion-dollar indulgence in luvvie heaven. I would oppose the breathtaking stupidity of ceding Australian territory to China even if the billions it raked in were being used to build the landing pad for the second coming of Christ.'

Greenwich added one to his column.

'Well boss, if we do that, and if the speaker holds, we win. But at what cost?'

Canberra

Harry Dunkley played with the volume on the car radio as he gazed out at the dark and glistening waters of Lake Burley Griffin. The night was quiet, but far from relaxing. The songbirds had gone silent; a few night creatures rustled in the bushes.

NewsRadio punctuated the night air. Parliament had descended into full-throttle chaos as the government and opposition traded punches.

'Mr Acting Speaker, the Honourable Member is a grub ...'

'Order! Order!'

It was closing in on midnight and Dunkley, having seen the damage to Celia's apartment, wasn't in a hurry to go home. He needed to make sense of the past few hours, of the violence that had been unleashed. He felt alone, rushing headlong into danger. He needed to put together the pieces of the puzzle. The ones he could see.

Eighteen months earlier he and Kimberley Gordon had been working on a story about Bruce Paxton. Dunkley had been following leads that pointed to the Chinese. Kimberley had apparently uncovered another strand. Then she was killed.

Now Celia had been threatened after she'd unlocked some of Kimberley's secrets.

This was a story people were willing to kill for.

He needed to delve deeper into this murderous affair. He owed it to Kimberley, to Celia.

He also needed help. He checked the time. It was late, but the fearful never sleep.

He fumbled for his phone, scrolled through his contacts, and punched on a recent addition.

It was an unpretentious apartment on the edge of the Yarralumla shops. Trevor Harris had been forced to downsize when his marriage collapsed. It was still lawyers at ten paces, but she'd kept the house and he'd taken refuge in this man cave.

It was spacious and messy: a trio of surfboards in baggy covers leaned against a wall while some serious-looking hiking equipment was heaped in a corner. Two leather lounges fronted each other, and a coffee table was layered in magazines – *Men's Health, GQ, Esquire, FHM*.

Harris explained that his oldest son was using the apartment as part home, part storage shed. 'I've told him to come and go as he pleases, which he does.'

Dunkley nodded. He only wished Gaby would visit occasionally.

Dunkley had arrived ten minutes earlier, feeling self-conscious. Harris was hardly a best mate.

'Sorry to barge in at this time of night.'

'That's okay. I don't sleep that well and, anyway, I'm running behind on a consultancy job.'

'Look, I appreciated our little chat the other day. In truth, I'm not sure where to go with this, Trev. But before we go any further, can I ask why you contacted me?'

'I thought long and hard before I did. I didn't know how much I could trust you.'

'Yeah, I felt the same way.'

'Well Harry, maybe it's time we both took a risk.'

Dunkley leaned forward and clinked his glass of red against Trevor's tumbler.

'Cheers to that, mate.'

'I don't think you appreciate how this game works, Harry. I worked for the signals directorate. We scoop up information from everyone. We work with similar agencies around the globe. Mate, we have bugged the planet. If we get interested in you, you have to assume that every move you make is being logged. Your mobile phone is a tracking device. We can turn it into a listening device. Every time you send an email, use an ATM, splash out on a credit card or surf the net for porn, we know.

'Harry, everyone marvels at what technology can do. They think it liberates them. But we've become slaves and chained ourselves to Big Brother.'

Dunkley thought of conversations he'd had with sources. How many had been monitored?

'Trev, you're making me nervous.'

'You should be nervous.'

Dunkley needed to reassure himself, to delve into Harris's past.

'So why did you leave DSD?'

'As politicians say, mate, that is a very good question.'

'Do you have a good answer?' Harris put his glass down. He thumped the arm of the couch.

'I was Ben's boss. He had access to some of the most highly classified material in the country. The means to tap into phones and computers. Usually if someone in that position dies in suspicious circumstances the intelligence community is all over it. That didn't happen.'

'Are you saying it was a cover-up?'

'I'm saying they didn't even do the basics. They didn't ask the usual questions. There was no inquiry. I kept pushing for one and was told the intelligence community was satisfied with the police report. It was made very clear to me that I should let it drop.'

'But you couldn't?'

'No. And in my own time, and in my own way, I began to look more closely at what Ben had been doing. He had been accessing deeply sensitive material on our system and was covering his tracks along the way. And he was very good at it.'

Dunkley smiled. 'Kimberley always bragged that she was one of the best in the business.'

'Almost as good as me, mate.'

'So what did you find?'

'I found myself on the dole queue. I was made redundant, with no explanation.' Harris paused. 'So what have you got?'

Dunkley pulled out the plastic crypto card.

'I've got this.'

Harris's pair of iMacs purred into life. One screen opened on a file of encrypted documents.

Harris smiled in professional appreciation. 'I trained Ben well. He put some serious effort into making this a hard nut to crack. I'm sure I can open them, but that's going to take some time. Let's have a look at what your girlfriend discovered.'

The two read in silence. It was quite a tale.

It was the late '60s, the height of the Cold War. Vietnam was escalating and Whitlam was making inroads into the national consciousness as a would-be prime minister.

A small cabal of Canberra mandarins was fretting at the prospect of Gough winning the 1969 election. So they took out insurance and formed the Alliance – its name a salute to the security pact that was their sacred text – and began to meet regularly with the serving American ambassador.

Names that had long vanished from the public gaze came tumbling out of Celia's summary: heads of Foreign Affairs, top-line spooks, Defence highflyers, prominent ambassadors.

'Wow, quite a line-up, Harry. They would have sunk some dollars into the Commonwealth Club.'

'Sounds like a cult, dreaming up coups over G-and-Ts, all very cloak and dagger. But how does it link to the present?'

'That, my friend, is another very good question.'

Canberra

The first hint of dawn crept into the House of Representatives, a scene of parliamentary chaos.

For fourteen brutal hours the Toohey government and the Brooks opposition had fought a war of attrition over the mental health reforms. The chamber, where the nation's laws were debated and written, may as well have been washed in blood. MPs were tired, emotional and impatient to escape the capital. A roster of speakers had struggled to keep order amid the pandemonium.

The previous afternoon, a successful ploy by the government's manager of business, Burt Crespo, to suspend standing orders had forced the MPs to stay. The Labor warhorse had delivered an impassioned speech, declaring, 'no one in this place should sleep soundly in their beds until this nation lives up to its duty of giving justice to the mentally ill'. But while Crespo had the numbers and the guile to ensure the House kept sitting, he didn't yet have sufficient backing for the legislation.

Labor had pulled every procedural trick in the book and filibustered the debate to keep the chamber running. Behind the scenes, the prime minister and his team fought to cobble together an alliance that would deliver victory. The manager of opposition business was counter-punching, trying to terminate proceedings as Emily Brooks schemed to kill the final vote.

285

Frantic whips from both parties had struggled to keep their unruly teams in check. Dallas Bairstow had been dragged back from hospital and was under house arrest in his office, with a Liberal and a National MP assigned to escort him to and from the bathroom. Every Labor MP had been instructed to stay awake and within an easy four-minute walk of the chamber, as failing to make a division before the doors were locked could spell disaster. Unfortunately it was difficult to stop exhausted and homesick MPs drinking, and some of the small-hour speeches had been train wrecks.

Around 4am there'd been a near disaster when the bells rang for a division and an eagle-eyed whip told Crespo that one of his charges was missing.

'Who?'

'Xavier Quinn.'

Crespo rolled his eyes. 'Of course.'

There were no prizes for guessing what the over-sexed education minister was up to, but the question was where? He should be able to hear the bells from anywhere in the building. Except …

'The Meditation Room!' Crespo yelled, unnerving nearby MPs as he sprinted from the chamber.

Crespo had been a useful rugby league centre in his youth and he hit full pace as he dashed along the glass-walled corridor that led to the marble-floored Members' Hall. He fixed his eyes on the call buttons of a little-used lift.

He hit 'UP' like an Olympic swimmer ending a race as he counted down the moments he had left to capture the errant minister and drag him back before they were both stranded on the wrong side of locked doors.

Elephant 200, elephant 199 …

Once inside, he pressed the 'M' button and moments later a soothing recorded female voice intoned 'Mezzanine'. The next female voice he heard didn't sound so relaxed.

'Yes! Yes! Xavy … ohhh!'

Crespo recognised the voice as belonging to Quinn's twenty-something press secretary, the latest in a long line. Happily they were so overcome with lust that they were disporting themselves within reach of the lift doors. Equally conveniently, the position they had assumed made it relatively easy to disentangle the MP.

'Hey! What the … I'm busy!'

It must have been the adrenalin. Somehow Crespo managed to manhandle Quinn into the lift before the doors closed, leaving a startled and semi-dressed press secretary in their wake.

'By my count you have eight seconds to get that thing back in your pants,' Crespo wheezed as he leaned on the elevator handrail for a breather. 'And when those doors open, you keep pace.'

'Ground floor,' the mechanical voice rang.

'Run, fuckwit!'

Crespo had hold of the libidinous minister's jacket as the two hurtled across the marble hall, Quinn trying to haul up his fly without inflicting permanent damage.

'Arrgghh!' Quinn stumbled as their footsteps echoed in the glass-walled corridor just metres from the doors. Crespo yanked on his lapel and the MP managed to keep his footing.

The two men collapsed into the chamber just as the sands on the four-minute hourglass ran out. The bells fell silent. The speaker intoned: 'Lock the doors.'

In the prime minister's office, the night was proving as expensive as it was long. The smell of a desperate government was like the scent of blood for a shark to a crossbench MP. And, like all commodities, the cost of a vote rose with the level of demand.

George Papadakis was charged with keeping a running tally of the promises as five of the seven crossbench MPs cycled in and out. At 5.30am he, Martin Toohey and Crespo took stock. The prime minister had handled the negotiations and was exhausted but pleased with himself.

'I think we're just about there, aren't we, Burt?'

Crespo had checked and rechecked the undertakings as the numbers shifted through the night. He nodded.

'Right now, if everyone holds we have seventy-four votes to their seventy-three. So there will be no reason for the speaker to have to use his casting vote. But if anything changes, if anyone goes missing and there's a tie, then he assures me he'll vote the bill down.'

Toohey turned to Papadakis who was nervously shuffling a pile of notes and looking every one of his fifty-six years.

'Didn't we even try to get him, George?'

'PM, as I said, I went round to his office and personally invited him to chat with you. He made some joke about not wanting to be swayed by your charms and repeated that his electorate would rebel if he supported the bill. Almost nothing would sway him.'

'Almost. You're holding out on me, aren't you?'

'It was absurd; I'm sure he was joking.'

'What did he want?'

'Ambassador to the Holy See.'

'And we can't do that?'

'Not if you want to retain a shred of dignity. But after tonight I'm sure dignity is also on sale.'

Stung, Toohey changed the subject.

'And what did Paxton want?'

'Nothing.'

'Nothing?'

'Yep. I visited his office at about 2am. He said he was voting with us because he believed in the bill and would I mind pissing off because he'd found a replay of the drawn VFL Grand Final in 1977. He said it was his favourite game for two reasons: the drama of the draw and knowing that Collingwood would lose a week later.'

'So what's the damage?

'After the Tasmanian left ten minutes ago with his pockets stuffed full of cash, the bill for this little exercise topped one billion dollars over four years, Martin.'

Papadakis didn't hide his distaste for the vote auction. He knew Toohey also felt sullied. The prime minister gulped a mouthful of water and wearily put the glass down.

'It's a small price, George; we're making history here. Think of the legacy.'

'I will. But I'm also thinking about the bill I will leave my grandchildren.'

The prime minister went fishing for a compliment.

'But George, the great negotiator sealed the deal again.'

'Martin, you can win over anyone when you give them everything they want.'

The government called on the vote at 7.22am and 147 exhausted MPs and a weary speaker trudged into the chamber. The public galleries were packed with people who had come from across Australia to cheer the landmark reform. Several activists were ejected when they called out 'Shame on you, Emily Brooks' as the opposition leader entered.

Toohey looked across the table that separated him from Brooks, caught her eye and glanced towards the speaker. They rose and walked into the small space behind his chair, out of range of prying cameras.

'Emily, trust you had a good night.'

'And you, Martin.'

'We have the numbers.'

'It looks that way.'

'You should back this bill, Emily. This is a historic reform that would really benefit from bipartisan support.'

'It's billions we don't have and I will never support it.'

'As you wish. But this will be popular and I will make you wear your opposition like a crown of thorns.'

'Do your worst. Oh, and Martin, if this vote goes down I will count it as a want of confidence in your government and begin calling for an immediate election.'

Before he could answer, she turned and walked over to the manager of opposition business who was standing nearby. Something was up. As Toohey returned to his seat he heard the speaker's call on the Third Reading vote.

'All those in favour say "Aye".'

Labor roared 'Aye' in unison.

'Those opposed say "No".'

The Coalition benches rang with 'No'.

'I think the ayes have it.'

'The noes have it,' called a group of Liberal frontbenchers.

'The House will divide. Ring the bells for four minutes.'

The clerk turned over the first of the three hourglasses that sat between the dispatch boxes on the table separating government and opposition. The prime minister was transfixed by Brooks, just metres away. He knew how hard she had fought to stop this bill and yet she was laughing with some of her frontbench colleagues. He motioned to Crespo, who was a handful of paces away, talking to the whips.

'Burt, do we still have the numbers?'

'Yes, just. By one. Seventy-four to seventy-three. Why?'

'Something's up. Brooks is too relaxed and was making threats about what she'll do if we lose.'

'There's no way. With Bailey out and her vote paired, seventy-four wins it.'

'Burt. That's it! Who's Bailey's pair?'

'Melanie Alexander.'

'Is she in the chamber?'

Crespo hoisted himself onto the green leather frontbench and searched the faces of the opposition. Then he saw her, tucked away in the National Party end of the chamber known as 'Cockies Corner'. With the pair withdrawn, the vote would be tied, and the speaker's casting vote would see the bill defeated. The Liberal MP's unexpected presence in the House had doomed Toohey's landmark reform.

Crespo jumped down and caught the eye of the manager of opposition business, then hissed in a stage whisper, 'You rat.'

Toohey grabbed his arm. 'Stop the vote.'

'I can't. The division's started.'

'But they've broken the rules.'

'There are no rules. It's a convention, a matter of honour. And they have none.'

Brooks smirked. Toohey's shoulders sank and he slumped forward on the table. He turned his head to the hourglass and could see his dreams running out with the sand. In less than a minute, his treasured bill, and Labor's last hope of redemption, would be lost.

It was the change in the chamber chatter that made him look up. The gossip of the MPs began to wind down and heads were turning towards the rear doors that led to the Members' Hall.

There, framed in the light, was the silhouette of a wheelchair. Toohey wondered if it was a protester. Then there was a gasp of recognition from one of the Labor MPs near the door.

'Catriona Bailey!'

The chatter faded to astonished silence as the foreign minister's electric wheelchair glided across the threshold as the hourglass ran empty.

'Lock the doors,' boomed the speaker.

The public galleries exploded in applause and cheers echoed ever louder despite the speaker's protest.

The messiah had risen.

Canberra

It was a dangerous and symbolic location. But there were no safe places now. Her every movement was being monitored.

So she had chosen Nara Peace Park deliberately, ignoring his pleas for somewhere more secluded.

The park edged down to the lake. It was a short distance from the Chinese embassy with its secretive sister compound taking shape behind razor wire. Weng Meihui had ventured several times to this lush square since arriving in Canberra, marvelling at the grace of its pagodas and sculptures.

Japan's Nara had forged a sister-city relationship with the Australian capital two decades earlier and presented this small themed garden as a gift to the people of Canberra. The garden's two huge stone lanterns symbolised the robust relationship between Australia and one of its largest trading partners – which also happened to be China's historic enemy.

Paxton arrived late, surveying the garden suspiciously. He pulled back quickly once they'd briefly embraced.

'Relax, my darling,' Weng whispered in his ear. 'Of course they are watching. They expect us to meet. I want to make it easy for them to see but not hear us.'

She led him to a gazebo where they sat on a timber bench. To the unsuspecting, they were a normal, loving couple stealing a moment.

Weng nestled her head on Paxton's shoulder, dropping her voice. 'I'm scared, Bruce. The ambassador is suspicious of me. He caught me asking questions about two men.'

She sighed. Paxton lifted her gaze to his.

'What did you want to know about these two men?'

'They were room-mates of Lin An, the man who drowned in the lake. They are both dead.'

'How do you know this, Mei?'

'He told me, the ambassador. He was warning me. I don't know all the details.' Weng straightened and pushed away. She looked careworn. 'Lin tried to defect and died in his escape. Nothing was handed back when we retrieved the body. But he was one of our best cyber-minds and he could have placed a lot of information somewhere. And knowing the man who questioned Lin's roommates, I assume they died at his hands.'

Paxton gazed out at the surrounding parklands: Canberra at its orderly best. Mothers strolled with their children across manicured lawns. On the lake, several yachts tried to catch a few wisps of breeze.

And in the midst of this, just a few hundred metres away, two men had been murdered.

He shivered.

'Do you think he might hurt you?'

'Yes Bruce, I know he will.'

Paxton drew her close again as he absorbed the horrifying news.

'We could call in the police, or I could make an official complaint through Foreign Affairs.'

'Your government will not take the risk of offending mine. If there is a controversy the state will drag me back. And if I'm sent home I have no future.'

He looked at her tenderly. 'Perhaps you should consider defecting.'

'Where could I go, Bruce?'

'Look, I'm no great friend of the Yanks. But I'll give them this. They don't have any problem standing up to China. I know their defence attaché well. We could get you out of the country. Soon. Mei, you would be a coup for them.'

She started to sob quietly. He held her tight, ignoring a couple walking past the gazebo just a few metres away.

They would make plans for her escape. Maybe he would join her, later. The risk would be great, but the risk of doing nothing was far greater.

Melbourne

Saffron Burgess and James Saville sat a few metres apart in front of a bank of computer screens flashing lines of technical data.

They were two of Vodafone's leading security boffins, paid to monitor the beating heart of the telco's vast mobile network. Each day, they and their team monitored the cellular base stations and network for hiccups, ensuring that customers got their money's worth.

The last two years had been the toughest in memory, a series of network crashes earning the ire of customers and management alike. Saville and Burgess knew the real reason behind the outages – a failure to invest by the Scrooge-like board of the British telco.

But that didn't stop the executive team giving them a kick up the backside every time they went to red.

'Have you been to that new laneway bar, Jimmy? The something Institute?'

'C'mon Saffy, those places are for you young types. Besides, Anna and I try to walk every night around the bay. Clears the head after—'

Saville pulled up quickly. 'Uh oh, we've got orange in the west.'

He traced his finger along a row of data to a pulsing circle that had suddenly changed colour: green to orange. That meant an overload of data traffic on one of the gateways.

And that meant customer access to the internet on mobile phones would be cut off.

'We got a position on this yet?' Saville asked his offsider.

'No. I'm trying to locate it right now. Looks like it's on the coast, just south of the CBD.'

Saville punched a series of buttons, trying to get an accurate picture of the network traffic levels. Something was amiss. A swift response was crucial if they wanted to avoid further outages.

'Mandurah, Jimmy.' Burgess spat out the name.

'Jesus, I thought we'd spent decent money upgrading those gateways down to Margaret River. Okay, let's divert some of this traffic to Rockingham.'

Garden Island, WA

As the first strains of 'The Star-Spangled Banner' rang out, Aubrey W Holland raised his right hand to his breast, eyes trained on the unfurled beauty of the American flag.

The four-star admiral had been appointed commander of the US Pacific Command just under a year ago. This was his first official visit to HMAS *Stirling*, the Australian navy's main base on the west coast.

It was just after 11am and an early sea breeze was softening a blazing summer's day. Holland had arrived in Perth the previous evening, and had several days of meetings lined up, primarily to discuss a series of joint naval exercises. He was also hoping to catch up with several old naval buddies, including an Aussie mate he'd met during his first tour of duty to Vietnam in '72.

It reminded him of San Diego, this naval base – the sparkling waters and friendly personnel. A small flotilla of vessels was moored at the dock, undergoing routine maintenance while their crews enjoyed several days of shore leave.

'Admiral, this way, sir.' He was guided up the gangplank of HMAS *Perth*, the youngest of the navy's fleet of ANZAC frigates, commissioned just seven years ago.

It was impressive, a descendant of the warship sunk by the Japanese during the Battle of Sunda Strait at the height of the Second World War.

Holland was ushered into a plush boardroom lined with photos of the ship and its crew. A waiter poured coffee as the admiral waved away a plate of pastries.

Michele Miller bounded into the room, flanked by an aide. She'd made history when appointed to command the warship in 2007, the first female sailor to do so. Holland considered her an impressive addition to Australia's naval elite, although her absence at his official welcome had been a tad mysterious.

'Nice to see you, Commander.'

'And you too, Admiral. You look well, sir. Sorry I missed the anthems. For some reason, Vodafone has decided to shut down our internet coverage. Again.'

Melbourne

Saffron Burgess straightened, trying to untangle the knot of her muscles. The pressure was building.

A small network hiccup had grown into a more serious problem. She and James Saville had tried to isolate the outage, but it had spread. Orange lights were flashing across her screen and Saville was increasingly frustrated at the time it was taking to put in place back-up systems.

Mobile internet connection was out of action from Fremantle to Augusta, hundreds of kilometres away. Vodafone's customer service lines were being overrun by scores of irate punters unable to access Google or Facebook.

More disturbing was the inexplicable claim that some punters couldn't make phone calls.

The data and voice systems were strictly separated. Voice was carried through radio waves, and data through internet IP.

Vodafone's diagnostic systems showed that the voice lines were fine.

Something didn't add up.

It was a PR nightmare and the operations centre was being harassed by management to get things right, pronto.

'We can't divert all this traffic to Perth. It will overload the network,' Burgess said.

Saville studied the network plan, the series of orange lights flickering their warnings.

'Have we got a fix on the problem here?'

'Not yet, boss,' Burgess fired back.

A team of technicians had already been scrambled across the south-west of Western Australia, but the remoteness and huge distances meant it would be hours before all the problems were diagnosed.

'Another one down, boss.' Burgess delivered the bad news without a glimmer of emotion.

'Shit, where this time?' Saville asked.

'Down at Albany, bottom of the state.'

'Right, so we've got problems from Freo right along the coast, and inland hundreds of kilometres.'

Burgess looked up from her screen. 'And it's about to get a whole lot worse.'

'Why?'

''Cause we've just gone to red.'

Patrick Fitzgerald's patrician voice boomed out of the speaker-phone. Since arriving from Britain two years earlier, the Vodafone CEO had spent endless hours defending the company's reputation.

'A new era of network investment and improvement' had been his mantra against claims the company was the telco equivalent of the Leyland P76.

But this was his greatest challenge. Vodafone's network in the west was collapsing and his technical crew had failed to isolate the problem.

Twitter was in overdrive – #notfunnyvodafone was starting to trend. The company was fielding media calls from local radio stations, while irate customers were flooding its Customer Care hotline.

The CEO was in a black mood. He'd ordered an emergency meeting of the crisis incident response team. They were scattered around Australia, patched in via conference-call technology.

'James, what's the latest?'

'It's not good news, Mr Fitzgerald. The IP network in the west is seizing up. We're scrambling to divert traffic, but the network is showing signs of system overload.'

'Have you got a fix on the source of the problem, James?'

'We're working on that, Mr Fitzgerald. I hope to have an answer within a few hours. But there seems to be a problem with our control-plane diagnostics. The read-outs don't match the calls we're getting.'

The CEO rubbed his eyes and sighed. Loudly.

'Not good enough, James. I want a report in half an hour. The problem must be solved. Network outage means bad publicity means loss of customers and revenue. Fix it. Now!'

Saville was livid. He'd been flat chat for the last four hours on this crisis and his CEO was treating him like an intern. It was always the same with the Brits. They sent out favoured sons who thought they'd lord it over you, only to find that running a mobile network in Australia was much tougher than it seemed from a distance of seventeen thousand kilometres.

'Saffy, you got the latest read-out for me, please?'

Saville was determined not to lose his cool with his team. They had managed to stabilise the number of outages, but he was worried about a report just handed to him by a network analyst.

'Vodafone network hit with 1.5Gbps D-DOS. UDP-based attack. Some form of botnet used, originating from India via Russia.'

Christ!

That alone meant Vodafone was in deep, deep trouble. He'd never experienced a botnet attack but, like most tech-heads, had read the literature. He knew how easy it was to buy a swag of infected computers and train them on a target.

The victim, this time, was Australia's third largest mobile phone network.

That kind of attack would explain the loss of data, but not of voice connections. Something else was wrong on the system's internal control plane. The adversary had got behind the firewalls.

'Jimmy, line 4 for you.'

He picked up the phone. It was the head of PR, calling from Sydney.

'Hi Jim, got a minute? We're in deep do-do. Channel Nine's called. They're going to air with a story on us. They reckon we've been hacked into ... by the Chinese.'

Canberra

Martin Toohey swept into the secure Cabinet Situation Room, a phalanx of advisers in tow. He was supposed to be entertaining a group of schoolchildren as a favour for an old Labor mate. Instead, he'd summoned the National Security Committee following Nine's 6pm bombshell. He was furious. Vodafone had made no effort to warn the government and he'd instructed his minister for communications to put a bomb up Patrick Fitzgerald.

The other television networks had swung into overdrive, attempting to play catch-up on a massive story that had serious implications – for Australia, for the Toohey government, for relations with China.

The prime minister had adopted a cautious approach to these cyber-attacks – until now. The court of public opinion was turning swiftly against the Chinese and the PM knew that he would be collateral damage if he didn't take firm and decisive action.

As he took his usual seat, he glanced around the room at his National Security Committee team. Every face was bleak.

'Right, what have we got?'

The attorney-general was on a video-link from Melbourne.

'Prime Minister, Vodafone has confirmed that it was the target of a highly sophisticated D-DOS attack. That's "distributed denial of service". This one was lethal. Usually when the network overloads, they shift traffic between gateways. Each time the technicians tried that, the point of attack shifted. No one in the company has ever seen anything like this before. But there was another, more disturbing, aspect to this.'

'What's that, Danny?'

'The attack should have only brought down data. This one also cut off voice.'

'Can they explain that?' Toohey asked.

'They think their control plane – that's the highly protected management system that runs the whole show – was infected by malware. An email opened by the CEO several weeks ago spread a virus. The D-DOS attack triggered it. Their systems were spitting out incorrect readings. Every move they made only exacerbated the emergency. Eventually they shut themselves down.'

Toohey demanded answers from the room. 'How many Vodafone customers are there in Australia?'

He was met with stony silence.

The PM turned to his chief of staff. 'George, how many are there?'

'Too many, Prime Minister – and most of them vote.'

The PM exhaled. The fallout would be devastating.

'Danny, are they back online yet?'

'Yes, they're limping back to full capacity, and the damage is restricted to the Vodafone network.'

Toohey corrected his attorney-general. 'No, Danny. The most popular television network in the country has linked this attack to our largest trading partner. Every other media outlet is following. The damage is much greater.'

Toohey turned to the defence minister. 'Brendan, has the signals directorate any clear idea who was behind this?'

Brendan Ryan picked up a briefing note he'd been handed moments earlier.

'We're still analysing it. DSD has no doubt that the last two cyber-attacks, on air-traffic control and the banking system, originated in China. But I note that the Vodafone attack originated close to the naval base at Stirling. And it happened just as it was welcoming the US Pacific commander.'

Toohey looked at the leaders of his national security agencies.

'Gentlemen, I asked you once before if you thought China was behind these attacks. Have you any doubts now that Beijing masterminded them?'

'No sir.' Jack Webster, chief of the defence force, answered for all. 'Not one of us.'

'Well then, we are effectively under attack. If I don't respond I will be failing in my duty to defend the nation.

'So we will deploy a squadron of planes to Guam. We will tell the Americans and the Chinese that they are being sent for "joint exercises".'

Toohey turned to his chief of staff. 'George, I want Ambassador Golding called back "for talks". I want the strongest of messages sent to the Chinese government. I will announce these measures after this meeting.

'I've had enough of being a softcock with our friends in Beijing.'

_____

Canberra

The diplomatic red carpet had been rolled up. The usual pleasantries had been dispensed with. There was not even the offer of a cup of tea. It was just the two of them in the office: not even a notetaker. Neither of them sat down.

Tian Qichen came straight to the point. 'My government is very displeased with your decision to send Australian war planes to Guam.'

Toohey stood ramrod straight, his ruckman's build towering over the ambassador.

'And I am very displeased that my country has come under serious cyber-attack – not once, but three times in the last month,' the PM responded.

He motioned to a sheaf of papers. 'My national security team says there is no doubt the attacks were launched from China. Frankly, I'm baffled. I have no idea what we've done to prompt this.'

Tian was resolute. 'Prime Minister, we deny it absolutely. You have no evidence that China is behind any of this. The Vodafone strike was routed through Russia and India, according to your own media reports. China does not attack its friends.'

'Ambassador, the evidence is overwhelming. Beyond that, your country has been increasingly aggressive since the beginning of the year. You have behaved maliciously towards your neighbours in the South and East China Seas, including Japan, Australia's good friend.'

'China is also your friend and major trading partner, Mr Toohey. You don't seem to value our relationship as highly as I thought.'

'We value it greatly. But we are not going to have our silence bought as you seek to shift the balance of power in the Pacific. I've been a good friend of China. I've publicly called on the US to exercise restraint and accommodate China's peaceful rise.'

Toohey fiddled with the knot of his tie before continuing.

'But your provocations make restraint impossible. If I'm to be forced to choose between trade and peace, then I choose peace. I implore you: withdraw the fishermen from the disputed islands. Close down the air defence identification zone. Propose talks to end this conflict before a fatal mistake is made. If China does that, I will ensure no Australian warplanes leave these shores.'

Tian bristled. 'China is not the aggressor in this conflict. We find ourselves surrounded by hostile forces. We are merely defending our territory, as you would defend Australia. America is determined to keep us boxed in.'

'I'm sorry you feel that way, Ambassador. But while you hold these positions I am bound to protect what I see as the interests of my nation. We will support our friends. And that shouldn't be taken as an act of aggression.'

Tian held Toohey's gaze as he unclipped his briefcase and reached for an envelope that he handed to the prime minister.

'This is a letter nullifying the heads of agreement between Sinopec and your government, Prime Minister. China will search elsewhere for gas.'

Toohey had been half expecting this response, but still wore the look of a man who'd just glimpsed his own mortality.

'I was assured by you, Mr Tian, that dealing with a Chinese state-owned enterprise was no different to dealing with a corporation from any country. You lied.'

Canberra

Two models of the F-35 Stealth fighter, locked in a mock dogfight, stood next to a plastic Collins-class submarine. An air-warfare destroyer, just over a metre long, had pride of place on a coffee table.

As Harry Dunkley passed through the defence minister's outer office, he recalled that Brendan Ryan had once confided to him that he'd never aspired to be top dog. The only jobs he'd ever craved were 'powerbroker' and 'defence minister'.

Now he had both.

Ryan was chewing into a donut as he rose to meet Dunkley.

'What's this about, Harry? I don't have much time.'

'I want to chat, off the record, about some stuff that's come into my orbit,' Dunkley began. 'You remember my friend Kimberley Gordon, who was killed. She was working on some important stuff just before she died.'

'Yep, I remember. We had a long conversation and I think we agreed that the Chinese were involved.'

'Well, here's the thing,' Harry said. 'I've got indications that the Americans have done some interfering in Australian politics. Deeper and for longer than I would have imagined.'

'How so?' Ryan was stony-faced.

'A group of mandarins was at the core of it. Senior defence and intelligence people in this town. I've got a list of names – old names – who were effectively running a shadow government in league with the US embassy. It stretches back to before Whitlam.'

'Harry, let me play devil's advocate. You're telling me that some former bureaucrats were talking to American ambassadors about how Australia is run and defended? Isn't that their job?'

'Brendan, this looks to be more than friendly fireside chats. I'm talking the real deal here. These guys have been interfering – quite maliciously – to get their own way.'

'That's a serious accusation. What have they done? And what evidence do you have beyond a list of names?'

'Well, we've got—'

'Hang on. You said "I" before and now you're saying "we". Who's working with you?'

'Don't worry about that, mate, just hear me out. I came across some material that had been placed on a computer Cloud. Stuff that a top-line security analyst uncovered – not long before she was killed.'

'Gordon? How did she come by this material? Did she steal it?'

'How she got the material matters less than whether it's fair dinkum.'

'How she got it matters a lot, but let's get back to my main point. What's this secret society doing and what hard evidence do you have?'

'Mate, there's the list of top-level officials who were part of this secret society. It includes former heads of ASIS, ASIO, Defence. And, like I said, US ambassadors ...'

'Oh, and who else? Robert Mugabe? The Pope?'

Dunkley ignored the jibe.

'They called themselves the Alliance. The whole thing stretches back forty years. Remember Whitlam's speech to parliament after he was shafted? He belled the cat. The Yanks were behind his demise. It's just that your mates mythologised the great man by claiming he was a victim only of Fraser's duplicity.'

'Harry, don't lecture me on Labor history. Whitlam had reason to be angry. The Yanks did get more involved than they should have.

'I told you eighteen months ago they were worried about Paxton, and they had every right. He was the defence minister and was cavorting with a Chinese spy.

'So of course the US kicked up a stink. They share intelligence with us. And yes, sometimes they get a bit pushy. But you're asking me to believe they were part of a shadow government running Australia. That, my friend, is a world-class conspiracy. Show me your evidence. Isn't that what your editor would ask?'

Dunkley was firm. 'I have evidence, but I can't share it yet. I'm not going to stop, Brendan.'

'Harry, you know I have the greatest respect for you. And I do remember our conversation. I told you about America's concerns. But when I told you that I feared our former PM was a Chinese spy, you accused me of peddling fiction. I'm sure you'll have something that will turn out to be a story. But if you came here hoping that I'd be able to confirm this extraordinary tale, you're out of luck. It's all news to me.'

The parliamentary bells started to ring. The Senate was dividing.

'Listen mate, I have to go, but look, I have a real story for you, one ready to print. I know you hate leaving here empty handed.'

He reached into a drawer and pulled out a sheet of A4 paper. Dunkley could only make out the words 'UMR Polling'.

'Harry, you can't have this or look at it. But I'll tell you what's on it. Usual rules, no reference to government sources – but you can report the ALP has been road-testing Catriona Bailey in marginal seats. Twice in the last fortnight. One in Sydney's west, the other in Brissie. A nice coincidence with her return to parliament, don't you think? And, my friend, the foreign minister is rockin' in the suburbs.'

Canberra

Martin Toohey could feel the noose tightening around his neck.

Within hours of his showdown with the Chinese ambassador, Sinopec had released a statement saying the Northern Territory gas hub had been shelved 'for the foreseeable future', citing finance problems.

It was another lie, but one Toohey would be forced to mimic to cover the crumbling relationship with Australia's largest trading partner.

The immediate problem was summed up in an AAP wire story. With the gas deal off, the rivers of gold to fund Toohey's ambitious social program had evaporated.

TOOHEY'S MULTIBILLION-DOLLAR BLACK HOLE

Chinese energy giant Sinopec has scuttled plans to build a gas hub off the Northern Territory, sabotaging the Toohey government's hopes of using the project's cash to fund mental health reform.

The landmark legislation scraped through the Lower House last week, with the stunning return of Foreign Minister Catriona Bailey tipping the balance in the government's favour.

Sinopec's decision is the latest disaster for Prime Minister Martin Toohey, with Ms Bailey's return reigniting leadership speculation.

One Labor MP described the Sinopec bombshell as 'the sound of the coffin lid being dropped on Toohey's carcass'.

The PM turned as he heard the door opening behind him.

'It's bad,' Papadakis said as he entered. 'I've been taking soundings with Caucus and the vultures are circling. I've got the secretary in the environment minister's office across the hall from Bailey's suite keeping watch. There's a traffic jam of suckholes down there. I've asked Brendan Ryan to start counting our numbers.'

'Does he have any idea how they stand?'

'It's close. If the Right holds we might hang on, but you know better than me that nobody really controls the numbers in leadership ballots. There's no block votes, just alliances of convenience. A cross-factional group is working with Bailey. Apparently they call themselves the Cardinals.'

The PM rolled his eyes. 'Really?'

'Really. You couldn't make this shit up. These people read too much Dan Brown. If only they'd put their vivid imaginations to good use.'

Toohey turned back to his computer and flicked through some of the dozens of articles that had been written about Bailey's 'miraculous' return. From the moment she'd glided into the chamber, Toohey knew her gravitational pull would suck all the light from his mental health reforms. But her reception had staggered him. News stories on her rare recovery, heroism, selflessness and courage had plastered the papers, the airwaves and online.

One pointy head at the *Guardian* had even dubbed Bailey 'Mother Courage'. Whatever she was called, Bailey and her plotters were a real and present danger.

'If she wants it, she's going to have to blast me out.' Toohey thumped the desk. 'I'm not getting spooked into calling a ballot based on plotting and whispering. They'll need signatures to force a Caucus vote. Let's see which mother has the courage to put their name to that.'

Papadakis nodded. 'Anything else, PM?'

'Yep. Tell Brendan to get down here so we can go through the numbers. I'm not making any calls or that will leak too. And when we're done with that, there's the minor matter of World War Three brewing on our doorstep.

We might want to discuss that at some point. I'm afraid the Yanks are about to do something that we'll all regret.'

There was a knock at the door and Toohey's senior media adviser opened it a fraction.

'PM, you got a minute? I thought I should let you know. The *Financial Review*'s been in touch with Standard and Poors. They're threatening to review our AAA credit rating if we push ahead with the mental health reform.'

'It would be easier spinning for Big Tobacco. Brooks is now so toxic she should come with her own health warning.'

Justin Greenwich ended the call to his girlfriend and scrolled forlornly through dozens of messages.

We're rooted.

Greenwich was a Liberal careerist who had risen from the ruck of Victorian state politics to make it to the big arena of Canberra. He'd arrived just as the Howard government fell and had been the media minder for three opposition leaders in six years.

It was the job almost universally acknowledged to be the most thankless in politics. He saw his role as the whipping girl's underpaid understudy. Years of ritual flogging at the hands of the media had hardened his hide. But he had never seen anything like this.

The decision to deviously revoke Catriona Bailey's pair would have been hard to spin on any day.

But to do it and then lose the vote … Gandhi couldn't survive that.

Liberal Party focus group testing showed it had cemented the community's many concerns about Brooks. 'Deceitful, heartless bitch' pretty much captured the mood of the mob.

Brooks had even been caned by radio shock jocks and the Right's online cheerleaders. All agreed that she should have been an unbackable favourite at September's election, but instead she was a drag on the Coalition's strong polling.

Let's face it, we were dead when the bondage video came out.

Greenwich picked up a media release he intended to get framed, to commemorate the moment when the opposition leader hit the point of no return.

SEX PARTY BACKS BROOKS

The Australian Sex Party will campaign for the re-election of Emily Brooks in her Queensland seat of Moncrieff.

Sex Party leader Robbie Swan said the party would direct preferences to the opposition leader in her Gold Coast electorate. Local sex workers would person every booth and hand out how-to-vote cards.

'She has done more to make bondage mainstream than *Fifty Shades of Grey*,' Mr Swan said. 'That should be rewarded.'

Yokosuka

'Sir, it's PACOM. Line 5. Admiral Holland's office.'

Frank W Vinson wiped his mouth with a white napkin, starched and embellished with 'FWV', and turned to his dining companions. 'Gentlemen, excuse me. You keep eating though, that beef is good.'

The one-star admiral was commander of Carrier Strike Group 5, an eight-ship flotilla whose flagship was the USS *George Washington*, one of ten nuclear-powered aircraft carriers that sailed under the Stars and Stripes.

The carrier was a floating colossus, measuring three football fields bow to stern, and twenty stories high. Two fourth-generation nuclear reactors could keep it steaming for eighteen years without refuelling.

More than five thousand crew were crowded inside. In the heat of combat, its four steam-driven catapults could sling one of its seventy-five planes into the air every twenty seconds. Each was a deadly war machine.

In blue water, the *George Washington* was a giant hub radiating deadly spokes. Its Super Hornets prowled the sky, the guided missile cruisers *Shiloh* and *Antietam* defended the sea, and the destroyers *Curtis Wilbur* and *Fitzgerald* protected the waters beneath. Two nuclear-powered attack submarines, *Tucson* and *City of Corpus Christi*, lurked ahead while the oiler USNS *Tippecanoe* tagged behind, carrying jet fuel and other supplies.

Vinson commanded an armada that combined more military muscle than most nations could muster. Moored in Japan, it projected American power to China's doorstep. When it sailed, it sent an unmistakeable message: we rule the waves.

It was 7.10pm in Yokosuka, which made it just after midnight in Hawaii. Something was biting.

Vinson had been expecting a call, but not from the man who commanded all US forces over half the world's surface. But he was ready for whatever might come: his group had been 'working up' to put to sea for days. They could sail within eight hours.

'Sir, what's my mission?'

'The president has ordered you to sail into the Taiwan Strait. He is determined to reassert America's right of free passage through international waters. I want you on the move by midday tomorrow.'

It was an extraordinary command. And it was high risk. Sending one of America's nuclear-powered warships into the disputed waters was akin to throwing a flaming rock at a swarm of angry wasps.

'Aubrey, that is quite a move. What are my rules of engagement?'

There was a slight pause before Holland spoke. 'You are to do what it takes to sail from one end of the strait to the other, north to south, and return to port.'

'What is my posture, sir?'

'Condition Zebra. I want you battle ready. Combat aircraft flying, electronic warfare systems up on all vessels.'

It was an extremely aggressive way to enter the strait. The Chinese electronic eyes would see a strike group ready for war.

'And if there's an incident? Do I escalate, or de-escalate?'

'You do what you have to do to complete your mission.'

Vinson was disturbed. The strike group was safest, and most formidable, when on the open sea. In the contained waters of the Taiwan Strait, he would be placing his crew in harm's way, well within reach of the People's Liberation Army's weapons.

If the strike group got into a fight they would face an overwhelming force with nowhere to retreat. But there were larger strategic considerations. Any miscalculation by either side could quickly spiral out of control. An accident could be misinterpreted and spark a regional war. Or worse.

'Sir, you know better than anyone that there are no protocols covering an incident at sea between the US and China.'

'I appreciate that, Frank. If something happens I can't reach for the phone and tell Admiral Leng Sha that we have no intention of picking a fight.'

'So all they can do is read our body language through their radar.' Vinson wanted his reservations underlined. 'And it will be screaming that we have kicked open the doors on the toughest bar in town armed with a broken bottle.'

'I understand all your concerns.' Holland sounded weary. 'And they are reasonable. But I have my orders and you have yours.'

'Yes, sir.'

'Thank you, Frank. Detailed orders and rules of engagement will be sent through asap, usual channels. Your trip will be announced by the secretary of Defence on *Good Morning America*. Now, m'boy, I'm going to get some shut-eye.'

Vinson sat back and exhaled. It had been four years since America had sailed one of its carrier groups through the Taiwan Strait. That had nearly ended in disaster.

The USS *Kittyhawk* had been shadowed by a Chinese attack submarine and destroyer, triggering a twenty-eight-hour stand-off.

This would be very different: a deliberate, public swagger through China's front door designed to show the world that there was only one superpower.

That really was taunting the dragon.

The admiral lifted a framed photo on his desk. His wife, Judy, still gorgeous despite the years, flanked by their extended family. The commander's diaspora. He loved this clan, and they loved him back.

He pulled a pad from the desk drawer and started making notes. He would follow his orders to the letter, even if the thinking behind this decision was hard to fathom.

Beijing

The outdoor broadcast vans from China Central Television had arrived early. A crowd of several hundred Chinese was already gathered on Liangmaqiao Road outside the Japanese embassy. They carried nationalist flags and chanted anti-Nippon slogans in the freezing Beijing morning. They were mainly young, enraged – and sanctioned by the state.

Ambassador Ito Sanetomi gazed down at the growing mob. Six months earlier, more than a thousand Chinese had demonstrated outside these same walls against Japan's rightful claim to the Senkaku Islands. They'd carried inflammatory banners that declared 'For the Respect of the Motherland, we must go to War with Japan'. A Toyota van had been torched – a pointless act of aggression.

The ambassador was taking no chances. Now that the United States had decided to sail the *George Washington* through the Taiwan Strait, all staff except for emergency personnel had been ordered to leave.

A crash drew his eyes to a mob who'd separated from the main crowd and were trying to scale the embassy fence. They were being forced back by riot squad officers. The defence was holding, for now.

But the ambassador knew this mob – and crowds like it throughout China – would only grow and become more aggressive. Sanetomi was anticipating a recall to Japan. He'd received a cable to say that he should expect such a directive if the situation worsened.

He'd ordered his wife to pack and prepare their two children. As he looked out at the violence below, he longed to breathe the peaceful air of his beloved Tokyo.

Jiang Xiu studied the material in front of him. He erased one sentence that was excessive, but otherwise he was pleased with the work.

China's Central Propaganda Department was in full swing and Jiang was barking instructions to a team of senior editors who'd gathered in his Beijing office.

'I want this out through the 50 Cent Party. Now!' The communist giant was mounting a public relations offensive against the West and Jiang needed every component of his propaganda arsenal primed and ready to roll. The 50 Cent Party was an informal network of bloggers paid a pittance to echo the party line.

'*Ming! Ming!*' he shouted at the editor of *China Daily*. 'When will this be online? Why the delay? Come on, let's move.'

Jiang studied the latest briefing from the CDP's Bureau of Media Statistics. It was sobering. The United States and Japan were winning the international propaganda war – he was starting well behind and at a big disadvantage. He did not expect to be able to quickly overcome the inbuilt jealousy and antipathy towards China in the international media. But here in the homeland he commanded the headlines and he could not afford to lose, even for a moment, the people's support. What had Mao said? 'Politics is war without bloodshed.'

This war would be fought – initially at least – through the internet, in newspapers and on television screens. He must not fail.

A woman entered his office, placing a mock-up of the *China Daily* front page on his desk. The headline was striking:

CHINA AND DPRK IN NUCLEAR PACT

The article outlined plans by China to assist North Korea with its peaceful nuclear expansion. A spokesman for the Foreign Ministry explained that the cooperative deal was designed to help North Korea generate the next phase of its nuclear power industry.

'All of this has been done within the framework of UN and Chinese laws,' the spokesman said.

The article went on to say that China was opposed to nuclear proliferation – but Jiang knew this line would be ignored as the West absorbed the story's tenor: the Middle Kingdom would meet acts of aggression by its enemies with unflinching resolve and veiled threats of its own.

'Xiu!' He turned to a familiar voice, that of Bo Gangmei, a long-time friend who, like Jiang, had worked hard to earn promotion through the party hierarchy. Two months earlier, Bo had been appointed editorial supervisor at Xinhua, the official Chinese news agency. His appointment had been strictly on merit, but this had not stopped a range of underground and dissident outlets from reporting his friendship with China's chief propaganda officer.

Jiang had told him to ignore the jibes. They were fuelled by petty jealousy and, besides, several of the critical ringleaders had been jailed.

Bo had been working on a top-secret project. Jiang pulled out a chair for his friend, eager to examine the details before they were released to the world.

'Oh! Very nice, Gangmei.' He read over the article to be released through Xinhua again.

China has advanced plans to sign a historic military co-operation agreement with the Democratic Republic of Fiji. The two countries are expected to formally enter the agreement within a month, allowing the People's Liberation Army to conduct formal exercises with the Pacific nation.

Fijian Prime Minister Commodore Frank Bainimarama is due to arrive in Beijing in a fortnight when he is expected to sign a pact with President Meng. China has also agreed to increase aid to the Pacific nation. This will reduce Fiji's reliance on Western countries, like Australia, which have been increasingly hostile to the island nation.

Jiang was satisfied. The evidence on the streets showed he had correctly read the mood of a people determined to see their country rise again.

America's decision to send the *George Washington* into Chinese waters was as predictable as the sunrise. Those fools in Washington had stumbled into the trap. Everything had been focused towards enticing the US to make an aggressive play. It had worked.

Now the world was watching. If the superpower retreated, China would make that giant leap forward.

And the world would shift on its axis. Forever.

Canberra

The newspapers lay unfurled across the kitchen table. Harry Dunkley cradled a cup of tea and munched on a piece of toast. He was in his element, the familiar black stain of newsprint on his hands as his exclusive screamed from the front page.

LABOR'S SECRET BAILEY POLL

Martin Toohey's leadership is under siege with Labor secretly road-testing Catriona Bailey as an alternative prime minister.

Internal party polling, details of which have been obtained exclusively by *The Australian*, reveals the foreign minister could save a swag of marginal Labor seats.

The polling confirms Ms Bailey – who made a triumphant return to parliament last week – is far more popular with swinging voters than Mr Toohey.

The prime minister's grip on power was yesterday rocked by the collapse of his multi-billion-dollar Northern Territory gas deal.

Critically, the polling shows that Labor could be returned if Ms Bailey is prime minister when voters go to the polls on 14 September.

Labor has been testing Ms Bailey's support in the key electoral battlegrounds of western Sydney and Brisbane.

The journalist knew his splash would ignite the simmering leadership speculation and dominate the day's political drama. He'd already fielded calls to appear on Sydney and Melbourne radio.

He glanced at the other front pages as the blare of the *AM* intro sounded on Radio National.

Tony Eastley plunged into Dunkley's story off the top.

'We now cross to our chief political correspondent in Canberra. Sabra Lane, I understand there has been an explosive development in the story leading the front page of *The Australian*.'

'Yes Tony, just minutes ago I took a call from Labor's national secretary, Gerry Tighe, who demanded air time. He's on the line now. Mr Tighe, good morning, I understand you say this story is an invention.'

'Good morning. Yes, it is. I admit Labor's struggling. Our numbers aren't good. But the story in *The Australian*, Sabra, is pure fabrication. I never usually discuss internal polling, but I can tell your listeners that Mr Dunkley's so-called scoop is 100 per cent wrong.'

'In what way, Mr Tighe?'

'Well, *The Australian* reports so-called internal party polling on Catriona Bailey. I can say this: we have not done any such polling. Dunkley has simply made it up.'

The online vultures started circling immediately, driven by a hatred of Murdoch and mainstream media. In just a few hours, Harry Dunkley had morphed from press gallery ace to the antichrist.

The social media lynch mob was whipping itself into a frenzy, their words laced with poison and relish. But the outrage spewed well beyond the twitterverse. Cabinet ministers were telling senior gallery figures that *The Australian*'s star scribe was a dead man walking.

'Dunkley's about as popular as Alan Jones at a Destroy the Joint meeting,' one female minister told a Fairfax journo, eager to plunge the knife into the News Corp hack.

In parliament, the Toohey government suspended standing orders so its chief headkicker, the minister for education and failed marriages, Xavier Quinn, could take a baseball bat to Dunkley. For fifteen ugly minutes, the South Australian MP laid out the case against the Murdoch employee, every word protected by parliamentary privilege.

'Politics is a tough business and we, in the government, respect the role that the fourth estate plays in holding those in power to account,' Quinn said. 'But this so-called journalist has crossed the line between reporting the news and being an activist. For on this occasion it appears he was intent on sabotaging a democratically elected government.'

Ease up, turbo. I got some polling figures wrong, okay? Toohey's still fucked. And I was set up.

The Greens and the independents were predictably linking the story with News Corp's alleged persecution of the Toohey government and the forty-third parliament.

'The "hate media" has overstepped the mark yet again in its unprincipled desire to bring about regime change,' Greens' leader Kiirsty Stanford-Long told reporters.

In his office, the journalist sat helpless as the assault on his reputation intensified. On the twittersphere, #DunkleyDoneFor was trending.

He'd desperately tried to raise Brendan Ryan, the man who'd fed him the figures and later verified the thrust of his now discredited scoop. There was no answer and his office said the minister would be busy all day.

His character was being shredded. Still, he could hardly complain. He'd built his career on being the hardest hitter in politics. He never shied from a tussle and worried about the diminishing pool of journalists willing to get their hands dirty.

'If you want to play in the big league, you've got to be prepared to take more hits than Joe Frazier,' was his advice to young guns arriving in Canberra.

This was no boxing contest, however. It was more like a one-sided UFC bout – and he was on the ground taking whack after painful whack.

Few of his colleagues had bothered to ask how he was faring. As if he should have been surprised. That was the nature of the press gallery. If you were on top of your game and filing scoop after scoop you received grudging admiration – but if you slipped up, look out. The bared fangs of jealous vipers were frightening.

His phone buzzed. It was Celia, the first time she'd rung since the big fright. He was heartened to see her name flash on his phone, but now wasn't the right moment to talk to her. He let the call go to voicemail.

Two minutes later, his phone rang again. And this time he had no choice about answering.

'Harry ...' *The Australian's* editor sounded as if she'd been lined up against a wall. As Dunkley would later discover, for the past thirty minutes she'd been trying to salvage the career of her political editor. She'd been outmanoeuvred, and forced by management into a defensive ploy, designed with one thought in mind – heading off a threatened media inquiry.

'I want you to take extended leave, Harry, a long holiday. The suits need a sacrificial lamb. I did my best, but ... well, the phrase "overplayed his hand" springs to mind.'

The reporter took a deep breath. He was about to be benched for the first time in a long and previously illustrious career – and it stung.

'Harry, I'm sorry. But things are fraught with the government. And it will be bloody hard to prosecute the case against this lot if you don't fall on your sword.'

'That sounds like I'm being fed to the wolves. Guess all those award-winning scoops really count for something, hey?'

'You know I'm your biggest fan, Harry, but these are difficult times and none of us are ... indispensable.'

'So I'm dispensable?'

'Yes Harry, don't make plans to come back.'

_____

ra

Dunkley was alive, but only just. He lay sprawled on a mess of a bed, ring at an upturned tumbler.

The day was half over, and he was trying to remember – through the dusty thud of a hangover – how he'd walked through these gates of hell. His mouth tasted of dirty copper and a faint scent of nicotine hung in the air.

Strange. I don't smoke.

It was a Thursday, sometime in March. 2013. Beyond that, he didn't have much of a clue. Then it slowly started to come back, thoughts he'd tried to drown in a lake of tequila. He sat up, a little too quickly, knocking his brain off its fragile mooring.

The previous day he'd been thrown to the wolves. News Corp's over-anxious management had discarded their gun political reporter.

Like other newsbreakers, Dunkley had been under constant pressure to bowl up stories that would cut through, sell newspapers and lure punters to cash-starved websites. He did it better than most – but News Corp couldn't afford a wide-ranging media inquiry.

'You want to know why fewer people are buying papers? 'Cause you bastards have got rid of all the decent reporters,' he'd told one executive who spent his days watching his back.

Bugger them all.

He dragged himself into the kitchen, searching for something to ease the tom-toms playing paradiddles in his head. Three Nurofen scratched at his throat as he reached for a chair, ignoring the mobile phone ringing somewhere in his flat.

Christ, you don't have the stamina for this anymore.

He'd drunk himself into a stupor of self-pity and self-loathing and was paying the price.

The phone was ringing. Again. Someone was determined to get through.

He stumbled into the lounge room and retrieved the device from beneath a cushion on the couch. Eight missed calls.

The SMH *offering me a job?*

Not likely. They'd cut to the bone and word was Fairfax management wanted another hundred staff gone to balance the books.

He flicked through the list. No Caller ID. No Caller ID. Celia. Jack, his brother. Celia again. He would talk to her, but his wounded ego screamed not yet. He continued to scroll down the calls. He stopped: Trevor Harris.

Wonder what he knows?

Dunkley eased himself into the shower, tilting his head as water rained down on his sorry skull. He stayed like that for five minutes, ignoring the nausea, until he felt half human.

Moving gingerly, he dressed in jeans and an unironed shirt, and picked up his mobile.

'Trevor. Harry Dunkley. How're you going? Feel like a coffee? Great. Hansel and Gretel in thirty.'

The cafe had attracted a decent lunchtime crowd. Dunkley ordered a double shot, his first for the day. His head still ached, but it was manageable pain. Like listening to Eminem with Celia.

A couple at a nearby table shot him a glance, exchanging conspiratorial whispers.

Yes it really is me. Mr Bring-Down-the-Government.

Harris was running a few minutes late, but that was fine. Dunkley had all day, and the day after. The waitress had just delivered his coffee when the former DSD analyst strolled through the door.

'Harry, you look a little worse for wear.' Harris was not about to paper over the bleeding obvious. He ordered a long black before turning back to Dunkley.

'So, you've taken the rap, Harry. Big time. I read about it in the *Canberra Times* – they seemed to quite enjoy writing about your … downfall.'

'I know, mate. I fucked up. Overreached. Was fed a dodgy bit of polling. Wrote it up. Hard. Front page of the broadsheet that matters. It was wrong. I was set up by a trusted source. And I've been executed. End of story.'

'I don't think so, Harry.'

'You don't think what?'

'That it's the end of the story. For you, that is.'

Dunkley appreciated the remark. Compassion had been in short supply.

Harris fiddled with his mug of coffee. He looked anxious.

'Harry, I need you to trust me.'

'I'm not sure I can trust anyone anymore, Trevor.'

'I appreciate that, but remember I'm going to trust you.'

Harris appeared to be struggling for words, and Dunkley knew from experience that the best course was to stay silent.

'Harry, when I came to you the first time I was simply handing over an email you were supposed to have. Then I said I would look at documents encrypted on Ben's Cloud. At no stage did any of that break the commitments I've made to keeping this country's secrets.'

Dunkley prodded. Gently.

'Has that changed?'

'What's changed is what I've found out. I've unlocked many of the documents that Ben hid on the Cloud. Harry, he stole some of this nation's most sensitive files. That is a crime. Trafficking it is a crime too.'

The shatter of glass on polished concrete made Harris swivel. An errant child had swept a cup onto the floor and a mother was fussing with the shards. Harris bore the look of a man who felt his every word could be overheard. He dropped his voice to a whisper.

'The files Ben collected are all top secret. AUSTEO: Australian Eyes Only. On top of that, Ben pieced together information from a host of classified sources to build a picture of the Alliance. If I speak to you about any of it, I am breaking the law.'

The analyst's face was agonised as he wrestled with his conscience.

Dunkley understood better than most the fine line that people were forced to walk between what was ethically 'right' and legally 'wrong'. He felt the public interest was best served by letting the sun shine on government. Folk like Harris thought secrets were essential to keeping the nation safe.

'What's the price of *not* telling me what you've found, Trev?'

'I'm not really sure. Perhaps my soul. I don't believe in God but I've always strived to do what I believe is right. I fear that if I stay silent, Harry, I'll be protecting people who see themselves as above democracy.'

'I suspect you might be right.'

'You already know part of the story, Harry. The Alliance was set up in the late 1960s when the Americans and our defence and intelligence establishment began collaborating, sometimes against the Australian government. It had a hand in Whitlam's fall. But it didn't end there.

'It's alive and kicking. RIGHT. NOW.' Harris emphasised the last words with two soft thumps of the table.

'You have the old membership list. Ben pieced together the current one. By his reckoning, the Alliance is now led by Jack Webster.'

'Webster? The defence force chief?'

'Yes. And it's an impressive list. Also on it is Brent Moreton, the US Ambassador, the secretary of Foreign Affairs and the heads of ASIS and ASIO. And one Labor politician, Brendan Ryan, the defence minister.'

The last name fell on Dunkley like a slap that snapped him awake. His eyes cleared as he saw how the jigsaw pieces assembled into a picture. It confirmed what he had suspected since his polling story had been disavowed. He'd been lied to, done over, to stop him exposing this powerful cult.

'Trevor, you've taken a risk. Now I'm about to take one. To do something I've never done before. And that's reveal a source. Brendan Ryan was behind the story that broke me.'

'I suspected as much.' Harris nodded. 'But thanks for the vote of trust.'

Dunkley caught his breath as he glanced around the cafe. A table of tradies was engaged in banter about women, cars and beer. Two young office workers held hands as they shared a pastry and the first shy blushes of a relationship.

Australians who worried little about how their country worked. Imagining in their apathy that the people they voted for ran the nation.

And in their midst, two outcasts drawn together by the murder of a friend that pointed to an extraordinary conspiracy. If they stood up and shouted what they knew they would be considered insane.

Yet Dunkley knew in his bones it was true. That everything he had believed in, right until that moment, was a lie.

The journalist rubbed his eyes and tried to compose himself.

'How do they work?' he asked.

'Harry, you have no idea how deeply embedded our defence and intelligence community is with America. You're a well-informed man, but did you know that B-52s based in Guam regularly fly training missions to the West Australian desert and drop live bombs? And did you know that the distance from Guam to that patch of Australian sand is the same distance as Guam to Beijing?'

Dunkley shook his head.

'Well, the Chinese know. And what do you think they make of that? And do you have any idea what Pine Gap is really used for? Among other things it watches every missile launch and nuclear test from North Korea to India. It's a vital cog in the US war machine.'

Harris kept glancing about, his voice barely a murmur.

'For all intents and purposes, the Australian defence establishment is an outpost of the US. Our generals and admirals like it that way. They call it interoperability, but it's really integration. China knows that. Is it any wonder they question our politicians who claim we can be an ally of the US and not pose a threat to them?

'Most of the time, all our defence establishment has to do is nudge the government of the day into line. Buying US military equipment. Ensuring that we can't operate with anyone else. Telling politicians that we need to go to war for "alliance maintenance". And governments, for the most part, are happy to comply. Even to think it was their idea.

'But sometimes the establishment needs to make a radical intervention, like in '75. And right now the Alliance is feeling so threatened it's decided to declare war against its own.'

Harris reached under his chair for his green shopping bag and removed a document, placing it in front of Dunkley. It was marked AUSTEO.

'Jesus, Trevor.'

'Read it.'

The cafe had emptied out, but Dunkley glanced around before he turned the cover sheet and exposed a three-word heading: THE LUSITANIA PLAN.

The document outlined how a false flag operation could be mounted in cyberspace. The plan was to stage a series of attacks on one nation's infrastructure routed through a third country in an attempt to hide the adversary's true identity. Potential targets included dams, electricity grids and traffic systems. But three specific targets leapt out: air-traffic control, banks and mobile phone networks.

'Shit!' Dunkley could feel the blood pumping in his temples as he struggled to digest the document's explosive implications.

'Harry, the attacks on Australia might not be coming from China. Maybe the Alliance is trying to shunt the government back into line. If Toohey believes China is the adversary, that forces him back into the arms of America ...'

Dunkley finally realised the role that he'd been playing in this great game. He wasn't a journalist. He was their stooge.

'And, Trevor, if every attack is reported as coming from China, then a government that didn't act would be seen as weak on national security. The people would turf it out.'

Dunkley knew he had been played by Ryan. But there was one other who had hung him on the hook.

Canberra

A red wall topped with gold-rimmed black tiles and a sliver of blue sky formed the background of Yue Minjun's famous painting. But it was the stark foreground that had first drawn Elizabeth Scott's attention.

Eight identical Asian men were divided into two groups of four. Those on the right were stripped to their underwear, while the others trained invisible rifles on them.

Scott loved Chinese contemporary art, but it was the title that really appealed: 'Execution'.

The print hung in her parliamentary office, a stark reminder of her brutal dispatch as opposition leader.

She pondered tweeting a picture of it today, as her executioner, Emily Brooks, took her place up against the wall. The aborted attempt to fix the numbers on the mental health vote had buried her.

But there could be no gloating in public and precious little in private. Scott had assumed the rebirth of her popularity would guarantee the return of the opposition leader's mantle. Her party had other ideas.

'The troops see you as too left wing.' The South Australian Liberal MP Steve Pitt had been walking the corridors. The ballot was at 11am and things looked terminal.

'How many by your count?'

'Twelve.'

That tallied with her own assessment, and she was shocked by how risibly low it was. She had loudly declared she'd be a candidate, so there would be plenty of humiliation to go around this day.

Scott wondered again why she didn't quit.

'Out of the eighty-eight Liberal MPs and senators, only twelve will back me. Who are the other seventy-six morons voting for?'

'They want someone new. And after experimenting with a wet from New South Wales and a dry-as-dust Queenslander, there's a strong mood for a Victorian. The one thing everyone keeps telling me is they want "a safe pair of hands". Barry Landry seems the most likely.'

Scott shook her head. 'The guy's a cardigan-wearing dill. My twelve-year-old labrador has more energy and appeal.'

'Well, maybe we need a drover's dog.'

The commercial television breakfast programs had moved their anchors to Canberra for the day, setting up marquees outside parliament. Sky and ABC News 24 had been cycling politicians, journalists, analysts and anyone else who could string a sentence together through their studios. The major print bureaus had rolled their Sydney- and Melbourne-based heavy hitters into town, and when they weren't crafting portentous opinion pieces, they were acting as network commentators. Radio talkback was filling the airwaves with chatter.

Security in Parliament House had been relaxed to allow cameras and journalists access to a junction of corridors about fifty metres from the opposition party room. The burble of live TV and radio crosses echoed through the building.

Excitement was rising. There was speculation, growing by the minute, that two leaders might fall before this day was done – something unique in the one hundred and twelve years of Federation.

Martin Toohey was resisting a call for a Caucus ballot. But a rumour was circulating that a petition was being organised for a leadership spill.

Ten minutes before the Liberal Party ballot, the first MPs and senators began running the media gauntlet.

Then the combatants arrived, faces fixed, acolytes in tow, to a barrage of shouted questions.

'Ms Scott, do you have the numbers?'

'We'll see.'

Barry Landry had indeed firmed as the favourite. Dull, but solid as a rock. He also had recent, real-world business experience, chairing a Victorian water business and turning its fortunes around.

'Mr Landry, can you win it?'

'Whatever happens, I hope it's for the good of the party and the country.'

Finally, Emily Brooks appeared. Alone. An act of defiance from a woman who'd been subjected to so much invective and ridicule. Determined to show her spirit was unbowed, she smiled as she passed the salivating media pack, their camera motor drives clattering through five frames every second.

'Is it over, Ms Brooks?'

'While there's life, there's hope.'

Justin Greenwich absorbed the broadcast, transfixed, camped in the opposition leader's office.

'Say what you like about Emily Brooks, she makes Thatcher look like Tinkerbell.'

Canberra

It was like walking onto the set of *Gone with the Wind*. Sweeping lawns cut by a circular driveway led to a grand Georgian-style manor replete with white-latticed windows set in a red-brick facade. Bruce Paxton half expected to see Scarlett O'Hara promenading on the lush grass.

Every Fourth of July the embassy hosted hundreds of guests. But today, on the spot where hot dogs and Budweiser were usually served, two men sat in deep and private conversation.

John Kowalski stubbed out his cigarette on the sole of his shoe and turned to face his Australian friend. 'Bruce, I'll say it bluntly. Why should we fly your Chinese mistress to the United States?'

Kowalski was the US defence attaché, a former Navy Seal who'd served with distinction in the first Gulf War. He'd forged a robust working relationship with Paxton during his time as defence minister, despite their occasional differences.

'Just think about this, John. The wife of a Chinese ambassador defects to your God-fearing country, armed with a heap of useful material for you to sift through. I would have thought that was a prize worth having,' Paxton answered.

'That's what I've always liked about you. You're a hopeless liberal, but you do have an eye for the main game. There'll be lots of red tape. Your government won't take kindly to the removal of a Chinese diplomat against the wishes of Beijing.'

Paxton smiled. 'John, this is one occasion when it's better to beg forgiveness than ask permission. Can you do it?'

'Well, Bruce, my Mom used to quote the Lord. "Anything is possible for those who have faith." I'll have an answer by close of business.'

At 7pm, Paxton fired off a text message to Weng.

Forster St. Hire car. 6.30pm. Tomorrow.

_____

Canberra

The ABC's chief of staff was the first to see the alert drop into his inbox. He yelled over the clamour of the newsroom. 'Prime minister. Courtyard. 1.50.'

The bureau had been busy writing obituaries for Emily Brooks, profiles of Barry Landry, cutting grabs for radio and TV stories and pumping out online copy. Editors were scouring for vision that evoked the drama of the moment.

For a few seconds everyone stopped as the significance sank in. It was 1.40pm and a prime minister under siege had called a snap press conference scheduled for ten minutes before Question Time.

The mid-afternoon sun scorched the prime ministerial courtyard and journalists crowded into a small oasis of shade. The camera crews laboured in the harsh sunlight, sweating under their heavy equipment as they prepared for Martin Toohey's arrival.

A podium, badged with a silver Australian crest, stood before two heavy timber and glass doors. Australian flags hung either side of it, each displaying a hint of the Union Jack and all of the Southern Cross.

A security guard pushed open the mighty doors and a perfectly groomed PM stepped into the glare.

'Ladies and gentlemen, thanks for coming. I'm going to make a statement and won't be taking questions.

'Forty minutes ago a delegation of Labor MPs came to my office, led by the foreign minister. They had a petition bearing the names of thirty-six party members calling for a special Caucus meeting to be convened next week, for a spill of positions and a leadership ballot.

'It is my prerogative as leader to call a ballot at any time. I have decided that this matter should be resolved today. These are serious times. We face serious domestic and international challenges. The Australian people deserve stability. The ballot will be held at 7pm.'

'Shouldn't you be on the opposition's payroll?'

It was four minutes to Question Time. Harry Dunkley had intercepted Toohey as he emerged from his office. He'd been camped outside, knowing that the PM would take that route to the chamber.

'I have to speak with you PM. It's urgent.'

'Mate, I don't have time or the wish to speak to you.'

Toohey was walking fast and George Papadakis was heaving along beside him. An AFP officer was eyeing Dunkley suspiciously, ready to step in if the journalist pushed too hard.

'Martin. You need to hear this. You've been set up. It wasn't the Chinese behind those cyber-attacks, it was the Americans.'

The prime minister stopped and fronted Dunkley. 'Sure, mate, sounds completely logical. If I haven't made myself clear, I don't trust you or that shit sheet you used to work for. I'm not interested in anything you have to say.'

Suddenly two metres of close personal protection stood between the prime minister and Dunkley.

Question Time was in full fury as Dunkley pulled up a chair at a near empty Aussies. He stirred his flat white, gazing at the televised theatrics playing out just a few hundred metres away.

A weakened Toohey was in no position to exploit the opposition's leadership change. Every question lashed the raw wound of his collapsed China gas deal.

'My question is to the prime minister. Can he tell the House where he will find six billion dollars a year to fund his mental health plan now that the Chinese have abandoned his misguided attempt to underwrite it by selling off the farm?'

The troops were in full voice, urging their new leader, Barry Landry, into the fray. Across the aisle, Labor MPs stewed sullenly. In a wide shot of the House they could be seen huddled in conversation, working out the numbers for the ballot that would come within hours.

Dunkley glanced at his watch. It was nearly 3pm and the more sedate Senate Question Time would soon be finishing. Dunkley contemplated how he might approach the man who had lied to him. The once trusted source who had destroyed his career.

The journalist hadn't thrown a punch in years, but maybe that would be a good way to start. He thought better of it as he approached the defence minister leaving the Senate chamber.

'Why did you do it, Brendan?' Dunkley's voice was soft, cold fury.

Ryan waved away his senior adviser and turned to front Dunkley.

'Mate, I thought the golden rule in journalism was to always check a story with multiple sources. What happened?'

'Fair point. Maybe I should be punished for that. But usually the starting point isn't a Cabinet minister lying to my face. I've always trusted you, Brendan.'

'Well, more fool you. Mate, you've been playing in the big league for a long time. You should know better than most that sometimes we do things that damage people. So be it. There are more important things than your front-page splash.'

Ryan jabbed a finger close to Dunkley's chest. 'You live for the thrill of the chase, Harry, and you don't mind who you fuck over to get a story. How many people have *you* hurt? How many careers have *you* destroyed? You thought you were doing the right thing. So did I. My job's to defend the nation and I take it seriously.'

'So I was a threat and you eliminated me.'

'If you say so. But try and get this past your ego. It's not about you. It's much bigger than you. Now I'm busy, and I don't have time for has-been hacks.'

_____

Canberra

The black Citroën appeared just after 6pm.

Harry Dunkley tensed as the greyhound-sleek figure of Charles Dancer emerged, camouflaged in the mundane suit of a bureaucrat. The spook checked his letterbox for mail, then slipped inside.

Dunkley waited five minutes before ringing the doorbell, his heart-rate rocketing, his right fist clenched white.

The door opened. Dunkley lunged. Dancer swayed like a boxer, let the blow pass and then pushed hard between Dunkley's shoulder blades. The journalist slammed into the cold tiles. As he rolled, a foot crashed onto his chest, pinning him to the floor. A gun was trained on his face.

'I've been expecting you, Harry. And yes, it's loaded.'

Dancer sat opposite the journalist, a fourth-generation Glock 17 on his lap.

'Didn't I say to you once before that you were out of your depth?'

Dunkley was hurting. His mouth tasted of blood, his hip and left knee ached. He wondered whether he'd broken his wrist.

'Charles, I've met some liars in my time but no one like you.'

'How have I deceived you, Harry? I showed you that Bruce Paxton was corrupt and dangerous. You proved that he was. I've shown you that China is a threat. That's beyond doubt.'

'Maybe, Charles. But you never mentioned the Alliance. It took our friend Kimberley to discover that.'

'Tell me what's wrong with a group of patriots looking at the long game. Yes, I work for them and I'm proud of it. They're the generals and I'm their foot soldier.'

'But whose side are you on? Australia's? The United States'?'

'Both. Don't kid yourself like some neophyte. We need the US, much more than it needs us. These are the most dangerous days of our lifetime. China threatens everything.'

Dunkley probed the inside of his cheek and felt a gash where his teeth had cut the soft inside flesh of his mouth.

'And you're prepared to bring down a government. A prime minister. To lie and scheme, just like your bosses have been doing, for what? Nearly fifty years.'

'No, Harry.' Dancer's voice was firm. 'I've made you an agent of truth, alerting the Australian people to the Chinese threat. This government's fate is now in its own hands.'

'What about the Lusitania Plan? Lives were threatened. Is that the work of a patriot?'

'No lives were in danger. We just showed a glimpse of the future. And make no mistake, our man in the lake, Lin An, was trying to warn us about the country he was fleeing. That embassy is a wormhole. China has tapped into our Five Eyes intelligence. Their stooge Catriona Bailey opened the door. There's a war going on, Harry, and the front line is here.'

Dunkley cursed himself as the reality of how badly he'd misread Dancer sank in.

'I've been your pawn.' Dunkley's admission was barely a rasp.

'You've played your role to perfection. And what do we do with pawns? We sacrifice them for the chance of victory.'

'Who else have you sacrificed? Kimberley?'

Dancer lifted the Glock with his right hand, as if he needed a shield.

Dunkley took a risk. 'Charles, I thought the three of us were working as a team.'

'She should have kept her investigation to Paxton's Chinese links. That was her job. Her duty. That's what we expected her to do.'

'But she didn't. You couldn't control her. She was an individual and asked uncomfortable questions. Like who would want Paxton eliminated.'

Dancer's hand betrayed him with the slightest of trembles.

'And now I wonder who would want to eliminate *her*?' Dunkley pointed at Dancer. 'Maybe you.'

Dancer stood and prowled the room, shifting his gun from hand to hand, avoiding eye contact with his captive.

'We are at war, Mr Dunkley.' His voice was harsh. 'The enemy is clear. Kimberley was never satisfied with accepting things as they are. As with her body, she forced them to fit her warped ideal. Her judgement was clouded. She threatened the project.'

Dunkley pushed harder. 'She threatened you. Confronted you with what you are. And you killed her.'

Dancer stopped. His head dropped and he inspected the gun in his right hand.

'I did.' The admission came as a shock, to Dancer as much as Dunkley. The killer turned to the journalist and his eyes shone with hate and fury.

'Every day I feel the guilt of that. But it was my duty. People die in wars.'

Dancer pulled back the slide on his pistol, dragging a bullet from the magazine into the handgun's chamber.

'And, Harry, never forget who got her involved. I pulled the trigger, but you loaded the gun. You didn't care that helping you compromised her. You were chasing the only thing that's ever mattered to you. A front-page story.'

Dancer aimed the Glock at Dunkley.

'Now you are a threat. And my job is to eliminate threats.'

Dunkley could see the fragility behind Dancer's facade. A man who hated himself and took out his rage on real and imagined enemies. But that was precisely what made him deadly. Dancer's masters used his self-loathing as their weapon.

Dunkley did not doubt his life was in the balance. A shudder of terror swept through him and his heart pounded. But he was surprised by the strength and defiance in his voice.

'Go on, kill me too.'

The spy dropped his hands.

'I don't have to kill you. You're already dead. No one will ever believe another word that you write. And you have no pages to write for.'

The truth of Dancer's words stung.

'I don't need a paper to expose your evil. I'll publish on the web. Everything I know. Everything.'

Dancer laughed, a rich baritone of ridicule, before throwing the Glock onto the lounge.

'And then, Harry, you'll be just another deranged nut job on the internet.'

Canberra

'It's a lovely view, isn't it, Brendan?'

The soft croak of her voice was nearly unrecognisable.

Catriona Bailey gazed out the window of a Senate office overlooking the lake. Her body had withered. She looked brittle, her skin like crushed paper, her hands reduced to tiny movements.

A battered rag doll in a motorised wheelchair.

Yet to Brendan Ryan she loomed as a grisly succubus. In his worst nightmares, the Labor warlord never dreamed he'd be having this meeting.

So this is what it's like to bargain with Satan.

Her left hand pushed a lever and an electric motor whirred as Bailey moved to face the defence minister. Her body might be broken but her eyes were a blaze of steel and resolve.

The eyes that had been her resurrection.

'They tell me you find it difficult to speak for long,' Ryan ventured.

324

'The tracheotomy did a lot of damage. I can talk for about five minutes. Then I have to stop.'

'Then this meeting will be mercifully brief.'

'It will, because your presence here speaks volumes. Doesn't it, Brendan?'

Ryan knew they were here to barter for the last of his dignity. He only wanted one assurance.

'The final matter to resolve is the date of the election. I will support you if you call it within a month of taking over as leader.'

'What's the rush? Toohey set September 14.'

'Frankly, I want to minimise the damage that you can inflict, Catriona. On the party and the country.'

'Yet the reason you want me back is to save the ship.'

'Don't kid yourself. The ship has sunk. I just want to stuff as many survivors as I can into the life rafts.'

Bailey's eyes, a stain of dark blue, held Ryan in their vice for a brief, uncomfortable moment.

'Done.'

Ryan stood transfixed by the view. The out-of-the-way office had been chosen to avoid prying eyes.

But he could not escape the glare of his conscience.

'What else could I have done?' he muttered, as he put both hands on the window sill to steady himself.

Ryan was an old-school right-winger, the son of a Victorian Catholic who'd stayed with the Australian Labor Party when the split had torn its heart out in the 1950s. His father had lost life-long friendships in the turmoil, so he hammered a set of principles into the eager boy. Old, unfashionable ideas like duty, constancy and, above all, loyalty.

'If a man isn't loyal then he isn't anything,' his father would say. 'You pick and stick, son.'

Ryan had settled his loyalties long ago. To his party, his country and its allies. Once he'd built those battlements, he'd declared war on his enemies. Life was about hard choices and a man had to realise he couldn't have everything.

But Bailey?

She personified everything he hated. A dictator who had hijacked and gutted his party, a vagrant Christian who shifted like a chameleon between denominations, and a multilateralist who embraced the impotence of the United Nations.

Above all, Bailey was a clear and present danger to the alliance that protected the nation's castle walls. Ryan had long suspected that Bailey was the human equivalent of a computer virus: a dormant but deadly infection.

One that had been cultivated by the Chinese.

He slumped into a chair and put his head in his hands. Martin Toohey was a decent man but had been a disaster as prime minister. Ryan blamed himself for part of that failure. He had pushed Toohey into rolling Bailey, not realising that the coup would kill both leaders.

Then again, Toohey had made plenty of his own mistakes.

He needed a cigarette and decided to have one, an act of defiance against another modern verity he despised. He pulled a packet from his jacket pocket and looked at the miserable image on it: a man with a gaping hole in a cancer-ravaged throat.

How appropriate.

'This is for you, Catriona.' Ryan stuffed a fag in his mouth and lit it. He drew in a deep breath and blew a long and gratifying line of smoke into the room.

He looked around for something that would serve as an ashtray before shrugging his shoulders and tapping the ash onto the carpet. He rubbed it in with the toe of his shoe, leaving a little grey smudge. A small sin compared to the mortal one he had just committed.

I have sold out to buy my party a few seats. A slim hope of redemption.

Ryan took another long drag and blew smoke towards the window. Out of sight, just off Kings Avenue to his right, he knew there was a statue of John Curtin and Ben Chifley, frozen in a moment from 1945 as they walked to the parliament.

Curtin, the leader who had turned to America in the nation's hour of greatest need. And the US had delivered.

Now Labor was turning away from America without understanding the consequences. His party needed time in the wilderness to reassess. But he didn't want to see it destroyed and, under Toohey, that was inevitable. Bailey was the only viable choice. It was a huge gamble, but a quick election would minimise the risk.

Once she had minimised the losses, he would bury her forever.

And all it has cost me is my soul.

Ryan threw the butt on the carpet, lifted his shoe to snuff out the ember, and stopped.

He decided to let it burn.

*

'I thought you'd be with me to the end, Brendan.'

Martin Toohey's voice was laced with sadness. The defence minister had hoped for anger. He could cope with a fight, but sorrow was more than he could bear.

'I had to do it. I had to make a choice between my friendship with you and my loyalty to the party.'

He forced himself to look at Toohey.

'Martin, we're doomed. The people have stopped listening to you. If you lead us to the election there will be a rout and it will take a generation for us to recover.'

Toohey's eyes gleamed. Like all leaders, he had an inflated view of his powers. He still believed he could turn the ship around.

'That's not true. We can claw our way back with the mental health plan. I can beat Landry.'

'Martin, even if we get elected we can't afford your huge welfare scheme. George, you know the truth. Tell him.'

Papadakis lifted his head and fixed Ryan with hate in his eyes.

'Truth. What would you know about the truth, Brendan? And don't ever mention the word "loyalty" again. You have betrayed us for someone you despise. And if she wins, what do you get? What promises has Bailey made to buy you?'

'I got nothing beyond a commitment to an early election.'

Papadakis snorted.

'You know your Bible, Brendan. "What does it profit a man to gain the whole world yet lose his soul?" I thought you were with us.'

'I didn't sign up so you could empty Treasury to build a welfare state. If you keep gutting Defence, you'll find your dreams mugged by reality. We're facing war in the Pacific and slashing Defence is endangering the nation.'

Toohey strode from behind his desk.

'Don't be such a fucking drama queen. The US and China can't afford to go to war. Their economies rely on each other. Both will come to their senses.'

Ryan shook his head.

'No one ever wants to go to war. No one can afford to go to war. But nations go to war when the alternative is unacceptable. The preconditions for war now exist. America won't be pushed back across the Pacific and China won't stop pushing.'

Toohey pointed to the map of the world on his wall.

'Then we need to sit where we are on that map. In the middle. As the calm heads at the table. Not to always fall in behind the United States. Those clowns started this fight, Brendan.'

Ryan waved at the briefs piled on Toohey's disorderly desk.

'What about the attacks on us? If a Chinese destroyer opened fire on an Australian ship, it would be an act of war. Yet Beijing has hit our airspace, banks and phones. Prime Minister, that is unacceptable.'

Toohey moved closer to Ryan.

'You know as well as I do that verifying that kind of attack is dicey. I'm not starting a fight without being certain who broke the windows.

'And is it any wonder that the Chinese see us as puppets of Uncle Sam? The Yanks keep dragging us into their fights. Maybe we need to reposition ourselves for the twenty-first century. To build a more nuanced set of alliances.'

Toohey's words confirmed Ryan's worst fears.

'Really? The next warning shot might be through your brain. Hitting air-traffic control was an act of war. And when did you decide to unwind the ANZUS treaty? When did that become Australia's foreign policy?'

'I do believe I am prime minister.'

Ryan checked his watch.

'Martin, I'll be supporting Catriona Bailey and I'll advise others to do the same. You will lose the ballot. I'm sorry about that. But the longer we've spoken this evening the more I'm convinced that it's the right decision. You're forgetting that your first duty is to defend the nation.'

Toohey put up his hand as Ryan turned to leave.

'One last thing. Something's been bothering me. I ran into Harry Dunkley and he had the most amazing conspiracy theory – that the US was behind those cyber-attacks, not China.'

The defence minister weighed his answer.

'Dunkley has been discredited. And, as I recall, you've never been a fan. It does sound like a wild theory. But some claim that Churchill dragged the US into World War I by allowing the *Lusitania* to be sunk. A thousand people drowned, but maybe millions were saved. The war ended. We won.'

Canberra

It had been a gift from her mother in celebration of her eighteenth birthday, her passage to womanhood. She'd packed the pink brush when she'd left

China; a link to a family and life left behind. Now it would go with her into exile.

Weng Meihui glanced around her room as she counted down the minutes.

What can you pack in one small bag when you are leaving your old life forever?

She brushed away a tear, trying to subdue a feeling of dread as she contemplated this flight from a life of certainty into the unknown. But her life was at risk if she stayed; the state would not hesitate to kill when her usefulness was spent. She had to flee.

It was 6.22pm. Eight minutes until the hire car was due. She would time her departure from the building to minimise the moments she'd need to wait on the kerb.

Her cover had been carefully thought through. The ambassador was at a parliamentary function. She was supposedly meeting the Canadian High Commissioner's wife for a drink at the Hyatt, a short stroll away. The driver had been instructed to pick her up around the corner from the Chinese embassy, opposite the rear entrance to the British High Commission. Bruce Paxton would be waiting at the airport.

It was time. She gathered her handbag and walked from the building. She nodded to the guard on the gate before turning onto the path that ran along the front of the complex.

Across the road three Falun Gong protesters were still camped under their banners. She turned into the crescent. The car was there, sporting the familiar 'HC' plates. She walked quickly to its rear door, her gaze lowered. She stepped in, collapsing into a comfortable leather seat.

Her heart surged with relief. She nodded for the driver to proceed.

The car pulled out from the kerb and indicated a left-hand turn. Weng knew the route well. They would pass in front of the Chinese embassy before turning left at the roundabout. In ten minutes, she would be pulling up at the airport.

She turned away from the embassy as they passed it on the left, nervously opening her bag to check that her brush was there.

Something was wrong.

'No. Turn left.' She waved in protest to the driver.

He said nothing as the limousine doors locked and the car glided up the dirt driveway to the new embassy building.

When he spoke, his voice was pure ice; his jet-black eyes were cruel in the rear-vision mirror.

'Ms Weng, where *did* you think you were going?'

*

'Mr Paxton, your flight is ready to board.'

Bruce Paxton offered a thin smile as the Qantas attendant handed him two boarding passes. It was 7.41pm and the final short-haul flight from Canberra to Sydney was about to depart.

He'd arrived at the Chairman's Lounge an hour earlier, ignoring the high-octane buzz of those Coalition MPs who'd managed to escape parliament and were heading home. The lounge was unusually empty because Labor's leadership showdown was still playing out.

That mattered nothing. His entire focus was on willing Weng Meihui to stroll into the lounge.

He had expected her forty-five minutes ago, positioning himself so he could nab her the moment she walked in. That was the plan. Hiding in plain sight and then a short walk to the gateway.

His phone calls had been unanswered and his fear began to rise with each empty minute.

Is she safe? Hurt? Has she changed her mind?

He was frantic. He left the lounge and looked down the escalators, hoping to see her rushing towards him.

A booming voice echoed through the cavernous space.

'This is a final boarding call for QF1494 ...'

Taiwan Strait

The glow on the horizon shimmered across the ocean as Frank Vinson surveyed USS *George Washington*'s flight deck from vulture's row, five decks above. The weather forecast promised a perfect day for flying, a breeze from the south, clear skies and a maximum of 69 degrees.

A Hornet thundered from the carrier, accelerating from zero to 165 miles per hour in two seconds. It banked as it climbed to take its place in the strike group's defensive bubble that stretched from the seabed to the heavens.

Two hundred nautical miles out from the carrier, a Super Fudd, the propeller-driven Grumman E-2C Hawkeye, monitored the group's battle space. From thirty thousand feet, its long-range airborne early-warning system kept watch for air and surface threats over a hundred and twenty thousand square miles.

Under water, ahead of the strike group, two USN attack submarines analysed the huge volume of underwater noise their sensors recorded, searching for surface and sub-surface threats. In the relatively shallow, noisy waters, hostile subs would be hard to find. Two cruisers and two destroyers formed the inner perimeter of the picket fence.

It was a formidable armada, but the 110-mile wide Taiwan Strait robbed Vinson's group of some of its defences. As large as it was, on the open ocean the strike group could disappear, moving from one point to another in a circle measuring seven hundred square miles in thirty minutes. But here there was nowhere to hide as it passed along the front fence of a nation that had developed 'area denial weapons' like the DF-21D anti-ship ballistic missile.

The carrier was sailing into danger.

Vinson could see the Pengjia Islet lighthouse blinking to port, just thirty-three nautical miles off Taiwan's northernmost tip. The fleet would sail south-west then turn towards the Taiwanese side of the cross-strait median, the imaginary line that delineated the territory controlled by Taipei and Beijing.

Two Westinghouse A4W nuclear reactors were driving the ship at a clip below twenty knots. At that speed it would take just over ten hours to pass through the Black Ditch.

The admiral caught the tang of salt on the breeze from the China Sea, a postcard of tranquillity, and wondered how long these waters would stay calm. Not since Bill Clinton had ordered the *Nimitz* and *Independence* to sail into the Strait in March 1996 – in response to Chinese missile testing – had the threat of conflict been so real.

Vinson turned his gaze towards the Chinese mainland, somewhere over the western horizon. He had never questioned America's role in defending democracy, not even when the fiction of George W Bush's weapons of mass destruction turned public opinion against the US.

But this? Something nagged inside.

He turned one last time to the ocean. An albatross passed close, flying north, a flash of white against a golden dawn. The admiral's spirit lifted. An omen, he hoped, that everything would be all right.

Hong Kong

First light began to brighten the Ngong Shuen Chau Naval Base, and preparations aboard the *Liaoning* were almost complete. China's first aircraft carrier was ready for its mission.

But Rear Admiral Yu Heng knew she was not ready for battle.

He looked along the carrier's flight deck with its distinctive ski-slope bow. The *Liaoning* had been transformed from a rusted Soviet hulk bought in 1998 under the pretext of it becoming a floating casino. At the same time, elite sailors were trained for the day the People's Republic launched its own carrier.

But like their ship they were not ready. The *Liaoning* was, in essence, *an aircraft carrier without aircraft.*

The Shenyang J-15 had been purpose-built for the *Liaoning*. Known as the Flying Shark, the fighter jet was a clone of Russia's Sukhoi Su-33. Chinese media proudly reported its top speed of Mach 2.4 and range of 3200 kilometres. But at this stage of China's carrier aviation development, the aircraft were purely for show.

Deception had always been one of China's weapons.

Exhaustive trials had shown that the J-15, like most carrier-borne aircraft, could not take off or land if fully fuelled and armed. But this jet's performance was much worse than anyone had expected. So they had a choice: a modest weapons load with almost no fuel; or a full load of fuel with almost no weapons. The compromise struck gave the combat aircraft an effective range of 120 kilometres.

In reality, the *Liaoning* was as yet only a training ship, not a fearsome fighting machine, and half the size of the *George Washington*.

At 0625, Admiral Leng Sha, commander in chief of the PLA Navy, phoned Yu with his final orders. He'd hand-picked Yu to command the *Liaoning*. His protégé would now carry the hopes of the navy and the nation on this dangerous assignment.

'Heng, you will sail in thirty-five minutes.'

'Sir, everything is ready. But you understand the limitations of our weapon systems. We can launch planes, but they are only capable of training sorties. They are not combat ready.'

'Yes, Heng. But your mission is not to engage the adversary. *Liaoning* is our flagship. You are to be seen to stare down the American strike group and make it retreat. Your systems won't be needed if it comes to a fight. Our mainland forces and our submarines can defeat the Americans. And they know it.'

'As you taught me, sir. The assassin's mace. A smaller force can wound a larger enemy if it is more nimble: with its weapons or its wit.'

'And the world will be watching. The most important weapon on this mission is the television crew. Are they on board?'

'They are, Admiral.'

'Make sure they get pictures of the planes taking off and landing.'

'Yes sir.'

'Good. America's retreat across the Pacific begins today.'

Taiwan Strait

The flag bridge of the *George Washington* was a scene of ordered apprehension as senior staff monitored intelligence and kept watch over a carrier battle group that stretched across more than a hundred miles of sky and ocean.

Jane Marsh, a naval intelligence officer, traced several lines of intel on her screen, reading it twice before reporting to Admiral Frank Vinson. 'Sir, the *Liaoning* has put to sea and is heading north. Into the Taiwan Strait. If it maintains its course, we will see her in less than five hours.'

The room fell silent as Vinson and his senior staff weighed the significance of the news.

'That ship is hardly fit to sail.' Marsh was incredulous. 'All our intelligence shows it is nowhere near ready to fight.'

The news confirmed Vinson's worst fears. His force was being drawn into a historic and extremely dangerous confrontation.

'That ship doesn't have to be able to fight. We're off mainland China. There is more than enough muscle to starboard and under us to overwhelm this strike group.'

'So why put the *Liaoning* to sea?'

The admiral stared toward the horizon.

'It's the David and Goliath image they want. China is making a statement that it is now powerful enough to stare down the world's only superpower.'

'So what will we do?' Marsh spoke for the group.

Vinson looked down at a screen that showed their position in the strait and weighed his options.

'I intend to complete my mission. But no one said how fast we have to travel. Alert the group, we're going to slow this operation right down. I hope the *Liaoning* commander has the sense to do the same thing. Get me PACOM. The president has to decide how he wants this to end.'

Canberra

The autumn cool had arrived at last. A light mist curled from the sky, barely skimming the ground baked flint-hard by an unholy summer. Across the lake, a swirl of lights sparkled from the walls of the National Museum.

Night had descended on Nara Park, transforming a row of trees into ghostly silhouettes.

A few days earlier, Bruce Paxton had perched on this same timber bench, comforting Weng Meihui as she poured out her fears. Now they were all too real, a waking nightmare.

For the first time in a long while, he was frightened.

A dozen desperate phone calls had gone unanswered. Mei had failed to make the rendezvous at the airport, vanishing without a trace. The hire car company said the booking had been cancelled with a phone call thirty minutes before the scheduled pick-up. By a male.

Paxton had asked his driver to cruise slowly past the Chinese embassy, hoping to pick up some clue. Nothing. Even the Falun Gong had packed up.

Mei had been tense, but excited at the prospect of defecting, of leaving her double life behind. They'd sketched out plans for the future. Had Paxton misread her? Had he, the great political schemer, been had?

Or had she simply backed away at the last moment, afraid of turning against a homeland that would pursue her to the grave, no matter where she went? Was he a fool for thinking she would discard the security of her past for an uncertain future?

Yet she had seemed so certain as she'd nestled into his embrace in this park, trembling as she told him of the deaths of her three compatriots.

Her fear was real. He was convinced of it. And he was certain that, if she had willingly changed her mind, she would have sent him a message. He knew enough of her to be sure that she would not want to torture him like this.

Then what?

Had the Americans betrayed him, tipped off the Chinese, or maybe his own government, unwilling to deal with the diplomatic stink?

The most likely explanation was that Mei had been discovered, intercepted.

Perhaps killed.

Was she lying somewhere below the black surface of the lake?

He shuddered and pulled his jacket tight. He rose and walked towards his ComCar.

Paxton was resolved. If Mei was alive, he would find her. If not, he would expose those who had harmed her. Nothing else mattered. He loved her, he realised, always had.

He quickened his pace, needing the security of plush leather, the reassuring idle of the Falcon's V6. Parliament House was just a few minutes away. He would take stock in the familiar surrounds of his office.

Then he would do what he did best. Plot. And exact revenge.

Canberra

The Cardinals had been sent out early. Catriona Bailey's damaged vocal cords restricted her public appearances, so the new prime minister's chorus of allies – all promised plum ministerial jobs – were out in force.

As one they trumpeted regime change and the promise of a turnaround in Labor's fortunes. The 'Bailey bounce' was already resonating with the television breakfast programs that had seized on suspect polling showing that she led the featureless Landry 55 to 15 per cent as preferred prime minister. The rest still favoured Elizabeth Scott.

The federation had never witnessed such political carnage: a prime minister and opposition leader fed to the sharks within hours of each other.

But the drama in Canberra was dwarfed by the first flashes of a showdown in the Taiwan Strait. The world's superpower was on a collision course with the rising titan of China.

Amid this maelstrom of news, Bruce Paxton decided to hold a press conference.

Just a handful of journalists gathered in the Senate courtyard, more out of duty than interest. Some defence correspondents tagged along to see if they could snag a decent quote on China to pad out their copy. None were prepared for the bombshell that followed.

'Ladies and gentlemen, thanks for coming. As a former defence minister, I know better than most that defending this country is the primary job of any government. I have grave fears about Catriona Bailey's capacity to do that job.

'It was Ms Bailey who green-lighted the new Chinese embassy down by the lake. I now have information that shows that building is a direct threat to national security.

'A month ago a Chinese national died as he tried to defect. Two other men have been murdered as part of a cover-up.'

Paxton took a deep breath.

'I also hold grave fears for the Chinese ambassador's wife, Weng Meihui. She was planning to defect last night, but has disappeared without trace.'

The *West Australian*'s defence writer broke the stunned silence.

'How do you know the ambassador's wife was planning to defect?'

335

'She was meant to be meeting me as part of that process.'

'How do you know her?'

Paxton stalled. His mouth was parched. He fiddled with his tie.

'We are … friends. A relationship was forged many years ago. We have warm feelings for each other.'

'Hang on, Mr Paxton, were these "warm feelings" going on when you were defence minister?'

'We shared no more than a genuine friendship.'

'What evidence do you have that two men have been murdered?' The questions were coming thick and fast.

'Ms Weng told me. And I believe her.'

'That's it? Can you back up your claim that Bailey has any link to this?'

'For that you will have to wait. I will be making a full statement to the parliament in the next session. But I call on the police and Foreign Affairs to investigate the murders at the embassy. And I plead with them to find Weng Meihui.'

Washington

Earle Jackson scanned the hard copy a final time. He'd already run through the autocue twice.

The US president was preparing to address the nation and every syllable had to be perfect. It was 8pm, primetime on America's east coast.

His throat was dry. The reality of the fire that he'd fanned was dawning on him. But he could see no way out without a massive loss of face. He had to stare down the Chinese.

The cameras rolled.

'My fellow Americans, as I speak to you tonight the USS *George Washington* is on a peaceful mission in international waters in the Taiwan Strait.

'For nearly seventy years our nation has stood guard over peace in the Pacific, allowing all to prosper.

'America is the brightest beacon for freedom and opportunity in the world and no one will keep that light from shining.

'The Chinese government is moving to prevent our peaceful mission by effectively blockading the strait, a crucial trade route.

'Make no mistake. If the George Washington is forced to turn back, then it will mark a new and dangerous chapter in world affairs. As your president, I will not allow that to happen.

'This is not the first aggressive act by the Chinese. Since the end of last year it has been increasingly pushing the boundaries of its power. Peaceful nations like Japan and South Korea are in dispute with Beijing in the East China Sea. China claims Taiwan. And to its south, China demands waters owned by the Philippines, Malaysia, Indonesia and Vietnam.

'These are not the acts of a nation that claims its rise to power does not threaten global peace. If the twentieth century teaches us anything, it is that those who stand silent when the first signs of aggression appear are condemned by history.'

The word PAUSE loomed on the autocue and Jackson took a breath before emphasising the next sentence.

'The United States will not stand silent.

'I call on President Meng to revoke China's ill-considered air-defence zone over the Senkaku Islands and to withdraw the fishermen who are occupying the main islands with his blessing.

'I call on him to talk to his neighbours, not bully them.

'And I call on him to let the *George Washington* sail unimpeded, as a sign that China genuinely believes in the right of civilised nations to freely navigate the world's waters.

'Good night. God bless you and God bless America.'

Beijing

The wash of applause from three thousand hastily assembled citizens rippled through the Great Hall of the People as Meng Tao strode onto the stage and took the microphone. He would be speaking not only to the gathering, but to his nation; his speech would be beamed via CCTV to a vast audience.

'Friends and comrades, these are dark and dangerous hours,' he began.

'The United States has sent a nuclear warship into waters just one hundred kilometres off the Chinese mainland.

'I ask the world to consider how President Jackson would react if he was in my position.

'But we do not have to guess. We know.

'In 1963 when the Soviet Union moved to station weapons on Cuba, one hundred and forty kilometres from America, President Kennedy said this:

The 1930s taught us a clear lesson: aggressive conduct, if allowed to go unchecked and unchallenged, ultimately leads to war. This nation is

337

opposed to war. We are also true to our word. Our unswerving objective, therefore, must be to prevent the use of these missiles against this or any other country, and to secure their withdrawal or elimination.

Our policy has been one of patience and restraint.

'Wise words from a wise president. I agree with every one of them. We are not the aggressors here. But we will not be bullied anymore.

'As a sign of goodwill, I have ordered the *Liaoning* to hold its position in the south of the Taiwan Strait. It will not advance, but it will not allow the American carrier to pass.

'America now has time to consider the wisdom of its actions.

'I call on President Jackson to order the USS *George Washington* to turn around and to go back the way it came.

'Today, like President Kennedy, I am drawing a line in the water.'

Canberra

Two Australian flags stood regally either side of a long low desk. A row of cameras crowded a small riser. It was 3.15pm. Catriona Bailey, fresh from a visit to the governor-general, had scheduled her first press conference as the nation's leader.

This was a make-or-break moment.

The PM had to prove that Labor was no longer a rabble but was back in business.

She had to contend with the threat of a war in the Pacific.

Above all, she had to convince a sceptical media pack that she was physically and mentally up to the job.

Flanked by the Defence chief, Jack Webster, Bailey scanned parliament's packed Blue Room, her wheelchair positioned dead centre.

'Ladies and gentlemen, it's good to be back. Last night I told my colleagues that Labor could win the next election. I firmly believe that with the right policies and leadership we can.

'These are dangerous times. They demand firm resolve, a steady hand and deep experience. I am the woman for this hour.

'Any questions?'

Bailey was assailed by two-dozen voices. She dismissed them all with a single word: 'Michelle.'

The press gallery doyenne opened with a question that every one of her colleagues wanted answered.

'Prime Minister, a week ago you lay stricken in hospital. For the past eighteen months you have been kept alive by machines. Are you up to it?'

'Michelle, I had a condition that kills most people. Almost no one recovers. I did. Am I tough? You work it out.'

Bailey's minders had briefed journalists that the press conference would be limited to twenty minutes. All desperate for a question, they yelled and gesticulated, hoping to steamroll the other voices into silence. Bailey ignored them, and simply worked her way through a roll call of names.

'Mark Simkin.'

'PM, President Jackson has called on America's allies to stand by its side during its stand-off with China. What role will Australia play?'

Bailey was resolute.

'War is not inevitable. Neither nation seeks war, so I believe it can be avoided. Australia does have a role to play as a creative middle power. This is what leadership is about.

'Because of my efforts we now have a seat at the UN Security Council. I have rung Ban Ki-moon and proposed a crisis meeting. He agrees. I will be flying to New York tomorrow to chair it myself.

'I have also called President Meng. He has warmly welcomed my intervention and invited me to Beijing for talks. Australia has a unique relationship with both the United States and China.

'I am determined to be an instrument for peace.'

For the first time, Bailey nodded in the direction of the grim-faced chief of the defence force.

'I have instructed Jack to revoke the order for a squadron of Super Hornets to be stationed in Guam. We treasure our historic alliance with the United States, but I feel that such a move at this time would be seen by the Chinese as provocative. And I'm sure President Jackson will understand.'

David Speers from Sky News called to Webster. 'CDF, do you agree with this decision?'

Webster shifted in his seat, a click of his tongue betraying a dry mouth.

'My job is to follow the orders of the government of the day. The prime minister has said the planes will not be deployed. That instruction will be followed.'

As the press conference was drawing to a close, one issue remained untouched. Karen Middleton from SBS went for the jugular.

'Ms Bailey, Bruce Paxton has made some extraordinary claims. That the Chinese ambassador's wife was about to defect and has gone missing. That two Chinese nationals have been murdered. And that you, as prime minister, risked national security by allowing the new embassy to be built with only Chinese labour.'

Bailey's disdain bled through every word of her reply.

'I literally do not have the breath to waste on this garbage from a disgraced former member of the Labor Party. Every word is a lie. And I note he offered not a shred of evidence to support it.

'One. The Australian government was never approached to offer asylum to any Chinese national. Two. The Chinese embassy has issued a statement saying the ambassador's wife has returned to Beijing to visit family. Three. They completely deny these absurd claims of murder. And, Karen, neither the Federal Police nor Foreign Affairs say they have any concerns. Four. I did give the go-ahead for an embassy extension that had been on the books for years. And Australia has reciprocal rights in Beijing. Last, there was and is no threat to our security from the new Chinese embassy. Is there, CDF?'

Webster leaned into the microphone. 'As you know, we do not discuss matters of national security. But I can confirm that Mr Paxton's claims are utterly without foundation.'

'And with that, folks, we have some serious work to do.' Bailey turned her chair to the door, gliding out of the room to the bellows of scribes and the machine-gun rattle of cameras.

'How the fuck did this happen?'

Every word was marinated with Jack Webster's anger. The CDF had just been reduced to a prop in a prime ministerial pantomime. But what really stung was the realisation that the fortress had been stormed. The enemy was in the castle.

Webster's office, on the fourth floor of Defence HQ, commanded one of Canberra's best panoramas, looking across the lake to the parliament and the Brindabellas beyond.

He had ordered two of the nation's most powerful bureaucrats to join him: the secretary of Foreign Affairs and the director-general of ASIO.

And one other. Matthew Whelan, the director of the Defence Signals Directorate. The 44-year-old public servant had enjoyed an unblemished career. Now he carried an indelible stain.

The Star Chamber was in session.

Whelan had spent a month trying to track down the source of the worst security breach in Australia's history. He had barely slept in the last forty-eight hours. Finally, his team had identified the trail. The news was horrifying, and he feared the messenger was about to be executed.

But the awful truth could not be avoided.

'The DSD systems have been compromised. All of them.'

Webster picked at the braid on his shoulder. 'You said that. What I want to know is how the fuck it happened?'

'The adversary has managed to inject a virus into our system. We're still analysing it. But it's the most sophisticated zero day program we've ever seen.'

DFAT's David Joyce spoke for all of the inquisitors.

'It's very important that you explain every detail of this. Clearly. What is a zero day program?'

'It exploits existing weakness in a system. Lies dormant until it is commanded to move. The moment it starts operating is zero day. In the very best of these programs the victim never knows there has been a security breach. And, as I said, this is the best we've ever seen.'

'How does it work?'

Whelan glanced at his notes. 'It's similar to, but much better than, the US National Security Agency's Quantum program. The NSA weapon is hardware. This one is software. Once downloaded, it hijacks the host hardware and uses covert radio waves to set up a highway of information outwards. More disturbingly it also sets up a pathway inwards. One that can be used for a cyber-attack. It's a work of genius. The only limitation is that the adversary needs to have a base station within ten kilometres to pick up the radio signal. But the receiver could be the size of a briefcase.'

'Or as large as a new Chinese embassy.' Joyce was shaking his head.

Webster asked, 'Why wouldn't they use the old one?'

ASIO's Richard Dalton interjected. 'Because it's hopelessly compromised, Jack, and the Chinese know it. I was part of the construction team in the '90s.'

Joyce got the questioning back on track. 'The question remains, Mr Whelan: How did the most secure building in Australia come to be infiltrated? Many of your systems are off the grid, not connected to the internet.'

'That's true. The adversary needed to jump the gap to our off-line computers. The only way to do that was to get someone inside to plant the virus.'

Webster jumped in. 'And who the fuck was that?'

Whelan's voice was a rasp. 'Well … we have a theory. Which I have to say seems unbelievable. But it's the only theory we have.'

'What is it?' Webster demanded.

341

'The only possible breach we can see dates back to September 2008. But as I say … it's inconceivable.'

'Just spit it out!' The CDF's impatience rang in his voice.

Whelan fidgeted with the pile of notes on his lap. 'It was at the height of the financial meltdown. The prime minister was visiting DSD for the first time. She was asked to turn in her phone at security and kicked up an enormous stink. Said she was expecting a call from the US Treasury secretary. Insisted on keeping her phone. I was called in. And … I relented.'

'What kind of phone was it?' Dalton asked.

'It was an iPhone, early model, and I hadn't seen that many of them.'

'So a sophisticated device capable of delivering a virus through a USB port,' Dalton said.

'Yes, sir.'

'But there are no USB ports inside DSD, are there?'

'Sir, there is one. In my office. We keep it for operational reasons. But it's in the most secure part of the most secure building in Australia.'

'Where was the meeting with the prime minister held?'

Whelan's head dropped. 'In that room.'

'And what happened?' Joyce's face betrayed the fury that was rising with every word of this briefing.

'Ten minutes into the meeting the call from the US came and Bailey insisted everyone leave the room.'

'Including you?'

'Yes, sir.'

'How long was she alone in that room?'

'Twenty minutes. Half an hour. Long enough.'

'Did you notice anything unusual when you were allowed back in the office?' Dalton asked.

'Yes, sir. Bailey had plugged her iPhone charger cable into my computer USB port. Claimed she was running low on battery. I protested and demanded that she immediately remove it. She reminded me, again, that she was the prime minister. But she complied. After she left we ran thorough system checks. Nothing unusual showed up.'

'Until now,' Webster said.

'Yes, sir. We believe the adversary left the virus dormant for years. Which is, in itself, remarkable. Our best guess is they activated the zero day program about three months ago.'

'The Chinese are very patient people. What have they got?'

Whelan's voice fell to a whisper. 'Everything.'

'How can we sanitise the system?' Dalton leaned forward with such urgency that Whelan flinched, as if expecting a blow.

'We'll have to shut everything down.' Whelan's shirt was damp with sweat. 'I mean everything. Every single computer in DSD, Defence, Foreign Affairs and the intelligence community is now potentially infected. Every terminal, every server. We'll have to clean them all.'

Webster, usually so clear-headed in a crisis, was visibly shaken.

He walked to his window and looked across the lake to parliament. He wondered, briefly, if it was his duty to speak out.

Should he, the most respected military figure in Australia, warn the people that their leader was a threat to national security? An agent of China.

If he spoke, she would be finished. Forever.

But so would he, as leader of a defence establishment that could not defend itself.

And what would the Americans do?

Webster shifted his gaze to the left. There, at the heart of the Russell Defence complex, an eagle astride a globe soared seventy-nine metres into the sky on an aluminium pillar. The Australian community had raised one hundred thousand pounds to have the American memorial built in 1954. The plaque at its base gave thanks for 'the vital help given by the United States of America during the war in the Pacific 1941–1945'. There was no more potent symbol of how deeply the alliance was embedded in Australia's defence establishment.

Now another Pacific war loomed and Australia would stand idle while the US took up the fight. Worse, his nation had blown a hole below the US waterline before the battle even began.

He turned back to the room.

'No one knows about this. Ever.'

_____

Canberra

Brendan Ryan had been waiting for an hour. It was the second time the defence minister had been summoned that day by Catriona Bailey, who had immediately reverted to type.

She had convened a National Security Council meeting for 9am and kept the entire defence and intelligence establishment in limbo for three hours. When she finally arrived, Bailey had launched into a dissertation about US–China relations before demanding a pile of briefs that Ryan knew she would never read.

It was now 6.48pm and Ryan's rage was rising with every minute. An electric hum finally signalled the arrival of the prime minister and the three staffers who trailed in her wake. She glided past Ryan without acknowledging him, continuing to fire off orders to her harried entourage.

'James, I need something to eat and a cup of tea. And where is that brief on Taiwan's defence capability?'

One adviser hustled off as Bailey barked at another.

'When can I expect the call from Park Geun-hye?'

'Prime Minister, we haven't yet been able to get a time confirmed with the South Koreans. Their president is in a meeting with her own national security committee.'

'I didn't ask for your excuses. Just get me a time.'

Bailey finally turned to Ryan. Her gaunt face was layered with makeup to lift the cadaver pallor of her skin. She stretched a thin smile.

'Brendan. You won't mind if I have a notetaker stay. My … condition … means I need an extra pair of hands.'

'Sure.' Ryan nodded. 'But before we go any further, I was surprised you didn't flag an election date at your press conference. As we agreed.'

'In case you hadn't noticed, the US and China are one mistake from war. Ban Ki-moon has personally asked me to mediate. Do you really think, in these circumstances, that the Australian people want an election?'

Bailey spat out the words.

'Our best hope of victory is to demonstrate that I am the only person capable of leading the nation through this crisis.'

Ryan wasn't surprised by Bailey's signature self-obsession.

'Don't kid yourself. Our best hope is that the bounce from your return lasts long enough for us to scramble a half-decent loss,' he shot back. 'Every day we wait we'll sink further in the polls. This is about the party, not you. And we had a deal.'

Bailey fixed Ryan with a don't-fuck-with-me glare.

'All bets are off.' The PM nodded to the notetaker. 'Put that brief where I can see it.'

She scanned a page and turned back to the minister. 'Brendan, I am reshuffling and offering you Human Services.'

'In the outer ministry?'

'Correct.'

'So you're turfing me from Cabinet?'

'Correct, again.'

'You've betrayed me.'

'Well Brendan, now you know exactly what it feels like.'

Power, a surge of power, unfiltered, coursed through her veins as she pressed her hands firmly on the arms of her wheelchair.

Slowly, painfully, she laboured and pushed until her body began to rise. Her legs, weak from months of stillness, moved. They joined the agonising task of trying to lift her body from the chair.

She stood, alone and unassisted, her staff banished from the office.

It was a triumph of the will. Her will to power. Power over herself. Power over others.

Her legs trembled under her weight. But they held. She focused her formidable will on moving just one foot. Her right. It slid forward.

Then the left. Her hands pressed on the desk to hold some of her weight. Her left foot moved and she took a small step forward.

She reached the end of the desk and lifted her hands from it. She shook but did not fall.

Catriona Bailey locked her eyes on the map she'd installed on the wall, the sole relic in this office from her first dynasty. She stepped towards it.

Five triumphant paces. Each surer than the last.

She stood before the map of the world.

Australia was now hers again. She loved its shape. The way it sat at the centre of the world.

She looked up at China, the nation that had beguiled her since she was a child. From the moment she saw the intricate genius of her mother's Ming vase. She'd spent a lifetime unravelling the mysteries of the Middle Kingdom.

Her gaze swept across the Pacific to the United States, the twentieth-century superpower. Unwilling to share the earth with its latest and most potent rival.

Soon she would travel to New York to chair a meeting of the United Nations Security Council. To mediate as the two angry giants threatened to shatter a fragile peace.

She had been born for this, had given her life for this. Everything she'd achieved had been to prepare for this hour.

She was the bridge between East and West. Cometh the hour, cometh the woman.

She began to fashion her opening address in her mind.

'Ladies and gentlemen, the world stands at a crossroads. It can once again choose the path of war and destruction. Or it can choose the path of peace. The lives of your children and grandchildren depend on the decisions we make here today. With my guidance ...'

'Prime Minister, are you all right?' The concerned tones of her chief of staff rang out, tearing at her, breaking her thoughts.

Bailey looked up, shaken awake, momentarily disoriented. She was still seated at her desk. Still locked in her wheelchair. Frozen by her illness.

Canberra

Harry Dunkley idled his LandCruiser down a narrow dirt track to a place that he'd last visited twenty months ago on an arctic morning. He had decided to revisit the place where his misadventure had begun, that day when a black-and-white photograph forever changed his life.

The same picnic table marked the end of the dirt road. An empty packet of Winfield Blue and a discarded insulin vial littered the ground beneath it, a sign that people sometimes visited this lonely clip of land. But today Yarramundi Reach stood empty.

It was late morning on a Sunday and Dunkley had nowhere else to be. It had been three days since Charles Dancer had trained a gun on him, while revealing himself as Kimberley's murderer. The memory of it still shook him, as did his impotence to expose the killer and his masters.

In his car, the mobile rang. He ignored it.

He'd lost Celia Mathieson. He'd returned her calls only to find she was merely checking to see how he was. As a friend.

He'd lost his job. No, it was more than a job. A calling. A crusade to hold those in power to account. Who would touch up the untouchable now?

And the one politician he had trusted without question had betrayed him.

He shivered in his shorts and T-shirt. A south-east breeze had picked up off the lake, chilly by comparison with the recent stretch of hot summer days. Soon winter would grip Canberra, a depressing prospect.

He had devoted himself to this city for most of his adult life. He loved it, the endless intrigue, the heady layers of drama and soap.

Now, he'd been nearly destroyed by it. He realised with a jolt that he barely knew how the game was played.

Why hadn't he, the great investigative reporter, seen the clues that in hindsight seemed so clear?

He had to consider what to do next. He'd fielded a couple of calls from suitors offering big bucks if he would sell his soul to work in public relations. He was appalled at the idea of becoming a spin doctor, angry with himself for even contemplating it. But he had to eat.

That one black-and-white pic had given him – what? One scalp. One cracking yarn. But at what cost?

His mobile rang again. He wandered back to the car and stretched his arm through the window. He checked the caller ID. It was the one person he was happy to speak to.

'Mate, I thought you'd be at church?'

He collapsed on the lounge, the emotion and pain of four brutal days washing over him.

'Harry, you look like shit. Scotch?'

'Yes, mate. A double.'

The Bailie Nicol Jarvie had an immediate effect, its warm medicinal balm washing the back of his throat.

'Jesus, Harry, sip it. That's my last bottle. Why don't you bring your drink over here?'

Trevor Harris motioned to the pair of iMacs. Dunkley settled into a chair as the analyst booted his machines into action.

'I've managed to decrypt the last of the files on Ben's Cloud. Mate, these are the most extraordinary of all.'

Dunkley was heartened by Harris's enthusiasm, but a large part of him was over the thrill of the chase.

'Just to get the timing clear at the start. The email you never received from Ben, the "shades of '75" one, was sent on Monday August 15, 2011. He died three days later, on 18 August. Three days is a long time and Ben wasn't idle. As I've told you, Harry, he stole a ton of information from DSD. But that wasn't all he did.'

Harris clicked on a folder.

'DSD's key role is to gather foreign signals intelligence. Its motto is "Reveal their secrets; protect our own". It taps into and listens to calls from across the Asia-Pacific. It's rarely allowed to tap domestic phones. But no one is better equipped.'

Harris swivelled his chair towards the reporter.

'Harry, Ben trained the intelligence guns on their masters. He tapped the phones of everyone on the Alliance list. *Everyone.*'

Dunkley took a long swig of whisky before tilting the glass upwards in mock salute. 'That's my girl.'

'No question about that, Harry. But they were onto him. While Ben was raiding the DSD safe, they were gathering intel on him … and you.'

'What do you mean, Trev?'

Harris seemed troubled.

'On 16 June, 2011, DSD got an order to open two domestic case files. One was on you. And the other was on Ben. It tapped everything: your phones, computers, bank accounts. You name it.'

Dunkley waved at the screen, still gripping the whisky tumbler.

'Did Kimberley find that?'

'No, Harry.'

'So how do you know about this, Trev?'

Harris sighed. 'Because I authorised it.'

A wave of nausea swept over Dunkley.

'You … what?'

The analyst's eyes glistened. His voice turned inwards. He seemed intent on reassuring himself as much as Dunkley.

'I was operating under strict orders. From on high. They claimed that Ben was leaking top-secret stuff to you.

'How was I to know how this would end? I have lain awake for hours at night wondering whether I should have done something different. Whether I was responsible for Ben's death.'

Harris pushed his chair back from the desk and stood up. He walked several paces before turning back to the journalist.

'Harry, on the night Ben died, a call came through to DSD asking for an exact location on him. We were tracking his movements using the signal from his mobile phone.'

'Christ, Trevor.'

'Yes … now you understand why I left DSD.'

He paused.

'And why I'm helping you. Even though I'm breaking the law.'

Dunkley studied the rim of his tumbler. The guilt he felt over Kimberley's death was still a raw wound. He'd sought redemption by pursuing the truth and had been abandoned by everyone. The admission by Harris had a perverse effect: Dunkley had found a traveller bearing the same burden.

'Trev, there's plenty of blame to go around. The only way we can make it up to Kimberley is to finish the job she started. What's in those files?'

Harris's face lightened. He nodded, moved back to his keyboard and clicked on an icon.

'Tapes, Harry. Hours of them. This one is from 17 August, 2011.'

The familiar voice of Australia's defence force chief sprang out of a pair of speakers.

'Brent, good news,' Jack Webster said. 'There'll be a story in *The Australian* soon, one that will blow Paxton out of the water. The defence minister is dead.'

For once, Harry Dunkley was early. It was nearly 5pm and he ordered a beer while his eyes adjusted to the dim lighting of the Kingston Hotel.

He wasn't a regular, but Dunkley had spent enough hours sinking his wages into pool-and-gin nights to know the Kingo's back story.

The hotel had been built more than seventy years earlier, and in 1963 it famously hosted a meeting of the thirty-six members of the ALP's federal conference. Labor's parliamentary leaders, Arthur Calwell and Gough Whitlam, were photographed cooling their heels in the street, waiting to be told what the party's election platform would be.

The trope of the 'faceless men' had been carved into the political lexicon right here.

Nursing his schooner, Dunkley moved away from the bar. He'd been told to look for a particular poster. It was in the furthest corner, a quiet nook disturbed only by the faint burble of poker machine music.

The wood-framed print carried the image of a Chinese beauty sitting on a chair. She had an open face and beguiling smile. The strap of a blue evening gown fell off her right shoulder. Her left hand was pulling back her hair. Foregrounded in the alluring scene were three packs of Golf cigarettes.

'Beautiful, isn't she?' Bruce Paxton stood by the poster, cradling a beer. 'The owner, Steve, tells me he picked it up in Beijing years ago for a song. Along with all the others.'

Paxton's gesture swept the room and Dunkley, for the first time, noticed the common theme of the artwork.

'Since I first came to Canberra, this has been my local. I always sit right here.' The MP hoisted himself onto a stool. His athleticism had faded, but he was still imposing. And his gloved prosthetic left hand showed he was not unacquainted with danger.

'Before we start, I need to get something off my chest.'

'You called the meeting, Bruce. Go for it.'

'I always had time for you in the past, but that story you wrote about me and that Chinese money was a stitch-up. I broke no laws and you destroyed me.'

Dunkley met Paxton's stare. 'Bullshit, Bruce. The article was accurate and fair. You knew you were doing the wrong thing, otherwise you wouldn't have hidden tens of thousands of dollars from the Electoral Commission. Your bad luck was that I tracked down your sidekick Doug Turner and he decided to rat on you.'

Paxton's drawl edged up a notch. 'I was set up, Harry. You know that.'

'That part is true.' Dunkley drank a generous pull of beer. 'And if it makes you happy, I was set up too. By the same people. So there you go. As you'd know, Bruce, it's a big wheel that doesn't go round twice. And I've sunk lower than you.'

'You have, mate. Welcome.' Paxton smiled and the men clinked their glasses.

'So why did you call me here, Bruce – to revel in my misery?'

Paxton shook his head.

'Actually, I thought that if there was one bloke who might understand my plight it would be you. I might be on the canvas but I've never ducked a fight. Neither have you. And clearly, Harry, you buy some outrageous stories.'

They laughed.

'Well, I've heard your story, Bruce, and it's pretty out there.' Dunkley turned sombre. 'Have you heard from the ambassador's wife?'

'No.' Paxton glanced at the poster. 'And if she could get in touch she would. Even if it was just to let me know she was okay.'

Harry lowered his voice. 'She was special to you ...'

'She was, mate.'

'I'm sorry.'

There was an awkward silence, broken by the ring of a jackpot and the clatter of a small wave of coins spilling into a metal tray.

'Do you have any evidence of these other murders?' Dunkley was happy to move from difficult emotional terrain to the more familiar ground of facts and questions.

'Only what Mei told me. But I'm sure she was telling the truth. She was terrified.'

'Yeah, that fits with one thing I know. The Japanese are convinced there's a killer on that compound. I have photos of him. Looks like a nasty piece of work.'

Paxton winced.

'Were you in Cabinet, Bruce, when Bailey gave China the go-ahead to build that compound?'

'No mate, outer ministry. But I do know that the brass were still whinging about it when I became defence minister. Maybe I should have listened to them. I'm changing my views about the threat China poses.'

'Well I've completely changed my view about your defence chiefs. But do you really think that Bailey is a threat?'

'I went to China in the '80s and Bailey was based at the embassy for six months. They tried to recruit me. And they failed. But if they tried with me, they would have tried with her.'

Dunkley drained the last of his beer. 'Have you heard of a group of bureaucrats called the Alliance?'

'The Alliance? Sounds like an insurance company. But the answer's no, Harry.'

'They're the ones who wanted to kill you off, and to scuttle the gas deal with China. Bruce, they won.'

'I have no doubt that the brass wanted me gone when I cut their cash. I didn't think there was a vast conspiracy, though.'

'Well, now it's my turn to tell an outrageous story. I think a bunch of mandarins has been interfering repeatedly to shunt the government into the arms of Uncle Sam.

'And this interference went so far as launching a series of cyber-attacks on Australia and making it look as though the Chinese were behind it. They even gave it a 007 code name: the Lusitania Plan.'

Paxton put his glass down.

'Fuck! Back up, Harry. I know about the Lusitania Plan. It's an Australian training project, based out of HMAS *Harman*, a few miles down the road. We wanted to develop the same kind of unit as Cyber Command in the United States. The Lusitania Plan was our test-bed. I ticked it off as defence minister. It's the sort of thing we should be putting our money into. It's twenty-first-century warfare, not the big ticket bullshit the brass is addicted to.'

The revelation floored Dunkley.

'Jesus, Bruce, I thought the US was behind this. A nudge to push us back into their tent. But this … these attacks … you say we had the capability to launch them from Canberra …'

'Well, it was the kind of capability we were developing.'

'If it originated here, it would be treason.'

'No, Harry. If they shot down a prime minister, it would be a coup.'

The two men fell silent as they pondered the unimaginable. Around them, the hotel bar drifted through the mundane rituals of a Sunday afternoon.

'So what do we know, Bruce? The Chinese are dangerous. The Yanks can't be trusted. And there are traitors in our ranks.'

'Harry, you know what they say: politics is the womb of war. In this world you need allies. Turns out the enemy of my enemy is my only friend. Perhaps we need to forge an alliance of our own.'

'We ain't holding many aces, Bruce. Neither of us has much credibility.'

'True that, Harry. But I do have parliamentary privilege and I plan to use it. So, what have you got?'

'Well, Bruce. Turns out that I've got tapes. And they tell quite a tale.'

A broad smile split the MP's face as he downed his last mouthful of beer. He placed the empty glass on the table, diverting his gaze to the Chinese beauty before fixing his one-time tormentor with firm resolve.

'Well then, Harry. Here's to the future. Let's publish. And be damned.'

BOOK THREE

THE
SHADOW
GAME

Sydney, February, 2015

Once more, he turned to the east where the sky was tumbling and growling, thick clouds rolling in from the coast.

Summer's crushing humidity had wilted people's spirits. Now, on narrow Sydney streets, they scurried for cover, anxiously glancing at a sky preparing to explode.

For the past few hours he'd wandered aimlessly in his stinking rags, a cask of cheap red coursing through his veins. His mind swirled like the clouds above as he weaved down Albion Street, the same verse nagging at his brain:

Hurled headlong flaming from the ethereal sky
With hideous ruin and combustion down
To bottomless perdition, there to dwell
In adamantine chains and penal fire.

He searched for a title but it had been lost, like so much else, in the months he'd spent living in parks, sleeping on benches, his soul adrift.

Sometimes he would wake not knowing where he'd been or where he would go. Always he would drift back to the Place, watching as they kept their distance, afraid of catching his virus, the sickness of desolation.

In the few moments of clarity he snatched each day, he would beg for money in the hope of settling the gnawing in his stomach. Mostly, though, it went on booze. It was never enough to drown the memories that clawed at his brain and pushed him to the edge of sanity.

He had to forget who he had been, how far he had fallen, how even his name had lost its meaning. If he was anyone now, he was the Hobo of Holt Street, the scornful epithet he knew they used to describe him.

A sheet of lightning turned the sky into a lake of fire, and a clap of thunder reverberated like a thousand angry drummers. The first drops of rain hit the pavement with staccato ferocity. The smell of ozone flooded his nostrils and momentarily lifted the fog in his brain. The sky flared again as a stab of light shattered a telegraph pole, showering timber and sparks across the street, snuffing out the lights in surrounding buildings.

Satan had come to claim him.

He threw back his head and opened his arms, screaming in the face of the tempest. Talons of rain drenched him, embraced him, cleansed him.

He was not ready to be taken. He turned and looked at the facade of the building behind him. The Place. News Corporation.

For the first time in months he had a purpose.

He strode into the semi-dark building, ignoring cries to stop as he dashed towards stairs that led to the editorial floors of Rupert Murdoch's most influential mastheads.

He bounded up to Level 2, where a sign in the shape of Australia told visitors they'd arrived at the national broadsheet. He kicked it hard, barely pausing as it crashed to the floor.

No one saw him emerge into the dim newsroom. He stopped, chest heaving, as he searched for a weapon. There it was, a sports editor's prized cricket bat.

His first swing was a square cut that burst a computer into a hundred pieces of plastic and glass. Sparks flew and the air filled with acrid smoke.

Heads turned and journalists froze at the sight of the intruder, his matted hair and beard framing a face contorted in a snarl, his eyes blazing with a dangerous light.

Staff fled as he cut a swathe of destruction through the newsroom, smashing his way to a glass-walled office where the heavyweights had gathered for an afternoon conference.

With a fearful swing he obliterated the door. Tiny missiles peppered the room's occupants as they cowered in a corner.

Only one was defiant. Editor-in-chief Deborah Snowdon stood in front of her troops like a warrior queen, flint hard and ready to confront the invader.

Their eyes locked as he raised the weapon above his head. This beast had a name, a past, a motive. She pointed her finger and uttered a single word, 'You!', as two burly guards crash-tackled him to the floor.

He woke to jackhammers in his head and the taste of blood in his mouth.

Gingerly he massaged his swollen face, then reached for his left shoulder which felt ripped from its mooring.

'Easy, mate.' He lifted himself onto an elbow as his mind sought to sift fact from fiction. His memory was grainy, but he recalled his head slamming into the News Corp conference table.

With some effort he forced his eyes open. The light was a hot poker into his brain. He closed and reopened them, trying to focus until he could clearly make out his surroundings.

The cell was small and clean, a steel-and-concrete tomb with a single bed, a washbasin and a toilet. Sunlight streamed through thick bars onto his face and he drew comfort from its warmth. An odd sense of calm enveloped him.

'Those with nothing have nothing left to lose,' he mumbled through a split lip, caring little for what happened next.

He looked for the time but his wristwatch was missing. Mid-morning, he reckoned. Should he call room service? He smiled. Some men feared jail but these were comfortable lodgings, the best in months.

A siren wailed nearby, another petty criminal on the loose. Then the clip of footsteps on concrete, getting louder, and the sound of a key in a metal door. The creak of hinges. He closed his eyes and lay still, yearning for solitude.

Someone was in his cell, treading softly towards his bed. He could feel a presence, the cast of a shadow.

Theatrically, the man cleared his throat. 'The once famous journalist Harry Dunkley, I presume.'

He stirred at the sound of a name he'd sought to bury. Lifting and turning his head was painful, and as his eyes opened all he could see was a black silhouette etched against the bright rectangle of the window.

'You're standing in my sunshine.' Dunkley's voice was thick.

The visitor stepped aside and Dunkley's eyes slowly readjusted to the daylight. He pushed himself up and sat in silence for a few moments as his mind grappled with what he was seeing.

'Well, well,' he croaked. 'The fallen prime minister, Martin Toohey. What the fuck do you want?'

'The same thing as you, Harry. Redemption ... and revenge.'

Sydney

Air Chief Marshal Jack Webster caught a satisfying glimpse of himself in the window of his Commonwealth car – ADF 1 – as his staff officer shut the door. He had been dubbed 'the four-star from central casting' by one women's glossy – with good reason. Standing six foot three in the old money, the 57-year-old military veteran had the chiselled features of a man half his age. Ramrod straight, his broad shoulders tapered to a waist taut from a lifetime of discipline. Inveterately vain, the chief of the defence force always had one eye on himself and the other on the enemy.

His career had been settled in the cradle. In a childhood short on sentiment, his father, a brigadier in the Australian army, was never to be called Dad, only Sir.

Webster had long ago given up wondering what his life might have been like if his mother hadn't died when he was twelve. But he often thought of the lessons his father had taught him.

'Nobody ever defended anything successfully, there is only attack and attack and attack some more,' the brigadier would say, quoting his hero, the American general George Patton, as he pushed young Jack through his daily pre-dawn fitness regime.

Convinced that Patton had been assassinated for threatening to expose Allied collusion with the Russians that had cost American lives, he had drilled another vital lesson into his son: trust no one.

How ironic, Webster thought as he double-checked the polish on his shoes, that *GQ* magazine had published their profile on him with the headline 'Hail to the Chief: Australia's Most Trusted Man'.

This muggy Sydney morning, Webster was opening a new wing of the Concord Repatriation General Hospital, for men and women who had suffered on the frontline and then succumbed to their mental frailties. He had championed the cause of military personnel with post-traumatic stress disorder and been instrumental in raising money for a specialised psychiatric ward.

A phalanx of dignitaries quivered with excitement as he was guided by the local federal MP to a makeshift stage. Bright TV lights shone in his face as he looked out at the audience of luminaries, doctors, nurses and patients. Already they were in his thrall.

'I too have felt the horrors of war,' he began in his measured, rich, powerful bass. 'I know the price that our people too often pay when they are in the midst of conflict they don't understand.'

Webster knew theatre and his voice lowered a notch as he dipped his head and recalled a painful memory.

'I will never forget the shock of seeing the blackened corpses of Iraqis whom I had a hand in killing when I was attached to a US combat group during the first Gulf War.'

He lifted his gaze to the crowd, his eyes now carrying a mix of pity and determination.

'I took no joy in it. My only comfort was knowing that I was doing my duty. This is what our country sometimes asks of us. This is the burden we agree to bear.'

Webster's eyes blazed as he warmed to his favourite theme.

'But we cannot be squeamish about fighting. Every nation, in every age, must have warriors. Perhaps the problem today is that we in the military are too good at our jobs, that the threats seem so remote that some folk believe that peace can be bought by purchasing a bumper sticker. One of the main dangers to the West is the fools in our midst who believe that talk of peace achieves peace.

'Peace is bought and maintained at the highest price: by blood, force and vigilance.

'We cannot be complacent about our democracy. It is constantly under siege, from within and without. We fighters, you and I, are democracy's frontline. We are charged with defending the liberties we enjoy. And everyone who lives behind the shield we build should remember that our nation's security trumps all other priorities.'

The small crowd erupted in applause and Webster let it wash over him. As he resumed his speech, his voice carried the weight of a terrible toll.

'Forty-one Australian soldiers died and two hundred and fifty-six were wounded in the desert wastelands of Afghanistan.'

He shook his head and slowly looked into the eyes of each patient in the room.

'But there are many more who carry invisible scars from their time serving this great nation. They are no less damaged, and no less deserving of our help.

'For those who find the burden too heavy, we must lend a hand. I will not leave my men and women on the battlefield. And if the horror of battle comes home with them, through minds tormented, then I will be there with them.

'That is what leaders do. It is both my duty and my greatest honour.'

Webster settled back into the soft leather seat of ADF 1 waving to the crowd as his driver merged into Sydney's traffic chaos. His phone rang, a call he'd been expecting.

'Jack,' cooed the familiar female voice, 'I was watching you on Sky News. It went splendidly and it's obviously money well spent. I'm glad you convinced me of its merit.'

'Thank you, Prime Minister.'

Elizabeth Scott was as besotted by Webster as everybody else: he was undoubtedly brave, handsome and charismatic, and he had something she craved – a genuine connection with the people. But while his popularity soared, hers sank.

Webster had moved effortlessly from triumph to triumph, watching as the nation's leader stumbled from disaster to catastrophe in her unhappy seventeen months in office. She was constantly in damage control and paranoid about those within her ranks who were feeding the media tales of dissent and disharmony.

As her position became more grim, her calls to Webster became more frequent. He had become her closest confidant.

'Jack, I like your idea about changing the honours system,' she said now. 'It will be a risk, but I agree that I need to reach out to the Right in my party.'

Webster smiled, but his voice was all concern and caution.

'You know, PM, it was just a thought.' The general exuded humility. 'I'm not a political adviser; I'm a humble foot soldier. You need to test the idea with your team.'

'Hah!' Scott could not hide her contempt. 'You mean the geniuses who dug the hole I'm in now. No, it's my decision, Jack; I'm happy to accept any credit, or blame, that follows. And I've hatched a brilliant idea to make sure that the public applauds me for it.'

Webster's face tightened to a grin. 'What is that, Prime Minister?'

'Arise … Sir Jack.'

Washington

The two bulls glared at each other across the desk, hard men whose careers had been forged in the toughest democratic battleground on earth. Neither wanted to display a hint of weakness.

President Earle Jackson suppressed a twitch in his shoulder as the enemy spat out his venom.

'If you run, you will lead us to an epic defeat,' the Chairman of the Republican National Committee growled. 'Our base is gone. You humiliated America; there's no way you can win back the people's confidence.'

Jackson was defiant as he slammed his clenched fist on the table.

'People have been writing me off all of my political life,' he seethed, his face set like a Rushmore statue, his voice squeezed out through his teeth.

'There will be challengers.' The chairman's hard eyes met the president's wrath. 'And no matter who runs against you they will win some primaries.

That will embolden others to stand. The vice president might even make a bid. How would that look? Our executive at war. As the good Lord and Lincoln said, "A house divided against itself cannot stand."

'It will be a repeat of the Johnson campaign in '68. Your last days in this office will be consumed by campaigning. And a series of bitter defeats.'

'What do you want? Spit it out.'

The chairman took a long breath. 'Do what Johnson did. Stand down.' His voice was calmer, but still determined. 'Say your health is shot. Say you want to spend more time with your family. For the love of God, say you want to take up painting. I don't care. But for the good of this party, for the sake of this nation, stand down and give us a chance at winning in 2016.'

For a long time the two were frozen in angry silence. Then the president dropped his gaze to the desk in front of him and ran his fingers along its edge.

'You see this,' he said, emphasising the point with two sharp raps. 'It's made from the timbers of a British ship that was abandoned and thought lost in the Arctic. It was found and sailed to America by a whaler. It was refitted and given as a gift to the Brits at a time when we once again stood on the brink of war. Then in 1880 part of it came back here as a desk, a gift from Queen Victoria, as a sign of the enduring friendship between our nations.

'Each day when I'm at this desk I touch this wood and I think of that ship's name. The *Resolute*. And that's what I intend to be.'

The president stood slowly, theatrically. He was a tall man who used his height and bulk to intimidate his opponents. He leaned across the desk into the chairman's space.

'You might be right.' His voice was controlled but steely. 'I might be humiliated in a primary battle with my own party. But I will not run from this fight.'

The Republican chairman was shorter than the president but as a sign of defiance he also stood and leaned across the desk to meet the challenge.

'With respect, Mr President,' – there was a sarcastic tone in his voice – 'it was running from a fight that got you to where you are now.'

Jackson balled his hands into fists and rested his knuckles on the *Resolute*'s timber. He resisted the urge to hit the chairman.

'Get out of my office,' he spat. 'Never contact me again. And when I win I will come after you.'

The chairman nodded, his face impassive. 'Mr President, I don't doubt your will or your determination. But you will not win. Remember I tried to warn you.'

Jackson remained standing until the chairman had left his office. As the door clicked shut, he sank back in his chair and flicked on the TV.

He knew he shouldn't watch Fox News, the broadcaster that gave voice to a generation of rabid conservatives and made Rupert Murdoch America's most powerful media baron. But like a moth to a flame he tuned to the high-voltage, high-rating *O'Reilly Factor*. As usual, the panel was in hyperdrive as the hawkish pundits tore into their hapless foe.

This time the victim wasn't some limp-wristed liberal trying to ban Nativity scenes in schools. The target was him, the highest profile Republican in the land: the forty-fifth president of the United States. The right-wing hit squad was united: the Grand Old Party would be best served if Jackson did the decent thing and resigned. If he didn't, then it was someone's patriotic duty to challenge the president in a primary run-off.

Just two years into his first term, Jackson had fallen further than Lucifer when he was cast out of Paradise. A single calamitous miscalculation had eviscerated him. He was now a national embarrassment, a lame duck leader whose fallibility and misjudgement had shamed America.

Sixteen months ago he had ordered the USS *George Washington* into the Taiwan Strait to demonstrate that America was the world's only superpower. Then, as confrontation with China loomed, he'd instructed the strike group to retreat.

He'd believed it was the right decision, that if the group had pressed on it would have been annihilated by the weapons that lined the Chinese shore. Then he would have had no choice but to declare war on China, a war America could not win and one where it would be seen as the aggressor.

But the spectacle of the Stars and Stripes being lowered before a rising Five-star Red Flag had recast the global order in a single, fateful afternoon. It was the retreat watched around the world, America's most humbling moment since Vietnam – but with much more serious implications. Vietnam was a setback; this was a shift in the tectonic plates of power.

Jackson knew all too well what he'd done to the American psyche. The damage was immense. A nation reared to believe in its invincibility was shaken to the core. The stock market crashed, consumer and business confidence were crushed – and forests had been sacrificed to explain what it all meant.

The electorate hated him for puncturing their mythology. His poll numbers fell to single digits and Jackson achieved the rarest of feats: uniting the Democrats and Republicans against a common foe.

Fox News was feasting on his corpse, the full-throttle character assassination showing no signs of letting up.

'"Jellywall" Jackson continues to stain the office of president of this great nation,' one panellist growled. 'He is a disgrace and should resign.'

Jackson punched his remote to end the torture. It would be easy to resign and fade into the shadows. But given the biggest mistake in his life had been to retreat in the face of a foe, he couldn't live with himself if he again cut and ran.

One of his few remaining friends had sent him a line from John Milton's *Paradise Lost*. He'd had it framed and it sat on his desk. He picked it up and read it aloud: 'Awake, arise, or be for ever fall'n.'

He smiled as he remembered the words of his mother. 'Yes Mom, that is what Jesus would do.'

He was still the leader of the free world and it was his solemn duty to put things right, to restore America's pride. He had triumphed against impossible odds before as he'd risen to become governor of Mississippi before storming the White House. He could do it again; he just had to have faith.

Brutal days lay ahead, but he'd be damned if these faceless backroom boys would tear him down. He was elected by the people and he would reconnect with them.

He would return to his roots, go back to making stump speeches in the hamlets. He would win back the country, town hall by town hall. He would speak in parks and on street corners to the real America. He would reach out to those who'd suffered the ignominy of unemployment as the economy shed blue-collar jobs. And he would speak of his plans to make the nation great again.

Like Teddy Roosevelt he would declare that his setback was not the end – because 'it takes more than that to kill a bull moose'.

He thumped his fists on the oak desk.

'Kiss my ass, Bill O'Reilly,' the president yelled, to no one but himself.

Sydney

The passenger's head was lowered, his eyes vacant in a grimy face. Clad in tattered jeans and T-shirt, he clutched a battered leather satchel containing his few possessions: a notepad, a coin purse and a lanyard printed with the seal of the federal parliament. It bore his name and told of his past: Harry Dunkley, *The Australian*.

As Martin Toohey sank into the front seat, his driver turned off the air conditioning and lowered all four windows, despite the stifling heat.

'Best let the air circulate, Mr Toohey,' he said.

Toohey nodded, acutely aware of the pungent smell of a man who hadn't washed in weeks.

It was nearly 1pm and the former prime minister had spent nearly two hours at the Downing Centre, waiting for a magistrate to hear the case against Dunkley, whose demolition derby in the News Corp offices had caused thousands of dollars worth of damage. Some of Murdoch's top henchmen had been keen to throw the book at their former employee. But common sense had prevailed and Toohey's offer to stump up for damages and legal costs, and to keep an eye on the man who'd once terrorised his government, had been accepted.

No one spoke as they crossed the Anzac Bridge before turning right onto Victoria Road, passing a derelict power station. As the turnoff to the Balmain peninsula loomed, Toohey contemplated the transformation of the once proud Labor heartland into a Green utopia where cashed-up, hand-wringing luvvies were replacing the horny-handed sons of toil and their hard-scrabble wives who'd given the place its working-class character and soul.

He shook his head as he recalled Neville Wran's dictum that Balmain boys don't cry. Now, the basket-weavers never stopped moaning about the perils of middle-class living: close-fit development, traffic snarls and the price of fair-trade coffee beans.

They crossed Iron Cove and the sweeping span of Gladesville Bridge before veering into Hunters Hill. The small shopping centre gave way to streets that recorded the Catholic Church's past colonisation of this now wealthy enclave: Matthew Street, Luke Street – the saints paraded by.

The car glided past the back of St Joseph's College and turned onto Mary Street. Just beyond the neo-gothic Villa Maria church they came to a halt in front of an old sandstone building.

'Marist Fathers' seminary', Toohey announced. 'My old digs. I studied here thirty-five years ago. They taught me many things.'

He turned to meet Dunkley's gaze.

'This will be your home for a while.'

Dunkley hunkered down in his seat.

'I am not going to doss down with a bunch of clapped-out God-botherers. I'm a tolerant man, Martin, and I have never held your weird superstitions against you. But I am a card-carrying atheist. So were my parents. It's an honourable family tradition.'

364

Toohey winced as he caught a blast of Dunkley's toxic breath.

'Harry, you've been released into my care. This is a genuinely safe house and they are good men. These are my friends, and they know how to keep a secret.'

Beijing

The morning sun had barely seeped into the Hall of Purple Light but it was already ablaze. Over a hundred artisans had been indentured to renovate the grand edifice that had stood at the centre of noble Chinese ceremonies for centuries. They worked with fierce determination, intent on maintaining a cracking pace in order to please their supreme leader, President Meng Tao.

Jiang Xiu stepped around some scaffolding and made his way inside. The propaganda minister had played an important role in building the profile of his president, but in truth it had been a remarkably easy job. Meng Tao exuded the certainty of those who are destined to rule.

Yet his path to leadership had been arduous. His father had been vice premier, but was purged and imprisoned during the Cultural Revolution. At fifteen, Meng left Beijing in shame, a 'sent-down youth' banished to seven years hard labour in rural Shaanxi Province.

Those years were the 'turning point' in his life, according to the official biography that Jiang had commissioned. What was not recorded was that it was there that Meng had forged enduring bonds with other sent-down princelings. The 'Shaanxi Gang' had risen from the wilderness to grasp four of the seven seats on China's supreme governing body, the Politburo Standing Committee.

Old hands had watched first in admiration, then trepidation, as Meng's influence grew. Step by step he was taking control of the Communist Party, the state and the military.

The president was also a micro-manager, right down to personally supervising the renovation of this monument of ancient power. He was ordering his palace as he ordered society – with the iron resolve of a budding dictator.

Not since Mao had a Chinese leader so dominated the party and combined power with the cult of personality. Meng made a display of his personal life and cultivated a connection with the masses to become the 'People's President'. He was married to a famous opera singer who travelled with him abroad. He sat cross-legged with rural peasants to eat dumplings, and carried his own umbrella. The *People's Daily* had even given him a nickname reflecting his exalted status: Meng Dada or Uncle Meng. Some China observers in the West had adopted a more sinister translation: Big Brother Meng.

Meng believed that Mao had done enormous damage by rejecting all of China's glorious past. This error had stunted his country, and Meng was determined to reconnect with Chinese history, to recreate it and bend it to his purpose. He liked to quote a motto he had borrowed from the Ming Dynasty: 'A society without ritual is like a plough without a blade.' The people lapped it up and courses in Confucianism flourished. Jiang was charged with reinvigorating the belief planted deep in the soul of the Chinese populace that their nation was the centre of all things. Having that snatched away by the West during the 'Hundred Years of Humiliation' had created a deep sense of resentment.

So it was no wonder that the defining moment of Meng's premiership had been when he forced the retreat of the USS *George Washington* from its mission to sail the length of the Taiwan Strait. It had driven his popularity to levels Western leaders could only dream of. It poured fuel on nationalistic fires and secured his freedom to make ever bolder moves in domestic and foreign policy. Chinese commentators had hailed it as the definitive end of the 'Hundred Years of Humiliation'. Once again the world's potentates were flocking to the Middle Kingdom, begging for an audience with its leader. In the minds of its people, China had returned to its rightful place, but Jiang knew that, for Meng, there was still a reckoning to be had. The humiliation would not go unpunished.

Jiang found the president surrounded by a cabal of officials carrying notepads and architectural plans, and whispering in the presence of their master.

Though Jiang dared not give voice to it, he had become fearful of what he saw in his president's unstoppable rise. He believed Meng saw himself not as a president, but as an emperor.

Canberra

It had been the Australia Day from hell.

Elizabeth Scott reached for the television remote to banish the barrage of ridicule that had assailed her all day.

Australia's twenty-eighth prime minister was alone in her office. She didn't need her staff's reproachful looks and redundant advice on how to dig herself out of this latest deep hole.

She'd disabled her Twitter feed to dodge the blizzard of digital excrement hurled by the masses. Social media had become the twenty-first-century pillory where the faceless and cowardly vented their spleen.

Scott's decision to bring back imperial honours had stirred the piranha pool into a feeding frenzy. What had started as a Twitterstorm had morphed into Twittergeddon, crowned with an uber-trending hashtag: #Knightmare.

What she'd thought would be a deft political play had backfired. The knighthoods were intended to be a sop to the restive conservative wing of the Liberal Party, a counter to their deep resentment of a string of socially progressive decisions. Now Scott, a lifelong Republican, was branded an out-of-touch, opportunistic hypocrite. The move confirmed the electorate's doubt about her character and judgement in one barbecue-stopping cock-up.

The only winner was the man she had honoured: Jack Webster.

Since he'd risen through the ranks of the RAAF to his current role as chief of the defence force, Webster had been the go-to man in every major crisis – from the war in Afghanistan to natural disasters.

Scott thought privately that Webster was one of the few safe pairs of hands working for her government. She clung to him in the hope that her low stocks would be dragged higher in his reflected glory. But the knighthood had only appeared to make her appear shabby.

Everyone agreed he was the right man – conferred with the wrong award. When door-stopped at a citizenship ceremony, the burnished and braided military leader had been humble and generous to a fault.

'The prime minister is a fine woman and a thoughtful leader,' he said. 'I am certain she did this for the right reasons. It was not my decision and I won't comment on your commentary about it. A military man serves at the pleasure of his leader and I accepted the knighthood to honour the warrior men and women I lead.'

'Do we call you "Sir Jack" from now on?' one reporter called.

Webster grinned. 'I'll always be just Jack. But if you serve under me, then it had better be "Sir".'

The reporters laughed. Everyone was laughing except Scott.

The decision had left her friendless, isolated and vulnerable. This was her nadir. She'd been dubbed the Accidental Prime Minister and the sobriquet had stuck because it was true. In seventeen months as the nation's leader, the PM had blundered her way from one self-inflicted disaster to the next.

Scott had regained the Liberal leadership in extraordinary circumstances. Her predecessor, Barry Landry, had lasted just a few months before he exploded in the only truly technicolour moment of his long beige career. It turned out that the man the Liberal Party had thought was Mr Safe Hands – and who had taken his party to a commanding lead in the polls – was corrupt to his brown brogue shoelaces. Labor's dirt unit had uncovered, and leaked, compromising details about his chairmanship of a Victorian utility.

In an exquisite piece of theatre, the Labor prime minister, Catriona Bailey, had timed her visit to the governor-general to ask for an election to the very moment that Landry was tearfully resigning as opposition leader.

Shattered Liberals were left with a Hobson's choice between two deeply flawed former leaders. Scott was considered far too liberal, and the ultra-hard-right Emily Brooks was haunted by the viral online footage of her spectacular sexual escapades.

'It's Bambi or the Bondage Queen,' one hardhead lamented.

Scott won the party room by a handful of votes, but the polling collapsed as the election campaign intensified. What had shaped as a Coalition landslide narrowed to a six-seat majority.

There was no honeymoon with a resurgent Bailey declaring that Scott would be a one-term wonder. Despite Scott's fierce intelligence, her radiant good looks, her Olympic past and her stellar business background, it now looked as though the Labor leader would be proven right.

The PM's phone rang and the screen lit with the name of the one person she was always happy to talk to.

'Looks like you are taking a lot of fire.' Jack Webster's voice was as comforting as hot chocolate on a cold night.

'Another bad day in a long line of bad days,' Scott sighed. 'Gets hard to tell them apart. Thanks for your support; I haven't exactly been run down by colleagues offering their shoulder.'

'I feel a little guilty. We'd talked about the idea but I thought you would run it through the political filter in your office.' Webster sounded genuinely concerned.

'Don't, Jack.' Scott was clicking through the news websites as she spoke. She was trending on every one. 'This is all my own doing.'

'It will blow over.'

'Maybe. But it might just take me with it.'

Sydney

Harry Dunkley glanced into the foxed mirror. A beaten face glared back, bloodshot eyes etched deep with the bitter past. The one-time political huntsman was ashamed of what he had descended to.

While he'd not touched alcohol for a week, he worried that he still ached for its false comfort. But the strength was returning slowly to his wiry frame, as was a sense of balance and calm. His appetite too was returning and he'd gained a kilo or more.

That morning he'd taken his first tentative jog around the seminary's spacious grounds that rolled over four hectares, sloping gently from Mary Street to Tarban Creek. The estate was a lush and secret garden dotted with gracious old sandstone buildings, and a couple of grey bunker monstrosities that hailed from the 1970s. The Marists had been the area's first white settlers, arriving in 1847 when land was cheap and Sydney was a boat ride away. Now, with the Catholic Church in seemingly irreversible decline in the post-Christian West, the fathers were preparing to administer the last rites on the seminary.

Harry was surprised by his sympathy for the priests. He had scant understanding of their beliefs, but it was clear they had toiled, within their lights, to make the world a better place. He respected that. As for their many flaws, who was he to judge?

He sighed, clouding the mirror in front of him. Carefully he pulled at his greying beard and sheared off a large clump of hair. Twenty minutes later his face was clean and raw.

He raised his eyes to a new reflection. Everything seemed a touch brighter.

'Welcome back,' he mumbled, ready to reconnect with a humanity that he'd been avoiding.

He ambled into the refectory, which was empty, as usual. Once the place had pulsated with life as dozens of zealous young men gathered to prepare their meals. Now just a handful of aged priests remained, eating their meals in a small room adjacent to the kitchen.

'Father.' Dunkley nodded to a priest who'd been particularly kind during his first days at the seminary. They were the only ones there and he set about making coffee and toast in silence.

A suite of newspapers was laid out neatly on a bench. Familiar feelings stirred in Dunkley as he picked up *The Australian*, the weight of the newsprint reassuring. But it was tempered by a pang of loss that he no longer had a hand in filling its pages.

Still, for the first time in months, he was taking an interest in the wider world. He turned his attention to Sydney's tabloid, which was revelling in Elizabeth Scott's most recent blunder. 'RIGHT ROYAL FOOL,' the *Daily Telegraph* thundered in hundred-point font.

Dunkley whistled and imagined how he might have written about this epic balls-up. He looked up at the priest. 'The PM's in all sorts of strife. But I guess you're a traditionalist, Father, and wouldn't mind a few new knights and dames.'

The priest gazed at Harry over the rim of his glasses. 'Why would you say that, Harry?' He contemplated Dunkley with a wry grin. 'The Marists were originally French and we all know what happened to their nobility. I'm from Irish stock, a lifelong Republican and Labor to the bootstraps.'

Dunkley laughed. The old man took a sip of his tea as Harry tried to guess his age. Mid-eighties? His mind was razor sharp and his hands were steady.

'And I like to think that it was my influence that won a young, impressionable Martin Toohey back from his Grouper father.'

Dunkley poured the last dregs of coffee into his mug and looked around at the uneven sandstone blocks of the dining-room walls.

'Father, it's not so bad this retreating from the world. I could spend a bit of time here. Not praying like you. But reading, thinking.'

'I read and think a bit too.' The priest held Dunkley in a long gaze. 'By all means, take the time you need to heal, Harry. You are a welcome guest. But don't misunderstand what this place was built for. We trained men to go out and take on the world.

'When you are strong again, you must leave. There is a lot of work left in this world for you. Harry Dunkley, you might just be our last missionary.'

'Morning, Harry. Welcome back to the real world. How're you feeling? You look a million dollars ... well, a few thousand anyway.'

Martin Toohey laughed and the two men shook hands awkwardly. Dunkley led Toohey into a sitting room lined with portraits of austere-looking priests.

'Any of them look familiar, Martin?' Toohey was studying the fading faces closely.

'Yeah, I remember him. Father what's-his-name. Nice old bugger. Taught canon law.'

Dunkley snorted. 'Now locked up by the Royal Commission for kiddie fiddling, no doubt.'

'I see you haven't lost your cynicism, Harry. Yes, the church has a lot to answer for, but these were good men. This is ... was ... a very liberal theological campus. Few of the teachers here would have had any truck with the arch-conservative types who became bishops.'

They sat quietly for a moment, then Dunkley asked a question that had been burning for days.

'Why, Martin?'

'Why what?'

'Why did you of all people reach out to me? Get me out of jail. Bring me here. After everything I'd done to you over the years; all the front-page hatchet jobs. We were hardly mates at the best of times.'

'Harry, they teach some strange things in this place. But the nub is this: do unto others what you would have them do unto you.'

Then he laughed.

'And taking a cricket bat to the *Oz*'s editorial HQ, now that's a very Australian act of revenge. I couldn't let them put you away for that.'

Dunkley smiled as Toohey paused and closed his eyes, as if searching out a painful moment of his own.

'Remember when you cornered me in parliament on the way to Question Time?' Toohey asked.

Dunkley's smile faded. 'Yeah, you told me to piss off and one of your goons got up close and personal.'

Toohey's eyes flashed open.

'You said that I'd been set up, that it was the Americans, not the Chinese, behind those three cyber-attacks.'

'Yeah,' Dunkley said. 'Then I teamed up with your old mate Bruce Paxton to show that the man behind that little war was Sir Jack fucking Webster. I had proof he was the mastermind behind the Alliance, those conniving puppeteers working in the shadows of government. But did anyone believe me?'

Toohey slowly shook his head, then surprised Dunkley by slamming the palm of his hand down on the armrest of the lounge.

'That was an attack on Australia, designed to mislead the elected government. My government.' Toohey's face turned scarlet. 'It was the straw that broke my back. It was a coup.'

Dunkley gave a mock salute. 'Australia's Allende, come on down. At least they didn't shoot you. That fucker damn near killed me.'

Toohey leapt up and paced about the room.

'Harry, I've thought about that conversation every day since I lost office. I didn't believe you then, but I believe you now.'

'Excellent. You can put it in your memoirs. I can even give you the title. Webster's code name for the deception was the Lusitania Plan. You'd appreciate the historical allusion to the Churchill conspiracy: let one of your own ships sink to suck America into World War I.'

Toohey turned to Dunkley, his voice now soft and pleading.

'I can't do this alone.'

'Do what?'

'Jack Webster.'

'What about him?'

'We can't let this stand. It's not just about me or you. It's about the country. It's about democracy. We have to expose this guy.'

A shudder swept through Dunkley.

'Are you insane? Haven't you been paying attention? I tried. Paxton tried. We had tapes that had him bang to rights. We published them online. He shut them down inside a day and sued. He released intelligence analysis claiming we fabricated the evidence.'

Dunkley's heart was racing as he relived the agony of his fall.

'What was left of my reputation was shredded. Webster took every last cent and there weren't many to begin with. Paxton was drummed out of parliament and they won't even give him a pension.'

Toohey eyed Dunkley earnestly.

'You know what's hammered into you when you join a union? There's strength in numbers. It's never been more relevant. I need you to help me get this guy.'

Dunkley shook his head.

'Webster's been knighted by Scott and he's adored by the public. He's the nearest thing we have to royalty. Webster is untouchable.'

'No one's untouchable.'

Dunkley snorted. 'Didn't you learn anything from what happened? You were mortally wounded by Webster. Then your Labor mates followed the blood trail, hunted you down and put that freak show Catriona Bailey in your place. Get it through your head, Martin. The bad guys won.'

'Harry, I have to believe that good can triumph. Otherwise what is there to live for?'

'Maybe it's just about surviving. You seem to be doing all right with your plush car and rolled-gold pension.'

Toohey paced the room again, clearly agitated.

'I got into politics to make a difference. God knows, amid all the shit, I tried. If I got turfed for my sins, fair cop, that's democracy. The Caucus and the people give you the job, they can take it away.'

He turned to Dunkley, his face alight.

'But in Australia the generals don't get to do that. Here the military obeys civilian orders. That's what makes us different from South America and Africa, even Fiji, for God's sake. Webster can't be allowed to get away with an attack on my government. We have to stop him. I thought you wanted to make a difference too. Surely if journalism has any purpose that's what it's for, trying to do your little bit for democracy.'

Dunkley smiled. 'Martin, great speech. If you'd given more like that when you were prime minister, you might still be in power. Christ, I might even have voted for you.'

'So, are you part of the team, Harry?'

'I'm enjoying being on the reserves bench.'

'We call it the interchange in AFL.'

'Call it what you want. The only thing I care about is my sanity, and that's only just coming back. Why the hell would I jeopardise that?'

Canberra

Charles Dancer woke to the suffocating still of the night. Another nightmare. Each was more intense than the last, and each ended with the same image of disbelieving terror as Kimberley Gordon looked into her assassin's eyes. It was something he'd been trying to erase each night since August 2011. The night of his ultimate betrayal.

Kimberley's death in Telopea Park had been easy to bury as just another gay bashing, but the residue of her last breath on that chilled Canberra night would not die.

Beside Dancer, the digital clock glowed green. 3.33am. One half of the devil's number. He sighed and rolled over.

Kimberley had been his lover, but her death had been ordered so he had killed her. He was a warrior, a partisan above all else. He'd had no choice.

Governments would come and go but the Alliance endured, and ensured that the realm was defended. Dancer was their foot soldier, ever ready to destroy any threat. Sometimes he was an invisible diplomat, erasing the footprints of his masters, fixing their messes. Sometimes he was a killer.

Until Dancer had brutally dispatched Kimberley he had never questioned the morality of what he did: the ends justified the means. Now, for the first time, he was beginning to question his orders. He had sacrificed Kimberley to protect the Alliance, but it was failing in its primary duty: to protect the realm.

It had begun with the plan to force Bruce Paxton from office when he'd threatened to slash the defence budget. The Alliance had leaked information about his past and successfully invited the media to destroy him.

Paxton was a 'panda', a left-wing ideologue, compromised by a Chinese spy, but not bent. His sins paled by comparison to Catriona Bailey's. She was the real threat, a genuine Chinese agent who had infected Defence's computer systems. The aim of Dancer's mission in inducing Harry Dunkley to destroy Paxton had been to ensure that Labor was forced from office and purged of its viruses.

But with the Scott government reeling, Bailey again stood within reach of the Lodge.

Dancer could not allow that to happen. He had implored Jack Webster to act against Bailey. His master had resisted, claiming the matter was in hand. Webster was resolute, but Dancer believed a real and present danger was being ignored.

Dancer turned again to the clock. 5.08am. The night was over; he was relieved. He swung out of bed and onto his feet with the fluid movements of an athlete.

Lean and muscular, Dancer was just a few years off retirement but could keep pace with men half his age.

Only one thing now animated him: to finish his mission.

———————————

Canberra

The full moon sat low on the horizon, casting a silver pathway across the lake.

Perched on a bench, Bruce Paxton whispered her name. They had huddled in this rotunda in Nara Park, mapping out their future together. She had clung tight, frightened by what she knew.

Nearly two years later, Bruce Paxton still couldn't envisage his future without Weng Meihui.

He'd searched for her, but never found her. No one would say if she was in Australia or had returned to her homeland. No one would say whether she was alive or dead. It was as if she had never existed and he was the only thing keeping her memory alive.

He shuddered as a sudden chill blew up from the lake and his mind shifted to another painful memory.

Paxton had used the only weapons he'd had to try to pressure the Chinese to hand over Weng, or reveal her fate. He had teamed up with

Harry Dunkley and used parliament to level an extraordinary series of charges.

He'd railed against a shadowy organisation calling itself the Alliance, naming senior military and intelligence figures as agents acting against the democratically elected government. He'd linked the former prime minister Catriona Bailey to the Chinese, declaring her a spy. And he'd accused the Chinese of kidnap, even murder, on Australian soil.

Paxton managed a grim smile when he recalled what should have been his moment of triumph. He had picked his mark well. The acting deputy speaker had been half tanked and nearly asleep when Paxton got to his feet to address an almost empty chamber. He'd been three minutes into the damning allegations before the presiding officer was roused by the frantic calls of a duty MP. The deputy had called on Paxton to resume his seat, but he'd ploughed on through his long list of allegations, even as his microphone was switched off.

The Serjeant-at-Arms was called and Paxton was dragged from the chamber.

Then the unthinkable had happened. For the first time in ninety-five years, the House expelled a sitting member.

Paxton was hauled before the bar of parliament on substantially the same motion that had been used against Labor's Hugh Mahon on 12 November 1920: 'having by seditious and disloyal utterances ... been guilty of conduct unfitting for him to remain a Member ... and inconsistent with the oath of allegiance which he had taken'.

Paxton was banished by a vote of one hundred and forty-eight to one. His Western Australian seat was declared vacant and he was briefly charged with treason before the case was dropped.

The retribution went deeper. His speech was expunged from Hansard, the entry now merely reading as 'a disturbance'. The tapes from the House monitoring system were erased. The media, on deadline as the speech was made, hadn't clicked to it until Paxton was being evicted. They were told the speech was covered by a Special Intelligence Operation order and they risked five years jail if they mentioned it.

Only one reporter even tried: Dunkley. He had posted a transcript online before his website was shut down. Then he was arrested secretly by the Australian Security Intelligence Organisation using its sweeping counter-terrorism powers, and held without access to a lawyer.

On his release, Dunkley was hit with a defamation suit by Jack Webster. It broke him, financially and emotionally. Dunkley's illusion that the truth mattered evaporated, leaving him bereft, rudderless.

The last time the two had spoken was on the steps of the ACT Supreme Court on the day Dunkley had lost his legal case. The journalist had been inconsolable and Paxton winced whenever he remembered the look of anguish on his face.

Paxton turned to the brilliant night sky and breathed in the sweet, clean Canberra air. He tried in vain to think of anything he hadn't done in his quest to find Weng.

He rose from the bench and crunched along a gravel path towards the carpark. A battered old Toyota waited for him. The ignition responded after a few false starts and he trundled onto the quiet streets of the city.

It was fifteen, perhaps twenty, minutes to his makeshift home, but he was going nowhere in a hurry. Not tonight, not tomorrow.

———————

Beijing

Meng Tao placed his morning's copy of the *People's Daily* on his teak desk, smoothing his hands over a front page that captured his nation's inexorable rise.

China's insatiable appetite for oil to turbo-charge its economy featured prominently alongside an article reporting on the record numbers of Chinese travelling overseas, each an ambassador for the Middle Kingdom.

Trumping them, though, was a picture story headlined 'A Night at the Opera'.

A prominent photo caught China's propaganda minister, Jiang Xiu, arriving at the National Centre for the Performing Arts with his glamorous wife. They were both perfectly groomed and stylishly dressed and the crowd seemed to part before them as they walked into the performance.

'She is so beautiful, so elegant. He is as handsome as the president,' gushed one smitten theatre-goer.

He'd read the article twice. It breathlessly described Jiang's growing authority within the politburo, declaring he was 'Meng Dada's strong and loyal right hand'.

That much was true. Jiang was his confidant, the indispensable ally who had helped wrest control of the Standing Committee from the fossils of the past as they forged the new China.

The president stared at the photograph once more before taking a sip of rich black tea. There was a knock at the door.

'Come.'

Jiang strode into the room, his face beaming.

The two men embraced warmly, Meng squeezing the shoulders of his loyal colleague perhaps a tad too hard. He stood well above Jiang and never missed an opportunity to demonstrate his physical superiority.

He motioned to a seat and offered tea to his friend who seemed eager to share an update on a crucial project.

'Good news. Australia's Cabinet has agreed to join the Asian Infrastructure Investment Bank.'

Meng clapped his hands. China had been expecting this decision, but it still sent a thrill through him. Another piece of the geo-strategic puzzle was falling into place. He had been planning this strategy for years, recalibrating the global financial order. The new China Bank would suck power from the American-controlled World Bank and International Monetary Fund.

Truly, Meng and his underlings were creating the financial, trade and military architecture to reshape the world. The shift of power from West to East had leapt a generation. With the humiliation of the imperial superpower in the Taiwan Strait, China had roared an unmistakeable message: it was again at the centre of all things. Meng and Jiang had capitalised on the moment, rapidly expanding China's economic and military footprint, pushing ever outwards while America reeled.

But in recent months Jiang had begun to urge caution, worried that some of their plans were perhaps too ambitious and risked a regional and internal backlash. He feared they would stumble if they tried to run too fast. Meng dismissed any hesitation, convinced that he was a once in a thousand years leader. To pause was to fail.

'Jackson is the weakest American president in a century,' Meng said now. 'He is our greatest ally. We must continue to act quickly.'

'Yes sir.' The minister nodded, but his expression belied his agreement.

Meng had been through this discussion many times and had begun to take note of the points at which his younger confidant would raise carefully worded objections. He motioned to the large map on his wall which displayed China as the hub of the world.

'We continue to push out in all directions and to bolster our defences,' he said. 'But as history teaches, states are destroyed by internal weakness. That is why you, as propaganda minister, are my most important colleague.'

'Thank you, sir, I understand.' Jiang nodded. 'The internet poses many challenges as you know. But it also raises many possibilities for keeping watch. We believe that we have all the monitoring and filtering systems we need. All the micro-blogging sites are covered. We have expanded the web surveillance teams. We have strengthened our control over universities.'

'All good, but we must not underestimate the value of making regular public examples of those who defy us,' Meng replied before turning back to the map. 'How are things progressing in the north and west?'

'As you know better than me, sir, we are well advanced on developing the New Silk Road from Xi'an,' Jiang pointed to central China at the heart of the map, 'through to Istanbul and then on to Europe.'

He swept his hand down to China's south.

'Quanzhou is the port where the Maritime Silk Road begins. It runs through the South China Sea then up through the Malacca Strait to Kolkata in India. It goes on to Nairobi, up around the Horn of Africa, through the Red Sea and into the Mediterranean before linking with the land-based Silk Road in Venice.'

Meng didn't need to be told the story but he loved encouraging others to extol his visionary policies. He leaned back and held up his arms as if trying to embrace the world.

'Through two roads, by land and sea, we will link three continents and once again we will be the Middle Kingdom, at the heart of the world of trade, power and culture.'

He smiled at his disciple.

'And we will arrive at our destination much sooner than you ever imagined, my friend.'

Jiang looked at his feet and nodded without making eye contact.

Meng adopted a fatherly tone.

'You are troubled,' he said. 'You know that you can speak freely with me. What is it?'

Jiang cleared his throat and glanced back at the map.

'The sea lanes to the south are the key to this,' he said softly. 'The South China Sea is ours, but other nations claim those waters. You demonstrated our power brilliantly when you turned back the USS *George Washington*. That is all we need to press for a negotiated settlement of our claims – to get everything we want without risk.'

'What are you saying?' There was a whiff of annoyance in Meng's tone.

'Militarising the islands in the South China Sea is courting disaster.' Jiang's voice was filled with urgency. 'We have bluffed the world that we are the equals of America on the high seas, but we know – and the Americans know – that it is not true. There is still a choke point in the Malacca Strait. We still do not have the fleet to sustain a presence in the Indian Ocean. If we overreach in the South China Sea and are defeated, then we will be set back years.'

Meng's eyes were both curious and reproachful.

'You surprise me, my friend. We were the ones who saw and seized the opportunity to humble the United States.' He swept his arm across the face of the world. 'This was our objective.'

Jiang seemed fearful of provoking Meng's ire; his voice was almost pleading.

'And we can have it, sir. We have demonstrated our power. Now let's show our wisdom. The regional players fear us. We can get what we want through diplomacy.'

Meng snorted.

'I don't have to seek permission from Vietnam, Malaysia, the Philippines. They are pissants, all of them. I will take what I want, what is my birthright. The South China Sea project is our Great Sea Wall. The islands we are terraforming will be unsinkable aircraft carriers and resupply ships. Once we have finished creating them we will claim all the waters around them. The world will have to beg permission to pass.'

Meng's voice softened, but his tone remained insistent.

'There is only one power that can challenge us and that is America. But it is ruled by a fool and a coward. Now is the time to act. If we pause, we allow the United States time to play itself back into the game.'

The president leaned menacingly close to his minister.

'The real threat … as it ever was … is internal weakness. It is your job to guard against that, not to be its mouthpiece.'

Jiang lifted his head and nodded. 'Yes sir.'

He bowed respectfully and left the room. Only the ticking of an office clock meddled with the president's thoughts.

Meng re-read the front-page article about the glamorous couple's night at the opera. Suddenly he lifted the *People's Daily* in both hands and tore it in two. He threw the pieces to the floor and picked up his phone. A female voice answered. 'Sir?'

'Send in the cleaners.'

Canberra

'You're playing Russian roulette with your life.'

The doctor unwrapped the blood pressure cuff from Catriona Bailey's right arm, jotting down a few notes before turning to the opposition leader who sat impassively in her motorised wheelchair.

'Five empty chambers is a fair bet,' Bailey said, the defiance in her voice matching the steel-blue coldness of her eyes.

Since emerging from the locked-in syndrome that followed the massive stroke she'd suffered in 2011, she'd engaged a specialist to visit her every month. Discreetly. Her recovery after twenty months of hospitalisation had been miraculous, testament to her fierce determination, but she was running on a dangerous cocktail of experimental drugs and unquenchable ambition.

She'd taken credit for the better-than-expected election result and had ruthlessly entrenched her authority. She'd forced a change to the ALP's rules to ensure her parliamentary leadership could never again be snatched by just fifty-one per cent of the Labor Caucus, neutering the faceless power harlots who practised the dark arts of political numerology. They despised her popularity, her power, her autocratic style that spurned their counsel.

But Bailey rode the heady heights of popular opinion. For the past year she'd held a commanding lead over Scott as preferred prime minister, and Labor was ahead in every poll.

She had followed Emily Brooks's playbook and simply obstructed the work of government. Bailey had never been an idealist, so she had no trouble abandoning policy for pragmatism. Scott might be right about repairing the Budget, ending industry handouts and signing free trade agreements, but Bailey didn't care. Every debate was reduced to one talismanic word: fairness. Every government entreaty met the same answer: no.

Budget cuts were 'unfair' because they slashed welfare. Cutting industry handouts was 'unfair' because of the loss of subsidised jobs in the economic badlands. Free trade agreements were 'unfair' to workers, farmers and protected businesses.

It was a message pounded daily in an endless parade of public and media appearances.

And Bailey's rise in popularity was given wings by Scott's hopeless tenure as she blundered from one prime ministerial disaster to the next.

In her few quiet moments, Bailey would imagine standing on the steps of Government House just after her ministry was sworn in: Catriona 3.0. But they would be mere decoration: she would have all the power and wield it ferociously.

The stern tones of her specialist jolted Bailey from yet another lapse in which she found it hard to distinguish reality from drug-induced hallucination.

'If you don't take my advice and pace yourself a little more, delegate some responsibilities to your colleagues and cut back on the travel, you may have just months to live. Or you could relapse and end up unable to move or speak again.'

Bailey's face, gaunt and layered with thick powder, slowly creased in a smile. Her right hand pressed a lever, swinging her wheelchair around. She glided towards the door.

'If those are my choices then I choose risk and a short full life over a long and empty one,' she said. 'I'll be prime minister next year. I'll worry about my health after that. Your job is to keep me upright until then.'

The lights of Parliament House sparkled as a gaggle of staffers and reporters boarded the Murrays coach. It was 4.30am and the early morning cool was forecast to give way to a summer scorcher.

It had been like this for more than a year. Every time federal parliament rose, the opposition leader would gather up a handful of colleagues and staff and embark on a blitz of electorates, the media trailing in the wake of the rock star political princess.

Bailey would usually fly to a state capital or regional centre, then board a chartered bus to continue a seemingly never-ending tour of safe and marginal seats alike. It was a perpetual election campaign, and Bailey would swat away claims that the public was tiring of the strategy with the riposte: 'Look at the polls.'

Today the Bailey Express was going local, leaving from the front of parliament and travelling across the ACT border into Eden–Monaro. The bellwether seat was held by the Liberals with the barest of margins.

Emblazoned with Bailey's campaign catchphrase, 'Advance Australia Fair', the coach was primed for a barnstorming three-day tour through this must-win electorate. The reception promised to be good because Labor's polling showed Bailey was well ahead, from the high plateau of the Monaro to the lush pastures of the South Coast.

At every town, she would spruik from a purpose-built platform alongside the bus. Bailey would doorknock the nation to win back the office stolen from her. Nothing had given her greater satisfaction than dethroning the usurper, Martin Toohey, but his demise had come too close to the election for her to salvage the Labor government. Now, with time and a relentless determination, the prize was again within sight. Just six seats stood between her and a return to government.

Her fingers gripped the canister that daily dispensed the cocktail of drugs that kept her functioning. Three pills, three times a day. She swilled them down with a cup of water before easing herself onto her bed, exhausted but satisfied after another relentless day.

It was 11pm and her touring party was nestled in at a modest Bega motel, but there was still work to be done. She took a sip of brandy and began typing a message on her mobile using Confide, the encrypted software app that sent self-destructing digital messages, keeping communications safe from the many eyes prying online.

Tonight she was continuing a conversation that had begun decades before.

I watch in awe as you go from strength to strength and I know that when I return to power we will do great things.

One minute later, a return message pinged its arrival.

We will.

_____

Detroit

He knew they were hunting for him.

The counter-snipers scouring the landscape always ran the same playbook: every window, every rooftop with a clear line of sight, was a threat.

The advance team had arrived two days before game day. He knew everything they would do, the checklist they would follow, how they would react to real and perceived threats. Twenty-four hours out their number had swelled as they set up a defensive bubble that radiated more than twelve hundred metres from the engagement zone.

By zero hour there would be helicopters in the air and gunmen stationed in the buildings around the target, searching for any signs of trouble through their scopes.

They were setting up a defensive screen for a shot that was rarely fired, an adversary who mostly didn't exist. They were searching for ghosts.

Multiply their task by a week, by a month, by years – and even the elite would be in danger of losing their edge. Their complacency was his friend.

Today the danger was real. If they missed him, they would live with it for the rest of their lives.

He had been planning this moment for weeks; when it came, it would be measured in heartbeats. Fifteen years of training would collapse into a few seconds and a shot that would reverberate around the world.

The monitor on his wrist showed his heart was beating at seventy. Normal for most, but twenty beats above his resting average.

He breathed in deeply, visualising his opponents' final preparations: the counter-snipers locking down buildings, starting with the one hundred per cent locations, the lairs from which even someone of moderate talent could not miss. Then they would fan out until all threats had been eliminated.

He'd chosen the impossible hide, high up and nearly two kilometres from the target, beyond what was considered the effective range of his weapons system. Only a handful of snipers could consider this position, and he was one of that handful.

Carefully he unpacked his favourite gun, a hand-made bolt-action British rifle, the Accuracy International PSR. His was a 'take-down' version: the barrel and butt could be removed from the rifle with a hex key, halving its size to fit in a rucksack.

He would be shooting .338 Lapua Magnum ammunition with enough power to punch a hole through body armour from one thousand metres. In the current atmospheric conditions, his bullet would slow from supersonic to transonic speed once it passed 1750 metres. That made it less stable, adding another variable to a multitude that he'd had to consider in planning the shot.

The first was gravity. From his eyrie, it would take the bullet nearly five seconds to reach the game. His Schmidt & Bender scope had been zeroed to one hundred metres, but at two thousand he was effectively lobbing the bullet, aiming nearly four metres above the target.

Then there was the Coriolis effect. As the bullet left the muzzle of the gun it would be leaving the face of the Earth, the planet rotating under its flight path. Beyond one thousand metres, if shooting west, the target would move up and towards the gun, so bullets frequently missed low. Facing east, targets dropped and moved away, so bullets might miss high.

And there was the wind, which channelled down streets and blew at a whim up and down the faces of buildings. Any city was a problem, this one more than most.

He reached into a pocket on his vest and pulled out his phone, checking the ballistics solver app restricted to those in law enforcement and the military. It was linked to his wind-velocity meter.

The final crucial variables were air density and temperature. An increase in air density meant more resistance, which would slow down the bullet sooner. An increase in temperature would make the powder inside the case burn faster and lift the muzzle velocity of the bullet.

Happily all those calculations were crunched by his software. Nothing was left to chance.

A flutter of movement to his left startled him. An errant pigeon strutting across the room. He smiled for the first time that day.

The building and the room had been chosen with great care. Like many in this dying city, the high-rise had long been abandoned and now stood as a 38-storey Renaissance-style tombstone for a more prosperous age.

The windows beneath the ornate green copper roof had been smashed by vandals and the walls were smeared with their profanities. Glass and rubbish were strewn across the floor. The stench of urine was overwhelming.

It was perfect.

The large open window gave him a clear view of the target and meant he could position himself deep inside the room. He was six metres back, lurking in contained shadow. There would be no Hollywood-style tell-tale barrel resting on the window's edge. All that was visible was a broken frame. His weapon was propped on the remnants of a table, which he'd turned on its side and secured to give him a stable platform.

The marksman was ready. He checked the time. Ten minutes to game time and the culmination of a lifetime serving with the very best in some of the very worst places on this wretched planet. In a world clouded by the lies and deceit of rulers claiming to speak the truth, the only absolute clarity was through his scope. Here everything narrowed to one pure purpose: the elimination of a threat.

His mind wandered back to another target. Afghanistan, eight years earlier. The tribal leader had been nearly two and a half kilometres out when he'd lined him up in the sights of his Barrett M82A1 .50 calibre rifle. The bullet took six seconds to strike.

In the elite enclave of military snipers, the Afghani kill was still spoken of with reverence.

He glanced over his shoulder to the open door behind him.

The danger in making any shot was that it revealed your position. The sound would be muffled, but not completely silenced, by his suppressor. Its main function was to diffuse the noise and make it difficult to assess where it had come from. From the moment of impact the clock would be ticking on being captured. Long practice had taught him to move methodically when the heat was on.

After confirming the hit he would drop to his knees behind the table. It would take him sixty seconds to dismantle the rifle and put it in his rucksack. There were three ways out of the building and he had investigated each one. If his escape was blocked through the quickest exit he would immediately shift to the next, and then the last. He would be on the street in three minutes, a long way from the immediate terror and confusion. Then he would blend with the crowd and vanish.

One last time he focused through his scope on the tiny lectern so far away. It was sharp and clear in the sight. It was a good day for hunting, bright with very little wind.

There was movement on the stage. The moment was close. He felt his heart rate begin to rise. Always he felt a surge of excitement as the game drew into the crosshairs.

There he was, familiar, waving at the crowd as he approached the lectern. The sniper waited as the crowd settled so the quarry could begin his speech. He would never get the chance.

The sniper breathed out slowly and squeezed the trigger. A crack echoed in the room.

His heart beat six times. Through his scope he saw the man's head rip to one side as the bullet exploded through the base of his skull.

He fell.

The president of the United States was dead.

Washington

Six heavily armed men burst through the door, the sergeant barking out orders to startled congressional staff.

'Everybody get down.'

They were a fearsome sight, wearing military-style helmets and body armour, their faces covered by balaclavas. Each member of the black-clad Containment and Emergency Response Team of the Capitol Police carried a short-barrel M4A1 assault rifle.

The staff of the speaker of the United States House of Representatives had been bunched around a TV and froze as they struggled to absorb what was happening. Only moments earlier they had been shaken by a shriek from an intern who'd been the first to see an unbelievable breaking news strap flash up on the screen: 'President Shot at Detroit Rally'.

The sergeant lifted his weapon to leave them in no doubt: he wasn't asking, he was demanding.

'Get down. NOW!'

As the staff dropped to the floor he raced to the office of Speaker Morgan McDonald, followed by two of his colleagues. Big Mac, too, was staring at a TV screen and swung around as the police burst into the room.

'Sir, you are coming with us.'

Big Mac raised his hands and didn't budge.

'Hang on, son, where are we going?'

'No questions, sir.'

The sergeant and another officer grabbed the speaker under each armpit and manhandled him out of the room. As they emerged, the team formed a phalanx round the trio, leaving the staff terrified and sobbing.

The unit moved at a trot like a deadly black spider through the corridors of the Capitol. Two in front, with guns shifting from side to side, eyes peeled for any sign of threat. Two supporting Big Mac, but scouring the corridors left and right. Two trailing, facing backwards and training their weapons on anyone who moved into their sights.

Minutes later, the team arrived at a fortified 'safe room' in the basement. The sergeant punched in a security code and a heavy steel door slid open.

Big Mac had never ventured this far into the bowels of America's legislature, but he knew this was one of a series of safe rooms that had been built after 9/11, in anticipation of a terror attack. Only when he was inside and the doors were shut tight did the two men remove their hands from under his arms.

Big Mac was a sweaty mess. His shirt was out, one of his braces had come loose. He'd lost a shoe somewhere along the way.

The sergeant spoke, his breathing laboured after the dash through the corridors.

'Sir, thank you for your co-operation. The president is dead. At exactly the same time he was killed, the White House was attacked by drone. It was shot down and exploded near the entrance to the West Wing. The vice president is in Air Force Two, about an hour out from Washington.'

Big Mac's heart was pounding and his head was swimming. It had been a long time since he had attempted anything more than a brisk walk and he was struggling to catch his breath.

'We believe this is a co-ordinated attack. After the vice president, you are the next in line, sir. We had to secure the leadership.'

'Thank you, son.' Big Mac panted as he struggled to regain some of his composure. 'Now, can you hook me up with STRATCOM?'

Air Force Two

'I don't care how many windows you break. Get there,' the voice barked inside the pilot's helmet.

Lieutenant Daniela Flores and her wingman turned their F-16 Fighting Falcons west and pushed them to Mach 2, just over 2450 kilometres an hour, crashing through the speed of sound.

Four F-16s from the 113th Wing, DC Air National Guard had been 'hot cocked' on the tarmac when news of the president's assassination broke. The 'Capitol Guardians' were in the air in less than five minutes.

As they screamed into the sky they heard a broadcast from Andrews Air Force Base – a message not used since September 11, 2001.

'Attention all aircraft monitoring Andrews Tower, this is a warning. I repeat: all aircraft monitoring Andrews Tower frequencies, this is a warning. All aircraft are warned to remain clear of Class Bravo airspace. Any aircraft intruding into Class Bravo airspace will be shot down.'

Two of the F-16s were now tasked with patrolling the skies over DC. Soon they would be joined by many more. Flores and her wingman had been ordered to charge towards the vice president's plane. At Mach 2, they would haul it in inside half an hour.

'Is America under attack?' The vice president was shaken. Although Mikaela Asta had always known that she was just one missed heartbeat away from becoming leader of the free world, nothing had prepared her for this moment. News of the president's death had been relayed to Air Force Two as she was flying back to Washington from a meeting in California.

Her chief of staff shook his head.

'We just don't know yet,' he said. 'But we have had two simultaneous attacks, one on the president and one on the White House. So we have to assume they are co-ordinated.'

Asta was conferring with a handful of staff inside her stateroom in the Boeing C-32. It was a surreal moment. For the first time since Kennedy, an American president had been assassinated – and she was the next in line. Mikaela Asta, mother of five.

Media commentators had dubbed her the Queen of the Tea Party when she'd arrived in Washington in 2008, and then called her a 'surprise pick' when Earle Jackson named her as his running mate in the 2012 campaign. But it wasn't a surprise to Asta. All those years ago, when she was curing homosexuals through her conversion therapy practice back in Minnesota, she'd known God had a plan for her.

She'd brought both feminine charm and northern cred to Jackson's decidedly southern Republican team. And as the president's support collapsed, Asta had been increasingly feted by the Conservative Right. Some on Fox News wistfully pondered whether she could restore American pride. Now they were about to find out.

But any sense of elation was crushed by the weight of the moment and the overwhelming feeling of vulnerability. Despite an unrivalled suite of on-board communications, they were flying blind on what this death meant. The vice president was demanding answers and there weren't any. If there was ever a moment to pray, it was now.

One of the stateroom phones rang and Asta's chief of staff picked it up.

'It's the speaker.'

'Morgan, thank God, what do we know?'

'Not much.' Big Mac's familiar voice boomed down the line. 'The drone attack on the White House was low tech; there were explosives on board but not enough to do any serious damage and there was no trace of chemical or biological weapons. The gunman who killed the president was a pro; the secret service and police haven't been able to locate the shooter's position, but it's likely to have been more than a mile from the park. Based on that, the shooter has to be ex-military, but that only narrows the enemy down to just about any group of whack jobs here or offshore.'

Big Mac paused and his voice dropped to a conspiratorial whisper.

'There was one other attack,' he said. 'On some of our military satellites.'

Asta struggled to get her head around the outrageous idea.

'Which satellites?'

'Two that circle the globe in tandem in a low orbit. Their code name is *Intruder* and they scoop up electronic intelligence. They eavesdrop on the communications, navigation and weapons control signals emitted by naval ships. They can pinpoint and track the position, speed and direction of all military ships at sea.'

'How do you attack a military satellite?'

'Turns out, just like you do in *Star Wars*. The satellites were hit with a directed energy weapon fired from Earth.'

'A what?'

'A laser, Mikaela. Our satellites were blinded by a laser. Strategic Command is still trying to work out if the damage is temporary or permanent. But one thing they do know: apart from us only two countries have militarised lasers – Russia and China.'

Asta glanced out the window and saw the comforting shape of an F-16 warplane pull up into a flanking position alongside what was now Air Force One.

'We are going to find the people who did this,' Asta said. 'And we are going to make them pay.'

'We are,' Big Mac echoed. 'But until we are certain that our nation is not about to be attacked, you're flying to Nebraska.'

Sydney

Harry Dunkley stumbled from a dream into words he struggled to believe.

'Just repeating, the American president is dead,' came the news from his bedside radio.

The former journalist wiped the sleep from his eyes, pulled on some clothes and shuffled over to the seminary's common room. His regular breakfast companion was standing transfixed in front of the TV, as CNN hit a near hysterical pitch.

The priest shook his head. 'Can you believe it? I remember when Kennedy was killed. I was still a young man, early thirties, just back from studying in Rome. Ah, JFK. We had such hopes ...'

'This might sound strange, Father, but it's one of my earliest memories. I was four. It was the first time I saw my mother cry.'

'I think we all cried that day, Harry.'

Dunkley pulled a couple of lounge chairs close to the set.

'He was a flawed man though, Father. Far from the saint many portrayed him as: the son of a ruthless tyrant, and a pathological pants-man.'

The priest laughed.

'That's what I like about you, Harry. You don't waste time on romance. But I've never prayed for saints to lead us. Just give me a halfway decent sinner.'

They were glued to the coverage, taking turns to dash to the kitchen before settling down with plates of toast and mugs of tea.

They saw a replay of the vice president's plane, escorted by two fighter aircraft, flying into Offutt Air Force Base in Nebraska. The base was the home of US Strategic Command, or STRATCOM. It was an ominous sign because it served as a transmission point for a presidential order for nuclear war.

Next, still pictures filled the screen, showing Mikaela Asta being sworn in as president by a local judge, then chairing an emergency meeting of the National Security Council via teleconference in STRATCOM's nuclear-proof bunker, before leaving Offutt for the flight to Andrews Air Force Base in Washington.

It was as the new president's plane was landing in Washington, and the countdown began to her address to the nation, that the first hints came of a disturbing new twist in an already deeply distressing day. Fox News began quoting 'congressional sources', saying that there had been a third attack on the US that morning, this one on a military satellite. That lifted the stakes from an attack by a terror group to an act of war by a foreign power.

At 7pm Washington time the networks all switched to the White House. An immaculately groomed Mikaela Asta was seated at the desk where Franklin Roosevelt had received the news of the attack on Pearl Harbor, and George W Bush had made his address on the night of September 11, 2001.

'My fellow Americans,' Asta began, her voice as steady as her gaze, 'all I have I would have given gladly not to be speaking to you from this office tonight.'

With an eye to history, Asta's speechwriters had chosen to begin by recasting the opening line of Lyndon Johnson's speech to the joint sitting of Congress in the wake of Kennedy's assassination.

'There are no words to express our grief and none to describe our quiet yet unyielding anger. Today was more than an attack on one man, it was an attack on a nation. If it was an attempt to frighten or intimidate us, then our adversary has grievously misjudged the character of the people of the United States.

'The search is under way for those behind these evil acts. We will bend the full resources of our intelligence and law enforcement agencies to find those responsible and bring them to justice, be they individuals or nations.'

Asta paused for a second, a neophyte president born for this moment.

'America has been through difficult times. There are those who say that our power is waning, who believe that our time as the pre-eminent nation has passed. I remind them that there is still only one superpower on Earth.'

The president's voice was calm, but her steel-blue eyes radiated anger and resolve. There was no hint of her usual Colgate smile today. This was her commander-in-chief moment.

'So whoever our assailants may be, I suggest they ponder the words of Admiral Isoroku Yamamoto, who led the attack against us at Pearl Harbor.

All you have done is awaken a sleeping giant and filled him with a terrible resolve.

'We have proven that we have the courage to seek peace. Perhaps our enemies have forgotten that we also have the fortitude to wage war.

'Tonight we mourn Earle Jackson; tomorrow we will avenge him.

'As Psalm 144 says: "Blessed be to the Lord my rock, who trains my hands for war, my fingers for battle."

'Thank you. Good night. And God bless America.'

'I dislike that woman, she is spoiling for a fight.' The priest pressed mute on the remote as the coverage returned to another studio panel parsing every word of the speech.

'That makes two of us,' Dunkley said. 'That wasn't a speech aimed at a lone gunman or a group of terrorists. Asta is preparing her nation for war, which must mean the Yanks suspect the assassination is state-sponsored.'

'It's more than that, Harry.' The old priest's face tightened into a grimace as he turned to the younger man. 'I met her, maybe thirty years ago, at a conference at the Graduate Theological Union at the University of California in Berkeley.'

Dunkley was surprised. 'I can't imagine the Tea Lady in Chief on a hippy campus in San Francisco.'

'It was a gathering that brought together every Christian group from the most liberal to the most conservative,' the priest said. 'Mikaela and her ilk were there because it's the kind of dialogue her type joins with the intention of destroying. When I met her she was an advocate of Dominion Theology: she believed that Christians should govern America. She is a dedicated theocrat and deadly dangerous.'

Dunkley shifted in his seat to get a better view of the priest.

'Father, without meaning to be impolite, all religions are dangerous in my view and responsible for most of the trouble and all of the wars in the world.'

'Really?' The priest raised a bushy eyebrow. 'Were you paying attention in the twentieth century, Harry? History's greatest criminals were Hitler, Mao and Stalin. Pol Pot could not match them for corpses, but did for evil. All erased religion and replaced it with the worship of a proselytising, messianic state. Bad men don't need God to justify mass murder.'

Dunkley felt a long-forgotten surge of competitive energy as he warmed to a debate he'd been having since he was sixteen.

'And how many deaths over millennia have there been because zealots decided to force their imagined gods on others? Your church was as brutal as any, not to mention the contemptible army of kiddie-fiddler priests you seem to have spawned. How can you live with that?'

The priest lowered his eyes and Dunkley felt a stab of guilt, remembering the kindness the man had showed him.

'It's a very fair question and I have no pat answer,' the old man said. 'The church is a human institution, and like all our endeavours it is flawed. At times I have despaired of it and its leadership. At times I think our slow death in the West is punishment for our many sins. Yes, the church has done great evil, but it has also done great good. And my faith is a different thing. It tells me to hope, even when all seems lost.'

'Father, you are clearly a good man. Don't you ever wonder? Don't you ever doubt?'

The priest looked around the room at the photos of the fathers now passed to dust.

'Of course I doubt. As Bertrand Russell said, the whole problem with the world is that fools and fanatics are always so certain of themselves and wiser people so full of doubt. But as I approach death, every day I ask myself just one question: could I have lived a better life?'

The priest shifted his gaze back to his companion, his eyes blazing with integrity and intelligence.

'And my answer to that is yes, of course. But with or without God, in or out of my frail and broken church, I will go to my grave knowing that I mostly did my best and tried to live a life for others. A life where hope always triumphed over despair.'

His voice softened.

'And you, Harry Dunkley? If you do not drink your life away, you have many years left. How do you intend to spend them?'

Dunkley slumped in his chair and stared up at the ceiling.

'I have no god to fall back on. So I have no idea what God's will is. I only have me, and just lately I'm a bit pissed off that I've been letting myself down. I don't have your luxury of a divinely ordained path.'

'Son, I like you. But you are chock full of the rote beliefs atheists have about people of faith. To put it in your language, you are full of shit. I don't pray for or expect a roadmap for my life. I have certain gifts and some strong beliefs. My strongest belief is that I have to make the most of those gifts. Harry, God's will is what you make it.'

The priest put his hand on Dunkley's arm. His grip was still strong.

'What will you make it?'

Dunkley exhaled in a long slow sigh before answering.

'I've lost faith in the institutions that run our country and the world. I used to believe that journalism was worthwhile and noble, that sunlight was the best antiseptic, that I was uncovering the truth. But I also learned to my great cost that it was an ego trip. As you say, all humans are flawed. I screwed up my marriage and now my daughter won't talk to me.'

Gaby, his only child. She was the one person he loved unconditionally, but six months ago she had cut him off and how could he blame her? When he was in his prime as a reporter he had all but ignored her and she had not coped well with his public fall from grace. Their last conversation had ended with her stinging retort: 'You are a pathetic disgrace.'

Of all his mistakes and misdemeanours, losing Gaby hit the hardest. How he wished he could hear the gentle arpeggio of her voice extolling his day's modest achievements. He wondered what she was doing now. Did she think of him at all, or was he just refuse locked away in her past?

He took a gulp of air, stifling an urge to cry.

'I've got more flaws than most. I got my best friend murdered, lost my job and nearly killed myself. So what will I make of what's left of my life? To paraphrase you, Father, that is a fucking good question.'

The priest smiled.

'Well, I trust you'll find a fucking good answer, Harry Dunkley. The world needs journalists like you. As Albert Camus said, a free press can be good or bad. But an unfree press is always bad.'

The saints were closing in.

Dunkley sat on a pew in the Villa Maria church, gazing up at a stained-glass window. The sun animated a colourful portrait of John or Joseph or some other Catholic hero. A marble plaque below the window asked people to pray for the soul of Father Placide Hault, who'd died in 1909 after a life caring for others. There were some good people here, those who laboured in the name of their God, even if he couldn't begin to understand their faith.

Dunkley had rarely darkened the doors of any chapel, but he'd grown to enjoy the contemplative ambience of this space. He breathed in the quiet of the sandstone building, feeling a renewed strength. For the first time in many months he was resolved. He lifted his hands and held them out in front of him. Steady. No trembling. He smiled to himself then took one last long sweep of the church. Built in 1871, it bore the scars of countless repairs. It had been extended, updated, patched and repatched over its 146-year life. But it was still standing.

The saints stared down at him.

He walked out into a glorious Sydney morning, fumbling in his pocket for his cheap phone. He scrolled through some recent numbers, then punched green and waited.

A familiar voice answered with a casual 'How are you, mate?'

Dunkley's response was instant. 'Martin, I'm in.'

Washington

Jack Webster had thirty minutes to prepare for the funeral of President Earle Jackson. The defence chief was in his preferred suite at his favourite DC hotel, the Willard, a short walk to the White House and a fifteen-minute drive to the National Cathedral on Wisconsin Avenue.

America was sombre, but Webster felt a small thrill as he began to dress. After all he was in Washington, the epicentre of global power, the New Rome. His spiritual home.

On this blackest of days, Sir Jack had never felt more alive.

He studied himself in his full regalia, pleased with what he saw, and his hand rose slowly in salute, his eyes never leaving the mirror. 'Sir!' The warrior was ready.

This nation feted men like him, and had made the military chiefs Washington and Eisenhower president. Here, he was among people who had real power and knew how to wield it. Ruthlessly.

Today the nation would pray for the soul of a slain president, but in reality Jackson was a flawed martyr who had damaged Brand USA. In this world no one respected the weak, and a vulnerable America was bad for the West.

The death of a president was a tragedy, but it was also an opportunity. A desperately needed chance to hit the reset button. The assassin had done America a favour.

'This is a sad hour in the life of our great nation. Earle Jackson won America's respect with his leadership, and he won our love with humility and goodness. He belonged to the people, and so to the people he will be returned, forever.'

Washington National Cathedral was overflowing with nearly four thousand mourners, many of them foreign dignitaries. They listened in silence as a black-clad Mikaela Asta paid respect to her predecessor.

For a week, the American people, who had too much experience in burying assassinated leaders, had mourned their commander in chief. Despite committing unprecedented resources to the hunt for the killer, the nation's law enforcement and intelligence agencies had made little headway in solving the case.

In a nation prone to wild rumour, conspiracy theories abounded.

In his seat fifteen rows from the front, Jack Webster dipped his head as the funeral entourage prepared to leave the grand cathedral. He had just turned to join the trail of mourners when he felt a firm grip on his forearm. 'Good of you to come all this way, Jack.'

The man who had been sworn in as vice president was at his side. Morgan McDonald had been Webster's close confidant for more than a decade.

'Of course I would be here, Morgan,' Webster said. 'America might have more powerful allies, but it has no better friend than Australia.'

Big Mac dipped his head in acknowledgement. 'I know. That is why we need to talk.'

In his office on the western edge of the White House, Big Mac was holding court, albeit with an audience of one.

'These are dark days, my friend, dark days indeed.' The vice president's southern drawl slowly caressed each word.

'Wherever you look around the world, the good guys are losing.' He waved at a massive wall map. 'In Africa, Boko Haram is on the rise and the Arab Spring has turned to a bitter winter that will last generations. The Middle East is aflame from end to end and Syria and Iraq are at the mercy of those infidel butchers from Islamic State.'

Jack Webster agreed with every word, and wanted to gauge Big Mac's direction and purpose.

'Europe is run by a pack of limp-wristed bureaucrats; it's a travesty of a state that provides false unity. In the north, the Russian bear is waking; it smells our weakness and is testing its strength.'

Big Mac looked from the map to his friend.

'And in your own neck of the woods, Jack, we have the biggest problem of all. An emboldened and aggressive China. A country determined to dominate the world.'

Webster nodded his agreement, leaning forward in his seat.

'Unfortunately, my friend, and I say this with great respect, our problem got a whole lot worse when the US cut and ran from the Taiwan Strait. That rolled forward China's plans for regional expansion by a generation. We needed that time to prepare.'

'Yes, Earle Jackson was a disaster as president. He should be buried in an unmarked pauper's grave to be pissed on for eternity by rodents. But don't misread the American people. We can criticise our own; others are not afforded that right. The people are angry that someone killed Jackson before they got the chance to do it at the ballot box. They are hurting and hunger for revenge. Turns out the best thing Earle ever did for America was die. We salute him for that. This is a crisis we must not waste.'

McDonald lifted his vast bulk from behind his desk and breathed out theatrically.

'It's time for us to shout to the world that we are still the only superpower on Earth. The murder of our president gives us a rare window of opportunity. We have reason to believe that the attack on our leader was not the act of a lone madman but part of a co-ordinated assault by a nation. We will take our time, but when we act it will be with a sledgehammer, it will come without warning and the world will shudder.

'Jack, this will be high risk. We will need our friends to be unwavering in their support.'

'You know you have it. We've been unwavering since you came to our aid in World War II. Australia does not forget its friends.'

'We need more than words, Jack, we need deeds. Concrete, unmistakeable signs that you are on our side in this scrap.'

'What do you want?'

'I understand you're in the market for submarines.'

'Yes, twelve of them. The biggest defence buy in our history.'

Big Mac smiled at Webster, revealing a gold tooth that made him look for all the world like the planet's shonkiest used car salesman.

'Well, I know a man who might just be selling some.'

Elizabeth Scott was surprised to find that she and the governor-general were being put up in two of the four adjoining townhouses in Blair House on Pennsylvania Avenue, three hundred metres from the White House front gate. With Washington groaning under the weight of world leaders, Scott had thought she would be well down the list of dignitaries vying for a spot at the president's official guest house.

Yet the American embassy had issued the invitation when the Australian travelling party was announced, and when Scott arrived there was a card waiting on the bureau in the entry hall. Inside was a handwritten note below the presidential seal.

'Elizabeth, I am sorry we are meeting under such sad circumstances,' it began, in copybook cursive script. 'But I hope that it will be the beginning of an enduring friendship. The alliance between our nations is one of the few rocks in an uncertain world. In such times, friends have to stay close. God bless, Mikaela Asta.'

She had read the note yesterday morning, but it seemed days ago. It was nearly midnight and jet-lag was taking its toll after a day of solemn ritual and a host of meetings with world leaders. There was one last crucial engagement before Scott could crawl into bed.

At least she wouldn't have to go far. Blair House's remaining two townhouses had been awarded to the Japanese prime minister and emperor, an arrangement not lost on other visiting dignitaries and Washington elites.

'They are ready for us, ma'am.' The bass voice of Jack Webster was accompanied by a sharp rap on the door.

Scott felt uneasy. Meetings between heads of government were usually secretive affairs, but few were actually held in secret. They took months to plan, were telegraphed in the press and attended by foreign affairs officials from both sides. Great care was taken that exact notes were kept, and agreed statements were issued at their conclusion.

This was a meeting so covert that not a single foreign affairs official knew it was taking place. It was scheduled for a time when both prime ministers were supposed to be asleep. And the layout at Blair House meant that no one outside would be alerted to the strange proceedings.

Just four people were present at the meeting. Two prime ministers and two defence force chiefs. Their mission was to cut a deal to spend $30 billion of Australian taxpayers' money on a fleet of twelve Japanese-built submarines. Defence usually spent years identifying which kit to buy. This deal would be sealed in hours.

Prime Minister Shinzo Abe wrote a note in Japanese and Scott penned one in English. The Blair House photocopier churned out one copy of each. Then they were exchanged and countersigned.

An exhausted Scott shook the hand of a leader who was determined to restore Japan's martial power and forge a chain of alliances to counter an increasingly aggressive China.

'So we are agreed,' she said. 'This project will be driven out of our offices. No one will breathe a word without the express permission of the other. This will take a lot of finessing behind the scenes in my country, Shinzo. The ship-building states will be up in arms. Literally.'

Abe chuckled. He hadn't shown a hint of emotion in two hours of tense negotiations, but now he beamed with enthusiasm.

'You are not the only one with domestic dramas, Elizabeth. The Diet and the bureaucracy will scream about handing over Japanese cutting-edge technology.'

'They are the best subs we can get for what we need; Jack has convinced me of that. In the end that is how we should judge these things. Beyond that, our mutual ally, as you know, is utterly determined that we should strike this deal.'

'Yes, they want the message to be heard loud and clear in Beijing that powerful regional partnerships are being built in response to the dragon's aggression in the East and South China Seas.'

Scott picked up her copies of the agreement, carefully folding them before handing one to Webster.

'And that's another reason we need time. There is a very delicate dance through a Chinese minefield lying ahead of us.'

It was a peculiar talent of the US security agencies: creating their own gridlock.

Elizabeth Scott could have strolled the few hundred metres from Blair House across Lafayette Square to the Chinese president's hotel in a matter of minutes.

But the Yanks had insisted on a motorcade that stretched the entire block from 17th Street to 16th Street, turning what should have been a simple walk into a half-hour melodrama.

The prime minister's patience was already in short supply as she'd managed barely three hours' sleep.

Truth be told, Scott was also nervous: there was a lot resting on this meeting with Meng Tao.

The view from the president's suite at the Hay-Adams was majestic, taking in the White House, Lafayette Square and St John's Church. Scott wondered what it was like for a Chinese leader who aspired to take America's place as author and arbiter of the world's rules to wake up and look out over the capital of his rival's empire.

Despite Scott's apprehension she soon found herself at ease with the communist leader. Meng was charming and businesslike, and most of their business was good news.

While China's growth was slowing, its demand for Australian resources was still high by historic standards. The free trade deal had been settled after a dozen years of often tortuous negotiations. Both countries were now happy with the terms.

Scott had just one uncomfortable issue to raise and she avoided it until the end.

'Mr President, we appreciate China believes it has extensive claims over the South China Sea,' she began, registering a slight change of expression on Meng's face as she waited for her translator to catch up.

'Australia does not take sides in territorial disputes, but we urge that there be no unilateral action, nor coercive action, and that all sides act in accordance with international law. We would, of course, be concerned by the artificial expansion of islands and the possibility that they might be used as military bases.'

Scott had managed to relay her entire agenda on the islands in three sentences. She would leave it to the foreign minister to do the hard policy yards at a later date.

Meng was silent for an uncomfortable age. When he responded it was in a measured tone. But his gaze had turned icy and his translator's words seemed more clipped.

'The most important expectation we have is that we need to respect each other's collective interests, accommodate any concerns and nurture a mutual trust. In this area, I have to point out that what Australia has done in terms of the South China Sea has jeopardised that mutual trust.'

As the president continued, his translator appeared to struggle, as if his finely tuned diplomatic mind could not cope with his master's directions. He did not translate the next sentence but seemed to ask for a clarification.

A dismissive flick of Meng's hand silenced the translator. The president turned to the prime minister and spoke.

'Madam Prime Minister.' Meng's English was perfect, with an accent that could have been minted in Oxbridge. 'Enjoy the embrace of the United States while you can; she clearly wants the world to know that you and the *Riben gou* are kept in the same kennel. But she is an old mistress who demands much but can offer little comfort in the future. The world is changing, returning to a truer order; soon you will have to make a choice. Do you cling to your past or embrace your future? Choose wisely.'

With a cursory nod, the president stood and swept into an adjoining room with his entourage in tow, leaving behind a group of bewildered Australians. Scott raised an eyebrow at her translator.

'Well, that message was clear, but what does "*Riben gou*" mean?' she asked.
The translator looked shocked.
'Literally, Japanese dogs.'

Canberra

The airport was modern, gleaming and near empty. It was just after 11am and Martin Toohey had arrived on a Qantas Dash 8 from Sydney, returning to the national capital for the first time in nearly a year. He'd called ahead for his former Commonwealth car driver who was now hustling for Silver Service. He spotted her immediately, holding court in a huddle of chauffeurs waiting on VIP fares.

They hugged and a familiar scent of stale nicotine closed over him.

'Linda, how wonderful to see you! How the hell are you?'

'Mr Toohey, very well. Good of you to drop in on us.'

He was happy to be back, genuinely happy. It had taken a long while to summon the desire to return to Canberra after he'd been punted by his Labor comrades. One of the consolations would be catching up with Linda. She knew Canberra, its intrigues and dark secrets, better than anyone. She was tapped into the city's best intelligence network: the VIP drivers who shuttled parliamentarians and captains of industry from the airport to Parliament House and beyond. Linda traded in gossip, and plenty of it.

They walked briskly to the underground carpark where Linda scooped up his bag and placed it in the boot of her Holden Caprice before theatrically opening a rear door, but Toohey had other ideas.

'No, I'm riding shotgun, so we can chat. So, what's been happening in the national capital? What have I missed?'

She smiled knowingly and for a while it seemed she would not answer his question, driving silently as the lake came into view. When she spoke it was in a soft, conspiratorial whisper. 'Some strange shit, Mr Toohey, some very strange shit.'

'Like what, Linda?'

'Well, seems we're top of the pops for some brash Yanks. Twice in the last month they've come in on a private jet – from New York, I think. Half a dozen of them, all tanned and impeccably dressed. Too much money, and very few manners. Strange thing is, they haven't been staying at the Hyatt or the Realm. I'm told they've been living it up out at Burra ... Well, here we are, Mr Toohey, the Kurrajong.'

'Thanks, Linda.' Toohey waited for her to continue, but she'd said her piece. 'Burra? Do you know where exactly in Burra?' Toohey wondered what the Americans could possibly find to do in the hamlet of hobby farms that lay fifty kilometres south of Canberra.

'That's the odd thing, Mr Toohey. The place they stay at belongs to Jack Webster. He spent a fortune on it by all accounts, must be planning to retire there. Guess he can afford it given the pile he gets paid and the fact that he gets his house, his food and his car for free.'

Toohey raised an eyebrow. 'Spending a fortune on a property just out of town makes him no different from your average senior public servant, Linda.'

She scoffed. 'Yeah, but name the winery that has security gates, cameras and a fence built for a fortress. That guy must be paranoid. And he's a creature of habit: goes out there every weekend when he's in Canberra.'

'Does he go alone when the Yanks aren't there?'

Linda gave a knowing wink.

'Not always.'

'Prime Minister Scott, how lovely to see you.'

She turned at his voice, radiant in her black Armani, chestnut hair a touch shorter than he remembered. Her grey-blue eyes sparkled with a wickedly playful light. A pair of silver pearl studs adorned her ears.

As Elizabeth Scott held out her hand and smiled, the deep oriental notes of her perfume washed over him.

'Martin, I heard you were coming tonight. Well, I guess some of this wonderful work is due to you.'

The prime minister motioned around the Anzac Hall, recently refurbished as part of a major upgrade of the Australian War Memorial, timed to coincide with the centenary of the Great War. The AWM's director had assembled a stellar cast for the opening of the new First World War Galleries and had personally rung Toohey with an invitation.

The former PM could hardly say no. He had approved the funding, and he wanted an excuse to return to Canberra anyway.

'Come on, Martin, let's take a quick look at G for George,' Scott whispered.

The Lancaster bomber, one of the War Memorial's most popular exhibits, had a mighty history, flying ninety bombing missions over Europe and being damaged more than twenty times by enemy fire during the Second World War. Somehow it had survived the torment of German Messerschmitts and had landed, forever, in this pantheon of Australia's military past.

'You look well, Martin. Retirement obviously agrees with you.' Scott smiled as they moved out of earshot of the knots of dignitaries.

'I'm busy, but not entirely content, Elizabeth.' Toohey looked up absentmindedly at the undercarriage of the bomber. 'I feel I had unfinished business in politics. But I have a few boards and a fair chunk of charity work. I might even find time to write a memoir.'

'Hah! You too! Let me know if you need someone to negotiate a big fat advance. Your story would be worth a bomb.'

'Yeah, there's a bit to tell …' Toohey said, his voice trailing off for a moment. 'But I still find it hard to describe what it feels like to be rolled as prime minister.'

He turned to her with an urgent expression.

'If you aren't careful, Elizabeth, you'll be one of a handful who'll find out just how much that hurts. Be wary of the counsel of those around you. Weigh up whether what they advise is in your best interests or theirs.'

Toohey glanced back to the swelling crowd.

'There are rats in your ranks.'

Scott, too, looked back at the crowd. It clearly wasn't a conversation she wanted to have and she returned swiftly to the safer ground of small talk.

'How's Mary?'

'Ah, not so good, at least with me. She's living in Melbourne and I spend most of my time in Sydney.'

'I'm sorry to hear that, I really am.' Scott gently gripped his shoulder and Toohey felt the small tingle of a pleasant memory.

The Embassy Motel, Deakin, 2007 …

'I think they want us to sit,' she said, breaking into his reverie.

They walked across to the head table. Toohey's search for his name tag was interrupted by a familiar voice.

'Mr Toohey, so glad you could join us on this auspicious occasion.'

He turned to the imposing figure of the defence chief, resplendent in his military finest. With his service medals gleaming, Jack Webster could have walked out of one of the display cases. His hand was extended and Toohey gripped it firmly.

'Sir Jack.' Toohey's voice was tinged with barely detectable sarcasm.

'I believe you're sitting next to me,' Webster said, pointing to a seat. Toohey edged his way around the table, taking his place between the defence supremo and the head of the navy.

'So how have you been, Martin? How's life after politics?' Webster was offering a bottle of white and a wide smile.

'Not bad at all. Less stressful than chairing the National Security Committee.'

Toohey contemplated his wine glass for a moment then leaned closer to Webster, a rich scent of cologne assailing his nostrils.

'Tell me, Jack, who approved the Lusitania Plan? Who really launched the cyber-attacks that helped sink my government?'

The CDF put his hand to his ear and spoke nonchalantly. 'I'm sorry, Martin, I missed that.' He placed his glass on the table and lifted his voice to signal the start of a new conversation. 'I hear Harry Dunkley's been released into your care after running amok at News Corp HQ.'

'You are, as always, well informed, Jack. Yes, he's working for me now.'

'A bit treacherous, wasn't it, the stuff he posted online?'

Toohey laughed, then turned a flat dark stare on the defence chief.

'Well, I suspect you know a little something about treason.'

Webster's shoulders stiffened slightly but his poker face registered nothing.

'What do you mean?'

'You know what they say: one man's terrorist is another's freedom fighter.'

The defence chief picked at an imaginary thread on his coat, then turned his back to the former PM. He exuded the carefree air of the powerful.

'... and now please welcome the chief of the defence force, Sir Jack Webster.'

As Webster stood to walk the short distance to the lectern, Toohey touched his sleeve.

'Give 'em hell, Jack.'

'Oh, I'll do that, Mr Toohey, I promise you.'

Canberra

Canberra South Motor Park was the kind of downbeat joint unlikely to trouble the folks at Luxury Travel.

A mishmash of red-brick units, caravans and camping sites, the facility on the outskirts of Fyshwick was home to a roll call of transient tradies, errant husbands and battlers addicted to welfare.

And one former federal minister of the Crown.

A mate from the building union had loaned Bruce Paxton a caravan with a canvas annexe. That came for free. The site rental was thirty-eight dollars a week, which was about as much as he could afford given that he was in dispute with the pen-pushers in Finance over access to his parliamentary pension. To keep the wolf from the door he'd been forced into battle with Centrelink to secure a modest disability pension as compensation for the left hand that he'd lost many years ago in a mysterious industrial accident.

He wasn't bothered by the simplicity of his digs. Paxton had enjoyed the many perks of his parliamentary career, but he hailed from a humble background and had loved, as a kid, travelling to similar caravan parks during the few holidays his family could afford.

Anyway, the '73 Franklin Regent had more character than the glass-and-metal palaces being built along Mugga Way, Canberra's version of Park Lane. He'd rolled up the sides of the annexe so it served as shade for his outdoor setting: a small plastic table, two plastic chairs. There he read and reminisced most hours of most days.

Now, returning to his abode from the amenities block on a morning threatening to soar into the high thirties, Paxton noted a well-dressed man seated in the annexe, most likely a bailiff serving a court order or a bureaucrat trying to explain why he had again failed to recover his parliamentary entitlements.

Paxton approached warily until he recognised the visitor, his initial surprise quickly turning to anger.

'Well, fuck me, the last time I saw you I was being banished from the parliament and you didn't lift a fat finger to help.'

'It's good to see you too, Bruce.' Martin Toohey extended his hand as he rose from the chair.

'What do you want?' Paxton asked aggressively, ignoring Toohey's greeting. 'It can't be to ask how I am; you had months to do that after you dumped me from the ministry. Oh, and that nice call after I was punted and my reputation trashed. Nothing. Fucking nothing. So you can't be here for my benefit.'

Toohey didn't blink during the tirade and offered no defence. Eventually he spoke.

'It's true. I hated you because you were just another burden on my government. Once you were gone I was too busy trying to keep the ship afloat to worry about the drowned. And when it sank the only survivor I cared about was me.'

Toohey eased himself back into the plastic chair and entwined his fingers across his chest.

'But that ship didn't go down on its own. We made plenty of mistakes, but the torpedoes that sank it were fired by those who were charged to defend it.'

Paxton glared at Toohey.

'Bravo on finally working that one out. The journalist Dunkley and I tried to tell that story. I didn't see you in the trenches when we got smashed. It was a cracker. I reckon we lasted all of fifteen minutes before we both had the shit blown out of us. We were firing muskets against their ballistic missiles. I was drummed out of parliament and ended up here. Fuck knows where Dunkley is; turns out he's a bit of a pisshead.'

Toohey put up a hand to shield his eyes from the sun.

'I found Dunkley in jail, in Surry Hills. He smashed up *The Australian*'s head office with a cricket bat.'

Paxton laughed, a long loud belly laugh. He pulled up the other plastic chair and sat down.

'That guy tortured me for years, eventually cost me my ministry. But once you get to know him, he's actually pretty decent. So what will he do now?'

'He's working with me at the moment.'

'You? Why?'

'Because he found we have a common enemy.'

'And who would that be?'

'Sir Jack Webster.'

Paxton whistled and slumped back in his chair.

'Well, that makes three of us.'

Canberra

The rap on the door was louder than it needed to be; not a request but a demand for entry.

Charles Dancer had been yanked from a tedious meeting in the Foreign Affairs building by an encrypted text message.

Your place. 15 mins.

The spy had excused himself then driven the short distance to his Manuka home. Now he opened his door to a thunderous Jack Webster who marched into the lounge room before speaking.

'Just what the hell is going on, Charles?'

Dancer shrugged, genuinely puzzled.

The chief of the defence force threw his hat onto the coffee table and slumped into a lounge chair, motioning for Dancer to do the same.

'Guess who I bumped into?' He didn't wait for an answer. 'Martin Toohey, that's who. I was seated next to him at a dinner at the War Memorial. He fronted me about Lusitania, would you believe, the lightweight, spineless dropkick.' Webster spat out the insult.

Dancer was used to Webster's foul moods and said nothing. It was pointless to interrupt and the fire would burn out quicker if it wasn't stoked. The defence chief gulped a coffee Dancer handed him, before lifting his gaze to his underling.

'How does he know about Lusitania, Charles?' Webster's voice held a hint of accusation, as if it was Dancer's fault that this precious secret was known to the enemy.

'Chief, my guess is he cottoned on to it through the ravings of Bruce Paxton in parliament. Harry Dunkley's also aware of it, and he and Toohey are now an item, are they not?'

Webster snorted. 'Seems they are.'

He wagged a finger as if he'd just lit upon a compelling insight. 'Charles, if he knows about Lusitania, what else does he know? And what are he and Dunkley up to?'

Webster's voice trailed off, leaving Dancer to fill the void. 'I don't know.'

'Well, I want you to find out. Find Dunkley then track everything he does; trace everyone he meets.'

Dancer didn't nod, didn't blink; he just held the military man in his gaze for several long seconds before he broke the silence.

'It's been nearly four years.'

Webster looked nonplussed. 'Four years?'

'Since you sent me into battle, remember? That picture of Bruce Paxton, planted so that Dunkley would become our dupe and do our handiwork by removing a meddlesome minister.'

'Yes,' Webster said. 'But that was necessary. Paxton was a threat to our national security.'

'There were other … casualties. Innocents. And the guilty, the most dangerous game, is still at large.'

Webster caught the note of reproach in his minion's voice. His eyes narrowed.

'Leave Bailey to me.'

'With respect, the last time Bailey was left in your hands the job was botched.'

Webster reached for his coffee cup.

'That dose should have killed her. And forgive me, but I do believe you assured me it would before I took her to lunch.'

'I underestimated her,' Dancer said. 'Her capacity for physical and political survival is unique.'

The spy didn't usually argue with Webster, whom he regarded as the one true leader in a nation led by harlots. He couldn't understand, though, why the defence chief didn't share his growing alarm at the possibility of Bailey's resurrection as prime minister. That was a threat that vastly outweighed any posed by Dunkley and Toohey.

'She's still in touch with Beijing. With the Coalition in disarray there is a very real chance that Bailey will be prime minister next year. We have to finish the job. That is the only game I want to track.'

Webster stood, signalling the audience was at an end.

'Bailey will never be prime minister. I will see to that. Your mission is to find out what Dunkley and Toohey are up to. If you believe they are a threat to our operation, you will eliminate that threat.'

The chief scooped up his hat and positioned it at the most flattering angle on his head.

'And that's an order.'

_____

Washington

Mikaela Asta laughed long and loud.

The forty-sixth president of the United States of America had stolen a moment to glance at the morning newspapers on her iPad. The reading was delicious.

America's liberal media was befuddled. The White House had its first female occupant and that should have been cause for celebration. But she was Republican, and their disappointment was palpable.

An article in the *New York Times* particularly tickled her. The Gray Lady typified the confusion of the chattering class: giving lip-service compliments to a woman who had finally reached the peak of American power, while being enraged at Asta's hardline stance against abortion.

The poor dears had got the wrong kind of woman. What they wanted was Gloria Steinem, but instead they were stuck with Boudicca. Just like the ancient warrior, Asta would lead America into battle. She needed a fight to prove her steel and was convinced America needed one to show it still had a spine. As the Israelis had told her on one of her many visits to that besieged land, 'Strike first and pretend you are sorry later.'

The president's most trusted adviser was Morgan McDonald. The former speaker had been sworn in as her deputy and the two met daily without staff. And Asta was just as hawkish as her vice president.

'Is there still nothing in the assassination of Jackson that links it to a state?' Asta asked McDonald, agitated at the lack of progress in the investigation of the former president's death.

'Alas, no.' Big Mac shared her irritation. 'We have nothing beyond the bullet that killed him. It's a specialist sniper's round, but one that is commercially available. Every terrorist group on Earth has claimed credit, none of them credibly.'

Although Jackson had been sliding towards electoral oblivion, the American people were outraged by the killing. Asta knew that was an opportunity. She could usefully direct the anger at a real or imagined enemy so long as she had a vaguely plausible chain of evidence. George W Bush had used the cover of 9/11 to attack Iraq, even though there was nothing to link the terror strike to that benighted state.

Asta wanted to strike while public anger was still red hot, fearing that it would cool as the days turned into weeks.

Big Mac swiped a donut from a teetering pile before him, halved it in a single bite and didn't pause in his analysis. 'The laser strike on our military satellite blinded it temporarily, but did no major damage. It could have been a test and, in any event, we can't trace the source.'

Asta was tired of pussyfooting around. 'As you said, it can only have been Russia or China and I don't buy the idea that the timing was a coincidence. 'It's still our best link to a state-based act of war and time is running out.

'Start building the case,' she ordered McDonald. 'Pull together anything that points to China. The fact that the assassination was so professional proves the killer had military training. Start there, then weave in the Star Wars strike.'

Big Mac shook his head.

'We have to have a credible motive. Why would the Chinese do it? The Taiwan Strait neutered Jackson. He was their patsy. They would have been happy if he'd won the next election.'

Asta smiled.

'You surprise me, Morgan. Establishing a motive is the easy part. He who controls the present controls the past and there is nothing the useful idiots in the media love more than classified documents. The best thing about them is that we never comment when they are leaked. Well, not on the record anyway.'

*

By the sedate standards of the *New York Times*, the report on the paper's front page the next morning was breathless.

CHINA KNEW OF SECRET PLAN TO AVENGE TAIWAN STRAIT

Dozens of top-secret documents reveal Beijing knew of Pentagon plans to provide military backing to the Philippines and Vietnam to help reclaim disputed islands in the South China Sea.

The covert plan was authorised by the slain president, Earle Jackson. He intended to mount the operation as he pushed for re-election, in order to regain the nation's confidence as commander in chief.

Senior government sources claim the secret plan explains why China is rumoured to be on the verge of deploying warplanes and other military hardware to the islands.

A spokesman for the White House said that it was the policy of the administration not to comment on matters of national security.

One senior White House official, who spoke on condition of anonymity, said the administration was furious at the leak, which has been described as the worst since former government contractor Edward Snowden released thousands of classified documents in 2013.

'But it might explain why someone would want to kill the president,' the official said. 'And the strike against our military satellites could only have come from a foreign power.'

Canberra

The speaker's face flushed scarlet as she bellowed to be heard above the din of the chamber, battling to bring it to heel.

'Order! Order! The leader of the opposition will cease interjecting or I will expel her under 94A.'

A rampant Labor Party could smell blood and couldn't contain its animal spirits. The target was the wounded prime minister, Elizabeth Scott. Her 'Knightmare' blunder had made her a national punchline. Her backbench was the antithesis of Labor's: the Coalition MPs were mostly mute, busying themselves with paperwork or flicking through phone messages as their leader was devoured.

'Madam Speaker, I was simply reminding the prime minister that any honourable woman should avoid one "knight" stands.'

Labor howled itself sick as Catriona Bailey smirked at her pitiful pun.

Elizabeth Scott had resumed her seat in the middle of answering a question as the speaker sought to calm the chamber. A two-metre-wide table separated her from Bailey, and Scott marvelled at her opponent. Close up, Bailey looked like a horror movie fiend: a pale and wizened witch on a motorised broomstick, her bloodstream filled with the drugs that kept her alive, all pumped through a heart made of ice.

Bailey caught Scott's gaze and mouthed 'You're dead' as she dragged her thumb across her throat.

It hurt because it was true. Scott had a fingernail grip on power. She led a divided and weak government, hamstrung by its mistakes and unable to garner the confidence of the people. If she kept trailing in the polls and her demoralised backbench could settle on a credible alternative, she would inevitably face a leadership challenge.

The attorney-general's face was frozen between astonishment and rage. Andrew North was a South Australian who had a colourful turn of phrase and a high-camp delivery. For once, he struggled for words.

'You can't ... I mean ... what were you thinking?'

'I was thinking of the security of this nation, Andrew.' Elizabeth Scott had decided simply to declare her hand in the Cabinet Room and slap down any resistance. 'The Japanese build the best conventional submarines in the world. Making them in Japan will save billions and the chief of the defence force recommended it.'

The attorney struggled to regain his composure.

'With all due respect to the CDF, he is not a politician and there are serious political considerations.' There was nothing flamboyant in North's tone now; Scott could see he was simmering with rage.

'Thousands of South Australian jobs are tied up at the Australian Submarine Corporation. And can I remind you that already your flat-earth, laissez-faire approach to Holden has ensured car manufacturing will shut down in my state.'

North held up the Cabinet-in-Confidence brief on the submarine plan before theatrically dropping it on the table. Scott had taken a risk by not circulating it before the meeting, but had wagered that Cabinet anger would be easier to handle than a pre-emptive leak.

'Is it your goal to lose every South Australian seat?'

'Don't be a drama queen, Andrew,' Scott snapped. 'Pick up the brief and read it properly. There will still be plenty of shipbuilding jobs in Adelaide.

More than at present, in sustainment and fit-out. Even guaranteeing that is against my better judgement because, frankly, I wouldn't trust ASC to build a canoe.'

The defence minister shuffled in his seat and cleared his throat. Scott knew this Western Australian would be weighing the ever-declining iron ore price in every word of his advice. His state was already suffering from a slowdown in Chinese demand.

'I think we all agree on that, although no one would ever be daft enough to say it publicly.'

His tone darkened as he continued.

'There are two deeper issues. This is a captain's call that commits $30 billion on our biggest ever defence build. You have made a mockery of the Cabinet process. Worse, China will see a Japanese build as a strategic alliance with a hated East Asian rival. Make no mistake, Prime Minister: Beijing will view this as an act of aggression.'

Scott gazed around the table at the sullen group.

'I understand the complexities, and forgive me if I have trampled on the niceties, but I think this is manageable.'

The prime minister had built her pitch around appealing to the national interest, but she feared parochial considerations would trump her. This would be a hard sell for any leader, but near impossible for one with no political capital.

'Our message is simple.' Scott struggled to suppress the pleading tone in her voice. 'We want the best submarine at the best price and our sole aim is protecting the legitimate maritime interests of the largest island on Earth. It is a defensive play, not directed at any country.'

She looked at each minister in turn as she pressed home her case.

'All we need to do is take our time, work out our strategy and then communicate effectively to both the Australian people and the Chinese. It can't be that hard.'

The attorney-general rolled his eyes and let out a pantomime sigh.

'You're right, of course, PM. Because we have done all that so well in the past.'

He folded his arms and leaned back in his chair, his voice dripping with sarcasm.

'And, dear leader, with you at the helm, what could possibly go wrong?'

Scott ignored the jibe and closed her folder. The meeting was over.

'The first thing is to ensure that not a word of this leaks until I hit the "go" button.'

She stood, rested both hands on the table and leaned towards the attorney.

'Can we at least manage that?'

As she walked across the corridor from the Cabinet Room to her suite, she consoled herself by reflecting that such an unpleasant day could not possibly get worse.

Her personal assistant intercepted her in the entrance lounge, wearing a cat-just-messed-the-floor look.

'Emily Brooks would like a word.'

'Perfect, yes, why not.' Scott threw up her hands, scattering top-secret briefs from her folder. 'Bring in the Jim Jones Kool-Aid and we'll make a party of it,' she said, as she slammed the door to her office.

Brooks was a head taller than Scott, standing an imperial six feet in her stockings. In heels she towered over many men and most women. She dressed impeccably, but her wardrobe consisted almost entirely of pants suits in navy blue and black. She kept her hair long, often tying it back in a ponytail, and dyed it just a shade above charcoal.

Her face was handsome but stern, and as she'd aged, lines from a lifetime of frowning had hardened it. She wore dark shadow around her deep-brown eyes which gave her a menacing countenance. Scott had dubbed her rival Morticia.

'Elizabeth.' Brooks swept into the room and Scott noted, again, that she never referred to her as Prime Minister.

'Another masterful performance in Question Time today. A few more days like that and we'll be able to fit the next Coalition party room into a Mini Cooper.'

Scott didn't bother to offer Brooks a seat. This meeting would be brief.

Brooks smiled, showing just enough of her teeth to look fiendish. Scott wondered if she practised in the mirror.

'I want you to know that I'm coming for you, dear. I want it to be the last thing in your pretty head when it hits the pillow each night and the first thing on your mind each morning. If I had a candidate who could walk without his knuckles dragging on the floor you would have been gone this week.'

Scott wasn't intimidated by Brooks, but she knew the threat was real.

'Well, you don't have anyone and you are too ... how can I put this delicately ... bruised by your exotic personal life to stand against me yourself. Puts you in a bit of a "bind", doesn't it?'

Brooks took a step closer to Scott, who didn't flinch at the approach. Scott had the build of the athlete she was, which gave her a physical confidence that matched her intellectual ego.

'My dear Elizabeth ...' Brooks lifted a strand of Scott's hair and rubbed it between her thumb and forefinger as she looked down on her, '... if things don't improve, then six months from now you will lose your job to an empty chair.'

Beijing

The underling was perched nervously on the chair, hands folded and head lowered.

For the past fifteen minutes Meng Tao had been absorbing her brief, flicking quietly through the pages. The president's face was serious, studious, impassive.

Finally, he placed the folder on the table, nodded briefly and spoke without looking at her.

'You may go.'

She rose, bowed, and as she left the room, Meng smiled. The minion had done as instructed. Her treatise was tailor-made for his plans.

All the evidence in the analysis pointed to one inescapable conclusion: weak-willed and internally divided democracies crumbled when confronted with an adversary that knew what it wanted and was willing to fight for it.

At the very moment China had risen confidently to its feet, the West was on its knees. Meng was ready to take the next decisive step.

'Sir, your next appointment ...' The secretary's voice rang through the phone intercom.

'Yes, send him in,' Meng replied.

The door opened to Jiang Xiu.

He sat by the president's desk as Meng lifted a beautifully proportioned but unadorned brown teapot made by the legendary potter Shi Dabin. He poured his colleague a cup and Jiang took a sip as he waited for Meng to speak.

'Xiu, our best analysts have compiled a report on what the assassination of the American president means for us.'

Meng pushed the document towards Jiang, clapped his hands and beamed.

'It is as I thought, and great news for us. Washington is in disarray. It cannot lift its head from the quagmire it created in the Middle East.

Russia is making it look like a fool in Syria and Ukraine. The Americans are weakened by years of trying to impose their will as the world's police force and the people are sick of foreign wars. The new president faces an election next year and she is behind in the polls. She will spend every day fundraising and campaigning.'

Jiang picked up the document and flicked through its pages as the president continued.

'I am accelerating our plans for militarising the South China Sea islands. I am planning to visit them and I would like you to accompany me, Xiu.'

The propaganda minister looked up from the report and nodded, but there was no hint of enthusiasm in his voice.

'Yes, Mr President. I will ensure my diary is clear.'

'We stand at an epic threshold,' Meng declared, his voice ringing with confidence.

'Our engineers are turning tiny reefs into islands that will sustain a population and will serve as unsinkable aircraft carriers. Our people are working diligently to ensure they are ready. They will be the talons on our hands as we grasp power from the delusional Americans.'

The president glanced at the map on his wall and his tone turned from triumph to menace.

'Japan, the Philippines, Taiwan, Brunei, Malaysia, Vietnam.' Meng spat out the list. 'They make foolish claims on the South China Sea based on incorrect data peddled by the Americans. We will not be dictated to by those who have no respect for our history.'

His face brightened.

'Jackson's death is an opportunity for us to move faster, push harder.'

Jiang continued to leaf through the report as he listened. He was frowning as he put the document down and tapped it with the forefinger of his right hand.

'Mr President, I do not doubt the skill of those who wrote this.'

He paused and Meng could sense he was wrestling with what he should say.

'But I do doubt their courage and their wisdom.' Jiang pushed back his chair a touch, and shifted uneasily.

'These people know what you want to hear and they shape events and their advice to reflect it. Everything they say is true. But no one can predict the way a wounded beast will react. The authors of this report should have included several possible scenarios in this paper. Including ... no, especially ... the worst.'

When Meng replied his voice was cold. 'My friend, surely you are not afraid to share your wisdom with me. What is the worst scenario we might face?'

'That the wounded beast will charge.' Jiang's words came in a torrent, and his eyes were urgent, pleading. 'The American president knows she is facing defeat. And she is more dangerous precisely because she is a woman. She knows she will have to work harder than any man to prove she is an effective commander in chief. The combination is lethal. If I were advising her I would feed those insecurities and tell her that she needs to engineer an explosive demonstration of her strength.'

Meng gestured airily at the document as he dismissed Jiang's critique.

'That is all in there; you need more time to fully study the paper. She has ordered increased airstrikes in Syria and is sending more military trainers to Ukraine.'

Jiang shook his head.

'That is meaningless; as the Americans would say, it's "nickel and dime" stuff. Asta needs a victory. She needs to pick a fight with the biggest kid on the block. And she has already started. She's trying to blame us for the death of Jackson.'

He leaned forward in his seat.

'Mr President, we have bluffed the world. It believes we have America's measure. Or at the very least that America cannot halt our rise. If we move with care, we can have everything we want. If we press too hard we risk losing it all.'

Meng waved his arm to silence his colleague.

'The lecture is over, Mr Jiang.'

His voice rose as he stared hard into the minister's eyes.

'America is weak. It has lost its leader and the new president is an untested and uncertain woman. She has neither the will nor the means to challenge us. America will not fight.'

His fist thumped the table, unsettling his tea cup and spilling liquid onto the teak surface.

'And as you have lost confidence in the mission you once championed you will stay at home while I travel to the South China Sea.'

The president pointed to the door.

'Go.'

Jiang stood and bowed. As he was leaving, Meng delivered a parting shot.

'It will be good for you to stay in Beijing. You can spend more time at the theatre with your lovely wife. The two of you seem so happy there in a world of make-believe.'

415

―――――――――

Lake George

It was a long drive into a painful past and an uncertain future.

Harry Dunkley had escaped Sydney three hours earlier, the city's morning rush giving way to quaint rural settings, roadside diners serving questionable coffee and B-doubles driving too fast and too close.

For the first time in a year he was receiving wages, after Martin Toohey had placed him on his payroll. Last week he'd sorted the paperwork on a loan for a fifteen-year-old Holden Commodore, still going strong after 180,000 clicks.

He had travelled down the Hume Highway onto the Federal Highway and now, across the flat low grassland of a long-vanished Lake George, an army of wind turbines rose into view, their blades frozen on this breathless autumn day.

A sign signalled Canberra was only fifty kilometres away and a nervous energy surged through Dunkley's body. The long sweep around the dry lake dragged him back to the bittersweet past. At the end of this road was the place where his best friend, Kimberley Gordon, had died. There he had confronted her killer, Charles Dancer. There he had been betrayed by the man he trusted, Brendan Ryan. There he had been dumped by Celia Mathieson, his girlfriend. There he had lost his job, his money and his dignity.

There, he knew, was a city where the man behind it all reigned as an uncrowned but unchallenged king. A national hero. Sir Jack Webster. Defence chief. Warrior. Fraud. Traitor.

Dunkley pulled into a rest stop, his heart pounding. His hands shook as he lifted them from the wheel.

He killed the engine and got out of the car. A few metres ahead of him the land fell down a rocky hillside to a billiard-table-flat expanse a couple of kilometres wide and a dozen long. The first time he saw this place, in the '60s, it had looked to his child's eyes like the sea, as water lapped the point he now stood on and the hills in the distance were so far off they could have been another country. That men had drowned out there now seemed absurd.

A wave of pain washed over Dunkley. He had been played from the moment he'd picked up the black-and-white photo of Bruce Paxton four years ago. They'd known how to reel him in, to make him feel that he had privileged access to a world of dark secrets. They had watched and listened to every move he'd made, and Charles Dancer had prodded him back on course any time he'd looked like straying.

416

When Dunkley uncovered the murky reality of Webster's shadow government, they'd sacrificed him like the pawn he was. Even having proof of their crimes had been useless. In the information age reality could be dialled up and down by the warlords of the web. The truth was what they decreed it to be.

Who was he kidding, this was a fool's errand. What made him think he could beat them now? What on earth was he doing? For a moment he contemplated turning around and driving back to Sydney.

Irritably, he arched his back, unknotting muscles unused to driving, then wandered over to read a sign explaining the naming of the rest area. He knew the stops along this part of the Federal Highway were named after Victoria Cross winners and wondered who had given his name to this particular dot on the landscape.

It was Major Peter Badcoe. He had been part of the Australian Army Training Team Vietnam. In February 1967 he had engaged in an attack across open ground, in the teeth of machine gun fire, to rescue an American adviser. It was just one of a number of acts of courage by the 'Galloping Major', who was killed in April 1967 by a burst of gunfire as he rose to throw a grenade at overwhelmingly stronger opposition.

His valour and leadership were in the highest traditions of the military profession and the Australian Regular Army.

The only true hero in Dunkley's battle had been Kimberley. She was meant to help nail Paxton, but when she'd found a deeper, more disturbing story, she had not hesitated in pursuing it. She'd found the conspirators in the shadow government, and she'd found the real Chinese spy, Catriona Bailey. Nothing was what it seemed.

What hurt Dunkley most, now that his grief for Kimberley was losing its acute edge, was knowing that he had allowed himself to fall into despair. He might have died but for the intervention of Martin Toohey, who'd rescued him from himself, from the police lock-up, and had overseen his rehabilitation at Villa Maria.

Dunkley, the great sceptic, had been saved in the company of a dying order of priests, whose church had been disgraced but whose faith remained undimmed.

He didn't share their creed, but he had rediscovered his faith in humanity and his belief that its abiding genius was its limitless capacity for hope. You could give up hope, but it could never be erased from the world. It persisted in every horror. It could survive death.

As Viktor Frankl had testified after the Holocaust, you don't get to choose what happens to you, but you do get to choose how you respond.

Martin Toohey had offered him hope, given him a job and a reason to live. Now he had a choice.

Dunkley looked up at Major Badcoe's sign again before walking back to his car. He had made mistakes. But so had they. They hadn't killed him. Yet.

Mischief Reef

The Boeing 747 had been flying for four and a half hours through the dark. For the past hour, two J-11D fighter jets had flanked the Chinese president's plane.

Now they were nearing their destination, the most extraordinary landing strip ever built, a testament to Chinese ingenuity, and the latest and boldest declaration of the nation's growing confidence.

For two years, an army of labourers had toiled on rolling 24/7 shifts, transforming an isolated atoll in the South China Sea into a fortress.

The landing was perfect, the plane decelerating smoothly before taxiing towards a hangar that had been completed just days earlier.

The captain's voice came over the intercom.

'Mr President, welcome to Mischief Reef.'

Pride and exhilaration surged through Meng as he prepared to disembark, but he would be careful to avoid any outward signs of hubris. Today's ceremony would mark just the start of a critical phase for China.

Not since the liberation of Tibet in 1950 had China been so successful in reclaiming its ancient lands, but even Meng acknowledged, if only to himself, that the expansion was a high-risk play. Beijing faced constant allegations that its 'creeping invasion' was the most provocative action by a nation since Germany's expansion across Europe in the late 1930s.

And Mischief Reef was but one pearl in the necklace being strung across the Pacific. Once it was complete there would be a continuous line of islands enclosing the South China Sea. Each would be declared Chinese territory, with the demand that the rest of the world steer clear of a twelve-mile exclusion zone.

Even while that weak fool Jackson was alive, America had been testing China, sending its warships close to what it called the Spratly Islands and declaring its right to 'freedom of navigation through international waters'. It had been a child's game because the Americans knew there was no military hardware stationed on the sites.

That would end today. This landing would show the world that the airstrip was operational. Beside the presidential plane on the tarmac were the two warplanes, the first of a squadron that would be in place by year's end. Missiles would follow on this and every other island.

The president descended a mobile gangway laid with a red carpet that tumbled down to a group of dignitaries flown in for this momentous event. Meng nodded at some and smiled at others as he made his way to a podium to address the workers standing obediently in ranks.

'Comrades!' Meng's voice rang unfortunately thin through the PA. 'As this day dawns so does a new era in China's peaceful rise. Through our ingenuity and hard work, the Nansha Islands are being transformed, but no one should misunderstand why this is being done.

'We are not expanding our borders or taking anything that is not rightfully ours.

'Three thousand years ago, pearls, shells and turtles from these waters were presented as tribute to the rulers of the Zhou Dynasty. Two-thousand-year-old Han Dynasty pottery shards were found on Taiping Island and we have documents showing China was mapping and patrolling these seas when the Roman Empire was nearing its end.

'The South China Sea has always belonged to our Middle Kingdom. We are just giving form to that reality. We have as much right to build here as we would to construct a new expressway in Beijing.

'It is our rights that are being challenged, our land that is claimed by others.'

Meng swept his arm in an encompassing arc.

'All this is being built to defend our core interests of sovereignty and territorial integrity. And make no mistake, we will defend them.'

He paused, looking proudly at the gathered workers and dignitaries. CCTV, the Chinese national broadcaster, was transmitting his speech live to the world. Right now, in capitals across the globe, world leaders would be in no doubt about the gravity of this moment.

His last sentence had been crafted for their ears.

'Friends and comrades, here we stand on the first parapet of the Great Sea Wall of China.'

As Meng finished to warm applause, a military band played the opening strains of the national anthem. Several hundred Chinese workers and the VIP guests united in full voice.

Arise, ye who refuse to be slaves,
With our flesh and blood let us build our new Great Wall.

Canberra

The Chinese nation faces its greatest danger
For each one the urgent call for action comes forth.

Jack Webster glared at his television screen as the last strains of the Chinese national anthem faded.

It was in Mandarin, but Webster was familiar with its meaning. He saw this moment as his own 'urgent call for action'. It was just after 9.30am in the national capital when the Chinese president concluded his extraordinary address. As the cameras pulled back from the podium, the parting shot was of two brand new J-11D fighter jets parked either side of the presidential plane.

The defence chief knew that the image was aimed directly at the specialist spectators in the worldwide audience. He glanced at a line of clocks on his wall: it was 5.30pm on the US east coast. Heading into the primetime news broadcasts. The communist leader knew how to pull an audience.

The White House Situation Room would be full. The Pentagon and State Department would have their Sino specialists crawling over every word of this speech; weapons analysts would be magnifying every frame of the final images.

In one sense it wasn't a surprise. The progress of the runway had been part of his intelligence briefings for the past two years. The US had been calling on China to stop terraforming islands in the South China Sea for at least that long and had routinely tested the Beijing-imposed twelve-nautical-mile limits. Even Australia had conducted fly-overs.

But the J-11D show of force proved that China believed the American threat was empty. The once mighty Stars and Stripes had been lowered in the Pacific by a pathetic president who had cut and run in the Taiwan Strait. Now, as the US struggled to come to grips with Earle Jackson's death, China was militarising its artificial islands.

This was Meng's one-finger salute to the West.

Webster grabbed his briefcase and called for his aide-de-camp. He had a short drive across the lake for a 10am meeting of Cabinet's National Security Committee, one he had advised the prime minister to convene just moments after the Chinese president had begun his Mischief Reef declaration.

Australia's defence chief wanted a robust response from the committee, but was expecting some resistance. That should be manageable, though; with the PM's backing, he was confident of carrying the day.

'As you know, we have long feared this moment.'

Webster's deep voice was calm, but his tone was grave as the group charged with defending the nation listened in respectful silence.

The Situation Room was full, and as Webster spoke all present – Cabinet ministers, defence, intelligence and police officials, notetakers and staff – turned to the two huge video screens running the length of the room, controlled by technicians in an adjoining suite, which flashed up a still picture of the Chinese president.

'Meng Tao has just radically changed the rules in the South China Sea. Until now his country's declarations about exclusion zones around reclaimed islands have been meaningless. The US has routinely breached the twelve-nautical-mile zone and we have flown over the air-defence bubble. It's been a game: they shout at us, we ignore them.'

Webster paused as he studied the attentive and anxious faces in the room. He was determined to exact every ounce of drama from this presentation.

'Today the game has become hard reality. We have the president's own words as evidence.'

Webster nodded and the image of Meng stirred, his words translated into English as he spoke.

'All this is being built to defend our core interests …'

Webster put up his hand, pausing the president's speech.

'When a Chinese leader uses the words "core interests" he is speaking of something he's prepared to wage war over. Once the term was restricted to Taiwan. Several years ago it was expanded to include Tibet and Xinjiang, two provinces with indigenous autonomy movements. From today it includes the South China Sea.'

Webster nodded again and the image pulled back from the podium to show the president's jet and the two warplanes flanking it.

'The president isn't making empty threats. Take a long, hard look at those fighters. They are next generation warplanes: the Shenyang J-11D. It's a Chinese super weapon and, ladies and gentlemen, this is the first time we have seen an officially sanctioned image. They have been flown in as the show stopper.'

The camera moved in slowly on the menacing wasp-like jet, its undercarriage bristling with advanced weaponry.

'Our intelligence reveals this plane has state-of-the-art stealth capabilities and vastly improved performance and electronic warfare systems. In short, it is the first Chinese fighter capable of taking on the US-made Raptor and Super Hornet.'

The image pulled out again to show an aerial view of the arrow-shaped island, with an airstrip that ran its entire length.

'Until today Beijing couldn't contemplate using this kind of jet outside the mainland because it can't be launched from China's sole aircraft carrier. The *Liaoning* is essentially a training ship and its planes wouldn't stand a chance in a shooting war with the US. Building a fleet of carriers that can compete will take a generation. But China has taken an audacious short-cut. Now advanced fighters, and missiles, can be launched from this unsinkable tarmac.'

The image pulled back further, to one taken from space by a spy satellite. It highlighted a series of dots that formed a ring enclosing most of the South China Sea.

'This runway is just the first of many. Soon there will be similar bases on all these sites. When they are finished, Chinese warplanes will rule the skies over all the sea lanes to our north.'

Webster studied the now grim figures around him: his words were having the desired effect, but he needed to hammer home the importance of swift action.

'There is some good news.'

The image zoomed back down to the Mischief Reef airstrip and onto the warplanes.

'The J-11D is still experimental and an expert analysis of the weapons systems concludes they aren't yet operational. Right now this is just a high-stakes bluff. We still have some time on our side. But it's rapidly running out.'

The image switched to a close-up of President Meng's face as Webster built up to his pitch.

'Beijing just set us a test. Based on how the world responds it will push harder or, perhaps, retreat. The next move belongs to the US. I understand that President Asta will soon be calling for an alliance of regional nations to send a flotilla into those waters to test China's resolve.'

Webster looked at the line of ministers, slowly engaging each in turn.

'We need to decide our course of action. Do we stand with our closest ally? Or do we step back, again, and allow China to bully its way across the entire South China Sea?'

The defence chief's voice was earnest, urgent.

'I believe we have no choice. We have to send the strongest possible message that this act of aggression won't be tolerated.

'I propose two steps: first, we send a ship to join the American-led flotilla. Then we send an unequivocal message about where our allegiance lies by permanently basing a nuclear-capable US B-1 bomber at Tindal in the Northern Territory.'

Like any good commander, Webster knew where his enemy lay and wasn't surprised when the attorney-general cleared his throat, signalling his intention to speak.

'CDF, we can't do that.' The attorney's voice quavered as he spoke. Webster fixed him with a contemptuous stare to ensure his next few moments would be as uncomfortable as possible.

'There is no possible advantage in either move and the downsides are enormous. Don't forget that China is our major trading partner and we are trailing in the polls.'

Webster couldn't help himself; he snorted and shook his head at the word 'polls'. The minister's voice became even more shrill.

'I'm not saying that China does not pose a strategic threat, but we have to be more nuanced in our approach. We need to use diplomacy, to use our influence to get China to recognise that these aggressive steps are not in her best interest.'

In Webster's view, the South Australian's spine was as weak as his mind.

'Mr Attorney, you sound like an editorial in *The Age*. Sure, China might pretend to listen, but it will see your calls for dialogue for what they are. Weakness. More empty words. Nothing will make her baulk except the real threat of real force. There is only one power in the world that can halt China's aggression and we can't let America stand alone.'

The room lapsed into silence as all eyes turned to the prime minister.

Scott was studying the brief and frowning. Webster noticed she was fiddling with her wedding ring, a sure sign she was troubled.

After a moment the prime minister looked across the table and locked eyes with the defence chief.

'Jack, I value the US alliance but I fear that their much-touted pivot to Asia is all talk and little action. And America is still bogged down in the Middle East – and will be for years. We are exposed here, terribly exposed,' she said.

Webster realised the need to tread carefully.

'Prime Minister, I don't think this will come to blows, but I don't believe we have a choice. China is testing how far it can push us. We have to draw a line at some point or there will be no end to it.'

Scott pushed back.

'And where will America's demands end? Surely China has a point when it says America and Japan want to ring-fence it. It's not in China's interest to stymie regional growth.'

Webster pointed to the video wall which had settled on a map of the region.

'Not now. But we are talking about what might happen and our long-term strategic interest. Ninety per cent of our trade goes through the South China Sea. We can't allow one country to dictate who sails through those waters.'

Webster's pitch lifted a notch.

'Need I remind you that Australia no longer refines its own oil. A blockade in those waters would see the bowsers run dry here in fifty days. Imagine the political consequences of that. We have to act.'

Scott shook her head and Webster tried to hide his irritation. He'd expected she would be a staunch ally.

'Who else is in on this armada?' she asked.

'The Philippines for sure,' Webster replied. 'Of course, others like Vietnam and Indonesia will be more wary and some will be swayed by what we do. Prime Minister, if the US can't get Australia to sign up then it will be dead in the water and they will react furiously.'

'What if China sees it as an act of war?' Scott was fiddling with her ring again.

'It won't come to that.'

Webster's tone was stern as he held the prime minister's gaze. The next move was hers. Eventually she cleared her throat and spoke.

'CDF, prepare a detailed analysis on the rationale, the benefits and the risks of sending a frigate to join a US-led flotilla and on basing a B-1 bomber at Tindal. I want every contingency covered. Every last one.'

Then Scott surprised him by turning to another senior official, the director-general of the Office of National Assessments. The ONA was packed with analysts whose job was to provide independent intelligence advice direct to the prime minister, but in Scott's time she had rarely used it, always deferring to the defence chief.

'I want the ONA to look at this from every possible angle,' she said. 'I want every risk to trade, defence and security thoroughly assessed.'

This was a significant power shift, which Webster knew would be noted by everyone at the table.

'I want you to play devil's advocate,' Scott said as the ONA chief nodded and took a note.

The prime minister put the palms of her hands on the table and spoke directly to Webster, emphasising every word. He listened like a dutiful servant, seething in silence.

'Let me make this absolutely clear: the decision of this meeting is that the committee is still considering its options. We are not saying "yes" yet. I am not going to be stampeded into action.'

She slowly gazed around the table.

'I don't have to remind any of you of the gravity of this. Remember, all decisions of the NSC are unanimous, no matter what disagreements we might have in this room.

'I do not expect to read about this in a newspaper.'

Canberra

Harry Dunkley pressed the doorbell of the townhouse and waited. Nothing. He rapped hard on the glass panel next to the security screen, straining to hear any sound from inside. Silence.

For the past hour, he'd been telephoning on a constant loop, but the mobile phone number had rung out. No message bank. Nothing.

He scanned the street for some sign of life. It was empty: a mute confirmation of the outsiders' view that Canberra was a suburban ghost town.

Dunkley knew looks were deceptive and turned back to the townhouse. There was a slight lifting of a heavy curtain covering a window. Someone was home.

He stepped up to the front door and rapped again.

'Trev, it's Harry … Harry Dunkley. Just need to chat with you.'

For a long moment nothing stirred. Then, from inside, the muffled sound of footsteps approaching the door. It opened a few centimetres, but the security screen remained shut.

Dunkley took a moment to focus. The face he could glimpse was roughened by a three-day growth and sallow cheeks, and the man's eyes held genuine apprehension. He recognised something of himself in Trevor Harris: the sunken look of a man who'd nearly given up. He spoke in a reassuring tone.

'Trev, how are you? Can I come in? We need to talk.'

Harris eyed him suspiciously, not moving.

'Please mate, I just want a few minutes of your time. It's just me; there's no one else here.'

Harris motioned to Dunkley's mobile, clutched in his right hand, and pointed to the car. Dunkley got the message, walked to the passenger-side door and put the phone in the glove box.

Harris said nothing as he unlatched the security door. Dunkley walked into an apartment in disarray. A stale smell hung in the darkened lounge room, where heavy drapes covered windows he guessed had not been opened for months. Papers were piled in drifts, unwashed plates sat on every flat surface.

They shook hands without conviction. Harris went to an ageing audio system and pressed play: the Bee Gees burst from the speakers in a slightly too loud rendition of 'Nights on Broadway'.

He finally spoke.

'Coffee?' he asked half-heartedly. 'I don't have milk, though.'

'Sure, black's fine. Mind if I sit?' Dunkley moved some books from a lounge chair. Engaging Harris wasn't going to be easy, but Dunkley had nowhere else to start.

'Go ahead.'

Harris crossed the lounge room to the open plan kitchen.

'So how was jail?' he called over the sound of a man making enough space in the sink to get a jug under the tap.

'Actually, it was the most comfortable digs I'd had in a while. Better than a park bench.'

Harris turned and offered a stiff smile, the first crack of a connection.

'I thought you might be dead until I read about your antics. Jesus, you cost News Corp a few grand in repairs.'

'Petty cash for Rupert.'

'Yeah, I guess.' Harris gave up looking for clean cups, pulled two from the sink and rinsed them.

'Harry, you shouldn't have come back to Canberra. You're in danger. You being here puts me in danger.'

'I know it's a risk, but I couldn't let it drop. Unfinished business.'

Harris shook his head. His expression was a mixture of curiosity and annoyance.

'What is it you really want?'

Dunkley contemplated the question for a moment. He needed Harris's help and got straight to the point.

'To bring down Jack Webster,' he said. 'To show the world what he really is.'

Harris laughed, a loud cynical rattle that unsettled Dunkley.

'You might as well try to remove Jesus Christ from the Trinity.' He theatrically thumped a clenched fist into his hand. 'He'll crush you. Again. You have no fucking idea how powerful that guy is.'

Dunkley stifled a mirthless laugh. 'I think I have some idea, mate.'

'You … that was nothing. Webster's influence stretches all the way to Washington. And people who are a nuisance to him seem to have a nasty habit of dying.'

Dunkley shifted on the lounge chair. 'Who?'

'You know one. Kimberley Gordon, when she stumbled into his little war. But she was a minor player, a pawn. This guy rubs out knights and castles.'

Harris picked up the coffee mugs and set them down among the clutter on a table. He pushed some papers off a chair, sat down and dropped his voice.

'Something happened in Defence, something big, about the time that Martin Toohey was rolled as prime minister. My mates in DSD told me that the director, Matthew Whelan, was hauled into a meeting with Webster and the heads of ASIO and DFAT.'

Harris glanced at the windows and the doorway to the entrance hall.

'Whelan returned from that meeting a changed man. Immediately afterwards, Defence started spending up big on IT.'

Harris stood and began pacing the room, his face creased in a frown that emphasised his gaunt features. He was clearly torn, as if he needed to talk to Dunkley but was wrestling with his fears.

'I know someone, Harry, someone who goes looking for missing treasure. He's told me a few things …'

Harris's voice trailed off, as if he'd changed his mind. He moved to the curtains covering the window and tugged at a tiny crack that was letting in light.

'Go on,' Dunkley urged him.

Harris let out a gusty sigh.

'My contact tells me that the entire Defence computer system was replaced – every server, every PC, every keyboard. A massive job. But, and this is the extraordinary part, it was apparently all done off the books. They hid it from government, burying the spending in big procurement projects.'

The former analyst turned around, his face a mask of anguish.

'Then people started dying.'

'Who?'

'Whelan, of a heart attack. Aged forty-six. Forty-six! He was a fitness fanatic, had just finished a run, Friday evening out at Stromlo Forest cross-country track. Left a wife and three kids.'

Harris was pacing wildly and speaking rapidly.

'Six months later, DFAT's David Joyce ran off the highway near Murrumbateman. He was alone; the police put it down to fatigue. He'd driven back from Melbourne.'

Harris stopped in front of Dunkley and marked off the body count on his fingers.

'So, that meeting I told you about, four people were there – Webster; Richard Dalton, the head of ASIO; Joyce and Whelan. Only two are alive – Webster and Dalton.'

Harris sat down, breathing heavily, as if the effort of telling the story had exhausted him. He reached out to grip Dunkley's arm.

'Remember when we first met, two and a bit years ago? I told you how the signals directorate scooped up information from everyone. How we had bugged the planet. The technology is getting better all the time. There's nowhere to hide. Absolutely nowhere.'

He took a sip from his coffee before continuing.

'That mobile phone in your car will be traced. Child's play. So they will know you're here. If you'd brought it in they would be using it to listen to us now. If they're really keen and have put a detail on you, they could have listened to our conversation at the door … well, your conversation.'

Harris looked over his shoulder and then waved his hands about, as if encompassing the room.

'I regularly sweep this house for wires. I have a lifetime of experience in surveillance so I know what I'm doing and this room is clean. But I also know what they can do.'

He pointed to the curtains.

'A tiny opening would let them listen to us with a laser microphone picking up the vibration of our voices off the glass. I could rig up that kind of unit on my kitchen table with twenty bucks worth of electronics. They spend billions. Now they have "through-the-wall" spying systems that use radio waves. The signal is weak, so they use cleaning tricks developed by NASA to decode signals from space.'

The pressure was etched on Harris's face.

'Don't think they haven't come after me, after helping you. I still have enough friends in the service to tell me when I'm on the watch list and I know the signs. My communications were tapped. My movements online followed.'

Dunkley noticed a slight tremor in Harris's hands and a twitch in his cheek. He felt guilty.

'I'm sorry,' Dunkley said. 'But this won't end unless we end it. I have to talk to your mate about what's been going on in Defence.'

Harris shook his head.

'Harry, let me think about this. I don't want to drag more people into your messes. You have a habit of leaving a trail of collateral damage.'

Dunkley put his hand on Harris's shoulder.

'If we give up, he's won. And you will be a prisoner in here forever.'

Canberra

The front page screamed a single word: BETRAYED.

It hung over an unflattering portrait of Elizabeth Scott, her mouth curled in a sneer and her fist raised as if she was preparing to strike the photographer. The story under the headline left no doubt as to the sympathies of the Adelaide *Advertiser*.

The paper's Canberra political correspondent had been leaked details of Cabinet's decision to abandon South Australia as the hub of the nation's naval shipbuilding industry, by purchasing submarines from Japan. The leak was an extraordinary breach of Cabinet confidentiality. It was also political sabotage.

The reporter didn't hold back as she tore into the prime minister.

Thousands of local jobs will be jettisoned and the state's economy torpedoed under a secret deal to buy Australia's next generation submarines from Japan.

Elizabeth Scott's backhander to South Australia is likely to see the closure of the ASC shipyards at Osborne. Furious senior government sources say it will also trigger a public backlash that will threaten every Liberal electorate in the state.

One Liberal Party elder familiar with the clandestine plan said it would see the party routed at next year's federal election.

'The prime minister is our very own suicide bomber. This is unbelievably stupid,' he said

'Pig Iron Scott has killed us in South Australia. The Labor Party will have a field day.'

Inside, the paper devoted four pages to dissecting the 'captain's call', while the editorial thundered that it had been made 'in total secrecy by a prime minister who lacks empathy with the working men and women who have made this nation great'. It encouraged voters to wield their axe at the ballot box.

Multi-millionaire Elizabeth Scott just doesn't get working people. This decision reinforces the view that the prime minister's silver-spoon upbringing clouds her ability to act in the interests of ordinary folk.

In her office, the prime minister slowly read through the online version of a paper that had near saturation coverage in South Australia. She reached for a tumbler of water, noticing a slight but discernible tremor in her hand as she lifted it to her mouth. She took a quick sip, then another, conscious of the small group of advisers gathered in her office.

Her primal instinct was to scream and rant, but common sense and the desire for survival said this was no time for hysterics. The prime minister was finding it difficult to know whom to trust, and an outburst could trigger another story.

She should have anticipated that the decision to buy the Soryu subs would be leaked. It was the latest in a long thread of strategic drops, from Cabinet and the party, that were a gift for the cartoonists who drew Scott at the helm of a listing life raft.

The acts of sabotage were coming more often, her authority eroded with every strategically placed article, every piece of bastardry.

What was so concerning about the *Advertiser*'s scoop was the level of detail provided by the minister, or ministers, who didn't seem to care that her fall would drag them down too.

Disunity is death: the maxim had never been more resonant as she contemplated which of her eighteen Cabinet colleagues was responsible. She stopped counting at nine.

Scott had never felt more isolated or less able to pick up the phone for a chat with a colleague. Her status as the nation's leader, as the most powerful person in the land, was illusory.

She scanned the room of hardened professionals, hoping for sympathy, encouragement, a thought. Instead she was met by wall-to-wall bemusement.

In the hours before her meeting with the Japanese prime minister, a month earlier, Jack Webster had convinced her of the merits of the Soryu submarines, the 'Blue Dragons' of the water.

They were a new class of diesel-fuelled attack submarine, powered by a Swedish stirling air-independent propulsion system. The Soryu was much larger than the earlier Oyashio-class boat and able to stay submerged for longer. The boat ticked two crucial boxes: Australia's geography demanded long-range subs and its politics demanded that they couldn't be nuclear powered.

Just as critically, the Soryus were furnished with American military and anti-surveillance weaponry, the latest in technology, which meant they were like underwater stealth bombers. It also meant that the subs would be interoperable with the US fleet, something her brass coveted more than gold.

Finally, the fact that the subs could be ordered 'off the shelf' meant they would save billions on construction costs. So the disaster of the locally built Collins class – a ship buried forever under a single tabloid headline: DUD SUBS – would not be repeated.

Webster said it was a no-brainer, but Scott had underestimated the depth of community support for local manufacturing, irrespective of the cost to the public purse. She'd ignored the advice of her industry minister who'd previously warned her that the protectionist streak ran deep in the Australian psyche.

'We might have torn down tariff walls, Elizabeth, but the punters still like the idea that we can actually build something here,' he'd counselled.

'Right, let's get down to business,' Scott said now to her despondent band of advisers. 'We can sell this. For starters, the story is wrong. The ASC will not be closed; there will actually be more maintenance jobs there in the future than there are now. We need to get the message out that we are procuring a better submarine while saving billions of taxpayer dollars. This is a good decision. It makes economic, strategic and military sense.'

Scott's principal media adviser was scornful.

'Then why did you make it in secret?'

Cooktown

It was hotter than Satan's sauna and Rafael Weiss was melting. The Labor pollster was three hours north of Cairns and the air conditioning in his rental had died without warning.

The bitumen on this Far North Queensland highway was blistering, the tropical air wet and humid. Cramped in his Hyundai, with another hour of driving ahead of him, the native Victorian tugged at a tailor-made shirt that stuck to his ample frame like cling wrap and cursed Catriona Bailey.

The opposition leader had dragged him from his comfortable Melbourne office to meet up with her manic, non-stop tour of electorates near and far. Campaign Insane, one insider had dubbed it. Today she was in the seat of Leichhardt; specifically, Cooktown. Population: 2330.

'There are more people in Fountain Gate on a Saturday afternoon than in that pissant town,' Weiss yelled out the window. 'Why. The. Fuck. Am. I. Here?!'

He knew why. Like everyone else, he was terrified of the former prime minister whose relentless pace had seen a mass exodus of staffers. The body count was now in the dozens. But in spite of her disability, she ploughed on, determined to visit every electorate before the next poll.

Weiss shook his head. Privately and grudgingly, he would admit that her campaign was working. The polls showed that. Bizarrely, the political cyborg was Ms Popular.

He picked up his mobile, bored by the track that was playing. He needed a dose of good old-fashioned rock; he needed Kiss. He wanted his favourite track from his favourite album.

The first few chords of 'Hotter than Hell' crashed through the stereo. Then the car speakers fell silent as its Bluetooth signalled 'No service'.

'Faaaarrrkkkkk.'

The Police Citizens Youth Welfare Association could hold four hundred people, but Weiss counted twenty-three. Of these, five were Bailey staffers and there was a youngish reporter from the *Cairns Post*.

The pollster had been told to wait until Bailey finished a question-and-answer session scheduled to run for twenty minutes.

That was ninety minutes ago, and Weiss noticed even the Labor diehards were drifting off to the toilets and not returning.

Then he heard the first cheerful words of the day: 'I think we'll leave it there.'

Weiss finally got his audience with Bailey at 10pm, but only after the Labor leader had cleared a list of appointments she deemed more important.

Despite the long delay, Bailey offered not so much as a 'Thanks for coming'.

'How are the tracking polls going?' she demanded, as she examined a print-out of the next day's schedule.

'I'm well thanks, Catriona, how are you?' Weiss replied.

'What?'

'Nothing,' he said, quickly adding, 'The polls are good, like they were a fortnight ago. You've maintained a consistent lead across all demographics since last year's Budget.'

Bailey was impossible to read. While she beamed in public, she rarely smiled in private; instead she exuded disdain, bordering on contempt.

Weiss had sometimes wondered why Bailey was a professional politician, when she so clearly despised people. Now he knew the answer: power.

'What about the focus groups?' she snapped.

'People think Scott stands for nothing. The knights and dames stuff killed her, confirmed their worst fears. They think she's never had a tough day in her life, but you … in that wheelchair … that alone shows you know what it's like to suffer.'

'Anything else?'

'Yes. People are getting very nervous about the state of the world. The rise of radical Islam and the aggression of China and Russia are really bothering the punters. In a dangerous world, they think Scott is weak on national security.'

'What makes people feel safe?' Bailey's expression changed almost imperceptibly. Clearly this shard of information was intriguing.

Weiss mopped his face with a drenched handkerchief.

'The cops. The army. Our alliance with the United States. Forget what the luvvies say about the Americans, most voters want the eight-hundred–pound gorilla at their back.'

Bailey nodded. Then without a hint of thanks or a farewell she glided from the room, driven by the whirr of an electric motor and the adulation of the people.

Weiss called out a piece of advice in her wake.

'So Catriona, whatever the question, the answer is "Back the Yanks".'

Canberra

The towering rust-red letters paid homage to the Australian expanse: WIDE BROWN LAND.

It was early evening and Harry Dunkley had driven to the National Arboretum for a rendezvous with a mate of Trevor Harris. He'd been given few instructions except to meet by this sculpture in the new botanical garden at the western end of Lake Burley Griffin, overlooking the city.

At first he thought he was alone, but as he neared the sculpture a slightly built man emerged from the shadows.

Dunkley thrust out his hand a little too forcefully. 'Harry Dunkley.'

'Yes, I know. Benny Hadid. Nice to meet you.'

Elfin-featured and pallid, Hadid looked like he'd stepped from a Tolkien novel. He was probably in his mid-forties, although an excessive comb-over may have exaggerated his age. Dark brows and deep worry lines hardened his face, and a nervous twitch hinted at a lifetime of avoiding other people's gazes.

Whatever his peculiarities, Hadid was considered one of the best forensic accountants at the Australian National Audit Office, a dogged public servant who loved to sniff around the financial entrails of big government deals. He'd risen to become the executive director of the Performance Audit Services Group, exposing numerous questionable schemes along the way.

Under his leadership, the group was charged with running the ruler over Defence and its multi-billion-dollar procurement budget. It was a rich field. Defence had been a notorious money pit for decades. After 9/11, the task of holding the military to account had become even more fraught as successive governments ladled ever greater amounts of public money into building Australia's national security capability. And the brass thought they were gods, above the reach of mortals and hostile to the scrutiny that Hadid believed was essential in a democracy.

Harris had said that while Hadid might appear timorous, when it came to defending his work he was fearsome and intense.

Dunkley was uncertain how hard to press this new contact, reluctantly given up by Harris. Flattery was usually a good way to start.

'Trevor tells me you're one of the best in the business.'

'Does he? That's nice of him.'

Hadid was fidgeting with a button on his coat, his eyes darting around the deserted landscape.

Christ, thought Dunkley, there's no one here, mate.

Dunkley had been in this dance for information many times. The first few steps were always awkward. Move in too hard and the waltz could end before the band warmed up. After all, they were little more than strangers. But there was one thing the veteran journalist was certain of: Hadid had shown up at the meeting. That meant he wanted to talk and sometimes the best approach was to say nothing and let the whistleblower lead.

On cue, Hadid broke the silence.

'Something doesn't fit, Mr Dunkley.'

'What do you mean?'

'What has Trevor told you?'

Dunkley realised he had to give this nervous tic of a man some assurances.

'Benny, if it helps, I've got no notepad, no tape recorder; I'm not working on a newspaper anymore. I'm doing some research for a former prime minister. I'm not even sure there's anything here to chase—'

434

'Oh, there is something here to chase, Mr Dunkley.' Hadid's eyes flashed a glance at Dunkley before darting away.

'Well then, Benny, perhaps you can tell me what that is. And please, call me Harry.'

Hadid buried his hands in his coat pockets. 'Air Warfare Destroyer. I presume you've heard of the program?'

'A bit … but defence procurement was never my forte,' said Dunkley. 'Always reckoned they had too much to spend and didn't give a rat's how much they wasted.'

Hadid smiled properly for the first time.

'The Audit Office conducted a formal audit of the AWD project throughout 2013, reporting in early 2014. The bottom line was that the $8.5 billion scheme to build three destroyers was well over budget, $302 million to be precise, and climbing. I qualified the audit, refusing to sign off on it.'

It sounded like a pretty boilerplate Defence overrun to Dunkley and he hoped he wasn't going to freeze to death as the bureaucrat relived every line of a multi-volume report.

His companion was getting more agitated as he spoke.

'That should mean something, Harry. There should be consequences. I was expecting that Defence would be torn apart at a Senate hearing. But no. On the day of the hearing, the departmental secretary came with defence chief Jack Webster in tow. I have never seen a performance like it; Webster was charming and staggeringly arrogant by turn. He had every member of the committee fawning over him. They waved his dodgy books through.'

Hadid moved his shoulders and shuffled his feet as he spoke. Dunkley thought that he had rarely seen anyone who looked so uncomfortable in his own skin.

'So I went back to the books. And conducted one of the most exhaustive audit processes I've ever done. I chased every dollar down every sinkhole in that department. I did it all in my own time: early mornings, late nights, every weekend.'

Hadid shuddered to a stop and for the briefest of moments he didn't move a muscle. He looked up from his feet and stole another glance at Dunkley.

'Billions!' His voice squeezed out as a disbelieving rasp.

'Billions of taxpayers' dollars are missing, all buried in a procurement project so long, so large and so complex that they could be hidden. My final report is almost done. What I believe we are seeing amounts to the biggest fraud in the history of the Commonwealth.'

'Where did the money go?'

'Most of it was ploughed back into Defence. The entire computer system has been rebuilt. What I don't understand is why. If it was necessary, they could have asked for the money and they would have got it. But it doesn't matter why they did it. It's illegal to procure money for one project and spend it on another. This time heads will roll at Defence.'

Despite his coat, Hadid shivered.

'And I believe it is worse than that. This time there will be no escape for the sainted Jack Webster. Several million dollars seem to have been siphoned off into an account for which he was the sole signatory. That breaks every rule.'

Dunkley was stunned and for the first time in many a long month he itched to be back in journalism. This was the kind of story he used to dream about, one that deserved a banner headline stretched across all eight broadsheet columns.

'Benny, if your report is nearly done and you have the authority of the Audit Office behind you, then publish. That will bring the whole show down.'

Hadid rocked from foot to foot, shrugged his shoulders and pushed his hands deeper into his pockets.

'I'm only telling you this because I'm not sure that my report will be published. I've done all this in secret. Recently I've been getting questions from higher up. My boss has been asking what I've been up to and I suspect he's been searching my files.'

Hadid shook his head.

'But I've told no one about this, other than Trevor. Now you. I knew how sensitive it would be and I want all the evidence to be bulletproof before I take it further. I've hidden the work deep in our system. How could anyone know about it?'

Dunkley looked out at the lights of Canberra.

'Believe me, Benny, there are no secrets here. You can't run and you can't hide anything from these people.'

The drive back to Canberra's CBD took barely ten minutes.

Dunkley hit a few buttons on his phone, keeping watch for the ACT's notoriously punctilious traffic cops.

'Martin, how are you? Dunkley here. Tell me, what do you know about the Air Warfare Destroyer?'

Canberra

The technician loved the room's blue glow. The ethereal light illuminated the nation's most powerful supercomputer, its performance measured in floating-point operations. This one crunched through a quadrillion per second.

The sealed room hummed as more than a quarter of a billion dollars worth of circuits kept watch, scooping up the communications signals of millions before distilling them into byte-size packs.

The supercomputer searched the sea of data for keywords that would elevate the watch from machine to man. 'Malware', 'terror', 'botnet', 'trojan' and scores of other words would trigger more urgent monitoring as the computer trawled through the communications of every person with a phone or a web connection.

Once a target was in its sights, there was no escape. Every internet search, every tweet, every conversation, every text – all were subjected to surveillance. The nation's secrets were logged, then distributed to the very few who had a right to know.

Her monitor flashed an amber alert the moment the call was made. An alpha target was on the line, and that demanded her immediate attention.

As he spoke, his words morphed into text on her screen.

Martin, how are you? Dunkley here …

Canberra

On the second-floor balcony of his apartment on State Circle, a deeply troubled Brendan Ryan nursed a gin and tonic.

The new puritans intent on taking control of society were making his life a misery. If they weren't moralising about Labor's stance on refugees then they were lodging petitions against its free market economic policies or its support for big media and big mining.

Ryan detested the green-tainted Left, seeing them as a plague of parasites gnawing away at the foundations of Western civilisation. They had perfected the culture of complaint and colonised social media as their own echo chamber.

All his hatreds and fears had coalesced that evening as he'd read a chilling article by Bret Stephens in the *Wall Street Journal*, titled 'In Defense of

Christendom'. In a compelling narrative, the journalist argued that Europe had swapped its belief in Judaism and Christianity for a raft of ephemeral ideals like 'tolerance', 'openness' and 'pleasure'. With its foundations gone, Europeans wondered why their house was falling apart.

Ryan shuddered and took a long swig of his gin. His beloved Labor Party had been white-anted by the same risible ideas and was also dying. The working class that had once sustained the party was now too engaged in the banality of TV reality shows or Facebook videos of cats sneezing to really care. Their apathy allowed the noisy few, the middle-class Left, to dominate. Perhaps when China closed the sea lanes in the South China Sea, denying Australians their modern opiate of cheap flat-screen televisions and Xbox games, they would learn the true meaning of the tyranny of distance.

Ryan still cared deeply about the party, about his nation and its place in an increasingly dangerous and unpredictable world. He cared about protecting the apathetic masses from online jihadists who were recruiting deep inside suburbia. As a key figure on parliament's Intelligence and Security Committee, he had received briefings on a new terrorist cell signing up would-be jihadists in Melbourne's outer south-west. The death cult was coming, of that there was no doubt. He laughed grimly at the irony of it. Finally, with Islamic State, there was a group who rivalled the intellectual Left in its hatred for the West.

But it wasn't a joke. Hollowed out from within and under attack from without, the defeat of everything that Ryan cherished was in sight. He could not, would not, let it happen. He would go down fighting, even if no one else knew that they were at war.

The intelligence and security tentacles of the state needed to be nurtured so they could protect the public. They had to be able to follow the enemy wherever it went, to chase it as it hid in its deep cyber-world burrows.

Australia also needed to be able to defend itself in the real world. It needed a strong army and navy and the reach provided by a sophisticated air force. Most of all, the small nation needed a big bully of a friend. America remained the only hope; that was why he was so committed to the alliance.

'Jesus.' Ryan let out a long slow breath.

Adding to his long list of troubles was Jack Webster's decision to accept a knighthood. The Alliance stalwart should have known better. 'Sir Jack' signalled that he was just like the rest, one of the elite whose first priority was himself.

And Ryan sensed something deeper. Webster was acting and looking more like a politician every day. The two had been friends for years, forging deep bonds in their membership of the Alliance. The whole idea of their union was to quietly ensure that Australia and the United States acted as one to defend the Western world. If governments strayed they would act, but their role was to guide, not govern, and to stay below the radar.

The Labor powerbroker looked to the brilliant skies above Canberra as he thought of his own leader, Catriona Bailey. She was the personification of the insurgency.

Ryan was one of the very few who understood the real back story to Bailey: the opposition leader had been recruited by Beijing in the early 1980s and was the glittering prize in the communist regime's worldwide web of operatives.

The Alliance had tried to remove Bailey, but she'd survived, against the odds, to again take her place at Labor's helm. Now with Elizabeth Scott hurtling towards oblivion, there was every chance Bailey would be PM some time next year.

The Liberals could change leaders, but they didn't have anyone who could beat Bailey.

Ryan knew there was only one man who could ensure a Coalition win, but he was not in parliament. Not yet.

Canberra

The sisterhood was out in droves. The Women in Media luncheon had sold out in record time.

Nearly three hundred of the national capital's movers and shakers were crammed into the National Press Club to hear what the PR bumpf promised would be a 'defining speech'.

The mood in the auditorium was electric as the guest speaker, Sir Jack Webster, rose and the cameras began to roll.

The military chief beamed his movie-star smile at the crowd before paying his respects to the traditional owners of the land and launching into his speech, his mellifluous tones washing over the expectant audience.

'I believe I am the first man ever to address a Women in Media event and that is an honour as great as I have ever enjoyed. I can never hope to fully imagine what it is to be a woman in today's chaotic, challenging world. I was born a man in this comfortable nation of ours, my parents were relatively well off, and I never experienced the institutional discrimination that I'm sure so many of you – here and watching on television – have been subjected to.'

Webster paused, fixing the room with a look of concerned indignation before continuing. 'When I joined the Royal Australian Air Force I had no idea that the military then, as now, had an endemic problem with recognising its inbuilt bias against women, at all levels and in all forms. I have long wrestled with the fact that the military really is a blokes' brigade, something which I am determined to change. My aspiration, my unwavering commitment during my tenure as chief of the defence force, is to achieve gender parity in our military, across all ranks, across all divisions.

'And might I add that should be a goal for every institution in our great nation.'

The audience stirred in appreciation.

'Of course, that is probably an unattainable state of perfection. But I have set tangible goals, my own gender KPIs if you will, against which I am willing to be judged.'

Webster was a picture of altruistic integrity. The room was poised, respectful.

'Today's military can never fully attain the goal of being truly inclusive until it can ensure that every enlisted woman has the opportunity of rising to the top, and is not fettered by some outdated model based on machismo, but is encouraged and assisted by one that does not discriminate against gender.'

The first hint of applause began in the back-left corner then washed across the room, a wave of reverential recognition that here, in the National Press Club, was a remarkable man seeking to make remarkable changes.

Webster could feel the crowd rising with him: the evangelist and his obedient flock.

'We in the Australian Defence Force have a special constitutional role. We train to achieve mastery in military matters and are entrusted and sanctioned by the government to employ extreme violence in support of Australia's national interests. But with these powers comes a tremendous responsibility. We must earn and maintain a high level of trust among our community, and never lose sight of the special place we hold in the hearts of so many Australians.

'That trust is enhanced when Defence ensures equality of opportunity. We are making great strides. One of our female fast jet trainees is in the final stages of her training at Williamtown base in New South Wales. She is progressing well.'

Webster lifted his head and scanned the room before nailing the punchline.

'Ladies and gentlemen, today I can announce that our first female fighter pilot will graduate within months.'

The room rose as one to the momentous news. Webster modestly acknowledged the rapturous reception, then sat down and sipped a glass of water as the auditorium kept up a torrent of applause, long and genuine. Elvis was in the fucking room.

Webster's speech had lived up to the promise of being a seminal moment in the history of the military. Now he had to field questions from those who bled scepticism for a living.

The first question from *The Australian* showed that the media was not about to be swayed by emotion.

'Air Chief Marshal Webster, that was an inspiring speech, but you failed to mention the one issue that is front of mind for Defence at the moment: submarines. Why should we turn our back on building the next fleet of submarines here in Australia, specifically in South Australia? Are we not potentially shooting ourselves in the foot by buying off the shelf from Japan?'

'That is a good question, thank you,' Webster said, radiating sincerity. 'As you appreciate, building submarines in Australia carries a forty per cent premium. Many say that is an unaffordable luxury. I am no politician and make no comment on that; this is a matter for Prime Minister Scott to decide.'

Webster parried away several other questions on submarines before an ABC inquistor rose.

'Sir Jack, your speech shows leadership and vision – something missing from today's politics. Would you consider a tilt for public office?'

There was scattered applause in the room. Webster shook his head.

'I was born into a military home, and I have always strived to serve the community in a military capacity. I am a humble servant of the people of Australia. I am grateful that you think of me as someone who would make the grade, but I really have not given any thought to changing my profession.'

Webster had just finished speaking when the voice of the club's chief executive unexpectedly filled the venue.

'Ladies and gentlemen, please don't panic, but I have received a text message advising there is a bomb in the room.'

Mayhem erupted. Screams rang out as the crowd rose as one and raced for the two exits, people stumbling and falling in the crush.

The commanding voice of the defence chief cut through the pandemonium, hushing the crowd as if by magic. 'Please be calm. Do not panic. Let's maintain order and leave methodically. Those closest to the exits will go first. Everyone else, please be patient. We'll all get out, swiftly and safely.'

That night the Press Club bomb hoax led every bulletin as the networks climbed all over the story.

The doyen of primetime news, the Nine Network's Laurie Oakes, sang the praises of the hero of the hour.

'Peter, I have been around this place for a very long time. This was an extraordinary day that highlighted the character of an extraordinary man. His calmness and authority in the face of an apparently genuine threat was inspirational.

'If only one of our so-called political class showed the same leadership, then this nation would be in much better hands.'

South China Sea

The grey hull loomed like a nightmare on the water. Jay Bawani wiped his brow as he gripped the *Nenita*'s wheel, his gaze shifting from the instrument panel to the steel monster closing in on his stern.

The Filipino captain had tried radioing the Chinese ship, but the signal was jammed. He'd turned his small fishing vessel to port, but the frigate immediately followed.

Now it was just several hundred metres away.

Bawani checked his navigational aids again. The *Nenita* was one hundred and fifty kilometres west of Subic Bay, doing what it did most days, putting out its nets to fish the tranquil seas off the Philippines for the crab, tuna and squid that were sold to the tourist resorts scattered around his home city of Iba.

His modest timber boat was in international waters. Something wasn't right. He'd heard reports of fishing vessels being pursued, but those incidents had taken place much closer to Scarborough Shoal.

Surely the *Nenita* was safe in these waters?

Chen Kuang-chi yelled instructions to his crew on the bridge. The captain of the *Yichang* had his orders and there was no room for sentiment. The Jiangwei II-class frigate was closing in fast, its twin diesel motors revving at a comfortable 450rpm, propelling it along at a shade over twenty-five knots.

The 112-metre *Yichang* was armed with sufficient firepower to sink a small armada, but Chen knew he'd have no reason to fire at the enemy.

442

He checked his computerised screen, calculating he had another three to four minutes before drawing level. He scanned the horizon, half expecting to see another vessel, but there was none. On this bright crisp morning, this clip of the South China Sea was clear to the horizon.

His chief radio officer had done his job. The Filipino vessel would have no chance to issue a distress signal, its paltry communications system disabled by superior Chinese technology.

The *Yichang* had stalked its prey. Now the catch was within easy reach.

The first deadly thud pitched the *Nenita* forward, the sound of splintering timber mingling with the whine of a small diesel engine labouring on overdrive. Bawani's hands were ripped from the wheel and he was nearly knocked off his feet. He broadened his stance and dug his soles into the slippery cabin floor, bracing for the next hit.

When it came it was overpowering. He turned in horror to witness the dull grey of the attack vessel's bow slicing through his deck with ease. He yelled to the four crew to man the lifeboat, but it was too late. The tiny vessel heaved to port, then it began to sink.

Canberra

Tian Qichen flicked through his papers as he waited in an anteroom near the prime minister's suite. He knew this would be a robust encounter, because he had been summoned like a naughty schoolboy for a dressing down.

The previous day, the *Nenita*, a Filipino fishing vessel, had gone down with all hands, while in the proximity of the Chinese frigate *Yichang*. Beijing claimed its ship had gone to the aid of a sinking boat, but added that it was operating illegally in China's territorial waters. The US and the Philippines disputed that version of events, believing the Chinese had targeted the fishing boat and maintaining that China had no claim over the sea where the boat was sunk.

The two countries had directed their Beijing-based ambassadors to hand-deliver protest démarches to the head of the Chinese Ministry of Foreign Affairs.

Canberra had not gone that far. Instead it had summoned the Chinese ambassador to a meeting with the prime minister, but had yet to issue a formal statement.

The summons to Parliament House sent the message that Australia was taking the matter extremely seriously, as a dressing down would usually be delivered by the secretary of the Department of Foreign Affairs. But it also showed that the nation's leaders wanted to bargain in private, not lecture in public.

In a detailed cable to his ministry, Tian had noted that Canberra was torn because it relied so heavily on China to underwrite much of the nation's economic prosperity. The strain of trying not to offend its major economic partner while simultaneously trying to please its key ally, the United States, was showing up as indecision.

His instructions from Beijing were clear. He was not to take a backward step. It was time to turn up the heat on Australia and force it to make a choice – for the future or the past.

Scott emerged from the Situation Room in the Cabinet suite and bustled across the hallway to her office with her chief of staff and foreign policy adviser in tow. An emergency meeting of the National Security Committee had run over time. It had heard directly from the United States under secretary for political affairs, his image beamed onto the room's TV screens from Washington. He had produced pictures from a US spy satellite that appeared to show the Filipino boat being run down by the Chinese military vessel.

The under secretary was insistent that Australia support a 'determined and robust response', to show Beijing that it could not be 'a global power of tomorrow by behaving like a regional cowboy today'.

It was a view that was strongly endorsed by Jack Webster. He'd argued time was running out for the region to make a stand against China's aggressive expansion. Inside a year, the terraformed islands of the South China Sea would be fortresses. He'd again pressed for Australia to join an international flotilla.

'Seven trillion dollars worth of trade passes through the South China Sea every year,' he'd thundered. 'If we lose freedom of navigation, if it is rationed or we have to bargain for access, then we will become a vassal state of China.'

Scott had her doubts. The Americans had overplayed the analysis of their intelligence before and she wanted to take a more cautious approach. She thought that China could be persuaded that what it was doing was not in its national interest. The businesswoman in her thought that ensuring the goodwill of the region was the best way to ensure the trade routes.

Webster had been terse.

'This isn't about money. It is about a much more glittering prize. What matters is power. As a politician, you should understand that.'

'Ambassador.' Elizabeth Scott held out her hand, offering a firm grip and a stern expression.

She motioned for Tian to sit as she settled into a lounge chair. Scott had ordered her staff to leave the room. This meeting was just for two.

The prime minister poured a cup of tea. Just one. She sipped from the fine porcelain, slowly put the cup back in the saucer, then fixed Tian with a cold stare.

'What exactly are you doing in the South China Sea?'

The ambassador leaned forward in his seat and motioned to the teapot.

'I assume it is self-service.'

He slowly poured himself a cup, spooning sugar into the too-milky liquid before meeting Scott's gaze.

'And good morning to you, Prime Minister.'

'This is not a time for pleasantries, Ambassador Tian. Your country has made a grave error of judgement. Your aggression threatens to destabilise the region. You cannot expect my government to allow such action to go unchecked.'

Scott picked up a folder of papers, skimming its contents before returning her unwavering gaze to Tian.

'My government—'

'Prime Minister, before you go on,' Tian interjected, but Scott raised her hand before slamming it on the table.

'You do not interrupt me, Mr Tian. Your bully-boy tactics might work at home, but they will not be tolerated in my country. Not now, not ever.'

Scott felt the blood rising in her face. She did not like being forced into this position. Nor could she understand Beijing's thinking.

She had always reasoned that the mercantile interests of China and the US would find their own level in the Pacific. They might elbow each other along the way, but in the end would come to an understanding.

The PM preached diplomacy over the 'kinetic action' preferred by the US: the drone strikes, the weapons sales and the secretive arming of insurgent forces. But China's barbaric behaviour could not go unchallenged.

It was one thing to push your elbows out across the 'nine-dash line' that China claimed was the basis for its territorial sea. It was quite another to sink a small, unarmed fishing vessel in international waters.

'Mr Tian, my government joins with other nations in condemning in the strongest terms China's actions. You cannot possibly hope to gain global respect and credibility with such behaviour, behaviour that quite frankly belongs in the Middle Ages.'

Scott spoke firmly, without missing a beat.

'If you persist in expanding and militarising those islands and enforcing an illegal interpretation of territorial waters you will provoke a region-wide backlash.'

Tian listened attentively, his expression almost indulgent. He contemplated his tea before placing it on the table.

'First,' he said, 'Beijing rejects the false accusation that we had anything to do with the sinking of that vessel. It was old and unseaworthy. Our ship tried and failed to save those men.'

Scott rolled her eyes. 'Please don't treat me like a fool, Mr Ambassador. I have seen the satellite photos.'

'Madam Prime Minister, you can choose to believe me or the Americans. But let's not forget the many famous American intelligence slideshows that were more worthy of Disneyland than Maryland.'

He smiled at his wit.

'But on this point, let us be clear. Our rights over those waters go back thousands of years. If the boat had not sunk, its crew would have been arrested.'

Scott drummed her manicured nails on the armrest of her lounge chair.

'I do not understand why you can't see that this unnecessary aggression is counterproductive. Economic power is Beijing's real might. Everything you want can be negotiated without building a fortress in the South China Sea. All you will do is ensure the region unites against you.'

Tian sat back in his seat and rubbed his right temple with his forefinger, as if the conversation was giving him a headache.

'Madam Prime Minister, if you really believed that economic security did not need to be backed by military might you wouldn't be signing agreements to buy submarines from Tokyo.'

Tian spoke the name of the Japanese capital with derision. Scott remained impassive as the diplomat continued.

'You might decide to support America in a parade of military force, Madam Prime Minister. You might eventually purchase your next class of submarines from the Japanese. Both decisions are entirely yours to make ... but, rest assured, they will be seen by my government as acts of aggression.'

'Are you threatening me, Mr Ambassador?'

'Certainly not, Prime Minister, just engaging in what you Aussies would call "fair dinkum" talk.'

'It sounds like a threat to me, Mr Tian, but then it seems you and your countrymen have become accustomed to issuing ultimatums. China has decided to play by its own rules, and to hell with the usual conventions.'

Tian gave a thin smile.

'Conventions are such a moveable feast, don't you think? They vary from country to country and are so often ignored by those who preach them.'

Tian paused as he reached for a folder, taking out a sheet of paper. He examined it before he continued.

'For instance, in your country, politicians tell the public that they play by one set of rules when they do very dark deeds in private.'

Tian put the piece of paper down on the coffee table. It was a photograph of Scott's old Mercedes with two people sitting in it. She recognised the time and place immediately and her skin went cold. She had met with a private detective whom she had paid to clandestinely spy on Emily Brooks. The PI had installed cameras in her Liberal rival's bedroom and captured the bondage session that entered online folklore and finished Brooks as leader.

'I have no idea what you are referring to, Mr Tian.'

'I think you do, Ms Scott. And in case there is any doubt ...'

The ambassador reached into his suit pocket and pulled out a USB. He held it aloft and gently shook it for effect.

'The audio is very clear ... and let me say your voice has never sounded finer.'

He rose suddenly and threw the USB on top of the photo on the table. He tucked his folder under his arm.

'Keep them, we have many copies.'

He moved towards the door before turning back to a frozen Scott.

'Think very carefully about what you do next, Ms Scott. My country is usually civil, but if we are forced into a battle ... well, there are no rules in a fight. There is only the survivor and the defeated.'

Canberra

The afternoon was bleak enough for dying. What had begun as a perfect blue-sky day had suddenly turned. The sky was now violent purple and a brisk wind had whipped up white caps on the lake.

Harry Dunkley picked up the pace to fend off the cold. He'd dressed lightly and for the past few hours had been cosy enough as he'd pored over old newspaper reports on the Australian Warfare Destroyer program at the National Library. He had been absorbed by his reading and was now running late.

Benny Hadid had chosen the venue for their meeting, the prime ministerial suite at the heart of the Museum of Australian Democracy, which now inhabited Old Parliament House. Dunkley arrived slightly out of breath to an empty room.

Dunkley was wary of the strange little man, having so recently been burnt by trusted contacts and still carrying the scars, but he was keen to know why Hadid wanted to see him again. What else had he uncovered?

From somewhere nearby, the recorded voices of an ancient protest offered a soundtrack to the clutter of offices and cubicles that had once been home to Whitlam, Fraser and Hawke. Dunkley wandered around the room to stand in front of the prime ministerial desk. A single Australian flag sat a little off-centre behind the large teak table, upon which sat an old-fashioned circular-dial telephone. A comfy-looking leather chair marked the seat of power for the leaders of yesteryear. Dunkley wondered what secrets this room had witnessed.

'A throne fit for a king, eh, Harry?'

Dunkley froze. He recognised the voice, as unexpected as it was unwelcome. He turned slowly and two words came coldly to his lips.

'Charles Dancer.'

The wiry spy stood in the doorway. The smile on his face held a hint of menace. The last time they met, Dancer had held a gun to Dunkley's head and admitted to killing Kimberley Gordon.

Dunkley wrestled with his emotions, hoping that his face and voice would not betray him. He desperately wanted to launch himself at this man, but knew from bitter experience that he was no match for him physically.

'It's okay, Harry, I'm just here for a friendly chat with an old friend.' Dancer's tone was faintly mocking.

'Skip the lies, Charles. Why are you following me?'

'Oh Harry, don't be so dramatic. Like you, I have come to worship in the cradle of our democracy.' Dancer gestured languidly around the room.

'Come,' he continued, beckoning Dunkley and disappearing into the hallway.

Dunkley followed, at a cautious distance. After a few steps he entered a larger room through a thick door held open by Dancer. There was no sign, but Dunkley knew this was the Cabinet Room. It was a relatively modest space dominated by a square timber table with a hollowed-out section in the centre.

'Whitlam had this room extended in 1972 to accommodate his expanding Cabinet,' Dancer explained, as if escorting Dunkley on an exclusive private tour.

'They soundproofed it, right at the time his Cabinet was leaking like a sieve. But, typically for Whitlam, they did a half-arsed job.'

Dancer pointed to an inlaid ceiling.

'Up there, Harry. The people who now run this place did some renovations a few years ago and guess what they found? The old press gallery was above this room and they found cigarette butts in the ceiling. The journalists literally had an ear right into the Cabinet.'

He turned to face Dunkley. 'You would have loved working here: all those juicy secrets to uncover; holding errant politicians to account – the noblest of causes, eh?'

'What's your point?' Dunkley felt a chill rush through him as Dancer stepped closer.

'You know, the thing about this place, Old Parliament House, is that they knew when to shut her down, to move on up the hill. They preserve the history, of course, or a sanitised version, at least. After all, history has always been a subjective glimpse into the past. Your history, Harry, is littered with the remnants of failure—'

'And unfinished business,' Dunkley cut in.

'Yes, Harry, and best to keep it that way. Shut it down. Move on.'

'Are you threatening me, Charles? Again?'

Dancer looked up once more at the ceiling.

'Mid-year, 1967. Holt was prime minister; it was a few months before he disappeared. His government was leaking like a rusty bucket too. One reporter, some nondescript type, was getting scoop after scoop, beating his rivals and thoroughly infuriating dear old Harold.

'Maybe he was up there, sitting right on top of the Cabinet Room, eavesdropping on every delicate conversation. So the Cabinet set up a fake debate on a hot topic and our intrepid journalist fell for it.'

Dancer turned a hard gaze on Dunkley.

'He was turfed to the wolves, just like you, Harry. Went off to a quiet retirement, never to be heard of again. Better for everyone, I would suggest.'

He smiled and spoke patiently, as if to a child slow to learn.

'You should have realised by now, Harry, that you can't hide. I see everything you do, know everyone you meet. You can let this drop. You can walk away. I gave you the chance once before. This is your last chance, I guarantee it.'

He strolled out of the suite, brushing against Dunkley as he turned, leaving the former journalist anxious and alone.

Dunkley's fingers were trembling as he reached for his phone, scrolling through numbers before hitting green. After a few rings, Benny Hadid answered, offering an immediate apology.

'Sorry, Harry, didn't you get my text?'

'No.' Dunkley's voice was cold and flat.

'I should have called, but I was about to leave when I got hauled in to see the boss. Something unexpected. Can we meet in a couple of hours perhaps?'

Dunkley felt like he was part of a jigsaw, a foreigner in a place he once knew well. He'd been rattled by Dancer's unexpected appearance; it confirmed what he had suspected: he was being tracked.

'I'm staying at the Kurrajong. Why don't we meet there?'

'I'd prefer somewhere a little less public.'

'Okay, I'll grab my car and pick you up outside the Burbury at five thirty. We can go for a drive.'

'Okay, see you then, Harry.'

Would he turn up this time? Dunkley wondered. And how much could he trust Hadid?

Dunkley raised his finger to his mouth as Hadid opened the car door, signalling for him to be quiet. He punched the start button on the CD player and Van Morrison began singing about the bright side of the road. If only, Dunkley thought.

He weaved the car up the familiar slope of Mount Ainslie, remembering the many frosty mornings that he'd nearly killed himself jogging to the summit. The first shadows of night were falling across Canberra as they reached the top.

Dunkley pulled up and got out. Dropping his mobile on the front seat, he motioned for Hadid to do the same, then walked towards the stone stairs that led down to a lookout. There was no one in sight.

'You're making me nervous, Harry.'

'Just call me cautious.'

Hadid was carrying a briefcase and wearing an oversized coat. As before, his shoulders were in motion as if he had a small colony of creatures living just beneath his skin that he was trying to shake out.

Dunkley couldn't afford to feel sympathetic.

'I had an unwelcome visit, Benny, from a man who once threatened to kill me. He came in your place.'

The auditor's face fell.

'Do you think he knows about me? About my work?'

'Obviously. I'm wondering about that too. Wondering if I can trust you.'

Hadid pulled his coat tighter. 'Harry, I've taken a huge risk talking to you. I'm only here because something is not right.'

He propped his briefcase on a stone wall and slipped out several pages that were stapled together.

'This is a summary of the work I've been doing secretly on the Air Warfare Destroyer and the missing billions. Apart from me, you are the only person with a copy. I'm giving it to you because I'm getting more concerned that it will never see the light of day.'

Dunkley contemplated the document.

'Why's that?'

'On the phone I told you that my boss called me into a meeting just as I was about to leave the office.'

'Yeah.'

'He asked if I was still working on the AWD brief.'

'And what did you say?'

'I lied, said I wasn't.'

The public servant's voice trembled.

'Harry, he didn't believe me. He told me to drop it, to do my day job. And in not so many words he gave me a clear message: tread carefully. I think he's genuinely concerned about what I'm doing and whom I'm taking on.'

'Why do you say that?'

'As he led me out of his office, he put his arm around my shoulders, pulled me in close and whispered two words: "Jack Webster".'

Canberra

Somewhere in the dark web of endless surveillance, Harry Dunkley needed a place to hide. He found what he was looking for in Kingston, a public phone box. He pushed his coins into the slot and punched out a number.

It picked up after two rings.

'Who's this?'

'Martin, it's Dunkley. I had a visitor. We have to talk. In person. I'm being bugged and tracked.'

'Righto. Let's meet.'

'Where, mate?'

'Why not out the back of my old place?'

'Where's that?'

'Harry, you're an investigative journalist. Work it out. And I'm bringing a mutual friend.'

National Circuit was all but deserted when Dunkley arrived at the rendezvous. High hedges hid the mansions of the diplomats and high-flyers who could afford to live in this wealthy enclave.

He parked fifty metres up the road and ambled to the rear gate of the Georgian-style mansion that had been home to prime ministers for nearly ninety years.

'The Lodge. Nice touch, Martin,' he said, as he greeted Toohey and another familiar form. He nodded to Bruce Paxton and the two men shook hands awkwardly.

Toohey waved at a guard who'd stepped out from the gate. He waved back as he recognised his former boss.

'So why here, Martin?' Dunkley asked.

'Because the front and rear gates of the Lodge are protected by radio signal scramblers that ensure a bomb can't be detonated using a mobile phone. The shadow stretches one hundred metres in every direction. Within that shadow, phones won't work and no one can monitor us with listening devices.'

Toohey reached into a plastic carrier bag and pulled out two small boxes. He handed them to his accomplices.

'Christ, a pager,' said Paxton. 'I haven't seen one of these since my early days as a union organiser.'

'It's a modern version of an old idea,' Toohey said. 'It's alphanumeric. It might be old school, but the signal is much tougher to track. Particularly if no one knows we're using them.'

Toohey looked up and down the street.

'So here's the drill. From now on when we need to talk, we meet. We'll meet where we can't be heard, and that's here or out the front of any other building that uses a scrambler. Like the US, British, Israeli, Russian and Chinese embassies. Type a message, leave cars and phones behind. But we'll need to keep these meetings short.'

His two offsiders nodded.

'So, Harry, what happened?'

'Jack Webster is onto us; well, me at least. I got a visit from his goon, Charles Dancer. Caught me by surprise while I was waiting to meet my contact from Auditor-General's at Old Parliament House. The warning was explicit … and I don't doubt it comes from Webster.'

Dunkley looked over his shoulder at a car that seemed to be passing more slowly than it should. He hoped he wasn't becoming as paranoid as the people he was mixing with in this town.

'Hadid, the guy from audit, reckons Webster's got his hand in the till. If we could prove that, then Jesus Christ couldn't save him. So what have you got, Martin?'

'Webster's turning his property out at Burra into some kind of fortress. He's spending a bomb on it. I'm told the Americans are involved.'

'Hang on, Martin.' Dunkley felt a surge of excitement as he made a connection. 'Hadid said Webster had siphoned taxpayer money into a private account. Maybe that's where he's getting the cash for that property.'

Dunkley took the pages Hadid had given him from his jacket pocket and held them so Toohey and Paxton could read over his shoulder.

'This is a summary of his investigation into the Air Warfare Destroyer blowout. It's a show stopper. We'd need to have more detail, but see, here he notes a bank account that he claims is operated by Webster. More than two million bucks has gone into it.'

Toohey let out a low whistle.

'This could be it, Harry. Remember, Al Capone wasn't done for being a gangster, he was done for tax evasion.'

He turned to Paxton.

'Mate, are you still talking with your building union comrades?'

'Martin, the bruvvers are the only people who've stuck with me. They gave me the caravan.'

'Great, then they can help us track down the builders, whether they're local or not. They'll have some idea what's going on out at Burra. Bruce, you find that builder. And Harry, follow the money.'

Dunkley smiled.

'PM, what are you going to do?'

'What I do best. Find more allies.'

Paxton slapped his good right hand on Toohey's back.

'Thank Christ for that, because the ranks are pretty thin at the moment for a war with a man who commands the entire defence force.'

Toohey nodded.

'Which is why we're off the grid now. Boys, welcome to the shadow game.'

Canberra

Jack Webster gazed across the lush lawns of Duntroon like an emperor surveying his realm. The morning's newspapers were neatly laid out beside his usual spartan breakfast.

Despite the early hour, Webster had already absorbed the media offerings. Nearly a week after the event, commentators were still writing about his speech at the National Press Club and his calm, decisive leadership during the bomb scare. The coverage was glowing.

He sipped his tea as he reread a particularly flattering editorial before checking the time: 0655. His driver would be arriving any minute to whisk him the short distance from his official residence, across Kings Avenue Bridge, to federal parliament. Elizabeth Scott had convened another meeting of the National Security Committee and Webster would go well armed as the government wrestled with how to respond to China's militarisation of the South China Sea.

This was no time for a limp riposte and Webster was prepared to take on the 'pandas', including the prime minister, if he had to.

His car pulled up and Webster settled back in the plush leather seat, gazing out at the Royal Military College as it sprang to life. He owed it to these budding warriors to make sure the NSC did right by those who were willing to die for their country.

He glanced up from his briefing notes as Parliament House came into view. He was early, as planned, allowing plenty of time for a brief discussion with some of the agency heads before the committee met.

His colleagues were already waiting in the Cabinet anteroom. He nodded briskly as he joined them. They were the cream of Australia's defence and intelligence establishment. It was critical – now more than ever – that they speak with a unified voice.

Webster was confident of their support. 'So gentlemen, here's the plan ...'

Elizabeth Scott swept into the Situation Room with graceful self-assurance, her chief of staff in tow. It was 7.28am and the prime minister had spent the past hour locked in meetings trying to resolve a raft of domestic woes. For once, though, there was even bigger trouble abroad.

'Good morning all. Let's get down to business. CDF, I might ask you to speak first on the defence options.'

'Prime Minister, thank you. If anything, our view has hardened since we last met. Then, we were debating our response to China's outrageous sinking of a defenceless Filipino fishing vessel in an unprovoked attack. And recall, five people drowned.'

Webster reviewed his notes.

'Our only decisions then were to deliver a lecture to the Chinese ambassador and to back the US in raising the attack at the United Nations Security Council. What did China do? It used its veto power to block any multilateral condemnation. Russia supported it.'

Webster's stern face matched the gravity of his tone.

'Ladies and gentlemen, the time for talking has ended. China isn't listening. We must act. We must act in tandem with our closest allies. Yes, there are risks – they are in our brief – but the biggest risk is indecision.'

The CDF tapped the table to underscore this point.

'Defence, and I do believe the intelligence chiefs agree, recommends that Australia join a US-led response.

'Yesterday, I spoke with the US Chairman of the Joint Chiefs of Staff. America is building a coalition of the willing to support an international flotilla that will patrol the South China Sea. This won't be a single exercise. It will be a permanent fleet stationed in those waters.

'The Philippines and Malaysia are on board. Indonesia and even communist Vietnam are giving it serious consideration.'

Webster maintained eye contact with the prime minister as he spoke.

'The Americans want us to send an Anzac frigate and for us to base one of our P-3 Orion surveillance planes and an air-refueller in the Philippines. As you are aware, the Philippines has reopened the old US base at Subic Bay. Soon they will invite the Americans to station one of their ten Nimitz-class aircraft carriers there.'

Ominously, Scott was frowning and fidgeting with her wedding ring.

'Jack, that is a significantly more aggressive response from Defence and a much bigger ask than we've had to consider before today. To be frank, I have serious reservations, but I will hold them until we've heard from the director-general of the ONA.'

Tania Varma was the no-nonsense head of the Office of National Assessments who'd risen through the ranks of Foreign Affairs before being appointed ambassador to Indonesia. She'd led the intelligence agency for just over a year and was considered a rising star.

'Prime Minister, you asked the ONA to forensically examine the potential fallout from Australia joining a single mission to enter disputed waters in the

455

South China Sea. I tasked my best people for this and I trust each committee member has read our exhaustive brief. I will stick to the key points.'

She glanced sideways at Webster.

'First, there is merit in what the defence chief says. On the surface, China appears determined to change the facts on the ground to force its will on the world.'

Webster offered an encouraging nod.

'But the risks are enormous,' Varma continued. 'To break it down into numbers that people can digest, two-way trade with China is worth over $16,000 per Australian household annually. More than two hundred thousand jobs are sustained by direct exports there.

'If you think the slowdown in the world's second biggest economy is a problem for us now, then try to imagine the disaster if it stopped trading with us altogether.'

Varma swept her gaze around the room until it was directed at Scott.

'Prime Minister, there is strong reason to believe that our diplomatic efforts are having an effect. There is active debate at the highest levels in Beijing about the wisdom of China's aggressive play. A recent Five Eyes intelligence report suggests that President Meng's closest adviser, Propaganda Minister Jiang Xiu, has been urging restraint.'

The ONA head turned to her right, where Webster sat.

'But all of that analysis was prepared before I heard just now what the US is actually planning. It was based on Beijing's possible reaction to a one-off mission by a US-led international flotilla. Unless I am mistaken, Sir Jack, what the US now proposes, and you support, is a blockade.'

Webster essayed his most charming smile, but shifted uncomfortably in his seat. 'I don't believe it will come to that.'

'What if it did?' Varma shot back. 'What if China tried to put weapons on those islands? What would your fleet do then?'

Webster responded a touch patronisingly.

'Then yes, of course, we would have to intervene. We can't make empty threats.'

Varma weighed up his words, then spoke directly to Scott.

'Prime Minister, I strongly advise against this course of action. It dramatically raises the threat of a conflict or a catastrophic accident. We'd be bringing the Cuban Missile Crisis to the South China Sea.'

As Varma spoke, an adviser leaned over her shoulder and placed a folded note in front of her boss. Varma picked it up and read it carefully before looking back at the prime minister.

'There is one last point. I think a vital piece of information is missing from our deliberations. When Sir Jack listed those countries that had agreed to sign up to the flotilla, I believe he omitted one. CDF?'

Webster managed to appear unruffled.

'It will be an unprecedented alliance,' he said. 'The Japanese will send a destroyer.'

The revelation rippled around the room as everyone recognised its historic import. For the first time since the Second World War, Japan would unshackle its military for action outside its own waters. It would be the biggest 'fuck you' the region could send to Beijing.

Scott stared at Webster for an uncomfortable few seconds.

'Something you forgot to tell us, Jack?'

Webster walked briskly along the blue carpet, nodding politely to several ministers. He left Parliament House through the ministerial entrance and strode to his waiting car, his driver holding the rear door open. The defence chief collapsed into the leather seat and briefly shut his eyes.

'Those fucking harlots.'

Canberra

The working-class nirvana was in full swing. It was Thursday night and Dickson Tradies was wall to wall with young men who hugged the bar and poured their wages into the pokies, their schooners perched precariously on the edges of machines hungry for cash.

The Construction, Forestry, Mining and Energy Union had built its empire in Canberra from gambling, using the dividends to pay for everything from workers' holiday cottages to Labor's election campaigns. The union was cashed up and in this small city of intimate connections, the local secretary, Dean Hall, was its emperor.

Hall was old-school union muscle, a former rugby league star who played by the rules. His rules.

Bruce Paxton jostled his way to a spare table and waited, knowing that Hall would be somewhere in his realm this night.

Two beers later he turned to a familiar voice. 'Comrade.'

Paxton rose from his chair to embrace one of the very few men who'd stuck by him when others fled. There was something about this union heavy that Paxton could relate to, a throwback to a simpler time with a simple creed: strength in numbers.

'How've ya been, Bruce?' Hall placed a reassuring hand on Paxton's shoulder. 'I've been meaning to call you, to chat about your living in that caravan. We can find you better digs, you know.'

Paxton took a long pull of his beer before answering.

'Nah, it's more than enough for me. Watertight, easy to clean, and the rent's a breeze,' he said with a grin. 'I'm not here looking for a handout, but I do need some information about a particular building project. And Deano, there's bugger all that you don't know about what's going on in this town.'

Hall smiled. Paxton's compliment had done the trick. 'Well then, Bruce, let's retire to the back bar and grab a quiet ale. My shout.'

The emperor was in firm command. With a single call Hall had tracked down the builder who'd overseen the Burra project and lined up a meeting.

It was mid-morning and Paxton had hailed a taxi for the short drive from the caravan park to a blue-ribbon address on Mugga Way.

The cab pulled up at a block the size of a football field.

Paxton marvelled at the building's footprint as a small army of excavators sliced into the hard Canberra clay. A big man wearing a hard hat and a mischievous grin lumbered over.

'You look like a former defence minister.' The builder thrust out his hand before motioning around the site. 'Welcome to the new home of one of the biggest tossers in this city. A public service bigwig who reckons a massive house can buy you class. And mate, he's one of the most difficult clients I've had the misfortune to come across.'

Paxton shrugged. 'Known a few of them. Always thought they were better than me.'

'I know.' The builder yelled a quick instruction to a driver, before turning back to Paxton. 'I understand you're after some info about another client of mine, one that makes this guy look like Snow White.'

'Yeah, that's right, a place out at Burra. You were in charge of the build.'

He nodded. 'I was. It was one of the toughest and most complex jobs I've ever managed. Took twice as long and cost three times as much as the original quote.'

'Why?'

'The owner kept changing the specs and was absurdly secretive. The place is chock-full of high-tech security. I understand you know this guy?'

Paxton nodded. 'I do. Jack Webster.'

'I know who he is. We had another name for him. The Big C.'

'Hah. So how do you get into this place?'

'You don't. Not unless you're invited. We did too good a job. It's got more security than most government departments. There are cameras on the gates and you need to swipe a security card to open them. The fence alone cost a million bucks and it has a laser alarm system mounted along the perimeter. Inside the fence there are trip systems and more CCTV.'

'Doesn't sound like he wants visitors.'

'No, mate – not unless you're American.'

'What do you know about them?'

'Not much. Webster had a bunch of Yanks swing by from time to time. All very cloak and dagger. Each time they arrived, we were ordered off site.'

'What were they doing?'

'Buggered if I know for sure, but it had to be something to do with secure comms. We set up some of the shells for that kind of stuff and they filled in the blanks.'

Paxton watched as a tipper swung into the dirt track of what would become the mansion's driveway.

'Anything else you can tell me?'

'Well, the most interesting bit is right in the guts of the complex. There's a conference room with TV screens on either side.'

'Like he's built a Situation Room? How can I describe it? Like something you'd see in a thriller about the American president?'

'Yeah, something like that. But he wasn't just interested in talking to people outside the room. He was keen to watch people in it.'

'What do you mean?'

'He had cameras installed in every corner of the room, trained on the conference table. We even hid two in the ceiling. So he can record whoever's in there in pristine high definition. Bruce, this guy doesn't trust anyone.'

Brisbane

The Oak Room had been booked for 10am. Just the two of them.

The Brisbane Club was whisper quiet on this glorious morning, but Emily Brooks needed a private suite for a very private discussion.

She was surprised to find the club's general manager on his mobile, sweating over what sounded like a romance gone wrong. 'Michael, how nice to see you,' Brooks purred. 'Now get the hell out of here.'

The manager scurried from the room, leaving Brooks to check a few notes before glancing at her watch.

He arrived on time and alone. She sized him up: tall, handsome, regal. Just what she needed.

'Well, Sir Jack, you are looking fine this morning. Please take a seat.'

Brooks motioned to a chair and set about stroking the ego of a vain man.

'Your speech to the Press Club is still making waves, Sir Jack, and not just with the feministas. I bumped into a retired general last night; he said it was the high point of your career. Must say, I agree.'

Webster smoothed a crease on his blue jacket.

'Thank you, Emily; yes, I've been rather pleased with the response. But it's not just talk. I'm determined to follow through. Absolutely determined.'

'I don't doubt that, not for a minute. I've always admired that about you. Your word is as good as its deed. I know some in Defence will resist it, but leadership is about doing what is right, not what is popular. You will no doubt upset some of the brass who are still fighting with pistols and bayonets. But you are looking to the future and you embrace the courage of your convictions. With your strength, I've no doubt that you will take the people with you.'

Brooks paused for a moment, clasping her hands winningly and leaning close to her target.

'We could use some of that leadership in the Liberal Party.'

Webster cocked his head in mock surprise. 'I would have thought the Liberal Party had a stable of leaders: you, the prime minister ...'

Brooks's response bled derision. 'Elizabeth Scott? Oh please. That woman is leading us off a cliff. She personifies the do-nothing, time-wasting style perfected by Malcolm Fraser, coupled with a bleeding left heart. She's lost our base and will lose us the next election if we don't do something drastic.'

'What did you have in mind, Emily? Resurrect Margaret Thatcher?'

'Hah! Yes, Jack, the Iron Lady is a role model. But we need someone closer to home, someone who understands the psyche of the Australian people, someone who can rescue this country from its meandering path to mediocrity.'

'Sounds like you should put your hand up again, Emily. I'm told the Right are feeling quite emboldened.'

'No, not me,' Brooks said, with an air of resignation. 'That sex tape cruelled my chances. We need a cleanskin, someone who can take us in a new direction, the right direction. Importantly, we need someone who can beat Catriona Bailey.'

Brooks arched her eyebrows knowingly as she arrived at the point of the meeting. 'You dabbled in party politics once, Jack; our side, right?'

'You know about that. It was a long, long time ago, during my young idealistic phase. The air force drove that out of me quick smart,' Webster said with a chuckle.

The Liberal warrior fixed the knighted hero with her piercing eyes. He blinked first.

'Jack, I am not joking. The nation is crying out for leadership; our party is aching for someone who can take the people with him, someone who is trusted.' She pointed at him. 'You could be that person.'

Brooks knew she was playing with one of the most vulnerable and dangerous animals on the planet: the male ego.

'I'm not even a member of parliament.'

'This state proved you don't need to be. Campbell Newman became premier from the outside ... though we'd be hoping for a better outcome.'

'Emily, in case you haven't noticed, we're on the verge of war in the South China Sea.'

'Yes, and I also note that your plans for action, and the only possibility of success, are being frustrated.'

Webster waited a moment. 'Those are matters for the National Security Committee.'

'No, Jack, we are talking about the security of this nation. We need a leader whose plans cannot be thwarted by some limp-wristed small-l liberal.'

The CDF checked his watch. 'I have to go, Emily; I'm due in Townsville at 1500 hours.'

'Townsville, hey? That's in Herbert. Solid north Queensland seat, full of Mr and Mrs Stringbag types. Rolled-gold middle Australia. You might like to think of it as a dry run ...'

Washington

Zero hour was approaching. Since the sun had set across the White House lawns, the US president had been walking a diplomatic high wire on one of the most sensitive military operations ever proposed by America.

Mikaela Asta stifled a yawn as she prepared to make one last call to slot the final piece into a fragile alliance. A single misstep could bring the whole house of cards tumbling down.

Weeks of groundwork had preceded these conversations.

461

Using her trademark 'strongarm charm', Asta had just secured the backing of South Korea's president for the international flotilla in the South China Sea, despite Park Geun-hye's reservations about the mooted inclusion of Japan, her country's historical enemy. But it had been a close-run thing.

And President Park had thrown Asta a worrying curve ball just as the conversation was winding down.

'I have one last question,' President Park had said.

'About what, ma'am?'

'Australia. They have followed your nation into every battle for eighty years. But my ambassador in Canberra tells me its leadership is divided.'

'Madam President, I assure you, Australia is fine.'

Despite her bravado, Asta was troubled. Morgan McDonald had told her that 'my man in Canberra' would close the deal so that when Asta spoke to Elizabeth Scott it would be a formality. She now feared it would be anything but.

The president rubbed at a knot in her neck as the call to Australia was put through.

'Prime Minister, thanks for taking my call.'

'Madam President, good afternoon – or should I say good evening? It must be late in Washington.'

'Approaching 11pm, Elizabeth. The day is but young.'

The two leaders briefly shared a laugh before Asta outlined the American plan. An armada of warships drawn from seven nations would sail into the South China Sea then through the twelve-nautical-mile exclusion zone around the Spratly Islands. It would be an unprecedented show of solidarity and send the most defiant of messages to Beijing.

And this would be no public relations parade. China had to be shown that the threat of force was real. So the US would establish a forward base for an aircraft carrier strike group in the Philippines, while other navies would rotate their warships through Subic Bay.

Any move by Beijing to stockpile weapons on the terraformed islands would be met with a blockade.

'But we don't think it will come to that,' Asta said. 'Beijing's hand is weak. We know that. More importantly, President Meng knows that.'

'How can you be sure?' The hesitation in Scott's voice was amplified by the speaker on the Oval Office desk.

'Our intelligence is solid. The combat systems on the experimental planes that China displayed during Meng's visit to the Spratlys are not ready. They won't be ready for years.'

Scott sounded far from convinced. 'With respect, Madam President, that's not the point. China will be forced to challenge any blockade, otherwise Meng would suffer a loss of face that would cripple his leadership. Like Kennedy in the Cuban Missile Crisis, you risk a high-stakes confrontation on the high seas. The slightest mistake could lead to war.'

'If that moment came we would prevail, just like Kennedy. China doesn't want war, neither do we.' Asta's voice rang with conviction, but Scott was unmoved.

'Most countries don't want war, but they wage war when the alternatives are worse,' Scott said. 'For Meng, losing face would trigger internal unrest and that would threaten his hold on power. Losing power at home is worse than risking war abroad.'

Each time the president raised a point, the prime minister objected. Asta hadn't needed or wanted a debate. It was now 11.28pm. She was beat and annoyed, but she couldn't afford to show it.

'Elizabeth, China is playing us because it thinks we don't have the guts to fight. If we don't make a stand now, we might not be able to in the future. Beijing knows that. So it will be delighted to pat your hand and keep you talking until it builds those islands into an unbreachable wall.'

Asta noted a long pause on the other end of the line.

'Mikaela, you are also asking for a nuclear-capable B-1 bomber to be based at Tindal in the Northern Territory. Its range is close to twelve thousand kilometres. It's half that distance from Tindal to Beijing. What message do you think that will send?'

Asta tried to maintain her calm. The entire mission – her mission – hinged on this phone call. If Australia baulked, the fragile coalition would fall apart.

'Elizabeth, China's ballistic missiles now have a reach of over seven thousand miles. One launched from Mischief Reef could land on your parliament. How would the Australian people feel if you allowed nuclear weapons in reach of their homes?'

She softened her tone a touch.

'This is about protecting all our interests. I hope that Australia will support us in this vital mission. We do not want to act alone, but we will if we must.'

The line went quiet and then Asta heard Scott taking a deep breath. 'Madam President,' Scott said, 'the situation for us is delicate. If you push me for an answer today ... tonight, then the answer is no – I need more time.'

Asta's response was immediate, and as frigid as a Minnesota snowstorm. 'I'm afraid you've run out of time, Prime Minister.'

Her sleep had been more restless than usual. In the month she'd been president, Asta had taken on the troubles of the world. Everywhere, nations cried out for help – and every time America responded it was pilloried and left to do the heavy lifting. The South China Sea was an exemplar: the entire region quailed before Beijing and called on Washington for protection. But when push came to shove, Asta had been abandoned by her closest regional ally. Australia's greed had trumped its fear.

After being rebuffed by Scott, she'd retired to bed, but her efforts to snatch some decent rest were in vain. She was up by four, in the Oval Office an hour later, and demanding to see the vice president at 6am.

'What the hell's she playing at, Morgan? You told me Australia was on board. You were wrong.'

The rumpled vice president, unusually, was at a loss to provide the right answers.

'Mikaela, I told you what Webster told me – "We've got your back." Clearly that did not translate into plain English for Ms Scott.'

Like the president, Big Mac had been working round the clock, hustling up the players in what would be a highly dangerous but calculated political gamble.

The play against China would be a declaration that Asta's presidency would restore American pride, a bold statement that there was still only one superpower. It was strategically vital too. Beijing's annexation of the South China Sea was threatening the security of a key trade route.

With an eye to next year's election, the move would also cement Asta's credentials as an uncompromising commander in chief, unafraid of deploying America's arsenal. This would be her Falklands moment. But it wouldn't be a squabble over a windswept waste with a bankrupt third-tier nation. This would be a heavyweight bout with the biggest thug in the world.

When she and Big Mac were mapping out the Chinese strategy they had spent countless hours on the 'hard asks': securing Japan, hustling Indonesia and Malaysia, cajoling Vietnam and South Korea. That Australia wouldn't play ball had never occurred to them.

Mystified, McDonald recounted his conversations with his close Australian ally.

'Webster said Cabinet would debate our request, but that a sign-off would be routine – and that is a direct quote. It seems someone's got in the prime minister's ear,' the vice president said.

'Yes, it appears someone has. And the B-1 bomber? Who asked for that?'

'It was Webster's idea. But no formal request has been made.'

Asta snorted.

'Well, it was very unhelpful. We should be solely focused on the flotilla. If I ever want to bomb Beijing from the air, I'll send the plane from Guam. And if I really want to nuke it, I will be firing missiles from Ohio-class subs parked just off its coast.'

The tense mood in the Oval Office reflected the gravity of the setback. America did not need the members of the international flotilla for their firepower; it needed them for their flags. Canberra's hesitation meant others were likely to pull out, and that was a risk they couldn't afford.

It was time to gamble everything on a 'Hail Mary' play.

'Morgan,' Asta said, 'let's drop the flag on Plan B.'

Canberra

They hunted in the shadows. Their headquarters were virtual, their operations ultra-secret, their preferred targets vulnerable government agencies.

They whispered through highly encrypted networks, managing to outrun and outsmart the cyber-police. Every assignment was different, every outcome the same.

A common routine was to send a document via email. Embedded within the PDF was custom code, undetectable and lethal. The email would bypass security checks before lodging at the destination. There it would lurk patiently, sometimes for months, until the bomb was detonated.

Then it would unleash its hidden code, exploiting a previously unrecognised system vulnerability, usually within Adobe Acrobat. Quietly the code would migrate into the Windows Explorer process, at the same time disabling antivirus software.

The infection would spread. As the host searched the internet, reaching out through legitimate connections to random files, it would be unwittingly unpacking and strengthening an army.

Periodically the invader would read and parse hidden code from a hacked webpage as data ricocheted back and forth across encrypted systems. Emails, usernames, passwords and other network tools needed to execute the attack would be extracted. Files on a network share would be poisoned and other users infected. The army would strategically position itself across the network, marching up the ranks towards the IT manager, moving closer to a zero day attack.

Once the network was breached, the manager's account would log into the area's domain controller. Hashed passwords would be extracted, then 'brute forced' offline. The malicious code would then masquerade as the 'administrator' of the domain controller. New accounts would be created, further compromising the system.

More network information would be exfiltrated. A domain account would then be able to log into the back-up server as an administrator. The back-up system would be altered, but only slightly. The system would believe it was duplicating certain files, but instead they would be empty.

On zero day minus one, all beaconing systems on desktops would self-wipe and delete, with the exception of the target endpoint. A logic bomb would be planted on a small number of servers that would, in a week, reinstall some malicious code. These systems would also self-delete, minimising the footprint and the chances of being caught.

On zero day, the target would be watched, and when it was time an innocuous document would be replaced with another that would throw the hand-grenade over the trenches.

The auditor-general's office was pristine in the early morning light. His personal assistant had arrived early to tidy up some basic admin before the daily mayhem, fussing with his diary notes before settling in to read his overnight email.

Most would be routine requests or briefing updates and she hummed a familiar tune as she dipped into his inbox.

Boring. Boring. A note from PM&C. Dull, dull ...

Oh! The invitation was glossy black and white, stylishly designed and presented. She enlarged it to fit the page, admiring the Art Deco lettering and illustration. For the past five years the auditor-general had received a personal VIP invitation to the Cancerians Ball. He'd been a key supporter since ovarian cancer robbed him of his wife.

This event was a must. She delved deeper into the PDF to check for dates and other logistics.

The Hyatt Hotel. Five-star elegance. August 22. Black tie, of course. Sequins, fur, feathers. How lovely. He would probably book his usual table of ten; she made a note to check. The RSVP closed on June 30. A silly date, what with the end of financial year and all. Still, the Cancerians Ball was an important occasion raising funds for a worthwhile cause.

She closed the file and moved onto the next email, from some nobody in Human Services. She stifled a yawn, then quickly checked her appearance.

Any moment he would stroll through the door, a model of public service efficiency, oblivious to the fact that his über efficient PA had unwittingly tripped the switch on a time bomb.

Beijing

Jiang Xiu paused as he studied his handiwork. The early morning ritual sustained him, the effortless grace of the brushstroke offering respite from the stresses of leadership.

He visualised the next stroke, dipped his brush in the oily liquid and gently tapped off the excess ink.

As he began an elegant curve his hand slipped, the brush sullying the Xuan paper. His discipline had deserted him. He had not been able to empty his mind of its burdens. Jiang put the brush down and stepped back to consider the error.

It was a small mistake, but it destroyed the whole work. The expensive paper could not be retrieved. It was a tiny augury of the giant blunder China was about to make.

Suddenly, he was resolved. He would confront the president once more with vigour and sound argument, seeking to dissuade him from pursuing his present course of action in the South China Sea. He ardently believed in the legitimacy of China's claims there. All he was asking for was time: taking a slower path to the same end.

It would be dangerous. Recently their relationship had soured. Though few words had been fired in anger, Jiang sensed that Meng Dada was far from pleased at being challenged.

He would take the risk, inspired by the Mao quote he had just besmirched.

'Firstly, do not fear hardship, and secondly, do not fear death.'

'No one lectures me, Mr Jiang. No one.'

President Meng spat the words at his propaganda minister. The two men stood facing each other, neither flinching.

Jiang had gambled, he knew that. His words had not been designed to provoke the president, but he could not hide his true feelings about the perilous course China was taking.

He believed it was not a matter of if but when America retaliated. Despite China's military advances, Jiang argued it was no match for the most powerful military ever assembled. He feared overreaching was about to undo all their achievements.

'Mr President, I am not lecturing you. I am hoping you will see merit in my argument. I only seek to offer you my counsel in order to avoid a ruinous confrontation. We know America is trying to build an international flotilla to block our path to the islands.'

'And we know it is failing. Not even its lapdog Australia will blindly follow it anymore.'

Jiang did not back off.

'Then it will act alone. All the signs point to military action.'

The president's face was twisted with anger and contempt.

'If it does, we will confront it with our navy. Again. And it will flee. Again.'

Jiang shook his head.

'On the high sea our aircraft carrier will be exposed for what it is, a training ship not ready for battle.'

Jiang's tone turned to pleading as he searched his leader's face for some hint of understanding.

'Mr President, all I am asking is that we move more slowly and with less aggression.'

Suddenly the president reached out and gripped his shoulder, hard. Jiang held his gaze as Meng strengthened his hold.

'I decide when this nation moves and, when I do, stenographers like you take notes on the history. You make records in ink, I write with my deeds.'

Jiang drew in the foul air of the president's breath, stale from the gold-tipped Huang He Lou cigarettes he devoured. He could see spittle on Meng's chin, and a vein protruding in his temple testified to his rage. The leader cut a much finer figure from a distance.

Just as suddenly, Meng relaxed his hand, patted Jiang on the cheek, smiled and returned to his desk, taking his seat before looking back at his comrade.

'Mr Jiang, I will think about what you have said. Perhaps I shall talk it through with others, with the premier and ministers. Yes, I should do that, test your assertions and your views.'

Meng made a note, as if resolved that this was the right course.

'Thank you for your honesty, my friend. Your value to the homeland cannot be overstated. Now I should prepare for my next meeting and you should go and continue your fine work.'

Jiang nodded then walked purposefully from the room.

Perhaps his efforts to persuade the other members of the standing committee would not have been in vain. Perhaps when Meng talked to them, they would no longer be the sycophants they had lately become, interested only in reinforcing Meng's belief in his infallibility.

Alone in his office, the president rubbed his hands over his cheeks, gently massaging his skin. He picked up the phone and issued an instruction.

Canberra

The prime minister's heart was pounding, her lungs burning, her body screaming for her to stop. So she pushed harder. Elizabeth Scott's Olympian frame could handle this kind of pain.

What tormented her was the pain she couldn't control.

She had stared down the leader of the free world, rejecting the US president's plea for Australia to embrace America's Asian escapade. Scott hadn't said no, but she hadn't signed up either, and while she hoped there was time for compromise, she feared there wasn't.

Scott tried to convince herself that asking Asta to delay had been reasonable, that the risk for her nation was immense. But the nagging truth was that she was being blackmailed by Beijing.

She was trapped between the hammer of the United States and the anvil of China.

As she turned towards the heights of Red Hill, the laboured breathing of her trailing security detail drew a rare grin.

Each of her close personal protection team had been ordered into special training. But they would never be fit enough to keep pace, as every morning Scott was motivated by her own yardstick: to outrun her 'wardens'. Because the prime minister felt she was a prisoner.

Every minute of every day she was monitored, watched, followed. Her home was a compound behind high walls and CCTV. A camera was trained on her desk at parliament. And when she ventured outdoors, her AFP detail swung in behind her. Public events were a three-ring circus: cameras recording every action, boom microphones snaring every word.

On the rare occasions she met with friends at a restaurant, security perched nearby and social media published every mouthful.

Then there was the mind cage. From the moment she was sworn in as Australia's twenty-eighth prime minister, she'd been urged to curb her small-l worldview to avoid alienating the dinosaurs who believed the Liberal Party still belonged to them. Like an actor, she was tutored to remember lines crafted by B-grade scriptwriters who claimed they were in tune with 'the punters'. In truth, their 'instincts' were honed by focus groups and professional pollsters.

More than once, Elizabeth Scott had felt she was playing the lead in Canberra's version of *The Truman Show*.

As Scott neared the summit of Red Hill she paused at a lookout to check on the progress of her detail. Fifty metres in arrears. A new record. She smiled and turned back to the view.

The rising sun lit the stainless-steel flagpole over Parliament House and shimmered across the lake. Mount Ainslie rose eucalypt green in the distance.

The capital lay before her: glorious, enticing, intriguing. Deadly.

It was 9pm, the fag end of another dismal day. Curled up on a lounge in her suite, Scott was leafing through a file, registering the tedium of another agricultural dispute, this one over sugar. The protectionists in the Coalition were seeking a retreat to the past. Again.

Her working day had begun with a media grilling over the most recent poll to show her government heading for oblivion, the latest in a very long line.

She'd delivered the rote defences, but she didn't believe them herself. If things didn't improve, she would lead the Coalition to an epic defeat; that is, if her colleagues didn't dump her first.

Her mobile pinged with an unfamiliar pulse, someone sending a self-destructing message. She grabbed the phone, touched the message and five orange bars appeared.

It was a welcome invitation.

Hi.
I know you're in the building.
Need to talk. Urgently.
Shake the cops.
And let's pray for your soul together. At 9.30.

Scott barely paused before replying.

I'll be there.

She packed away the file and checked the time. A few minutes to freshen up.
Her private bathroom was an oasis of tiny luxuries. The PM brushed her
hair and touched up her makeup. Leaning into the mirror, she thought the
lines around her eyes and on her forehead were getting deeper. This job was
ageing her. She sprayed a hint of Joy on her neck.

Scott walked briskly from her suite. As she passed the security post, the
lone guard sprang to his feet.

'Prime Minister, are you going somewhere?'

'To stretch my legs,' she said, motioning for him to sit. 'Do me a favour,
don't rat on me to the AFP.'

'Well, PM, if anything happens … it's my job.'

She patted his hand reassuringly.

'I'm taking a short stroll inside the most secure building in Australia.
There are police with automatic weapons outside. I'll be fine. Twenty
minutes.'

'Okay ma'am, but please, no more than that.'

She turned left and walked along the ministerial wing's blue carpet then
swung right into a wide corridor, her high heels echoing on timber. She
pressed the button on a lift door near the Senate entrance, then entered
and hit 'M'. The doors opened to one of parliament's secret nooks: the
Meditation Room, a small multi-faith chapel sandwiched between the first
and second floors. Few people knew its location. Even fewer went there to
pray.

Scott stepped out to softened lights and a tall, handsome, grinning figure.

Martin Toohey bowed mockingly. 'Prime Minister, my party thanks
you. Keep up this excellent work and Catriona Bailey will be rolling her
wheelchair over your body in a year.'

'Thank you, Martin. Screwing up is now part of the incoming
government brief. We found your template.'

Toohey's laughter was soothing.

'I deserved that,' he said. 'Come sit with me for a minute.'

He took her arm as they stepped into a small booth and sat on a bench.
Toohey nodded towards a tiny glass plaque on a window ledge, inscribed
with an arrow pointing north-west.

'If you think Allah might help, Mecca is that way.'

Scott shrugged. 'High Church Anglican. Anyway, my faith has been shaken by experience.' She looked searchingly at Toohey. 'How's yours?'

'My faith was battered by the job, but it survived. Unlike my marriage.'

'I'm sorry about that.'

'Don't be. It's better for both of us, and happily Mum didn't live to see her eldest son facing divorce. How's Brian?'

Scott leaned back against the wall and looked at the ceiling.

'Distant. The media might think it's amusing to dub someone Denis Thatcher, but it gets tired very fast. Let's face it, we haven't been close for ages. He rarely comes to Canberra and when I'm not here I'm on the road.'

Toohey placed his hand on Scott's, sending a tingle up her arm. This simple act of intimacy brought a lump to her throat.

'Marty ...' She paused to compose herself. 'I don't know who to trust. I've lost my confidence and that frightens me.'

Toohey searched her face, as if looking for the scars that came with the office.

'Well, I'm one of the few people who can honestly say I know the feeling.'

He looked away and when he caught her gaze again there was urgency in his eyes.

'That's why I came. You're in more trouble than you think. Your greatest threat isn't even in your party.'

Scott frowned. 'What do you mean?'

'You said you didn't trust anyone. Does that include Jack Webster?'

'Well, no ... yes ... I mean I did trust him. Without question. But recently I've begun to worry about his advice. He's pushing hard on something, and that disturbs me.'

'Let me guess. He wants you to join a Yank-led pissing contest with the Chinese. Just like he did with me.'

'Martin, you know that I can't speak about what goes on in the NSC.'

'Well then, let's deal with the known knowns. Webster's speech at the Press Club wasn't just about shoring up his feminist credentials. That guy's running for office. There's only one job he wants, Elizabeth ... yours.'

Canberra

Benny Hadid's right foot was tapping like a madman's as he booted up his PC. It was just after 7am and the Australian National Audit Office was creaking to life.

For the past week he'd barely slept and the sharp angles of his face were accentuated by a darkness beneath his eyes. The pitch of the pressure had risen as he'd applied the finishing touches to his secret dossier. It was his best work and it was bulletproof. After a final polish, he would present it to the auditor-general, with whom he'd requested a meeting. The findings could not be ignored and would set wheels in motion that would run down Jack Webster.

He mentally ticked off the work that still had to be done. The audit of the $8.5 billion Air Warfare Destroyer program had been immense and complex. Hadid had forensically pieced together a string of suspicious transactions. He'd chased down every dollar, checked and rechecked critical data entries and calibrated the language of his report to reflect the seriousness of the key findings.

The Audit Office would red flag the project, the police would be called and it would unleash a political shitstorm.

Hadid had hidden the report deep in the Audit Office mainframe. He had also sent a copy to CDC2, one of the three Commonwealth data centres located around Canberra. The centres were giant hubs that collected the trillions of gigabytes sent daily through the 882-kilometre 'dark fibre' network known as ICON. The Auditor-General's Office had been an early signatory to the Intra-government Communications Network, which now had links to nearly ninety agencies, including key defence and intelligence bureaus.

Hadid contemplated another coffee as he opened the report's folder. He sped through some preliminary remarks, scribbled a few notes on a pad then jumped to the main game: 'Air Warfare Destroyer Program. Overall Conclusions.'

His body skipped a beat and his world began to collapse.

His mouth parted in silent horror as he absorbed what was before him. Someone, something, had been in the file, changing and deleting large sections of it.

'Jesus.' He rubbed his eyes, blinking hard, grabbing at the mouse, scrolling down the page, looking for some sign of forced entry. None.

He backtracked, saved the file to the shared drive, then reopened it. The same. His right hand trembled as he searched for the contents page. Deleted. The Introduction. Deleted. Recommendations. Deleted.

Two years of his life. Deleted.

He retraced his steps from yesterday. He'd worked on the file till 7pm, then headed home for a meal and an early night. Then till now: twelve hours. He scrolled through the file's properties, searching for a clue. Nothing. Then he went back to the Word document, reading carefully to try to get a handle on exactly how much had been changed.

'Morning, Benny.' A colleague had arrived at his workstation next door. 'Um, mate, are you all right?'

Hadid lowered his head. 'No'.

The results were horrendous. Months of painstaking work, sifting through layer upon layer of Defence bullshit, checking every dollar, every balance sheet entry, and it had all been deleted or substantially amended.

The audit into one of the most expensive procurements in the history of the Commonwealth was now useless and the criminal's footprints had been erased.

But Benny Hadid wasn't the only officer in the Auditor-General's Department with a problem and his wasn't the only Commonwealth agency under attack. News was filtering in of other agencies that had lost reams of work. Back-up files had been deleted too, and teams of technicians were scrambling to limit the damage.

Hadid slowly shook his head as he listened to the auditor-general briefing the executive team on the fallout from the cyber-attack. The agency's IT manager had confirmed that key files had been destroyed or severely damaged, internal back-up systems had been erased and the fallback – the Canberra Data Centre computers – had been infected. Hundreds of thousands of hours of irreplaceable work was gone for good.

That other public servants had also lost precious work was of little comfort to Hadid. He was convinced the entire attack had been aimed at him.

He felt the buzz of his mobile phone, pulling it from his pocket as the screen lit up.

Walk to your desk. Answer the landline.

There was no caller ID.

He did as instructed, weaving through the office, the ring of his phone getting louder as he neared his desk. Suspiciously, he scanned the room, but he was alone.

He eyed the receiver for a few seconds. Finally he reached down to pick it up. 'Hello?'

Silence. Nothing but the faint hum of the air conditioning.

Then a calm voice spoke.

'Walk away from the AWD audit, Mr Hadid. Walk away and don't look back.'

Canberra

'Let there be no doubt. This is one of the most significant cyber-attacks in the history of the Commonwealth.'

Jack Webster towered over the lectern in the theatrette on the bottom floor of R1, the epicentre of the Russell Offices Defence complex.

'We are still assessing the damage, but it's clear that this attack has compromised Centrelink's database. As you would be aware, the agency holds highly sensitive personal and financial details of many Australians.'

The Australian's defence correspondent fired a question.

'Can you tell us how many Centrelink files are involved?'

'I'm sure we can get you all the numbers, but do the maths. From memory, there are two and a half million aged pensioners and almost a million people on Newstart and Youth Allowance ...'

Five kilometres away, Harry Dunkley took an air swing at the television screen. He was angry, but not surprised.

'This is total bullshit.'

Jack Webster was sounding like the pompous knight that he was, detailing the cyber-attack that had hit almost every Commonwealth agency, including Defence.

He had been sent out by a weak defence minister to try to explain the magnitude of the attack and minimise damage to the government.

Dunkley didn't buy it for a moment. Webster had orchestrated and was ramping up the attack for his own political ends. Dunkley had seen this shell game before and that time he'd been the dupe. Now he watched helplessly as history seemed to be repeating itself.

'Yes, it bears the hallmarks of a state-sponsored attack.' Webster's jaw was set like an Easter Island statue as half a dozen reporters vied for the follow-up.

'CDF, the Chinese apparently stole millions of files in their recent cyber-attack on the US government. Did this attack come from China?'

'It's a good question. I don't have a precise answer for you yet. What I can tell you is that we will find out and pursue whoever committed this act of war.'

'War?' the questioner shot back.

'What would you call it? Millions of dollars worth of damage has been done, sensitive information stolen. An attack on a nation, be it through conventional weaponry or cyber-warriors is an act of war, at least in my eyes.'

The defence chief leafed through a sheaf of papers before continuing.

'As you know,' Webster intoned, his words carefully chosen for the television audience, 'I have long pleaded for more investment in cyber-security. There are many agencies using the ICON network that don't encrypt their files. Perhaps more than half. That is unacceptable.'

The ABC's reporter interjected.

'Are you criticising the government, Sir Jack?'

'That is your commentary, not mine. Now, ladies and gentlemen, if you'll excuse me I have a meeting to attend and the prime minister does not like to be kept waiting.'

Dunkley slapped his right fist into his open left hand.

'Trevor, this is laughable. Webster's about as credible as a street market hawker. I can't believe he's getting away with it. Again. We can't let him—'

'Harry, for fuck's sake, shut up. Please.'

Slumped on a lounge chair, Trevor Harris raised his hands in supplication. An hour earlier he'd been told of Benny Hadid's admission to a private mental health facility. Details were sketchy, but Harris believed the breakdown was linked to his dealings with Dunkley.

'Come on, Trev, you don't buy that China cyber-bullshit – do you?'

Harris was in no mood for a Dunkley lecture. The former journalist had reverted to type: everything revolved around him. The chase, the story, the scoop – no matter how much collateral damage he caused.

Hadid was just another body on the pile.

'Harry, for once, just once, think of someone other than yourself. Seriously, mate, Benny's been admitted to a psych ward. You ... me ... we helped to push him over the edge.'

Dunkley felt a twinge of remorse, but rallied.

'C'mon, that's unfair. Benny was already chasing Webster and wanted him to answer for his crimes just as much as we do.'

'No, Harry. As *you* do. You pushed Benny, just as you're now pushing me. Your return draws a target on everyone you meet.'

Harris stood and took a few paces before turning to face Dunkley.

'Mate, you leave a trail of destruction and broken relationships every time you get involved with Jack Webster. Look at the tally. You asked

Kimberley Gordon for help; she gets murdered. You enlisted your former girlfriend and she gets death threats. Bruce Paxton lost his seat and now Benny Hadid is in the nuthouse.'

The torment was written on Harris's face as he dropped his head into his hands.

'And me.' His voice quavered as he spoke. 'Since I helped you my life has collapsed. I'm entombed in this fetid little hole. I know they're hunting me. I defend myself as best I can, barricade the doors, spend my days peering through the curtains.'

When Harris looked up, his eyes were moist.

'Harry Dunkley, you are a dangerous friend.'

They fell into silence as Dunkley looked around at the clutter, the piles of books and unwashed dishes, the flotsam and jetsam of a once vibrant life. When he spoke it was with quiet resolve.

'Webster started this war, not me. There were no conscripts on our side; we were all volunteers. Webster used me. And he used you too, right down to you telling them where to find Kimberley on the night she was murdered. That was why you reached out to me. Remember? It was your call to help.'

Dunkley stood and grabbed Harris by the shoulders.

'If we don't fight this guy, we lose. There is only one way for this to end. For you to escape this tomb and for me to get my life back. We either get this megalomaniac or we die trying. We owe it to Benny Hadid, we owe it to Kimberley Gordon, and we owe it to ourselves.'

Harris met Dunkley's gaze, slowly shook his head and sighed.

'If we're going to do this, we'll do it properly. Get that bloody phone of yours.'

Qingdao Port, China

'Sailor take warning,' the rear admiral muttered as he scanned the livid red sky.

Yu Heng had picked up the old English naval lore while studying at the British Joint Services Command and Staff College in London.

The admiral stood on the open deck above the bridge of the *Liaoning*, gripped the rail with both hands and breathed in the bustle as the port came to life.

Like so much of the new China, the naval base, on the south side of the Shandong Peninsula, had grown rapidly. In the space of a year, three and a half thousand people from six villages had been relocated to make way for the North Sea Fleet, which patrolled the waters surrounding Japan and the Korean Peninsula. The base was also the home port of the *Liaoning*, the nation's only aircraft carrier, strategically located less than two thousand kilometres from the US overseas naval base in Yokosuka, Japan.

Even from his vantage point, Yu could see only a fraction of the sprawling base which ran from the waterfront to mountains hollowed out to house missiles, chemicals and armouries.

The admiral shook his head. 'Too much, too fast.'

Yu was a proud member of the Communist Party, but had begun to question the wisdom of his leaders as he watched China's breakneck development. He dreaded his regular trips to Beijing where he could not find the sun in the smog-heavy sky and the stench was nauseating. The oriental beauty of the old city had been buried beneath gleaming Western-style glass-and-metal towers. And, as in the West, the streets were choked with traffic.

It was all a gilt facade that papered over the many blemishes that arose when ambition outran wisdom. As with the ship he commanded, looks were deceptive.

The *Liaoning* was conventionally powered by four 50,000-horsepower steam turbines that combined to push it along at a top speed of 32 knots over a range of 3800 nautical miles. It had a crew of 1960 and an air group of 626 who serviced twenty-four 'Flying Shark' warplanes. The carrier bristled with other weapons too: four air-defence missile systems, each with an 18-cell launcher, and a pair of ten-barrel, 30-millimetre cannons, both fed by dual ammunition boxes holding a combined one thousand rounds.

The *Liaoning* was the hub in a mighty circle of steel designed to project China's power far into the blue waters of the Pacific. When it sailed it was flanked by four Luyang-class guided-missile destroyers and two 054A frigates. A Shang-class nuclear-powered attack submarine glided beneath it.

Yu commanded a carrier group that China had declared was a match for American naval might. Two years earlier, the communist power had boasted to the world that the *Liaoning* had forced the retreat of the USS *George Washington* in the Taiwan Strait.

But the admiral knew that it was a public relations stunt. His group could not threaten the Americans. The trick had been to lure the enemy into a deadly bottleneck.

Once inside the Taiwan Strait there had been no room for the *George Washington* to manoeuvre and what it feared was not the *Liaoning* but the sophisticated array of area-denial weapons that lurked a hundred kilometres away on the Chinese mainland.

Weapons like the Dong-Feng 21D anti-ship ballistic missile. US intelligence dubbed it the 'carrier killer' and painted a disturbing picture of its capability to shift in flight while moving at hypersonic speed. It carried a conventional warhead large enough to destroy an aircraft carrier in one hit, and America had no defence against it.

That explained the *George Washington*'s retreat. The American president hadn't been prepared to risk the loss of a carrier strike group with all hands. That would have forced him to declare war on China, a war he couldn't hope to win without a massive loss of life.

The experienced sailor instinctively ran his eyes along the ship's deck, looking for any sign that something was amiss. He knew every line and every limitation of the *Liaoning*, which was why he was so troubled.

He had been commanded to sail the strike group deep into the South China Sea as a warning to the US and its lackeys that Beijing would repel any move to test the twelve-nautical-mile exclusion zone around the Nansha Islands. His superiors were gambling that the Americans would rattle sabres but would not fight.

Yu reached into his pocket, pulled out a packet of Zhonghua cigarettes and lit one with a deft flick of the Zippo lighter he had bought on a trip to Washington. He inhaled deeply and blew a long line of smoke into the still morning air.

The light on the clouds was fading from red to pink as the sun rose, but the warning had been writ large and he would heed it.

This time the Americans would be ready. He could feel it. They were wounded and angry and that made them dangerous. This time they would meet on blue water where all the players in this deadly game knew his group was no match for even a fraction of the US Pacific Fleet.

He took another long draw on his cigarette.

Once the only reason for charting the Nansha Islands had been to warn sailors to avoid their dangerous shoals. They were much more dangerous now.

The admiral knew the islands had many names. The Americans called them the Spratlys. Another name for the largest island was 'Storm'.

It was apt. A tempest was brewing and Yu was sailing right into it.

Canberra

It was a gleaming billion-dollar shrine to the truth that Big Brother was actually watching you. Born in an era when fear was driving a national security boom, the ASIO headquarters rose six levels to form a sleek crescent on the edge of the Russell Offices Defence complex.

It was the heart of Australia's domestic spy network. More than two thousand carefully chosen and highly trained agents fed their intelligence into this building to be analysed, dissected and acted upon.

For a spy movie junkie like Brendan Ryan, this was Shangri-la. The Labor MP felt a schoolboy's excitement as his ComCar pulled up in front of the brand new edifice. Despite massive cost overruns – and rumours it had been compromised by the Chinese – Ryan had ensured that Labor's support for this state-of-the-art spy headquarters never wavered.

Ryan was asked for photo identification before receiving a lanyard holding a temporary pass, then a blue-tagged key for a locker in which to store his mobile phone.

'And your Fitbit, if you have one, please,' the guard added.

Ryan snorted; the idea of wearing any kind of device designed for a fitness regime was abhorrent to him. As was the idea of fitness.

It turned out to be just the first layer of security. Ryan followed a junior officer to a glass door where she swiped her pass then held her thumb to a wall-mounted scanner. The door slid slowly open and they entered a transparent holding pen. The officer turned to Ryan as the door closed.

'Welcome to the Tiger Trap. The far door can't open until the one behind us closes and I swipe and have my thumbprint checked once more.'

Emerging into a long corridor they moved to a bank of lifts where the young spy swiped her pass again.

Exiting the lift, Ryan noted that a vast atrium stood at the centre of the building, anchored by a ground-floor cafe. An array of security cameras was set into the ceiling, monitoring his every movement.

The officer led him to a heavy metal-set door designed to withstand a bomb blast. It opened to a boardroom that looked across Lake Burley Griffin to the High Court and Parliament House.

'Magnificent, isn't it?' Richard Dalton, Ryan's long-time friend and director-general of this vast palace of intelligence, stepped forward to shake his hand.

'It is, Richard,' Ryan agreed. 'It's great to know you're keeping an eye on us.'

The two men pulled up chairs facing the window, exchanging small talk on the current list of security concerns. The rise of homegrown terrorism was number one.

Suddenly Dalton's demeanour changed and he swung around in his chair so that he was facing Ryan.

'Brendan, I called you here for a reason.'

His shoulders slumped as he seemed to shrink into his chair.

'What I am about to tell you I have confided to no one else. You are never to breathe a word unless something happens to me.'

'Like what?' Ryan was bemused by the abrupt turn in the conversation.

Dalton's face was anguished and he looked searchingly at Ryan, as if trying to impress upon him the gravity of his words.

'If I should die. Unexpectedly.'

'Mate, you're freaking me out. It's not like you to play stupid games. What are you talking about?'

'I'm talking about the leader of the Australian end of our little project. Air Chief Marshal Sir Jack Webster.'

Dalton's voice dropped as if he feared being overheard even in this most secure point of a secure fortress.

'Forty years ago, good men on both sides of the Pacific lost faith in the political class to look beyond the next headline. These men of vision, drawn from intelligence, the military – and rare political figures, like you – foresaw an ever more dangerous world. So they forged the Alliance to ensure the long-term security of both nations.'

The ASIO head paused as if trying to convince himself of the righteousness of his extramural cause.

'Its aim was to guide our democracies, not usurp them.'

He rapped the table to emphasise the argument.

'We have only acted … *should* only act … to correct the errors of politicians who are driven by the winds of the day. Very rarely we have acted to remove those, like Bailey and Paxton, who posed a direct threat to our security.'

Ryan was confused and wanted Dalton to end the speech and get to the point.

'And Richard, that is what we have done. In hindsight, Paxton wasn't in the clutches of the Chinese but he might as well have been the way he slashed the defence budget. Bailey is still a clear and present threat to national security. So far, the mad fucking witch has proved impossible to drown. But I haven't given up hope.'

Dalton shook his head, his voice now a whisper.

'She is far more dangerous than you know. When she was prime minister she managed to compromise the entire defence and intelligence computer network. It was shovelling out information to the Chinese for about three months before we discovered the wormhole and shut it.'

Ryan was stunned.

'Jesus, Richard, why are you only telling me this now?'

'Webster. When he discovered the breach he was petrified Washington would cut off our access to Five Eyes. We grilled the poor bastard responsible, Matthew Whelan from the signals directorate. There were just four people in that room: Whelan, Webster, David Joyce from DFAT. And me.'

Ryan noticed a tremor in the intelligence chief's right hand as it rested on the table.

'Webster's parting words are carved in my memory: "No one knows about this, ever."'

The spymaster shifted uneasily.

'Brendan, he meant it. Three months later Whelan died from a heart attack, a fitness freak in his forties who dropped dead during a gentle jog. The toxicology report from the autopsy disappeared. Six months later Joyce died in a car accident.'

Ryan gazed out at the familiar and tranquil vista of the national capital, wondering if the stress of work was pushing Dalton over the edge. His extraordinary tale could not be true.

'You think Webster killed them? Come on, this is Canberra, not Moscow.'

Ryan touched his friend's arm, trying to reassure him.

'I'm certain he did.' Dalton was unmoved. 'There were four men in that meeting and two are dead. And they are not the only ones, Brendan. Do you remember the security analyst who was murdered in Telopea Park some years back?'

'Yes, Kimberley Gordon. You told me the Chinese killed her. That's what I told her mate Harry Dunkley.'

'It wasn't Beijing, it was Webster.' Dalton was shaking his head. 'He has an acolyte in ASIS. Charles Dancer. Acts as his garbage collector and enforcer. The night Gordon was murdered, the ASD sent a message telling Dancer exactly where to find her.'

The spy chief put his hand inside his suit jacket and pulled out a thumb drive.

'It's all on this.'

He placed the USB on the table, then pushed it towards Ryan.

'It was pulled from the gut of a Chinese defector who drowned in the lake. He'd downloaded a trove of information which he wanted to use to barter with the Americans for asylum. That's how we discovered the wormhole.'

Ryan picked up the USB and rolled it in his fingers as Dalton continued.

'But I have added many more chapters to it. Everything I've gathered on Webster, using all the resources at my disposal. Like his hero, George Patton, Webster has an unshakeable sense of destiny. He believes he was ordained to rule, so killing those who threaten him isn't just necessary, it's moral.'

Dalton pointed at the memory stick in Ryan's hand.

'What you hold would destroy him in an afternoon.'

'What do you want me to do with it?'

'Keep it. And if I die … if I get hit by a fucking meteor … then you'll know that Jack Webster's murdered me. If that happens, I want you to kill him with that.'

Ryan placed the USB back on the table, eyeing it as if it were a nuclear fuel rod.

'This is way over my pay grade. Why give it to me?'

'Because you are the only one left I can trust.'

Ryan weighed up the words of his friend. He was still deeply sceptical, and even if it was true, the last thing he wanted was to be dragged into a power game where people got killed.

He reluctantly picked up the USB, put it in his pocket and stood to leave.

Dalton rose with him.

'By the way, my friend, how safe do you feel?'

Canberra

The codebreaker had a plan.

For the past few hours Trevor Harris had cleared the clutter from his office as a way of cleansing his mind. Now, he opened a folder of newspaper clippings and pulled out a glowing *Good Weekend* profile of Jack Webster, written after his Press Club address. In it, the defence chief had spoken of his admiration for General George Patton and revealed that his most prized possession was the US war hero's 1909 Patek Philippe pocket watch.

A simple search showed that the timepiece had been sold a month earlier by Heritage Auctions in New York. Another search found the auction house's website. It was as Harris had suspected: you needed to create an account to purchase items online.

'Bingo!'

Harris had prepared well. He'd loaded message-encrypting software onto Harry Dunkley's phone then asked him to contact Martin Toohey to check if the former prime minister had ever received an email from Sir Jack's private address.

Dunkley had delivered. Harris had scribbled the address across the statesmanlike full-page shot of Webster that formed the cover of the *Good Weekend*: airwebster@gmail.com.

He scrolled through icons on the first of his pair of iMacs, clicking on 'John the Ripper Pro'. The program cracked passwords with brute force, running a super-fast exhaustive search using every combination of letters, symbols and numbers.

If Harris had to find both a username and password the search could take months. But he was confident Webster's email address would double as his username, because that's what ninety per cent of people did. That left the password. And Harris knew that humans were creatures of habit.

As he keyed in instructions to 'John the Ripper Pro', he was reminded of the advice he'd often given budding government hackers.

'Everyone hates having to remember multiple passwords and that laziness is our best friend,' he would tell them. 'The place to start is the target's partner's, child's or pet's name, followed by a zero or one, because most systems demand a numerical component. If that fails, then try – and I am not kidding – 1234 or 123456 and so on, depending on the length of the password required by the site administrator.'

Then he'd add the kicker: 'You'd be shocked by the number of senior public servants who simply use "password".'

Harris reckoned he already had the basis of Webster's password: George Patton. But the defence chief would have been repeatedly warned that he needed to reinforce its security by adding embellishments. The simplest trick was to swap a letter for a number or symbol: a '3' for 'E', '@' for 'a', and so on.

The former analyst keyed in a series of options then set his brute force program running. He wanted the grunt of one computer devoted to that single task, so he turned to the other iMac for the hunt that would require his guile and finesse.

Again, the expert codebreaker had an advantage. He had repeatedly raged about the Commonwealth's lax cyber-security. One of his pet hates was ICON. The Intra-government Communications Network had been set up in 1991 when the Department of Foreign Affairs ran a cable between its old headquarters in the John Gorton Building and its new premises in York Park, in order to connect its teletype machines. From small beginnings in what now seemed an absurdly innocent age, it had grown into a network that provided 'secure communications' across four hundred buildings in the capital.

'And the security on it is shit,' Harris mumbled as his fingers stabbed at his keyboard.

There were more than a thousand manholes around Canberra where ICON's cables were protected only by a plastic cover secured with a padlock. Telstra maintenance crews routinely used bolt-cutters instead of keys to open them. Then they would fit a new lock to cover their laziness. Harris had pictures of sites littered with the discarded brass locks.

If the physical security was bad, the virtual security was worse. A Finance Department audit had shown that most agencies failed to encrypt the information transmitted on ICON's fibres. Even a novice hacker could break in.

Trevor Harris was no novice. Today he was going to put the cracks in the system to the test.

The Commonwealth's problem was gateways: there were corridors from one agency to the next and ICON left the front door wide open. Once inside, Harris was sure he could plot a pathway to the nation's most secure files.

He walked easily through the front door then set his course for the weakest link.

Harris was aware that those who design security systems often fail because they think of them as individual units rather than one part of a larger entity, like cells in a human body. Millions of dollars were poured into forging cyber-shields for sensitive sites. But putting steel-cap boots on your feet matters little if your body can be infected by a paper cut to your hand.

Within minutes the Bureau of Meteorology site lay open. Valuable intellectual property that could have been sold to foreign governments lay within easy reach, but this was just a way station on Harris's journey.

As weather forecasts are vital in military operations, he knew there would be a pathway to the Defence complex at Russell Hill. And the people in need of this specialised weather data? The commanding officers. Child's play, thought Harris.

He quickly found the one commander he was looking for: 'WebsterJ'.

'Follow the yellow brick road.' Harris smiled as the computer next to him pinged.

The 3DR SOLO Smart Drone hovered above the oval, the high-pitched whirr of its four props barely audible.

The operative monitored its flight path through a smartphone connected to the remote console. A hundred metres into the sky, the GoPro camera add-on was transmitting crisp high-resolution images of the nearby townhouse.

The drone had cost $1800 online, but attached to its small chassis were tens of thousands of dollars worth of sophisticated circuitry, developed after tens of millions had been ploughed into R&D.

It was mid-afternoon and the oval on the edge of Yarralumla Primary was near empty. A couple was wrestling with an errant pup and a few schoolchildren had wandered towards the operative, fascinated. He smiled politely, then ignored them.

The target had demanded specialist skills and equipment. The brief said he was a pro, and his behaviour proved it. His online connections were scant and random. When he was on the web, he used the strongest armour. And when he went offline, he disconnected every cable.

The operative had never seen a better set of defences. But nothing was impregnable.

There was one routine. Each day the target walked to the nearby shopping centre to pick up basics: milk, bread, newspapers. The round trip took fifteen minutes. It had been more than enough time.

The front-door lock had been picked in a moment and the back-to-base security system easily disabled.

The operative had walked through the mess to the two iMacs in an office facing the street. It had taken him barely a minute to prise open the power board, set his device and close it. He'd reset the security system and left. He'd checked his watch: less than five minutes.

In that short time he'd established a link that used a covert channel of radio waves. It would be activated when the computers were turned on, irrespective of whether they were connected to the internet.

It was the US National Security Agency that had found a way to crack 'air gapped' networks. Code-named *Quantum*, the technology was shared with only the most trusted of allies. Australia was one.

Now, as the afternoon sun shimmered on the nearby lake, the drone picked up a strong pulse. The target was active. The operative touched an icon on his smartphone. Five seconds later he began transmitting to base.

The routine of the day was punctured when the technician's monitor flashed amber alert. The target was online and trawling. Expertly, she linked to *Quantum* which was already pumping out bytes of data.

The target had broken into a remote system and was downloading documents at breakneck speed. She was peering over his shoulder, impressed that he'd managed to gain access through a maze of connections.

The computer spat out the entry point: ICON. It jumped to the Bureau of Meteorology then moved up the chain: Russell Defence Weather System; Defence Internal; Secure Network; Commanders.

The targeted profile flashed on her screen.

She grabbed her phone and punched a name on speed dial.

'Sir, we have a serious problem.'

The iMac motors were in overdrive, and every second on the inside raised the risk of being caught. Trevor Harris moved with the calm precision of a practised expert: quick, clean, no fingerprints.

He had stalked many dangerous prey in his career – but this one was deadly.

Once he'd reached Jack Webster's profile, cracking his security wall had been ridiculously easy. The username was public service boilerplate. Harris's second iMac had unearthed the defence chief's auction house password: G3orgeP@tton4. It had been created two months earlier, so Harris had simply changed the last digit to '6'. He was in.

Then he tunnelled deeper, sifting through Webster's shared drives until he reached the prize: the desktop. Harris knew any gold would be stored on its hard drive.

Within seconds he was in and began downloading every document. A thin white line moved left to right across the top of his screen, marking off the precious seconds to completion as the files marched from Webster's world into the cyber-hacker's clutches.

All he needed was another five minutes.

'System breach. Shut down your computer.'

Charles Dancer's voice barked in Jack Webster's ear, jolting the defence chief from his perusal of an intelligence brief.

'Shut it down. Now!'

'Hang on.'

Webster strode to his desk with his phone in his left hand and tapped the keyboard with his right. His PC demanded his username and password before unfolding to the usual bland landscape of icons.

'I can't see anything wrong.'

'Doesn't matter. You've been compromised. Every second raises the threat.'

Webster moved the mouse, but the cursor didn't budge. He tapped the keyboard again.

'The screen's locked,' he told Dancer.

'Pull the plug. Quickly!'

The defence chief put down his phone and wrenched the screen to the right, scrambling to find the power cord. A tangle of cables disappeared down a hole at the back of his desk.

He tore the screen from its mooring and lifted it above his head before bringing it crashing down on the black box of the central processing unit. Metal twisted and glass showered across his desk.

The office of the most powerful military man in the land filled with smoke.

The connection was broken.

There were many possible reasons, but Harris feared he'd been seen. He immediately shut down his system and yanked the power board from the wall.

Only then did the codebreaker feel the stress of the past hour. He was drenched in sweat and his head was pounding.

Think. This man is deadly and he commands an army.

Harris had to assume that someone would come after the data. Or him. Or both. He was confident he'd left no fingerprints, but couldn't risk going online again.

The stolen documents had been backed up on a thumb drive and also sent to a secure cloud server. But his adversary was ruthless and skilled. No matter what happened, the data had to survive.

Harry Dunkley was right: they had not started this fight and they would only find peace when the warlord was defeated.

There is a way. An old pathway, but reliable. Hiding in plain sight.

Harris put the thumb drive in his pocket and stood up, stretching his back, trying to relieve the stress. A quick walk to the shops would be therapeutic, then back to work, sifting through files offline.

He'd call Dunkley if he found anything useful, but he knew from bitter experience that you had to pan a mountain of dirt to find an ounce of gold.

He stepped from his dark townhouse into a dazzling day.

Canberra

Harry Dunkley's phone shook. There was a note on the Cryptocat secure messaging system. Trevor Harris had scoffed when Dunkley told him Martin Toohey used Confide.

Need to talk. My place.

Harris's message was promising, but Dunkley was in Canberra's deep south having his car serviced.

He punched in a reply:

Give me an hour.

It was an easy drive from Canberra's outskirts and Dunkley followed an ACTION bus as he cruised the last few kilometres to Yarralumla, a smudge of smoke drifting to his west.

He veered off Adelaide Avenue towards Hopetoun Circuit, the bleached white walls of the Saudi Arabian embassy looming into view. He slowed as he approached a pair of speed bumps at the local school, then turned into Harris's street and a scene of pandemonium.

A pair of police cars, their lights flashing, cordoned off the street, one at either end of a hundred-metre strip. Three fire engines were parked in a ragged row, their tentacles in a tangle as they ran from nearby hydrants.

The townhouse was gutted, smoke stains vivid around windows cracked by heat. The roof had partially collapsed and its charred wooden rafters looked like broken black fingers clawing at the sky.

As Dunkley watched in horror, ambulance officers carried a black body bag to their vehicle.

A small crowd had gathered in the quiet street, their voices lowered in respect for the dead. Dunkley scanned the faces, but they were all unfamiliar. A surge of grief forced him to his knees.

A fireman who had been mopping up hurried over to him.

'Mate, are you okay? Was he a friend of yours?'

'Yes.' Dunkley nodded as he wiped his face with his hands.

'Sorry, mate,' he said. 'We did our best.'

'What happened?'

'Well, it's hard to say, there'll be an investigation. But – and I don't mean any offence – the place was filled with old newspapers and other rubbish. It was a fire trap. That's how accidents like this happen.'

Dunkley looked at the blackened townhouse.

'This was no accident.'

Northwest Pacific Basin

Frank W Vinson felt the cool, salty breeze wash over him from an opening in the ship's hull. He was exercising alone in the hangar-deck gym of the USS *George Washington*, just twelve feet above the waterline.

It had taken the rear admiral some time to gain confidence on the Woodway Curve treadmill, but he could now sustain a cracking pace. He was in the groove and this was his meditation. A punishing fitness regime had been the commander's salvation following the humiliating retreat of his carrier strike group in the Taiwan Strait.

Congress and the press had demanded a scapegoat. He'd been hauled before the House Committee on Armed Services and all but labelled a coward.

Despite being cleared of misconduct, Vinson was damaged goods and his health had deteriorated.

'Get fit,' a naval doctor had urged him. 'You need to do something that you can control. The fitter you are, the better you'll be able to cope with the pressure.'

So Vinson had promised himself two things: he'd get in the best shape of his life, and he'd never retreat again.

He'd resisted offers of a quiet desk job in DC. This sailor would not fade away.

Besides, atonement might lie over the horizon that he was running to catch. His orders were to sail to the Philippines.

Canberra

His eyes were haunted, stone-grey blank instead of blue.

Martin Toohey sat down beside Harry Dunkley, who sat hunched over a cafe table, pondering a half-eaten slice of cake and the death of Trevor Harris.

They sat in silence until Toohey's espresso arrived, then Dunkley raised his head.

'We are in fucking danger.'

The former prime minister nodded. He was the ringleader of this circus and was again experiencing the heavy burden of leadership.

'What do you know, Harry? What did the police tell you?'

'Nothing,' Dunkley responded, his voice frail. 'I got a message from Harris, telling me to come to his home. That's it. In the space of an hour his house burned to the ground and he was dead.'

'But the police say there were no suspicious circumstances.'

'Yeah, and they also said Kimberley was the victim of a gay bashing. What do you reckon?'

Dunkley ticked off a list.

'Celia Mathieson, my former girlfriend, is frightened off. I'm threatened with a gun. You are punted from office. Benny Hadid is in an asylum.'

Toohey searched Dunkley's face as he contemplated his response. He could see how vulnerable the journalist had become and worried that he might return to the easy embrace of alcohol and despair.

'Say what you suspect is true, that Webster had your friend murdered. Do we run?' Toohey asked.

Dunkley stabbed the table with his fingers.

'We can't win. Webster commands an army, and is ruthless. He's beaten us to every turn and his henchmen found Trevor before he had a chance to tell us what he'd discovered.'

Toohey shrugged.

'You might be right. Maybe we can't win. You run back to Sydney and leave all this behind. But could you live with yourself? You could hide from Webster, but you couldn't hide from your conscience.'

He searched for a reaction, for a sign that his words were having an effect. There was nothing but the stricken stare of a man fast losing hope.

Beijing

She slept serenely, effortlessly. He nestled into her back, careful not to wake her. She had what he craved. Peace.

Jiang Xiu and his wife lived in House No 2 in the middle of Beijing. The ultra-exclusive enclave was heavily guarded, but the propaganda minister felt insecure. He had drunk several whiskies to calm his growing trepidation, and yet he lay restless and overtired.

China was forging ahead under President Meng, but the satisfaction that Jiang once felt had been extinguished. Where there once was elation, he now sweated fear.

He gently stroked his wife's hair, longing to share his concerns. But that would only frighten her.

The state can only be strong when it's in harmony with the will of the people, Meng often said. In truth, the president had marginalised and usurped the state. Such men arise in all cultures when they are allowed to. And such men are lethal.

Meng had marginalised Jiang too, despite his loyalty and selfless counsel. He had misread his leader and now feared he was dispensable.

Silently he stretched out under the covers, seeking a comfortable position. He needed to wake fresh and alert. In the weeks and months ahead, he would need all his strength.

'*Xiànzài jiù chuànzhou.*' The shrill demand to rise was accompanied by a sharp jab to the ribs, puncturing the grogginess of his mind.

Rough hands grabbed his shoulders, but he shook them off. They came back, rougher than before, and his body took another blow.

He panicked and threw out his right arm. A warm crease in the linen marked where his wife had been lying.

'Where is she?' His demand was met with a slap to the face.

He was hauled from the bed, hitting the tiled floor hard. Pain jarred his shoulder. A bright light shone in his face. He was yanked to his feet and his hands cuffed together.

'Where's my wife?' he screamed, but there was no reply, just the jab of cold steel on his neck as they dragged him from the room.

Canberra

Brendan Ryan could sniff the change of season in the crisp morning air. The national capital was edging towards winter and the temperatures were tumbling.

He hugged a cup of coffee as he took in his favourite view across the parliamentary precinct from the balcony of his comfortable unit in Deakin.

Today was set to be a tangle of high-level meetings, including a confidential briefing with intelligence chiefs. Being deputy chair of the Parliamentary Joint Committee on Intelligence and Security ensured his access to some of the nation's most important secrets.

Tomorrow, Australia would commemorate the centenary of the Gallipoli landings and Ryan had secured a privileged position for the service at the Australian War Memorial.

He was looking forward to the commemoration, the massive crowds with heads bowed in quiet reflection.

A whiff of something burning shook him from reflection.

'Oh shit ...' He'd forgotten the toast. He shuffled into the apartment and eased two blackened corpses from the toaster.

ABC NewsRadio was reciting the morning's headlines. '... survived by his wife, Judy, and three children ...'

Ryan froze. He pumped up the volume but it was too late, the host had moved on.

'Fuck!' His phone, where had he left it? He raced to the balcony but it wasn't there. He ran into his bedroom and found it on his bedside table. He picked it up, hands shaking, and rang his friend.

'You've called Richard Dalton. Leave a message.'

But it would be futile.

The nation's most powerful spy was dead.

Canberra

Elizabeth Scott gazed at the solemn mass of humanity spilling from the lighted parade ground into darkness.

It was one hundred years since the Gallipoli landing. Record crowds surrounded the Australian War Memorial and edged along Anzac Parade towards the lake.

On the one day that united the nation, the prime minister had never felt more alone, more captive to her precarious tenure, which had forced her to cancel her long-anticipated trip to Anzac Cove.

The VIP enclosure had been full for an hour, jammed with the nation's political and military elite. In the front row, Scott looked over a plinth in the Memorial's forecourt, with its words carved in stone: *Their name liveth for evermore.*

More than one hundred thousand hardy souls were expected at the service, each wanting to pay homage to the men and women who had made the ultimate sacrifice. In the pre-dawn, many held candles as their ancestors had held the hopes of a young nation.

What was it about Anzac Day that resonated so deeply, Scott wondered. Why did the nation pause with such reverence to recall distant blood-soaked beaches where young lives had been sacrificed for an uncaring imperial master?

When Scott was a teenager, this day had been mocked and some had even forecast its demise. But in recent times Australia's youth had embraced this piece of history with a fervour that stirred the prime minister's pride.

This resurrection had not been driven by authority. Instead, young people had gone in search of a foundation story that defined them and the country they loved.

What particularly touched Scott was that Anzac Day commemorated a defeat. There could be no triumphalism in such industrial-scale death.

What endured was hope, the notion that there was life and light beyond defeat, that it was not the end. Many of those who survived Gallipoli had been ordered to the killing fields of France, where their spirits never bowed amid the carnage.

Yet Scott had all but given up, and that shamed her.

A single tear slowly trickled down her cheek as a lone bugler played the haunting melody of the Last Post.

Canberra

The request for a meeting took Martin Toohey by surprise. Brendan Ryan had once been his close ally, but his loyalty had turned with the polls and the Labor numbers man had been instrumental in rolling him as prime minister. That was nearly two years ago and they had not spoken since.

'It wasn't personal, it was politics,' Ryan now explained in the opposition private anteroom in Parliament House.

'I was prime minister. You betrayed me. It doesn't get more personal than that.'

Ryan put out his hands, imploring Toohey to understand.

'I was trying to save the party. If you'd stayed on we would have been routed.'

'So you put a psychopath in the Lodge.'

'For a heartbeat, Martin, a couple of months. Anyway, we have more pressing issues.'

'Like what?'

'Jack Webster.'

Toohey didn't trust his former ally but he caught a hint of fear in his voice and noted the glistening of sweat on his upper lip.

'Why?'

'Because my life depends on it.'

*

For old times' sake, Martin Toohey wandered along the corridors of the House of Representatives. A place he'd last haunted in 2007 before he was elevated to the ministerial wing. He'd arrived an optimistic neophyte, determined to change the nation for the better. And he had done great things, but everything had been overshadowed by his fall, which left him broken and embittered. He paused outside the office he'd occupied when he was first elected and eyed the latest nameplate.

That dickhead.

He backtracked along the photo gallery of former speakers, their faces immortalised in black-and-white and, more recently, colour.

'Mr Toohey.' A voice called from the Clerk's Office. The former PM recognised the face, but couldn't place the name.

'Mate, how are you?' he replied enthusiastically.

'Good, Mr Toohey. I'm glad I caught you. I was just about to forward a letter to your Melbourne office. Here it is.'

The attendant handed over an Express Post envelope. It was addressed in neat blue ink.

Harry Dunkley
c/o Martin Toohey
Parliament House
Canberra ACT 2600

Toohey turned it over. There was no return address.

'Probably just a nuisance letter,' the attendant said. 'But you know what they say: "Neither snow nor rain …"'

Harry Dunkley turned up late and reluctant.

The death of Trevor Harris had sent him perilously close to tumbling back into the hole he'd crawled from just a few months earlier. The hope of progress had been crushed by another tragedy. Only Martin Toohey's energy and determination was keeping him in the game.

He entered the National Security College, built in the post-9/11 security boom, and found his way to the conference room.

He pushed open a heavy metal door and stumbled into a space that looked as if it had been conceived in the vivid imagination of a Bond movie scriptwriter. The oval-shaped room was fitted with honeycomb-relief patterned walls, and a massive elliptical light hovered like a flying saucer over a conference table that could seat thirty. A microphone rose in front of each high-backed white swivel chair.

There was a huge screen at one end and at the other a curtain divided off a section of the room.

Sitting at the head of the table was Toohey.

'Very theatrical, Martin. How did you score this?'

'Only cost the taxpayer twenty million bucks.' Toohey grinned. 'The dean is a mate. She claims spooks need somewhere to hold secure conferences. ASIO sweeps this place every month and the walls are electronically secure. In trade talk it is a Sensitive Compartmented Information Facility. In English that means we can talk here. Safely.'

Dunkley slumped down next to Toohey, suddenly exhausted.

'Not much to talk about, Martin.'

Toohey's smile evaporated.

'Don't quit on me, Harry. I can't do this without you. We know Jack Webster is a traitor who's misappropriated millions, maybe billions of dollars. He might even be a murderer.'

Dunkley groaned.

'Perhaps, but we don't have any proof. Even if we did it wouldn't matter. People think this bloke is God.'

Toohey shook his head.

'Not God. Icarus. He's flying high, but veering too close to the sun.'

Toohey paused, carefully weighing his words.

'How far would you go to get Webster? Who would you deal with?'

'Would I dance with the devil?' Dunkley shrugged. 'Well, my standards are pretty low.'

Toohey glanced at the far end of the room.

'What about him?'

Dunkley stiffened as a familiar rotund form stepped out from behind the curtain.

'No. No fucking way,' Dunkley snapped.

Brendan Ryan threw up his arms. 'I told you,' he said.

Toohey put up his hand. 'Shut up for a minute, Brendan.'

The former prime minister turned back to Dunkley, his eyes pleading. 'Listen, he can help us.'

Dunkley shot up from the table, moving menacingly towards Ryan.

'I did listen to him. I trusted him. With everything. We were friends, I thought. Then he fed me a story that ended my career.' Dunkley spat out the words as he relived his fall. 'And you expect me to trust him?'

Toohey shook his head.

'No, Harry. Trust me.'

Dunkley realised that he was shaking. His right hand had balled into a fist and his heart was racing. He took a deep breath.

'Sit down for a moment. Please,' Toohey said, pointing to the chair.

'It was more than fifteen years ago,' Ryan began.

Positioned safely at the other side of the conference table, Dunkley thought the Labor powerbroker looked pale and drawn, older than he remembered.

'I was a pup, thrilled to be invited to the Australian American Leadership Dialogue. I met a Republican congressman, Morgan McDonald. We hit it off immediately. He couldn't believe that someone from the Labor Party was as committed to the alliance between our nations as he was. He hooked me up with others, including an up-and-coming RAAF officer, Jack Webster. I was recruited then—'

'To do what?' Dunkley scoffed.

'I believed what we were doing was defending Australia.'

'No. You were an insurgent!' Dunkley snapped, pointing his finger at Ryan. 'You were the eyes and ears of an anti-democratic cabal undermining both countries. You were its lapdog.'

Ryan's eyes flashed.

'You do understand how this world works, don't you, Harry? It's power that nations respect. The threat of force buys us peace. We need the US. Now more than ever. Yes, it makes flawed decisions. But America remains a force for good and stability in a chaotic and dangerous world.'

Toohey glared at Ryan.

'But we're not talking about America, we are talking about your cabal of despots. Your shadow government launched an attack on my democratically elected one. We're talking about treason. And we're talking about murder.'

Dunkley jumped in.

'You told me the Chinese killed Kimberley Gordon. She was murdered by Charles Dancer, who was working for the Alliance.'

Ryan looked genuinely distressed.

'We never ordered that. I had never heard of the guy until recently. You have to believe me. It wasn't the Alliance running him, it was Jack Webster.'

He kneaded his fingers, then pulled at his ruddy face. His usual facade of confidence was gone.

'Webster's out of control. I know that now. He's a dictator who's been using the Alliance.'

Dunkley could see that Ryan was struggling. Some of his initial anger dissipated.

'Well, Brendan, bravo. I'm glad we're on the same page,' Dunkley said. 'Big question though, pal: how do we expose him?'

Ryan reached into his pocket and threw a black USB onto the table.

'With this.'

Dunkley looked at the memory stick and shrugged. 'And?'

'This is a record of every crime Webster's committed. Every time he's acted without authority. It's an extraordinary story.'

Ryan turned to Toohey, who was eyeing the USB.

'Martin, did you know that our Special Forces were used to protect US interests in Nigeria?'

'No.'

'Well, it happened on your watch. And Webster ordered it. They were flown in on a plane provided by a US contractor. Bought and paid for by the CIA. Meant no one in the US ever had to answer hard questions in a congressional hearing.'

Dunkley was still sceptical. 'Where did you get it?'

'From the only man who could compile it. Another member of the Alliance, Richard Dalton. The late head of ASIO.'

'Why would he do that?' Toohey asked.

'Because he was frightened. He'd been tracking Webster's every move. Now he's dead.'

Ryan leaned forward, resting his forearms on the table.

'But that USB holds more than just ASIO's work. Remember that Chinese spy who washed up in the lake two years ago?'

Dunkley nodded. 'Yeah. He was trying to defect.'

'Well, he wasn't coming empty-handed.' Ryan picked up the USB. 'This was taken from his gut. It holds thousands of files. Some were easy to crack and translate; the rest took ASIO months. The Chinese took a very keen interest in Webster. And it explains in detail how Beijing recruited our very own Catriona Bailey, recruited and trained her. It also identifies the man who was running her.'

'Who?' Toohey and Dunkley spoke at the same time.

'Always had impeccable connections, our Catriona. It was Meng Tao.'

Dunkley whistled. 'The Chinese president.'

'Got to hand it to her, she could always spot the people best able to help her,' Toohey said.

Dunkley looked at Toohey and then Ryan.

'That's a great story, Brendan. But I have one big problem. The last time I trusted you I was destroyed. What was your experience, Martin?'

Toohey nodded. 'Same.'

'So I'm not making the same mistake twice. You said that USB had files about Webster. Does it spell out your role in the Alliance?'

Ryan reached for a glass of water and took a sip. He didn't look up when he spoke. 'Yes. It does.'

Dunkley leaned forward and took the USB from Ryan's grasp. He pointed it at the politician as he spoke. 'So, Brendan, if this ever became public you would be toast.'

Ryan didn't respond. He didn't have to.

Dunkley dropped the USB on the table and clapped his hands. 'Then I want copies of everything. Right now. Call it an insurance policy.'

Toohey smiled and looked at Ryan. 'Sounds reasonable to me.'

After the barest pause, Ryan nodded.

'Good,' Dunkley said. 'Martin, does this *Star Wars* theatrette have a printer?'

It was a motherlode of treasure. Ryan had left Toohey and Dunkley reading a ream of documents. They'd printed out several dozen and copied the thousands of files onto two USBs begged from the dean. Dunkley tapped a page. 'This is extraordinary. If I was still in the trade I'd be leading the pack for years.'

The former prime minister held up an A4 sheet. It was one of more than a dozen that had been captured in a keyword search: 'Burra'.

'Seems that Dalton took quite an interest in Webster's little Burra venture too. Even planted ASIO technicians in the building teams, called them "plumbers".'

Dunkley smiled.

'Didn't you guys do the same thing when the Chinese embassy was built in the '90s?'

'Well, the Hawke government approved the builders who bugged it. Seemed like a better use of our intelligence resources than planning coups. Oh, by the way …'

Toohey reached into his jacket pocket and pulled out a folded yellow-and-white envelope.

'This is for you. I picked it up at parliament.'

Dunkley checked the address, flipped it over and then tore open one end. Another memory stick slid onto the conference table.

'Never rains but it pours,' Toohey said. 'Who do you reckon sent it?'

Dunkley picked up the stick and pondered for a moment.

'Trevor Harris.'

'What do you think is on it?'

Dunkley put it down and looked at Toohey.

'Something that Jack Webster is willing to kill for.'

───────────

Philippine Sea

The eight officers snapped to attention as Frank W Vinson stepped into the command centre of the USS *George Washington*.

'Please sit.' The rear admiral pulled up a chair at one end of a conference table. Two large television screens were at the other, set above a line of clocks displaying time zones from Beijing to Washington.

He looked inquiringly at his intelligence officer.

'Sir, the *Liaoning* passed through the southern end of the Taiwan Strait an hour ago,' she said, as a map on the right-hand screen pinpointed the Chinese carrier strike group.

The left-hand screen displayed a close-up image, tagging each Chinese vessel.

'Its strike group includes four Luyang-class destroyers: the *Guangzhou*, *Wuhan*, *Xi'an* and *Changchun*. There are also two frigates, the *Xuzhou* and *Huangshan*, and a Shang-class nuclear-powered attack submarine.'

Vinson closely studied the formation. Something vital was missing.

'Where are the supply ships?' he asked.

'That's the intriguing bit, Admiral. There are none.'

Their absence was telling. Despite the billions poured into the People's Liberation Army Navy, China had been unable to forge a strike group that could sail far from port because it lacked logistics ships.

'Can they resupply the strike group from the Spratlys?'

'Perhaps from Mischief Reef, but their stores are limited,' the intelligence officer said. 'Whatever they have planned, they can't stay at sea for long.'

Vinson pondered the mismatch. He had studied the *Liaoning*'s Admiral Yu Heng and respected him as a thoughtful commander.

Right now he would be a worried man. His ships were no match for the American strike group, and the planes he carried could only fly short distances with a full complement of weapons.

The Stars and Stripes held another ace. The Pentagon had developed electronic and signals intelligence that would take China a generation to match.

Since the height of the Cold War, America had been filling space with spy satellites. Among the most secretive of these aerial networks was the Naval Ocean Surveillance System.

The twinned low-Earth-orbit satellites, code-named *Intruder*, scooped up signals from every warship at sea and beamed them to four ground stations positioned strategically around the globe: in Germany; at Diego Garcia in the Indian Ocean; just north of the Misawa Air Base in Japan; and at Vandenberg Air Force Base in California.

America had also spent billions developing technology to analyse the operating frequencies and transmission patterns of every warship on the planet.

The positional and fingerprint data could be married, then relayed within minutes to any US warship anywhere on the globe.

It was akin to placing ankle bracelets on naval adversaries and gave American commanders a complete real-time picture of everyone in their battlespace.

In Vinson's mind it was instructive that these were the satellites that had been hit by laser fire on the day President Jackson was assassinated. If the Chinese were planning a confrontation at sea, Beijing knew it had to take out America's huge intelligence advantage.

That strike had failed. So wherever the *Liaoning* sailed, Vinson would see its every move, while he would lurk in Yu's blindspot.

Canberra

Elizabeth Scott held her mobile to her ear. 'You're absolutely certain? The Brisbane Club. What date? What time?'

The prime minister scribbled notes as she listened intently. 'Thanks.' She ended the call, glancing at the time before dialling her EA. 'How long? Okay, thanks.'

The meeting had been called at short notice. He was due in five minutes. She summoned her chief of staff. 'I don't want to be disturbed. At all.' She pointed to a CCTV set in the ceiling. 'And switch that off.'

Right on time, Jack Webster, in full military regalia, his chest festooned with medals, strode masterfully into the prime ministerial suite. Scott realised she'd never seen him in civvies. His every public moment was an opportunity to boost his status and ego.

'Please have a seat.'

Webster nodded, dropping his hat carelessly onto Scott's desk.

'I was surprised that your diary secretary called my executive assistant,' he said. 'You usually text or call me personally. And she must have misheard because she said you were ordering me here.'

'I was. You do recall that I am the prime minister. You answer to me.'

'I have never questioned it, and frankly, Prime Minister, your tone surprises me.'

Scott ignored the hint of aggression.

'Who do you think is leaking information from the National Security Committee, Jack?'

'Do you have to ask? One of your colleagues, as ever.'

'It's a breach of the Crimes Act.'

'I know, and no one will be happier than me when you jail the attorney-general.'

Scott rose from her chair.

'I don't think it's the attorney,' she said softly, stepping towards him. 'I think it's you.'

His face flushed with anger as he, too, rose to his feet.

'That is an outrageous accusation.'

Scott didn't flinch.

'No. It's the truth. Worse, my chief military adviser has pushed me into buying Japanese submarines in haste, bypassing all the usual procurement guidelines, triggering an unnecessary confrontation with China.'

'It's the right call. The Soryu are the best option. And the Americans want us to seal that deal.'

Like the class fencer she was, Scott lunged at the opening.

'That's it, isn't it, Jack? Pleasing the Americans. Always doing Washington's bidding. But you don't work for them; you work for me ... or do you just work for yourself?'

Webster bristled. 'This is absurd.'

'Really? What were you talking to Emily Brooks about at the Brisbane Club?'

For a moment Webster was blindsided and Scott recognised she'd scored a hit.

502

'We met by chance. I am constantly talking to politicians, from all sides.'

'A chance meeting that went for an hour.'

'What are you accusing me of, Prime Minister?'

'Of conspiring with the enemy.'

'Bullshit.'

'If you want my job, you'll have to resign from the one you have now.'

Webster picked up his hat.

'This demeaning conversation is over. I will try to forget it ever happened.'

Scott stepped in front of Webster, blocking his path.

'Air Chief Marshal, I am not asking for your resignation, I am demanding it.'

The CDF's face boiled with rage, and for a moment Scott feared he might strike her. When he spoke, his voice was cold and deliberate.

'If you want me gone you'll have to sack me but it would be the final act in your pathetic career.'

Scott moved to her desk and picked up a sheet of paper.

'Your resignation letter. Sign it.'

Webster moved close, towering over her.

'And I will say you sacked me after I discovered you were compromised by the Chinese, that they recorded your illegal surveillance of a colleague for rank political gain. That the prime minister of Australia is whoring herself to Beijing.'

Scott's face was ashen.

'Have you been following me, Jack? Bugging me?'

Webster put his hat on, and pushed past the prime minister. He turned his head slightly and spoke over his shoulder.

'You are going to announce that you are sending an Australian frigate to join the US-led flotilla in the South China Sea. You have forty-eight hours. Or you can deliver your own resignation to the governor-general.'

Elizabeth Scott had glimpsed her own mortality. She stood frozen, staring at the door.

In the cut-and-thrust of the corporate world, Scott had played as tough as anyone. But here the stakes were not measured in profit and loss; they were measured in careers.

Scott's was now on the line.

She slumped back into her chair, ignoring a nagging desk phone. Instead she reached for her mobile, scrolling through a list of names.

'Hi. I need you here. Now.'

'Martin.' She bounded across the room, threw her arms around him and held him close for a few seconds.

'Elizabeth, you'll ruin my reputation as a hard Labor man. Try to recall we are mortal enemies.'

She pushed him back with a shaky smile.

'Comrade.'

'Now you're just being silly. What's so urgent?'

Scott walked to her desk, distractedly picking up her handwritten notes that recorded the defence chief's deceit.

'You were right about Webster. He's hatching a plan with Brooks to put him in the Lodge.'

Toohey nodded. 'It might just work. Webster has the profile, and the public adores him. And Brooks knows she can sell it to your colleagues because it would be their best chance of hanging onto their seats. As I learned, that's all they care about.'

'I know, but it gets worse. Much worse. Webster knows something that could blow me away.'

'Like what?'

Scott put down her notes before turning her back on Toohey. When she spoke, her voice was barely audible.

'Webster knows that I was the one who brought down Brooks using the sex tape.'

'Really?'

She turned to face Toohey, but could not look him in the eye.

'The Chinese know too.'

'Jesus, Elizabeth, you've grown in my estimation. You've mastered black ops. They say you can judge a person by their enemies. You've hit the jackpot.'

Scott slumped onto the lounge.

'Maybe I should just resign.'

'Elizabeth, if you resign, he wins. We can't allow this mongrel to keep taking out prime ministers. That is the real crime.'

Scott sighed loudly. 'Yes, but what can I do to stop him?'

Toohey's grin was the tonic she needed. 'Prime Minister, I'm already working on something. You trusted me; now I'm trusting you.'

He reached into his jacket pocket and pulled out a USB.

'This is Webster's death notice. Read it carefully and when the time comes you'll know who to share it with.'

He pointed to her iPhone.

'Don't go anywhere without that and don't let your staffers answer it. Sometime soon you'll get a text from a number you won't recognise … It will begin "Embassy Motel" and you'll know it's from me. When I call, you'll need to act immediately. Will you promise me that?'

Scott thought for a moment. There were few options.

'Sure. What will you want me to do?'

'Send in the cavalry.'

South China Sea

The *Liaoning* was tracked as it pushed deeper into the South China Sea. The Chinese strike group moved into a holding pattern fifty nautical miles north of the Spratly Islands, on the edge of the China Sea Basin where the ocean plunged to depths of sixteen thousand feet.

At the same time, the USS *George Washington* strike group cruised down the east coast of the Philippines and into the Celebes Sea. It reached the near perfect circle of the Sulu Sea and waited close to the island of Palawan as the *Liaoning* took up its position to the north.

Then, under cover of darkness, the American armada sailed through the narrow Balabac Strait between Palawan and the northern tip of Borneo. The Spratly Islands lay two hundred nautical miles to Admiral Vinson's north. The *Liaoning* was a further hundred away, well within his 600-nautical-mile battlespace.

Everything was ready for the trap to be sprung.

Canberra

An expensive vase lay shattered on the floor. Enraged, Jack Webster paced his office, glaring from his fourth-floor window at the distant parliament.

Charles Dancer arrived to find a secretary cowering at her desk. He nodded casually as he sauntered into the defence tsar's lair.

'The meeting went well, then.'

Webster's eyes blazed with fury.

'I am going to bury that harlot,' he thundered, emphasising each word with a pump of his fist.

'The prime minister, I assume. You should know that Ms Scott called Martin Toohey moments after you left. He is in her office now.'

'What are they talking about?' Webster demanded.

'I think we can guess, don't you?'

Webster's eyes hardened as he spat his reply.

'Your job is to find out.'

'I'm surprised you called me here,' Dancer said as he poured imported mineral water into a crystal glass. 'It is irregular and unwise.'

'The game has changed. There are new threats.'

Dancer sipped from the glass, appreciating the subtle taste.

'You overestimate Toohey and his little band of washed-up pissants,' he said. 'Catriona Bailey remains the real threat. She can't be allowed to win the election. She was the original mission. We need to finish it.'

Webster snorted at his henchman.

'I'll decide the mission. You will follow my orders. I have Bailey in hand; she can beat Scott at the election – but she can't beat me. I repeat: there are new threats for you to deal with.'

Dancer put down the glass. 'Are you ordering me to kill a former prime minister?'

'I didn't say that.'

'But you didn't deny it.'

Manila

The spit-roasted pig dominated the main table at the Philippine Exporters Confederation lunch in the Solaire Resort's vast conference room.

Experience had led Benigno Aquino to hold low expectations of the food served at such gatherings, so this was a pleasant surprise. But he wasn't here for the *lechón*.

'Ladies and gentlemen, please welcome the president.'

Aquino dabbed a napkin to his lips and stood to polite applause.

He began his speech with the usual pleasantries, and moved smoothly to the main game for this business audience: trade. He reminded the listeners that the South China Sea trade routes were the Philippines' arteries and that China's aggressive island building threatened to clog them.

Then he launched into the part of his speech that was the real reason for his presence. It had been drafted in close consultation with his key ally.

'I'm a student of history and I'm reminded of how Germany was testing the waters in the 1930s and of the weak response of other European powers,'

Aquino said. 'The South China Sea is our Sudetenland, which was seized by Adolf Hitler prior to the Nazi invasion of Czechoslovakia.

'Unfortunately, even after Hitler annexed the Sudetenland and, eventually, invaded Czechoslovakia, nobody said "Stop". What if somebody had said "Stop" to Hitler, to Germany, at that point in time? Could we have avoided World War II?

'We are a small country, but I believe, on behalf of the free world, that we should now cry out "Stop" to the annexation of the South China Sea.'

The president paused to allow the weight of his comments to sink in, and to add gravitas to the punchline. He gripped the lectern with both hands and leaned forward.

'Soon we will send naval ships to the Spratly Islands. They will be on a peaceful mission in international waters. I expect our ships to pass unhindered.'

The response from the Chinese Ministry of Foreign Affairs was immediate and furious.

'Mr Aquino is an amateurish politician who is ignorant of both history and reality,' an official told a press conference in Beijing.

'His remarks are inflammatory and we urge him not to take any foolish steps that will interfere with China's core interests. Let us be clear. The Philippines has started a small fire. It should not pour fuel on the flames.'

The following day, in Washington, the White House press secretary strongly defended the thrust of Aquino's speech, although he noted that the reference to Nazi Germany was 'his choice of words, not ours'.

'Language aside, President Aquino is just stating a fact,' the press secretary told the crowded room. 'Those are international waters. America will fly, sail and operate wherever international law permits. We will do that at the times and places of our choosing. There's no exception to that. In the case of our allies, we will use our power and influence to enforce and defend their rights.

'Can I remind you that last year President Jackson signed an Enhanced Defense Co-operation Agreement with the Philippines, our closest ally in Asia.'

Within hours of the Australian Cabinet's national security meeting, word began to spread among Coalition ministers and senior staff of a telling exchange between the prime minister and her chief military adviser.

Those who had been present noted a significant deterioration in the pair's relationship, which was once considered too close by some ministers.

Elizabeth Scott had raised the row between the Philippines and China and the danger to the region, saying, 'We have to do something.'

Jack Webster's reply had dripped with sarcasm. 'What, exactly, Prime Minister? Issue another hollow statement?'

Canberra

It was the culmination of months of bubbling anger against a hapless prime minister. *The Australian* had taken aim at Elizabeth Scott and fired every gun.

SCOTT SCUTTLES FREEDOM FLEET

Prime Minister Elizabeth Scott has rejected a personal plea from the US president to join an unprecedented regional alliance to press navigation rights in the South China Sea.

Well-placed Australian defence sources say Washington is incensed by Ms Scott's decision, which has all but sunk plans to assemble an international flotilla to challenge China's militarisation of disputed islands.

'You have to wonder why the prime minister feels she cannot offend Beijing but can snub Washington,' one senior military source told *The Australian*.

The broadsheet's stable of battle-hardened columnists had been let loose in pages of fearsome and excoriating commentary. And the editorial thundered that Scott 'risked an alliance that has been the foundation stone of peace in the Pacific for seventy years'.

Emily Brooks savoured every poison-dipped word as she scrolled through the coverage on her iPad. The discord in Coalition ranks had been building for months, but the conservatives' natural instinct was to give their leader every chance.

The revelation that Elizabeth Scott had scorned the US president would rattle even the prime minister's most steadfast supporters.

Brooks hadn't been idle, relentlessly undermining her rival. Soon another whispering campaign would begin, circulating the name of an extraordinary candidate.

The well-rehearsed ritual of the political assassination of an Australian prime minister was afoot.

_____

Adelaide

The yellow-and-blue flags fluttered in the light early morning breeze, proudly displaying a stylised map of Australia overlaid with the white stars of the Southern Cross.

Several hundred members of the Australian Workers' Union had been whistled up as stage dressing for the latest act in this political play. Hard hats and high-vis vests were on display for the dozen bleary journalists gathered outside the front gates of the ASC shipyards at Osborne.

The Bailey Express had hit Adelaide.

Right on cue, the bus arrived at 7am. A riser was assembled before the star emerged and a microphone wailed to life.

'Being a leader isn't easy,' Catriona Bailey began in her rasp of a voice. 'You might remember I faced the rough end of the pineapple once or twice when I was PM.

'But, fair shake, some things should be easy. Ensuring national security is the first line on page one of the job description.'

A smattering of polite applause rose from the crowd. The opposition leader's folksy charm still worked with the masses.

'Friends, national security means a lot of things. As I rock around the country, one thing you good folk tell me is it means fighting for job security. And no prime minister with a heart should ever allow Australian jobs to be shipped offshore. It's just not fair.'

A murmur of assent rippled through the workers. Several yelled 'Blood oath'.

'And, you know something? It means protecting economic security. No prime minister with a brain should threaten that by striking a foreign submarine deal designed to antagonise our major trading partner.'

The crowd rose with the rhetoric. One unionist yelled 'Scott's a moron' to general merriment and Bailey waited for the cheering to subside.

'But let's call a spade a spade; Beijing does need to be warned against militarising the South China Sea. So no prime minister with a spine would humiliate our key ally by refusing to join America's peaceful protest mission.'

Applause thundered, cheers echoed and some stamped their feet as Bailey's language sharpened to deliver the grab that she knew would lead the primetime news.

'Elizabeth Scott is the clown from Oz. She is a heartless, brainless coward. And her lack of spine is threatening every aspect of our security.'

Canberra

They gathered in the shadows of Canberra's most heavily guarded building.

The Israeli embassy had been chosen because its electronic dead zone stretched across the road into the park where the conspirators were convening. All phone and radio signals were scrambled; they could not be overheard.

Bruce Paxton arrived after walking from the nearby American embassy while Harry Dunkley had been lurking outside the Polish mission. The ringleader turned up in a taxi, walked briskly to the meeting place, then drew the others into a huddle.

'Gentlemen, it's time to launch Operation Icarus,' Martin Toohey said.

'What's the drill?' Paxton asked.

'We head to Burra tonight.'

Toohey pointed at the former union strongman. 'Bruce, you're in charge of the technical side of this operation. We'll need a sparky and someone who can handle telecoms in the dark. Have you been in touch with your building union mates?'

Paxton nodded. 'Hall's Heroes are ready to roll. Again.'

Toohey pulled a sheet of paper from his jacket.

'Okay, they'll need to get their heads around this. ASIO's "plumbers" did good work.'

He turned to Dunkley. 'You and I will meet at 6pm—'

'1800, mate,' Paxton interrupted.

'Whatever floats your boat, comrade. 1800. Harry, bring your phone and make sure it's fully charged. Bruce, leave yours in the caravan.'

Dunkley cut in. 'How do you know Webster will be there?'

'Harry, Webster has every eavesdropping device known to science. But I have the oldest and the best: people I trust. He will be there. And, if his plans change, I will hear about it. Right, any questions?'

'Yes, a fairly significant one,' said Dunkley. 'What do we do once the gates open?'

'We go inside.'

'And then what?'

Toohey smiled.

'You leave that to me.'

South China Sea

At 1200, the *Liaoning* was alerted to two ships sailing from the Philippines' naval forces facility at Oyster Bay on Palawan's coast, heading due west.

On the bridge, Admiral Yu Heng studied the Chinese intelligence brief. The vessels were reported to be moving at a steady clip of twenty-five knots. Only two ships in the small Filipino fleet had that capacity: BRP *Gregorio del Pilar* and BRP *Ramon Alcaraz*. At their present speed, the US-built Hamilton-class cutters would breach the twelve-nautical-mile limit around Mischief Reef inside five hours.

The commander pushed away his light lunch of fish and rice and gazed out at the calm waters shimmering to the horizon. His orders were to prevent any foreign vessel from entering the exclusion zone around Mischief Reef. And he was authorised to use force.

If either Filipino warship crossed that invisible line, they would be crushed – just like the *Nenita*.

Canberra

The Falun Gong had packed away their protest banners, driven home by temperatures that had dropped as rapidly as the sun.

At exactly 1800, Harry Dunkley arrived at the Chinese embassy, clad in a black tracksuit and dark woollen beanie. Moments later, Martin Toohey strode down the slight incline from the Hyatt Hotel. He wore jeans and a black leather bomber jacket, and a Special Forces baseball cap pulled down tight over his greying curls.

He was in high spirits.

'You look like Phillip Adams,' he told Dunkley, laughing.

'I feel like I'm about to be done for break-and-enter.'

'Well, you nailed the dress code. Did you bring the camera?'

Dunkley pulled a Canon IXUS from his tracksuit jacket.

'One hundred and twenty-five bucks from Ted's.'

'With thanks to our friends across the road,' Toohey said, motioning to the Chinese embassy.

The arrival of a pair of white Commonwealth cars interrupted their banter. The late-model Holdens turned into Coronation Drive then pulled up opposite the embassy gates.

Toohey pointed to the lead vehicle. 'Righto mate, give your mobile to the driver; mine's going in the other one.'

Dunkley nodded as he handed over his phone. The first ComCar pulled away, turning left into Commonwealth Avenue, heading towards the lake. The second turned right.

'If anyone's tracking us, then for the next few hours we are wherever those cars are,' Toohey explained.

A horn blast sounded as a well-worn LandCruiser lumbered around the corner and rattled to a stop in front of them. A small woman with brown hair and a cheeky grin jumped from the driver's seat and bowed theatrically.

'Your chariot awaits, Mr Toohey.' She slapped the bonnet. 'Picked it up today for two grand. Goes well enough, though.'

'Thanks, Linda, I left your car outside the Hyatt gym.'

They exchanged keys.

'Hop in, Harry.'

Dunkley fought with a misbehaving seat belt that locked each time he tried to drag it over his shoulder. As he finally coaxed it towards the buckle, he noticed a slight tremble in his hands.

His throat was dry as he looked across to Toohey who adjusted his seat before the engine rumbled to life.

Dunkley marvelled at the vagaries of circumstance that had paired them in a crusade against a vicious killer. As the Toyota crunched through the gears the journalist feared they were badly outgunned, boys going to war against a man who had spent his life training for it.

It would be a short drive from the bush capital to the enemy's stronghold.

———————

South China Sea

The first warning was issued at 1628 by the Chinese. In English.

'This is the Chinese navy, this is the Chinese navy. Filipino vessels, you are approaching Chinese sovereign waters. Change course now or we will consider your intentions hostile.'

The BRP *Gregorio del Pilar* and BRP *Ramon Alcaraz* were thirty nautical miles west of Mischief Reef.

The *Liaoning* had used the VHF maritime mobile band, because all vessels monitored its international distress channel.

There was no response. A second warning was issued. Nothing.

Admiral Yu Heng calculated the warships would breach the twelve-nautical-mile zone within thirty minutes. If they crossed that line his orders were explicit.

The Chinese commander lifted his cap and rubbed his forearm across his brow. The strike group under his command vastly outgunned the Filipino frigates, but opening fire would be an act of war.

He checked his watch again. The Shenyang J-15 fighter jets could intercept the ships in less than ten minutes. There was still time.

He grabbed the microphone from the radio operator.

'This is Admiral Yu Heng aboard Chinese aircraft carrier *Liaoning* to Philippine navy vessels. Please respond. If you do not change course immediately we will launch action to defend our territory.'

The radio remained silent. Five minutes later, Yu issued an order to deploy two warplanes. They were instructed to fly towards the Filipino ships, but not to fire unless fired upon.

Yu hoped their radar signal alone would be enough to force a Filipino retreat. As he watched the warplanes scream down the flight deck and off the ski-jump bow, he felt a deep foreboding.

The *Liaoning*'s fatal flaw was that it had no catapult to slingshot its warplanes into the air with a full payload. They could carry heavy weapons or a full fuel tank, but not both.

Minutes later, Yu's spirits briefly lifted as the VHF band crackled to life.

'This is Admiral Frank Vinson, commander of the USS *George Washington* to the *Liaoning*. We are escorting two Philippine navy vessels in a joint exercise on a peaceful mission through international waters. Recall your planes. If you do not, I will assume we are under attack.'

Yu felt the skin on his scalp tighten. He had sailed into a trap.

Frank W Vinson had dropped the flag on Operation Nemesis.

From high above the flight deck, the commander of the USS *George Washington* watched as the most sophisticated and deadly weaponry ever assembled burst into action from the most dangerous work environment in the world.

The roar from vulture's row was deafening as jet engines and steam-driven catapults combined to hurl warplanes skywards from zero to 165 miles an hour in two seconds.

First off the deck were two EA-18G Growlers. Built with the DNA of a fighter, the Growler's trump card was its ability to manipulate the electronic spectrum. Its battlefield was the shadow world of radiation frequencies and it wrought havoc by firing radio-, infrared- and micro-waves instead of bullets.

The Chinese would be rendered blind, deaf and dumb.

The Growlers were the point guards for the more conventional F/A-18F Super Hornets, surveillance planes and helicopters that would follow in the blackout. This was electronic warfare on afterburners, way beyond anything the Chinese could muster.

Vinson checked his watch.

Within two minutes the Growlers would activate their weapons systems and Yu would lose visibility of the battlespace.

The Chinese pilots would be operating in the dark, unable to even communicate with each other.

The most fateful play in China's recent history would be in their hands.

If they fired, the US admiral had issued clear instructions. Shoot them down.

Old Cooma Road

They drove through a tunnel of darkness, the road illuminated by the weak beam of headlights burrowing into the night.

Empty paddocks swept by as they rattled down the winding, narrow road into the sprawling rural parish of Burra. The two men travelled in silence, Toohey focused on the road, Dunkley seeking to draw comfort from the aged vehicle's familiar rhythm.

The night held an edge. Four years of Dunkley's life had collapsed into this single encounter with the dark.

What hath night to do with sleep?

The voice in his mind was so clear that Dunkley turned to Toohey with a start.

'What did you say?'

Toohey glanced at his companion.

'Me? Nothing. Too noisy in this rattler to talk.'

The memories came in a vivid torrent. Dunkley was swept back to the streets of Sydney, his mind a blur of booze and despair with fragments of John Milton echoing in his head.

He stared hard at the darkness. Everything in this routine landscape was sinister. A stand of gum trees bleached to death by ringbarking stood as a symbol of man's casual brutality. Dim moonlight cast demonic shadows on the blighted land.

Dunkley felt panic rising from the pit of his stomach and reaching up to squeeze the air from his lungs. This was a fool's errand that would destroy them all. He had to fight the urge to scream at Toohey to turn back.

The journalist closed his eyes, took a deep breath and dug past the horrors in his mind to summon another line from *Paradise Lost*.

Long is the way
And hard, that out of Hell leads up to light.

Toohey slowed the vehicle, then pulled to the side of the road, checking their bearings with an old-fashioned map and torch.

'Not far now, and right on time.'

Two hundred metres on, he turned left into Urila Road and drove for another half a kilometre. Then he stopped the car and killed the engine.

Ahead, a brightly lit compound shone like a beacon in the darkness, imposing and out of place.

'Welcome to Fort Webster,' Toohey muttered.

They were parked about a hundred and fifty metres from a pair of front gates. Beyond them, a row of pencil pines marked a long driveway that led to the residence.

The compound was guarded by a three-metre-high fence made from steel posts set close together like bars in a jail cell. Four CCTV cameras monitored the gates and driveway entrance.

Toohey turned to his friend. 'Need to stay well out of shot of those, mate.'

Dunkley could see two laser security poles mounted on pillars either side of the gate. Paxton had warned them about the network of invisible light that would sound an alarm if its beam was breached.

Against the high-tech fortifications of this sinister and powerful warlord, Dunkley felt completely inadequate. Worse, he was scared shitless.

'All right. So what now?' he asked, trying to mask his fear.

'We sit tight and wait for reinforcements.'

Ten minutes later the hum of an approaching car broke the silence moments before its headlights lit the narrow bush road.

A white van pulled in behind the LandCruiser. Another black-clad figure clambered out of the passenger-side door.

Bruce Paxton ambled over to Toohey and held out his right hand.

'Here's the burner phone you wanted; you owe me fifty bucks.'

515

Toohey chuckled. 'I'm good for it.'

'So where's the pit?' Paxton asked.

'This way.'

Paxton signalled to the van and two men emerged. They followed Toohey for fifty metres towards the gates. He took a folded sheet of paper and a small torch from his jacket. He checked his bearings and then walked slowly into the long grass by the side of the road. Minutes passed as he searched before he signalled to the group and pointed his torch at a metal rectangle obscured by a tangle of weeds.

A pair of bolt-cutters sliced through a hardened steel padlock guarding the telecoms hub. The two tradies hefted the cover to one side then poked a torch into the pit. One disappeared into its maw.

'The back door, Harry,' Toohey whispered. 'The ASIO "plumbers" installed a bypass to the security system so they could get access from outside. Let's put it to the test.'

Two minutes later, the technician emerged from the pit and gave the thumbs up.

'Ready to roll when you are.'

Toohey nodded, and a moment later the tiny red lights on top of the security cameras went out and the massive metal gates guarding Webster's domain smoothly parted.

'*This horror will grow mild, this darkness light,*' Dunkley whispered as he stared into the void.

South China Sea

A storm of disorienting electromagnetic noise washed through Captain Song Bo's helmet and the instrument panel on his Shenyang J-15 fighter jet had gone haywire.

The Chinese pilot had lost communications with his ship and his wingman. The two planes were wingtip-to-wingtip and the other pilot's hand gestures confirmed he was also flying blind.

In the moments before his equipment was scrambled, Song had locked his radar onto the lead Filipino warship. His instruments were now useless, but he gambled that his anti-ship missile's onboard radar seeker would still find the target.

His orders were clear: to fire, if fired upon. It was obvious he was under attack.

He flicked off the safety switch on his joystick and launched one of his missiles.

The 3M54AE's cigar-shaped canister dropped from beneath the wing and glided for a few moments. Then the nose-cone fell away and the missile inside was ejected.

The weapon deployed wings and tail controls, its turbo-jet engine engaging as it screamed towards the ocean. It would fly at subsonic speed twenty metres above the water as it homed in on the target. At terminal phase it would kick up to supersonic velocity and skim just five metres above the waves.

Captain Song dipped his wing to watch the weapon's flame disappear below, then he righted his plane and scanned the horizon.

The Filipino frigate stood no chance.

Major Jennifer Mau yelled out a warning as the red alert of a hostile missile launch flashed in her helmet-mounted cueing system.

'*Ramon Alcaraz, Ramon Alcaraz*. Incoming cruise missile closing at subsonic speed. Launch your countermeasures.'

The US Growler pilot engaged her weapons and turned her head until the enemy warplane hit the crosshairs in her visor. Mau locked her radar onto the target, shouting 'Fox Three' as she launched an AIM-120 Advanced Medium-Range Air-to-Air Missile.

The weapon dropped from her port wing. Its rocket engaged, banked right and vanished. The AMRAAM would reach Mach 4 as it closed in on the target.

As the missile blasted from the Growler, its signature was picked up by a Northrop Grumman E-2D Advanced Hawkeye aircraft. The turboprop-driven eyes-in-the-sky was operating at 25,000 feet, the huge grey disc mounted on its back monitoring every inch of the battlespace for the USS *George Washington* carrier strike group.

In the deadly game of aerial cat and mouse, the Hawkeye would ensure the odds were stacked with the hunter. It would transmit targeting data to the US missile, allowing it to manoeuvre in flight as the Chinese J-15 took evasive action. In the missile's terminal phase, the target would be caught in the web of the AMRAAM's own radar field.

In the wide blue skies above the Pacific, Mau knew there was nowhere the adversary could hide.

_____

Burra

They moved swiftly in the dark, keeping to the fringe of the red gravel drive to muffle the sound of their footfall.

Martin Toohey motioned to his two improbable accomplices to stay locked in close behind him. The driveway, lined with its two neat rows of pencil pines, ran dead straight from the road. A small rise partially obscured the residence, which they estimated was more than one hundred metres inside the fence line.

They reached the top of the rise and stopped. Before them, a vast neo-colonial mansion was illuminated by a bank of security lights trained from every corner. A wide verandah that looked as if it had been ripped from the American deep south wrapped around the building. Light streamed through coloured glass panels either side of a grand entrance.

'How many banks did the fucker have to rob to pay for this?' growled Paxton.

'Just one. The Treasury,' replied Toohey.

They crouched in semi-darkness just beyond the light cast by the security beams. Thirty metres of open ground lay between them and the verandah. Two late-model BMWs were parked in front of the house.

Toohey turned and whispered, 'Stay low, stay quiet.'

The three figures scampered from the shadows to the cover of the nearest vehicle.

A waft of classical music came from inside the fortress.

Toohey pointed to a pair of floor-to-ceiling windows to the left of the entrance. A ribbon of light was shining through a gap in thick curtains.

'Thanks to your builder mate, Bruce, we know that must be the "state room". You two stay put. I'm taking a look.'

He crept towards the verandah, prowling quickly up the steps and dropping to all fours between the windows. He peeked through one quickly. Then again, this time for longer. He shook his head, scrambled to his feet and hustled back to the other two, fixing them with a broad grin.

'Well, fellas. The lights are on and everyone's home.'

'What now?' Paxton inquired.

Toohey reached into his jacket and pulled out the burner phone. He punched in a number he'd scrawled on a slip of paper, then looked at his companions.

'We call in the cavalry.'

South China Sea

The warning from the Growler bought vital heartbeats of time.

The crew of the *Ramon Alcaraz* had been battle-ready for hours, but now counted their lives in seconds.

Moments after Major Mau's alert, the Filipino warship's Mark 36 Super Rapid Bloom decoy system started blasting out chaff rounds in a bid to confuse the Chinese missile. Then, when the weapon was just over two kilometres from its target, the warship's close-in defences locked onto the missile as it kicked up to its terminal speed of Mach 2. The ship's cannon began automatically firing 25-millimetre projectiles at the rate of two a second. Even at that furious pace, only six rounds could be fired before the missile would strike.

At one thousand metres, the missile was on target to blast into the stern, and the crew of the *Ramon Alcaraz* braced for impact. Then – at five hundred metres – the missile erupted in a thunderous flash.

Shrapnel travelling at twice the speed of sound hailed into the hull and the deck, cutting through steel, glass and flesh.

Fifty kilometres to the north, the two Chinese fighters were banking, jinking and swooping in anticipation of an attack from over the horizon.

Both had engaged their jamming signals, but still couldn't communicate with each other or their carrier.

First Lieutenant Yang Gan was working through a well-practised drill: pulling hard, left and right; shunting up and down.

It would have been exhilarating if it wasn't a dance with death.

The pilot saw a flash to his left before he was rocked by the shockwave as Captain Song's jet disintegrated. Fragments of China's most advanced naval fighter threw long ribbons of orange and black as they plummeted towards the ocean.

Instinctively, Yang corkscrewed his plane downwards, flattening at fifty metres above the waves before shooting up almost vertically. The bladders in his G-suit inflated, tightening around his muscles, forcing blood into his brain as acceleration and gravity combined to press like a giant boot on his chest.

He banked and flattened out again at one thousand metres, then turned back to where his commander's plane had fallen.

He scanned the ocean for any sign of life, but all he could see was the debris from his comrade's plane scattered over several hundred metres. There was nothing else: no beacon, no parachute.

Nothing except the sun flickering on the waves.

America's domination of the battlespace was near complete.

Admiral Frank W Vinson had deployed every weapon in his extraordinary arsenal. Four Growlers and sixty conventional F/A-18 Hornets prowled the skies, while MH-60R Romeo helicopters pinpointed the enemy's submarine.

By wiping out the Chinese communications, superior US technology had disabled the *Liaoning*'s strike group.

Admiral Yu had wisely not launched any more warplanes, but Vinson wasn't prepared to take any chances. Nor could the American commander afford to overplay his hand. Vinson intended to humiliate his enemy, but knew that he must limit casualties.

This next move carried the greatest risk. A Hornet would target the *Liaoning* with a long-range anti-ship missile.

Vinson looked to the heavens as he prayed that it would disable but not sink the carrier.

Then he would deal with the airstrip on Mischief Reef.

Burra

Three black vans roared through the open gates and down the driveway, screeching to a halt just metres from Webster's lair.

An elite team from the Australian Federal Police Specialist Response Group poured from the vehicles. Three heavily armed officers dressed in military-style uniforms and carrying assault rifles fanned out to the left, each dropping to one knee as he raised his weapon. Another trio covered the right of the entrance.

In the same instant, an agent wielding a black metal battering ram raced across the driveway and dashed up the steps. He reached the doorway and in one fluid movement launched the heavy steel weight at the lock of the double door. It splintered apart and a trailing officer quickly leapt through the shattered opening, followed by his colleagues.

Seconds later a blinding flash of light accompanied a loud bang as a stun grenade detonated in the state room. Screams erupted within the mansion as officers barked 'On the floor!' Then there was silence.

Watching from a safe distance, Martin Toohey turned to his astonished companions. He motioned to Dunkley.

'Camera ready?'

'Yes boss.'

'Great, then follow me. This will be priceless.'

Toohey led his rag-tag team to the verandah and pointed to a plum position. 'There.'

Dunkley was firing off a shot to check the camera's flash as the first two officers emerged. A naked man was being dragged between them, yelling protests at the indifferent agents.

A short while later two young women were escorted from the house, their modesty protected by blankets. The officers kept a light grip on them as they were led to the waiting vans. They stopped dead in their tracks as an enraged howl erupted from the doorway.

Handcuffed and clad only in a pair of tight leopard-skin briefs, Australia's military chief was threatening to end the careers of his captors.

As Dunkley's flash blazed, Jack Webster snarled and flailed in the policemen's grasp. Toohey waved: 'Smile for the camera, Jack.'

The defence chief continued to wrestle with the officers as he issued a string of questions and demands.

'This is private property. You have no right to be here. Don't you know who I am? What am I being charged with?'

From beneath his balaclava, an agent offered one word.

'Treason.'

South China Sea

Admiral Yu Heng paced the bridge of the *Liaoning*, moving anxiously from station to station as his crew battled to restore the carrier's eyes and ears.

For the past thirty minutes the pride of the Chinese navy had been sailing blind. The enemy had launched an attack across the entire electromagnetic spectrum, bringing down radio, radar and navigational equipment.

The admiral's worst fears had been realised: China's overzealous leaders had picked a fight they were bound to lose. Yu had grounded the carrier's air wing, unwilling to risk the lives of pilots by ordering them into a black hole.

'Admiral …' A technician beckoned him to a radar screen that was a mess of static.

'Still nothing?'

'No sir—'

The sailor's mouth froze and his face was twisted into a mask of horror as he was catapulted across the bridge. The admiral's head was slammed against an instrument panel as he tumbled to the floor, opening up a deep gash that rained red across his combat uniform.

The brutality of the blast was amplified in the confines of the bridge. As the air around him compressed, the oxygen was punched from Yu's lungs and pain screamed in his ears.

He staggered to his feet, slipping in his own blood, pressing the heel of his right hand into his head wound. He stood deafened and breathless as smoke clouded the room.

As the admiral's hearing returned, the screams of the wounded and dying reached his ears.

The *Liaoning*'s first and only battle was over.

First Lieutenant Yang Gan flew over the crippled hulk, struggling to comprehend the scene below.

Thick black smoke bellowed from a massive hole blasted above the waterline in the carrier's hull.

The *Liaoning* had been hit amidships on its port side. Planes lay smashed and scattered along a torn and ruined flight deck. Crew were battling fires and tending the wounded. Others lay bloodied where they had fallen. Yang presumed they were dead.

As he flew close, one of the aircrew waved him off, not that he'd had any intention of landing on the wreckage.

Yang checked his fuel gauge. He had to land soon or ditch in the sea. With his navigational equipment still disabled, he checked the sun and his watch, then turned towards the point on the horizon where he hoped salvation lay.

If it hadn't been for the smoke, Yang would never have found the tiny island.

From the air, it resembled a sand-coloured arrowhead pointing south-west. Its highest feature rose just metres above the water. A channel had been cut into the broad northern end, terminating in a square-shaped port dug into the reef. On the eastern edge there was a cluster of buildings linked by two roads.

An airstrip flanked the entire western side of the atoll. Its runway was large enough to land a 747, but it would be a long while before it operated again. Yang counted eight craters along its length.

None of the reef's buildings had been touched and he couldn't see any bodies. He assumed the island's workers were holed up in shelters. He wondered at the grim lives of those who'd been sent to pile up dirt to turn this remote place into a Chinese fortress.

He circled the tiny atoll, a pin-prick of land in the wide blue ocean. This is what had triggered a war. Mischief Reef hardly seemed worth the fight.

He checked his fuel again. Out of options, he lifted his altitude a touch and dropped his speed, then pulled a lever next to his seat. The canopy blew off and he felt a jolt as rockets catapulted him from the cockpit.

As Yang glided beneath his opened parachute, he watched his plane arc into the sea.

Canberra

At 8.16pm AEST the *Canberra Times* splashed the story of Jack Webster's arrest.

DEFENCE CHIEF CHARGED WITH TREASON

In five punchy paragraphs on its website, the ninety-year-old broadsheet told how Webster had been marched from his Burra retreat by elite Australian Federal Police officers shortly after 7pm. A slightly blurred photo of a handcuffed Webster being pushed into a black van accompanied the article.

It carried the byline: *Special Correspondent, Harry Dunkley.*

The veteran journalist had dashed off the copy on a laptop borrowed from the technicians. Martin Toohey had phoned ahead to reassure a sceptical editor.

'Trust me, it's rolled gold. Elizabeth Scott will confirm everything. She's expecting your call. Dunkley will send the copy soon.'

The journalist hit 'send' as the four-wheel drive rattled back down the Old Cooma Road towards Canberra. The final words of the article held a tantalising promise: 'More to come'.

Rarely had the paper – as old as the national capital itself – landed such a scoop, and Dunkley's copy sent newsrooms around the country into a frenzy.

Editors, reporters and producers were dragged from their Friday night revelry as word of Webster's demise ricocheted around the web.

Just after 8.30pm, an alert was issued by the prime minister's office:

PM Press Conference. Blue Room. 9pm.

At the same time, Elizabeth Scott's squad of spinners began calling senior gallery scribes to reinforce the story's grunt.

When pressed for detail they merely replied, 'Read Dunkley.'

Despite the late hour, the Blue Room was crammed with journalists agog with anticipation. Their hubbub subsided as Elizabeth Scott swept in, accompanied by the attorney-general.

'Ladies and gentlemen, thank you for coming. I will make a short statement and won't be taking questions.'

She checked her watch.

'Two hours ago, Australian Federal Police executed an arrest warrant at the rural residence of John Reginald Webster, the former chief of the Australian defence force.

'Webster will be charged with treason, misappropriation of public monies, improper use of telecommunications services and the wilful destruction of Commonwealth government property.

'Commonwealth security agencies and the AFP have shown me detailed and compelling evidence that supports each of these serious charges.'

The PM put aside her notes and looked into the lenses of the cameras at the rear of the room.

'On a personal note, I counted Jack Webster as a friend and trusted adviser,' she said, her voice tinged with anger. 'Can I say that I am shocked and saddened that a man charged with defending this nation has so wantonly betrayed its trust.'

She ignored a flurry of questions and silenced the room by holding up her hand.

'I have another serious matter to address. Just minutes ago I spoke with the President of the United States. Mikaela Asta informed me that earlier today there was an exchange of fire between American and Chinese warplanes in the South China Sea.

'The president tells me that the Chinese triggered the conflict by firing on a Philippine navy vessel that was being escorted through international waters by the US carrier *George Washington*. The Americans returned fire, damaging the Chinese carrier *Liaoning*.'

Scott gazed at the shocked faces of the journalists who were trying to process this second bombshell.

'Early reports suggest the Philippine navy suffered casualties. It appears there are Chinese casualties as well, although details are sketchy.

'The *Liaoning*, I am informed, is sailing back to its home port and is being shadowed by the *George Washington*.

'This is a serious and regrettable incident. It is vital that it is contained and that cool heads prevail. Australia urges these two great nations to peacefully resolve their dispute.

'I will be calling on the United Nations to urgently convene the Security Council. And I will be discussing this grave situation with the Japanese prime minister when he arrives in Canberra on Monday. Thank you and good evening.'

Canberra

He sat coiled in front of the two screens as he clenched and unclenched his right hand, a metronome of anger and despair. Charles Dancer read the *Canberra Times* newsflash online while watching the prime ministerial pantomime on TV.

As he absorbed the scale of the defeat, his surge of anger and despair was itself a failure. He had spent a lifetime disciplining his mind and his body, stripping away all feeling in order to focus coldly on each mission. Fear, anger, love – all were weaknesses.

Just one person – Kimberley Gordon – had pierced his armour, awakening shameful desires.

He'd followed the order to kill her without hesitation. But in death she had awoken another long-silent voice – his conscience.

Jack Webster had issued the command. Dancer's trust in the defence chief had been absolute. Webster understood the nature of the world, the extent of its evil, and knew that hard and disciplined warriors were needed to man the gates. Without soldiers like Dancer, chaos would reign.

He rolled his shoulders, trying to shake out the tension. He needed to calm himself so he could think clearly. He closed his eyes and took a deep breath.

The general had fallen and left his foot soldier alone, vulnerable – but defiant.

Soon the trail would lead the enemy to him, but there was time. He would not fail like the others. The standard-bearer would be the last to fall, and his going would be glorious, leaving a blaze of light across the heavens.

Washington

It was 0800 and the cameras were ready. Asta checked her notes as an assistant secured a stray hair. This special address to the nation would be the defining moment of her presidency, played out in front of a global audience.

'Okay, let's do this.' She nodded to the crew.

As the red light on the camera signalled she was live, Asta knew she had to strike a tone of measured authority and convincingly establish that China had been the aggressor. After outlining the clash in the South China Sea, she advised that she had recalled the US ambassador from Beijing, while the Chinese ambassador to the United States had been given forty-eight hours to leave the country.

Her delivery was perfect, and as she built to her finale she knew she had the country in the palm of her hand.

'America is a peaceful nation. For seventy years we have been the guardians of peace in the Pacific. We will not allow China to continue militarising the South China Sea and we will not countenance the daily cyber-attacks on US government and industry.

'China says that it wants a peaceful rise, but its actions do not reflect that. If it wants to play a larger role on the world stage, then it must obey international laws. And it should never doubt that America has the resolve to enforce them.

'My fellow Americans, there are difficult days ahead. I am sure that we can resolve our differences, and the starting point must be that Beijing shuts down its naval bases on contested islands in the Pacific.

'I thank you for your time. I wish you a good day and God bless America.'

Beijing

Meng Tao exploded with rage as he hurled ten pages of text in the air. The president had demanded elegant prose; instead they had delivered dross.

'These words are trash,' he barked. 'You make me sound like a peasant. You have failed to convey my thoughts. Fix it. You have ten minutes.'

The emperor had gambled and lost. Meng had wagered that America would retreat as it had in the Taiwan Strait, and that he would emerge victorious. Instead, the Chinese people would soon learn that his promise of global military might was a lie.

Too late, the president realised that he should have heeded the words of his former propaganda minister. Now Jiang Xiu was gone, and Meng was surrounded by peons.

A makeup artist dabbed at his face to remove the shine from his forehead as he prepared to address the nation. The Hall of Purple Light had been turned into a makeshift television studio. Meng strode to the lectern bearing the distinctive red-and-gold emblem of China, took a last gulp of water, and nodded.

'Ladies and gentlemen, friends and comrades. Today in the South China Sea our aircraft carrier the *Liaoning* was attacked without warning.

'The missile was fired by a plane launched from the American carrier, the *George Washington*.

'It was cowardly, unexpected and unprovoked. Because the *Liaoning* was on a peaceful mission our brave flagship did not have its defences in place.

'Despite this, it managed to return fire, hitting one of the vessels in the aggressor's fleet.

'To show that China is determined to forge peace in the Pacific, I then ordered the admiral to cease battle and return to port.

'Yet we cannot let this act of war go unanswered. I have expelled the US ambassador and recalled our envoy from Washington. All diplomatic and ministerial contact with America will be suspended immediately.

'We will work to resolve this dispute, but we will protect our core interests in the South China Sea, waters that China has held for a thousand years.

'But, my people, be in no doubt. If we cannot have peace on our terms, then China is not afraid to make war.'

Canberra

'Congratulations, Harry, you are making world news.'

Martin Toohey shouted the bar as the National Press Club erupted in a late-night ovation for Harry Dunkley. In several hours of frenetic scribbling, the *Canberra Times*'s newly recruited correspondent had punched out a front-page lead, a breakout and a piece of commentary.

Every sentence was a revelation and Dunkley's scoops were being reprinted around the globe, mostly without credit. In Australia, too, he was being slavishly copied by all forms of media, which were desperately playing catch-up.

Toohey, Dunkley and Bruce Paxton commandeered a pair of lounges in an alcove, retreating from the crush of boozed-up sycophants.

In his pocket, Dunkley had the Australian equivalent of the Pentagon Papers, a vast trove of Chinese and ASIO intelligence data. He also had thousands of Jack Webster's personal files and Benny Hadid's outline of his forensic audit into the Air Warfare Destroyer project.

Life, indeed, was beautiful.

'How much have you been able to read?' Toohey asked.

'A fraction, mate,' Dunkley said as he sipped a mineral water. 'There are four thousand documents on the ASIO thumb drive alone, along with a couple of thousand pictures and videos. I limited myself to searching for Webster, but there's a rich rogues' gallery in there.'

'Speaking of rogues, I can't shake that one image,' Paxton said, throwing some snacks into his mouth, 'of the last person out the door at Webster's mansion.'

Dunkley agreed. 'Jesus, that was a shock. It's seared on my brain. Emily Brooks in a black corset and red stilettos.'

'See, Harry, maybe there is a god after all.' Toohey laughed before raising his glass to Paxton.

'And we couldn't have done this without you, Bruce. Well done.'

'Martin, you know I've always had your back.'

Toohey nearly choked on a mixture of beer and nuts. When he recovered he offered another toast. 'To the great flawed fucking wonderful democracy that is Australia.'

'Cheers to that, Martin,' Dunkley said, but his mind was elsewhere.

He turned to Paxton. 'Bruce, you got a minute?'

'Sure, what's up?'

'No, not here.'

Dunkley led Paxton through a door into the Press Club's boardroom. It was lined with photos offering a glimpse into Australia's political past. A roll call of prime ministers hung in a neat row, Martin Toohey's visage frozen in its customary grin.

Dunkley pointed to a chair. 'Take a seat, Bruce.'

Paxton was puzzled. 'What's going on?'

Dunkley sighed.

'I did search the USB for one other name: Weng Meihui.'

Paxton's face was sombre. 'And?'

'ASIO had been tracking her, as you would expect. There's a note about the night the two of you planned to fly to the United States. And … well … there is no record of her ever leaving Australia.'

Dunkley stalled, struggling.

'Bruce, they believe Meihui was killed that night.'

He reached out and rested his hand on Paxton's forearm.

Paxton nodded. 'I guess I've always known that. But I had to keep searching, just had to. More than anything I just wanted the whole damned truth.'

'Mate, there's something else …'

Paxton drew back. 'What?'

'ASIO had files on her going back several decades. Detailed records of every posting, every time she met anyone of import, including you.'

'Of course they were tracking us. So what?'

Dunkley fiddled with a drinks coaster as he considered how to break the news.

'Meihui … she had a baby. The father was Caucasian.'

For a long while Paxton said nothing, then asked: 'When?'

'She was born in November 1982. You were in Beijing that year, weren't you?'

The union hard man lowered his head. When he looked up there was the hint of a smile.

Canberra

It would be celebrated as one of Australia's most memorable tabloid headlines.

BUNGA BUNGA AT BURRA BURRA

Sydney's *Daily Telegraph* had whipped itself into a frenzy over the sordid escapades of Jack Webster and his harem of nubile accomplices.

The sub-head left nothing to the imagination.

Big brass caught with pants down

Without crediting Dunkley, the paper had reprinted the photo of Webster being dragged into a black van. It had conveniently got its tabloid paws on a high-definition video of a sex romp, recorded by the secret cameras Webster had installed inside his fortress.

The footage of Emily Brooks, starring in all the wrong ways, had gone viral.

While the Sydney tabloid was predictably lurid, *The Australian* cleared five pages to dissect the fall of Australia's military boss at a time of global crisis. The broadsheet was torn on whether to lead with the arrest of Webster or the exchange of fire between America and China.

In the end it married the two in a headline blasted across the entire eight columns of its front page.

WEBSTER FALLS AS WORLD REELS FROM MAY DAY WAR

But they were all playing catch-up to Dunkley who had documentary proof to back every explosive claim – and an apparent hotline to impeccable contacts.

As the morning papers were being opened, the *Canberra Times*'s ace new correspondent was on the move again, filing an online story with the smoking revelation that one of Webster's high-priced escorts was just sixteen.

Dunkley also reported that Brooks had been questioned by police, but released without charge.

He had largely left the sex romp to the tabloids and focused instead on the political charges the Liberal powerbroker had to answer. He quoted high-level sources claiming there was a secret plot by Brooks to recruit Webster to parliament to topple the prime minister.

The journalist wrote that Brooks and Webster had been conspiring to release 'concocted information' suggesting that Scott had commissioned the infamous Brooks sex tape.

ASIO had examined material purporting to show the PM's involvement, but declared it fake, he reported.

'There is no gutter too low for Brooks and Webster,' the source told the *Canberra Times*.

Canberra

The Glock was reassuring, its familiar weight nestled into the left side of his chest, the holster strapped around his shoulder, pulled in tight.

He looked up at the sky. The morning was sombre and grey, threatening rain. Above the parliament, the Australian flag rustled in a slight breeze.

The forecourt was alive, ready to formally welcome the Japanese prime minister. It was 0955 and the official party had assembled in front of the main doors. The former prime minister Martin Toohey was a special guest.

The warrior scanned the crowd. The head of the AFP's Close Personal Protection Unit – a friend – had been thorough. Uniformed and plain clothes agents mingled with the onlookers and he mentally mapped their positions.

He'd called last night and his friend had welcomed the offer: it would be good to have one more set of eyes.

Across the forecourt, five cannons stood poised to fire a 19-gun salute for the Japanese leader. The Federation Guard was assembled in neat ranks, awaiting inspection. He knew there was not a single round in any of the gleaming chrome-plated magazines on their L1A1 Self-Loading Rifles.

Two Australian Federal Police officers stood at a distance of twenty metres either side of the official party, armed with Heckler & Koch G36 NATO battle rifles. And these ones were loaded.

He blended with a cluster of staffers and media standing just behind the official party. He glanced at his watch. Precisely 1000. The bollards at the right corner of the courtyard lowered, allowing Shinzo Abe and his entourage to drive the short distance to the waiting dignitaries.

Dressed in a dark suit, the beaming Japanese leader emerged to be greeted by Elizabeth Scott, vibrant in a flattering blue dress. She introduced him to the official party before the acting chief of the defence force guided him through the ranks of the Federation Guard.

As the Japanese anthem began, the warrior drifted closer. When the first strains of 'Advance Australia Fair' sounded, he placed his hand over his heart, his fingers resting on the gun beneath his jacket.

There was a command from the edge of the forecourt. The first of the cannons roared.

He saw the blaze from the muzzle and the puff of smoke as the second boom sounded.

Shot number three. Without fuss, he moved a few paces nearer.

The target was in sight. Shot number four.

He reached into his jacket and gripped the Glock's handle, pushing open the release on his Kydex holster as the fifth shot fired.

It was time. As the sixth shot roared he pulled the Glock from the holster, stepped in front of the dignitaries and fired.

As the second bullet ripped through the target's skull, his ribs were crunched. He hit the gravel hard, but rolled to his feet, gun in hand. Screams rang out as someone yelled 'Everybody down'. To his right, a rifle cracked twice.

Charles Dancer had always wondered what death would feel like.

'It is my sombre duty to announce that the leader of the federal opposition was pronounced dead at Canberra Hospital a short time ago.'

Elizabeth Scott bore the evidence of Australia's first federal political assassination. Her dress was torn and smeared with blood and a bandaged elbow showed where she'd struck the ground.

'Many things divide us in politics. Most are trivial. Australia is a great nation because we settle our disputes with arguments, not weapons.

'That changed today. We are the poorer for it, but great nations are not dictated to by events. They meet challenges and overcome them.

'Whatever our differences, Catriona Bailey was a proud Australian and a fine and visionary leader of her party. She will be accorded every honour.

'Ladies and gentlemen, this was the act of a lone madman. Charles Dancer had served as an Australian diplomat. At this stage we don't know what his motivation was and I will not speculate.

'Prime Minister Abe is safe, and after discussion he has agreed that his trip will proceed as planned.'

As Scott turned to leave the press conference, a reporter yelled out, 'Prime Minister, you tackled the gunman. Are you a hero?'

She stopped for a moment.

'This isn't about me.'

The front page profile of Charles Dancer spilled to page 5, and ran to nearly three thousand five hundred words.

Among a host of explosive claims, Harry Dunkley reported that Dancer was an active Australian agent who'd answered directly to the disgraced former defence chief, Jack Webster.

Recruited straight from university to the Australian Secret Intelligence Service, Dancer had caught the attention of the up-and-coming air force officer in the late 1990s.

In 2000, Webster had penned a secret report, arguing that the emerging threat to the West was Islamic terror and it demanded a unique response. He recommended the establishment of a cross-discipline unit drawn from the Special Air Service Regiment, Special Forces and intelligence agencies.

They would be the nation's licensed assassins.

Soon after 9/11, the plan was ticked off by the defence minister without reference to the prime minister. Dunkley explained that this was unusual, but not exceptional: it gave the leader deniability. The only people in the know were the minister and his four defence chiefs.

The ultra-secret Reconnaissance Liaison Branch was born and Dancer was one of its first recruits.

Quoting 'Air Chief Marshal Jack Webster's personal files', Dunkley detailed Dancer's many missions and his unique qualities.

The agent's psychological assessment showed he was a patriot with exceptional intelligence. It cautioned that he was 'driven by rage', but that neatly fitted with the purposes of the unit, because 'he will carry out any order'.

At the end of the long feature, Dunkley had insisted on a special and unusual tagline: *Research by Trevor Harris. May he now rest in peace.*

Canberra

'Yes mate, yes mate – might be getting ahead of ourselves, though. Are the unions on board?'

The powerbroker's animated conversation reached Harry Dunkley's ears as he opened the Labor senator's office door.

Brendan Ryan motioned for Dunkley to enter, then signalled he needed a little more time.

'Well, check it out. We'll need 'em before we get serious.'

Ryan dropped his phone on the desk and clapped his hands.

'Ding dong, the wicked witch is dead. Now maybe we'll get a decent leader.' He winked. 'Bit of support coming my way.'

Dunkley placed his iPad on the desk as he took a seat.

'Glad to see you're not overcome by grief, Brendan.'

He laughed, shuffled out from behind his desk and slumped onto a leather lounge.

'Come on, Harry, everyone hated Bailey. The game is wide open now and the comrades are talking about generational change.'

The journalist laughed. 'Downer was generational change. People in here are always talking up generational change. But nothing really changes.'

The Labor hard man was insistent. 'You know me. I could make a difference.'

Dunkley met his eye. 'You're right. I do know you.'

He opened his iPad and handed it to Ryan.

'I was wondering if you could have a read of a story I'm working on.'

The story chronicled the exploits of a Labor leadership aspirant who was part of a secretive shadow government called the Alliance. The cabal comprised senior defence, intelligence and political figures. For years it had been manipulating Australian governments to march in lockstep with the Stars and Stripes. Its mastermind was Jack Webster, who'd orchestrated a series of cyber-attacks on Australian government agencies that had been attributed to the Chinese and had contributed to the fall of the Labor prime minister Martin Toohey.

An ashen-faced Ryan put down the device.

'I'm thinking of going to print tomorrow. What do you reckon, Brendan?'

Ryan lumbered to his feet. 'I helped you nail Jack Webster—'

'Only because you thought Webster was going to kill you,' Dunkley responded. 'Nothing before that bothered you.'

'Webster was a demagogue who used the Alliance for his own ends,' Ryan shouted. 'And don't pretend this nation doesn't face real threats and needs a powerful friend.'

'You know, Brendan, I don't doubt that. But I prefer to leave our foreign policy to the democratic roll of the dice.'

Dunkley picked up the iPad.

'So do I press send or delete?'

Ryan's face hardened as he spat out his words.

'What do you want?'

'Genuine change. It's time for you to go quietly into that good night.'

The fallout from Harry Dunkley's reporting ricocheted around the world.

Powerful men who had thought themselves immune to prosecution began to tremble.

Daily, the journalist revealed the names of the mandarins in the Five Eyes intelligence community who'd been conspiring against their own governments.

In London, the head of MI6 was hauled before the Intelligence and Security Committee of Parliament to answer claims that he had been acting without proper authority.

The director of the Canadian Security Intelligence Service was arrested and charged with breaching the nation's Official Secrets Act.

Across the Tasman, New Zealand's chief spy was stripped of his office after he was found to have acted against the national interest.

But the biggest scalp was in Washington, where the vice president was hauled before the Senate Select Committee on Intelligence. In front of a packed congressional hearing televised live, Morgan McDonald delivered a tour de force, railing against the liberal media and its 'endless undermining of the state's ability to protect itself'.

In a moment endlessly replayed on American primetime, the flint-hard career politician was captured slamming his fist into the table as he hollered his defiance.

'I am a patriot. At all times I have worked in the best interests of this nation and within its laws. This hearing is an insult to me and the men and women who stand the watch.'

Big Mac's strident defence divided America's media. The right-wing cheer squad at Fox News swung in behind him, arguing that he had no case to answer. But the liberals at CNBC and the *New York Times* demanded the appointment of a special prosecutor.

The president wasn't immune either. Appearing at a county fair, Mikaela Asta was peppered with questions about her deputy.

'I have every confidence in Big Mac,' Asta told reporters, quickly adding: 'At this time.'

The next day the *Detroit News* splashed with a sensational headline.

FBI PROBES VP LINKS TO JACKSON ASSASSINATION

A shaky iPhone recording from a local meeting of the National Rifle Association had been anonymously sent to the paper. It showed a member boasting that he had shot Earle Jackson, because he was 'a coward who betrayed the nation'.

A crack investigative team had spent a month examining every element of the claim.

They'd identified the speaker as Leroy Porter, a former Navy Seal sniper who'd served with distinction in Iraq and was credited with the longest range confirmed kill in Afghanistan.

The reporters found Porter had access to sophisticated weaponry and had developed a serious drug and alcohol dependency. He'd agreed to an interview and not denied the claims in front of two reporters.

'I was following orders,' he explained.

They'd initially thought him delusional and handed over the material to the FBI, which had already linked Porter to the vice president's chief of staff.

The agency requested that the paper hold off publication until it was ready to move.

That afternoon America recorded another iconic moment in its colourful and chequered history: the vision of a vice president being led from the White House in handcuffs.

Morgan McDonald was charged with being an accessory in the assassination of a president, a crime that carried the death penalty. He was also charged with helping to orchestrate a drone strike on the White House and with fabricating reports of an attack on a US military satellite. Every network saturated the airwaves with coverage of Big Mac's demise and every talking head agreed: the disgraced vice president could not have acted alone. Other heads would roll.

While the West shook, the East trembled as the rise of the communist power was checked.

Meng Tao's humiliating defeat in the South China Sea had shattered public confidence in his leadership and sparked a series of tremors.

Dissidents hacked into a cable television network and broadcast anti-government slogans and images of tortured prisoners. Fifty thousand people took to the streets of Beijing to protest against the relocation of a chemical plant in the biggest demonstration in a decade. And China's economy stumbled, with nervous investors wiping one-third off the Shanghai Stock Exchange in a week.

As his popularity plummeted, the president resorted to the time-honoured tricks of panicked despots.

The prosecution of Jiang Xiu was broadcast live. The former propaganda minister had been charged with a litany of crimes and blamed for every one of China's recent setbacks. Numerous senior officials were accused of being part of the 'Jiang Gang' and arrests mounted across the Middle Kingdom. Meng released an official statement, saying 'I am saddened at the betrayal of the People's Republic by a man I once considered a friend.' Another high-profile prisoner was Yu Heng, the now disgraced ex-commander of the *Liaoning*.

As a desperate president used repression to cling to power, Western scholars speculated that Meng was facing a revolt from within the ranks of the People's Liberation Army.

One made a chilling prediction: 'The next uprising in Tiananmen Square won't just involve students and it won't be quashed by the military.'

Sydney

It had taken one hundred and twenty-four years, but the Labor Party finally had what it had always craved. A martyr.

On a crisp autumn morning, the comrades gathered to pay homage to one of the toughest individuals ever to sit in federal parliament. In death,

Catriona Bailey had achieved what she'd never managed as leader: she had united the party's many factions.

Sydney Town Hall was bedecked with images of the former prime minister as the ALP prepared to do what it does best: honour its fallen.

George Street was cordoned off as large crowds formed ahead of the ceremony. Bob Hawke, a little stooped but with his silver mane still glistening, was received like a hero, and the applause rang even louder when Paul Keating walked into the historic building.

A few minutes later Martin Toohey arrived to a polite, but noticeably less enthusiastic, reception.

In a rare display of bipartisanship, the Liberal prime minister received a rousing welcome. Elizabeth Scott had been lionised for her heroism – and her poll numbers had soared.

Just minutes before the service began, Brendan Ryan arrived in a ComCar to find his path blocked by a wall of media.

His resignation from parliament had shocked pundits. Ryan had rehearsed his lines well.

'What happened to Catriona vividly demonstrates that politics exacts a heavy toll and life is short,' he said solemnly. 'My doctor has advised that I take some time to smell the roses.'

Broken Hill

The cemetery on the edge of town was near empty. Rows of neat headstones stood under a blazing sky while nearby the Barrier Highway rumbled as a B-double rig departed Broken Hill, bound for Adelaide.

She scooped a small handful of dirt from the hard ground as she stood above the pit marking his grave. The preacher had never met her brother, whom she had not seen for twenty years. She had once loved him, but now realised she had never known him.

Blessed be the God and Father of our Lord Jesus Christ ...

She felt sorrow for his death, but anger at the shame he had brought to the family. Most of all she was pleased that her parents were not alive to experience this humiliation.

... the Father of mercies and the God of all comfort, who comforts us in all our affliction ...

The preacher nodded to her. She sprinkled a fine coating of red dirt on the coffin.

537

'Remember, man, that you are dust, and unto dust you will return,' she whispered.

Miriam Dancer wiped the soil from her hands as she walked from his grave. She would leave it unmarked.

Canberra

Perched on a swivel chair, Harry Dunkley stabbed at a keyboard and looked out across a hundred empty desks. The once proud *Canberra Times* resembled the journalistic killing fields, legions of reporters discarded on the edict of short-sighted Sydney bean counters.

Still, Dunkley couldn't complain. He'd been treated like royalty since his appointment as special correspondent, and his daily scoops were being syndicated across the Fairfax stable.

Tonight he'd already punched out an 1800-word feature revealing how Jack Webster had hot-wired his Burra retreat by siphoning off wads of Defence money to install a secure and direct link to Washington.

He'd also revealed that Burra was connected to a cyber-warfare centre at HMAS *Harman* on Canberra's south-eastern fringe. The high-tech naval intelligence facility – run by a member of Webster's elite Reconnaissance Liaison Branch – had been the source of the recent cyber-attacks against the Commonwealth.

One of the few remaining sub-editors was giving Dunkley a hand on a special weekend report that would detail Webster's many other crimes and misdemeanours. Among a long list, the defence chief had staged the Press Club bomb hoax to burnish his leadership credentials.

The journalist was polishing the lede when his phone rang for the umpteenth time that night.

He'd been avoiding most calls as they were mainly requests from one-time press gallery 'mates' desperate for a drink and a catch-up.

But it was late and he was still hoping his ex-girlfriend Celia Mathieson would get back in touch, so he answered.

'Harry? Harry Dunkley?'

The voice was somehow familiar and resonated with authority.

'Yeah. Who's this?'

'We met some years ago, briefly in Washington, then more recently in Canberra, the night of the News Limited Awards. I think you received a commendation.'

Jesus.

Here he was in this lifeless newsroom, the time was half-past dead and Rupert Murdoch was on the line.

'Mr Murdoch, hi. Um, sorry about that little misunderstanding at *The Australian.*'

'Forget that. We need to talk.'

Washington

Mikaela Asta swirled a fine Napa Valley white in an expensive tumbler and kicked off her shoes. The hour was late and the West Wing had emptied to a skeleton crew of housekeepers and secret service personnel.

The president reflected on where the scandal that had engulfed her deputy would sit amid the long litany of White House travails.

Morgan McDonald faced life in a federal prison – if his lawyers managed to stay his execution.

Asta had spent the day duelling with the heavyweights of American television. CNN had hounded her over her claim that she had no knowledge of Big Mac's deception.

She had skilfully argued her innocence, emerging triumphant and with her leadership enhanced. Each interview had pivoted from accusations to acclamation for her dramatic intervention in the South China Sea.

Fox News had hailed her a hero for 'restoring American pride', while even the liberal media had conceded that she had recast the international order.

Around the globe, the May Day War was being met with a mix of outrage, admiration and dread. That pleased Asta. She had long subscribed to Machiavelli's view that it was better for a prince – or princess – to be feared than loved.

Tomorrow a new vice president would be sworn in; tonight she would bask in the glory of a campaign that defined her as this generation's Iron Lady.

She poured another small glass of wine. Something had been nagging at her and on a whim she reached for her phone and dialled a number.

'Madam President! I wasn't expecting this call. I didn't—'

'Elizabeth, I need to get something off my chest.' Asta assumed the stern tone of a scolding teacher. 'Your pre-empting my announcement on the South China Sea action broke every protocol.'

Asta could feel the line go cold.

'What about the protocols – and laws – that were shattered when your vice president engaged in an act of treason with my defence chief?'

539

A long moment of silence was broken by the president's laughter.

'You are right. We were both let down by our leading men.'

'I suspect not for the last time.'

Asta smiled. It sounded like the Australian leader had relaxed.

'What's the time in Canberra?'

'Approaching midday, Madam President.'

'Elizabeth, please, it's Mikaela. By the way, I saw the footage of you tackling the gunman. It was very courageous.'

'It's funny. I don't remember even thinking about it. I saw his gun, heard the shot and the next thing I remember is hitting the ground. Instinct, I guess. I trained as a fencer.'

'Well, now the world knows you're a fighter.'

'As they do of you, Mikaela.'

Asta paused before responding.

'The world is a dangerous place, Elizabeth. I would like a fighter on my side. One that I can trust.'

'Our world is more treacherous than I ever imagined,' Scott replied. 'And trust? That has to be earned.'

Canberra

The Chairman's Lounge was bustling with late afternoon trade as the three men settled into five-star comfort. They'd arrived just after 5pm then spent twenty minutes fighting their way through a conga line of one-time colleagues and enemies, all keen to shower praise and good wishes.

'Nice.' Harry Dunkley eased into a chocolate-leather chair. 'Clearly being an ex–prime minister carries a few perks, even for one as disgraced as you, Martin.'

Martin Toohey passed a champagne flute to Bruce Paxton, then one to Dunkley.

The journalist smiled as they clinked glasses. He knew that, like him, the others felt relaxed and safe for the first time in ages, able to enjoy the day without having to glance over their shoulders. Though deeply saddened by the deaths and devastation that had befallen so many who had helped him, it felt good to reflect on the rare justice of bad men facing the consequences of their actions.

He scanned the luxurious lounge, quietly nodding to some nobody MP who'd once threatened to commit unspeakable acts against him.

Only a few months ago he'd been scamming the streets of Sydney, living each day in a daze of self-pity and delusion. Now he was enjoying the perks of fine living. More importantly, he had recovered something priceless, his dignity.

The journalist turned to the former defence minister. 'This must feel good, Bruce, after the downbeat digs you've been living in?'

'I guess so, Harry, though I never went in much for gilt-edged living. I was always happy dossing down with the common man. Still am.' Paxton motioned round the room. 'Too many thieves in here, in this town, pretending to do good work when they're really only concerned with one thing: themselves.'

'As self-righteous as ever, Bruce,' Toohey chipped in, offering a broad smile to his mate. 'What about your entitlements? Has Finance finally sorted them out? I'm reliably informed the department had a bomb put under it.'

'Yep, things are looking good on that front, Martin, no doubt thanks to you.'

'You heard from the clerk?'

'He rang me today to confirm the petition to reverse my expulsion from parliament. I'm not sure whether it's a help or a hindrance that Elizabeth Scott and the new opposition leader are co-sponsoring it. I'll be relieved when it's done, but it ain't the most important matter in my little world right now, not by a long shot.'

Paxton gazed out the window as an aircraft lifted in a graceful arc towards the heavens.

A respectful silence fell over them, broken when Toohey softly spoke. 'You think you'll manage to track her down, Bruce? Hong Kong's a massive place.'

'Yes, I think so, mate. She's family, right? I've got to find her. What are we if not the heritage of the past searching for a better future?'

'Very poetic,' Toohey said appreciatively. 'Hemingway?'

'No, cobber, Bruce fucking Paxton, shitkicker laureate.'

The three men laughed heartily, their mirth eventually interrupted by a Qantas steward. 'Your boarding pass, Mr Paxton.'

He nodded and gathered up his travel bag and paperback, a proud man embarking on a mission to track down a daughter he'd never known, a precious link to the only woman he'd ever truly loved.

'Well boys. Showtime.'

He embraced Toohey, then Dunkley; solid embraces that lingered, that said all that needed to be said.

'I hope he finds her.' Toohey looked solemn.

'Yeah, me too,' Dunkley said, but he was absorbed in his own thoughts. His daughter had telephoned and asked to meet him in Sydney.

'Martin, a simple yes or no. Did you contact Gaby?'

The former PM looked sheepish. 'Might have.'

'I wondered how she got my phone number.'

'Well, as Bruce said, family is important.' Toohey fell into silence, gazing out at the lengthening shadows.

'You okay?' Dunkley inquired, placing his hand on his friend's arm.

'I am. Just got a bit on my mind, that's all.'

'It's been a tumultuous time, I grant you that.'

Toohey fiddled with his glass as if pondering what to say. 'That phone call on the drive out here, that was from the prime minister.'

'Jesus! Not offering you a knighthood?'

Toohey chuckled. 'No, thank God, they've been consigned to the dustbin. No, Elizabeth wants to see me. To talk about a job and a few other things ...'

His voice trailed off, but the slight blush on his handsome face said it all.

Dunkley was genuinely pleased for his friend.

'Remember when you dragged me out of the lock-up? You said you were motivated by redemption and revenge. Well, you got your revenge, but much more importantly you redeemed all of us. You're a good man, Martin Toohey, and in the opinion of this atheist, you deserve a sainthood.'

Toohey smiled, then caught the journalist in a bone-jarring hug.

They were interrupted by the steward. 'Mr Dunkley, your flight is boarding.'

The journalist picked up his leather satchel, a long-ago gift from Gaby that he'd carried in good times and bad.

'You've got lots of offers, Harry. What are your plans?'

'Not sure. But you know, for a long time I always put my career first. This time I won't be making any decisions until I've had a good chat with my daughter.'

He turned to leave, then stopped.

'Rupert wants to fly me to New York, you know.'

The two men roared with laughter as they walked through the lounge. As its sliding doors opened, Dunkley placed his arm around his mate's shoulder and offered a conspiratorial whisper.

'You never know, Martin, I might just write a novel.'

ACKNOWLEDGEMENTS

Over the course of crafting our three novels, dozens of people have volunteered advice, helping us research and write these political dramas. Some have allowed us to formally acknowledge their support while others prefer to remain in the shadows.

Firstly, we'd like to acknowledge our magnificent editor, Amanda O'Connell, who has managed to kill our darlings without crushing our spirit.

Mary Rennie, Anna Valdinger and Jeanne Ryckmans helped steer us through to publication, never losing patience.

Shona Martyn, a publishing dynamo, took a gamble on this odd couple of Australian journalism, and was a steadfast supporter from go to whoa.

We couldn't have written these three novels without the wise and generous counsel of many experts. In particular we would like to acknowledge Hugh White, Alastair MacGibbon, Dr Carl Ungerer, Ben Turnbull and Rob Woods. The chapters on the USS *George Washington* could not have been written without the expert guidance of Admiral (Ret) Ronald J (Zap) Zlatoper, a former commander in chief of the United States' Pacific Fleet. Rear Admiral (Ret) Brian Adams, AO, former deputy chief of the Royal Australian Navy, made patient corrections to the drafts.

A serving US Air Force pilot provided expert guidance to help us write the chapter on flying the B52 out of Guam. Patrick Siu was generous in helping the authors understand the beauty of Chinese calligraphy.

Many others were generous in reading draft chapters, and giving constructive feedback.

Finally, we want to give thanks to many politicians, staffers, senior public servants, members of the defence and intelligence agencies, both here and in the United States, who enthusiastically offered ideas and corrected draft chapters when they veered too far from the truth.

For the record, we have kept a detailed log of every conversation, every email, every text. Be afraid.